I0781074

BOOK THREE OF THE

NOSS SAGA

RELINQUISHED REALMS

JOAQUÍN BALDWIN

Library of Congress Control Number: 2025900442
ISBN: 978-1-961076-08-2 (e-book)
ISBN: 978-1-961076-09-9 (paperback)
ISBN: 978-1-961076-10-5 (hardcover)
ISBN: 978-1-961076-11-2 (audiobook)

First Edition, 2025.
Los Angeles, California.
NS3-P1.0

"For small creatures such as we
the vastness is bearable
only through love."

— Carl Sagan

UNTHAWING OCEAN
Elanúbril
Khaar Du Tribes
TESLURKATH
Baysea Beyenaar
Tesz Bay
FJORDSULF
STELM NEDROSS
Klad Mohnjaun
Dragonkeep Bay
Spine Bay
Fjordlands
Southlock Strait
Needlecove
STELM
Abandon Bay
Koroberg
Isdinnklad Sea
Zovaria
Isdinnklad Lake
Moordusk
Zovarian Union
Nebush
Muskeg
STELM CA'ÉLI
Varanus
Old Karst
Klemes
Klad Senet
New Karst
Fel Varanz
Free Tribelands
QUIESCENT OCEAN
Vel Baribol
Yanan
STELM ANKROV
Allathanathar
Sajal Crater
Brasha'in Scablands
STELM SAJAL
USHERKA RANGE
Dunewaar
MOUNT LOOR
Yenwu
Unclaimed Territories
Yenmai
Lhambor Di
Esduss Sea
Yenwu State
Aksas Di
Azurean
Navar Mat
Bay of Hashmun
Kingdom of Bauram
Kizad
Gulf of Erjilm
Ashen
Bauresht Sea
Ngau Tor
Taring
Nisos
Normouth
Republic of Lerev
Nisos
CAPRICIOUS
Loorian Continent
Berjan Continent

NOSS

Khaar Du Wastes
Ash Sea
Dathereol Princedom
Therimark
Falbagrish Range
Eel Fjunno
Loorian Continent
Jerjan Continent
Khaarkadesh
Unclaimed Territories
Bergsulf
Da'Aju Caldera
Stelm Khull
Brimstowne
Fractured Range
Lequa
Lequa Sea
Wujann
Anglass
Negian Empire
Eel Svelknob
Witurvale
Anglass
Shaderift
Wyrnwash
Ophidian Sea
Heartpine
Thornridge
Hestfell
Ultad
Bayanhong Tribes
Farjall
Kayamur
Montano
Stelm Rilgéreo
Kalford
Caerlye
Brinelaar
Bighorn
On Khurderen
Sharzi
Laaja Jerja
Dorhond Tribes
Stelm Rilganesh
Stelm Tai-Du
Oskirin
Bay of Negórmea
White Desert
Azash
Tsing Empire
Tarpits
Archstone
Elmaren Queendom
Stelm Mokyo
Shusnukran
Hashan
Moonrise
Shash
Nargara
Graalman Horde
Doralghon
Sharr Helm
Tharma Federation
Alommo Sea
Scoria
Mount Alvforg
Korolok
Sundhollow
Cape Artok
Tumultuous Ocean
Kingdom of Afhora
Ocean
Illenev
Austral Sea
Druhal
Wastyr Triumvirate
Farkhalum
Seafaring
0   100   200   300   400   500   Distance in Miles   1000

Quiescent Ocean
Isdinnklad Sea
Char Forest
Decapod Sanctuary
Fel Shim
Fel Evar
Fel Evar
Radula
Dormant Bay
Oton Forest
Mo'ogu
Radda Jungle
Fel Angul
Fel Syric
Taciturn Fort
Quiet Forest
Arahu Mill
Stelm Ajuur
Timma
Stelm Verj
Eiju
Duasi
Macu
Feal-Ni
Thicket Island
Bolgir Timberland
Klad Eramar
Stelm Trodaari
Uniss Jungle
Keldu Lekra
Turaan
Ommo Naj
Fel Vazihus
Fel Brokken
Laaja Gunnari
Consecrated Wilderlands
Khiben
Esduss Sea
Stelm Ajiira
Angu
Strangle Mountain
Dregger
VARANUS DOME
KRUWENDROLOMS
Fel Varanus
Reeflen
Davit
Hermitage
10   20   30   40
DISTANCE IS MILES

Löögan
Dorvir
Tyevoids
Serumein
Unclaimed Territories
Malawe
Mount Argente
Dorhond Tribes
Paukk Ruins
Stelm Rilgéreo
Plunnwek
Oirnos Sanctum
Laajus Glacier
Tibaloë
Semeria
Desolation of Zen-Zagárro
White Desert
Speleo Sanctum
Yesshun
Mount Oiâv
Waliowa
Anilo Glacier
Dorhond Range
sklan Barrows
Lallaga
Zech-Ryah
Quas Endur
Pistai
Pistea-Nir
Sulltilg
Kaelmat Prairies
Perikat
Sullanee
Ommo Praw
REST FOREST
Raks
Gulassüe
Quthot
Ismaltaar
Saba-Nir
Perath's Menhir
Njmm
Fal Fad
Tivelo Forest
Kithra
Munno
FOREST
Plinf
Terrin
Tembarr
Ew
Udera Anticline
Barrabaul Trenches
SERENN FOREST
Ushwelmath
Vulle
Seniiro
Goob Mesa
Lianis
Wou'Gaast
Teala
Arevuur
Krao
Graalman Horde
Amo Arch
LEO TOMB
Skyward Arch
SHADDO FOREST
Tsenhanuur
Lektte Mesa
Scorrve
ARCHSTONE DOME
Kandorf
ALMELDROLOM
FIELDS OF THE THIRD LASH
Road of Arches
Tera Arch
Zajiv
Saruun Arch
Gate of Juk
Ruuvo
Talus Spoils
Rapier Arch
Ewoolt Arch
Senduura Desert
Ford Arch
um
0   10   20   30   40
DISTANCE IN MILES

FJORDLANDS DOME

NAGRADROLOM

AZUREAN DOME
QUAJUDROLOM
Doird
Urallach's Fortress
Dendokar
NARAATU BATTLEFIELD
Allath's Well
STELM HABAD
Ausentia
JANGGU RUINS
Huss Di
Safur
STELM CUBJOOLT
Grelras
COBALT DESERT
SERENITY WOODLAND
Ennél
Grelith
Ansira
Klad Jín
Onnáthu
ares Mat
Ta-Gu
CHAIL TRODESH
Trod Eino
Trod Jík
Asra
Trod Garr
Mikkagolm
Udurával
Navar Mat
Agalgan
Tarin
Klad Chach
Ulóki
Wuahak
Mishan
Sirur
BUURA RUINS
Keldris Khesúra
NAMITUS CHASCRETKES
Drin
Faramon
STELM INUTH
Sarkhum
DARGON'S TOWER
Ienaff
CERULEAN DESERT
ESHTEA RUINS
Oora
Listus
Tala-Ena
Taciturn Bay
Malverte
MOUNT NGE
0   10   20   30   40
DISTANCE IN MILES
BARROWLINDE
ar Juv
NAGUR MINES
Aesjavar
MOUNT GLIRJIL
QUAS SEJAAR
Uinn
Scantus Di
MOUNT CUVVO
ZAHIR'S SEPULCHRE
STELM GLIRJIL
Soman
Yivv
Adafa

NISOS DOME
OKRIDROLOM

's Rest
Noraa
Mex Lands
Den-Drosa
Tompali
Elmaren Queendom
Carran Twins
Carran Amel
Wiley Desert
Desert
Jayra Peak
Nala Mines
Talos Peak
Fel Woods
Erkhyan Peak
Haven's Pass
Telm Ashanyu
Stelm Sevra
Knav Forest
Glaalv Woodlands
Pheno Ruins
Mines
Golkennah
Ommosu
Stelm Fau
Minnsar
Tserof
Islad Vindri
Wyndendale
Maargo
Maldin Forest
Kujo
Crescent Point
Ncur Rest
Maples End Forest
Annok
Hofrr
Gusnuch Tower
Karl Isle
Falodin
Zergu Beacon
Dorst Forest
Shard Peninsula
Azash
Nighby
Tros Cowon
Cy Tower
Novra Monolith
Qik Cove
Moongap
Seeres Bay
Bay of Negórmea
Yorrick's Perch
Fel Arvits
Fel Crow
Wagnas Forest
Teles Finds
Brombe
Fel Noit
Kenn Braus
Eira
Keldris Gwom
Herva
Fuiv
Fel Avathan
Tirva
Siwbir
Welt Forest
Uovel
Alluver Plateau
Aun Falles
Moor Anbe
Islad Mily
Klad Ismalt
Daenn
Vairrelno
Sepir
Gulas Ash
Teros Tomb
Gulas Quorga
Mefalt Forest
Stelm Khar
Erne Du
Ommone
Garovit
Ilaadrio Wastes
Keldris Ervo
Tumultuous Ocean
MOONRISE DOME
GWONLEDROLOM
0   10   20   30   40
DISTANCE IN MILES

Stelm Wujann
Unclaimed Territories
Stelm Khull
Sinkvoids
Lurr's Abyss
Teraff Craters
ANGLASS DOME
URGDROLOM
Ruins of Hu-Samiil
Lappan
Aulth Ruins
Neshgliig Fehen
Death Forest
Gulas Ihaast
Juviel
Mayanno Cliffs
Urgólloth
Kenn Scerr
Eruudea
Nokhlo Ruins
Nerokholm
Stelm Vaus
Druke Forest
Ianoi
Stelm Nil
Dormendal
Trod Pecuv
Laaja Khuaga
Blood Fore
Gaast Mar
Field Mill
Stules Forest
Sataai
Gwolm Ebsost
Stelm Obb
Laahúm
Gumma Forest
Stiss Mira
Waggath
Basgrul Jol
Gwolm Chail
Stelm Road
Brälvo
Es Krus
Anglass
Stelm Farre
Ebjelt Forest
Farre Wastes
Negian Empire
Stiss Malpa
Malfa Mill
Old Pilgrim's Road
The Four Bastards
Yauvirr's Egg
Erratu
Foxglove Forest
Free Tribelands
Lunk
Noria Camp
Easter Forest
Dimbali
0   10   20   30
DISTANCE IN MILES

Perifall
Vathereol Princedom
Ljarmallen Peninsula
Foen's Tomb
Agulum Forest
Thimbell
Voresea
Shatter Harv
Dismal Shores
Car Alla Vei
Cranus Isle
Pelesh Quincsh
Fir Isle
Fel No
LEQUA DOME
KROSTDROLOM
Lequa Sea
Cossta
Tib's Tower
Fel Erius
Fel Shisen
Tunfss
Isdinn Kimen
Quagro
Eskis
Sull Drenih
Bramble Flat
Ushwen Krost
Kruss
Almoth Bay
Bay
Apini
Lith-Leo
Aldavi
Shiorelg Forest
Galassue Forest
Seaborr
Khaliv Forest
Loompool
Munn
Ferr-Noh Ruins
Stelm Ampen
Khanotamba
Erne Goro
Dier
Lash Spain
Calbor
Durg Namba
Ifen
Klad Jilo
Yango
Jianmu
Cowomu
Ruins of Eixaon
Stelm Oath
Khai
Ommuv
Trod Bumro
Mount Vox
Erath
Stelm Astar
Fort Hio
Shaderift Aqueduct
Tunhau
Tonhond
Forest
Dejian
Bayanhong Tribes
Birelm Forest
Klad
Spire Falls
Mireinfield
Shaderift
Naysayer's Crypts
Amatto Dier
Negian Empire
Vezza Bay
Fel Add
Wyrmwash
Ayrch
Ophidian Sea
Wyrm Core
Haulfr's Covenant
Zerren
Fel
0   10   20   30   40
DISTANCE IN MILES

Table of Contents

Author's Note

Hello reader; I'm glad you made it to Book 3 of the *Noss Saga*! This one is a lot more action packed than the first two, so I hope you'll enjoy the shift to a grittier mood. As with the previous installments, I have a few recommendations before you get started:

Maps and illustrations

There are several new maps for this book. To properly read all the details on the maps, I recommend you view them at full resolution and in color. Visit the link below to find all the maps, illustrations, and other goodies.

Guides & glossary

Characters, locations, and common Miscamish words can be found in the appendices at the end of this book. Previous guides, such as the pronunciation guide that was included in Book 1, or the guide to the Eighteen Clades from Book 2, are not printed in this installment, but they are available on the link below alongside even more extras.

Supplemental Materials

Follow this link to access all the Supplemental Materials, including the color illustrations, maps, glossaries, lists of characters, locations, and more.

JoaquinBaldwin.com/book3/extras

The Story So Far

The *Noss Saga* is a complex tale. It's easy even for me to forget all that happened in previous books. While I try to remind the readers of the preceding events along the way, I recognize the need for a full-on refresher.

The following is not a comprehensive synopsis, so it will not make much sense unless you've read the previous books in this series (you should not be here if you haven't read them yet, either way).

Thank you for joining me for the next part of this queer and epic journey. I hope you enjoy your return to Noss.

May the moon light your path,

— Joaquín Baldwin

Book 1 - Wolf of Withervale

Lago Vaari is entrusted with Agnargsilv—the mask of canids—by a shapeshifting elderly woman named Sontai, who asks him to take the mask to her grandson, Bonmei. Lago tricks Chief Arbalister Fjorna Daro of the Negian Empire, who had been hunting Sontai to acquire the mask. Fearful of the mask and the soldiers pursuing it, Lago and his best friend Alaia hide it away in a coal mine. After his father kicks him out of his home, Lago gets a job at the Mesa Monastery, delivering packages for the Havengall monks and helping Professor Crysta Holt with the monastery's telescope. He falls in love with the stars, the planets, and the moon. A dire wolf, a species thought extinct, is killed near Withervale. The creature is much larger than any in fossil records, and the recent collapse of the Heartpine Dome's roof seems to be related to the giant's appearance.

Six years later, Withervale is attacked by Fjorna Daro and General Alvis Hallow. Lago escapes through the coal mine and retrieves Agnargsilv, aided by a scout from the Free Tribelands named Ockam Radiartis, who considers Bonmei his adopted son. Alaia and Lago's pet dog Bear join them. Lago learns how to see the threads of life with Agnargsilv but knows there are more powers the mask is hiding. Shortly after they arrive at the Thornridge Lookout, Fjorna's squad attacks them, killing Bonmei. Lago defeats Fjorna's soldiers by using Agnargsilv's powers, which let him see in the pure dark and foresee the attacks of his enemies. Platoon Commander Jiara Ascura also joins their party, and the five of them flee by using Agnargsilv to penetrate the wall of vines that surround the Heartpine Dome, hoping that taking the mask away from the Free Tribelands will avert a potential war.

After being imprisoned for some time with a handful of survivors from her squad, Fjorna and her team escape to warn Alvis Hallow. When they find him, Alvis is already in possession of the mask of cervids, which he stole from the Anglass Dome. With Artificer Urcai's aid, Alvis finds his elk half-form. As the Red Stag, he kills the weak Emperor Uvon dus Grei and takes the throne of the Negian Empire under the title of Monarch Hallow.

Inside the Heartpine Dome, Lago and his friends discover that the Negians exterminated the Southern Wutash tribe who lived there. They find strange quaar artifacts at a broken lattice located in a temple at the dome's trunk, and also encounter Safís, a white wolf shapeshifter who is the spirit of canids. They help her escape the dome and then head north, searching for the Firefalls—also known as Minnelvad—where they hope they might find the surviving "cousins" of the Wutash.

After a steamy visit through Brimstowne, they venture up the hot creeks of the Firefalls, where they are struck by a blizzard. Lago is caught in an avalanche and overcome by the toxic fumes of the falls. He hallucinates a huge golden bear coming to save him. He wakes up in a cabin and meets a corpulent giant named Banook, who rescued him and his friends. Lago quickly grows fond of the mountain of a man.

Banook, who is the spirit of ursids, tells the wayfarers the story of the Downfall, and how the domes were grown to protect the eighteen chosen clades from the cataclysm. He reveals that the dome of ursids was never grown, causing the demise of the Northern Wutash tribe. Banook also teaches them about the Nu'irgesh—animal spirits of each major clade—and tells them that the mask of ursids, Urnaadisilv, lays buried under the icy caldera that engulfed the city of Da'áju. He promises to take them there once Winter is over.

With Banook's aid, Lago finds his timber wolf half-form and is gifted with the name of Sterjall, as well as with a dagger named Leif, which Banook and Ockam crafted from a lattice segment and dire wolf fang that Lago took from the Heartpine Dome. Lago-Sterjall and Banook fall in love but are fearful of their future because Banook will not be able to join them—he can only travel where other bears reside, and the bears only live in the mountains of the north.

During an excursion into Brimstowne, Banook sees that Negians are searching for the mask Lago-Sterjall wields. He meets with a ranger named Ardof, who tells him that the Red Stag may be readying to attack Withervale.

The Red Stag has ransacked the Anglass Dome and reshaped the Negian Empire's politics. He captures and mindlocks Sovath, the cervid Nu'irg, forcing her to join his army of enslaved cervids, including the megaloceroses (giant elk) and cervalces (giant moose). The Red Stag ventures to the Lequa Dome. With the aid of Fjorna, he acquires Krostsilv, the mask of musteloids, and gifts it to General Jaxon Remon. He also gifts him with caged jarv wolverines—vicious, bear-sized creatures he captured in the Lequa Dome.

Throughout Winter, Lago and his friends train with Jiara, preparing to journey into Da'áju. Once the Thawing season arrives, they leave Bear in the cabin with two bears who will take care of the mutt, and venture into the Da'áju Caldera. They find the ice-buried temple of ursids and rescue Urnaadisilv from its forsaken depths. Ockam becomes the wearer of Urnaadisilv, although he is not yet able to shapeshift. From a rock-carved map, they learn that there was once another dome in a volcanic desert known as the Brasha'in Scablands; they do not know why it is no longer there. They decide they should travel west, to the Moordusk Dome, in hopes of finding a Miscam tribe who might know why the domes have not opened as they were meant to open, and who might know how to defeat the Red Stag.

Upon exiting the glacier, they spot an orange glow in the distance: Withervale is on fire. Lago-Sterjall needs to help Crysta and his other friends in the city. Banook tries to follow them to Withervale, but once he is too far from his bears, the Nu'irg withers and turns feeble. Unable to follow any longer, he kisses his precious cub goodbye.

BOOK 2 – MASKS OF THE MISCAM

After leaving Banook, the wayfarers hurry to Withervale to save their friends, but the Red Stag breaches through the ramparts with his megaloceroses and conquers the city with his army of cervids. Lago-Sterjall is attacked by General Jaxon Remon, a wolverine general wearing Krostsilv, who kills Khopto and breaks Sterjall's arm. During the Winter months, the Red Stag had traveled east to the Lequa Dome, where he enslaved the local tribe and took the mask of musteloids for his general; he now faces Sterjall, flanked by Fjorna's arbalister squad.

Taking a feral bear form, Ockam saves Sterjall, but dies from his wounds aboard the catamaran sailing them toward the capital. Jiara becomes the steward of Urnaadisilv.

After Ockam's funeral, they travel to Zovaria to meet with Balstei Woodslav, an artificer who studies the aetheric elements. Kedra (a scout who has been helping Crysta) betrays them and calls for her uncle, Admiral Grinn, to seize the masks. Balstei helps them escape Zovaria. They journey through the bogs and enter the Moordusk Dome, where the Laatu Miscam live. They meet Khuron Aio-Kulak, Nelv (the felid Nu'irg, a clouded leopard), and Blu (Aio's smilodon companion). During a Laatu council, they decide they need answers and determine that Mamóru, the proboscidean Nu'irg, might have them—if he is still alive.

To prepare for their adventure, they train with an allgender shaman named Sunu, who has an azure-hooded jay herald named Olo. They learn about hot crystals of aetheric sulphur named *brime* and scout the perimeter of the dome to prepare for the threats they may encounter. Sterjall takes Kulak outside the dome to see the stars, and Kulak takes Sterjall to see fireflies. They begin to develop feelings for one another, fearful of being caught by the strict Laatu.

The wayfarers venture out of the dome to the Brasha'in Scablands to locate Mamóru. Jiara finds her bear half-form while climbing among redwoods; she receives the name of Kitjári. In the volcanic desert they find Mamóru, who tells them the true story of the Silvesh, that Noss themself is truly conscious, and that the Silvesh were used to speak to Noss in times before the Downfall. He recounts the story of Jiu Zezi, who discovered the comet that would later cause the Downfall. Mamóru's entire story is written upon the walls of lava tubes, a story he intends to preserve for the future. He explains that the threads the mask-wearers see with the Silvesh are consciousness, and that the masks control the force of empathy itself. Mamóru helps them retrieve the proboscidean mask from the collapsed temple, for which he himself will be the wielder.

They battle their way back into the Moordusk Dome, with Mamóru taking the form of a mammoth. At a council they decide to open the Moordusk Dome and agree that their new goal is to gather six Silvesh, the minimum needed to speak to Noss, who may have the answers that Mamóru is unable to provide. While Balstei travels with the Laatu and felid migrations with the intent of transcribing Mamóru's petroglyphs, the rest of the wayfarers sail west to the Fjordlands Dome aboard a ship named *Drolvisdinn*.

Through Olo, Lago sends a message to Crysta, asking her to travel to the Moordusk Dome before it fully opens. Crysta replies that Banook is now with

Safís, the canid Nu'irg. The white wolf has claimed that the Anglass Dome is slowly growing out of shape, causing them to fear for its future. Crysta rushes to the Moordusk Dome accompanied by Hefra Boarmane, her naturalist friend. After exploring the Laatu lands for some months, Crysta and Hefra decide to follow in Balstei's footsteps. They reunite with him in the new Laatu colony hundreds of miles away, south of the scablands.

The Red Stag is amassing an army of cervids, planning to strike the Jerjan Continent. Crescu Valaran, second-in-command of Fjorna's squad, is promoted to general and given the title of Silv-Thaar Valaran, taking over Jaxon's legion. He finds his half-form of a raccoon, but a rift forms between him and his old arbalister squad. The Red Stag crosses the Ophidian Sea and breaches the Bighorn Dome, using giant pipe segments to keep the vines open, enabling his entire army to flood into the dome. Two Ikhel Miscam factions inside Bighorn are at war with each other. Luhásu, chief of the Western Ikhel Miscam, helps the Red Stag defeat the Eastern Ikhel, and as a reward is granted Rilgsilv, the mask of caprids, becoming Silv-Thaar Markhor. With the aid of a caprid army, the Negians take the Bayanhong capital of On Khurderen. The Red Stag decides to split his efforts, sending Silv-Thaar Valaran and the arbalisters to take the Moonrise Dome while he secures the Archstone Dome.

To the far west, the wayfarers sail into the Fjordlands Dome, land of the Puqua Miscam, where they recruit Prikka-Nalaníri (a skilled chef, wielder of Nagrasilv) and Captain Siffo. Nalaníri sets the dome to open and boards *Drolvisdinn* to sail away with the wayfarers, followed by *Fjummomurr*, Siffo's vessel. They are attacked at sea by Admiral Grinn and Kedra, but defeat their enemies and enter the Varanus Dome, where the Mo'óto Miscam once lived, though they have all died from a terrible disease.

From a sunken palace the wayfarers retrieve Kruwensilv (the mask of reptilians) and befriend the Nu'irg, Ishke'ísuk, whose primal form is that of a double-crested basilisk. Sterjall sets the Varanus Dome to open. Ishke'ísuk wants Sunu to become the wielder of Kruwensilv, and although under Laatu Miscam law allgenders are denied such honors, Aio-Kulak vows to change the laws. The prince also openly declares his love for Lago-Sterjall, causing his Laatu followers to desert him. While Sterjall cares deeply for Kulak, and they finally have a moment of passionate if somewhat disconnected sex, the wolf remains hesitant to reciprocate the prince's feelings, haunted by the greater love he feels for Banook.

With six Silvesh in their possession, the wayfarers initiate an audience with the Noss consciousness. The planet tells them that the Noss of old is dead, and that only a patchy memory of those times past remains. Noss also claims that many more memories reside in the domes that are still sealed, urging the wayfarers to travel on, some toward the southern domes, others to return east and open the domes the Red Stag ransacked, before they begin to collapse in the way Heartpine has. Noss teaches the Silvfröash how to take their feral forms and encourages them to seek the aid of the Nu'irgesh to aid them in the war that is certain to come.

Mamóru dies, using the last of his energy to tell Noss as much of the history of the last hundred thousand years as he can recall. Momsúndosilv turns inert.

Kitjári and Nalaníri choose to venture toward the Negian Empire aboard *Drolvisdinn*. Sterjall, Kulak, Sunu, and Alaia choose to go south aboard *Fjummomurr*. Before parting ways, Sterjall writes a letter to Banook and asks Kitjári to deliver it to him.

The two ships sail their separate ways.

RELINQUISHED REALMS

PART ONE
FORSAKEN DESERTS

CHAPTER ONE

THICKET ISLAND

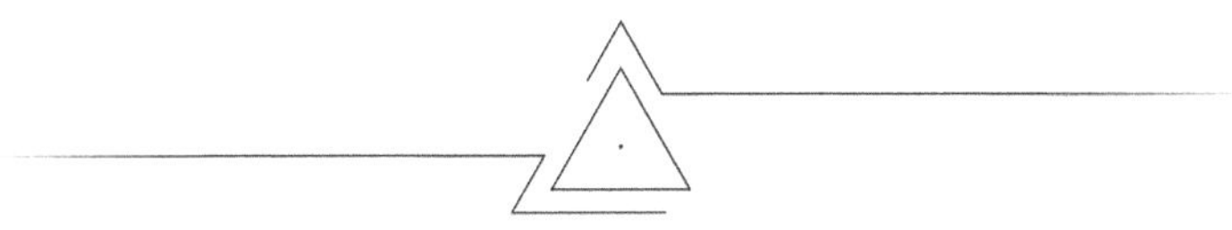

Black sails billowed.

The bone-white hull of *Fjummomurr* sliced through the salty sea, weaving among the dragon-like vines of the Varanus Dome.

"Land ahead! To d'east!" Captain Siffo called out from his ship's forecastle. He held his bulky frame still, standing on the railing right above the narwhal figurehead. The narwhal's silver-painted tusk shimmered brightly, always pointing forward.

Sterjall stepped beside him, holding a map tightly in his handpaws to prevent it from blowing away. "According to Grinn's map, that must be Thicket Island," he said. He tapped the map with a claw. "There should be a passage that cuts straight south through it."

"Aye," the captain replied. "We shell find d'route, then we'll fullow d'winds toward d'ocean."

They had sailed through the unruly walls of the dome during the night and had finally reached the outside world. Although most of the smaller vines had been receding with the dome's ongoing opening, the wayfarers were not entirely out of danger yet: the larger vines were still curling around everywhere, like partially submerged sea serpents.

The Puqua sailors adjusted course, directing the ship along a careful path that circumvented the vines, keeping Thicket Island to starboard. The volcanic island rose vertically, leaving sharp cliffs facing the water, with barely any shore to speak of. Most of the island had been overtaken by the long-reaching fingers of the untamed dome, which unraveled as thorny arches and tangled tendrils from the heavens to the unseen depths. Farther east on the island, a narrow, sandy beach glittered beneath the overcast skies.

"Dragons," Sunu pointed. "Along the shore."

There they were. Varanus dragons, just like the ones they had seen prowling within the dome, were patrolling the shoreline in search of food.

"This dome seems to be opening faster than the others," Alaia commented. "The dragons found their way out so quickly. I wonder how long it'll take for them to spread over all of Fel Varanus."

"Will we find mour dragons in d'dome we're a-heading to?" Siffo asked.

"My scalp doubts it," Kulak said. "Unless there are marsupial dragons."

"I don't know nothing 'bout marsupials, or 'bout d'lands uf Bauram we're a-sailing to, but mine crew is ready fur d'challenge anyhow. Right, hogs?"

"Aye!" the Puqua sailors roared.

Captain Siffo led the singing of one of the many sea shanties they had been belting out while on their voyage. Sterjall had heard them sing before, but always from a distance as he had been traveling aboard *Drolvisdinn*. He felt merrier with the Puqua than with the Laatu, as the Laatu did not sing while at sea—the liveliness of this crew was invigorating.

Siffo's voice was deep, rumbling, and full of exuberant trills. The responses of his sailors were energetic and playful, even if a bit out of tune.

Grind yer tusks n'stow that tail.   *-Weigh!*

   Light-ho d'kenzir stone.

Rig a jig d'blackened sail.   *-Weigh!*

   Bright-glow as cold as bone.

   Weigh-a-weigh d'kenzir stone,

   D'fjords await, d'winds are blown,

   D'Puqua sailors leeward bound,   *-Hey!*

   Weigh-a-weigh d'kenzir stone.

Hold d'hull, outlast d'squall.   *-Haul!*

    Light-ho d'kenzir stone.

Drink n'hold yer alcohol.   *-Haul!*

    Bright-glow as cold as bone.

    Haul-ee-haul d'kenzir stone,

    D'fjords await, d'winds are blown,

    D'Puqua sailors leeward bound,   -Yo!

    Haul-ee-haul d'kenzir stone.

Where's d'cap'n? Where's d'chief?   *-Reef!*

    Light-ho d'kenzir stone.

Where's that scum, that wretched thief?   *-Reef!*

    Bright-glow as cold as bone.

    Reef-oh-reef d'kenzir stone,

    D'fjords await, d'winds are blown,

    D'Puqua sailors leeward bound,   -Wee!

    Reef-oh-reef d'kenzir stone.

Up ye go hogs pigs and boars.   *-Board!*

    Light-ho d'kenzir stone.

Haul them foresheets, stow them oars.   *-Board!*

    Bright-glow as cold as bone.

> *Board-oo-board d'kenzir stone,*
> *D'fjords await, d'winds are blown,*
> *D'Puqua sailors leeward bound,   -Oar!*
> *Board-oo-board d'kenzir stone.*

> Jibe-ho signal coming soon.   *–Boom!*
> *Light-ho d'kenzir stone.*
> Blown aloft homebound to Krûn.   *–Boom!*
> *Bright-glow as cold as bone.*

> *Boom-ay-boom d'kenzir stone,*
> *D'fjords await, d'winds are blown,*
> *D'Puqua sailors leeward bound,   -Hoo!*
> *Boom-ay-boom d'kenzir stone.*

Captain Siffo snorted a loud chuckle. "I love them tone-deaf sailors to death," he said, leaning his bulky body against the railings. His tailcoat suit fluttered in the sharp ocean breeze, while his wiry mane remained tucked under his colorful tricorne hat. He scanned a nearby cut in the island. "That seems t'be d'channel we're looking fur. N'look at them arches go!"

At the eastern end of Thicket Island, the landmass was split in two. The largest portion lay to the west, ending abruptly in a rocky shore; a mile to the east, the smaller island of Fel Erkhus rose; over the channel between the two, a tangle of vines braided itself into knotted arches that bridged the skies. The vines seemed like a purposely constructed series of sky bridges, yet the elevated path was slippery and covered in deadly thorns, and no animals other than small rodents and lizards would dare cross it. Plants, however, grew eagerly over the arched vines, dangling lianas and colorful ivies.

Fjummomurr veered south into the funneling gap, sailing under the striped shadows of the monumental arches.

"My scalp ponders what is to happen when the large vines recede," Kulak mused. "Do they shrivel where they stand? Maybe fall down and crush mountains, like in Agnargdrolom? Or perhaps they snake back slowly, like scared earthworms."

"Let's hope they simply crawl back to where they came from," Sterjall said. "Too much of this land has already been damaged."

The wind blew colder outside the dome. Sterjall wrapped his gray-and-black cloak around his shivering body, fastening the Sceres-shaped brooch to keep it tight. He lifted the hood up, letting his pointed ears poke out of the holes cut into the fabric.

A Puqua scout atop the crow's nest yelled a warning in their guttural tongue.

Siffo looked up. "Sails to d'south!" he interpreted.

"Shit. Where?" Sterjall asked, hurrying to the captain's side while pulling out his binoculars.

Siffo pointed a hoofed finger. "Them be docked. Port side island, near d'pine forest, where d'vines connect into d'cove."

Sterjall aimed the glass southward. "Zovarian. Lodestar guide us. Two warships, a few smaller ones as—wait a moment." He lowered the binoculars, squinted, then placed them back over his muzzle. "Those look like the same ships we encountered before. Is that Admiral Grinn's ramship?" He handed the binoculars to Siffo, who struggled to line up the device without bumping it on his tusks.

"Aye, them look like d'same sea wings we clipped."

"I don't see Kedra's trimaran," Alaia noted.

"Should we turn around?" Kulak asked.

Siffo shook his warthog head. "Much long it'd take us, n'we'd be a-struggling against d'wind. Them ships are not expecting us. I say we fly by n'flash our tusks at them plain-skinned cowards."

"But they'll chase after us," Sterjall objected, leaning over the narwhal figurehead to get a better view.

"Them only caught up to us last time 'cause d'wind was in them favor," Siffo noted, "n'*Drolvisdinn*'s keel got snagged un d'vines. *Fjummomurr* sails faster. If we keep due southwest, we'll remain ahead."

"They won't catch us," Alaia said confidently. "We'll leave them in the dust this time. Or spray."

Fjummomurr's black sails were fully extended. Before they got close enough to see faces, they heard a tolling bell, then spotted movement on the decks of both Zovarian ships and a scrambling of soldiers at the shore.

The channel tapered further, shifting *Fjummomurr*'s course closer to their enemies. A compact port clung like a cluster of barnacles to the edge of the island; a Zovarian settlement spread behind it, which Sterjall guessed was used as a repair or supply stop for ships traveling between the mainland and Fel Varanus.

"Yes, that is definitely Admiral Grinn's ship," he confirmed, peeking through the binoculars once more. "I bet he'll be happy to see we made it out okay."

As they passed by the docked ships, they saw the admiral leaning over the taffrail of his ornate vessel. Alaia climbed the ratlines to make sure Grinn could see her, then yelled, "Suck on my nub, fucker!"

Fwip! Fwip! she heard right by her ears.

"Get down!" Sterjall called while pulling her to the deck. "Arrows!"

Alaia took cover behind the kubanochoerus bones of the ship's skeletal hull. *Thud! Whap!* More arrows rained upon them, piercing the sails and splintering the deck. But soon *Fjummomurr* had drifted too far away to be reached by projectiles, and the crew was safe to leave their cover.

"Well, maybe he was not so happy to see us," Sterjall said, then approached Siffo, who was dislodging an arrow from the forecastle while directing his crew to mend the sails. "We might need to reconsider our course," he said to the captain. "We should consult the maps once more."

Siffo snapped an arrow in half and tossed it overboard. "Aye, let's all go to mine quarters t'discuss."

The wayfarers entered Siffo's rustic yet comfortable cabin, where an oval-shaped table was placed beneath the cold light of a pharolith chandelier. Logs crackled in an iron furnace by the raised bed, with a fur rug spread in front of it, making the space cozy and welcoming.

Sterjall spread open the maps they had stolen from Admiral Grinn's ship: one focused on Fel Varanus, another showcased all the continents, albeit with much less detail. He looked to Siffo. "How long do you think it'll be before we reach the Azurean Dome?"

Siffo pulled off the pharolith rings and caps decorating his four tusks, so they would not blind him in the dimmer light. His brow creased. "If d'winds keep up, n'yer map scales are correct, I'd guess we'll reach d'dome in 'bout a week or two."

"As long as we stay clear of the northern shores," Sterjall said.

"Why are the northern shores a problem?" Kulak asked.

Sterjall pointed at the northern tip of Fel Baubór and said, "The problem is that the Zovarian Union is enormous. This portion here is not part of the Kingdom of Bauram, but of Holv-Yanan, one of the sixteen Zovarian states. Grinn's logbook said a Zovarian fleet is stationed there. We could push west around it, then turn south into the Quiescent Ocean. From there we could enter the Azurean Dome through this bay." He tapped on a curving body of water that led straight to the dome.

"We shell aim to stay far frum d'shores," Siffo said. "Zovarian or utherwise. If we are spotted, we'll aim t'outsail them."

They left Siffo's quarters and gazed north. Thicket Island was still looming, with its dark peaks and dragon-like tendrils, but the Zovarian settlement was now too far away to be seen.

"I wonder what Kedra and Grinn will do next," Sterjall pondered.

"At least we know they won't be chasing after Kitjári and Nalaníri," Alaia said. "They'll have an easier way making it back to the Fjordlands Dome."

Sterjall nodded. *I wish Kitjári was here to help us,* he thought as he inhaled the cold ocean breeze. *She'd be decisive. She'd know what to do.*

"How long do you think it'll take them to reach Banook?" Alaia asked.

Eihnk-eihnk! Olo called from Sunu's shoulder.

"I wasn't asking you," Alaia replied.

Eihnk! the jay insisted.

"No, something is wrong," Sunu said. "Olo, what did your eyes see?"

Eihnk! Olo repeated as he flew upward. Sunu followed his path with their violet-cast eyes and spotted a flutter way above the bird. "Enemy heralds, following us."

"Shit," Alaia said. "I see three of them. And they're not following us… But…"

The magpies overtook them, flying ahead of the Puqua ship.

"They are going south," Sterjall said, "to warn the Zovarian fleet at Yanan."

SAILS TIGHT

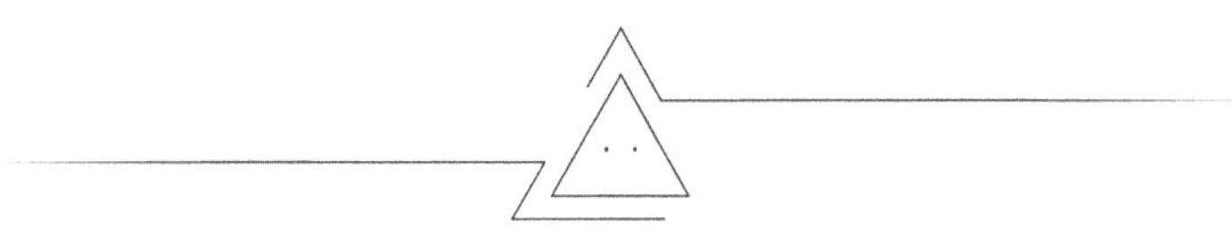

The wayfarers encountered the first signs of trouble three days into their voyage, as their ship tried to cross the wide sea separating Fel Varanus from Fel Baubór.

"*Flummo swaømig, naxest irv!*" a Puqua sailor called from the crow's nest.

"Be ready fur trouble!" Siffo yelled out, his tone more encouraging than warning.

Sterjall hurried to the foredeck and scanned with his binoculars—five masts were rising over the horizon: one directly ahead of them, the others to its left and right, separated by a few miles of open water.

"They are in formation," Sterjall said, "making a wall across the sea."

"Line abreast them come, but we hold d'weather gage," Siffo replied confidently. "Gwullmonn's breath shell propel us 'tween our enemies, n'we shell sail faster than any ships them eyes have e'er seen. Ready yer long-range weapons!" He turned to his crew and yelled commands in Puqua.

Kulak, Alaia, and Sunu assembled their quaar blowguns, and Alaia put her quaar helm on. Sterjall picked up a bow and quiver; even though he did not feel comfortable shooting arrows, it was better than standing around like a fool, holding a dagger. The Puqua sailors kept short and long bows at the ready while a small crew loaded the harpoon cannons atop the forecastle.

They changed course to sail *Fjummomurr* between two trimarans, which Siffo knew were faster and more maneuverable, but much less threatening than the ramships. Being leeward, a trimaran trying to ram into them would have to be suicidal. The enemy could, however, match their speed for long enough to board; and the Zovarians were preparing to do just that.

As they neared the line of ships, the two trimarans repositioned themselves to make full use of the northeastern winds. Two ramships changed course as well, one to port and one to starboard, forming a choke point right in their path.

"We could try to circle around them," Sterjall recommended.

"That we won't, wulf Lorr," Siffo said, attuned to the winds. "Any loss uf speed or change in direction would put mine ship in jeopardy."

The ramships were sluggish, but they had plenty of time to tack and drive themselves directly into *Fjummomurr*'s path. Their hulls were iron reinforced, and although *Fjummomurr* was solidly built with kuba bones and could sustain a strong impact, any additional water weight from a hull breach would slow its pace, leaving it as an easy target for the ships that would follow.

"Full speed ahead!" Captain Siffo commanded.

The first ramship approached their port side.

"Veer not! Sails tight!" he called, crossing his arms over his belly.

The ramship encroached ever faster. *Thud! Whap!* Arrows began to rain upon them.

"Hold yer shots!" Siffo ordered. "Waste not yer arrows un them!"

The Puqua lifted round shields to protect themselves—the very shields they had stolen from Admiral Grinn's soldiers when they battled before entering the Varanus Dome. Flaming javelins accompanied the next barrage of arrows, which were also set aflame. The crew hurried to put out the fires, dangling from the lines and swinging to protect the sails from the blaze.

The first ramship had gotten close but had no chance of making impact with *Fjummomurr*. The second ramship, however, was farther away, and had more time to alter its course. A collision seemed imminent.

"Cap'n! We must veer or them'll crash into us!" the ship's quartermaster urged.

"Stay d'course!" the warthog replied. "If we lose speed, mour ships will soon gather upon us. Full sails ahead!"

The ramship inched closer, aiming to pummel them on their starboard side. A scream came from above them, followed by a cracking sound at the main deck as a Puqua barrelman toppled from the crow's nest, a burning javelin stuck in his chest. More flaming projectiles pierced their hull, but kuba bones did not burn as easily as wood.

"Take cover un d'port side, now!" Siffo commanded.

Fjummomurr nearly avoided the collision, but the Zovarian ramship pushed on until its brass-tipped bowsprit dug into the bone-white hull, tore a piece of the quarterdeck off, and snapped up, tossing splinters and cables about *Fjummomurr*'s stern. The shattered remains of the bowsprit snagged and tensed, still attached to the ramship's bobstays and forestays, pulling like a titanic fishhook. Sunu rushed to the back of the ship, jumped over the shattered planks of the quarterdeck, and swung their halberd to cut the ropes. They ducked just in time as another flight of arrows hit the stern.

Fjummomurr was free and sailing ahead.

The fires were put out as they continued onward. Ahead of them, the two trimarans moved with the wind. They were smaller ships, much more maneuverable, and they were clearly trying to synchronize their motions so that they could board *Fjummomurr* from both sides at once.

"Wait… is that…?" Sterjall asked, watching the trimarans approach.

"It's Kedra," Alaia muttered, recognizing the petite figure of the scout who had once worked for Crysta, and who had betrayed them by handing the masks over to her uncle, Admiral Grinn.

"Reef your sails!" Kedra bellowed from the trimaran, barely audible against the wind. "There is an entire fleet ahead! If they sink your ship, the masks could go down with it."

"They would not be any better in your hands, you traitor!" Alaia yelled.

"Don't be a fool. Do not gift this battle to the Negian Empire. If we work together, we can—"

"Take them down while d'wind is in our favor!" Siffo called out.

His crew released their arrows, aided by their elevated position at the forecastle and by the power of the wind. Kedra scurried to cover. A few arrows pierced Zovarian soldiers, while many others lodged themselves into the sails and decks of the trimarans. The Zovarians waited, shields and blades in hand, ready to board and fight.

"Aim fur d'masts!" Siffo called to the crew at the harpoon cannons. Once the trimarans were within range, the harpoons released with a metallic *clang!* The ship on the port side took the most damage, with the harpoon piercing through the triangular sail and deep into the mainmast, shattering its side and making the entire rig unbalanced. Sails toppled over the soldiers waiting to board, who hurriedly hurled their grappling planks and hooks. The planks missed, but the hooks caught their teeth on *Fjummomurr*'s railings. Sunu sliced the ropes before the trimaran could pull closer to board.

At the same time as the mast of the ship on the port side was falling, Kedra's trimaran to starboard managed to lock its planks and ropes.

As the Zovarians boarded *Fjummomurr*, a small flash of green and yellow darted between the two ships. Ishke'ísuk had launched himself as a lined gliding lizard; right before hitting the trimaran's deck, he shapeshifted into a gargantuan saltwater crocodile, landing atop three soldiers and tail-whipping a dozen more.

"Release the mindrégosh, now!" Kulak yelled.

From below deck, Pichi and Blu came roaring, flashing their fangs. The smilodons were drowsy from the sea voyage but could still fight and intimidate. As they tore the flesh and armor from their enemies, the Zovarians cowered in terror. It could have been a fair fight—one ship against another, with similar crew sizes—but having witnessed two ferocious smilodons, an enormous crocodile, and now the approaching figures of a black-faced wolf, a human-shaped feline demon, a drove of pig-headed freaks, and a black-masked witch spinning their halberd, the hopes of the Zovarians entirely evaporated.

"Stop!" a familiar voice called out once more. "Stop or the spur fucking gets it!" Kedra had climbed unseen up to *Fjummomurr*'s quarterdeck and was holding a dagger to Alaia's neck, holding her tight with a chokehold.

"Listen to me, and stop this madness," Kedra demanded. "You've won this battle already, but there is no way for your ship to continue past our fleet. We have countless more ships ahead. We know where you are headed."

"Let her go!" Sterjall said from the bottom of the quarterdeck's steps. Behind him, a few Zovarian soldiers were still battling, but he paid them no attention now. "Kedra, you are getting nowhere with this, why do—"

"Will you fucking listen?" Kedra yapped. "There's no point in what you are attempting. Even if you manage to get through us, the Baurami will never let you sail into the Azurean Dome. We've warned them to keep an eye on the Quiescent Ocean, and even to block the sea routes into the Taciturn Bay. If you make it past us, you will sail straight into their hands."

"Why would the Baurami listen to your demands? We won't believe anything you—"

"Zovaria and Bauram agreed to work together in this war. We have allied with them."

"Allied?" Sterjall mocked. "Did you even tell Bauram about the masks, or did you hide that detail so you can keep them in your power?"

Kedra deflected the question, simply saying, "Bauram will get the northern state back, as they have sought for decades. And Zovaria will tear the Negian Empire down. Think this through. You could be our allies as well, instead of rushing to your deaths."

"It's that simple, is it? Allies. Like Grinn wouldn't simply kill us after taking the masks. No, actually, he'd likely torture us first. You already sold us out once, because you have no morals, because you are blinded by power, just like Hallow." He took a tentative step up toward her.

"Stop right there, runt," Kedra demanded. "One more step and this bitch gets it. I have nothing left. My crew is dead, my ship wrecked, and my uncle won't come in time to save me. I'm only doing what I know is right for our Union. For the future of all realms. And you… You have a chance. You can still do what is right."

Sterjall climbed one more step.

"I'm not fucking bluffing," Kedra snarled, pushing her blade tighter, drawing blood from Alaia's neck. Sterjall froze, seeing Alaia shake her head, and spotting a fearful yet decisive tension in her expression. *No*, he thought. *Don't risk it, don't do it.*

While pretending to try to loosen Kedra's chokehold, Alaia snuck her hand into her overalls front pocket and pulled out a dart. The needle-thin tip was so minuscule and sharp that she might have been able to prick it into Kedra's knife arm without her even noticing. But Kedra saw the movement, flinching back just enough to prevent all of the venom from entering her veins.

"You bitch, you—" she gasped, pulling hard to tighten her grip, perhaps to sink her blade into Alaia's trachea, but instead her arm swung limply and her knife clinked to the deck.

Alaia bent down to grab the weapon, but Kedra's knee slammed into her jaw. The strike was so hard that it knocked Alaia's quaar helm off and sent her tumbling backward.

Sterjall rushed to aid his friend, but as Alaia toppled, she grabbed onto Kedra's coat, pulling her into her fall. They plowed into the bulwark and spun overboard, splashing into the sea as one.

Alaia kicked at Kedra and tried to swim away, but the scout grabbed onto her suspenders. To Kedra, Alaia was no longer a negotiating chip, but a way for her to enact one final act of revenge.

"Let go!" Alaia screamed, her last word bubbling up as her head submerged. Even with her small frame and single working arm, Kedra overpowered Alaia and used her to keep afloat, attempting to drown her.

Alaia thrashed about, trying to gasp for air but only swallowing cold, salty water. "Useless fucking spur!" Kedra yelled, holding her down. Alaia could see Kedra's distorted face yelling at her but could not break free of her grip.

"We could've saved the Union! All you had to—"

Alaia stopped trying to push away and instead pulled Kedra toward her. A wet *crack* resounded as she smashed her nub into the scout's forehead, making her twist backward. Alaia used the momentum to place herself on top, already holding a new dart in her hand. She punched it into Kedra's chin, sinking the tip and fletching into her flesh. She had not been able to tell which kind of dart she had picked, but as Kedra began to foam at the mouth, she realized it had been one of the deadly ones.

Kedra gurgled a rabid screech, and in one last effort tried to take the Oldrin down with her. But her muscles suddenly loosened, then her eyes went blank.

"Cunt," Alaia coughed out, kicking the body away as she swam back toward a rope ladder Sterjall had tossed down for her.

"Are you hurt?" Sterjall asked, helping Alaia back on board.

"I'm fine," Alaia said, shaking the nerves and water off.

"You are blee—"

"I'm fine!" she insisted, holding her throat and walking away. She looked around. A handful of Zovarians were still fighting, dying in the name of courage and foolishness. The smart ones had jumped overboard, hoping to be rescued by the pursuing ships. She sat on a bone-carved bench, watching as the ropes tying *Fjummomurr* to the enemy's trimaran were severed and the broken vessel was left to drift away.

"Here," Sterjall said, handing her a clean cloth soaked in water.

"Thank you," Alaia said, pushing the cloth to her neck wound to prevent more bleeding. "It's not too bad," she added. "You better help with those who are truly injured first."

"I should've done more to protect you. If I had—"

"Sterjall!" Captain Siffo called. "We got two live ones here. Both surrendered. What shell we do with them?"

"Go deal with that." Alaia said. "I'll be fine, I swear."

Sterjall nodded, then rushed toward Siffo. "Tie them up," he ordered. "We'll need to change our plans. And they might be the only people who can help us find a way out of this."

Once the prisoners were secured, Sterjall first unsuccessfully tried to gather information from the one they'd tied up at the ship's stern, then he stepped up to interrogate the one they'd bound to the foremast, who seemed particularly terrified of his black face, amber eyes, and sharp fangs.

"What is your name?" Sterjall growled.

"Please," the man sobbed. "I have a-a-a f-family, I didn't hurt anyone!"

"I asked for your name," Sterjall demanded, squatting next to the blubbering soldier.

"Al… A-Alid."

"Well, Alid, you are going to tell us exactly what Zovaria's plan is, and where they have the sea routes blocked. Do you know a woman named Reija? Green eyes, slender—"

Alid's eyes lit up in fear. "Reija? What did you do to her?"

"She's tied up at the back of the ship. As alive as you are. For now." He pulled out Leif and placed the senstregalv blade uncomfortably close to Alid's nose. "I already asked Reija the exact same questions I will be asking you. If your answers don't match hers, you can guess at what I will cut next. I'll be right back with a map, and I expect you to cooperate."

Sterjall strode to Siffo's cabin at the quarterdeck. The wall to his left and part of the ceiling were missing, having been pulled apart by the crashing ramship. He was glad to see that the maps were still waiting at the oval table, secured by heavy paperweights.

"Hey, hold on," Alaia said, hurrying behind him, holding a bandage that Sunu had wrapped around her neck. "What is it you plan to do with that dagger of yours?"

"Make him talk. What else?"

"And if he doesn't talk, you'll start chopping off pieces? Is that what—"

"Of course not," Sterjall said, grabbing a map. "Just play along. He's scared shitless. And Reija wouldn't tell me anything, I'm just pretending. Now let's go find out what their plan is."

Alid told them everything that he knew, but Reija still would not speak; she was not scared of Sterjall's face and could see past his ruse. It took a bit more persuasion to get her to cooperate—Blu helped with that.

The captain's shattered cabin was still too windy, so instead they gathered at the 'tween deck to discuss their next move. Siffo spread open the petals of a pharolith lamp as they sat on the planks and placed the map upon a wooden crate.

"We will never make it into the Azurean Dome by sea," Sterjall said, "not with the entirety of the Baurami fleet waiting for us. I doubt we'll even make it past the Zovarians waiting just a bit ahead."

"What is it we can do?" Sunu asked, who had been too busy dealing with the wounded to be present for the interrogations.

"We'll do what they would not expect us to do. We are changing course. Instead of sailing over the Quiescent, we'll take the Esduss Sea straight south."

Sunu studied the map. "There is no access to Quajudrolom by this sea."

"There is none," Sterjall agreed, "but we can dock in the Cobalt Desert, as close to the dome as possible."

"How will our scalps know where to dock?" Kulak asked.

Sterjall pointed at the shores east of the Azurean Dome. "I guess once we see the dome in the distance, we find any safe spot on these shores. It will be a long walk over the desert. But hey, you once told me you wanted to see blue sand dunes—you'll definitely get to see them now."

"My eyes still want to see them. As long as we do not die."

"Alid mentioned the Zovarians are guarding the north coast, all the way to this point here." He tapped a claw on a triangular landform on the southeastern end of the Lilac Basin. "The city of Orobet, at the border of the Zovarian state. He said that after the city, there's mostly just desert. There are a few settlements by the shore, but they are smaller, and from independent duchies. All the big cities of Bauram are on the west coast."

"We should stay deep at sea," Sunu said, "away from shores until the time to sail west comes."

Sterjall nodded his approval. "Let's hope the winds keep blowing in our favor." His claw moved south, beyond Orobet. "We should aim to move past Lhambor Di, the biggest city on this coast, and find a place to dock beyond it, somewhere hidden. We'll spend a lot of time crossing the desert and back, and by then the Zovarians will have figured we took a different route. They could be expecting us when we return."

"Then let's look fur a secret cove," Siffo said, nodding eagerly. "*Fjummomurr* can hide like a black-winged swallow 'tween steep walls."

It was dark out by the time they exited the 'tween deck. The ship's black sails looked particularly eerie against the starlight, much more so now that all of the pharoliths had been covered to make their new course invisible to prying eyes.

"You didn't say a word during the meeting," Sterjall said as he followed Alaia to the bow of the ship.

"Sounded like a sound plan," she said tersely, staring at the gloomy sea ahead. The wind was cold and unsteady.

"Is your neck—"

"It'll heal, it wasn't that deep, doesn't hurt at all. Sunu patched me up, don't worry."

Sterjall leaned closer, feeling the warmth of Alaia's body without touching her. He probed with his mask, feeling that Alaia was indeed in pain. He slowly took some of the pain into himself, just enough that she would not detect his intrusion.

"She deserved it," he mumbled.

Alaia didn't respond.

"If anyone deserved it, it was her," he righteously added. "We wouldn't have had to escape Zovaria if she hadn't turned us in. We wouldn't have been running away. Wouldn't have lost Abjus, Givra, Fulm, any of the sailors. I wish I had cut her throat before she even got close to you. But you were brave, you did what you needed to do."

"Did I? Maybe if I had waited, instead of playing the hero, she would've given up. She had nowhere to run, no way to defeat us any longer. I was reckless, I was angry, and… And I didn't mean to kill her. I grabbed the wrong fucking dart. I didn't want to kill anyone."

"We are at war. It was going to happen, sooner or later."

"It doesn't make it any easier."

"No, it doesn't," Sterjall murmured, half to himself. "Not… Not the first time. That first time hurts." He held still in the wavering breeze, not wanting to dwell on the image of the first person he killed. Instead, he pictured a pearlescent-white brightness—a glow that enveloped him and pushed through him and became one with the sea itself.

"We must stop our enemies without losing ourselves in the process," he recited.

Alaia glanced curiously at him.

"It's something Mamóru told me. And perhaps I should've better listened to his advice. I still get… angry. I just want these assholes to pay for what they've done, but… But you are right. We need to be better than this. Sometimes there is no choice, but we still need to try to be better than them."

"He was a wise old mammoth."

"That he was," Sterjall sighed, breathing out the words as he placed a comforting arm around her. "I just hope we can make him proud."

CHAPTER THREE

SUNU'S VISION

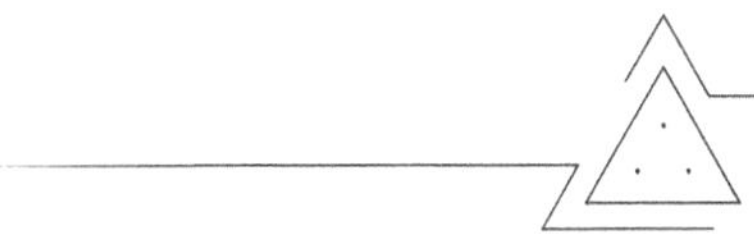

Fjummomurr changed course, taking refuge in the vast blueness of the Esduss Sea. They sailed day and night without disturbance, until the top of the Azurean Dome became visible on the far southwestern horizon, although it was still barely a dim, curved haze.

It was their first day with direct sunlight since they'd left the Varanus Dome. Lago was shirtless, enjoying the flowing breeze next to Aio. They were sitting atop the quarterdeck, which had been hastily repaired by the crew.

Aio had taken his shodog off to more fully relish the breeze. He kept his kilt on, but that did not impede the breeze from cooling off all his smooth, hidden places. "How far does your scalp think it is?" he asked Lago.

Lago put the binoculars down. "Maybe two hundred miles? The domes are so tall that, on clear days like this one, you can see them from that far away. Crysta once told me there's something of an optical illusion, a kind of mirage, which sometimes lets you see the domes from even farther. I hope that's not what we're seeing."

"Optical illusion? Like a ghost?"

"Something like it. It's the way the atmosphere refracts the light coming from the dome, like how boats sometimes seem to float above water when they are very distant."

"Or why Sceres flattens when she sinks into the water?" Aio asked, pointing west. The waning crescent held weightless near the horizon, like a scimitar cut from jade.

"I think so. It's all related somehow."

"She also changes colors, sometimes, my eyes have seen. Close to the horizon, she warms herself."

"You should see her during an eclipse, when her atmosphere glows deep magenta. Do you know what an eclipse is?"

"No. You have not shown me eclipse."

"I've only seen eclipses of Sceres, but not of Sunnokh, not a full one, at least. But Crysta's seen it happen twice. They are very rare. Sunnokh is much farther from us than Sceres, and sometimes they line up so that Sceres blocks his light and casts her shadow straight on us, and that's when we get an eclipse. The sky turns black for a long moment, and so does Sceres. But around her she gets this vibrant ring as her atmosphere turns a bright magenta."

"Is it because Sunnokh sets behind her and wraps her in sunsets?"

"Exactly! She gets a sunset all around her at once. But unlike our sunsets, which are orange and red, hers is more purple. Crysta says that likely means that the sky in Sceres is not blue, but closer to green, like the color of her atmosphere. Can you imagine that? I very much want to see that someday. An eclipse, I mean. I don't think I'll get to see the skies of Sceres."

"Me too," Aio said. "There is much I still want to see, with you."

They held hands and leaned back, letting the breeze cool their necks.

I am so glad to have you with me, Lago thought, and wondered why he did not say so out loud.

He closed his eyes for a relaxing moment. When he opened them again, he looked up to the crow's nest. Sunu was sitting there, cross-legged, eyes tightly closed. Olo was drifting above them effortlessly, like a kite.

"Do you think they are asleep?" Lago asked.

"Maybe. Sunu sleeps weird. But sometimes not asleep, sometimes meditating. They are having a hard time finding out who they are."

"I always thought Sunu would have it easier. Shamans are so in touch with animals already, I thought they'd know exactly what to look for."

"Sunu is not normal shaman. Normal shaman does not take life, does not hunt. Sunu chose different path. They are good teacher, but they also need time to learn their own lessons."

"Are all Laatu allgenders like them? I mean… During the ritual, when they entered naked into the circle, it's like they had both sexes in one."

"That is rare, too. I never knew until that day. Like they always lived two lives—one we know about, one which is hidden."

Lago bounced his eyes between Sunu's solemn figure and Olo's flapless wings.

Sunu kept Kruwensilv between their crossed legs.

Sunu dreamed.

Their legs were tired, their back ached. They walked through a valley of green rocks and red rivers. In their right hand they held Kruwensilv, but the mask was made of water, though somehow they could still hold it as if it was solid. They walked steadily upon the green rocks, which seemed too regular, broken into diamond-shaped bricks. The valley narrowed into a box canyon, as a slit between two green walls. Sunu had to scrape their small breasts to fit through. Red waters gurgled by their feet, as cold as the snowmelt of Stelm Humenath, sending a crawling chill up their spine.

As they reached the end of the confined passage, they found themself on a cliffside overlooking a distant, enormous eyeball, which protruded from the green valleys and canyons and reached miles into the heavens, like a glossy dome. The starry sky illuminated everything in dim but sharp clarity, reflecting itself in the eye, turning it into a scintillating star map. The slitted eye turned to look down upon Sunu and saw that they were naked. Sunu felt the eye in her slit, in his penis, in their breasts, questioning Sunu's ambivalence and self-deprecation.

Sunu looked down in shame and saw blood dripping between their legs. They reached down and pulled from themself a mangled fetus; incomplete, reptilian-looking, with downy feathers glued to its body. There was no heart-beat, no life. The fetus turned to dust, leaving Sunu with nothing but loneliness. They held Kruwensilv in front of their crotch to cover themself, but the watery substance only refracted and mixed their confounding pieces even further. Sunu put the mask on their face to hide their tears—the droplets became one with the reptilian Silv, adding to its essence.

The slitted eye glared. The elongated pupil dilated, threatening to suck away all light. After a condemnatory pause, it blinked its third, translucent eyelid. The motion of the enormous nictitating membrane was of such scale that it spawned a hurricane, lifting Sunu off the green cliffside and tossing them into the blackness of space. As they floated away from the eye, they saw the rest of the mountain they had been standing on: the slot canyon was merely the space between two scales of a continent-sized alligator. The dome that was its eye became smaller in the distance and paled in comparison to another dome: Mindreldrolom, which the alligator wore upon its back like a turtle's shell. The gator whipped its tail and floated away into forgetfulness. Sunu saw it all, refracted through the mask, as if underwater.

They heard a *crack* as they landed on a bed of branches and fuzzy feathers. They found themself inside an inverted dome made of twigs. It smelled like shit. Right next to them were two other domes, smaller, smoother, light blue, dotted with brown specks; they were the two halves of the egg they had just hatched from. Sunu looked up and saw their own face looking down at them. Their other, larger self reached into the nest and grabbed the smaller Sunu, in the same way they had once taken Olo from his nest. The larger Sunu squeezed a berry in their fingertips and fed them the acrid pulp, then squatted down. Sitting on the large hand, Sunu saw a requiem of splattered feathers on the mossy ground: blue and black. Was it their mother? Or was it their father? They could not tell.

The larger Sunu plucked an earthworm from the ground and let it snake into the smaller Sunu's belly. They enjoyed it, and swallowed it whole, feeling it wriggle inside of them. Then the larger Sunu lifted their hand up into the sky and released them, and then they were gone. Sunu was left alone in the air once more, letting their blue feathers catch the warm currents.

It felt so good to fly. It felt right; it felt comfortable. It gave them distance from the rest of the world. They screeched *eihnk-eihnk!* and landed atop a tall banyan tree, taking off their watery mask to turn back to their human self. *But that is not who I am*, their mind said, in the first person, surprising itself. *I am not a bird. The mask that chose me is that of reptiles. I wish I could be a bird, but that is not the path given to me.* They lifted the mask and drank it, gulping until the form disappeared into their belly and not a drop was left.

They felt the conflict bubble within their veins. They felt their legs weaken and fail. Blood began to seep from their pores. They fell upon the white sand of a familiar beach, with legs bleeding, broken, half eaten. Near them they saw two varanus dragons fighting, blood streaking from their pink gums. They thought the beasts looked grotesque, malicious, impure. The dragons tumbled in clouds of white sand until one snapped the other's neck. The victor walked toward Sunu, with a flicking tongue scenting the iron in their dripping blood.

The dragon chewed on the remains of Sunu's torn legs, then began to eat their ribcage. Sunu took a poison dart from their sleeves and lifted it to defend themself, about to pierce it into the dragon's neck. The dragon stopped and looked at them with cold eyes, thinking nothing, knowing nothing, feeling nothing. Sunu held the dart tightly, then brought it to their own neck instead. They took one last breath of satisfaction as they died, knowing they had spared the vile creature's life.

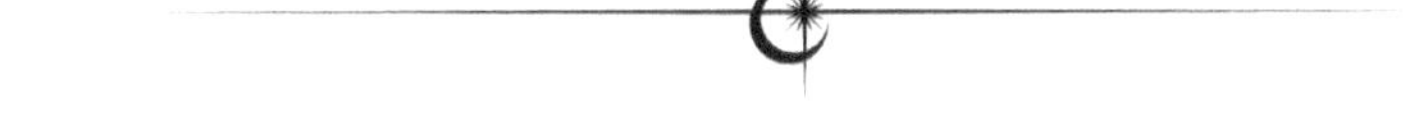

Sunu woke up gasping for air.

The breeze evaporated the sweat on their purple-tinted scalp. Their eyes gazed upward, toward Olo, who still floated above them, like a shadow that would follow them anywhere.

Cobalt Shores

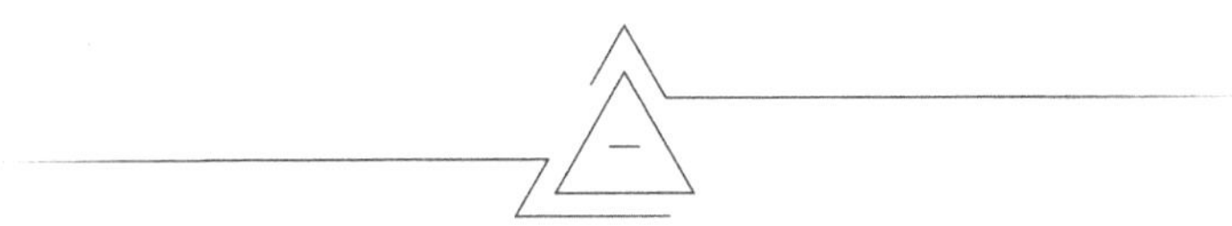

"Still nothing. We should be seeing land already," Sterjall muttered as he leaned on one of the harpoon cannons, trying to get a good look at the western horizon.

Siffo stood next to him, scanning with the binoculars. "Nothing t'see but d'dome's snowy top so far."

The sun had just risen, tinting the top of the Azurean Dome in orange flames. The dome's reflection smeared itself in the choppy waters. They hit a rolling wave, which threw Sterjall off balance as the harpoon cannon tilted forward on its carriage, almost dropping him into the sea.

"Watch out, wulf Lorr," the captain said. "Flip that lever to lock it in place."

Sterjall locked the ancient-looking harpoon cannon, then examined it more closely. It was meticulously ornamented, yet had no pharoliths embedded into it, which was the primary way the Puqua added decorations to their most luxurious possessions.

"Do you have a lot of whales in Nagradrolom?" he asked.

"Not very many. Some belugas, beaked whales, narwhals. Them say in d'past, whales were as big as *Fjummomurr* itself!"

"They still are! The kinds you mentioned are quite small, but near Withervale, I've seen humpback whales and killer whales, though only a few times. Blue whales are the biggest. I've never seen one, but they would be bigger than this whole ship."

"So them survived d'Downfall? I'd love t'see one mineself someday. What a wunder t'behold! N'fret not, m'lad, fur this 'ere 'poon cannon is not fur hunting. Whales are precious, smart creatures. That's why we named this ship d'*Tusked Whale*. Our ancestors used t'hunt them with these weapons, but we've changed our ways."

"Then why have harpoon cannons at all?"

"These beauties are antiques, frum times before d'Downfall. *Fjummomurr* is not that old, but we keep some relics like these fur sports. Such as a-hunting fur Negian ships!" Siffo elbowed Sterjall and bellowed a heavy chortle. "Have ye ever participated in a 'pooning regatta?"

"I have no idea what that is," Sterjall confessed.

"That's what these 'ere 'poons are fur. It's d'greatest pastime in Nagradrolom. Very competitive we are. Each port joins with one ship. Frum Atêmmo, to Gmunnog, Liyam, Zichee, Arho, Skrummo, n'several uthers, including them cheating plain-skins frum Nibsal. *Fjummomurr* plays fur Ôllomuy. We all meet at d'port uf Birlénno n'sail together, seeing who can hunt mour buoys."

"Buoys? Like floating markers?"

"Aye, 'fore d'race starts, hundred uf buoys are set afloat around d'islands where d'Keldris Klannath n'd'Keldris Allastirg meet. It's a race t'see who can pick d'most uf them. D'largest ones ye can only pick with 'poon cannons like these, worth mour points. Smaller ones can be caught by any sailor with hand-hurled 'poons. There are even some secret buoys weighed down by anchors, hard t'spot, worth mour points than any uthers. We must launch d'poons through d'water to snatch those, or swim under t'get them."

"That sounds really fun. Must take a lot of coordination."

"It is. It does. That's why ships like this one are built fur speed, we've been a-working un it fur a long time. We've won d'regatta four times thus far. I could boast all day 'bout mine crew n'mine lovely *Tusked Whale*." Captain Siffo glanced proudly toward the shining tusk of the narwhal figurehead.

"I think I see something up ahead," Sterjall warned, pointing toward the dome. Where the dome met its reflection, in a mirage of white caps and soft haze, a dark line appeared.

Siffo nodded, tightening his tricorn hat over his pointed ears. "Land ahead, at last."

"How close to Lhambor Di do you think we are?"

"Hard t'tell without better measurements n'a mour detailed map. It could be north uf us, or south. Might as well head straight t'shore n'see what we find."

A bizarre landscape was gradually revealed as they approached the great island of Fel Baubór. There was no shoreline, but only a length of vertical cliffs hundreds of feet tall. The sea stacks and walls reminded Sterjall of the chalk cliffs of Needlecove, near Crysta's old home; these were not white formations though, but glossy black, with dark-blue bands crossing through their centers. The blue striations sparkled and had more striations of their own, in shifting tones of indigo, cerulean, and hints of turquoise.

Siffo ordered his crew to veer to port and follow the cliffs. "There's nowhere t'dock among them walls. South we go, till a shore we find!"

For miles they continued, finding no place for the ship to rest. The cliffs remained as impassable as they were unwelcoming. As they came around a promontory, they saw to starboard a lighthouse that had been hidden from view. It was shaped like a five-sided pyramid, blue and black in color, emerging from the rocks like a glassy spur.

"T-that's one of the lighthouses from Lhambor Di," the prisoner Alid called out, still tied to the foremast. "If you let us jump here, we can swim to safety, and we won't bother you, we won't say a word."

"What d'ye think?" Siffo quietly asked Sterjall.

"We can't. Not until we return from the Azurean Dome. They would give away too much information." He walked over to Alid and squatted by his side. *I wish we didn't have to treat you like this,* he thought, feeling through his mask just how much the prisoner was suffering, how much he feared him. "Sorry, Alid," he said, "but you'll have to stay with us until we are ready to move on. We'll make you and your friend a bit more comfortable, but you'll still be tied up."

Alid nodded in a voiceless mix of disappointment and gratitude.

They kept parallel to the cliff until they found themselves before a bay flecked with fishing ships of all kinds. Farther in, the bay ended in a blue-sand beach, and just past the beach, the natural cliff walls had been carved into an architectural wonder of windows, statues, arches, and colonnades. Two wedge-shaped towers soared over the sandstone formation, tapering toward their sparkling blue tops.

"Keep moving past the bay!" Sterjall urged. "We don't want all those eyes on us."

They crossed the bay as fast as possible, reaching a twin lighthouse that framed the mouth of the inlet.

"D'ye think any uf them saw us?" Siffo asked.

"Can't be certain," Sterjall replied, "but if any of those fishing crews spotted these black sails, they'll have enough tales to tell for generations."

A few dozen more miles ahead, the cliffs' impassable edges broke apart into a series of headlands, arches, canyons, and coves. They found no signs of habitation or any safe place to dock, but Siffo pointed to a teetering formation that showed promise.

"That arch yonder seems t'open into a river canyon. It could offer cover, fresh water, mayhap a place to dock."

With utmost care, *Fjummomurr* sailed beneath the blue curve and entered the canyon beyond it. They meandered around goosenecks until, about a mile in, the channel expanded into a cove. The dark sand had eroded into a soft beach, making the waters too shallow to travel. They dropped anchors and lowered the cockboat.

At first, the beach seemed composed entirely of black sand, but as the cockboat slid into the shallows and cut through the granules, it revealed a piercing blue beneath the black. The travelers disembarked, leaving bright-blue footprints atop the black surface, then climbed up an eroded bluff in search of a vantage point.

The flatness above had no trees, but the colorful sands were sprinkled with dune grasses, short shrubs, and tracks of small animals. The travelers plodded up to the highest point they could find and looked west. The edges of the vibrant Cobalt Desert spread before them for uncountable miles. It was a landscape of infinite blueness, teeming with outlandish succulents and cacti. On the horizon was a band of black and blue, cutting across their view: an elongated mesa, creating an almost too perfectly flat base for the Azurean Dome to seemingly rest upon. But the wayfarers were not fooled; they knew the dome did not actually sit upon the relatively close mesa, but lay about a hundred miles beyond it.

"My eyes see no sand dunes," Kulak remarked. "Only sandstone and cracked grounds."

"There's a lot we can't see beyond that mesa," Sterjall said. He poked at a spiraling succulent with his footpaw. "At least there seems to be plenty of life around here, even if it's of unusual kinds."

"I shell send scouts t'explore d'canyons n'headlands," Captain Siffo said. "Let's gather by d'map n'make some plans."

The Puqua scouts returned after a few hours, having found no human tracks or signs of danger. They decided the cove would be a safe place for *Fjummomurr*, as there was good fishing, a few edible plants, and even some strange-looking rodents and birds they could hunt. Although the scouts had not found a source of fresh water nearby—the canyon's water was too brackish to drink—they still had plenty in their wooden casks, and they also had plenty of strong braaw to keep the water from growing moldy, or to replenish the crew's spirits every now and then.

It was decided that Captain Siffo should stay with his crew to wait for Olo, who would fly a message to let him know once the wayfarers had reached the dome, and another at the time they began their return. Sterjall and Kulak would travel atop Blu, and Sunu and Alaia atop Pichi. They would carry limited supplies: mostly water, munnji cakes, dried foods, and their weapons. Ishke'ísuk was glad to go as well, and he would perch wherever he saw fit.

"One hundred miles does not sound like too much for our swift cats," Sunu said, "but we should remain cautious, for we know not what lies beyond the blue mesa."

They estimated their travel time, packed their gear, and prepared one last feast for dinner. At the break of dawn, they would begin their journey across the Cobalt Desert.

What had seemed like flatlands from afar were anything but. The top surfaces were flat, but the land cracked open in confusing canyons filled with soft sand. There was no way to traverse the canyons other than to slide in and then crawl out on the opposite sides, but with the sandstone being less tightly compacted at the eroded edges, it was difficult for the cats to use their claws to climb back up.

Though the day was not particularly warm, Sunnokh was unrelenting in the cloudless sky, draining their energies. At midday, worn out from all the sliding and scrambling, they took shelter in a secluded gully. The cats went out to hunt. Pichi returned with a straight-horned antelope with gorgeous black-and-white patterns on his face and legs.

"Great catch!" Sterjall said. "I didn't expect such large animals to be found in the desert."

"What is this creature?" Sunu asked.

"It's an oryx," Alaia answered.

"Pichi says she picked it from a herd one hundred strong," Kulak informed them. "Though she knows not how to count. It is just expression for large numbers."

They grilled the oryx, burning dried-up cactus skeletons for a fire. After they enjoyed the mild and finely textured meat, they let the cats take a well-deserved nap.

Kulak was resting on Blu's belly when he noticed Sterjall following an invisible trail in the gully, searching. His tufted ears perked up.

"Don't mind him," Alaia said. "He's searching for a stoneleaf."

"What is stoneleaf?"

"A plant we used to have at our place. A ruby-flecked stoneleaf, to be precise, that's what Lerr Holfster called them. They were born here in Bauram, where the plants grow. Stoneleaves look a bit like a smooth stone."

Kulak immediately stood and began to search as well.

Sterjall was exploring a dry wash sprinkled with river rocks when he sensed the caracal behind him. His ears pivoted, but his eyes kept probing the sand.

"Is this the plant your eyes seek?" Kulak asked, holding up a thornless, disc-shaped cactus.

"How did you know…" he began to ask, then saw Alaia rummaging through a pile of rocks nearby. "No, that's a cactus. The ones I'm looking for look more like dark-blue pebbles split in half, with red dots all over them. And they are much smaller."

Kulak's whiskers slumped with disappointment. He replanted the cactus back where he found it and moved on.

"I swear I'll find one before you do," Alaia said, standing up and shaking the dust off her overalls' legs.

"What is so special about these stone plants you seek?" Sunu asked, strolling next to Ishke'ísuk while the Nu'irg hunted for insects. "What ailments do they cure?"

"They are not medicinal, as far as I know," Sterjall replied. "They only grow in blue sand and are very hard to take care of, and I had done a respectable job of growing one for six years in Withervale. It's just a good memory from those days. I would like to see one in the wild, where it truly belongs. The one I had was a gift a good friend gave me, a kind botanist who sold plants near my school."

"Sold plants?" Sunu asked, fondling the fire opal octahedron that dangled from their neck—what the Laatu used to sign ledgers instead of trading Qupi chips. "Why do your people sell or buy plants?"

"Because they are pretty. Succulents like the one I'm looking for we consider exotic, and it just made me happy to have one. We don't have weird plants growing out of every crevice like you do in your dome."

"Your people are strange," Sunu muttered.

"This one looks kind of like it," Alaia said, pointing at a pebble-like succulent.

Sterjall leaned down to inspect it. He had to agree; it was very similar to his old stoneleaf, but it was black as quaar and did not have red dots over it.

"That is a stoneleaf alright, but not the right kind," he said. "Kulak, check this one out, that's how they should look, sort of."

They kept searching among the whimsical plants, but could not find the one Sterjall's memories treasured.

The cracked flatlands stretched beyond sight, populated by sparse yet diverse oases of life where all manner of sneaky rodents hid, predatory birds hovered, and intimidating arachnids set their traps. On their journey west they discovered tasty cactus fruits they could eat as long as they first burned the hair-like spines, as well as a blue tuber that tasted like a salty watermelon, but many other plants they chose not to risk eating. Their Silvesh helped them find hidden life underground, and soon they also discovered a freshwater spring that flowed several feet beneath the blue sandstone—they were able to bathe in it, after Pichi clawed her way down to make the water sprout up like a fountain.

"This might be our last chance to find food and water," Sunu warned, covered in dark-blue mud that was turning a lighter blue as it dried over their smooth body. They heeded the shaman's warning and refilled their waterskins, bags, and bellies before moving on.

Sunnokh had just hid behind the crest of the Azurean Dome by the time they reached the blue mesa. Alaia looked up at the sandstone wall; it was covered in striations of black and dozens of tones of blue. A hint of purple also streaked there, though only in dim strands. "How are we going to get up this wall?" she asked.

"We can worry about that tomorrow," Sterjall said. "Let's camp here. The dome's shadow has brought with it a sudden chill—it's going to be a cold night."

Sterjall struck the brime on his bracer, shooting out a lingering constellation of white sparks. The dried-up cacti caught fire quickly. They cooked the blue tubers, wishing Nalaníri was there to prepare them in a truly special fashion.

That evening, as the bonfire sputtered and died, the last hints of warmth evaporated so abruptly that they could almost hear it happen. Sterjall pulled out a blanket and cuddled up between Kulak and Blu. Alaia borrowed Pichi's enormous arm for a pillow and sank herself into the smilodon's chest fur. Sunu slept sitting up, resting their back against the mesa's cold wall.

It was a crackling-cold morning, with Sunnokh still napping in the east, when Sterjall awoke to muscles tight from the cold. He had not had a good night's sleep, and he was not warm enough to want to rise, but a darkening beyond his heavy eyelids told him to open his eyes. "What is it?" he asked as he found Sunu squatting next to him and poking at his side. Their freckled face held an expression that urged Sterjall to stay quiet.

Sterjall pushed his blanket over Kulak, then slowly sat up. Sunu used their lips to point at something farther along the base of the mesa, where Sterjall spotted four dog-like figures staring in their direction.

"Sunu believes they feel Agnargsilv," Sunu whispered. "They have been waiting there for nearly an hour. Unmoving, like the statues in front of Ommo ust Mindrel."

The strange canids were at the edge of Agnargsilv's perception. It was still too dark for Sterjall's eyes to see much more than their dim silhouettes. He got up without disturbing Kulak or Blu. The canids shuffled their feet, ears attentive, heads rising over outstretched necks.

Perhaps I'll finally figure out how this works, Sterjall thought, still embarrassed that he'd not yet learned how to mindspeak. He had managed, many a time, to express emotions to other canids, to tell them he was a friend, or not to fear, or to give thanks to them, but he had yet to breach that last barrier of full comprehension. He did what he knew how to do and projected toward the figures a sense of friendliness, of welcoming warmth, of acceptance.

The four canids felt Sterjall's call and came rushing to the camp, emitting high-pitched chirps that sounded like a mix of bird calls and the whining of a young dog. Kulak, Alaia, Pichi, and Blu all scrambled to their feet. The pack stopped, terrified of the big cats.

"What's going on?" Alaia asked.

"Shh, stay still," Sterjall replied. "It's a pack of... What are they?"

Alaia craned her neck for a better view. "I think they are spotted wild dogs," she guessed. "I saw a drawing of them in Hefra's books once. Look at those huge ears!"

"Blu and Pichi won't hurt them," Kulak said to reassure Sterjall. "Call for them, they seem friendly."

Sterjall took a careful step forward. "It's alright, you can come closer."

The wild dogs trotted to him, chirping and whining. They rubbed their wet noses, their enormous, round ears, and their black, yellow, and white marbled fur all over Sterjall's legs and handpaws.

"They make really weird sounds," Alaia said, "but they do look gorgeous. Are you practicing on them?"

"Yeah. Sorry," Sterjall said distractedly. "They seem friendly. Can't hurt to have them around."

They ate a slim breakfast while the spotted dogs watched. Sunu tried to share some of their food with the dogs, but they cared not for cold tubers or munnji.

"I guess it's about time to get going," Sterjall said, looking up the mesa's wall. "Let's follow south until we find a way up." He glanced at the dogs. "Come on, you can follow along if you like."

As they walked parallel to the wall, Sterjall kept looking up at it, thinking of ways to overcome the obstacle.

Wrong way, something deep in his mind told him, just as a honking sound brought him to a halt. Sterjall turned to see that the dogs had stopped. One of them made the odd sound once more; it reminded Sterjall more of a goose's honk than a dog's bark.

"They seem tense," Alaia said. "What do they—"

"Quiet," Sterjall said. "Hold on." He looked up at the wall again and let his mind wander into a reflexive self-dialogue. *I need to get up there,* he thought.

Wrong way, the voice in his head explained again, though it was more of a feeling than the two specific words. This time the voice, the thought, was clearer.

But that's where we must go! he thought, trying to recall how it had felt when they had communed with Noss. That had been mindspeech of a sort, but Noss was a different kind of intelligence, and Sterjall had not been himself then, but six consciousnesses in one. Yet he *had* learned something from that experience, and this feeling now fizzing in his gut felt similar. *We must reach the top of the mesa,* he insisted within his mind.

A dog honked—or barked—once more.

«*Wrong way,*» the voice that was not a voice said again, and this time it was oddly directional, orienting itself toward the pack of wild dogs, and it carried much more meaning than two words could. It carried fear within it, it delivered silty scents, the essence of blueness, a twinkle of starlight, and a biting cold.

Can you hear me? Sterjall probed from the depths of his self, reaching into the marrow of meanings, into the threaded connections that words, life, consciousness, matter, and mind shared. «Can you understand me?»

«Yes,» all four dogs mindspoke as one.

"I did it!" Sterjall yapped, scaring the dogs, and even making Blu flinch by his side. "I can mindspeak!" He rushed toward the dogs, who seemed a bit disconcerted by his outburst, and perhaps embarrassed for him. "It's like they are in my head, in my bones, like we are, like—" He squatted, squinted, and clearly communicated, «I am Agnargfröa.»

The dogs blinked, puzzled as to why something so obvious needed to be stated.

«We are searching for a way across the desert, for a path to the Azurean Dome,» he tried to explain, but the desert was the entire world for the dogs, and the dome only a distant form as abstract as the horizon, as unreachable as the stars; they did not grasp what he meant.

Sterjall felt frustrated, so he tried a more polite approach. «What are your names?» he asked, but the dogs became even more perplexed. Their scents, their sounds, those were their names. Could the Agnargfröa not smell them? Had he not heard their voices?

Sterjall turned around. "They, they don't seem to understand what I—"

"It is confusing with wild animals," Kulak explained. "Easier with Blu, Pichi, companion species who fed from idshall-munnji. But keep trying, your scalp will understand. Do not speak your words, let them feel you, let them know you."

Sterjall focused again, this time forgetting about sentences, about making a request, or even about having a conversation. Words were human things, and the less he thought about them, the closer he came to understanding the animals in front of him. He sensed their thoughts were scattered, yet there was a simplicity there he could grasp. There was a sense of need, of warmth, of family emanating from them.

«Pack and wolf are of one heart,» he mindspoke, if not in a sentence. But the feeling, what the words truly meant, that was communicated clear as glacial waters. Young and old, large and small, frail and strong—he was himself and he was them all.

«Yes,» one of the dogs replied. «We are pack. We take care of one another.» She expressed it almost like an invitation.

«This… This is my pack,» Sterjall replied, not having to look behind him to convey his meaning. «I want to protect them,» he said, «but we have to… to find a way to a place far away. Can I tell you our story? Can I share why we are here?»

The dogs agreed to listen, even if they could not fully grasp the complexities of the situation; what mattered was that they felt the urgency, and that they understood that this new pup needed shelter, needed guidance.

An hour later—although to Sterjall's mind mere moments had elapsed—he concluded his conversation and related to his friends how much progress he'd made with his mindspeech. He'd found there were two separate modes for 'hearing' the canids. One was active, as he tried to feel the emotions of the dogs. In the active mode, he found that one dog was hungry, one was tired, one felt terrified of the smilodons, and one was bored and wanting to move on—they were not saying those things to him directly, but Agnargsilv read the threads of those core emotions in the same way it could read anyone else's emotions, but with more clarity when it came to creatures of its own clade.

The other mode was passive for Sterjall, requiring an active involvement from the dogs themselves. In this mode, Sterjall simply felt in his mind what the dogs consciously wanted to tell him, with the thoughts oftentimes taking visual or olfactory forms. It was more than a process of listening, more akin to interpreting emotions and imagery that came with their own jumbled non-syntax. It reminded him of how he could think of multiple ideas at the same time but not necessarily be thinking of the words that represented those ideas, or how he could recall a location in a dream yet couldn't see individual details of the location, but only muster the general impression the location etched in his memories.

"I'm so happy you have it figured out," Alaia said. "Can you imagine what it'll be like to talk to Bear this way? No, actually, it would probably be quite dumb."

"I miss Bear so much," Sterjall said as he scratched one of the spotted dogs along the neck. "I'd listen to him mindspeak about whatever he wanted. For hours. I swear." His eyes drifted to the cold sand.

"Have you asked them how to get up onto the mesa?" Sunu inquired.

"I did. They told me there is no path up the way we were headed, not for a very long while. But there's something, a space, hollow… It's something vertical… I can feel it, but what's the word—a box canyon?" As soon as he thought of the idea of a box canyon, it was as if the message the dogs had been trying to communicate found a match. The meaning became clearer, and the mental image attached itself to the corresponding words. "Farther north, there's a cut in the sandstone that leads up. They are asking that we follow them."

The spotted dogs led the way.

Some miles north, the wayfarers reached a stack of toppled boulders that piled over a silty, dried creek. The dogs went under the jumble of rocks, while the cats carried the riders over the obstacle, as they would not have fit in the tight spaces below. They dropped into a wide crack that kept narrowing, with the walls stretching straight up. Turquoise pebbles and rounded boulders poked out of the darker substrate, revealed by millennia of water and wind erosion; Pichi's thick body dislodged the rocky inclusions as she scraped between the sandstone walls. Blu had to twice push his head against Pichi's behind to help her fit through the narrowest spots.

The box canyon split and turned, but always ascended, revealing new, colorful strata as they reached higher elevations. When they at last reached the top, they did not find the flat ground they were expecting, but a gentle slope. What had looked like a flat mesa in the distance was actually a diagonal uplift of land. From its peak, the uplift dipped westward in a shallow incline, until at the very bottom it merged with pristine, curvaceous sand dunes.

"There they are," Kulak said to Sterjall. "Blue sand dunes, like you promised me."

"And black ones too," Alaia added. "Quite the opposite of the White Desert of Dorhond. It is so vast…"

The dunes went on forever, and far beyond them, despite the long journey, the Azurean Dome did not yet seem any closer.

Sterjall explored with his binoculars. "There are other formations past the dunes. Pointed hills of some sort."

«Badlands,» said a voice in his head, communicating fear and uncertainty. Sterjall looked down at the spotted dogs, listening.

"They are telling me we should stay here. There's food here, but only death in the dunes, death in the badlands beyond them."

"Ask them if there is a way to avoid death," Kulak suggested. "An easier path."

Sterjall communicated the question, but he imbued it with all manner of emotions, gravity, and even perceptual details he wasn't sure the dogs could grasp. They mostly understood.

«No,» was their concise reply. «Only desert lies beyond, nothing more. Dogs do not venture there.»

Sterjall could feel the dryness and heat in their non-words. "They are saying they do not know of a way across," he interpreted. He then mindspoke to the dogs while also speaking the words out loud. "We have to go that way," he said, pointing to the dunes. "We need to reach the dome." He found it easier to focus on what to say this way, as his spoken words set his mind in the right space.

«Desert is death,» the dogs said as one. «Stay. Good food, shelter. We feed you, protect you. We can be pack here.»

Sterjall shook his head, only then realizing the dogs would not understand the gesture. "Thank you for showing us the way, but that is where we must go."

The dogs held still, uncertain, worried for him and his friends. The leader of the pack shook her ears and turned. Without another mindspoken thought, the dogs returned to the box canyon.

They did not look back.

CHAPTER FIVE

THE BLUE DESERT

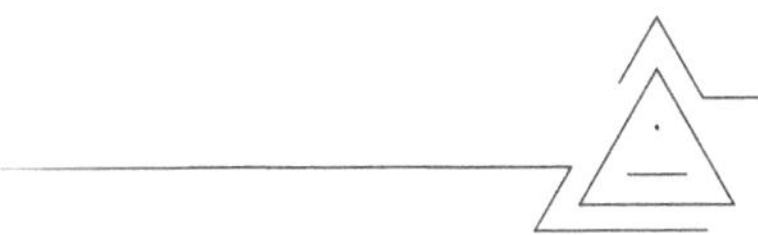

The sloped mesa ended abruptly at their feet, the blue sandstone sinking beneath a pristinely black dune. As the cats stepped onto it, the surface crunched and broke apart, as if held together by the most brittle of crystals. Blue sand sparkled underneath, just as it had beneath the ebony sand at the beach. The wayfarers climbed atop the dune, with the wind at their backs, and followed the serpentine crest, leaving blue paw prints behind. They noticed that the leeward slipfaces of the dunes tended to be bluer, while the windward shoulders picked up more of the black granules, though some dunes were black to their cores or purely one of many variations of blue.

Their progress was sluggish and tedious. The crests offered the best view ahead and the most solid surface to trudge upon, but it made their trek longer and windier. They tried for a while to follow the slacks between dunes, but the sloughing sands were so soft that they nearly swallowed the cats whole.

When night came, they could find no shelter other than the slope of a tall dune where the wind did not strike them as harshly, yet it constantly dropped sand on them from the dune's crest. The gusts blew noisily, bringing with them the deep cold of the desert in Umbra. They cuddled up next to the cats and awoke half-buried in sand.

They slogged on toward the remote dome, which remained distant no matter their efforts. They slept in the cold once more, unable to make a fire due to the wind, having to hold on to their brime cubes for warmth. The next day was warmer, which felt comforting in the morning but dreadfully hot by the afternoon.

"Do you see that?" Alaia asked, shielding her eyes as she squinted toward the dome.

"It's just a mirage," Sterjall said, scouting with his binoculars as they let the smilodons rest. The dome seemed to float on an ocean, with the dark sands rippling their heat underneath it.

"No, not that. There's something brighter between those two dunes." She pointed.

The focusing ring on Sterjall's binoculars ground against accumulated sand, but he was able to resolve the sparkle in the distance. "It's... It looks like a buried building. Ruins!"

"Forsaken temples hidden under sand," Kulak said with a grin. He tapped on Blu's shoulder. "We go! My eyes need to see what hides within them."

As they hurried toward the ruins, the shadow of the dome began to encroach upon the desert. It was getting too cold, too windy, the sound of the blowing sand roaring as it drifted sideways and upward, finding its way into every crevice.

The first sign of remnants they found was a small triangle of white protruding from the side of a dune. Sterjall hurriedly wiped off sand to uncover what seemed to be a square-carved brick, perhaps the corner of a building. They soon found more bricks and realized the white rocks were the capitals of dozens of columns from a long colonnade, which together marked the path toward the building they had spotted earlier. As the dunes dipped lower, the columns were further revealed, leading them to a marble staircase so bright and crisp among the black and blue sands that it looked as if it was painted on with a palette knife. The steps invited them to climb a narrowing structure where a wedge-shaped doorway yawned darkly. The front face of the building was mostly uncovered, and so was much of the roof, but they could not guess at how much more slept beneath the sands.

A blue dust devil was twirling at the bottom of the steps, playfully fiddling with flurries of sand before banishing them to the skies. They squinted at the blown dust as they approached the steps. The tall, temple-like face of the structure was ominous yet seductive. Cryptic glyphs were carved into the white walls, all filled with different colorations of deposited granules.

"We can take shelter in there!" Sterjall screamed over the howling gusts. The dust devil slapped them left and right, then twirled to the side as if granting temporary passage. They hurried up the steps and through the tall portal, and once inside, fully opened their eyes for the first time in hours.

"The wind does not sing through," Sunu noted. "Only one opening."

They took out their pharoliths and followed their cold light deeper into the building. Sand was piled up in every corner, but some of the complexly tiled grounds had been spared. Past an ornamental arch, the space widened into a square room with steps leading down—but the stairs only descended to a sand-filled pit.

The chamber echoed the howling from outside, yet the air within barely stirred.

The other three sides of the room also had steps sinking into the central chamber, as well as arches leading beyond. Alaia held a pharolith up and looked at the curved ceiling, which was decorated with geometric forms rising and falling in polygonal coffers replete with ancient carvings and diagrams. It all looked too alien, too sacred, too complex to understand.

"Whatever was down here is buried now," she said, stepping down into the sandpit. "I wonder how many treasures hide right here, right under my feet."

"I bet it has all been looted by now," Sterjall said.

"We will have to find out," Kulak added with a grin.

They hastily explored the remaining three passages. The ones to the left and right led to plundered shrines, where pottery shards lay scattered alongside pieces of marble from broken pedestals. Remains of an old campfire darkened one corner. The doorway directly across from the entrance burrowed deeper before splitting into multiple passages, most of them with spiraling steps leading down to nothing but sand.

"We could spend days exploring these tunnels," Sterjall said, running a handpaw over the images carved on a toppled monolith.

"Not wise to do," Sunu advised. "We have limited water, little food to spare. We came here not for ruins, but to reach Quajudrolom. Let us go back before we find ourselves lost."

They returned to the main chamber and settled down in the sandpit to make camp.

"We'll be safe here for tonight," Sterjall said. "At least we won't have to suffer those winds anymore."

"What if the whole place gets buried while we sleep?" Alaia asked.

"There's no way that much sand will shift in just a few hours. The doorway is too high. We'll be fine."

It was still early. The sun was behind the dome, not yet at the horizon, but the howling winds made it unpalatable to consider anything but taking shelter for what remained of the day. With their stash of dried cacti, they made a small fire. After an early, meager dinner, Sterjall reached for his bedroll and began to unroll it in a corner of the pit.

Kulak placed a handpaw on his shoulder. "I like the circular room in the other tunnel," he said. "We can make our beds there, then explore deeper before we fall asleep."

Sterjall's ears perked up. "Sure," he said.

"Ishke'ísuk and Sunu will go with you," Sunu said, "in case danger lurks."

Alaia intervened. "What about me? I need protection more than they do. Stay here, Sunu. I don't want to be left alone."

Sunu hesitated, then seemed to understand, and sat back down.

Kulak grabbed a pharolith lamp and led Sterjall into the tunnel.

The young men dropped their bedrolls in the circular room near the archway, then held handpaws as they ventured into the ruins. Much farther in, they entered a chamber that dropped lower, one which had not yet been completely swallowed by sand. They took the white steps down, careful not to slip on the blue granules of sand.

"You know," Sterjall idly commented, "I don't need to use my mask to read you right now, I only need my nose."

"What do you mean?"

"I may not be as good as Kitjári, but I have a much keener sense of smell than you do. When you are aroused, I can smell it on you."

Kulak turned to look at the sunken chamber, trying to hide his smile and embarrassment. "I smell bad?"

"No, you smell great. It arouses me, too," Sterjall said, and reached below Kulak's kilt, fondling his short tail.

Soon the lamp had been dropped, and the two were hurriedly undressing each other. The light of the pharolith bounced off the sand, tinting everything from their fur to the white marble columns and the glyph-covered walls in soft blues.

They had not enjoyed much privacy for a long time; *Fjummomurr* had offered a bit, but Puqua sailors tended to drink their braaw in the hold to unwind, leaving them no room to truly escape. At last, they were far enough away that no one could hear them, where no other Silvesh could spy on them through walls, where there was nothing but blue sand, their hurried breaths, and their tangled bodies.

Sterjall lifted Kulak and carried him to a pillar as they kissed. He leaned him against the stone and pushed his sheath between the caracal's legs, partially sliding inside him while still standing. "My legs are tired," he said through a chuckle, trying to hold Kulak up while also balancing and keeping his erection from slipping free.

Kulak grinned and leaned forward in a forceful kiss, making Sterjall drop tail-first onto the sand. The sudden bump made Sterjall's cock grow and tie them together, as they'd only been tied once before. Rather than yelp from the pressure or surprise, they both laughed.

"Stay in me," Kulak said, still sniggering.

"You tighten every time you laugh!" Sterjall half-complained. "You're going to make me finish if you keep doing that."

"Not finish yet," Kulak teased, trying to keep from laughing. "Hold me, like this."

They rolled onto their sides, face to face. Rather than pushing harder, Sterjall simply relaxed, feeling Kulak's warmth around him.

Kulak purred, feeling the knot pulse within him.

"What does it feel like?" Sterjall asked.

"Like you become part of me. Like you are holding me tight, and I have to give myself fully, and accept you, sharing your heartbeat. What does it feel like to you?"

"It feels like I'm probing deeper, expanding beyond my control. Like it is not me, but your desire that controls me. It feels good to let go, to give in to it."

Kulak's triangular nose was pressed against Sterjall's larger one. He stared with sly eyes. "Would you like to try it and learn how it feels?" he asked.

Sterjall's cock swelled simply from the thought of it.

"My tail thinks that means yes!" Kulak said as he laughed, not helping the situation.

"P-perhaps we could try it," Sterjall said reluctantly, forcing himself to unfocus his thoughts before he went too far. "But yours is… smaller. And not shaped in that way."

"That is not what I mean." Kulak did not blink. His dilated pupils were not oval shaped now, but perfectly round. "I know your scalp thinks about it, too."

Sterjall knew what he meant, and the excitement from the idea made his cock throb inside Kulak once more. The caracal winced and held his breath. "My tail hears yes once more," he said with a devious smile.

"It's… Yes, I've thought about it. But at the same time, the idea scares me."

"Why it scares you?"

"For starters, it's yet another thing the Miscam would want to kill us for."

"They have enough of those reasons, one more will make no difference."

"Do you think anyone's ever done it?"

"Not that my scalp knows. The Silvesh were kept apart. Different tribes, different lands, not mingling. Lives of the Silvfröash, always too public, too dangerous. But my scalp also feels the other fear, the one you have not mentioned."

Despite Sterjall's excitement, his fear had made his erection wane. Kulak released him without losing eye contact.

"I don't think the masks were meant to be swapped and shared," Sterjall began. "The first time I became Sterjall, it was as if Agnargsilv reshaped my mind, and I *became* Sterjall, whether I was wearing the mask or not. I still feel that way. I feel I am a man, a wolf. Not a felid."

"My scalp shares the same emotion. But perhaps it will be more like feeling not as yourself, but feeling as another. You will feel like Kulak feels, but you will not be Kulak, and you will know that." Kulak propped himself up on one elbow. "My scalp wants to know what it is like to be Sterjall. Perhaps only for one night. Perhaps more, if we both like it." His eyes glimmered.

They both sat up. Sterjall shook the sand off his ears as he considered the request. "Muh-maybe just once. And we shouldn't tell Sunu, or even Alaia. Assuming it will even work."

"If we try, we find out." Kulak shifted into Aio and removed Mindrelsilv. He sat there naked, his smooth skin glistening, his small erection still pulsing with eagerness. "Have you thought what forms you might become with other masks?"

"Many times. I think the first time must be the hardest, but by now I know what to look for, or more specifically, what the Silvesh look for. What do you think you'd be with Agnargsilv?"

"My scalp knows, but does not want to spoil the surprise." Aio tapped under Sterjall's muzzle, then pointed to him with his lips.

Sterjall shapeshifted into Lago, placed Agnargsilv on his lap, and sat nervously, nearly trembling. Aio handed him Mindrelsilv, then took Agnargsilv from him. Lago tensed as his mask left his hands.

"At same time?" Aio asked, lifting Agnargsilv close to his face.

Lago swallowed. "You do it first. Just in case something goes wrong. I want to be able to help you out of it."

Aio nodded. "Hold my hand."

Lago took the prince's hand and squeezed his fingers.

Aio placed Agnargsilv on his face. He felt a slight rush of pain, given that this Silv differed slightly from the one he was used to, yet it took him but a heartbeat to bring the pain under his control. He looked at Lago through the dark eyeholes, and in his mind he saw not Lago, but Sterjall. He felt the kinship toward the canids, a kinship he had shared only with felids before.

He visualized then the time he had found his caracal form. He was alone, walking aimlessly in a forest, still uncertain of his own felid nature. He stopped, suddenly entranced by a pattern of light above him. The leaves in the canopy were weaving in the breeze, revealing pockets of light that sparkled and vanished in pearlescent colors, showing him glimpses of the domed sky he knew so well. The shifting shapes became hypnotic. Aio kept his gaze upward and remembered times long, long before; times when he'd been just a baby, and his mother—as a tigress—would hold him in her arms and make him stare up at the light filtering through the leaves, as it was the one certain thing she could do to make him quiet and lull him to sleep.

Aio found himself back in the temple of blue sands. He clutched to that memory and tightened his grip on Lago's hand. With eyes never wavering or disconnecting, his body began to shimmer coldly in the light of the kenzir stone. The refracting cloud grew around his smooth body. His erection throbbed as threads extended from it to a larger shape. More threads connected, from nails to claws, round ears to triangular ones, button nose to a slenderly pointed muzzle. Lago felt the smooth hand he held turning rough and leathery, felt a pointed claw dig into his skin. The smoke coalesced, revealing the shape of an angular canid.

"You are magnificent!" Lago exulted. "Look at you!"

The furred figure stood, admiring his new body as he turned around, trying to catch a glimpse of his own back and tail. His fur was terracotta and ochre, with touches of yellow on the undersides, bleaching to white by his sheath. A prominent, black marking stretched over his back, striped with textured whites. A black-backed jackal.

Kulak, or Aio—he knew not what to call himself after this new discovery— looked around the room. It seemed darker than when he had been a caracal, but felt fuller. He let go of an excited mixture of a whine and yip. The loud sound echoed through the chamber and told him of the room's shape and size, as if he could feel the walls without seeing them. He rubbed his leathery paw pads together and became confused when he could not retract his claws.

He dropped on his tail again, facing Lago, and let blue sand cascade between his fingers, hearing every grain fall, sensing every rustle against his textured fur. Lago watched with a smile, not wanting to interrupt Kulak's discovery, letting him savor it all.

"Diff… Deesh… This veels worrderfool," Kulak struggled to verbalize, contorting his black lips into unfamiliar positions.

"You look beautiful," Lago murmured, surprising himself with his words. He leaned in and kissed the jackal's pointed muzzle.

Kulak smiled through the kiss, eyes and ears wide open, still scanning the space around them.

"Yeeou shell try nowgh," he said.

Lago's anxiety had not waned, yet he was a bit more hopeful now that he saw Kulak in his new form.

Kulak nudged him with raised brow whiskers. Lago picked up the felid mask. He closed his eyes, then opened them again to find the jackal staring too intently at him.

"Just give me a moment," he said self-consciously. He gazed down at the mask and studied the filigreed tendrils of black upon black, trying to make sense of the labyrinth of forms. His grip tightened. He exhaled a broken sigh, then placed Mindrelsilv on his face. The jolt of pain he felt was stronger than the one Aio had felt. Tensing up at first, he then relaxed, letting the pain run through him like a cold creek. He swallowed the discomfort, making it vanish quickly as he internalized it. With the mask adapted to the forms of his face, it felt the same as it did to wear Agnargsilv, except for the shorter muzzle, which did not hinder his sight as much.

The jackal took both of Lago's hands in his handpaws. Lago then noticed—as Aio had right before him—how Aio-Kulak was truly a felid, despite his current canid form. He felt the jackal's connection to Mindrelsilv, the pull toward the mask—yet the jackal also felt true, in place, and natural.

Lago tried to focus on an image, but it came to him too jumbled. It was a mixture of flowing water, of spiraling leaves, and swirling sand. He recalled the anxiety he had once felt around Banook during the days of trials before he had found his timber wolf half-form. The apprehension bubbled within him and took hold. His heart pumped faster, his mind drifted, now thinking of Banook, hearing the mountain song while his heart moved far and away from the sunken ruins. He tried to repeat Ockam's litany in his mind but couldn't even remember it properly. *A young fish I am. No, a young tree. A young tree I am, the vast ocean. Shit.* His breathing turned ragged. *Pack and wolf are of one heart, pack and wolf are of one heart, pack and wolf are of one heart...*

"I—I can't," he stammered, taking the mask off and looking away. Sweat streaked his forehead. "I can't focus."

He rose to his feet, then offered a hand to help the jackal up. "But I want you to be able to enjoy it. Don't worry about me. I also want to get a better look at you," he said, making Kulak spin around, lifting his furry arms, measuring his bushy tail. Kulak's body was as sensual as ever, even if a bit less rounded.

"Now my scalp undeerstanf what yew said earrlier," the jackal mumbled. "A jac-ckal alsso hassa vetter nose. As yew looked at my vody, I c-could ssmell your exccitement, your lusst."

Lago agreed with a look. He caressed the jackal's fur, letting his hands drift down to lightly rub on his balls. "I don't need to hide it. You look incredible. And I wasn't entirely sure, but I guessed you'd be either a red fox, or a jackal. I think a jackal suits you best."

"My scalp thinkks dso too," Kulak replied, already better understanding his canine mouth. He once again kept an unabating stare.

Lago knew what he wanted. He caressed the angular muzzle, the pointed ears, then kissed the jackal. He then dropped to his knees and carefully pulled the sheath back from the jackal's cock, grasping the widening knot at the base until Kulak's new length was fully revealed. He smelled him, tasted him, then, with equal amounts of eagerness and playfulness, tackled the jackal to the ground. They rolled over each other, once again laughing, exploring, sharing their newfound passion.

Kulak reached over to his side. "Wear the mask," he said, placing Mindrelsilv in Lago's hands.

"I… I really can't do it."

"As Lago, wear it as Lago. To see us better, to see us together."

Lago did as the jackal asked.

Kulak pushed Lago onto his back, holding on to his hands and pressing them into the fine sand. He brought his furred body over Lago's and looked down at the feline mask that stared back at him. Mindrelsilv prevented them from kissing, but Kulak's eyes could penetrate deeper than his tongue. He stared into Lago's soul as he guided himself into his lover.

Lago winced at the pain, making Kulak pull back. "You are bigger," he whimpered. He took deep breaths, then slowly nodded for Kulak to ease back inside him. He stopped the jackal again, his eyes darting around.

Kulak held still, waiting. Once Lago's eyes focused back upon his, he said, "Let me become part of you, Lago-Sterjall. Give yourself, fully."

His eyes were hypnotic, demanding, unrelenting. Lago noticed how tense all his muscles were and made a conscious effort to relax them, sinking deeper into the sand. "I'm ready," he lied.

Kulak pushed forward. Lago groaned, his neck and back arching. Kulak buried himself deeper still, holding on to Lago's hands.

"Give yourself," the jackal urged.

Lago tensed up more, his sphincter tightened.

"Give yourself," he said again, his lolling tongue dripping on the felid mask.

"I… I can't… It's too…"

"Give yourself."

Lago whined and twisted his body beneath the jackal's, but his eyes could not escape Kulak's gaze.

"Give yourself," the jackal insisted, as he pushed all the way into Lago and hardened to his full size.

As their bodies tied into one, Lago let out a repressed moan. He let it out loudly, with anguish and ecstasy, with fear and lust. As he let his tension release, the moan rumbled into a roar. He shapeshifted instantly, roaring as a mountain lion while he orgasmed completely under the prince's control.

The jackal finished at the same moment, then dropped his relieved body on top of the mountain lion.

Sterjall began to purr, without knowing how.

"That is what it feels like, to me," Kulak whispered. He kissed the mountain lion's bewhiskered cheeks, then dozed off.

OUT OF THE SHELL

Sunu dreamed.

They dreamed they were a young boy and girl who lived inside a warm shell. It was their personal dome, extending a deep, enveloping curve around them. The boy and the girl looked up. They could see a spine and ribs above, while beneath their bare feet the shell merged into a flattened sternum. It was so warm and safe in there, and terrifyingly lonely, despite them being two, not one.

Sunu peered at the opening at the far end of the shell and saw a slitted, green eye staring back at them. The eye seemed evil, but Sunu knew it not to be malicious, only misunderstood. The boy and girl who were Sunu held hands and walked to the eye, feeling the chill breeze from the opening.

"I don't want to go," they said as one.

"Me either," they replied to each other.

Their twin heartbeats drummed in echoes of themselves. "Hold me," they said, and took a step toward the slitted eye.

They left the shell behind and welcomed the cold.

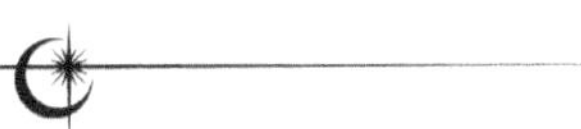

Sunu awoke.

They had been slumbering like a dark-masked statue, sitting on the blue sand at the very center of the abandoned chamber. They had not felt the warmth being drained from their blood, not until that moment.

They opened their eyes and looked at the patterns carved onto the curved ceiling. They felt stranded. Ishke'ísuk and Olo had both nestled in Pichi's deep fur for warmth. Alaia was snuggling with Blu. Sterjall and Kulak had gone their own way, to do things Sunu was forbidden to do.

Sunu stood in perfect silence, walked up the steps, and strode confidently toward the exit. The wedge-shaped doorway aimed east, where soon the glow of the new day would saturate the horizon. As they walked down the hallway, they dropped their shodog, kilt, and necklaces to the ground.

Only Ishke'ísuk saw them leave, but he remained still, holding fast to Pichi's warmth.

Sunu exited the ruins, fully naked except for the reptilian mask clinging to their face. The winds had ceased their howling. Overnight, the sand had crawled much higher up the steps, almost reaching the entrance.

It was dead still, and quiet. The cold of desert night was all-encompassing. The Galactic Belt cut across the skies like a pathway connecting two disparate worlds. All the stars were out, and some of the planets too. Iskimesh, the Enchantress, shimmered greenly to the east.

A prominent dune breached the horizon, slicing an arc from the black-blue ground into the inky blue heavens. Sunu walked down the few white steps, then up the dunes. As they climbed, their body turned colder, but their feet felt warmer; the sand still held some of the heat of the day within it. Sunu reached the top and looked around the starlit expanse. The new moon had not yet risen.

They felt the warmth between their toes and the cold in their marrow. They sat at the crest of the dune, and at the steep, east-facing leeward slope they lowered their smooth, freckled body, swaying back and forth until the sand opened up and slowly pulled them in. Their legs sank in first, then their back. They slithered downward until blue sand covered their crotch and filled their slit. They kept swaying until their arms were gone, then pushed down until their shoulders disappeared as well. The sand soon flowed over their chest and covered their purple-pigmented scalp.

Sunu finally stopped moving, their body at an angle that was half standing, half laying down. Only their stiff nipples, their tight erection, and the toothed muzzle of the reptilian mask protruded from the sand. They absorbed the warmth of the dune as they gazed upon the eastern horizon. The winds picked up again, blowing whirlwinds of blue over their head. After several immobile hours, Sceres rose in front of them as a thin slit of Jade green. Sunu stared at her, and Sceres stared back.

"Sterjall, Kulak!" Alaia's voice called with strained urgency.

The two woke up instantly. They were in a small room not too far from the sandpit, where they had set their bedrolls before exploring the ruins the night before. The jackal and mountain lion almost left their private room in their new forms. They quickly traded masks, traded forms, and ran down the tunnel to the main chamber.

"What is it?" Sterjall asked.

"Sunu is gone. I woke up and could not find them. They are not in any of the rooms to the sides, I checked already. They left their halberd right there."

"Did you see where they went?" Kulak asked Blu and Pichi, mindspeaking at the same time. But the smilodons had not seen the shaman leave.

Sterjall searched for clues, while Kulak grabbed a pharolith and headed toward the exit.

"Their clothes are up here," Kulak said, picking up the shodog abandoned in the corridor. "But… the exit, it is gone."

They all rushed to Kulak. No light other than the pharolith's shone down the passage—a wall of sand was blocking their path.

"Blu, Pichi, can you help us dig?" Kulak asked.

They worked together, though Pichi excavated most of the sand on her own. They soon felt a chill breeze, and not long after, saw a patch of pre-dawn sky. The winds were tenacious outside the ruins, birthing dust devils of blue and black. Once Pichi made the hole large enough, they all exited the building.

"We won't find any footprints like this," Sterjall yelled over the howl of the wind, covering his eyes from the blown sand. "Why in Noss's name did they leave us?"

Most of the columns had been buried, but the ones still showing led their eyes eastward, toward a tall dune. The thin slit of Sceres was rising over it, already dimmed by the first glint of pink sunlight seeping through a hidden horizon.

From the crest of the windswept dune, a silhouette rose. Their shape was confounding, unreadable due to the distance and the curtains of sand blowing between them. The figure slid down the tall dune and ambled over the buried colonnade.

It was not a smooth, freckle-skinned allgender who approached, but a reptilian form covered in tight scales, walking upon two clawed feet. Sunu lumbered forward, dragging their long, heavy tail over the dunes, drawing a snaking pattern of blue and black that was quickly erased by the roaring wind.

Sunu sampled the air with their forked tongue and stopped in front of their friends. The polychromatic aura of Kruwensilv was vivid through their body, shifting liquidly in countless lilac, pink, and violet hues. They were a varanus dragon now, although they were also still Sunu.

The dragon bowed, then walked into the portal to take cover from the abrasive sand. As soon as they were inside, Olo flew to their right shoulder, while Ishke'ísuk climbed to perch on their left. The dragon let themself be examined by their curious friends.

Kulak lifted his whiskers into a smile and said, "You look beautiful. You look dangerous." He greeted Sunu with a tap of their right temples. Olo pecked at Kulak's ear tufts for intruding on his space.

Sterjall had never had a close relationship with Sunu, not enough to feel comfortable reaching for a hug or anything of the sort, but he could not keep himself from sliding his pads over the folding, armored skin of their scaled arms. It felt cold. He scrutinized the colorful transitions of scale colors, which varied from greens to cold grays, ochres, and even turquoise blues.

"I thought you hated varanus dragons," Sterjall said.

"We dith," Sunu replied. "No mourr… We werrr wroungg." Their slow, breathy voice came from somewhere deep. The edges of their maw were less flexible than the lips of mammals; most of the enunciations were produced within the pink folds of their complex palate and gums.

"Hey, your scalp pigments are still showing!" Alaia exclaimed, tiptoeing closer to inspect the flat top of Sunu's head. "The drawings are all distorted, though. But the colors are nice."

The top of Sunu's head had many purple-tinted scales, in a pattern resembling their scalp pigments but reduced to something like a mosaic, with each scale either picking up the purple hues or remaining entirely in their natural colors.

"Whoa, watch out!" Alaia yelped as she tried to inspect Sunu's thick tail. "You are going to break our legs if you keep swinging that around." She stepped back to safety in front of Sunu. "How does it feel?" she asked. "The scales, the tail, the claws."

"They ffffeeel… like anotherrr… like not ourssssself. Yet like mourr offf usss. There isss cold, warmth, wholenessss."

Alaia smiled, then cocked her head, noticing that Sunu's breasts were entirely gone now; then her eyes dropped lower, toward the vertical slit in Sunu's crotch. "Sorry to get too personal here, but… Are you a girl now?" she asked.

"No. There isss mourr withinn, even mourr than we had befourrr. We arr bouth, as we have alllwayss beennn."

They all shamelessly gawked at Sunu as they ate their breakfast, which they prepared in the long hallway in order to keep an eye on the entrance and make sure it did not close up on them again. The pink immensity of the dragon's maw was frightening. Sunu had put their shodog back on with not much trouble, and the split in their tailcoat kilt seemed to work well for their thick tail. Their sandals, however, they had to attach to their belt, as their footclaws were oddly shaped and needed no protection in any case.

"Now I wish we hadn't left that tail armor at the ship," Sterjall said, still entranced by Sunu's alien figure. "You should've told us you'd be a dragon! Imagine how much more powerful your tail will be with quaar plates and a spiked end."

"We dith not knoww. We dith not ecssspecct."

"Hey, why are you saying 'we' instead of 'Sunu'?" Alaia asked.

"Beecausss we finally unnderssstand that we are mourrr than one, we have alllwayss been mourr. We acceptt ourssellvess this way."

They left the safety of the ruins and rode slowly for the rest of the day. Sunu had swapped places with Alaia on Pichi's saddle, so that their wide tail was not in the way. Careful with their sharp claws, the dragon held on to Alaia's overalls straps.

The winds had abated, but they would sporadically return. That evening, the wayfarers found no shelter, but before the winds picked up, they enjoyed a decent meal around a fire. Sunu and Ishke'ísuk had left the camp to stare at the Azurean Dome. Sunu's training as a shaman had made it easy for them to mindspeak with the Nu'irg, who perched like a gargoyle upon their left shoulder, listening. Sunu was disappointed that even after taking their varanus dragon half-form, they still could not mindspeak with Olo. Soot would allow them to communicate, in a different way, but the mask of reptilians only truly spoke to reptiles.

"You seem happy," Alaia said to Lago as they sat by the small fire.

"Just making myself presentable for the ceremony," Lago replied, mixing up a fresh batch of fingernail lacquer. The last time he had painted his nails was nearly a month ago, before the conversation with Noss, when he used a transparent lacquer. This time he chose green.

"Seems like more than that," Alaia said. She stood, gave him a kiss on his curly hair, then went to find more dry material to toss into the fire.

"Cannot hide a thing from her," Aio murmured next to Lago. "But please, tell not about last night. Let it be our secret, just for us."

"I won't tell, don't worry."

Sunu returned to the camp and sat in front of the dying embers, curling their tail around their legs.

"I wish we had a bigger fire for this," Lago said.

"My scalp wishes the same," Aio concurred, "but it will have to do."

Alaia tossed in the few scraps of tinder she had found, struck her brime cube to add more sparks, then sat with them.

"Sunu," Aio said, "while you talked with Ishke'ísuk, we also talked. Before new day comes, we want to grant you your honors. We are not shamans, we do not know proper words, but our scalps think we have found a good name."

"The name was Alaia's idea," Lago added, glancing proudly toward her.

"And I remember some of the words for the ritual," Alaia said, "from when you said them for Kitjári. I mean, I got the gist of it, at least."

"Words are not important when intentions are clear," Sunu said. "We made up words for Jiara-Kitjári, as we did not remember many of them. We would be honored to have our friends gift us with a name for when our body is one with that of the Kruwen." Sunu's reptilian voice was clear now, yet it still rumbled eerily from the back of their throat.

"Let me try, then," Alaia said. "Lodestar guide me." She shook the anxiety from her fingers, cleared her throat, then rose to her feet. "We are honored to have you, Sunu, as the voice of the lizards. We—"

"Reptiles," Lago corrected.

"Voice of the reptiles. We've chosen a name for when you are in this amazing new dragon form. Among the eighteen Miscam tribes, and whatever Lago and I happen to be—"

"We are Toldask Miscam, remember?" Lago interrupted again.

"Oh, that's right. Toldask Miscam indeed. Anyway, among however many tribes, you shall be known as Lummukem, like the legendary dragon who could turn into a human, except you are the other way around. Do you accept this name, and something something about the laws of the Silvesh?" Alaia shrugged, unsure of how the invocation ended.

"We accept," Sunu replied serenely. "Like the winged dragon who now flies among the stars, we shall be a guardian for all life."

"Then rise, Lummukem," Alaia continued with a deeper voice. "Rise and be many. Rise and be your entire self."

Lummukem rose, feeling proud of their new name, and gazed toward a snaking line of stars. They held their slitted gaze on the constellation, then wiped their violet-cast eyes with a foggy blink of their third eyelids.

BADLANDS

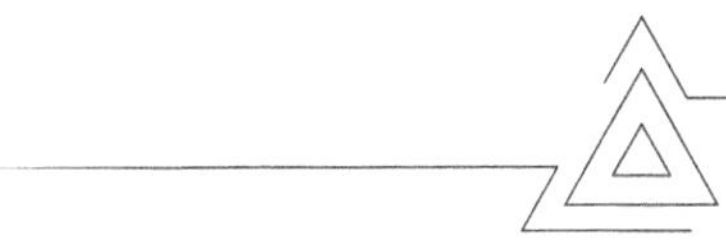

"We are almost at the badlands," Alaia said as they neared the pointed hills they had seen from afar. From this shortened distance, the spires seemed to rise taller and steeper than they had envisioned.

By early afternoon, they reached the end of the sand dunes to find a flatland composed of a silty clay of blue, purple, and black. After a long trot, they entered the first ravine of the badlands through a passage cut between extensively eroded walls. The simple drainage path was flat and easy to navigate, providing them with a false hope that crossing the ravaged country of picturesque pinnacles would not pose a challenge. After many miles, the ravine ended in a crackled butte.

"Let's climb to the top to see which path to take next," Sterjall said.

The cats pawed and clawed their way up the eroded cliffside, though making progress was difficult for them; here they slid back down even more easily than at the steep dunes. Dislodging sheets of crust, they at last reached the crest of the wall that connected to the flat top of the butte. As they balanced on the saw-toothed divide, the silt broke under their weight. Blu was in front, trying to reach the butte before he lost traction. As he began to slide, Pichi charged forward to help him, but their combined weight shattered the powdery crest. The cats tumbled down the opposite side of the butte, then shook the silt off as they regained their footing.

"By the Crone's tits!" Alaia cursed, spitting out the salty, purple clay that had wedged in her mouth.

"At least we made it to the other side," Sterjall said, wincing as he rolled a bruised shoulder.

They found themselves in a sheer gully with another flattened path at the bottom that was much narrower than the one before, yet still easy to traverse. After the cats shook off the colorful dust, they followed the canyon.

"Which direction is the dome?" Kulak asked. "My eyes have not seen it for a while."

"From the angle of the shadows, I think it's that way," Sterjall said, pointing ahead of them.

The canyon gave way to deep gorges, then to eroded canals where steep walls met, leaving little room for the cats' huge bodies. After scraping through a tight bend, they arrived at a clearing of blue silt where drain water from the gullies must have flooded from time to time, letting Sunnokh shrivel the mud to leave a blue playa of cracked sand—the crust made a sound like that of fracturing eggshells as the smilodons traversed it. From this wide playa, dozens of potential paths opened up before them.

"At least we can see the dome now," Alaia said. "But which path do we take?"

"One path seems to go straight to it," Kulak mentioned.

"*Seems* is the right word," Sterjall said. "But we might as well try that one."

For the rest of the day, they followed the maze, never able to travel in the direction they wanted, only able to follow the paths predetermined by erosion and forces too ancient and unknowable. It was getting late, and though there was not much wind when compared to the sand dunes, the badlands were equally cold.

"There's an opening up ahead," Sterjall observed. Blu and Pichi trotted forward excitedly, and soon entered a blue playa of cracked sand.

"Is this… Fuck," Alaia said. "It's the same place! We've gone around in a circle."

"We better rest," Lummukem said. "Tomorrow we will better plan our path."

In the morning, they let Blu and Pichi rest while exploring on foot, paw, and claw. With their lesser weight, it was easier for them to climb up the eroded walls. After much tumbling and sliding, they reached a mesa surrounded by purple hoodoos. From the top, they looked at the path behind them and the path ahead, and their hearts sank.

"We've barely entered this area and we are already lost," Sterjall said. "How are we going to cross all of that?"

"We make a map, like old times," Alaia suggested. "Pinpoint key structures, try to reach them, then move on to the next one."

"They all look the same to my eyes," Kulak said, "but we can try."

They did not have Ockam or Balstei to draft precise maps, so Sterjall drew this time, trying to estimate a path through the labyrinth of gullies and canyons. The butte they stood on was high, but not nearly the highest point in the surrounding area—many of their possible paths lay hidden to them.

With the map drawn, they returned to the smilodons, then chose an opening near the one they had taken the day before and continued west until the path chose to take them in other directions. Lummukem sent Olo up to help them, describing specific formations they had scouted earlier, and having the jay hover with his beak pointed toward their sought destination. They did not always succeed in using Olo this way, however, as most of the spires and hoodoos looked the same.

That night, they camped in a ruthlessly eroded gulch, then set off again in the early morning, having had little to drink or eat. The fogs of Umbra had enveloped the badlands overnight, clinging heavily even after dawn. Unable to use Olo for guidance, they resorted to Ishke'ísuk, who took the form of a spiny-tailed lizard and scouted for paths the cats could follow. But even the Nu'irg was unable to find trails the smilodons could traverse, and the wayfarers had to turn around so many times that it became hard to gauge how much they had gone forward or backward. The cats were getting hungry and thirsty, so most of the food and water went to them, leaving the four riders parched and ravenous. For another night they stopped to cower from the cold, then continued again at first light.

By midmorning, they saw a hopeful sign ahead: an open area from which they could perhaps find a clearer path. After two days lost in the foggy maze, they were happy to find any respite. They rushed to the clearing and found a blue playa of cracked sand.

"Fucking cockgobbling Khest!" Alaia yelled. "We are back at the same place! It's been days and we've gotten nowhere! And our water is almost gone!"

"Calm down," Sterjall said, trying to keep his own frustration out of his voice, "you are making Pichi upset." He hopped off Blu. The others followed.

"Rest for a bit," Kulak told the smilodons. "We will look around."

They circled the misty playa, finding their own prints at the paths they had taken before. At least a dozen more possible routes were available, but the wayfarers did not have the time or energy to try them all.

"What is this?" Kulak said, pointing at the ground by a dry creek. "These are not our tracks."

"A bird's foot, it seems," Lummukem said, using the tip of their tail to flip flakes of crust around the three-toed print. "A very large bird. Fresh prints, no more than a day."

"Like an ostrich?" Alaia guessed. "If there are creatures that big around here, they either know the way in and out, or they know where there is food and water."

Sterjall looked up, trying to sense the angle of the sun through the fog. "This path goes south," he said. "We need to travel west."

Alaia shook her head. "Our last path went west, and it was nothing but a convoluted circle. This bird is the best chance we've got."

Kulak whistled. Blu and Pichi begrudgingly rose to their feet and approached them, and soon they all began following the three-toed tracks along the southbound path.

"Told you," Alaia said when they spotted the first signs of life they'd seen in a long while: a handful of bushes and sharp grasses, most of them shriveled dry, but still better than nothing.

The tracks climbed over hills and pinnacles, where they guessed the bird had had a much easier time than the cats. It was growing dark by the time they entered a purple canyon of nearly vertical walls, but at least the fog had mostly cleared. The bottom was flat, dry, and the avian prints were clear even in the dim light. As they turned a corner, Kulak held up a handpaw.

"Stop," he whispered. "Quiet." He silently told Blu and Pichi to back off, then shifted into Aio. "Hide your Silvesh. There is a man ahead."

They hid their masks in their bags.

"He was in the dark," Aio said. "He could not have seen us like my eyes saw him."

Lago nodded. "He could show us the way out if we don't scare him. Let's walk in front of the cats, so that he doesn't fear us."

They approached with caution, but purposely made some noise. They heard a rustle ahead and the sound of a blade being drawn. Only the smilodons could see the man, who backed off slowly.

"*Tsan-fai gollo met aru-bi?*" a voice queried.

They stopped.

"*Sneiv? Ush… ushma…?*"

"Do you speak Common?" Lago asked, then a breath later, "*Chienn enuss Miscamish?*"

"Baurami. Common, little. No Mishkhamen. Who comes?" The man glanced behind him while clicking his tongue. A long-necked bird, almost eight feet tall, stomped her way forward to stand next to him. He held on to her side, ready to hop on and flee.

Lago signaled for his friends to wait, placed Leif to the ground, and walked forward with his hands up. "We are lost," he said. "We need help."

"You bring Fau-Lawar, beasts from Void of Khest, clothes from Zevvieren. Why are you desert? Why help?"

Lago wished he had thought up a story beforehand, but it was too late now—he would have to make one up as he went along. He remembered the name of a city near the Azurean Dome, one Alid had marked on his map, called Navar Mat. A trading town between two desert lands, the prisoner had said.

"We are traders, looking for the city of Navar Mat," Lago tried. He could barely discern the vague silhouettes in front of him, but he discerned the smaller figure untense his taut shoulders. "We can pay you for your troubles if you help us reach it. My name is Lago." He quickly regretted using his real name.

"What pay you, for Navar Mat?"

Lago turned to discuss with his friends. They had almost no food or water left, their weapons were too important to trade, and soot might make the man suspicious, as it was often used to scam traders by selling low-quality powders to those who did not know better. They thought they could spare one of their pharolith lamps, as they had four with them and dozens more aboard *Fjummomurr*. It would be an artifact of indescribable value to anyone outside of the Fjordlands Dome, a treasure the stranger could certainly not refuse.

Lago approached with the closed-up lamp. The man pointed his sword at him.

"It's okay. We can pay with this," Lago said, rotating the base of the lamp to make the petals blossom, sprouting the cold light of the kenzir stone.

"*Gnam-oube, fon wai kenzir-elo ma-pur…*" the man mumbled, the light revealing his disbelieving face.

He was tall, slender, wearing a sleeveless cloak of all colors over his yet more colorful tunic. His clearly Baurami-blue eyes were framed by a draping headcloth. The bird standing next to him was of a muddy color, with thick blue legs and a bald blue face. The bird twisted her head back and forth to stare at the lamp, using one eye at a time.

The man reached a tentative hand forward. Lago pulled the lamp back.

"If you take us to Navar Mat, you can have it."

The man swallowed. "Serdein is name. Serdein Humuen-Vok sar Ashil ill Lhambor Di. I show path, *Ngorr*." He bowed.

They made a fire with dried brushes and a bundle of charcoal Serdein was carrying. He lit the charcoal atop slabs of slate to keep the heat from dissipating too fast, then cooked a couscous paste that he shared with the group, though he shared none with Alaia. Lago let him hold the pharolith as they talked, though they could not understand much of what they were saying to each other.

To make his story more believable, Lago claimed they were merchants from the north, coming from the Holv-Yanan state of the Zovarian Union, looking to sell precious wares at Navar Mat. Serdein did not question them much, and instead smiled with an air of complicity and understanding. There was an unspoken implication that something as valuable as a kenzir stone must have been stolen from a palace, or from a powerful general. He likely thought the travelers were fugitives who had fled into the desert with stolen treasures, trying to save their hides. Serdein asked to see what else they were selling, claiming he could find the right buyers, but Lago refused to show him what else was in their bags.

Serdein was a quiet man. He kept to himself perhaps more out of an unspoken respect than because of his limited understanding of the language. He said tomorrow he would show them the way, covered himself with a blanket, and slept right on top of the sand.

Before the sun rose, they were loading their gear onto Pichi's saddle. Aio brought a bowl of water for her, and then passed it on to Blu, making sure not a drop was spilled.

"How much water? Food?" Serdein asked them.

Lago did not mind showing him that—their resources were dwindling.

"*Nahuul-rit*, Navar Mat far," Serdein said. "Big cats die. Eat cats, sell fur."

Aio ground his teeth. "No, cats stay alive. They are friends."

"You thirst, you die," Serdein insisted.

Lago shook his head. "If you cannot show us a safe way, for all of us, we will find our own way instead."

Serdein's blue eyes narrowed. He turned away and considered for a long while. When he faced them again, his expression was stern, unreadable. "Another path, secret water. I show, but you pay more." He looked at Lago's belt, locking his eyes on the quaar hilt of Leif. "Dagger, for water," he said. "Cats not die."

Lago refused, claiming the pharolith lamp was worth more than anything Serdein could've dreamed of, and knowing Serdein knew this to be true as well. Serdein huffed and tightened his lips, but agreed to take them either way.

"I show secret water. Two darks away." He hopped onto the large bird, which he called a *moa*, and led the way, wrapping his headcloth around his face to protect it from the sand, sun, and wind.

Two more nights they spent in the badlands. Their water supply had been exhausted, and only a few munnji cakes remained. Serdein kept insisting the 'secret water' was close, but the journey had taken longer than he'd estimated, as his moa could easily cross over obstacles the cats had to struggle through.

That evening, he did not stop.

"How much farther?" Lago asked, unable to keep the desperation from his voice. He felt his skin shriveling, his pores plugged by sand, his eyes dry and crusted.

"Water. Close," was all Serdein would say.

"Please, we need—"

"Close."

The Ilaadrid Shard shone fiercely that evening, making their path clear. They rode under the green-and-white moonlight, casting sharp shadows on the purple silt. Their hunger and thirst hurried them onward.

A sandstone bluff loomed ahead, of a hard material different from the clay-like eroded cliffs found along their trail so far. A concave hollowness in the blue rock demarcated a shallow cave, with toppled boulders obscuring it at the bottom.

"Secret, do not say," Serdein demanded of them, then hopped off his moa and walked behind the boulders.

A large slab of rock leaned against the sandstone wall. Despite its size, it was thin, and Serdein easily moved it out of the way. Behind the slab was carved a wedge-shaped doorway.

The moa stayed outside, but the cats came in, crouching to fit through the passage. Lago held up one pharolith lamp and Sunu another. Serdein immediately noticed and turned to face them, utterly perplexed.

"Two kenzir, how?"

"One will be for you, and the other is ours to sell," Lago said.

"Serdein knows Duchess Hilid Kei. She buys treasure. I meet duchess and you, for price."

"Maybe. We can negotiate that after we are out of here."

"Sell big cats. Big price. Ten, twenty moas each, maybe more. I help you sell Duchess Hilid Kei. For price."

"Cats are not for sale," Aio croaked through his dry throat.

The hallway ended at a round room where five other rock-carved tunnels connected. The architectural style and the look of the glyphs adorning the walls told them it was from the same pre-Downfall civilization that had built the sand-buried temple they had recently explored. Each of the six doorways had white marble trimmings, and the floor was mosaicked with pictorial scenes.

"Lost city. Old," Serdein explained. "Many lost in sand. Follow."

He picked a doorway to his right and led them through a set of maze-like tunnels and empty rooms, into a larger square chamber with dozens of engaged columns projecting out of the sandstone walls. The room was entirely empty, except for a central dais scorched black from old campfires.

"Water, close. But stay secret, *Ngorr*," he repeated. He approached one of the embedded columns, which was made from hefty wedges of marble. He grabbed one of the segments and swung it sideways, revealing a metal bar behind a hollow compartment, then pulled on the metal bar and removed it. A metallic sound reverberated, as if a mechanism had unlocked. He took the metal bar to a sandstone wall and stuck it in a perfectly shaped hole hidden among glyphs. He then pulled hard on the bar, and the entire segment of wall began to roll. The wall was an enormous disc, hiding its curves behind the columns, and its edges had been rimmed with metal and ridged with even bumps, like an enormous gear.

The heavy slab rolled slowly, then locked into its carved slot. Behind it was a round portal and a small, cozy room. Serdein cast a pinch of gold sand at the portal to ward against unwelcome spirits, then invited them in.

The room was stacked with crates. Most of them were empty, but some held caches of dried food, textiles, and other inexpensive items that became priceless when need arose in the middle of a desert. In the back of the room was a water pump that dug deep into the rock, following an invisible spring. Serdein picked up a ceramic bowl and began pumping until purple-blue water came spilling out. Pichi rushed toward it.

"No!" Serdein hissed. "Wait!" He spilled the water into a drain and resumed pumping until the water turned clear. Only then did he let Pichi drink, and then filled more bowls for the others.

"Thank you, thank you…" Lago gasped through cracked, shriveled lips. Even his eyelids were chapped, clumping with sandy granules. He drank so fast that he convulsed and threw up.

"Slow," Serdein said, not having taken a sip of his own yet.

After their thirst was quenched, they sat on dusty cushions and lit a small fire. The ceiling was curved, with a small hole at the very top for smoke to escape through. They watched the smoke rise as they waited for the water to boil. Serdein brought out dried meats to cook, as well as a perfumed blue rice which he tossed into the water. He chewed on a strip of jerky as he prepared the meal.

"We will need more, for the cats," Aio pleaded.

Serdein looked at Lago's blade once more, his eyes demanding compensation. Lago reached for the pharolith lamp and handed it to him. "I cannot give you my dagger. This lamp is worth enough. You can have it now, it's yours"— he picked up the other pharolith they had opened—"and you can have this second lamp later, once we reach Navar Mat. But we need you to share more food, or our cats will starve."

Serdein seemed suspicious of the offer, but he simply kept on chewing as he poured the stew-like meal into a larger pot, then added more dried meat and rice. As he waited for the meal to cook, he played with the pharolith lamp, opening and closing the petals, making the light shine directionally when he opened them only partway, aiming the beam around the chamber.

Once the meal finished cooking, he tasted it, sprinkled some salt in, and tasted it again.

"No good," he said, then rummaged through crates in a corner of the room. He brought back a shaker and sprinkled copious amounts of a red powder over the meal. "Burns good," he said. "Secret spice of Navar Mat."

He first served a generous portion for the cats, then smaller ones for each of his guests, although none for Alaia, who had to serve herself while staring daggers at the man. Serdein chewed on his strip of leathery meat as he watched them eat.

"This is delicious," Lago said, eyes tearing up. "Even if a bit too spicy."

"I think it's just the right amount," Alaia countered, enjoying the added pain.

Sunu pulled the bowl close to their face, letting Ishke'ísuk eat at the same time. Olo did not care for the meaty meal, but he had swallowed a handful of seeds earlier, and would not starve.

Serdein poured water in small bowls for all but Alaia.

"I think he believes you are our slave," Lago told her in Miscamish.

Alaia responded in Miscamish as well. "Just because I like his food, it doesn't mean I like *him*. He's too distrustful."

"I've already offered him a second pharolith, that's more than fair. Maybe he expects we'll try to trick him."

Alaia felt drowsy from the heat of the meal. "Maybe," she replied, wiping droplets of sweat off her forehead. "Could I have more water?" she asked Serdein. He looked away.

She stood up to reach for the jar on her own but slipped, barely catching herself. She lifted the jar, but it fell from her fingers as she poured, cracking on the ground and turning the fire into a plume of white smoke. The cats were asleep and did not notice the loud sound. Ishke'ísuk fell from Sunu's shoulder, landing on their kilt. Sunu tried to stand and lost control of their legs, sending Olo flying to perch on a crate.

Serdein backed away into the shadows.

"Stop… him," Lago mumbled, losing his voice. He tried to get Aio's attention, but Aio was sprawled on his back with his eyes closed. Lago tried to crawl. With blurred eyes, he watched as Serdein sifted through his bag and pulled Agnargsilv out. The man stared at it in wonder for a long moment, then stowed it back inside the bag. Lago whimpered.

Stop, he thought, unsure if he had said the word out loud.

His eyelids weighed on him, his consciousness faded, and he collapsed onto the cold marble tiles.

CHAPTER EIGHT

ARCHSTONE

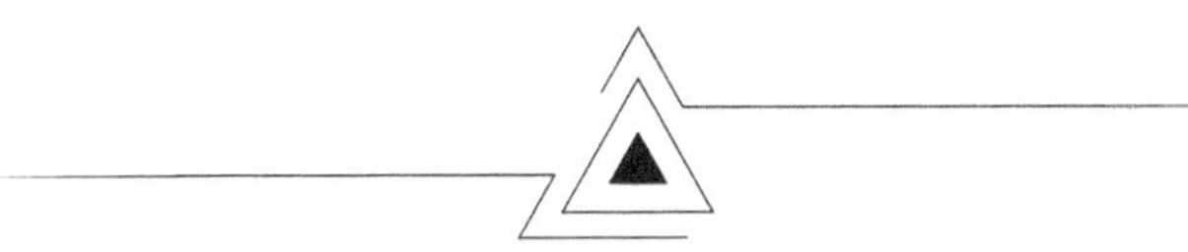

"I'm sending two additional shamans with you," the Red Stag said to Silv-Thaar Valaran. "I want you to keep me informed at all times."

The raccoon general nodded, his white whiskers bouncing over his dark-furred cheeks. "I will, Monarch Hallow. We are almost ready—once Shea is done readying the fleet, we'll march to war. She'll provide a helpful distraction as we approach by land."

The Red Stag's army had long since left the ravaged lands of the Bayanhong Tribes. A smaller force had remained at On Khurderen to protect the resources of the capital, while the Red Stag marched south toward the Archstone Dome, where the monarch expected to take control of Almelsilv, the mask of perissodactyls.

They had stopped for the night near the Dorhond city of Oskirin. Inside a lamp-lit pavilion, the Red Stag and his Silv-Thaar planned their next moves.

The Red Stag traced a hoofed finger on a map. "Once we take Oskirin, we should clear the city entirely. I don't want to leave any troops there. From there, we'll head our separate ways."

Valaran squinted uncertainly. "But we are still marching together for a while longer," he noted.

"We are not. Oskirin is where we part ways. I've chosen to lead my legions across the White Desert. Once we're through the desert, Silv-Thaar Markhor's caprids will help us traverse the Dorhond Range. We'll enter the Archstone Dome through the mountains, to scout it from high ground."

"But Lorr... You can't move enough supplies through the desert sands."

"The Oldrin slaves we'll capture at Oskirin will help with that. Besides, the alternate route would take much too long and drag us through Graalman territory. I do not wish to fight the Horde until we have secured the new mask—their horse-mounted cavalry is their most powerful asset, and they could easily set a trap for us."

"You won't be able to maintain a healthy force by the time you arrive, nor will you have enough water for your soldiers."

"Let me worry about my legions, Valaran. You worry about your own. We'll have more than enough resources once we enter the dome, where we'll recruit more soldiers to make up for the ones lost along the way."

Valaran tried to hide a scowl behind a forced grin; he found it sickening the way the Red Stag dismissed the value of his own soldiers' lives, yet in the long run, the monarch seemed to always come out ahead.

"Trust my strategy, like I trust you, Valaran," the Red Stag said, sensing Valaran's disappointment. "What you are doing will also go down in history. Make the Empire proud, and inform me as soon as you have secured the pinniped mask. I won't need your soldiers to conquer the Archstone Dome, but once I leave it, your archers might be necessary to flank the Horde, who are already digging trenches to protect their perimeters."

"Yes, Monarch Hallow," Valaran said through a sigh. "I will follow your strategy."

The Oldrin captured at Oskirin became indispensable guides to the Red Stag while he crossed the desert of pearl-white sands. But even though the slaves showed him the best paths over the dunes, his army was not ready for the torturous journey. He lost countless humans, cervids, and caprids, yet he pushed on. With so many bodies left to rot in the sand, the morale of the marching soldiers was shattered. Despite their broken conviction, they had nowhere to flee to but certain death, so they followed their leader hoping there was some strategy they were blind to.

The month-long treacherous journey through the dunes finally ended at radiant mountains of white rock streaked with pale greens: the Dorhond Range. As a wall of darker green, the imposing curve of the Archstone Dome framed the rising peaks. No arches of sandstone teetered in these lands, which were unlike the southern territories that gave the dome its name.

With the help of Silv-Thaar Markhor's nimble-footed caprids, the army climbed up the pale range until they reached the dome's wall. The Fourth Legion, under the command of General Gino Baneras, was the first to arrive. Gino's troops carefully hauled pipe segments through the mountains, aided by the power of the Red Stag's cervids, including Sovath, who most often was forced to assume the form of a megaloceros.

"We need to enter this wretched place, fast," Gino told the Red Stag. "I lost too many soldiers, and the rest are parched. They've been so thirsty they've been drinking blood from the dead animals. I've told them it'll make them sick, but they do it anyway."

"At least they did not starve," the Red Stag said. "But I hear you, Gino. Once the pipes are installed, we'll have a paradise to conquer. It won't be much longer. In the meantime, we must hasten and scout the best point of entry."

Since Fjorna Daro and her arbalisters had followed Silv-Thaar Valaran and were not present to act as the Red Stag's personal guard, he instead took Silv-Thaar Markhor, General Gino Baneras, General Korten dus Fer, as well as his two captured Nu'irgesh, and ventured into the dome.

Almeldrolom—as the Miscam called the Archstone Dome—was vast and picturesque, teeming with sandstone arches, hoodoos, buttes, and spires that rose from fertile grasslands and lakes, giving form to meandering canyons, verdant valleys, and trout-filled creeks. Clouds of dust lifted from the prairies, where herds of horses, rhinoceroses, tapirs, and long-thought-extinct ungulates roamed. The Red Stag glanced over the landscape and analyzed its resources, content with the value it provided.

"Takh have mercy, what are those monsters?" General Korten dus Fer muttered, aiming a spyglass toward a herd of giants at the shore of a lake.

The Red Stag took the instrument and surveyed the creatures. He felt a jolt of excitement mixed with fear. "Behemoths," he answered. "Urcai warned me we might find them in here. The largest creatures to ever roam Noss. But they seem much heavier than the pre-Downfall texts described, at least twice as tall as my megaloceroses."

"They could tear us apart," Gino Baneras said.

"Not if we take Almelsilv before they strike. And that is just what we will do."

The behemoths, also known as paraceratheriums, had been one of the Alampaari Miscam's companion species, who had grown bigger, smarter, and more long-lived thanks to the special diet from the core vine's blood. Like giant, hornless, long-necked rhinoceroses, the behemoths towered twice as high as any mammoth ever did, and had no natural predators, for no fangs could pierce their thick, armor-like hides.

Silv-Thaar Markhor grunted, then nodded her screw-shaped horns toward the giants. "Big, make trouble," she said with her limited but improving Common. "Too big. Pipes not too big, pipes too small."

"She's right," Korten said. "If we capture those monsters, they won't fit through our pipes. How are we planning on taking them out?"

"It's more complicated than that," Gino said while tying his long hair in a ponytail. "We barely have enough segments to build the entry pipe—we won't be able to construct an exit tunnel to the south as we planned."

The Red Stag ground his teeth, thinking.

"We move," Markhor said decisively, resting her ice axe over her armored shoulders. "Ikhel and caprids thirsty, dying. Where building pipes?"

The Red Stag turned to his officers, weighing his options. They were atop an elevated mesa of white and green rock, with a good view of the landscape below, but also in a position that provided little cover for his massive legions. He could see a handful of human settlements far below that posed no threat, but the cliffs that loomed higher than their position gave him pause—if there were any Alampaari Miscam up there, they would spot his army making their way in. The mesa had plenty of water and abundant life to exploit. The only resource lacking was time.

"Let's ready the pipes," he directed. "This mesa could hold about half of our army. The troops will need to take turns moving in and out. There shall be no fires, and the soldiers are to remain away from the cliff's edges. We must keep our presence a secret for as long as possible."

It was a mistake.

The Negian invaders avoided further death from thirst and exposure, but despite their efforts to remain concealed, they were soon spotted from nearby peaks. The Alampaari tribe knew an army when they saw one, as they themselves had their own skirmishes and wars between rival clans and had long ago been one of the fiercest warring tribes on the Jerjan Continent. They did not know these foreign infiltrators, but they found the way the Negians mistreated their cervids and caprids sickening, and they saw the mask wielders not as Silvfröash, but as corrupted manifestations of gods from before the Downfall.

The Almelfröa was promptly warned of the intrusion. Her name was Hud Ogampal, and she had the half-form of a kiang, a mountain wild ass. Together with Estriéggo—the woolly rhinoceros Nu'irg—she hurried to the northeastern end of her dome to observe the army that was pouring in. From high ground, safely behind cover, they studied the enemies' strengths and weaknesses.

Once the arudinn began to dim, quiet as a nighthawk's whiskers, the Alampaari Miscam moved their herds to the edge of a cliff overlooking the swarmed mesa.

Ogampal climbed a rope ladder dangling from an enormous garrison horse, a heavy-hoofed breed that was one of their sapient companion species. Garrison horses were so large that they could comfortably hold four riders upon their muscular backs, but Ogampal always rode alone. She settled in the saddle, then looked down at a chief who had thick gray skin like a rhinoceros. "Gwuro, it's time," she said to him.

"My troop is in position," Gwuro replied, stomping with one foot. "None of the invaders will make it out of the mesa alive." He took his leave, issuing commands to a group of soldiers possessing various perissodactyl traits; some were long-faced and maned, some dragged silky or leathery tails, some had armor-like skin like Gwuro himself, or wielded sharp horns and hooves that could easily shatter Negian bones.

«Make sure the companions rush to the chokepoint as soon as they hear your signal,» Ogampal mindspoke to Estriéggo. «Go now, and may the strength of a thousand hooves thunder within you.»

The Nu'irg tipped his enormous horns and was about to trot away when a sight in the distance made him stop cold—two giant creatures had appeared in the enemy's encampment, creatures that had not been there heartbeats earlier: an antlerless megaloceros and a thick-horned bootherium.

«Nu'irgesh,» Estriéggo mindspoke, dread filling his heart. «Sovath. Beiféren. My friends. I know them. I see them.»

Hud Ogampal felt the anguish boiling within the mindspoken thoughts. She felt her own heart shrivel and weep.

"What is the matter?" a plain-skinned shaman asked.

"The demons have captured Nu'irgesh," Ogampal said, flattening her long ears in disgust. "Estriéggo… he says… that they are not themselves. That they are enslaved to the corrupted Silvesh. We must rescue them."

Briefly, in thoughts that conveyed sadness and hopelessness, the Nu'irg told Ogampal the story of Däo-Varjak, the pinniped Nu'irg who had once suffered a most wretched fate when a mad prince stole Gwonlesilv, then used the mask to mindlock her and force her to perpetrate unspeakable atrocities. Hud Ogampal relayed the direness of the situation, begging the chiefs not to attack Sovath or Beiféren, for they were not guilty of the actions they would be forced to commit.

«Patience,» she told the woolly rhino. «Patience, old friend. We shall rescue them from this evil. And soon you three shall gallop through the Käelmat prairies as one.»

Estriéggo snorted decisively, then trotted away. As he made his way down a hidden canyon, he shapeshifted into a harmless dwarf horse, then entered the Negian camp, acting like a lost foal searching for his herd.

Soldiers noticed the tiny creature and stared curiously; a few pulled out daggers to snatch an easy dinner. Once at the center of the camp, Estriéggo shifted into a behemoth even taller than those who had been drinking at the lake, and swung his long neck to swipe at dozens of soldiers at a time. He then bellowed a terrifying call that echoed through the very bedrock.

The Alampaari charged.

Behemoths led the assault in a cloud of dust and splintered tree trunks, followed by Hud Ogampal and her legion riding atop garrison horses. Close behind them came the slower but deadly anisodons, another of their companion species, who looked like long-armed horses or overgrown gorillas, muscular and almost bipedal.

The first behemoths to arrive took care of dismantling the only exit. They reared up on two legs and dropped their weight atop the segmented pipe, collapsing it with a white spray of torn vines. Slowly but surely, the vines encroached to cover the space the pipes had left behind.

While the battle broke all around him, Estriéggo trampled away in his primal form, slamming his enormous horn against shields, skulls, and ribcages, making his way toward his enslaved friends. Sorrow filled him when he witnessed Sovath and Beiféren helplessly killing Alampaari soldiers, killing perissodactyls, killing his own kind. He tried mindspeaking sense into them, causing the two enslaved Nu'irgesh to slow their attacks and stare back in recognition, looking shameful and tired behind those dead eyes. Their muscles spasmed, as if struggling between two competing commands. Estriéggo was speaking deeper into their minds, trying to bring his friends back to their senses, when a red-painted cervalces slammed into his side and pushed him down a slope, making him lose sight of them. He tried to regain his footing but was quickly overwhelmed by too many cervids, who swarmed on him like ants over a dying grasshopper.

Hud Ogampal dangled from the enormous saddle of her garrison horse, slamming her war club at the invaders. Her troop followed in a sharp formation, carving a wedge into the enemy forces. The Red Stag's army was not only split and unable to communicate—with half of them still outside the dome—but they were also fatigued and terrified, unable to properly wield their weapons. Those who could tried to flee from the mesa, only to be pushed off the cliffs by the perissodactyls. All around the Negian troops were dwindling— no escape could they glimpse, and their morale was shattered.

Ogampal swooped back and forth like a pendulum, searching for the enemy officers. But she was unprepared for the cruelty of the Red Stag and Silv-Thaar Markhor, who cared not for the wellbeing of their mindlocked creatures and sent them in waves to overwhelm the Alampaari, breaking antlers and horns in piles of sacrificial meat. Buried under a mass of mangled ungulates, she spotted Estriéggo. She was fighting hard to free him when she heard a command shouted by the enemy.

"Fall back!" the Red Stag ordered his officers. "To the wall!" He took cover from the rain of arrows behind his quaar shield and began to withdraw, abandoning his doomed army.

«You must stop them,» Estriéggo told Ogampal, struggling to push the cervids off him. «Stop them, lest they take the Nu'irgesh out with them. Kill any of the Silv wearers and their enslaved Nu'irg will be freed, and they will join our side. Go, now, do not delay.»

Ogampal spotted the retreating stag. "I will not let you get away, demon," she said through grinding molars.

Under the protection of Sovath and Beiféren, the Red Stag and his officers backed into the wall of vines, using their masks to form a new passage by which they could escape. Before the opening narrowed too tightly, Hud Ogampal forced it open with her own empathic focus and hurried her horse toward it. "The Nu'irgesh are not yours to corrupt!" she bellowed through the gallop.

The Red Stag sent Sovath to block the way, but Ogampal had called for a behemoth's aid, who tumbled with the megaloceros in a rock-shattering quake. Ogampal's horse leapt over the cloud of dust.

"Markhor!" the Red Stag called. "Stop her!"

Markhor mindspoke a command to Beiféren. The bootherium charged, ramming into Ogampal's horse. But Ogampal had foreseen the strike. At the moment of impact, she jumped off, landing atop a rhinoceros and scrambling to hold on to his horn.

As the rhinoceros entered the vine tunnel, Ogampal lifted her war club high, spiked end eager to strike. "Death comes to you!" she screeched. She savored the fear she saw reflected in the Red Stag's eyes as she swung her weapon toward his disbelieving face.

She heard a sharp whistle, then felt a mighty jolt as the rhinoceros twisted violently and threw off her aim. From within the dark depths of the tunnel of vines, General Gino Baneras had let a single arrow fly from his longbow, carving a path through the rhino's eye all the way into his brain.

As the beast fell, his body rolled over Hud Ogampal, crushing her and burying her under mounds of gray skin, dirt, and heavy bones. The chief could feel her legs bent out of shape, but she still had the strength to pull herself out from under the corpse. As she strained to free herself, she saw the opening leading toward her dome closing, and in that narrowing iris was Estriéggo, breaking the vines with his mighty horns.

«I will free you,» the Nu'irg mindspoke. «And together we will take our revenge.»

As the wooly rhino tore his way in, he was rammed once more by Beiféren, who then took the form of a mountain goat and dashed through a gap in the vines, then Sovath followed through the tightening passage in her primal form. The vines had closed too far by the time Estriéggo returned. He stood there breathless, terror filling his eyes, feeling a rabid panic boil within him as his hope drained, as he recognized his own enslavement would soon come, as certainly as the end of Almeldrolom would.

Ogampal watched Estriéggo's blurry image vanish, replaced by two cloven hooves standing by her side. As she looked up, the last thing she saw before her skull was crushed was Silv-Thaar Markhor's fast-swinging ice axe.

☾

"Damn that ass and her cursed animals!" the Red Stag spat, kicking at the mask still attached to the fallen Almelfröa. "Scorch her flesh sixteenfold. She almost took everything from us!"

"Monarch Hallow, be careful!" General Korten dus Fer urged, holding up a shaking lantern. "We got what we came for, there's no need to damage the artifact!"

"Don't be a fool, Korten, they cannot break." The perissodactyl mask detached limply, revealing a young and fierce-looking woman with a drooping face—although her half-form had been that of a kiang, Ogampal had been born with aspects of a mountain tapir.

The Red Stag squatted and sneered at the sight of the partial half-form. "Silv-Thaar Markhor, is this what I think it is?"

"Half-blood," Markhor confirmed. "Happened in Rilgdrolom few times. All Alampaari, half-blood. Sinful, better with skull cracked."

"Damn horse fuckers. But why is she not an ass, like when she was wearing the mask?"

No one had an answer for him, so he picked up the mask and shook the dirt and blood off. "We lost half our bloody army. And there were already too few of us after Valaran took his share of the soldiers."

"The little water we brought out won't last long," Gino Baneras warned.

"I know. We have to go back in soon, or we'll all rot in these mountains."

"But now we can control those huge beasts they have," General dus Fer said. "And as ugly as this dead woman here is, her brain-splattered face gives me some hope. If they truly are half-bloods, do you think… maybe Almelsilv could control them as well?"

The elk looked down at the fallen Alampaari chief and poked at her flaccid, trunk-like nose with his hoof. "If what you posit proves correct, Korten, it would offer us more than just an advantage. There would be no need to fight them at all, only to approach them and take them for ourselves. I'll get this mask to one of our shamans straight away. Perhaps Heraz, or Keurvak—they have both shown great promise."

"If I may," Gino interjected, stepping closer. "I do not mean to impose, but I have splurged some of my earnings on soot in times past and know full well what the effects feel like. And growing up in the Great Steppes, I captured and trained wild horses for a living long before joining the army. This mask speaks to me. Let me try it on, and if I don't learn fast enough, then give it away to the shamans."

The Red Stag considered the offer. In his mind, Almelsilv was meant to be granted to either Gino, Korten, or even Behler, while the shamans were to be given a chance at the remaining masks only after the generals. But right now, time was of the essence, and he knew the shamans could learn quicker. Still, there was an issue with the shamans that had been bothering him—their allegiance. Despite Urcai fully vouching for them, their interests were always in question, for they were paid mercenaries, and this mask was much too powerful to risk on someone who might defect.

"Your arrow saved me from this Miscam ass," the Red Stag said to Gino. "I guess you earned this one. I hope you know what you are doing, Gino, and I hope you do not make us wait. Learn to use it at once, and the mask is yours."

He put Almelsilv in Gino's hands. The equine mask was strangely long-faced, resembling a horse but with a nose that drooped more like that of a tapir, and two stubby but sharp horns that granted it an air of power and severity.

"I will learn fast, Monarch Hallow," Gino stated. "The Archstone Dome will soon be yours, and the tribe inside will pay dearly for what they've done to our legions."

CHAPTER NINE

WILD HORSES

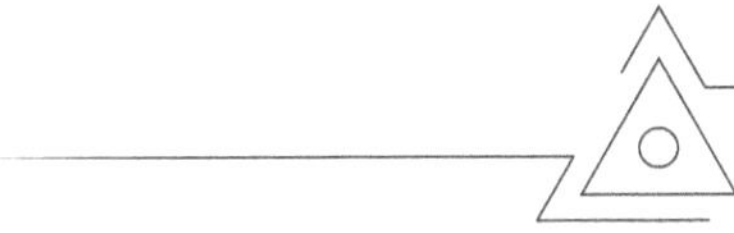

General Gino Baneras kept his promise, but not without struggle.

Almost immediately, he learned to internalize the pain shared by Almelsilv. It was a rather simple dilemma to him: either learn to wield the mask and use it to take the resources he and his legion desperately needed, or die in the mountains. That did not make it easy, however. Gino suffered more than he ever thought possible, but he pushed himself, more for the sake of his own soldiers than for the sake of the Empire.

Under Silv-Thaar Markhor's tutelage, he learned how to focus his mind, and it did not take him long to learn the art of shapeshifting. Gino found his half-form of a steppe wild horse—known as a takhi among the tribes of the plains—like the ones he used to catch and train on the Great Steppes as a young boy. Strong-jawed, thick-limbed, well-hung, and dark-maned was he, now assuming the title of Silv-Thaar.

Silv-Thaar Baneras practiced his mindspeech on the surviving horses from their decimated army, who were easy to manipulate, to coerce, and to command. He soon mastered the insidious art of mindlocking and told the Red Stag he was ready to march back in to take control of the giants who lived within the Archstone Dome.

"They will be waiting for us when we breach," the Red Stag said to his Silv-Thaars. "If we encounter any immediate threats, we must force the tunnel closed, then regroup. Are we clear?"

Markhor nodded her spiraling horns. Baneras simply squinted with determination as he finished tying his mane, then grabbed his longbow.

They were deep within the pipes that led into the Archstone Dome, waiting by the final pipe segment, the one that the behemoths had demolished during the battle. The debris was now strangled by vines, and the interior of the dome remained beyond sight.

A troop of shield bearers tightened their formation around Monarch Hallow, his Silv-Thaars, and a handful of shamans, creating a perfect shell to protect the officers from projectiles, then advanced slow as a tortoise.

The vines parted, ever so slowly.

"I see movement," Baneras said. "I hear them, too."

He scanned with Almelsilv's sight, and past the opening vines sensed a dozen humanoid figures. They were hiding behind a newly constructed stone wall pocked with arrowslits.

"Hold," the Red Stag ordered. "They are well aware of us now." He visualized the threads and felt something more than just a new wall. "They dug a moat. There is water and spikes between us and them."

"If I could make one of the half-bloods aware of my presence, I could take them," Baneras said. "Let me try."

He borrowed a shield from a soldier and carefully stepped forward, opening the vines so that he could see past the moat, directly into the arrowslits.

An eager arrow immediately found his shield, bouncing off the magnium-reinforced plate. Baneras kept advancing until he was certain the warriors within the fortifications could see him, until there was a clear empathic link between them. He then reached with his mind to ensnare, to take control of the unsuspecting, half-formed humans who waited beyond.

Five arrows slammed into his shield with enough force to nearly topple him to his back. A sixth was more carefully aimed, striking the one portion of Baneras's body that had been briefly exposed: his hooves.

"Fuck!" the horse yelped, quickly closing the vines before more projectiles found him. "They fucking got me!"

"What happened?" the Red Stag asked. "Why did you not command them to stop?"

"I tried," he said, reaching down to break the arrow, leaving the sharp tip wedged in his calcareous hoof. "I could not mindlock them. I could not see into their minds like I can with our horses!"

"Pity," the Red Stag said. "Perhaps they are not half-formed enough to be controlled."

"If I may, Monarch Hallow," one of the shamans interjected.

"Speak your mind, Heraz," he said to them.

"Wastyrian philosophers have long speculated about the loss of our true voices, the human mind's ability to mindspeak. Our scholars believe it is within that ability that the key to mindlocking resides. Those half-formed beasts in there have no Silvesh over their heads, they are still human, as beastly as they might seem. In the case of Baneras, Markhor, and yourself, it is your Silvesh that grant the ability, not your forms. I believe the attempt was soundly founded, but it will not lead to the sought outcome."

The ground suddenly trembled, and then shook again and again, with a pounding beat like a war drum within the ground itself.

"The giants," Baneras said with a long smile. "Those idiots called their giants for aid." He rushed to take his position back in front of the group.

"Wait, Baneras," the Red Stag said.

"I'm doing things differently this time, Monarch Hallow," the horse replied, and he began to will the vines to open once more; this time not straight ahead of him, but up at an angle, forming a tunnel that once fully opened looked into the dome's sky. And there, silhouetted against the distant, pastel-white light of the arudinn, he saw a neck long and thick as a tree trunk, and above it a head like that of a hornless rhinoceros.

Baneras whistled. The behemoth stopped, turned his head, and with that alone, his fate was sealed.

"You are mine, beast," he whispered, burrowing into the giant's mind like a wasp laying eggs inside a live caterpillar. "And you shall do my bidding, from now till the Endfall swallows all lands."

His first order was direct and clear: kill every Alampaari within eyesight, then demolish the barrier.

The colossus complied, and then the invasion began.

One by one, the odd-hoofed animals fell to Baneras's merciless trap. One after the other, they rushed to trample the fortifications the Alampaari tried to shelter behind.

With the added power of the perissodactyls, the Red Stag's army flourished once more. And the Alampaari Miscam, too honorable and stubborn to surrender, had no choice but to flee or be slaughtered

PART TWO
BOARS AND BEARS

CHAPTER TEN

SUID REUNION

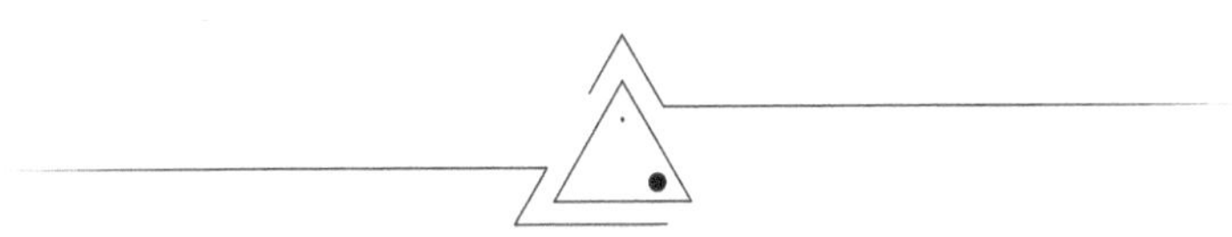

Drolvisdinn's green sails shone brightly with the blessings of the morning sun, the lines casting vein-like shadows over the leaf-shaped canvases. Ever since the ship had sailed out of the Varanus Dome, the days had been gray and the visibility low due to the mists of early Umbra, but today the first blue skies brightened the crew's fur and skin, and even Sceres had come out to rejoice in the warmth.

"Her colors are much too beautiful," Nalaníri remarked, her head tilted up, floppy ears bending backward. "She was purple d'day we left Nagra-drolom. Now she's a-turned d'color uf fresh watercress sprouts. A good omen I take this is."

"It's the unavoidable changing of her seasons," Kitjári explained, her eyes also on the Jade moon, who was merely a waning sliver, but indisputably green against the brightening sky.

Nalaníri shifted her gaze toward the mainmast. "Cap'n, how does d'path look?"

"Waters are clear!" Hud Ilsed informed them. The Laatu chief climbed down from the crow's nest, her red kilt billowing like flames. She landed gracefully and added, "Our sails will deliver us to your dome's wall by this afternoon." She walked over to stand next to the boar and bear as she collapsed the spyglass stolen from Admiral Grinn. "This device confuses my scalp, but is much too useful." She rubbed her eyes as she handed it back to Kitjári.

"You might be able to buy one at the city of Koroberg," Kitjári said, "east of the Fjordlands Dome. They'll be happy to trade goods for soot. Or once you return home, you can buy them at big cities in the Zovarian Union, as long as they hold no quarrel against your race."

It had been a bit over a week since they had split ways from Lago-Sterjall, Aio-Kulak, Alaia, Sunu, and Siffo. *Drolvisdinn* had struck a headwind while traveling northeast, so their journey had dragged on longer than expected. Now they were at last nearing the dome of the Puqua tribe—almost a month had passed since Nalaníri had set it to open, and even at a glance, it looked strikingly different. The monumental structure still looked solid, but the smaller vines had shriveled away, leaving dark holes throughout the surface. When the wayfarers finally arrived at the wall, they did not need to use their Silvesh to open passages. *Drolvisdinn* sailed right in.

It was past midnight inside the dome, and the arudinn that would light the vines in the morning were still fast asleep, yet the interior was awash with an otherworldly brilliance. Shafts of light from the afternoon sun shone through the cracks in the dome like heavenly roots, making the sea glow like emeralds and sapphires wherever they touched down. Slim tiles of blue sky were visible in the roof of the dome, like shards of a broken vase. Day and night would be mixed in this land for many months to come, until all that remained was a spiderweb of the thickest structural vines, which would take a long time to unweave themselves.

They made their way north past the islands and fjords, toward Birlénno, the port closest to the capital city of Krûn. There was an odd shimmer in the air, like a shattered haze.

"What is that?" Nalaníri asked in wonderment, pointing at the branching top of the trunk. The beams of sunlight near it had become sparklingly brighter, shifting in marbled patterns of luminance.

"The snow at the dome's summit is falling through," Kitjári answered.

"It's beautiful. Like a mist uf gold."

As she finished saying that, a few flurries reached them, incongruous and gelid. The flakes melted instantly upon touching their faces.

By the time they entered the Birlénno fjords, the trunk was beginning to light up, while outside the dome Sunnokh was ablaze in yellow and orange, stretching horizontal beams of sunset across the eighty miles of the dome. Nalaníri seemed nostalgic watching the spectacle, nearly mournful.

"We've got company," Kitjári muttered, snapping Nalaníri out of her spell.

Nalaníri glanced toward the approaching city, then snorted. "Them are not Puqua ships at d'port," she warned. "Zovarian?"

Kitjári shook her head. "They look Khaar Du. Probably trading ships. I guess the economy is moving already, not wasting any time. But keep your eyes open in case you see ships with pink sails."

They docked at the port of Birlénno.

Nalaníri asked for Puqua volunteers to help *Drolvisdinn* sail to the Moordusk Dome, as she did not want to force the sailors who had helped operate the ship to continue on this journey if they did not want to. Unsurprisingly, everyone in the crew felt eager to explore the worlds beyond and would not allow others to replace them.

"My scalp offers its thanks," Hud Ilsed told the sailors and Nalaníri. "You fought bravely with us, helped sail our ship away from danger. We carry differences hard to overcome, but my heart treasures your courage, and my scalp admires your kindness."

Nalaníri grunted her acknowledgment.

"Thank you for carrying us in your mighty ship," Kitjári said to Ilsed. "Now return safely home and tell Ierun Alúma all that has happened."

Kenondok stepped closer and stood by Ilsed's side. "And my eyes will search for the Nu'irg ust Mindrel," the monolithic weaponsmith said, "and deliver Khuron Aio-Kulak's message to her spotted ears. My oath stands." The brawny man still openly showed his disdain for the Puqua and anyone else who did not follow the Laatu ways, but he was a man of his word.

Kitjári and Nalaníri disembarked, then watched *Drolvisdinn* sail away. Sunnokh was now below the hidden horizon, illuminating only the top of the dome. The highest vines glowed a deep magenta that merged with the spreading pastel whites of the trunk.

It was very early morning for the locals. Many had traveled to the borders to see the New World, leaving the docks mostly deserted. Nalaníri spotted a merchant she knew, working at a fishery. She greeted her by rubbing noses and asked, "Do ye know d'whereabouts uf Probo?"

"Aye Lurr, I hear d'Nu'irg's a-helping d'suids migrate through d'northern mountains, by d'city uf Claoth. Shell I send an envoy t'get him?"

"Nah, we'll travel t'him. But if ye could hold that kuba who's about t'depart, we would much appreciate a ride to Krûn."

"I'll see to it, Lurr."

The kubanochoerus had been loaded with gifts to be delivered to Krûn, brought by Khaar Du traders who were looking to make themselves rich by being among the first to trade commodities for kenzir stones. Kitjári and Nalaníri rode the mammoth-sized suid up the Stelm Shäerath, following the lodestone trails, and stopped at the Guildhall of Krûn, where Nalaníri was very glad to find Malnûvi, the elder chief of Onbar.

Malnûvi explained that most of the chiefs had taken the pilgrimage with their citizens, while regents had been volunteered to maintain order in the cities. Nalaníri asked Malnûvi to gather as many representatives from the provinces as was possible.

"I will send birds fur them," the long-snouted elder said. "We can have 'em regents here within a day or two."

The regents made haste and arrived by the following day. Once gathered at the guildhall, Nalaníri explained how she and Kitjári had a mission to travel east to open the domes the Red Stag had sacked. The regents offered warriors to protect them, but Nalaníri declined their aid, as they would need to travel fast and remain unnoticed. She did, however, accept an offer of fresh supplies, particularly Winter parkas; the end of the year approached, and with it the heavy blizzards of Hoartide would arrive.

Kitjári traveled with her scouting backpack filled with survival equipment, including her quaar rope. Nalaníri brought her tusked axe, as well as her multipurpose chef's knife which had a blade laminated in rose patterns and a solid ironwood handle. She also carried a cumbersome—but in her mind, indispensable—amount of cooking supplies and flavorful spices. To help with the journey, Malnûvi recruited the two best companion suids left in the Tricolored Mountain.

Nalaníri's ride was Gufrok, who was of a giant suid species known as a *celebochoerus*. Gufrok had long caramel-colored fur striped in white; he brandished four enormous upper tusks, which extended sideways like the horns of a longhorn highlander.

Kitjári would be riding Nupáll, a giant domestic pig of wiry gray fur with bright-pink skin underneath. Nupáll had a wide nose that probed everywhere she went. Both suids were roughly the size of horses, albeit a bit shorter and a fair amount thicker. Their mounts were readied, and soon the two wayfarers departed north in search of Probo.

"Can't venture far frum home with no honey truffles," Nalaníri explained as they made a brief stop in the Slømmon Forest. She hopped off Gufrok and looked up at a black-topped hoodoo. "I can't possibly survive fur that long without them, them are a necessity fur mine heart's wellbeing."

The forest looked very different now that the leaves had fallen. The ground was covered with piles of reds and browns, and sprinkled with fresh snow.

"Mayhap this one over here," Nalaníri said, approaching a tall hoodoo. "It's shaded un d'north side. Them are mour likely t'grow in d'shade."

"Not that one," Kitjári said. "Come this way, I can smell them. This shorter hoodoo has a bunch of them, I'm certain of it."

Kitjári was right.

"I'll show ye how t'tie d'rope around yer waist," the boar offered, but the bear would have none of it.

"It's a curious technique, but too easy to slip. I'll show you how it's done, with a proper rope."

Nalaníri snorted derisively, tucked her rope away, and crossed her arms. Kitjári swung her quaar rope over the top of the hoodoo, tied it with a practiced move, and used it to expertly pull herself up while using her foot claws for traction.

"See? Told you," the bear called as she ascended the rust-colored column. She plucked a dozen small but ripe truffles from between the red and black layers of rock, tossed them to Nalaníri, then climbed back down. "And I didn't even fall my ass on you when getting down," she said as she reached the ground and wiped off her handpaws.

Nalaníri pretend-smiled, stowing the truffles away in her vest pockets.

"Yer nose will come in handy," she finally acquiesced as they got back on their mounts. "If Probo's a-going with us, we'll need yer skills, as he's most demanding n'too lazy t'find his own share uf food."

They followed the lodestones down the northern slope of Stelm Shäerath, finding lodging at the town of Cazze for the night, then continued north all the way to the edge of the dome, not too far from the kenzir mines of Erne Brumm, where Nalaníri had lived until her early teen years.

They slowed down as they came upon a group of travelers who were headed toward the vines. "Have ye hogs seen Probo?" Nalaníri asked.

"Lurr Prikka-Nalaníri!" a babirusa-headed man called out. "Glad t'see ye returned!"

A mostly plain-skinned teenager popped up from behind him. "D'Nu'irg went north 'round d'Keldris Klannath!" she said excitedly. "He's been a-showing d'herd where t'move to. If ye fullow d'shore n'them hoof prints, ye'll find him."

Nalaníri thanked them, then she and Kitjári moved on. When they reached the wall of vines, Nalaníri stopped and turned around, taking one last look at Nagradrolom. The arudinn were turning dark, leaving only the largest of the vines and the splitting trunk still alight. As night settled into her old home, so did part of the New World's morning, piercing dozens of horizontal light beams from east to west, as Sunnokh found his way in through cracks and crevices. The Tricolored Mountain glowed, alight in soft whites from above and a reddish-orange beam from the side.

Nalaníri watched her two worlds blend into one. "I shell miss these fjords, these mountains," she whispered. "N'mine Puqua people too. I've had mine share uf problems with them many a time in d'past, but I love them thick-headed suids. This land will be much different by d'time I return. *If* I return. N'so will its people."

Kitjári saw her friend's eyes sparkling orange with tears. She wanted to ask Nalaníri whether she would also miss her two children, but there was a disconnect there, an unspoken sore spot the boar had never opened up about. Kitjári nudged Nupáll to inch closer to Gufrok. "Before all this began," she started, "I traveled extensively through the New World, from Bergsulf's frozen shores to the Sajal's boiling lakes. Then I saw the dying wonders inside Heartpine, the buried mysteries of Da'áju, the endless greens of the Moordusk Dome. And then I briefly got to see your magnificent fjords, and even the terrifying beauty of the Varanus Dome. Each has been a blessing, and each new wonder drives my thirst to see more. And despite all this, I can't wait for the day I return home to the forests of Farsulf, the vastness of the Klad Senet, and the jagged cliffs of the Pilgrim Sierras." She drew in a long breath, then exhaled slowly. "Your land is beautiful and unique. I wish I had seen more of it."

"Mayhap once this is all over, ye'll show me yer homeland, n'I'll show ye what remains uf mine." Nalaníri wiped her eyes and turned toward the vines. "Let us hurry now. We must a-find that bothersome Nu'irg."

Traversing the wall of vines was a surreal experience. The holes the vines had left behind were now filled with sap, which they had to avoid by taking circular paths around the many craters. The largest pools were all liquid, with yellowish crystals beginning to solidify on top; the smaller holes had mostly dried up, at least on the crusty lids at their tops. The entirety of the half-lit space reeked sharply of sap.

They exited the dome to find snow had fallen on the outside world. It wasn't much, merely a fresh covering that would soon melt, but it was a portent of more to come. The tracks the suids had left were easy to follow, tracing a muddy path around the shores of the Keldris Klannath. The hoof prints took them through new fjords and headlands, then bent toward a compound of ruins where Puqua droves had been gathering to barter and trade with Khaar Du caravans.

"We need to stay away from those crowds," Jiara said, stowing Urnaadisilv away. "That road connects the lands of the Khaar Du with Koroberg, which is part of the Zovarian Union. We don't want any Zovarians spotting a conspicuous couple and reporting it to the capital."

"There's plenty uf suid-faced Puqua among them," Nalaníri retorted. "And ye as a bear don't look much different."

"We are not taking any risks. Your mask."

Nalaníri reluctantly shapeshifted, put her mask away, and combed her short hair back.

"Jis' till we're out uf them sights," she griped as Prikka, unhappy to be back in her pink-and-black-patterned human skin.

Farther east, the suid tracks trampled away from the main road, heading toward a fertile headland where almost no snow had accumulated. Thick and ancient trees grew around the many glacial-fed creeks, while vast open fields stretched south toward Spine Bay, which the Puqua knew as the Keldris Klannath.

Once far from any passersby, they returned to their half-forms and followed the tracks to a field sprinkled with glacier-deposited boulders, where they spotted a herd of babirusas, bushpigs, javelinas, and wild boars. The suids were working together, methodically plowing the ground in a coordinated manner. There was even a sounder of kubas at the periphery pushing enormous boulders to create a wall.

"What are they doing?" Kitjári asked, but before Nalaníri could answer, she was interrupted by a distant squeal. The herd parted, and bounding out of the group hurried Probo in his javelina primal form, sprinting and slipping in his excitement. As he closed the distance, he jumped at Nalaníri and in midair shifted into a pygmy hog so she might catch him.

"Ye filthy, lovable, rotten gourd. I missed ye. There's much I have t'tell ye about. Ye've met Gufrok n'Nupáll before, haven't ye?"

Probo grunted twice, then scurried away and crawled onto the saddlebag on Gufrok's hind side, digging around with his wet nose until he loosened the top flap.

"Get uff, ye pampered swine!" Nalaníri said, shoving Probo to the ground. "Them honey truffles are fur cooking, not fur inhaling. Them have to last us fur long roads n'cold nights."

Probo squealed his discontent, staring up at her dejectedly.

"N'a filthy mouth too! But I tell ye what… If ye show us a good place t'camp, n'if ye bring me some fresh tubers, I may consider inviting ye fur lunch. Mayhap even dinner."

They removed the saddles from Gufrok and Nupáll, setting their camp next to a calm creek. Probo soon returned with fresh ingredients.

Nalaníri prepared a roasted rutabaga dish with shaved honey truffles and pepper. While they ate, she explained to Probo what had happened during their trip and what their next mission was. She spoke out loud to the Nu'irg, who nodded along.

"I thought only Banook and Mamóru were able to understand our languages this well," Kitjári observed.

"Oh, he's dense as a turnip, don't ye worry. He doesn't understand mine words, but I'm mindspeaking t'him at d'same time. I'm saying d'words out loud fur mine n'yer sake, not fur his."

She carried on with her conversation with the Nu'irg. Kitjári paid close attention to their rosy, opalescent auras, and could see the way the empathic focus made them entwine with the threads around them in a clear flow. It was pure meaning without syntax being communicated, and though she tried to tap into it, she could not, as her ursid qualia did not match that of suids.

"I need to learn how to do this," Kitjári said, "but I haven't seen a single bear since I began to wear Urnaadisilv."

"Ye'll get t'practice soon. In d'morrow, we'll find us some good ol' bears."

Some hours before sunset, Probo left them to help his herd, organizing the lines of suids and making sure they dug in the right spots. Kitjári and Nalaníri climbed atop a boulder to watch them work.

"Probo told me this is d'first herd that left d'dome," Nalaníri said. "Them had been scouting fur weeks till them scented this fertile soil. Them've been working d'land to plant key species that are important fur them survival n'fur Noss's health, so that them will sprout eagerly in d'meltwaters uf Thawing."

"How do they know what to plant?"

"Our shamans told him n'our companion species. Noss had precise instructions fur d'time uf d'reopening. Animals can easily move about, but plants cannot. Some will die, some will thrive, n'some are too essential to risk. This 'ere seems like a perfect land t'begin d'spread, with no plain-skinned humans around t'bother them."

"They certainly seem smarter than the wild boars we used to... chase, back in the Free Tribelands."

Nalaníri pondered for a moment. "Ye know what? This would be a great time t'show Probo our new secret."

"Secret?"

"What Noss taught us. I have not told him 'bout this yet, I've been wanting t'surprise him. Mind if I go mess with d'herd fur a moment?"

"Not at all. I'll be watching from up here. But don't try doing that when you are on your own."

"I know, m'dear, I'll have ye close-by in case I get too lost in d'feeling. N'Probo, too, I trust him."

Nalaníri hopped down from the boulder. Kitjári smiled at the sight of her bouncing, tufted tail springing up and down as Nalaníri rushed to the side of the creek and undressed.

With no hesitation, Nalaníri dropped onto all fours and shapeshifted into her wild boar feral form. She snuck around the boulder and seemed to tiptoe, if that was possible to do with hooves, and was about to go join the herd when Kitjári called from above her, then jumped down beside her.

"Hold on. If you want to be sneaky, this will give you away too soon." She reached for the boar's glowing nosering, unscrewed one of the shining beads, then slid the ring off. "Now go, scare that filthy beast, and have fun." She slapped the boar's buttocks, then climbed back on the rock to watch.

The boar approached Probo carefully. She stopped next to the javelina and waited.

Probo stood still, feeling uneasy. He turned and scanned around, gazing right past the suid in front of him, searching for something that seemed misplaced. Nalaníri grunted, but Probo still looked past her, scenting something familiar. He then glanced down and recognized the fur pattern on the boar, smelled her nose, then squealed so loud that all the suids around him jumped.

Kitjári chuckled as she watched Probo chase after her friend. The two ran in circles, dirtying their fur, stomping over freshly planted seeds, and scaring a litter of dumbfounded piglets.

"Just graceless swine is all you are," Kitjári thought out loud. "And how happy you look."

Once they tired, the pair walked about leisurely, mindspeaking to the other suids. Then they went on exploring the headland until they ran too far from Kitjári's sight.

It was getting dark.

Kitjári set to hang pharolith lamps around their camp. A bit unnerved, she stopped her work, then looked around and called, "Nalaníri? Probo?" No response. *What trouble are those two getting into?* she wondered. She grabbed a lamp and went to explore the headland. "Hey, have you seen those two idiots?" she asked a dozing kuba, hoping the companion suid would understand her words. The giant suid knew enough Puqua to get by, but not Common, so she snorted back a non-reply.

"Probo? Nalaníri?" Kitjári tried.

The kuba grunted wetly, tilting her head to point her forehead horn toward a copse of birches. Kitjári hurried to the trees and found the boar and javelina slumbering on top of each other on a grassy mound, covered in mud, branches, and leaves.

"Okay Lurr Sty, I think you've had enough," she said, shaking the boar awake. "Let's get you cleaned up."

The boar heard the words, but barely understood them. Probo awoke as well, noticed her hesitation, and mindspoke a nudge until she came to her senses, until she remembered the other aspects of herself. The boar grunted twice and shifted back into her half-form, indifferent about her nakedness and her mud-splattered, wiry fur.

As they walked back to the camp, Nalaníri held a contagious grin on her snout. "Thank ye fur letting me do that," she said with a giggle. "It was a magical experience. I haven't jumped 'round like that since I was a piglet. Can Nu'irgesh get heart attacks? I think mine trick gave Probo a big one."

"You two were delightful to watch. I can get dinner started while you go wash. The creek is very cold, though."

"Cold water has never stopped a Puqua before. I'll be back in a few moments t'warm up."

Kitjári struck her brime cube to start a bonfire, then lit a smaller cooking fire to the side, where she set water to boil. She wanted to prepare the last of the isopods before they went bad, but as she looked through Nalaníri's bag, she could not find them, so she went to the creek to ask about them.

She did not find Nalaníri, but Prikka, up to her thighs in cold water. She sidestepped behind a rock to watch. Prikka was filling Nagrasilv with water, emptying it over her short hair, letting it roll down her hairy armpits and muddy back. She had seen Nalaníri naked a few times before, but never Prikka. She stared at the spotted patterns of pink and black skin, at the portly body, at the curved hips, and the small flushed breasts, until she became uncomfortable with her shameless peeping.

"Do you know where the quoll-quolls are?" she called out, pretending to be just arriving.

Prikka jumped and turned to face her. In an unexpected display of modesty, she covered her breasts with one arm and placed Nagrasilv over her crotch. "Ye scared me! Some privacy, if I may?"

Kitjári averted her eyes and asked the question again.

"Probo got to mine bag earlier. Them quoll-quolls were lost to his selfish snout. Give me jis' a moment, I'll dry out n'help ye. I was a-thinking uf cooking d'sweet potatoes t'night."

After Prikka was done bathing, they ate their sweet dish as they warmed up by the fire. Jiara was relaxing in her human form, feeling the warmth caress her skin. She downed a gulp of cold water from her canteen, then handed it to Nalaníri. "I'm sorry I scared you earlier."

Nalaníri took a sip, then snorted. "Not scared… It's jis'… I'm a bit shy when it comes t'mine human form. I shell've warned ye."

"You don't seem shy at all in your other forms though."

"Nah, this plump boar body I'm much proud uf," she said, patting her belly. "But unlike yerself, I'm not much happy when mine fur goes away. It's not a pretty sight."

Jiara felt compelled to vocally disagree. She shook her head and mumbled, "I-I don't understand why you think that."

"It's one uf d'reasons I was picked t'be d'Nagrafröa. D'way our tribe works… worked, is peculiar. I have no suid traits uther than mine odd-colored skin, n'even that can be seen as jis' a skin condition. We Puqua treasure suid traits so much that frum very young we are made t'believe that if we are plain-skinned, we are ugly n'lesser than uthers."

"That's terrible! Anyone should be happy in their own skin. But… if being plain-skinned is seen as negative, why would they pick you as the Nagrafröa?"

"When d'Puqua decided t'break d'Miscam rules, them vowed t'make sure that all families would be given d'chance to breed in, so that d'blood uf d'tribe would remain strong. Puqua who already have many suid traits are 'wasted' by a-wearing Nagrasilv, as them have already been bred in with uthers like themselves, meaning them are more closely related to Noiu-Lømappor, d'first Nagrafröa t'have fertile, partially suid children."

Nalaníri tightened her jaw, then continued. "Mine family is not so closely related to old Lømappor, making us uf a lesser caste in d'eyes uf d'tribe. Mine mother had spotted skin, n'mine father was plain-skinned as a mole rat, so we were poor n'worked d'kenzir mines like d'other plain-skins in d'village. 'Twas a great honor to mine family when d'chiefs chose me t'be d'next wielder uf Nagrasilv."

"How did they pick you?"

"Mine mother was a friend uf d'chief uf Gwur Innalv. Ye've met him. He took to like me n'recommended me fur d'role. Each pruvince provided one candidate, n'I was d'lucky winner." Nalaníri leaned back and reached into her bag. She brought out a small bottle filled with a most potent rum-braaw, which was meant for cooking and not for drinking. She allowed herself a small sip, then handed the bottle to Jiara.

Jiara capped it without drinking. "If I met that chief… Do you mean that man who showed up at your home before we left the dome, with your children? I can't recall his—"

"Odask. That's him. He's d'one who—" she absentmindedly rubbed her heart-shaped nose, noticing something missing. "Mine nosering."

"Sorry, here," Jiara said, retrieving it from her pocket.

Nalaníri pushed the ring through her septum, then continued while she screwed the bead back on. "I was a-saying, Odask is d'one who gave me mine nosering. It's how d'Puqua show that them are married. When I accepted Nagrasilv, I didn't know I was accepting t'be bred by Odask. As soon as I turned fifteen n'learned t'take mine half-form, after d'celebration with mine family, Odask took me to his bed. N'many a time again thereafter. He kept saying he was doing it fur d'sake uf d'tribe."

Jiara tried to prevent an awkward silence, but only made it more awkward by stumbling on her words. "Why would—that's not, not even right to… I—"

"Them give us no choice," Nalaníri went on. "If we want t'keep d'mask n'not lose that half uf ourselves, we must bear at least two children. N'so I did mine job."

Jiara wanted to scoot closer to comfort her friend, but did not know how to do so. Her tongue tied a few times before she finally managed to say, "That's… I'm sorry. I could not imagine what that must've been like. When we first got to know the Puqua, their openness to different ways of living was inspiring. We thought they… we thought you all were more forward-thinking, I guess. But it seems like all cultures figure out a way to make themselves go backward and allow for unnecessary suffering."

"We have many things t'be proud uf, n'some things t'fill our hearts with shame. But we must let d'pride outweigh d'shame. That's what I think, that's what I try n'live fur. But it makes me feel bad, fur mine children. I love Rushun n'Pau, but I could never love them as much as them deserved. I never wanted children, but I still wish d'best fur them both. N'I never want another man t'touch me, not after Odask."

Nalaníri stood and ambled toward her bedroll. "So there ye have it, mine plain-skinned friend. That's why ye may find this boar maiden a bit apprehensive at times. N'I appreciate ye holding yer curiosity at bay n'letting me a-tell ye under mine own terms, but don't feel like I'm unapproachable. I'm happy t'talk about any uf mine dreams or fears with ye. Jis' don't go spying un mine furless arse again."

Chapter Eleven

Urnaadi's Emissaries

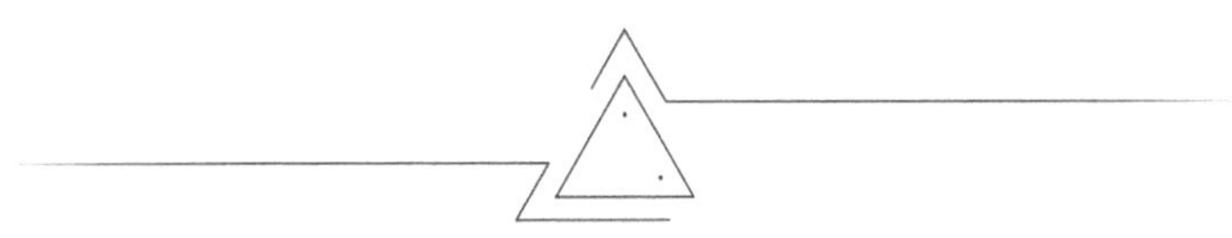

"Do you think Probo will miss the sounder we left behind?" Kitjári asked, watching the Nu'irg lead the way while she kept a handpaw on Nupáll's wiry neck fur.

"He's taught them all them need to know to carry un with d'planting n'spreading," Nalaníri confidently replied, riding on Gufrok. "He says he's happier fullowing us un this mission."

Probo stopped, carefully studying the path ahead, then looked to Nalaníri.

"He says t'cross d'road here, to fullow d'valley east, not south."

"Better if we move far from this road either way," Kitjári said. "Bears don't venture south of the mountains, and it's the bears we are after."

Probo checked the road—still clear—then grunted and trotted across onto a hidden path.

"D'Puqua used t'live all across Fjordsulf n'd'Stelm Nedross before a-taking residence in Nagradrolom," Nalaníri said. "This is Probo's land. Fur thousands uf years he explored these mountains, valleys, n'fjords. There's no better guide than him."

Probo proudly pranced ahead. Kitjári watched his oversized testicles as they bounced obscenely, like udders, as the javelina led them to a river-cut valley. They followed a white-capped creek that meandered toward a distant, snowy peak: Mount Punwok. A few miles into the valley, they entered a verdant forest of thin, tall stalks that shifted in the breeze like a sea of green.

Nalaníri scanned the tubular plants. "What are them giant asparagus trees? N'mour importantly, can we eat them?"

"They aren't asparagus. They are bamboo. And you can eat the younger shoots if you cook them properly. We should cut some for lunch. I'll show you how to prepare them."

Probo was ahead of them, enjoying the gentle wind while weaving a path for them. He suddenly stopped, then huffed. On the mossy ground in front of the Nu'irg was a creature lazily munching on bamboo leaves. Five more were behind the first, one up a tree and the others on the ground eating or sleeping, including a young one small as a human toddler.

Nupáll and Gufrok stopped behind Probo.

Nalaníri cocked her head as she eyed the animals. "What un Noss's dearest face are them fuzzy creatures?"

"They're pandas!" Kitjári exclaimed. "It's a kind of bear. Banook told us they lived far in the western mountains, but I've never seen one."

Nalaníri listened to Probo's thoughts, then said, "Probo says them didn't live in these forests back when he roamed these lands. He says them lived far east across d'Ash Sea. I think that one wants t'say hello to ye, d'little darling." Indeed, the panda nearest Kitjári hesitantly stepped forward, eager yet confused, sensing something he felt closely bound to, yet having no memory of it.

Kitjári hopped down from her giant pig and approached the panda. He was a sizable male, and though he seemed intrigued, he also seemed too lazy to do much about it. Kitjári squatted in front of him to squeeze his round, black ears.

"Hey buddy. Our friend Banook told us a lot about you." The other pandas slowly approached and sat near them. The cub began to chew on Kitjári's dark-walnut cloak.

Nalaníri dismounted and inspected the funny creatures. "I've never seen no bears uther than yerself. I thought them'd be a bit… fiercer. N'faster-moving."

"There are other kinds you'll get to meet soon enough."

"Well, these black n'white loaves aren't going t'be running away frum us— ye might give it a try at mindspeaking with them. Someone's gotta tell them t'move them arses south."

Kitjári sat on a mossy mound and watched as the pandas ripped the bamboo leaves and slowly munched on them. One of the adults rested on his side and began to snore. The cub rolled around, trying to grab his own nubby tail.

Kitjári tried to focus, aiming to find some common ground with these creatures, but they still felt so alien to her. She had met black bears, brown bears, kiuons, spectacled bears, and sun bears, all of whom she could somehow relate to. She tried to commune with the pandas for a while, sometimes with her eyes closed, uncertain of how much time had elapsed.

"Do ye think them float?"

"Huh?" Kitjári snapped out of her trance.

"Do ye think them balls uf fluff can float? How buoyant are them? I don't see them a-taking a hike through d'mountains with us. D'best we could do fur them is toss 'em into d'Isdinnklad n'hope d'currents carry them south."

"Don't be so mean! How can you say that when they are so adorable?"

"Ya, in a most useless sort uf way. Carry un, I'll collect them bamboo shoots while ye try t'talk some sense into them."

Kitjári strained herself to communicate with the ursids, but she had no luck. It was merely her first attempt, and she did not quite understand how to approach it. She did catch the attention and curiosity of the pandas, but she guessed that had more to do with the presence of Urnaadisilv, not with any skills of her own. She heard Nalaníri approach with her bamboo harvest, and suddenly felt awfully hungry.

Hhrruuff, the large panda huffed next to Kitjári, handing her a handful of bamboo leaves. Kitjári stared at him. "Thank you," she said. She took the leaves from the panda's paws, noticing a faint connection that slipped out of her mind before she could grab a hold of it.

Kitjári taught Nalaníri how to peel, cut, and braise the bamboo shoots. It took a while until lunch was ready, as they first needed to boil out the toxins and bitterness, but once that was done, Nalaníri worked magic with her spices and served their meal.

Wholly satisfied, Probo led the way once more. He was quite proficient at finding paths through the mountains, even if the trails he had known in times before the Downfall had been overgrown and eroded. By the sixth day of Fog-dawn, they arrived at the southern base of the mighty Mount Punwok, which was fully blanketed by fresh snow, its summit hiding behind the Umbra mists.

They had encountered more pandas along their journey, as well as black bears and brown bears. Kitjári had kept practicing, feeling a wisp of a connection now and then, but her attempts at mindspeech had borne no fruit.

They camped in a cold maple forest that had forsaken all its leaves, where they lit a bonfire underneath two toppled tree trunks. Jiara had shot a ptarmigan, which they'd just finished eating. She tossed the leg bones into the snow behind her, then shimmied closer to the flames.

"Fire always feels much better when I have no fur on," she said. "It's more direct. I feel each flick of the flame at the moment it happens instead of merely feeling the warmth seep slowly into me."

Urnaadisilv rested on her left knee, as if watching the flames with intent. She poked at the fire with a long stick. "You should try it too."

"I can feel it over mine bare nose."

"That's not the same, and you know it." She quieted for a prolonged moment, then tried once more. "I'm not Puqua. What you look like as Prikka is what we are used to seeing every day."

"It's not mine best self," she countered.

"Who cares? We can be all of our selves."

Nalaníri's lips lifted ever so slightly over her tiny tusks. "Maybe fur a little while," she conceded. Her wiry fur and long snout turned smoky and translucent, but did so slowly, as if she was savoring the transformation, as if it was something she hadn't done many times in the past. Her hoofed hands ran over her vanishing fur, over the liquid smoke that was somehow a solid, exploring the smooth transition. Her glowing nosering sank into the refracting forms as they turned black as coal and coalesced into Nagrasilv. Prikka lowered the suid mask onto her knee, mimicking Jiara. She pulled her sleeves up and let the warmth caress her pink-and-black skin, then closed her eyes for a moment.

She looks beautiful, Jiara thought. *And she cannot see it.*

Prikka slightly opened her eyes, conscious of Jiara's stare. "Well, it does feel nice, but I miss mine tusks," she hurriedly said, then put the mask on again. "It's a-getting colder too. It might snow t'night."

"Seems like it. Will Probo be able to find his way in the snow?"

Probo was nuzzling between Gufrok and Nupáll, keeping warm. He lifted his head and grunted softly.

Nalaníri nodded. "Easily. Snow would not stop him. He can find his way even in d'dark."

"The Stelm Nedross are not too bad, but farther east we have to deal with the Stelm Wujann, which are much taller. The only pass I know into them is on the south side, too close to the Zovarian roads."

Nalaníri had a brief conversation with Probo, then turned back to Jiara. "He's not worried. We could take d'path through d'Laaja Khem mines. It was long abandoned in his times, n'it connects d'valley uf Da'áju with a great lake west uf d'mountains, or so he says. Do ye know about that underground path?"

"I've only seen the volcano from far away. The lake Probo mentioned must be the Klad Mahujann, which is frozen year-round, although Banook once told us it didn't use to be frozen before the Downfall. Those paths all fall within the Unclaimed Territories, so it's unlikely anyone knows about them."

"Then them are a-waiting fur us t'rediscover them! D'path under d'volcano used t'be an obsidian mine, Probo says, d'best uf its kind, mour durable than any uther that could be found."

"This might be where Banook got the senstregalv for Leif, Lago's dagger. He mentioned he got it from a volca—"

A familiar bleat mixed with a low hum rumbled behind them. Jiara put her mask on and shifted into her half-form. At once she could see them, and now that she was Kitjári, they saw her too. A pair of kiuons had quietly snuck up behind them to pick at the bones they had discarded in the snow. The dog-sized bears dropped the scraps they were fighting over, bleated their low hums, and came trotting over to Kitjári.

"Kiuons!" she yelled, dropping to her knees to receive them as if they were old friends. The little bears ran circles around her as they wagged their short tails up and down. Kitjári caressed their yellow-and-brown marbled fur, making them drop and expose their bellies, humming all the while.

"What manner uf noisy beasts are these now? Are them bears as well?"

Kitjári let one jump into her arms. "They are, the smallest kind of them. Fast and ferocious, however. They hunt in bigger packs, so more of them must be lurking nearby."

"As long as them don't like swine meat, them look fine to me."

"They won't bother our friends. They can see we are all together. Don't you boys?"

Their short tails wagged something fierce.

They settled back by the fire as Kitjári attempted to communicate with the kiuons, who were more attentive and energetic than the pandas had been and even seemed to make an effort to aid her. Still, she could not find a way to bridge the gap. She tried for a while, until they all grew tired, curled up next to each other, and fell asleep.

The kiuons were gone when Kitjári awoke. She got up and followed their tracks through the frozen forest, then crested a hill. Down in a misty meadow, twenty or so of the creatures were rolling in the snow and dried-up reeds. She recognized the two she had already met, but they didn't notice her peeking at them yet. She focused with flattened ears, squinting and tensing her jaw and neck, sometimes holding her breath.

"Still a-trying?" Nalaníri said, approaching behind her.

"Huh? Yeah, sorry. They don't seem to hear me at all. I can't figure this out."

"First uf all, them need t'be aware uf yer presence, m'dear. If them are not, there's no connection, n'them won't ever hear yer thoughts."

"Shit. Yeah, I knew that. But they are having a good time down there. I didn't want to be a bother."

"It takes time. Fur me it was several weeks before I could mindspeak even a grunt." She rubbed a knuckle on her tusks as she considered an idea. "I think I know what ye need," she said after a pause. "Ye are a-having a hard time a-thinking like a bear. What ye need is to let yerself go, m'dear. Meet yer friends in yer feral form, that way ye will unly have a bear's mind t'think bear thoughts with. Things will seem much clearer that way."

"I'm a bit afraid," Kitjári confessed. "When we tried it at the Varanus Dome, you seemed very in control. But for me, it was hard to come out of it."

"I'll be here t'help ye, jis' listen t'mine voice. It's time ye begin t'spread d'word among yer kind, 'fore we travel much too far. Go, do what ye must, but don't furget t'enjoy yerself while yer at it."

"Okay," Kitjári agreed quickly, excited by the prospect despite her fears. She dropped her clothes atop a rock and, without delay, shapeshifted into her feral form, bouncing down the hill to greet the pack.

Nalaníri watched as the kiuons surrounded the cinnamon-furred black bear, jumping and bleating all around her. They rolled in the snow, chased after each other, and stalked unsuspecting prey. Kitjári was not good at hunting with them—she was too big, too slow, but the kiuons let her try anyway.

Probo came to sit next to Nalaníri.

"Look at them fools," she chuckled. "We must've looked jis' as silly d'uther day. But wasn't it worth it?"

Probo grunted twice.

After a few hours had passed, Nalaníri yelled for her friend to make her way back. Down the hill, the bear turned, sat on her nubby tail, and looked up with unfocused, beady eyes. The bear then turned back to her pack and play-fully bit at the neck of one of the kiuons, who rolled on his back and flashed his claws. The bear heard the strange sound again and looked up. She saw Nalaníri sliding down the snowy hill and recognized her. She was her friend, her companion. She loved her, and would listen to her.

Nalaníri squatted and rubbed her fingers on the bear's round ears. "Ye've had enough fun, m'dear," she said.

The bear licked at Nalaníri's snout, pulling up her lips in an even wider smile. She smelled Nalaníri's arms and chest, noticing the scent of honey truffles somewhere in the pockets of her vest. It was all so familiar, though more intense than she remembered. She sniffed around, scenting something else; she placed her muzzle on Nalaníri's folded legs then pushed her nose farther down into—

Nalaníri stood up and held her at arm's length. "Come un girl. It's time fur ye to turn back. Ye can do this."

The bear remembered words. They tasted soft and shimmered bright now, like petals covered in dew, but she picked up on their meaning. She huffed, closed her eyes, and balanced on her hind paws. Slowly, her proportions changed, although her fur stayed the same.

"There ye are. Welcome back."

"I think I get it now," Kitjári said. "I've been doing this all wrong." She turned to the pack of kiuons and in her mind said, «Hey!» The syllable wasn't truly a syllable, but all the meaning was conveyed in an instant.

The kiuons stopped their thrashing and stared at her. They all listened now.

The entire pack followed them to the camp.

"Do you see it too?" Kitjári asked Nalaníri, looking at the attentive bears that sat in front of them.

"Ye mean them glowing?"

"Yes. Their aura. When they all listen together, when they work together, they get that soft glow about them, just like Sterjall once described to me. It's like I'm talking to one big creature instead of many."

"I've seen it happen with large sounders, but it's not much cummon. Them kiuons seem t'listen mour intently. Them are smarter than uther creatures we've met. Certainly smarter than them foolish pandas."

Kitjári tried to explain to the kiuons why she needed them to move east and south, but she could not make herself understood; many of the abstract ideas had no obvious ways of being translated.

«Red Stag, a general, emperor, I guess. Do you even know what that means? Anyway…» She got stuck in her own thoughts, suddenly portraying too much dread and uncertainty, but not any cohesive call to action. She tried again. «Migration, travel, like geese. You know geese? *Honk.*» Her mindspeech somehow perfectly conveyed the sound geese make, surprising her, but it only bewildered the kiuons, who were not migratory creatures and could not fathom what birds had to do with all this.

«Confused,» one of them conveyed, although it seemed unnecessary to do so.

"What helps fur me," Nalaníri interjected, noticing her struggle, "like ye've seen me do with Probo, is t'simply talk out loud as ye would to a human. Don't try t'have them listen to yer words, them won't understand them, but as d'words make it out yer tongue, yer mind will set in d'right place. Ye can do it without saying it out loud, uf course, but then it would be awfully quiet fur me."

Kitjári followed the recommendation, and out loud she told the kiuons their story. It soon became second nature to her—even if she slurred her words or spoke them too quietly, the connection was made, and the kiuons heard Urnaadi's voice.

Nalaníri listened in, feeling proud. Eventually she called out, "I can prepare breakfast if ye'd like. But fur two, not fur twenty."

"Thank you. And sorry, I'm almost done telling them everything. They seem receptive, even thrilled to help us. They are so smart, perhaps too smart. And one of them has met Banook and has told the pack about him. I told them they should listen to Banook as well, so that they can all follow the plan even if I'm not around to guide them."

After the entire message had been conveyed, Kitjári let the kiuons run back to their meadow.

They finished their breakfast, packed their gear, and rode the giant pig and celebochoerus up the hill. "Hold up a moment, I just want to make sure they understood all I said," Kitjári said, feeling uncertain how well the information she provided had translated. The pack had been hunting in the meadow and was now feeding on an unlucky caribou. Kitjári whistled, and all twenty of the kiuons rushed up to meet her.

She talked with them to see if they had understood; they had, and also seemed miffed by her having to check on them like this. Kitjári apologized, making sure they knew it was not mistrust, but merely caution that prompted her to double-check.

The kiuons repeated her instructions in a wordless series of thoughts. Despite the lack of proper syntax, Kitjári could feel that the essence of the message had been clearly communicated. The kiuons said that after they had finished their meal, they would travel fast to the east, tracking down all the ursids they could and asking them to move south, and then follow the waters toward the rising sun in search of new lands beyond the mountains. They would avoid humans, if possible, not interfering with their matters, their crops, or their cattle. If they encountered Banook, they were to listen to his commands, and let him know the Urnaadifröa was coming to meet with him, and that their migration would open a path for him so that he could travel without bounds. Once they reached the Great River, some bears were to continue east toward the domes, while the rest were to cross the river to settle in the sister mountain ranges, prairies, steppes, and meadows of the south. They would need to expand their territory as far as possible, until they reached the endless shores of the snaking Ophidian Sea. That would be the end of their journey, as the sea was too vast to swim across—any resettling into the Jerjan Continent would have to occur at a different time.

«Migration. *Honk,*» one of the kiuons said with good humor, making Kitjári laugh. Then another of them continued the explanation, conveying that they would recruit other kiuon packs to deliver the exact same message, some of whom would travel west and north so that the entire ursid population of the northern lands of Fjordsulf, Teslurkath, and even the Khaar Du Wastes could be made aware. The kiuons understood the terrain and the distances to the places to which they were to venture, as if the mental map Kitjári held in her head had become part of their collective consciousness.

Not all bears would need to travel away from the mountains, but a large-enough number from each species would be necessary to settle the new lands. Pandas had been exempted due to their particular diet, while polar bears would be told to remain within icy regions, although the kiuons warned that they were known to be stubborn. Kitjári, too, would mindspeak to all bears she found along her path, deliver the same message, and recruit new kiuons as emissaries to spread Urnaadi's voice yet farther.

"They are ready," Kitjári said with full confidence.

The wayfarers rode eastward, letting the kiuons finish the rest of their now-cold meal. About two wicks later, they saw the pack rush past them, trotting over a trail that veered to the north. They vanished out of sight, humming ahead.

"They are definitely fast," Kitjári said. "I think we are in good hands now."

CHAPTER TWELVE

ONE BIG PUSH

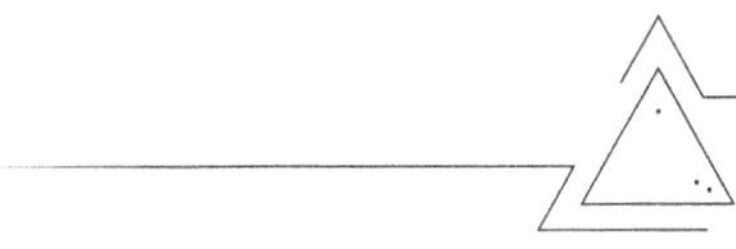

Over the course of many frigid and perilous days, Nalaníri and Kitjári crossed the vastness of the Stelm Nedross, until they reached the hollowed cones of the Galewrath Craters, which Probo claimed had not been there before the domes closed. Past the last of these craters, the frozen Klad Mahujann extended to a remote horizon over which the Stelm Wujann sharply poked, capped by a cloud of dark smoke. Mahujann was a deep blue with white cracks that sliced jaggedly to reveal its textured translucency. Unlike the glacier of Da'áju, however, Mahujann was not shattered by crevasses, but was perfectly flat.

Northwestern winds blew dagger-sharp. Nalaníri tightened her fur-lined hood and tucked her hands under her armpits. She wore no boots, having had no need for them before, but now found that although hooves could withstand the cold quite well, they were not so good for traversing slick ice, as Nupáll and Gufrok were also discovering. Both of the companion suids skidded and stumbled with every other step. Probo, too, was having trouble, but he seemed to be enjoying himself.

"Our hooves are not like yer claws," Nalaníri complained to Kitjári. "We can't a-drag our hides over ice as ye would."

"We can follow the northern shore," Kitjári suggested. "It won't be as direct a route, but snow will be better than ice."

And so they did, following the perimeter of the icy lake while battling the freezing gales. The incessant winds blew fresh snow, but they were so constant that they never allowed any snow to accumulate over the glassy blue ice of the lake. Laaja Khem drew nearer every day, its billowing clouds of ash blackening the snow at its sharp peak.

"That looks a bit too treacherous," Kitjári said, bringing them to a stop at the end of the shoreline. They were close to the east end of the lake, but their path was interrupted by serrated rocks; Kitjári might have been able to traverse them with the help of her quaar rope, but they would be impassable for the suids, Nalaníri included. Behind the jagged cliff that stopped them, steam billowed; the far shores seemed to be as icy as they were boiling.

"Probo says d'entrance to d'mines is hidden behind this shorter range. He used t'swim through here before d'lake was frozen, or hitch a ride in canoes."

"Is there a way around it?"

"He knows uf one, but it goes north n'up d'mountains, n'it would be several mour weeks uf travel."

Kitjári dismounted Nupáll to explore the ice and rocks. "We might have to slide over the ice from here on. It's not too much farther. Can the suids handle that?"

Nalaníri left her saddle and asked Gufrok to give it a try, patting his huge rump encouragingly.

Gufrok failed miserably, toppling over like a drunken sailor, then struggling to get back on his hooves. He tried to use his long tusks to propel his body as if they were oars, but only managed to spin himself in place. Nupáll snorted and did not even care to attempt the crossing.

"Probo has an idea!" Nalaníri said abruptly. "A stupid one, that is, but that's the kinds uf ideas he has. Show us, m'boy. Go on, do yer daft trick."

Probo crept toward the ice-stranded celebochoerus. He was better at keeping his balance, spreading his legs wider, but he still floundered. He stopped halfway to Gufrok, then his shape grew in a smoky cloud until he towered above the ice in the form of a kubanochoerus. Once Probo's transformation was complete, he vocalized a whale-like, oscillating pulse in rising and lowering trills, making the ice sheet shimmer as snowflakes lifted from the reverberations of his call. A kuba's limbs were adapted similarly to those of a mammoth, providing excellent traction; he planted his broad cloven hooves and set across the ice near effortlessly.

"He's doing quite well," Kitjári admitted. "He could carry us, but what about Gufrok and Nupáll?"

"That's where d'stupid part uf his plan comes in," Nalaníri said. "Show her, m'boy!"

Probo stopped in front of Gufrok, leaned down, and with a swing of his tusks pushed the suid farther onto the icy lake. Gufrok squealed as he slid like a smooth pebble. Nupáll took a step back as she watched, emitting the tiniest of snorts.

For several humiliating miles, Probo shoved his suid friends across the ice, making a sport out of it, while Nalaníri and Kitjári held tight to his wiry mane. It was a slow-going method, but it allowed them to cut a perfectly straight path to their destination.

The shoreline was nearly a stone's throw away now, its edges steaming into whiteness that rose to meet the dark clouds of Laaja Khem.

Probo emitted an intense, pulsing vocalization.

"He says it's d'last toss! He thinks he can make them reach d'shore with jis' one big push."

Probo positioned himself carefully. He aligned Gufrok and Nupáll in the perfect spot next to his tusks, then swung them both at once, demoralizingly hard. The two suids glided and skidded almost all the way to the shore, losing speed until they softly touched the frozen black pebbles at the beach.

Probo was ecstatic. He hooted a tremolo of pulsing, low notes, then performed a little prancing dance that was not quite little enough. The ice below him cracked, a metallic sound reverberating as a warning.

"Ye careless swine!" Nalaníri warned. "Save yer celebration fur later. Yer going to—"

The ice gave in, shattering in thick shards. The cracks expanded, shearing a polygonal chunk of ice at the kuba's hooves. The women held on to his fur, but Probo could not keep his balance, now standing at one end of an icy raft which tilted and turned over, dumping them into the lake.

Kitjári felt a sharp coldness, then immediately felt as if she was burning. The ice had been thin only due to the hot springs that flowed underneath, making her fear they might all be cooked alive. But it was merely a shock reaction to the temperature change—the waters were barely lukewarm. Probo remained in his kuba form, able to stand with his head above the broken ice. He waded to his friends, who climbed onto his protruding cheekbones, then held tight to his forehead horn.

The kuba sloshed and cracked his way to shore, crushing the thinning ice beneath his columnar legs. He dropped his friends onto the pebbles, turned back to his preferred javelina form, and shook the warm water off.

Kitjári got to her feet, still in shock. "I thought we were going to freeze. Then I thought we were going to be boiled. And I don't know if suids can do that, but Nupáll and Gufrok seem to be grinning with satisfaction."

"Quiet yer tusks, ye two!" Nalaníri said, taking her parka off to wring it out. She turned to Kitjári. "D'disrespect frum them two, unbelievable. Ye shell be glad ye can't hear them thoughts."

After drying their clothes and fur by a fire, they continued over a flow of basalt which soon turned to pumice and shards of dark glass, similar to the deadly sharp rocks Kitjári had encountered at the Brasha'in Scablands. Luckily, this had been a trade route, and the volcanic glass had been flattened to make it walkable, even if it was overgrown with thorny shrubs and covered in a thin blanket of snow.

"Probo claims d'entrance to d'mines is still a few days' journey away," Nalaníri said.

"It's getting quite cold," Kitjári replied, holding on to Nupáll's wiry fur. "But I'm still not sure about walking into a volcano. Could it not be filled with lava by now?"

"D'mines aren't *in* d'volcano, but around it, in dried up flows that turned to black glass. D'place has been dry fur thousands uf years, since before Probo first pranced his testes through here."

Black and gray were the formations along their path, sometimes streaked with fibrous tendrils that seemed fuzzy and soft, but could pierce skin at the slightest caress. Remains of forsaken structures surfaced from the snow, collapsed by the pressure of centuries of disrepair, offering them scant shelter at nighttime.

The day they arrived at the Laaja Khem mines, they did so amidst a howling blizzard. Unable to see their path, they trudged onward, tightening their parkas till only their muzzles poked out from their furred hoods. Probo bounced confidently ahead, leading Gufrok and Nupáll through the storm.

The path ended in a wall of obsidian that rose to lose itself in the whiteout. The smooth glass had a triangular crack wide enough to fit three kubas shoulder to shoulder, or five high if they could balance atop each other. It was a natural break in the mountain, but it had also been sculpted with utmost delicacy, enhancing the triangular opening with engaged columns and twirling motifs.

"These aren't Miscamish runes," Kitjári said, running her claws over characters carved into the glass. They were circular in nature, unlike the sawtooth writings of the Miscam. The runes were easy to discern, as the snow had clung in the crevices to draw clear patterns of white atop black. "These look like the runes we saw at the Emen Ruins. It's a place Banook took us to once, a lava tube that ends in a cavern of magical hot springs. The Dorvauros, if I recall correctly, was the name of the tribe who built it."

Probo turned his head at this and grunted, recognizing the name.

"Probo was a friend uf them," Nalaníri said, "that's how he learned about these mountain passes. Golden hair like yers, he says them had. He says d'tribe used t'live in d'southern continent, near d'lands uf d'Acoapóshi. Them were cast away to d'north, settled these lands fur millennia, n'then vanished with not a sign."

The wayfarers dismounted their suids and walked into the triangular tunnel, relieved that the cold winds would trouble them no longer. The snowdrift piled up at the entrance, but once they ventured deep enough, they were sheltered in a perfectly black and reflective hallway. Nalaníri looked up at the wall and saw the reflection of her glowing axe at her belt, and of her heart-shaped nose illuminated by her nosering.

They spread open the petals of their pharolith lamps. The cold lights reflected everywhere upon the black rocks, lighting up their faces and reflecting them back onto myriad facets; a penumbral hall of mirrors.

"Skeletons, over here," Kitjári said, kicking a grinning skull. "More in that corner." A dozen frozen bodies huddled in a sad pile.

Kitjári sniffed at the stale air, but no smells remained. "Dorvauros?" she asked.

"Doubt it." Nalaníri leaned down to examine the corpses. "These here mines were abandoned centuries before d'Downfall. No Dorvauros were left by then. Probo says there were no dead bodies last time he was here. Them probably froze when d'Enduring Winter came."

"No. Look at how this one is leaning." Kitjári shook some of the ice crystals off the body. "There's an arrow between the ribs. There was a fight here. I wonder what happened."

The triangular cut on the rock ended in a flat wall. A narrower passage opened there, oval-shaped, like a curious, feline pupil.

As they ventured into the narrow tunnel, they heard a clang behind them. They turned to see Gufrok stuck at the entrance, his wide tusks unable to fit through. Nupáll pushed him out of the way, as she had no tusks to stop her, yet she stopped just after her head went in—her shoulders were too broad.

"Oh, Probo, ye should've seen this a-coming!" Nalaníri scolded the Nu'irg. Probo fit just fine as a small javelina; it had not occurred to him this would be an impediment. They exited the narrow passage once more.

"Are there any other ways in?" Kitjári asked.

"Not un this side uf d'mountains, he claims. D'main entrance, that through which d'obsidian blocks were taken out in wagons, is un d'northern side. That's d'spot he mentioned would be un a detour several weeks away."

"I guess we'll have to say farewell, then. We couldn't have used such conspicuous mounts once we arrived in Negian territory either way. But will they be able to find their way?"

"Them say not t'worry. Probo described d'northern path n'places where them could dig up food n'take shelter, free t'adventure where them wish. Them seem rather pleased—we were a bit uf a heavy burden."

They thanked Gufrok and Nupáll for their speed, endurance, and friendship through the last several weeks, said their farewells, then ventured into the oval-shaped opening.

CHAPTER THIRTEEN

THE ARC OF THE NIGHT SKY

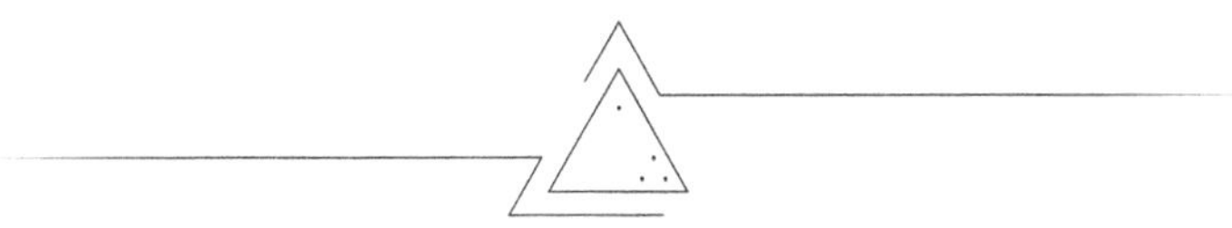

"These mines are breathtaking," Kitjári said as she admired the delicately carved walls.

"Them tunnels don't jis' seem carved fur practical purposes," Nalaníri said, "but fur d'sake uf beauty itself."

"It's more like a temple. Even the floors are exquisite." She dragged her claws over the glassy walls, making them lightly screech. "How long do these mines go on for?"

Nalaníri checked with Probo. "It'll take us a handful uf days t'cross to d'side uf d'caldera."

"We have just enough food for that, so we better hurry through."

"Ye heard the bear," Nalaníri said to the Nu'irg.

Probo grunted approvingly, flicked his tail, then bounced his balls ahead. At each intersection, Probo showed them which path to take, navigating the splits of a maze that would have been impossible for them to negotiate without his help.

A few hours into their somber walk, they entered a great hall of lustrous darkness. The ceiling converged into a sharp angle, and even the dark columns were set askew, mimicking the acute triangle of the chamber. More bodies lay scattered about, these with no ice crystals to keep them company or with much weathering to decay them.

"These definitely died from starvation or cold," Kitjári said.

"Perhaps them were looking fur shelter, n'whoever was inhabiting d'mines didn't let them in."

"Could be. Perhaps that old tribe returned to claim their mines?"

Probo sniffed the aged bones, probing them with his snout.

"He says none uf them are Dorvauros," Nalaníri interpreted. "Something else a-happened here."

"Well, it's a bit grim in here, but there's plenty of room, and it must already be late night outside. Want to spend the night with some skeletons?"

They slept in the ominous chamber, then continued through endless tunnels once their bodies assumed morning had arrived.

"Here's one uf them bears fur ye," Nalaníri said, entering a shrine with an obsidian-carved statue at its center.

"Looks more like a wolverine to me," Kitjári said, touching the sharp claws of the effigy, which was standing on two paws and towered to twice her height. Thirty-six concave circles drew a larger circle around the figure, some filled with crackling wax, some with dust from offerings that had disintegrated.

Probo smelled the dark sculpture and grunted softly at it.

"Neither bear nor wolverine, m'boy says. A honey badger named Muri, d'Nu'irg ust Krost. Old friend uf his, who d'Dorvauros used to worship." She looked straight up. "Big hulking badger."

"I don't think it's meant to be life-sized. It's so strange that the tribe abandoned all of this and just disappeared."

"We Puqua did d'same, n'd'uther Miscam tribes too, leaving our cities behind t'settle in our domes."

"Yet still, they had no dome to go to…"

Probo hurried them ahead and continued through the labyrinth that seemed to never end.

"This looks out of place," Kitjári said, as they reached a collapsed barrier that had once blocked the path. "A barricade. They were definitely trying to keep these fighters out, but it doesn't seem like they managed. At least not entirely." They stepped over the toppled wall, then past a pile of bones, and continued for a stretch of time they could not guess at, resting when needed, climbing up and down steps, always thankful for the light of their pharoliths.

"Now this is looking more like a proper mine," Kitjári observed hours later as they entered a chamber as expansive as the entire Guildhall of Krûn. It was rough and unfinished, replete with wooden support beams, makeshift lifts, and broken-down machinery for cutting, sorting, polishing, lifting, and smashing. Blocks of obsidian slept atop abandoned wagons, where more skeletons kept guard.

Kitjári lifted her pharolith to better take in the massive cavern. "What did they build with so much obsidian?"

Nalaníri asked the Nu'irg. "He says these would be d'discarded blocks. Them are d'trash ready to be taken out. If ye could see d'north side uf d'mountain, it's covered in blocks like d'ones in these wagons. Them were a-digging fur seams uf senstregalv. Them had t'move a mountain uf glass t'find a single vein uf it."

They tiptoed around the edges of a collapsed balcony, slid down a drainage shaft, then followed a passage that led to a more upscale set of tunnels where every crevice was embellished with circular runes. The space widened abruptly into a barrel-shaped chamber dozens of strides across. Although the top was visible, reflecting their pharoliths like two lonely, distant stars, the bottom dropped into a void of blackness. An obsidian bridge, wide and imposing, cut across the chasm to connect with an archway on the opposite side. Too many dead bodies cluttered the black platform, some dangling over the stone parapets.

"They died on the bridge?" Kitjári thought out loud. "And what are all those holes?" she added, eyes cast on the curved wall of the room, which was covered in circular burrows, spaced evenly, reminiscent of a giant honeycomb.

"Tombs," Nalaníri replied, voicing Probo's thoughts. "Them are Dorvauros tombs."

As they made their way across the bridge, Kitjári noticed a rope tied to a thick obsidian baluster, dangling limply into the void. The rope's fibers disintegrated at her touch, casting its remains into the darkness. Her eyes followed the vanishing form and spotted something glistening in a hole a few levels down. "Look!" she said, tightening the beam of her lamp and shining it down. "That hole is much larger, like a portal, and it has a landing."

"N'also mour dead bodies. Grave robbers?" Nalaníri guessed. "Probo says d'exit is across d'bridge."

"No, hold on a breath. Something is amiss. All these corpses, the dangling rope. If they were here trying to survive the Downfall, why bother risking this chasm just to loot some dead Dorvauros folk? And why did so many of them die in battle?"

Nalaníri squatted next to a pile of bones, pulling at the shaft of an arrow. It was lodged in a dried femur, yet the serrated obsidian tip did not shatter when she pulled it out. "Why does it shimmer like it does?" she asked, holding the sharp glass in front of a hoofed hand.

"Huh?"

"Mine threads, them align to d'arrowhead."

Kitjári stepped closer and took the arrow. "Well, that is something," she murmured in awe. "This must be made of senstregalv." She put the arrow on the ground and slammed the tip with the steel pommel of her sword. The pommel sparked, but the arrowhead did not shatter. She scratched the arrow's tip against the obsidian floor, leaving a thin cut in the black tiles. "Sharp as the light of the Ilaadrid Shard. There could be more of these around. Help me find them."

They quickly searched the bodies, finding only two more senstregalv tips among dozens of regular ones.

Probo grunted restlessly from farther across the bridge.

"Quiet your impatient tusks," Kitjári said to him as she pulled her quaar rope out of her backpack. "There's more here that needs to be uncovered. I want to find out what's down in that tomb."

"Ye ain't a-dangling down there like that! What if ye fall?"

"This rope can hold up Banook and then some. It's as safe as can be. The landing is not too far down, I have enough to belay us both down and up again."

"Yer demented! I'm not a-going!"

"If you can climb up hoodoos to get honey truffles, you can dangle down a death pit to help me solve this mystery."

"But what if we fall? There's no need fur—"

"Truly, it's safe as can be. The balusters are solid, the rope unbreakable, and I know very well what I'm doing. Here, let me show you."

Kitjári helped Nalaníri down first, with Probo as a pygmy hog tucked in her parka, expertly lowering the two of them until they were at the level of the landing.

"Swing to the platform, then tie the rope to that column."

"How am I supposed t'swing with nothing t'push frum?"

"Just… um, swing!"

It took Nalaníri a dozen clumsy attempts until she finally propelled herself far enough to reach the ledge. Kitjári lowered herself right after, secured the rope, then led them into the ample passageway of dark glass, which was so flawlessly round and polished that their pharoliths reflected around them as perfect rings, suspending them in circles of light.

"Much wider than the other holes," Kitjári observed, pausing to admire the beauty of the corridor. "Not just any peasant's crypt."

They collected more senstregalv arrows as they passed, pulling them from skeletons they could not help but step on as they lurched along. At the end of the passage was a heavy double door made of a sparkling blue metal. A pile of grinning corpses littered the bottom half of it, as if they had been trying to pummel through using their last breaths.

Kitjári banged on the metal doors, but they were unyielding. There was no keyhole, no knob, nothing to pry open. She kicked at a wooden shield. "Well, I guess this will have to remain a mystery."

"Not so fast. Fullow me." Nalaníri pulled on Kitjári's shoulder and walked her back along the hallway. "Probo has a smart idea. He gets them, sometimes."

The javelina stood between them and the heavy metal doors. He scratched his cloven hooves against the floor, lowered his head, and charged. He picked up speed, and as he neared the doors, he leapt and shifted into his kubanochoerus form in midair, barely fitting in the tunnel. His forehead horn slammed right between the twin doors. There was a *thud!* like a thunderclap, then Probo fell to the ground, crushing dozens of skeletons under tons of fat and fur.

The entire hallway was blocked by the kuba, but as Probo shifted back to a javelina, he revealed the wide-open passage in front of him. He returned to them with a smug trot, took a tumble to one side, then found his balance once more.

"Easy, don't show uff so much. Look at ye," Nalaníri chided, crouching next to the suid. He had no forehead horn in his primal form, but where the single bone would've been, there was now a splatter of red and a deep cut. "Ye poor turnip. Kitjári will take care uf that."

Probo huffed and turned around, confident he didn't need any aid, and led the way through the open doors. The bar locks on the inside had buckled, splintered, and exploded.

They entered a palatial chamber of opaque glass. It was six-sided, with each portion colored for one of the seasons of the moon: yellow, purple, green, pink, pearl, and then the most tenebrous black. The mosaic of obsidian that covered the walls and columns was marbled with impurities, imbuing them with their distinctive colors.

"By d'Tricolored Mountain," Nalaníri whispered. "It's like we entered d'heart uf Sceres herself."

The room sparkled sixfold. Even the dust of ages could not contain its radiance. A calm gurgling sound permeated the chamber, from a glacier-cold stream that flowed across the floor following concentric paths that described orbits of celestial forms. The indentations the water was meant to run through had mineralized in places, spilling the stream into mirrorlike pools that grew mounds of crystals at their edges. The air inside the sepulcher was stale. Bodies littered the ground here too, most of them spread radially away from the metal gates, having been hurled outward by Probo's explosive entrance.

"Maybe this is the royal crypt," Kitjári said quietly. "Did the Dorvauros have kings and queens? Emperors?"

"Probo doesn't know. Them didn't talk t'him like I can talk t'him, n'he cares not fur d'politics uf humans. He's never seen a chamber like this one."

They stepped in further, trying not to disturb the pools of water. Kitjári kicked at a tangle of dried legs encrusted with minerals and said, "These warriors are all dressed the same as the ones on the outside. They were fighting with each other. And look at all these supplies." She approached a stack of crates piled at the edge of the room and pulled one down. It was filled with rotten food, so old that it had mostly turned to dust. "I guess they tried to hoard supplies in here and trapped themselves inside. But what were they fighting about?"

"M'dear, I think them might've been a-fighting over this," Nalaníri said, headed toward the center of the chamber, where six raised sarcophagi glimmered in the six colors of the moon. The stone lids had been pulled down on their sides as makeshift barricades, all pitted by projectile impacts.

They approached the carved tombs in awed silence, peering into the yellow-colored one first. Their lights sparkled over the remnants of an ancient hero of the disappeared tribe, who was dressed in regal clothes woven of gold and silver filaments decorated with precious stones.

Nalaníri leaned in. "Golden hair, jis' like yers. Maybe them were yer ancestors."

"They look like rulers, but also like warriors," Kitjári said, now peering over the figure inside the purple-colored sarcophagus. "But… All the precious stones are still there, untouched."

"Jewels wouldn't have served much uf a purpose t'people trying to survive d'Downfall."

Kitjári then noticed ornamental mounts on the sides of each sarcophagus. "Weapon holders," she deduced. The mounts on the first two tombs—which were decorated with citrines and amethysts—were empty. The third tomb, verdant and translucent, was the largest of all, and from its mount dangled a massive, unwieldy polearm. The weapon was leaning halfway off the support, and its green-scaled leather scabbard had been pulled off. Kitjári crouched down to touch it.

"Piss sprites have mercy, a senstregalv glaive," she said. The grotesquely oversized glaive was fitted with a disarming hook at the ornamented, bladed end. It was as heavy as it was impractical.

Kitjári stood up again, staring at the heavy-boned hero resting in the green tomb. Emerald beads decorated the entire length of the figure's golden hair, like translucent serpents. "If you were able to wield this monster, you must've been quite a monster yourself," she said with earnest respect.

She left the unsuitable glaive behind and approached the fourth tomb, one with a much smaller skeleton resting within. The sarcophagus was rosy-pink, and there was no weapon to be found on its side. The fifth tomb, however, had a pearl-encrusted scabbard dangling from its mount.

"Look at the details on this thing!" Kitjári said, gawking at the iridescent sheath. She probed the velvety interior with a claw, then sighed. "But no sword. It must've been quite a weapon to deserve this scabbard." She looked for it around the tomb, then along the sides of the nacre-armored skeleton inhabiting it, but she found nothing but pearlescent jewels.

"No sword here either," Nalaníri said, already examining the sixth and final tomb, one made of purely black obsidian. "But look at this a-grinning beauty."

Kitjári trotted over and peered inside. The obsidian void sucked out all the light, but the bones shone resplendent. The skeleton seemed restful and somehow virtuous. Its golden hair was tied in a dozen braids that spiraled galaxies across its chest. Topazes were embroidered into its dark robes, tracing flickering constellations.

"You must've been magnificent," Kitjári murmured.

She heard a *crack*, followed by a grunt.

"Probo, don't mess with them remains!" Nalaníri complained, shooing the Nu'irg away from the body of a warrior who was perpetually taking cover behind a sarcophagus lid. Stacks of empty quivers piled next to the calcified body. "Seems like this hapless hero took out most uf them soldiers un d'outside," she ruminated, tapping a hoof against the crystals Probo had shattered, which had built up over the skeleton like a cocoon. "What a legend. Too bad not a soul survived t'tell yer tale."

"Hey, but what is that? Is this…?" Kitjári started, observing the dead body with Urnaadisilv's sight. A peculiar glimmer hid within the crystalline chrysalis. She pushed at the salt-like buildup until it cracked, dug her claws in, and out from the crust she pulled a night-colored recurve bow. She shook a scapula off it, then grinned sharply.

"By Lømappor's seed n'd'four mighty tusks uf Lûrrumaag," Nalaníri exclaimed, snout agape. "By d'light uf d'kenzir n'd'glory uf d'Tricolored Mountain."

"It's… It's a quaar bow," Kitjári whispered, her mahogany eyes wide and dazzling. "And not just the bow, the bowstring, too. Marvel of the gods!" She grinned down at Probo. "Bless your turgid testes, you wonderful Nu'irg."

"M'dear, this is no ordinary bow…"

"Of course it's not. It's made of quaar!"

"No. I mean, there's unly one quaar bow in d'ancient myths. Ye are a-holding d'legendary Dunokh Sull, d'*Arc uf d'Night Sky*, which was once wielded by no uther than Lerr Mauvenel themself."

"Sounds mighty impressive," Kitjári said, inspecting the bowstring; it looked like the fibers on her quaar rope, but much more intricately knotted. "It's quite compact for a recurve, and so oddly constructed. Where does the bowstring even attach? And why does it loop back and forth like this?" She tested the weapon's power, and it released with unforgiving speed and in perfect silence. Instead of bouncing in an endless resonance, the bowstring settled back in place almost at once, as still as the void between the stars. "This is outstanding. This string has been sitting here for centuries, yet it has no abrasions, no loss of tension. And the bow weighs as much as a breath of cold air."

The bow was as masterfully constructed as their Silvesh. It did not have an aura, as it had not been created for an intelligent purpose, yet it had been crafted with the same kind of crystal-like structure and filigreed details.

"But this… This is not a Dorvauros weapon, is it?" Kitjári asked. "Miscam runes are etched on the limbs. And if it's quaar, it must've been crafted by the Acoapóshi."

"Mayhap. I don't know its origins, but it's spoken uf in many Puqua stories."

"Tell me more about this Dunokh Sull, if you please? I heard Lago mention its name once, in a constellation or something."

"Them say those who wielded it could take a kuba down in one shot. Them say d'string would never tear, never slacken, n'that it could shoot arrows as fast as one could pluck strings frum a harp. Legends speak uf d'bow being birthed at d'heart uf a star, n'say that if it loosed an arrow toward d'horizon, it would eventually fly uff into space in search uf its home, as d'planet is much too curved fur d'straight path d'arrows fullowed."

"The legends might exaggerate a bit, but by Noss's shriveled tits, this is a wonderful weapon." Kitjári caressed the bow reverentially, then looked to Nalaníri as if searching for approval.

Nalaníri rolled her eyes. "Yes, uf course ye can have it. I'm no archer, I couldn't hit Probo's enormous balls if them were a-bouncing right in front uf us. Dunokh Sull will be safer in yer paws."

Kitjári grew happy dimples beneath her fur. "Thank you. I will take good care of it. Now it makes sense, somewhat, what these people were fighting over. Weapons like these could turn the tide in a war."

"Unly two out uf six," Nalaníri observed. "But we haven't yet looked through d'entire place."

They searched the crypt carefully, making sure to inspect every dead body, every rotting crate. They found no more legendary weapons, but they did find dozens of senstregalv arrows, most with shafts too aged and brittle to be useful, so they snapped them off to keep just the tips.

"I guess that's it," Kitjári said, dropping the last loose arrowhead into a leather pouch. They had discussed taking some of the gemstones that adorned the Dorvauros skeletons, but they found it distasteful to directly disturb their remains; Kitjári was already feeling guilty enough about taking the bow, but since she hadn't been the first to remove it from its mount, she didn't let her guilt overpower her needs. She looked around, debating in her mind. "Well, maybe I'll take just one more thing."

She approached the largest of the sarcophagi again and inspected the monstrous glaive.

"Ye ain't a-carrying that tree trunk with ye, m'dear. It must weigh more than ye do."

"Not for me. For Banook," she explained. "It will fit like a toy in his hands. Though I'll regret having to haul it." She chanted a Free Tribelands prayer of gratitude and respect to the weapon's previous owner, covered the obsidian-rimmed blade with its green scabbard, then negotiated a way to balance the polearm over her shoulders.

With their fruitful looting concluded, they exited into the circular tunnel, and once at the landing, used the quaar rope to pull themselves back onto the obsidian bridge.

"My back is already hating me for this," Kitjári said as she tied the glaive to her backpack. She lifted the gear over her shoulders and nodded. "Let's go. Probo, show us the way out."

Past the bridge and the tombs, the mountain's innards changed drastically. No longer were the tunnels carved from obsidian, but from a mix of other volcanic rocks. The scents were siltier, the flat surfaces non-reflective, and their echoing footsteps less sharp. Long they traveled, resting when they thought night might be darkening the outside, walking again when they felt the exhaustion leave their bodies.

Turning a sharp corner, a sudden brightening nearly blinded them. "Daylight!" Nalaníri barked.

Handspans
Khamam
Seleria
Junneg
Harl-Eavish
Numbion
Lancari
Fin

Chapter Fourteen

The Dorvauros Refuge

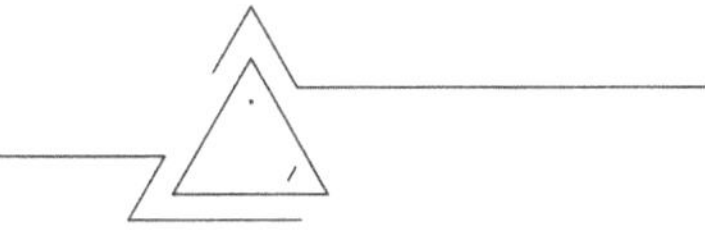

Threateningly cold was the weather when they exited the Laaja Khem mines, and it would only worsen in the coming days.

The smoky sky was gray; so was the snow, and as they traversed it, they left behind a striated track where snow and ash had accumulated in thin layers, now broken to reveal the history of past snowfalls.

"We are at the edge of the Da'áju Caldera now," Kitjári observed. "I didn't miss this chilled air."

Nalaníri buttoned her parka and pulled her furred hood up. "How do we get to Banook's cabin?" she asked.

"Ask Probo if he knows about the Emen Ruins. Hmm… Actually… That was not the place's real name, just the name Banook gave it. It's a Dorvauros cave full of hot springs. It overlooks the Stiss Khull's tributaries, deep in a lava tunnel. Should be east of here. If he can get us to those hot springs, I can find the way to Banook's cabin from there."

"He's familiar with them," Nalaníri replied after a moment. "But he says there are dangerous glaciers to cross, n'it's a long way away. As a kuba he could carry us, but unly frum time t'time, fur he spends mour energy in his larger forms n'needs t'eat mour. Even mour than usual. N'I don't see much t'eat 'round here."

"Couldn't he fill his belly in a smaller form and then take the larger one once satisfied?"

"That's jis' not how things work, m'dear. But he shell do his best t'help us."

Probo shapeshifted then, taking his kuba form much too quickly, unleashing a wave of gray-streaked snow onto the women.

Nalaníri shook the snow off and climbed on. "D'ride won't be comfurtable without a saddle, but jis' hold tight to his neck fur," she said, helping Kitjári up the giant suid's back. Probo then trotted forward, carving a narrow path of white into the gray snow.

For days and nights they had to lean their bodies into slapping blizzards, rush for shelter against freezing rains, and negotiate pathways across icy crags. Probo carried them as often as he could, but when the path was too narrow or brittle, the women went on foot. Eastward they trudged, following the courses of ancient riverbeds and glaciers.

"See that line of white on the horizon?" Kitjári asked, pointing south past the blue ice of the Crescent Glacier.

Nalaníri had just stopped to fix the straps on her bag and to tighten her hood. "D'flat past them peaks?"

"That's it. The Da'áju Caldera. That's where we found Urnaadisilv. That cloud that grows from it is steam, from hot springs under the ice. It all looks flat from this far away, but the ice is filled with crevasses and seracs." She stared, losing herself in memories. Her fur shook in the wind. *Like aspen leaves,* she thought. After a long pause, she continued, unable to keep her sudden melancholy out of her voice, "It was Ockam's mask back then. We spent so many good times together. I wish he could've been with us through all of this. He would've loved the mines, particularly the treasures within that tomb."

"Sounds like ye loved each uther dearly. Were ye two together?"

"Together? Oh, no, not like that. He was a great friend from our time at Klemes, when we were both merely teenagers training for the Barujan War. He flirted often with me, but well…" She trailed off, uncertain about how to proceed with the story. She was hoping Nalaníri would ask, *Well what?* to give her an excuse to let it all out. But her companion did not inquire further.

"Anyway," she continued, trying to escape the awkward silence, "Ockam even made advances on my sister one night, when he was nearly passed out drunk. He thought she was me, and that whore let him fondle her! And then pretended it had been me all along the next morning! That graceless tramp."

"Ye have a sister? Never told me 'bout her."

"Older sister, always kept at least one rank above myself. I bet she's going mad trying to find out where I disappeared to. She's a handful. But anyway, no, Ockam and I were just good friends."

"I don't blame ye. I'm sure he was a good man, though most men I don't trust much. Like I once heard Alaia say, *Men are all pigs.* No disrespect to ye, m'dear Probo, or to mineself fur that matter."

Kitjári saw a chance and took it. "Damn right they are. Pigs. Men, I mean," she fumbled her words disingenuously. "So, you're not, I mean… You don't get along with men very much, I take it?" She immediately regretted the vagueness of her words, but hoped they would suffice.

"Odask was plenty n'enough," she restrainedly replied.

Kitjári felt her beating pulse beneath her cheek fur. She forcefully drew her threads inward to prevent her emotions from being read by her friend. *Khest, you clumsy cuntwad, just say it. Tell her you are lurrkin, say the fucking words.* The compulsion to be courageous boiled within her, but her courage faltered. Despite the ambiguous clues she had received, she could not figure out a follow-up question that would not make her stutter and look utterly inept. *Just open your filthy muzzle and say it!* Lips tight, she kept on walking.

That night, a howling gale prevented them from lighting even the smallest of fires. They leaned against an icy rock and bundled themselves close to each other, holding their brime cubes to steal as much warmth from the aetheric sulphur as possible. Probo slumbered as a pygmy hog within Nalaníri's thick parka. A few hours into their restless sleep, Nalaníri made herself more comfortable by pulling Kitjári closer, keeping an arm wrapped around the bear.

Kitjári nearly stopped breathing; she could sleep no more after that. She dared not move.

Despite her confident irreverence at taverns and other sleazy places she used to frequent, now that Kitjári was next to a friend she earnestly liked, she found her will utterly frozen.

Once the morning light brightened the snow, they dislodged their frigid bodies from the rocky shelter and continued on their journey.

"Look, kiuon tracks," Kitjári said. "Maybe they could help us find food." They hadn't seen bears or any sizable creatures since before they had entered the mines.

They stopped by the toppled boulders the tracks led to, and Kitjári crouched down. «Hey, you silly fuckers,» she mindspoke through the ground, unsure if the proper meaning was being conveyed by that last word. It was, in a way. «Would you come out from hiding? I need a word with you.»

The kiuons reacted immediately, recognizing the Urnaadifröa as soon as she mindspoke to them, and came out humming and bleating excitedly. Kitjári told the bears that she and her companions had run out of food and were unfamiliar with these lands. Despite the Silvesh's powers, all they had managed to catch since leaving the mines was one scraggly hare. The request left the kiuons dumbfounded, seeing the plump javelina who traveled with the wayfarers. Kitjári explained who Probo was, but the kiuons insisted he'd still make a good meal.

The small bears led the two women to their hunting ground in a hidden meadow. Kitjári was ecstatic about testing out her new bow. She chose to use regular arrows instead of the ones with senstregalv tips, too afraid of losing the precious arrowheads in the snow. Hiding behind a wall of blue ice, she sniffed the air and listened. She could smell a rabbit's den and hear a soft rustle upon a hill when the breeze quieted. She spotted movement, white upon white, nearly invisible behind the falling snowflakes. She slid an arrow out of the quiver, lining the nock upon Dunokh Sull's bowstring, then pulled. The tension felt solid and smooth, as if her claws were gliding over ice. She felt the fletching caress her cheek fur, aimed carefully, then released. The arrow flew faster than a diving falcon and struck the target with such power that Kitjári had to dig the rabbit out from the crater of snow it had created. She recovered and cleaned her arrow, then brought the rabbit to Nalaníri.

"This thing is a beast," she said, sitting down to admire the bow. "I swear, the arrow released with much more power than my arms could pull that string with. It seems to store the energy somehow as you are pulling. There must be something in how the bowstring is constructed, some hidden, microscopic alignment of all the quaar threads."

"Fascinating," Nalaníri said flatly. "Can it be used t'skin a rabbit?"

"I don't know how you'd use it to—"

"Then get yer claws over here n'help, m'dear."

After their much-needed meal, Kitjári thanked the kiuons, delivered to them her carefully memorized message regarding the migration they were to help with, then let them go about their day.

"This area seems remotely familiar," she observed as she took in their surroundings. "Those five peaks to the east, they are the Drann Trodesh. I think we might reach the Emen Ruins before evenfall."

The sky had cleared, bringing with its blueness the coldest day of their journey thus far. Frigid and tightly bundled, they arrived at an angled, circular opening framed by three broken columns. Kitjári immediately recognized it, despite the ice and snow that covered it.

Sunnokh had recently set; his distant warmth was replaced by a gust of inviting, warm air that wafted from the portal. Although the top of the entrance was frozen, instead of icicles it was rimmed by stumps of broken ice.

"Banook must've been here recently," Kitjári said, leaning toward the entrance.

"Hold it, m'dear. Look at yer feet. Wulf prints."

"It's alright. I think I may know these wolves—I hope they still remember me." She stepped inside.

"Ye aren't going in there t'feed a pack uf wulves, m'dear. Take yer weapons out."

"Relax. It will be fine. I'd rather be mauled by wolves than have to stand in this cold one heartbeat longer. Stay here until I call for you."

Kitjári carefully walked down the ice-encrusted steps. Before reaching the bottom, Urnaadisilv showed her the figures of five large wolves as well as four pups. They were standing alert. As soon as they saw her come through the threshold, they growled and approached with their gums exposed.

"Easy, it's me. Remember me?"

The wolves continued to growl, snapping their jaws in the air.

Shit, shit, how stupid of me, she thought. *Of course they don't remember.*

She shapeshifted into Jiara, removed her mask, and pulled her hood down, draping her ash-blonde hair over her right shoulder. One wolf stopped growling, but the others continued their threatening approach. The friendlier wolf barked and whined at her pack, making them stop. She hesitantly trotted toward Jiara, smelled her hands, then returned to the corner to calm the pups down.

"Thank you," Jiara said. "I hope you don't mind, but I brought friends. And I mean *friends*, plural—the javelina is not dinner." She knew the wolves would not understand her words, but she was getting used to talking to animals out loud; it seemed to calm her nerves.

When Nalaníri finally stepped inside, the wolves were all huddled in a corner, ears following her. When Probo came slipping down the steps, their tails began to wag, and a tongue or two flicked out of their maws.

"Not for eating. Please," Jiara repeated. "You don't want to mess with this one, it's not a fight you are likely to win."

Jiara opened a pharolith lamp and led Nalaníri into the circular passage, following the warm air current.

Probo was familiar with the lava tunnel and trotted ahead of them. There was a distant splash, then a happy squeal.

Jiara delightfully presented every chamber they passed, recounting the story of what had happened during those seemingly distant days, although she avoided discussing Lago-Sterjall and Banook's steamier escapades, still uncertain of how a Nu'irg having a relationship with a human might be perceived by Nalaníri.

"Jis' like at Laaja Khem, d'Dorvauros did an outstanding job carving these tunnels," Nalaníri said, eyeing the circular runes adorning the trims that followed the ceiling and floors.

"Banook maintains the place. He comes here a few times a year to clean up, fix any broken pipes, redirect newly sprouting springs, and make sure the pools flow in the proper way."

"N'this room is warm as an overmitt! Even them stone benches are warm."

"And the floors too. There are pipes with hot water running through them. This is the room where we once set our camp. But the true marvel of this place waits just around the corner."

"Ye've aroused mine curiosity enough," Nalaníri said, dropping her bag inside the heated chamber. "We can't let Probo have all d'fun without us." She unashamedly dropped all her clothes, then followed the steam wafting through the hallway, carrying only a pharolith lamp.

"Wait for me!" Jiara said, struggling to get her leather armor off. She dropped her undergarments, took her half-form, then grabbed a pharolith before hurrying behind her friend.

"Hold on, let me get that for you," she said, reaching an icicle-barred portal that had stopped Nalaníri. Probo had broken some of the frozen bars off, but only at the bottom, so she finished the job by making an opening just wide enough for them to fit sideways.

"Magnificent…" Nalaníri whispered as she ventured in, her breath materializing more solidly than her softly spoken words. "Them pools are like rainbows, like d'bow uf Hêshoggo."

The hot springs fumed, revealing the colorful pools only sporadically, coming and going at the whims of the air currents. Probo had already been enjoying the waters, sampling each of the pools one at a time.

"Careful, the higher pools are very hot," Kitjári warned. "And the one by the far window is icy cold." She led Nalaníri across the chamber so that she could see the veil of water that shot out of the sheer drop at the end of the lava tunnel. Farther north, the vaporous stream gave birth to the Stiss Khull, bathing the Telm Klannath with life.

"Ye can see d'whole world frum here," Nalaníri said, careful not to get too close to the edge. "But mine tits are getting frostbitten in this breeze. Which pool shell we try first?"

"Take your pick."

Nalaníri chose a medium-heat pool to try out first. As the two of them slowly lowered their bodies into the water, Kitjári snuck a peek at the boar's bare chest and belly, holding her breath while each of the dozen teats slipped into the water. A freezing-cold drop landed on her wet nose, making her flinch and avert her eyes.

She wished that Sceres was out already, so that the pool chamber would be lit in Jade, but Sceres would not show her face until after midnight. The light of the pharoliths was cold and harsh, casting sharp shadows from the columns holding together the domed ceiling of rock, but the steam softened the light and set the space aglow in diffused tendrils of mist.

After an awkward pause, the bear said, "Time has moved so strangely. I was just trying to figure out how long it's been since we came to these hot springs. We were here for the Day of Renewal, so it's been eleven months now."

"A long adventure," Nalaníri murmured through a contented sigh.

"B–but I'm glad. To be back. Here, I mean, it's a wonderful place."

"Anuther true beauty frum d'New World," Nalaníri replied, leaning back to look at the darkening sky through the five round holes in the cave's domed ceiling. "Thank ye, m'dear friend, ye've granted me quite a blessing. We have hot springs in Nagradrolom, near d'Laaja Deulmosk, where I grew up. But them don't compare to even one uf these mystical pools."

They loosened their muscles and soaked their bones, watching the patches of twilight sky transition from deep blues to star-studded blacks. Nalaníri seemed utterly relaxed, but Kitjári was trying hard not to shake. She could not stop thinking that it was here that Sterjall had kissed Banook for the first time. *There's not a more romantic or perfect place than this,* she told herself. *And we'll be leaving in the morning.* If she didn't make a move now, she was afraid she'd be too embarrassed to try anything ever again. *Even that tail-wagging wimp was intrepid enough to do it, why can't you?* she scolded herself.

Nalaníri had her eyes closed. Sweat glistened on her black-and-white fur, her pink snout. Her glowing nosering dripped sparkling sapphires. The tips of her hair had frozen the condensation, growing icy crystals that twinkled like a sharp halo in the cold light of the pharoliths. She was within reach, elbows resting on the edge of the pool in an invitingly open posture.

Kitjári was glad the bubbling and dripping sounds obscured her unsteady breathing and heartbeat. She lifted her handpaws out of the water and let her furry arms steam freely, then combed her fur with her claws, fidgeting to kill time. Her nervousness was too glaring. She could not open up to Nalaníri so clumsily, not like this; it had to be under her own terms. She focused on her threads and made sure they were carefully tucked in.

Please, don't let her see the nervous wreck I am.

She opened her muzzle and closed it, then opened it again and said, "Y-you know, there's something I haven't told you about yet."

Nalaníri's brows rose, but her eyes remained closed. "N'that would be?" The kenzir stone right behind her cast a heavy shadow over Kitjári's side of the pool.

"Well, it's a bit of a secret. Not with everyone, but sometimes, I mean, it's… I guess it depends on who I'm comfortable enough telling." She regretted the clumsiness of her words at once.

Nalaníri shrugged, nonplussed. "I feel like we already share secrets deeper than any mere mortal would dare t'carry. One mour shell not shock me, n'I know how t'furget things I'm meant to keep quiet 'bout."

"N-not an easy one to *furget!*" she spluttered with an embarrassing chuckle, then quieted sharply. *I wish we could use these masks to mindspeak,* she thought. *It would be so much easier. But no, you have to keep using your clumsy mouth and turn into a blubbering brat in front of her. I wish she could just read my thoughts.*

Although the Silvesh did not pry as far as she wished, Urnaadisilv told her that Nalaníri was tense even though she looked relaxed, but she could read no further. *Is she tired from the trip?* she wondered. *Am I making her uncomfortable?* Something in the quality of her threads seemed off, too hard to perceive.

"Well. The secret… I am… What I was wanting to s-say is t-that…" Kitjári stammered. She quieted for too long a moment, panicked, spotted an exit, and took it. "Did Lago ever tell you about him and Banook?"

"Uf course, he talks about Banook all d'time. To d'point I feared it might make Aio jealous." She chortled at her own joke.

"Well, you might not be too far off."

"What d'ye mean?" she asked, opening her eyes.

"Lago and Banook were a couple, before Lago and Aio got together. I guess they are still a couple, though they are far from each other."

Nalaníri sat up straight.

"Ye mean that boy? With a Nu'irg? How is that possible?"

"Sorry, you seem bothered by this. I didn't mean to—"

"Ain't bothered. Who am I t'judge who anyone else loves? Lago is a precious n'brave young man, n'what I've heard 'bout Banook tells me he's jis' as good a companion. Good fur them, I say. Not bothered, unly surprised. Wait till Probo hears about this." She looked around the room, but Probo had left to dry off.

"I'm glad you are so open-minded about it. We keep quiet about this because some Miscam tribes might not take to it as kindly. It's hard to tell what some people will tolerate or feel insulted by."

"Nothing t'worry 'bout with this here boar. But I have a hard time a-picturing it. Isn't Banook something like eight feet tall n'wide as a barrel?"

"Nearly nine. And more like two barrels."

"Must be quite d'sight seeing such curious a couple. Jis' how in d'twelve great fjords did something like that come t'happen?"

Kitjári swallowed. "How it happened, well, it's a long story involving their adventures across these very mountains, traveling through the cold snow. They fell for each other, wanted each other, but for months did not dare to take that step. B-but then, about one year ago, for the Day of Renewal, Banook brought us all here, as a surprise."

Kitjári placed an elbow at the edge of the pool to feign relaxation, but almost immediately pulled it back and massaged her neck. "I was asleep when it happened, but Lago told us about it later. They were in this very pool. It's their favorite since it's hot but not too overbearing. Lago followed… Well, actually, it was Sterjall. Sterjall followed Banook here in the middle of the night, and they had a conversation about their hopes and dreams. Banook had been hesitant to pursue anything with Sterjall—he thought it would be unfair since we all had to continue on our journey without him soon."

Nalaníri was halfway lost in the glowing mist, listening. She nodded for Kitjári to continue.

"So, that night, as they talked about what they really wanted for each other, Sterjall mustered the courage to tell Banook how he truly felt. He stood up and planted a kiss on the big man's lips. What happened after, he's purposely vague about, but one just has to imagine."

Nalaníri wiped her dripping brow. "How wunderful. Sterjall was clever. He chose a great place t'make his move."

Kitjári couldn't tell whether her friend's smile was due to the pull of her tusks or something else. She was inaccessible. *Is she also hiding her emotions?* she wondered.

She hesitated a bit too long, afraid she'd already missed the perfect opportunity. *Kiss her before it's too late. Why are you so afraid?* She noticed Nalaníri had closed her eyes again, and her brow had tightened.

Suck it up, you coward. Do it.

Her claws trembled under the water.

Now or never.

She leaned forward and—

Splash! A wave of colder water from a nearby pool sloshed upon them.

"Watch it, boy!" Nalaníri barked. Probo climbed out of his pool and jumped in the one they were sharing. He grunted happily at them.

"Well, it's a-getting hot in here," Nalaníri said. "I think I'll try d'frosty one by d'big opening." She stood to leave. Kitjári's dark eyes timidly stared as the rows of pink nipples rose, one by one. Fresh out of the hot water, they were now much more vibrant, plump, and flushed.

They left a trail of steam behind them.

CHAPTER FIFTEEN

TO THE CABIN

Dinner was quiet and awkward. *She's really upset,* Kitjári thought, never look-ing directly at Nalaníri. Between the way she'd left the pool and the tension afterward, she had to conclude that Nalaníri had noticed she was about to kiss her. *She did you a favor. She left so that you wouldn't have to feel even worse about it. Be thankful you didn't fuck it up all the way.*

They had slept close for warmth during the previous nights, but tonight they had a warm room, so their bedrolls were set far apart. When morning arrived, they found two dead pikas near the doorway. They heard the bicker-ing barks and whines of the wolves nearby.

"A selfless bunch them are," Nalaníri whispered, picking up the small lagomorphs.

They decided to bathe once more after having the pikas for breakfast. Probo stayed with them the whole time, making it impossible for Kitjári to even consider making any moves or inquiries. She was certain she would not have dared either way, so Probo's presence reassured her.

They packed up, and found the wolves cuddled up by the entrance. Kitjári thanked them by placing down one of her blankets in a corner, then said her farewells. The wolves said nothing, following them with their eyes.

"Can Probo carry us the rest of the way?" Kitjári asked.

"He hasn't had much t'eat. Mayhap fur a few hours here and there," Na-laníri replied dismissively.

"The land is more fertile farther south, he'll be able to dig out plenty. But let's not bother him till tomorrow, at least." Kitjári tightened her hood. "It should be three days' walk to Banook's cabin."

"N'ye left them wulves one uf our nicest blankets."

"The pups will appreciate it."

"By tearing it t'pieces."

"Whatever makes them happy!" Kitjári said a bit too snappily. She breathed in, then added, "We are close, we'll be much cozier soon enough. Just hold on to your brime cube and keep your parka tight. I can't wait for you to see Banook's cabin—it's a wonder."

Kitjári talked to a few more bears they found along their way, but did not say much to Nalaníri, afraid of embarrassing herself with another tense conversation. On the first day of Hoartide, just as the sun was setting, a blizzard struck them. Kitjári knew they were close to the cabin, so she pushed on despite the draining pain of the cold.

"Did ye hear that?!" Nalaníri shouted through the slapping gusts of snow.

"What?!" Kitjári replied with her fullest voice.

"D'howling! It's not d'wind!"

Kitjári stopped, listening to the howling sounds. She looked around, but through the dimming light and streaking snow, she could not see very far. The howl returned. Probo perked up and huffed, seeing a brown-and-white shape jumping through the snow. The form passed right by him, as if not even seeing the javelina, rushing to Kitjári.

"Bear!" she screamed with unfettered joy as the mutt jumped into her arms and whined ecstatically. He smelled her, licked her, certain it was his old friend even if she looked a bit different. "Look at you! You are as slobbery as ever!" She looked at Nalaníri and screamed through the wind, "This is Bear, Lago's dog!"

She placed the yipping mutt on the ground. Then, as if she had always been standing in front of them, a white tundra wolf materialized from the snow. Probo blinked, cocked his wide head, then jumped toward the wolf, rebounding around her in excitement. The wolf may have been equally happy, but she wasn't about to demonstrate it in such a graceless manner.

"Nu'irg ust Agnarg!" Nalaníri hollered, sensing Safís's oceanic-blue aura.

"And there's a bigger one incoming!" Kitjári yelled over the storm.

From the whiteness, a mountainous form slowly revealed itself.

"Bear! Safís!" the rumbling voice called. "Where have you gone to? Come back!"

Probo rushed toward his old friend and jumped into his arms.

"Probo?!" they heard through the storm. "How did you? This must mean that…" Banook stepped close enough to finally spot the snow-plastered figures, seeing no more than two muzzles poking out of heavy parkas. His bearish nature told him one of them was the Urnaadifröa.

"Ockam?!" he called, stepping forward.

"It's me, Jiara!" Kitjári shouted. "Let's get in the cabin!"

"But Lago, Ockam, Alaia, they will freeze out here. We need to get them first!"

"They're not traveling with us. I'll explain when we're inside! Get us to the cabin before we all freeze!"

They pushed through the snowy meadow until they found the stone steps that led down to the cabin's terrace. Banook opened the wide doors to let them in, ducked beneath the entryway, then closed the doors against the forceful winds.

They all shook the snow off themselves and dropped their bags, weapons, and Winter gear. Bear hurried straight to the fireplace, curling up atop his favorite deerskin pillow. Probo followed him, clacking his hooves next to Safís.

Jiara placed Urnaadisilv on the kitchen table, then hurled herself into Banook for a proper hug, savoring the soft belly and wide arms that embraced her. Without letting go, she said, "This is Nalaníri, the Nagrafröa. And it's obvious you've met Probo."

"A true pleasure, voice of the Nagra," Banook intoned, enveloping her hoofed hand in a disproportionate handshake. "I am Kerjaastórgnem, as Jiara must've told you. And yes, I've met Probo. I'll lock my pantry while you explain to me what is going on."

After Banook had brewed fresh coffee for them, they sat on the comfortable couches in front of the fireplace, where Lago had once woken up from his feverish dreams. Jiara struggled to begin her story, but once she organized her thoughts, she carefully explained all that had occurred in the past year. When she spoke of Ockam's death, Banook covered his mouth and shed tears, but did not say a word. He listened without interrupting, except for when he needed to refill their mugs, or when he had to toss a new log into the fire. He silently relayed the story to Safís, who listened intently.

"—that's when we heard a howl, and Bear came running through the snow. And then you found us."

Banook took a long moment to process it all.

"My dearest Ockam. The protector," he mourned. "He kept his word. I will be thankful to him and honor his memory till the Endfall. And Mamóru's as well. I felt it, as he passed away, like a shard of glass stabbing my heart… And I knew he was gone. All of us Nu'irgesh felt it."

Safís and Probo blinked slowly.

"But I am glad to hear my cub is safe, and Alaia too, and that so much progress has been made. I was aware of your coming, as I saw many kiuons pass by on their way south. They told me the Urnaadifröa had commanded them to leave the mountains. I thought they were referring to Ockam, so I was waiting for his arrival. As the sun set and the blizzard wailed, Bear became uneasy and began to whine, smelling something familiar. He darted out and got lost in the storm, so we hurried out to find him."

Banook scratched Bear's neck. The mutt's tail slammed percussively on the couch's leg. "Jiara, you still have not told me why you are here. Why have you traveled back to these glorious mountains? Though I would not hold it against you if you came only to rejoice in their beauty once more."

"There was a particular request Noss made when we conversed with them. They are concerned about the domes the Red Stag has conquered. If they go the same way as Heartpine, part of Noss's locked memory will be lost forever. Not to mention the innocent animals who would perish."

"Them asked us t'open them Negian domes before it's too late," Nalaníri said quietly. "Them said we shell recruit d'help uf d'Nu'irgesh, n'venture east."

"You've worked smartly," Banook said. "The kiuons are swift as swifts, bright and sharp as the shard. The first pack passed by here long ago. They have already opened a path for me to take, and though the mountains will forever be my home, I will gladly join my friends in this quest. You need not ask twice. If there is no immediate urgency, we could depart here in a few days. How does that sound, my dear Urnaadifröa?"

"Every extra hour I could spend in this cabin, I would treasure," Jiara replied. "We are exhausted, but before we depart, we could use comfortable beds, your nourishing smiles, and your unmatched hospitality."

"And I shall provide," Banook assured them. "We can speak more tomorrow, once Sunnokh warms the summits of the Wujann once again. You must rest now."

Banook claimed the guest bedroom for himself while offering his large upstairs bed to his two friends.

"I think I shell sleep down here instead," Nalaníri said, averting her eyes from Jiara. "I'd like t'enjoy this fire before them embers run cold." She made herself comfortable on the ample couch.

Jiara walked up the steps alone. As she reached the top landing, she saw Banook returning, bringing a bearskin blanket to Nalaníri. She could see in his eyes that he sensed something was wrong, but he did not inquire.

Jiara sat on the bed, placed her mask on the nightstand, and curled up under the fur blankets on one end. The bed felt enormous. She felt so warm, so comfortable, so… alone. But she was too tired for her troubled thoughts to stop her from falling deeply asleep.

Before the visitors had stopped snoring, Banook was up and ready with a copious breakfast. The savory fragrances awakened the wayfarers and dragged them to the kitchen table, ready to fill their bellies as they watched the fresh snow brighten outside. The storm had subsided. The landscape was serene.

After breakfast, Banook cleared the terrace of snow, wiped the outdoor furniture, and invited them to join him. The women bundled up for the cold and followed him to bask in the splendorous views.

"That is Lago-Sterjall's favorite chair," he remarked to Nalaníri as she sat down. She wasn't sure whether the comment meant she shouldn't sit there, and almost stood up, but Banook tapped her shoulder reassuringly. "And these views," he continued, leaning on the handrail, "these were the views we'd enjoy most mornings. He's such a precious cub. I miss him as I've never missed anyone before." He suddenly became aware of his openness and conspicuously stepped to one side, next to the chair Kitjári had claimed. Holding still while his eyes darted around, he mindspoke, «Does she know about my cub and me?»

Kitjári flinched in surprise. She was so used to Banook as a human that she hadn't even considered they could now mindspeak to each other. «Yes, she knows,» she silently replied, «and she is perfectly fine with it.»

Banook turned on his heel and cleared his throat. "But anyway. It might be hard for you to notice, Jiara. I mean, Kitjári, my apologies. But take a look at the Anglass Dome. If your eyes are as keen as your nose must now be, you may notice that the vines are in slight disarray. As slowly but as surely as the glaciers breathe, the dome has been changing."

"I can't see the difference from this far away," she admitted. "Must not be so bad yet, not compared to what we saw at Varanus. We got your message regarding what's happening at Anglass, the one you sent to Crysta. That was smart of you, even if *Luras Varum* wasn't the most subtle name to use for Lago. Crysta had further nuggets of information, and said the Negians were thinking of evacuating the dome, fearing it might fall on them. But I doubt their greedy-ass generals would let them off so easily—we should assume it's still infested with vermin in there. We'd be better off planning our moves with care rather than rushing straight into a fight." She got to her feet. "That reminds me. I'll be right back."

Kitjári soon returned and handed a cloth-wrapped object to Banook.

Banook unwrapped the cover, then suddenly exclaimed, "Dunokh Sull!" staring in disbelief at the mighty recurve bow. "Gift of the heavens, birthed by the night sky itself!" He held up the mythical weapon with reverence. "It is weightless as birdsong. The bowstring taut as a rattlesnake ready to strike. The limbs curved and dark as a black cat's arched back. Do you know what this is?"

"Indeed, Nalaníri told me ab—"

"They say a stray arrow from it is what split the Loorian and Jerjan continents, carving the entire Ophidian Sea. The ancient priests of the Kingdom of Afhora claim that whenever its nightly string is plucked, a star implodes to balance the enormous energies created. I heard legends that the great hero Lerr Mauvenel themself once put their feet upon its strings, pulled with their arms, and flung themself around the entire planet in one uninterrupted swing."

"Well, those are all new to me," Kitjári chuckled. "I'll have to try the trebuchet launch someday, perhaps if we are trying to besiege a castle. But truly, it's a mighty weapon, and we gathered senstregalv arrowheads that are the perfect complement. I just need to craft shafts for the loose tips. And don't you think I forgot about my favorite bear." She handed Banook the oversized glaive.

"I was going to ask about this monstrous thing you hauled in with you," he said as he took the weapon out of the green leather scabbard and admired the edge of black glass. "The light shines darkest in the sharpest end of the glass," he quoted. "Outstanding craftsmanship, just like the ancient Dorvauros style. Wait... It *is* Dorvauros."

"It is indeed. We rescued it and my bow from the Laaja Khem mines."

"That is where I found the bit of senstregalv I used to craft my cub's dagger, but I didn't encounter weapons such as these. I never ventured inward too far, for the mines seem endless and much too dark and frightening."

"It wasn't so scary with pharoliths to light our way, and with Probo as our guide. He's the one who found the bow, although I think he was just trying to eat a crusty skeleton. Maybe we'll all explore those mines together someday."

Banook took two steps to the side and spun the glaive in a spiraling dance, with movements so elegant and controlled that they seemed incongruous with his bulky frame.

"Whoa, hold it there, big man!" Kitjári exclaimed. "I didn't know you could wield a polearm in this way. I was picturing you slamming the flat of the blade like a hammer—which would be equally deadly, just less stylish."

"I'm not that brutish, most of the time," Banook said, twirling the long shaft in his massive fingers. "But I've had time to practice with multiple weapons. Most swords feel like daggers to me, so polearms always fitted me best."

"Ye must've fought in many a war," Nalaníri observed, "if ye've lived fur so long."

"It's not something I'm proud of, even if the fights were necessary. Most wars I fought with maw and claws alone, as I have not been a man for too long—only a few thousand years."

In a controlled swing, Banook lined up the blade to the scabbard and locked it in safely.

"Thank you for this," he said, voice thick with gratitude. "I might need it in the battles to come. It's a beautiful weapon, made with exactly the—"

A crashing and shattering sound made them turn their gazes toward the cabin. A hungry hog was standing atop the kitchen counter.

"Probo!" Nalaníri yelled as she stood up.

"I'll deal with him," Banook said. "I've known this pest for much longer than you. It's just his way of saying that it's time for me to start preparing lunch."

A squealing blur landed in a poof of snow. Banook closed the door and prepared the kitchen for a slow-cooked lunch.

COOKING LESSONS

While Banook kept busy in the kitchen, Kitjári took the time to show Nalaníri around the wonderful cabin, visiting its hanging bridges, secret cellars, and multiple additions across the treetops. It was easier to talk to her again this way, because the conversation was merely about the place, about things Kitjári was familiar with.

They returned to the terrace in time for lunch. The table had been cleaned and set. With only thin clouds and barely a breeze around, it was the perfect chance to enjoy a meal outdoors.

"Caribou… casserole," Banook intoned, pausing between the two words with theatrical emphasis. He lifted the large pot's lid to let the steam find its way into everyone's attentive noses.

"Mouthwatering!" Nalaníri said. "Do I smell bay leaves n'dried cherries?"

"My! That's a good nose, mayhap too sharp. You smell them indeed, plus a secret ingredient, which I won't reveal, as it's my most—"

"A pinch uf lingonberry sugar."

Banook glared at Nalaníri with a mix of admiration and vexation.

"I know jis' what'll make this dish a-perfect!" Nalaníri said. She unbuttoned one of her vest's many pockets and pulled out a glass shaker with a dark powder.

"Don't you dare!" Banook warned her. "The casserole is perfect as it is, there is nothing in this world that—"

Nalaníri uncapped the shaker. A few particles caught the air and wafted to Banook's perceptive nose.

"H-h-honey truffles?" he salivated.

"Not fresh, unfurtunately. Them would've spoiled during our long trip, so I dried up n'ground d'last one to a powder. Kitjári picked them fur me, at d'Slømmon Forest."

"I haven't tasted honey truffles for nearly two millennia. That fragrance, that pungent sweetness… I… I'll… I will let you sprinkle some in *my* casserole, but don't you go taking credit for it afterward."

After they devoured the perfectly spiced meal, Banook carried the empty pot into the kitchen. He took care not to be seen as he wiped the bottom with a fat finger and savored the last drops.

Banook agreed to let Nalaníri cook lunch the next day so that *he* could teach her a thing or two in the kitchen. He tried to follow along and provide advice, but quickly found himself lost in the complexities of her technique, in the speed of her chopping, in the exuberance of her choices. After too many confused moments, he took a break and stomped grumbling out to the terrace. Kitjári saw him exit and followed behind him.

"I've never seen you act like this before," she said, leaning on the handrail next to him.

Banook ignored the comment. "Last night, I noticed you two seemed to have some… issues. A tenuous tension, positively palpable. And I'd been meaning to ask you about it, but there's no longer any need. I see the problem now—she's infuriating!"

"Excuse me?"

"Just because she brought exotic ingredients, it does not mean she knows what to do with them. Anyone could—"

"Banook, Banook, listen to yourself. Hey." She rubbed his hairy, log-thick forearm. "You are adorable when you get envious. I wish you could see your pink cheeks right now."

Banook huffed, but he let a tiny smile escape before he could turn his head away.

"Come on, big bear. I have something else that will lift your spirits. I've been waiting until we had a moment alone." She reached into her pocket and pulled out a wax-sealed envelope. "Lago gave me this, moments before we said goodbye."

Banook gasped. He took the envelope and sat down. Kitjári kept leaning on the handrail, looking toward the landscape to let him have his privacy.

Banook's hands were trembling. "He stamped the wax with the bear and wolf carvings I made on Leif's pommel. Did you notice?"

"Oh, I noticed."

He tenderly caressed the blue wax with his enormous fingers. "I… This may sound silly, but I don't want to break the seal. I want to keep it intact."

Kitjári used a claw to carefully cut the side of the envelope and handed it back, then turned away once more. Banook pulled out the letter and read it to himself:

> Dear Banook,
>
> Today is the twelfth day of Dewrest. Do you remember that date? It's the day Sterjall was born. I'm one year old today, though I feel much older (truth be told, I'm writing this as Lago, because Sterjall's claws and fur get in the way of handling the quill). It's been one year since you helped me find myself, since the day I first saw you fully and knew I loved you completely.
>
> I hope Kitjári and Nalaníri found you without much trouble. I wish you could've been there to see Jiara's first day as Kitjári. Isn't her cinnamon fur just exquisite? And I believe you'll end up liking Nalaníri quite a lot: she's a magnificent chef, and a most kind-hearted and humble boar. Ask her if she has any honey truffles with her—they are only found in Nagradrolom, and I believe you'll love them. I think Kitjári likes Nalaníri; she acts a bit goofy when she is around. I mean "like her" as in she wants to suckle on each of her twelve teats (I saw Nalaníri naked today, and counted them).
>
> I will miss them both. In a few more days, we will sail our separate ways. Jiara was there for me all along, never faltering, selfless and courageous as no soul other than Ockam. I'm sure she's told you what happened by now… There's so much I could say about him, but my chest hurts from the memories. And there's also Mamóru. As I write this, he's still talking with Noss, but we know this will be the end for him, even if not the end of his knowledge. I see why you loved him, and I will be broken once this is over. But I'll have to find the strength to carry on.
>
> There are too many goodbyes, too many departures. I feel lost some days. I feel like I try to find a sense of home and all I can do is think of you and sing the Mountain Song. I keep picturing the day we can be together again…
>
> …But I don't mean to make you feel sad. I am not alone. Friends old and new are here with me. Alaia keeps my heart in the right place and understands me better than anyone; I'm so

happy she's sticking with me through this. I have Sunu, the fiercest shaman warrior, whom we met at Mindreldrolom. They are now the new Kruwenfröa, though they haven't found their half-form yet; it's making us all burst with anxiety and curiosity. There is also Captain Siffo, who commands a magnificent ship with a Puqua crew as unrelenting as the winds of the Tumultuous Ocean. And I also found Aio, whose name is Kulak when he is a caracal, and who I've come to care for very deeply.

Ask Kitjári to tell you more about Aio-Kulak's story, but I wanted to tell you a part of it myself. I'm honestly trembling as I write this. I don't want you to feel jealousy. All I want is to share the happiness I've found. Aio and I have been together for a little while. He loves me. He finally came out and said it the other day, in front of everyone. I was terrified. I think I love him too, though not in the same way I love you, and that makes me feel guilty. At least Alaia is helping me reconcile these emotions.

I know you told me this would be okay, but it still feels strange, as I don't have you near me to talk about it, to share with you. And I wish you could meet Aio too, however awkward that might be; I believe you two would like each other.

I wanted you to know this because, despite all the struggles, despite the deaths we've experienced and the despair that still lies ahead, I am happy. I'm happy because of those who are with me, those who've left, those who will soon leave, and those I will meet next. I am happy, for I carry the hope of the days to come, knowing I'll see you and Bear again. The world is more beautiful the more I get to know it, and each new day fills me with wonder and joy.

I had this idea I figured you might like. I thought I could continue the Mountain Song from where you added me to the poem. I'm *really* trying, and I'm not as good or fast as you, but this is what I have so far:

The wolf cub takes the poet's quill and dips the tip in verse,
His paw is nowhere near as skilled, yet hopes he'll be no worse.
Their tale in rhyming couplets grows alongside best of friends,
Though he'd be happier writing prose, a quatrain next he pens.

Wayfarers leave the cabin's sight and turn away from home,
Da'áju's vast and endless ice caldera they must roam.
Between crevasses deep and cold, they reach the ancient room,
Urnaadi's mask, as legends told, departs its hallowed tomb.

I keep changing it all the time. I'm working on the next quatrain. It is about our goodbye, when we saw Withervale burning, so it's been hard for me to write. I thought I could keep adding to the poem as I continue on this adventure, and once we meet again, we could finish it, together.

I love you. I will be thinking of you, always.

- Lago-Sterjall

"Oh, my dear Lago," Banook whispered. He wiped his eyes and let out a broken sigh. "Thank you so much, Kitjári, for bringing me this gift."

Kitjári turned to face him again. "So? What does it say? You know I was going to ask, eventually. Might as well ask you now."

"Many things. Among them, it says you are eager to suckle on Nalaníri's twelve teats. Is that correct?"

"Pardon?!"

Banook flashed a playful grin. "I guess I don't mind if you read it. I think you will find it charming, and you will love to hear his voice once more. Here."

Kitjári took the letter and read it, unable to hold back a chuckle once, and a few tears a bit later. She folded the letter, pondered with a paw over her muzzle, and suppressed a snort.

"That stupid kid could not keep his pen quiet," she grumbled.

"You'll have to tell me more about this Aio fellow, like the letter suggested. But there are more pressing matters at hand now. Tell me about these twelve teats you yearn for so."

"Oh, you stop it right now! I… I was thinking about telling you, maybe. I'm not sure. I screwed up, I think. That friction you noticed between Nalaníri and I, yes… It's because I like her."

Banook peered over his shoulder to make sure Nalaníri was still busy in the kitchen.

"I'm afraid you'll have to explain yourself, dear Kitjári."

While keeping an eye on Nalaníri's movements, she told him about Nalaníri's past life, her ambiguous comments, their moments alone in the mountains, and her fear that she had been misinterpreting everything. Then she told him all that had happened at the Emen Ruins, and how her fear had gotten the best of her, and how she had turned a beautiful moment into an awkward and tense situation.

"I thought… It worked for Lago, didn't it? But he was assertive, determined, and didn't screw it up the way I did. And you knew he was lorrkin, while I still don't even know if Nalaníri likes women… or bears."

Banook pondered. "It is true that being assertive worked for Lago-Sterjall. My cowardly self would not have taken that first step, and without his courage, my heart would have remained incomplete. But what is true for one does not need be true for another."

"It's just… The Puqua's ideal of beauty is tied to suid traits, which I lack in either of my forms. I'm not sure we fit together, we are so different in many ways. Maybe I'm trying to make something work that isn't meant to be. I always wanted to find that other half, the one that fits perfectly with me, *meant to be with me*, and I'm going out of my way to make it complicated."

"Other half?" Banook questioned. "But you must understand, each of us is but one piece among thousands of shattered pieces of a much larger puzzle. Some of those pieces may fit perfectly alongside you. Some can be forced to fit in angles you hadn't considered. Some shove their way in and bring pain with them. And some others—the rarest kind—were never meant to fit together, yet align in such an unexpected way that they create a magic all of their own."

"You are no longer talking about Nalaníri and I, are you? I can see it in your eyes."

Banook smiled. "I will get to know Nalaníri better as we venture out together, and I'll do my best to understand her. If there's something I find that might clear up your uncertainties, I will let you know, as long as it does not cause a breach of trust among us." He put a hand on Kitjári's shoulder. "And with that, my cinnamon-furred friend, I shall go make sure she's not burning my kitchen, and I will perhaps learn a bit more about why she exasperates me so."

Kitjári thought it would be better to leave them alone. She picked up her bow and quiver, then hollered for Bear, who followed her to the backyard meadow. She readied an arrow on Dunokh Sull's string and set out to hunt. Bear snuck around, trying to find his own food, and even caught a mouse hiding in the snow.

There was more game here, perhaps too much so, making the hunt too easy. After hitting a hopping hare in midair, Kitjári practiced on non-animal targets, getting used to Dunokh Sull's perfectly balanced weightlessness. *I need to get used to this level of precision,* she thought. *And the power, too. Every shot reaches much farther than should be possible.* She tried her luck on dangling acorns and falling leaves, and was almost always on target. Luckily, the shots she missed did not split the land into new continents, nor did they fly off into outer space to bring forth the Endfall. She recovered all of her arrows and returned to the terrace in time for yet another feast.

"Could you tell Bear to drop that at the cleaning bench out back?" Banook asked Safís, seeing the dog proudly carrying the hare Kitjári had shot. "I'll take care of it after lunch."

"Is this the same Bear from before?" Kitjári asked. "Can't be, because I saw him catch a mouse."

"Good boy!" Banook said, directing his voice toward the proud mutt. He turned back to Kitjári. "Sabikh and Frud taught him how to hunt! He fends for himself now, somewhat, though he is still a spoiled child." He placed the last few dishes on the outdoor table, then announced lunch was ready.

Kitjári sat and served herself a generous portion of the cedarwood-plank-grilled gar, which had been stuffed with nuts and mushrooms and fired with a fresh juniper bough that charred into aromatic ashes on top.

Banook sat next to her and pushed a gar onto his plate. "She burned a perfectly good plank of cedarwood to cook these," he muttered, as if Nalaníri wasn't present. "I told her we have a grill for that, but she would not listen."

Nalaníri smirked as if she had received a compliment.

"Is this cassava?" Kitjári asked, reaching for some side dishes.

The chef nodded. "Roasted with tea seed oil, lime juice, n'sprinkled with honey truffle powder n'a few uther herbs. Quite simple, really."

Banook reluctantly served himself the roasted cassava. He tried it together with the fish, failing to hold back an ecstatic sigh.

Lunch was devoured quickly, with glee. Probo and Bear partook of the feast as well, but Safís did not care for cooked meats. The meal had not been of great proportions, particularly for Banook's size, yet it left him fully satisfied. He leaned back, unbuttoning his shirt to better rub his hairy belly. After some time sucking his teeth and considering whether he should confess the thoughts on his mind, he said, "You've proven me wrong, Nalaníri of the Nagra. Every choice you made brought this meal closer to true perfection. I apologize for my earlier doubts—I have cast them aside."

"Ye are as sweet as d'figs uf Ôllomuy during their second season. I think there is a lot we can learn frum each uther during d'long adventure ahead uf us."

"And it's time we decide on our plans for those days. I shall bring out the map." He retrieved a map from inside, then stretched it over the table, and they began to plan their route.

"The snow will only get worse," he said. "Today's sky is clear as a dragonfly's wing, and it seems like it will be the same tomorrow, but any later than that, no oracles can predict. I suggest we leave in the morning and take the pass at Minnelvad, the same one you know so well, Kitjári. The other option is going east toward the Stelm Khull, then directly into the dome, which would be a quieter road to traverse, but we would miss Brimstowne entirely."

"We have all the supplies we need," Kitjári said. "I don't think we need to bother with Brimstowne."

"Perhaps. But I have a friend there who might have useful information for us."

"You mean that ranger you met last time, when you went down for Winter supplies?"

"The same one. I also saw him when I traveled to the Wujann Observatory to send Safís's message to Crysta. His name is Ardof. There is a chance we might find him in town."

"D'ye know him well enough to trust him?" Nalaníri asked.

"I believe so. He already knew about Lago and Agnargsilv, as he has contacts within the Negian forces. He knew another mask had been spotted, meaning Urnaadisilv, but kept all of that a secret from the kind woman who runs the Wujann Observatory. He knows which secrets to guard, which to reveal, and which to trade for bigger secrets."

Kitjári squinted. "How much more did he find out through you?"

Banook frowned at the question, but mostly out of shame. "Well, he's quite a persuasive individual. We talked, extensively, as we walked together down Mount Fogra. I might've told him a bit too much. But I trust him, truly. He is doing this for the right reasons, from the kindness of his heart. He may prove a worthy ally."

He turned to look at the white-topped Anglass Dome. It did not look out of shape from this far away, but he could feel something in disarray. He glanced back down at the map.

"Well, dear friends," he concluded, "this will be a treacherous journey, but I'm excited to at last travel through lands I have not seen for centuries. My heart will feel incomplete without the mountains, but there's a much larger hole in it that needs to be filled."

He straightened up, drew in a bountiful breath of fresh mountain air, then said, "Follow me now. We better get to packing."

PART THREE
BAURAM

Stolen Light

"… Need… get up!" a muffled voice called.

A thrumming headache. A lethargy that sank to the bone.

"—sten to our voice, Agnargfröa. Liste—"

Why are they screaming? Just… let me…

A splash of cold.

Lago opened his eyes, but it did not help. The darkness was complete.

"Where…" his lips drooped, his eyelids too.

A slap on his face. His shoulders shook.

"Up, Lago-Sterjall, awaken!"

He recognized Sunu's voice.

"You must fight. Open your eyes!"

Eihnk-eihnk! came a distressed call from the dark.

"Olo, do not fear."

Lago heard Alaia mumble something. He couldn't pinpoint where the voice had come from. He looked left and right, seeing nothing, then felt around him with cold fingers, sensing someone missing. *Where is Aio?* he thought. "Where is Aio!?" he screamed, and the desperation jolted him from his stupor. "Aio! Is Aio okay?" he called out, then crawled along the ground to find him.

"He still sleeps," Sunu answered. "His breathing is forced."

"What… happened?"

"Poison. Serdein poisoned our food. Ishke'ísuk brought us back to consciousness. He has been searching for a way out."

"The poison blinded me. I can't see anything."

"Your eyes are fine, but there is no light. Serdein took our bags, took the kenzir stones, took the Silvesh. The sliding door is sealed."

Lago instinctively reached for his belt. Leif was gone too. He tried to stand but lost his balance.

"Save your energy," Sunu said calmly. They put a hand on Lago's shoulder, slid it down to his own hand, then directed it down to a smooth, barely breathing chest. "Help Khuron Aio wake up, while we help Alaia. The drug wears off."

Lago felt over the cold body until he found Aio's smooth head. He crawled next to him, kissed him in the dark, and whispered, "Aio, wake up." But Aio did not respond.

"Please, I need you. Wake up, we need to get out of here. Please…" he caressed Aio's lips with his fingertips, then tried to spread open his eyelids.

"Try this," Sunu said, tapping Lago's shoulder with a bowl of water.

Lago's mouth was dry, so he drank some water first, then spilled the rest over Aio's face. Some dripped into Aio's nose, making him sneeze.

"Ashaskem…" Aio wheezed, then fell back down.

"It's me, it's Lago. Wake up, Aio."

Aio fell silent again.

"Please, come back," Lago pleaded, shaking his shoulders.

Aio drew in a jagged breath.

"Please Aio. Don't leave. Please, I love you, I can't lose you. Please, Aio, Kulak, I…"

"Ashaskem… Ashas… La… Lago… What happened?" Aio pulled himself up to his elbows. "Why is it so dark?"

Lago kissed his lips. "You are alright, thank Noss. Stay with me. It is dark, but keep your eyes open. Stay with me. Don't fall back asleep."

The three of them helped wake Alaia up next, who vomited violently before gasping into consciousness. It took them all a while to recover their senses, but the pounding headaches and disorientation would last for much longer.

"That backstabbing thief," Alaia croaked. "We need to… Have you found the door?" she asked the darkness.

"It is locked," Sunu replied, "it will not roll. The metal bar must be latched outside."

They heard Blu and Pichi stir and moan.

"Be strong," Aio comforted the smilodons. "We will get you out of here."

Eihnk-eihnk! Olo called once more, terrified of the darkness.

"Patience, Olo," Sunu said as they searched around. "Find something dry for us," they told the group, "something that will burn, something to keep a fire alive. Lago, your brime bracer, is it still there?"

Lago patted his left forearm: the innocuous-looking arm bracer was still there, with the row of brime cubes still attached. With so many other treasures to gawk over, Serdein had overlooked it. "It's still on my arm," Lago answered, feeling around until he found a piece of broken ceramic. He scraped the shard over his bracer, shooting out a blindingly bright rain of white sparks. They lingered on the ground like a shattered meteor, giving the group enough light to see by for a dimming moment.

"Try that again," Alaia requested once the light had faded. Lago splashed starlight onto the ground a second time. "This should do." She tossed a bundle of wool and splintered wood over the burning sparks. Soon they had a decent fire burning in the center of the room, with enough wood from the crates to last for a while.

They scoured the chamber for other supplies. Serdein had left them with no bags and few weapons. Sunu and Alaia still had darts in their pockets, and Sunu's bone halberd had also been left behind, perhaps because it was too long and cumbersome to carry.

There was no exit other than the spinning doorway. Ishke'ísuk approached it, turned into an alligator a bit too large for the cramped room, and slammed his tail against the rock. It did not crack, nor did it move a hairbreadth, even after a dozen consecutive slams.

Ishke'ísuk suddenly vanished in a vacuum of air, having shapeshifted into a tiny leaf-tailed gecko. He crawled around the secret door, trying to find a pocket large enough to fit through, but the construction was precise; unless he could turn paper-thin, he would not fit. Next, he shifted into a banded coral snake, wrapping himself around Sunu's arm. He hissed, then twisted around their bald head and hissed again next to their ear.

"We cannot understand him without Kruwensilv," they said. "We feel lost."

Ishke'ísuk hissed again.

"What are you trying to tell us?" Aio asked.

Ishke'ísuk let go of Sunu, slithered to the fire, and whipped his black and orange tail against a log, causing a shower of sparks to rise. His eyes followed the movement of the sparks, and he spat upward for emphasis.

"I know!" Alaia exclaimed, eyes on the twirling pillar of sparks. "The hole in the ceiling, where the smoke filters through. Ishke could fit through there!"

"It is very high," Aio fretted. "How are we going to reach?"

"Why doesn't he just crawl up?" Lago questioned. "He could, as any of the sticky-footed lizards." He picked the snake up and lifted him to a wall. Ishke'ísuk seemed frustrated with the gesture, but he demonstrated the problem: he turned back into a gecko and began to crawl up the wall, but as soon as he reached the ancient dust and buildup at the higher portions, the particles dislodged, and his sticky feet became useless. He fell, and Lago caught him.

"Too brittle," Sunu said.

"Just hurl him up?" Alaia half-joked.

"Maybe we can lift him," Lago countered, more sensibly.

"Bring the crates," Aio suggested. "Blu, can you help?"

They moved the fire a bit to the side, then built a pyramid of crates at the center of the room. Blu balanced on the crates and stretched his neck up. Aio climbed on top of Blu's head and, extending Sunu's halberd, reached its sharp tip to where the ventilation hole opened above them. Dust and thin sheets of carbon broke away and fell into his eyes as the halberd scraped against the sides of the opening.

"Ishke'ísuk, climb, now, before my feet lose balance."

But Ishke'ísuk did not comply. Instead, he shifted into a frill-necked lizard, expanded his cartilaginous spines to expose the frill of skin around his neck, and hissed at the fire burning on the ground.

"Too much smoke. He'll need to breathe," Alaia deduced. "We'll have to lose the fire. Aio, can you find the hole in the dark?"

"I can try," Aio said, lowering the halberd to rest his arms. "Blu, stay still."

Sunu placed a ceramic bowl over the fire to contain the smoke. They waited until enough smoke filtered out of the room, then tried again, with Lago creating new sparks from his bracer to provide fitful lighting.

The lizard climbed the crates, scaled Blu's legs and back, clawed his way up Aio's body, and followed the halberd's shaft all the way to the sharp tip, until Aio felt his weight on it no more. Aio lowered his arm and listened to the crumbling sound of particles falling from the hole above him.

They all sat down to wait.

"Will he be able to use that metal handle on the other side?" Alaia asked.

"I think so," Lago replied. "He has many forms with claws that could pull on that secret panel and hold the bar. I'm more worried if he'll be able to find his way in the dark. There were many other tunnels we took before finding this room."

"He will find us," Sunu assured them. "He remembers. And his tongue can catch scent almost as well as Sterjall's nose."

About an hour later, after a smoky climb to the top of the mesa, sliding down a sandstone bluff, finding the secret cave and entrance, and following the dark tunnels aided by his sense of smell, Ishke'ísuk found the doorway and began to scratch at the walls, searching for the hidden mechanism.

"He's here!" Alaia said. "Light the fire again!"

Lago struck his bracer. The chamber reformed warmly around them.

They listened eagerly, hearing the Nu'irg probing at the walls in the next chamber. There was a screech, then something fell and shattered. Then there was the sound of something heavy and metallic falling onto the ground, followed by more scratching. Next came a solid *clang!* and a low rumble.

"It's unlocked!" Lago cheered. "Let's help him open it!"

The four of them flattened their hands onto the rolling wall and used the friction to make the circular stone begin to roll open. The heavy disc picked up momentum and rolled the rest of the way on its own.

The Nu'irg rushed into the room, climbed onto Sunu's shoulder, and wrapped his basilisk tail around their neck. Perched there, he fell asleep—the climb and successive form changes had drained him.

CHAPTER EIGHTEEN

DOUBLE-DEALING

With cushion covers and cheap rugs that had been left in the room, the way-farers constructed makeshift bags into which they loaded all the food left in the crates. The pots and waterskins they filled with water from the pump.

"Why would Serdein abandon all these supplies?" Alaia asked.

Lago chewed experimentally on old nuts, then tossed a jar of them into his new bag. As he crunched, he answered, "What is all this junk worth to him now? With even one of our pharoliths he can live like a king, as long as he finds the right buyer. He won't be traveling the desert anymore, that's my guess."

"Makes sense. That lowlife didn't even care to kill us properly, just locked us in here to starve and rot. He knows he won't need this hideout anymore. Good way to bury the evidence."

As Lago filled his bag, he suddenly felt lightheaded. He dropped the bag and sat on the ground, leaning against a wall.

"What is wrong?" Alaia inquired, squatting by his side.

"I... I feel so empty," he confessed. "It's like he stole a part of me. I feel drained, angry, and scared."

Aio sat next to him. "My scalp feels the same. But it is not the distance from Mindrelsilv that makes me feel lost, it is only the fear of losing it." He held Lago's hand, then tapped on Lago's chest. "Ster-*jall*. Agnarg is in here. He did not take Sterjall away, or Kulak, or Lummukem. We will find our Silvesh."

He helped Lago to his feet.

"We must hurry," Sunu said. Their eyes looked dim, sunken within heavy bags. "Serdein's bird is faster than our mindrégosh, and we know not for how long we slept. We must follow before his prints are wiped away by the wind."

They cleaned their bodies and drank as much water as they could, then packed their bags atop Pichi's harness and left the ruins. Blinded by the afternoon sun, they followed the moa's tracks. They were much clearer now, thanks to the added weight the bird carried.

"Sluggish and encumbered the bird must be," Sunu said. "Perhaps we will catch up."

They allowed little rest for Blu and Pichi, but granted them generous amounts of water and food. For three days they followed the tracks, encountering Serdein's cold camps along the way, where he had burnt no fires—he was being cautious.

"The dome is so close," Lago remarked at one point, staring at the imposing wall that kept growing closer. "It's like Serdein has been heading straight for it."

"We will find our masks and venture in soon," Aio promised him.

Lago held on tighter to his chest. "I'm just so afraid. What if we don't get our masks back? What if—"

"No. You must stay strong. There are more adventures awaiting, so much to explore."

Lago quieted, mulling over something, then mumbled under his breath, "My long homeward journey must come to an end."

"What do you mean?" Aio asked, looking over his shoulder to try to read Lago's expression.

"Nothing. I was reminded of a song, of a poem, from a book. But no, this is not the end. We have to keep going, we have to find him and take back all that he stole from us."

They climbed up a silty wall and at last exited the maze of the badlands. The tracks ended there, on a wide road of compacted sandstone a mere couple of miles from the Azurean Dome. The azure- and lilac-tinted vines of the dome were sunken into mountain-sized dunes of blue, purple, and black. The higher the vines reached, the more they lost their oceanic hues, until a mile or so up they entirely traded them for the more familiar, waxy greens.

Sunu examined the last of the prints left on the silty sand. "The bird tracks turn slightly left before the road. Serdein must have traveled south." It was their only chance to find him, so they continued southward on the hard road.

The desert grew more fertile near the dome, with plant life similar to that which they had found along the shores of the Esduss Sea: short and spiky, ornate and outlandish. They soon spotted farmlands and sandy trails leading to sandstone-carved huts.

"My eyes see the moa!" Aio cried out. "Hurry ahead!" he told Blu.

It was not one, but three moas, walking in a line toward them. As the birds got closer, they veered off the road. Their veil-faced riders drew long daggers and screamed unknown obscenities in their Baurami tongue.

The cats stopped. Lago tried to ask questions, but the moa riders either did not know his language or were simply too afraid. He tried a name instead. "Serdein? Do you know Serdein? Serdein Humuen-Vok."

One rider seemed to recognize the name. The three exchanged words quietly, with their eyes constantly darting to the south.

"No," the rider said and began to move away, dagger still held tight.

"Hold on!" Lago said. "What about Navar Mat?"

"Navar Mat!" the rider exclaimed, pointing his dagger south, then fled north at full speed, followed by his friends.

The wayfarers passed by more moa riders on their way: some who turned around and hurried back south, some who threatened them but didn't dare approach, some who tried to follow at their sides until they were spooked by Pichi's hisses.

"If Navar Mat is the largest trading city around here," Lago said, "that is where Serdein will try to sell our belongings. We go in, find him, then escape through the dome. What was the name of the buyer Serdein had there?"

"Duchess Hilid Kei," Sunu answered. "She sounded like an important person."

"She may be. Let's not use our real names. Listen to me, and play along when the time comes. Here's what I'm thinking…"

The road had been flanked by dunes on either side, but as they approached Navar Mat the landscape hardened and became pierced by buttes and spires, all carved with doorways and windows. The prominences became more numerous the farther they traveled, until they merged into the larger form of a mesa, forming a striated wall in their path. Like the coastal city of Lhambor Di, Navar Mat was carved straight into the sandstone, in multiple levels, each of a different-colored rock. The wedge-shaped entrance echoed the style of the ruins they had found in the Cobalt Desert, though this gate was a few hundred feet tall and tightly guarded.

Before they got too close to the city, a troop of moa riders three dozen strong formed a circle around them. These riders were armored beneath their sleeveless cloaks—even their moas wore barding on their heads and around their necks. The riders pointed silvery lances and arrows at them.

Their leader moved forward on a silver-armored moa, and said, *"Tsan-fai gollo, irve Navar Mat?"*

"Do you speak Common?" Lago asked.

"I speak it," the woman answered. *"Ushmahiel, ter varia dino.* What manner of beasts are these you ride? Where have your colorless eyes brought you from?"

Lago had thought of what to say in this situation, though he still had to improvise.

"We come from Zovaria, in search of profitable trade. My name is Luras."

"May Sceres's light brighten your trails, Luras ill Zevvieren."

"May the stars guide your heart. As you have probably heard, the Moordusk Dome recently opened, and from it many animals like these came forth." He tapped on Blu's shoulders. "We captured these two and are looking for a buyer. They are tame, yet still deadly, as they obey only their masters' orders."

"Zevvieren is far from Bauram. Why not sell them in the pink capital?" the leader asked, pushing closer within the circle to examine the smilodons.

"We were promised a better deal in Lerev," Lago replied. "But as we traveled the Esduss Sea, we hit rocks near the shore. A merchant pointed the way for us, telling us Navar Mat has wealthy traders, and that Duchess Hilid Kei might be interested. Perhaps for the price of one, we could buy a new ship to continue toward Lerev. The Republic will still be happy with the purchase of the remaining beast."

"Lhambor Di is where you find ships, not Navar Mat," the woman questioned. Yet she considered, measuring the potential profitability of the situation. "But perhaps we can make a deal. I am Commander Vaalag Feallanor-Vok sar Gelleth ill Navar Mat, in service of Duchess Hilid Kei and the Duchy of Blue Stone. Will your beasts behave if we let you enter the city?"

"They may hiss, but they will not attack," Lago replied. "We want no trouble."

"Then follow us," Vaalag said.

The moa riders escorted them under the massive gate. The road tunneled south underneath the city to cut through the mesa, but as they passed under the gate, Vaalag diverted them to a ramp to their left, then hurried ahead to inform the duchess of the incoming visitors.

They followed their escorts up the ramp, traversing the multiple levels of the sandstone city. The first level was black, hollowed by a maze of windows and tunnels. The second was adorned by turquoise-colored striations, and there the road opened into a wide plaza and marketplace where a lively population of colorful locals cooked and devoured fresh and greasy street foods.

Alaia was surprised to see many Oldrin among the crowds, who were as far from their homeland of Dorhond as any Oldrin could be. But she was not surprised to see they were all servants, likely slaves. The Oldrin who inhabited these lands had prominently decorated spurs painted in different shades of blue and purple. Alaia wondered if it was a way for them to make themselves more beautiful or simply a way for their masters to tag them.

Their escort tried to conceal the smilodons from the public, but rumors had moved fast, and now too many eyes were upon them. More soldiers appeared to push the crowds away, with violence where they deemed necessary.

They crossed through another black level, and then came upon a dark-blue one where it seemed most of the inhabitants made their homes, where clotheslines bridged the streets like rainbowy banners of an unending celebration. After yet another black level—this one equipped with parapets, towers, and other defensive structures—they reached the top of the mesa, where dozens of white marble buildings rose. Blue banners slapped in the wind above the palatial structures, each adorned by a black star with a white vertical wedge at the center—the sigil of the Kingdom of Bauram. Beneath those banners waved slender pennants with striations in the same colors as the levels of the city, flying in the name of the Duchy of Blue Stone.

The wayfarers were led through a colonnade much like the one they had found buried in the desert, then stopped in front of the gates of a palace. Vaalag was there, waiting for them next to her fleet-footed moa.

"Duchess Hilid Kei has agreed to meet with you," she said. "You will need to leave your weapons and beasts out here."

Lago looked around and hesitated. "These cats are too valuable to us. We need your assurance that they will not be bothered. They will attack if you try to carry them away."

"Our duchy is one of honest trade, so you mustn't fear. You say the beasts answer to their masters only. It would be unwise of us to force them to move—my soldiers' lives are much too valuable. The beasts will be protected out here while you are inside."

They had no other choice, so they dismounted their cats. Lago spotted a figure observing them from a high balcony, wearing robes of blue, black, and nacreous white. The figure withdrew from the balcony and closed the doors.

Sunu surrendered their halberd to Vaalag, who handed them a black cloak. "We must display modesty in front of the duchess," she explained, also handing a cloak to Aio, who put it on with no complaint. Sunu complained with their face but put the cloak on to cover their small breasts. Olo and Ishke'ísuk, who'd had to dismount Sunu while they donned the cloak, returned to perch upon their respective spots.

"The slave will stay with our guards," Vaalag ordered, eyeing Alaia's nub. A few of her soldiers approached, but Lago jumped in front of them.

"Stop! She comes with us."

"As you wish," Vaalag demurred, "but her impertinent eyes must remain on the floor. She is not properly trained." Alaia scowled, but Lago placed a hand on her arm and with a stare asked her to comply.

Vaalag led them up the steps of the marble palace. Halfway up, she looked at Lago and remarked, "You do not seem aware of the proper greetings or manners of our people."

"We are not," Lago confirmed. "I apologize."

"Follow my guidelines, lest you disparage those higher born than you." She eyed Lago carefully and made sure he was paying attention, then with a friendlier tone continued. "Only one of you must speak. The duchess will not speak until the visitor has first greeted her properly. You must call out *ushmahiel*, and bow without breaking eye contact. Wait for her answer, and only then may you speak. Common will do, as you don't seem familiar with our tongue. Never place a hand behind your back. Never stand with your left foot in front of your right. Never face away from the duchess, not even when you make your exit. Do your colorless eyes understand?"

"Yes," Lago confirmed, repeating the instructions in his mind.

Vaalag looked at the others. "The rest of you, not a word, unless you are directly spoken to. And you must keep your eyes on the ground, unless your tongue is moving."

The palace doors opened silently as they approached. Vaalag guided them through a long hall decorated by illustrated tapestries of sizes unsurpassed in any other realms, then signaled to a guard who opened a door that seemed to be made of pure gold. In the smaller room beyond the door, Duchess Hilid Kei waited, wrapped in the colors of the Baurami flag. She stood tall and still as an obelisk next to a wide, pompously ornamented chair. Her eyes were bright as sapphires, her hair darker than the tar in the caves of the Stelm Glirjil.

An attendant stepped to the side of the duchess, facing Lago's group. She performed an elaborate curtsy and intoned, "*Ushma hajiel, Charud Hilid Kei Ushtamin-Vok sar Gwahir ill Navar Mat, ushma tai-helv.*" She scurried away to stand attentively nearby.

Lago walked in front of his companions. "Ushmahiel," he said to the duchess. He bowed, feet well aligned, not breaking eye contact, not even blinking.

"Ushma tar-viv," the duchess replied, bowing as well, though not as deeply. She settled into her chair while servants quickly brought four more chairs for the guests, followed by glasses of chilled water.

"Please, do sit," the duchess invited with the rough voice of one who had partaken in far too much mistleaf. The wayfarers complied; soldiers stood at guard directly behind their seats. "What is an acolyte of Havengall doing so far from the nearest temple? And one so young, at that?" she asked, perspicaciously eyeing Lago's copper bracelet.

"It is but a family heirloom," Lago lied with determination, forcing himself not to look at the bracelet that Khopto had gifted him so many years back. "I'm not a monk."

"I know. Your hair tells me so." She kept her expression blank as a marble block as she scanned Lago's face, his clothing, his posture, as if hunting for a lie. Even though Lago could not see his own threads without Agnargsilv, and he did not believe the duchess could see them either, he forced himself into the mental state Aio-Kulak had taught him, pulling his threads inward to make his feelings inaccessible to others.

"Commander Vaalag informed me of your travels," the duchess continued, "and of your tame beasts. I saw them from my balcony. They are larger than the mountain lions of Wastyr, and seem more obedient. Speak your name, and tell me—is it true that the beasts came from within the dome of the moorlands?"

"It is true," Lago answered. "My name is Luras, Luras Varum. The Moordusk Dome's opening brought a lot of these beasts into our lands."

"So I have heard, Luras Varum. And I have heard of the battles being fought at the dome's perimeter. My cormorants' wings are wide, they keep me well informed. I have also heard that no Union citizens have been able to tame these beasts—they are ruthless." She stared at the nearly entirely faded pigments on Aio's scalp, then at his sapphire pendant. Though the precious stone was highly valuable, it was nothing to the duchess, but her keen eyes still took note of it. "News from afar tells me that these people who control the beasts— the Laatu, they are said to be called—have no hair, and they paint strange sigils upon their glossy heads."

Lago had expected that news of the Laatu would've traveled this far, given that it had been nearly two months since the Moordusk Dome began to open. "You are well informed, and observant," he replied, keeping his composure. "This is why we can control the beasts. My two friends have forsaken the Miscam tribe to join me, as I have promised them riches they could never have dreamed of within their confined dome. I have a contact in Lerev who says the Republic will pay generously for the two smilodons. That is what the beasts are called."

"I know their names, Luras Varum-Vok ill Zevvieren. Like the giant beasts of epochs past, though yours do seem much larger. Their fossils sleep in our dunes, waiting to be uncovered from between blankets of blue and black. Pray tell, how do you make these smilodons so tame?"

"That is the information we've come to sell, more than the beasts themselves. The Miscam's sacred words will turn them to your favor. We can offer you the knowledge of the sacred words as well as one of the smilodons, but we still must travel to Lerev to sell the other. The price Lerev is willing to pay is much greater than we'd be comfortable asking of you." He swallowed, uncertain if his words had come off as a friendly tease, a challenge, or an insult.

The duchess narrowed her eyes almost imperceptibly. "You speak dangerous words, as Bauram and Lerev are not on good terms. You are double-dealing, young acolyte, overstepping your bounds."

"That is the nature of any good deal, otherwise it's pocket change. I'm not here for Lodes or Quggons."

The duchess laughed, charmed. "A heart of ambition may speak truth, but only when the truth serves it. Tell me, Luras Varum-Vok ill Zevvieren, what has the Republic of Lerev offered for your smilodons? What do they have that is so precious?"

"We were promised a kenzir stone, a pharolith," Lago stated.

The duchess repositioned herself in her wide chair. Her face could not hide the surprise or the sudden distrust, though distrust seemed to be her primary predisposition.

With a flick of a finger, she summoned a servant who offered her a tray. From it the duchess grabbed a minute pipe of gold and copper, already lit for her. She inhaled deeply and observed her guests carefully. "This is too much of an odd coincidence," she murmured as she exhaled the heavily spiced smoke. "Do you know why I say this?"

"No Lurr, I do not."

She rolled the small pipe in her fingertips. "A merchant from Lhambor Di came offering one such stone, only days ago. Do you know who I speak of?"

"No. If I knew where to find one here, I would not be traveling as far as Lerev to get one. He's likely lying—no one has seen those stones for ages."

The duchess waved at another servant, who leaned in close to her. She whispered in her ear and the servant hurried out of the room.

"Perhaps. I, too, thought he was lying," the duchess said. "Yet he showed me proof."

The servant returned with a tiny wooden box. The duchess opened it and plucked out a knapped shard of a pharolith. It looked like an insect's iridescent wing, but one that shone with a light of its own. Lago did not need to feign surprise, as he *was* surprised, only in a manner different than the duchess guessed.

"So, you have one?" he asked.

"No, I do not. The merchant asked for far too much and clearly lied about how he had obtained it. The man is currently undergoing interrogation, as bringing such a precious item to these lands—an item which was likely stolen—could also bring us an unwanted war. He has hidden it somewhere, but he won't reveal the location." She shifted in her chair, assuming a more graceful posture. "So, it's true then? The rumors that Lerev still holds one of the ancient pharoliths? Does it still shine?"

"That is what I've been told, though I have not seen it myself."

"And you trust the Republic to keep their word?"

"I trust my contact. My dealings with Lerev are my own to worry about. But what if…" Lago hesitated, unsure of his strategy. "You say you don't want the trouble the kenzir stone may bring. If the rock is hidden somewhere, and I can find it, I can take it away. And in exchange, you get to keep both smilodons, and we will teach you the sacred words to control them. It will save me trouble, as I will not have to travel to Lerev after all, nor will I have to feed those beasts any longer."

"A kenzir stone that may be cursed in exchange for two beasts," Duchess Hilid Kei pondered. "It may be a fair deal."

"The stone, and safe passage back to the Esduss Sea," Lago added, extending the negotiation to make it seem more plausible. "And enough Qupi to board a ship that can take us back to Zovaria."

"Your further requests are easily within my reach. You seem brave, young man, but the man in our custody does not wish to speak."

"My Laatu friends know of ways to make any prisoner cooperate. Let us try. If we succeed, you get not one, but two of my beasts, and the Republic of Lerev gets none. And you get rid of the pharolith, if it does indeed exist."

The duchess called for Vaalag. They discussed the issue in their tongue, yet still quietly enough for the guests not to overhear. After a stretched moment, Vaalag returned to stand behind Lago's seat.

The duchess rolled her small pipe, as if meditating. "I'm not certain what sort of gamble you think you are playing, Luras Varum-Vok ill Zevvieren, but I'm willing to play along. Vaalag will escort you to our prisoner, but I must warn you—you have everything to lose if you try to deceive us. One wrong move and you will be chained in the next cell. If we can't control the smilodons then, I will make a rug with their precious furs. You best know what you are doing."

"I know exactly what I am doing," Lago replied. "I will make him talk, and I will find out where he's hidden the treasure."

CHAPTER NINETEEN

THE BROKEN PRISONER

All including the guards walked backward out of the chamber, never showing their backs to the duchess. Once outside the palace, Commander Vaalag let them ride the smilodons one level down to where the sandstone was a matte black. Blu and Pichi were left to wait on a heavily guarded barbican. From there, a tunnel led toward the prison.

"The duchess has authorized me to let you into the merchant's chamber," Vaalag said, "but one of our guards will supervise you." They walked in front of cells secured by metal doors, with small hatches at eye level to allow the guards to keep their eyes on the prisoners.

Agonizing screams seeped out from some of the cells. Alaia had to cover her ears. Vaalag noticed her discomfort and smiled mirthlessly, then stopped near the end of the hallway, where the prison warden was waiting. "*Ishma, Tanurr,*" he barely whispered to Vaalag, although his distrustful eyes did not leave the wayfarers. He pulled out his keyring and unlocked a heavy door.

Inside the cell were the tattered remains of Serdein. His arms were splayed wide by heavy ropes that suspended him against the cold sandstone wall. He was naked, covered in cuts and bruises, dripping piss and blood at his feet. He could no longer hold his weight up with his feet and instead dangled limply, further damaging his overstretched arms. His eyes were shut, and he was so exhausted that he did not even glance at the people entering the room.

"You may do anything you require to our prisoner, except kill him," Vaalag instructed, eyes locked on Lago. "I can provide you with no weapons, but I don't think they'll do you any good. We've tried everything with him already. I hope your Laatu friends know what they are doing." She signaled for one guard to step into the cell. "Keep an eye on them," she said in her clearest Common, then repeated the instructions in Baurami, walked out, and closed the door.

The barred hatch swung open loudly, and through it Vaalag's voice announced, "You have four hours. Or knock on the door if you are done before your time has elapsed."

The door was locked from the outside. Footsteps receded down the hall.

Lago approached Serdein and was about to lift his chin up when he heard a muffled cry from behind him. He turned to see Sunu slowly lowering the guard's body to the ground, a paralyzing dart buried deep in her neck.

"Sunu! Fuck!" Alaia whispered hoarsely.

"It would have been necessary, sooner or later," they said. They took the guard's sword for themself and handed her knife to Lago. "Cut him free."

As Lago sliced through the ropes, Serdein regained his senses. He spotted the guard's body on the ground, then lifted his head and saw the young man with a knife next to him, immediately recognizing him. He began to scream.

Aio rushed to cover Serdein's mouth.

"It does not matter if he screams," Sunu noted. "They are expecting screams."

"True," Lago said, "but we don't want them to hear anything else." He finished cutting Serdein free while Aio tried to calm him down.

Sunu took off their borrowed cloak and wiped Serdein's wounds with it. Aio then offered his own clean cloak for Serdein to wear, making sure he understood to remain quiet. Serdein did.

"We are here with a proposal," Lago began, squatting next to the pile of a man.

Serdein nodded resignedly through cracked teeth.

"The duchess is not yet willing to let you die. She wants to keep torturing you until you talk. She *will* kill you, but only after you tell her where you hid our belongings." Lago spoke slowly and clearly, repeating his words when it seemed Serdein had a hard time interpreting their meaning.

Serdein began to sob and plead.

"Stop. Be quiet." Lago continued, "We have a better offer for you. We will help you escape if you tell us where you hid our bags. We will set you free away from the duchess's soldiers, and you may live, as long as you are able to run away from them. Do you understand? We help you escape, you give back our things, you live. Or do you prefer we hand you back to the duchess's torturers?"

"No, please…" Serdein whimpered. "Understand. I help. *Sanirr, faul negga, sanirr…*"

"Where are our bags?" Lago demanded.

"Near road."

"Where exactly."

"Sleep in sands, hidden. Have to show."

"How far from here?"

"Five miles. Near road. Take me."

"We will. We will have to ride, fast. No moas, just big cats. You will have to hold tightly to the saddle. You will point where to go. If they catch us, we all die. Do you understand?"

"*Sanirr,* understand."

"We can't leave through the main gate, too many soldiers. Do you know a safer way to escape the city?"

"Badlands. Escape badlands, I show you. Out prison, up mesa top. Run east, slide down cliff into badlands. Moa will not follow."

"If he's telling the truth, we could lose our enemies there," Alaia said. "But we are high over the ground."

"Very high, yes," Serdein said with sudden energy. "High, sand below. Good, dangerous, no moa follows. Only escape. Jump. Live."

Lago helped Serdein up to his feet. "You will need to run with us until we get to the cats. Can you handle that?"

"Help. I try."

"Okay," Lago said. "Aio, help me carry him. Alaia, take the knife and protect us from behind. Sunu, you and Ishke'ísuk open the way ahead."

They moved the paralyzed guard out of the way and stood to one side of the door, hiding flat against the wall. Sunu inhaled a dose of soot from their pendant, mindspoke a few secret words to the basilisk Nu'irg, then knocked on the door.

"*Tsan-umin?*" a voice came, but the door remained closed. Sunu knocked again. The small hatch slid open. "*Tsan-umin, Khalof?*"

They could sense the warden peeking through, and they knew he could see the ropes had been cut.

"*Khalof!*" the warden called out, louder now. Ishke'ísuk jumped through the hatch, landing atop the man's headcloth, then shifted into a blue coral snake. The slender reptile looked harmless with its minute jaws, but they were big enough to bite around the warden's pointed nose. The potent venom made his nerves fire all at once in a spasm of horrifying screams. The screams went unnoticed among those from the prisoners, and soon stopped as the man collapsed to the ground.

Ishke'ísuk changed into a monitor lizard and pulled at the keyring by the warden's belt. He had only his jaws to work with, for his claws would be of no use with such a delicate object. He carried the keyring to the lock, fitting a key in and trying to turn it. Wrong one.

"Tsan-hamuk? Eish-melal?" A soldier approached from the end of the hallway, seeing his friend on the ground and a strange shadow slithering by the door.

Ishke'ísuk fit another key, then another, with no luck. The soldier inched closer, saw the lizard, and drew his spear. The fourth key turned just as the soldier thrust his weapon forward. The monitor lizard shrunk into a rainbow skink too tiny for the attacker to spot, slinked underneath him, then shifted into his enormous alligator form, launching the man upward to smash his head into the hard ceiling.

The cell door opened, and the wayfarers fled, following the alligator. Two more soldiers rushed into the hallway. Ishke'ísuk snapped his jaws down on both of them at once, nearly splitting them in half. The screaming, rumbling, and gurgling were distinctive now, alerting more sentinels.

Ishke'ísuk filled the entire width of the hallway as he stomped ahead, taking down anyone who stepped in front of him. Alarm horns were blown, and more enemies approached, but these were more sensible, and in their terror ran away from the incoming teeth.

One of the soldiers they had trampled over had gotten back to his feet and was now behind them. He charged toward Alaia with a scream, spear in hand. She only had a short knife and knew she could not fight him. Instead, she hurled the knife, piercing the attacker's leg, who tripped and fell to the ground cursing.

They exited the prison and hastened straight to the barbican, where Ishke'ísuk swiped his tail and chomped at the moa riders surrounding Blu and Pichi. Both smilodons immediately understood the situation and slashed at their captors as well. Sunu hurried ahead, brandishing their stolen sword until they found the soldier keeping hold of their halberd. They returned the stolen sword by piercing it through the soldier's chest and traded it for their own weapon.

Lago and Aio helped Serdein onto Blu's saddle, holding tightly to the broken man, who could not support his own weight for long. Ishke'ísuk hurried ahead of them to open a path of broken bones. Some Baurami simply jumped out of the way, cracking their bones more safely on the level below.

The Nu'irg could run as fast as the cats in this form, but only in short bursts. He helped them reach the top level, then turned back into a basilisk and held on to Sunu's shoulder once more.

Blu and Pichi rushed eastward, dashing through palatial gardens adorned with every conceivable species of desert plant. For a moment, shocked by the madness and bloodshed, Lago recalled the image of the soldier he'd killed inside his own home in Withervale. He could smell the blood soaking into the spilled blue sands, and saw his precious ruby-flecked stoneleaf lying on the ground next to the body. He wiped the image from his mind and held on tight to Blu.

Many guards patrolled the gardens and the parliamentarian-looking marble edifices, but they were not soldiers of war, and though they held lances in front of them, they did not know how to attack the incoming felines. The real threat was behind the fugitives, where dozens of moa riders had just crested the top level and were giving chase with legs twice as nimble as those of the smilodons.

The first moa rider approached too confidently. Sunu swung their halberd, slicing the bird's head off, armor and all. The headless bird careened forward at full speed, its rider still mounted, until they crashed into a white marble wall.

"Over wall! Jump!" Serdein pointed and yelled, as loud as his broken lungs could manage.

Moas encroached on every side, some now in front of them. Pichi swung her claws as she ran, taking two down, making others trip and stumble behind them.

A troop of moas rushed ahead and formed a feather-and-steel barricade in front of the marble wall, but the cats charged directly at them. Ishke'ísuk jumped off Sunu's shoulders to the top of Pichi's head, and from there propelled himself yet faster, turning into a lined gliding lizard. He flew ahead and in midair tumbled sideways as he turned back into an alligator, all the while spinning into a death roll, taking five moas with him and snapping at the legs of those who dodged the attack.

A small gap had been cleared by the Nu'irg. Pichi and Blu took the chance and jumped over the wall, finding nothing but air to hold them on the other side.

The riders pushed off their saddles in midair. They hit a slope of purple clay and tumbled, bouncing gracelessly down the soft silt. The angle soon became less steep and settled into a bed of powdery blue dust.

"Not again," Alaia muttered, recovering her breath. "Pink walls in Zovaria, blue walls in this damnable desert. I'm sick of these jumps into sand." An arrow thudded by her leg, then a lance dug into the sand.

"Hide, closer to the wall!" she warned. They scurried away from the projectiles and flattened against a sandstone wall, catching their breath.

Eihnk! Olo complained, confused and uncertain if it was safe to land again.

"Where is Ishke?" Aio asked, and as he did so, he noticed a green form smoothly gliding down through the air.

Ishke'ísuk landed expertly atop Sunu's shoulder. He had not suffered severe injuries, yet he was weak, drained from all the forms he had taken in such short a time. He tried to hold on to his friend but collapsed; Sunu caught him before he hit the ground. In their hands, the unconscious gliding lizard slowly shifted back to his primal form.

"Ishke'ísuk worked too hard," Sunu said, cradling the basilisk in their hands. "It is our turn to protect him." They tucked him between blankets in a comfortable bag.

Bruises and scrapes abounded, but the wayfarers had no time to properly check for injuries. Serdein had broken an arm, but he had many other wounds in any case, most of which had begun bleeding again. They got back on their saddles and bolted away before more arrows could be loosed at them.

"Point the way, fast," Lago ordered Serdein.

Serdein could read the erosion lines of the badlands as clearly as the oracles of Allathanathar could read the sixty-six cards of the Deck of Sands. He swiftly called out confounding directions, keeping them safe and away from any roads.

A few miles deeper along the pathless path, Serdein yelled, "Here! Behind!"

A toppled hoodoo leaned at the edge of the road. It had left scars on the bluff on its way down, now further deepened by the wind erosion.

"Hide," Serdein said. "Under rock."

They dismounted, then followed Serdein. The toppled hoodoo was much lighter than it seemed for its size. They helped Serdein push it out of the way, then he dug into the silt. Pichi shoved him away and dug much faster. Her claws caught on a strap, and out came Lago's old and trusty delivery bag.

Lago quickly opened it. His heart skipped a beat as he pulled out Agnargsilv.

"Mask. Quaar?" Serdein asked. He'd had time to examine the masks after stealing them, and knew them to be precious, but had no idea how truly precious they were.

"Yes, it's quaar," Lago said absently. He put the mask on and immediately shifted into Sterjall. The wolf sighed deeply, feeling whole and rejuvenated.

Serdein backed off, horrified.

Aio's and Sunu's bags came out next. Kulak and Lummukem took their forms. Serdein whimpered against the bluff, unable to back away any farther.

Alaia pulled out her haversack last. She put her quaar helm on and remained Alaia.

They unhooked the makeshift bags they had been using from Pichi's harness and secured their own bags in their stead. All four pharoliths were there, as were their weapons.

"Do not leave," Serdein implored them.

"You will be safer on your own," Sterjall advised. "They will chase after us. We left some food and water in those bags. Take them and hide. Your secret cave is still there, if you can find it."

"Yeah, and scorch your flesh sixteenfold, you murderous thief," Alaia added. "Let's get out of here."

They left the bleeding man in the dust, searching for a safe path through the bluffs and toward the Azurean Dome.

Chapter Twenty

Moa Riders

"Hold," Sterjall warned. "There are five more coming."

They had found a low ridge that overlooked the road to Navar Mat while still within the safety of the badlands. The sun was now behind the dome, though it would not set for another hour.

Lummukem lifted their flat head and scanned the road. "Should we wait for night to veil us?" they asked, spotting dozens of moa riders on patrol.

"Too risky," Alaia said. "If we don't move soon, they will catch us from behind. We left clear tracks."

The Azurean Dome was merely a mile past the wide road, through a field of sand and striated buttes. They could make it all the way in one final rush, but they had to be mindful of the chasing birds, as they were twice as fast and could handle the desert sands expertly.

"The two buttes in front of us," Kulak said, "the ones that protrude from Quajudrolom's wall—we should aim for the canyon between them."

Sterjall's sharp ears rotated as they perceived a tongue-clicking sound.

"Shit," he said as quietly as he could. "I hear them, around the bend we just passed. We can't go now, there are too many on the road. Pull back. Let's take care of the ones behind us first. Can Ishke help us?"

Lummukem checked inside their bag, where the basilisk was curled into a green ball. They tried to mindspeak to him but could not, for the Nu'irg was fully unconscious. "He needs rest. We will fend for ourselves."

Kulak stayed with the cats in the middle of the canyon, while the others returned to the bend and waited to ambush their pursuers. The Silvfröash could see their enemies through the silty walls, riding on their birds. The soldiers saw the cats as they turned the bend. Kulak held on to Blu's saddle and spoke to the smilodons, making them pretend to flee. The soldiers clicked their tongues and gave chase. As soon as the birds were in sight, Lummukem hopped out from behind cover, swinging their bone halberd above and their heavy tail below, smashing the legs of four moas at the same time. Their riders tumbled to the ground. Two more moas evaded the attack and tried to circle Lummukem, but Alaia used her blowgun to paralyze the birds. The moas were left squawking on the ground, kicking off dust.

Six Baurami soldiers recovered from their falls, back on their feet with weapons in hand. One of them was Commander Vaalag.

"Tell your soldiers to lower their weapons," Sterjall told her, stepping forward. "We don't want to hurt you."

Vaalag spun her sword and faced Sterjall while keeping an eye on Lummukem, who prowled to her side. She had no idea what these creatures were, but she recognized Alaia. "What sort of demons of Fau-Lawar did you summon, slave witch? Stay back! Where is your master and his Miscam allies?"

"I poisoned them with my spit and swallowed their bodies," Alaia replied. "And with their entrails, I gave birth to these monsters. And I'll do the same to you, if you try to attack." She lifted her hands and struck her brime cube with a knife, shooting up a torrent of angry sparks. All six soldiers flinched, sinking their heads between their shoulders.

The smilodons and Kulak approached behind her. Lummukem opened their jaws and hissed, spitting sticky fluid from the depths of their petrifying pink throat. Sterjall pointed Leif at Vaalag. "Return the way you came, and do so quietly, and we might let you live."

"That voice…" Vaalag began, but got distracted by Lummukem's halberd, which was hovering uncomfortably close to her face; she parried pointlessly, making sparks fly. She looked at her friends, hesitated for just one more breath, then ran with them back the way they had come.

"Shit, shit, that burns like the netherflames!" Alaia yelped, slapping at her shoulders as if trying to swat a swarm of ants—some sparks had landed on her. "They were burning through my clothes this entire time!"

Sterjall laughed. "Poison spit? Swallowed our bodies? What was that about?"

"I thought it'd creep them out," she said through a blistered shrug.

"It creeped *me* out."

Lummukem stepped close to the four moas they had injured. Two had received severe cuts, losing their legs, and would soon die. With twin swings of their halberd, Lummukem cut off the agonized birds' heads, right beneath the armored plates. The other two moas had broken legs from the tail swipe and would likely live. While Olo watched with curiosity from their shoulder, Lummukem kneeled next to the moas and used their empathic focus to take some of their pain away.

The dragon stood back up and mounted Pichi, right behind Alaia. Kulak helped Sterjall up on Blu, then directed the smilodon to climb back onto the silty wall. He flattened his tufted ears and spied over the ridge.

"Go, now," Kulak said, seeing a potential opening. "Quietly."

Blu and Pichi slinked over the silty wall and dropped onto the opposite side, dragging a cloud of cracked and powdered clay behind them. As soon as they hit the ground, they bolted forward, crossing the sandstone road and jumping onto the desert sands. Not too far down the road, moas were alerted, emitting a series of hums and shrilling squawks. The birds galloped after them, fast and steady as sandstorms.

Blu and Pichi hurried over the dunes while the speeding birds closed the distance. A pair of riders caught up with them, one armed with a sword, one trying to nock an arrow without losing grip of his moa's reins. As the soldier began to draw his bow, a dart from Alaia hit his bird's chest. The darted moa tumbled sideways into the other, taking both soldiers down with them.

"Take out the ones with bows first!" Alaia yelled, readying another dart.

More riders caught up, threatening to flank them. Alaia and Kulak aimed for those wielding bows, and Pichi slammed her heavy body against any who came too close, all while Lummukem swung their halberd and chopped off limbs in bloody sprays.

"Monsters! Demons!" a rider screamed. "Cast them back into the nethervoids!"

The wayfarers entered the canyon between the two buttes, with the wall of vines rising not too far ahead of them. "Keep going!" Sterjall urged. "We'll lose them at the vines!"

But the birds were faster and had surrounded them, and more yet came from behind—too many to fight against.

Sterjall focused on the threads, sensing a moa rushing toward Blu. The rider swung his sword, but Sterjall blocked the attack with Leif. The rider reared back and immediately attempted the strike again, but Kulak blew a dart into the bird, making the moa lose their footing and slam against Blu's side. The impact did not deter the smilodon, but it twisted the saddle, hurling Sterjall off. He reached out and caught the edge of the saddle with one handpaw, then tried to pull himself back up, but the saddle only spun further.

"Hold on to me!" Kulak cried out, trying to retain his balance while reaching a handpaw down. Sterjall was still holding on to Leif, so he tried to sheath it before reaching for Kulak, but a rock in their path slammed into his hips. He tumbled into the dunes.

"Gwoli!" Alaia screamed as Pichi nearly trampled Sterjall. Before the smilodons could react, Alaia had jumped from her saddle, landing in the sand right next to the wolf.

Kulak held tight to the loose saddle. He asked Blu to turn back, but the smilodon was too busy defending himself from more attackers, having just reached the wall of vines.

"Khuron, stay with Blu and open the vines!" Lummukem commanded, directing Pichi to turn around.

Alaia was helping Sterjall to his feet. "Get up!" she yelled. "We are almost there, keep running!" Disoriented, Sterjall stumbled up to follow Alaia's lead, just as two mounted soldiers attacked—one from each side.

Pichi charged forward and pounced at one of the moas. Even before her fangs dug into the bird's neck, Lummukem had leapt off the saddle and soared in an arc above Alaia and Sterjall, taking the other moa down in a cloud of dust. But the rider had dismounted the bird right before the strike and was now running toward Sterjall, sword ready to swing.

"Run!" Alaia shouted.

"Wait, Leif!" Sterjall replied, taking a step back to reach down for his dagger. But he was still too stunned from his fall and fumbled his grip.

Alaia screamed. As the sword flashed on its way down to the wolf's neck, she lifted her arm and deflected the strike with her blowgun. The blowgun took no damage, but it had no crossguard. The sword sparked down the length of the quaar conduits and sliced through Alaia's left thumb, sending her digit and weapon spinning down into the sand.

Before she could even feel the pain, Alaia kicked the soldier in the hips. He recovered quickly and swung again, but both his arm and sword abruptly twirled upward, cleanly sliced off by Lummukem's halberd. The dragon helped Alaia and Sterjall hurry forward, with Pichi slashing a barrier between them and the incoming attackers. "Hold your wound tight," Lummukem said to Alaia. "Keep pressure."

"*Alun-harath!* You are surrounded!" one soldier yelled. "Where are the other fugitives?" she asked, uncertain of how to address the monsters before her.

Kulak had opened a small tunnel in the vines, with Blu's body blocking the soldiers' view of it. While the enemies paused, the wayfarers rushed into the vines, then Blu and Pichi slowly backed into the opening.

"What is this? Stop!" the leading soldier commanded, seeing their enemy being swallowed by an opening that had not been there before. "Stop! Attack! Stop them!" she ordered her troops, and the moas were about to rush them, but Sterjall scraped his brime bracer and let out a stream of sparks as dazzling as lightning, making them hesitate.

The birds were better at attacking on the run and from the sides, not in a frontal attack like this. They stomped clumsily forward, rearing every time Sterjall released a Brime Strike. A handful of soldiers dismounted and pursued them on foot, entering the tunnel that was now five strides deep, but Blu and Pichi stopped them cold with their terrifying growls.

"Run, now, or you will be trapped here," Sterjall told them, hoping they understood Common. Most of them gave up and ran, but one held his ground for a breath too long. The remaining soldier looked back and saw the vines closing on him. He sprinted and tried to leap through the narrowing hole, but his cloak snagged on the thorns and stopped him, bringing him down upon the closing vines. From the darkness of Quajudrolom's walls, they heard the soldier's wails, then silence.

"You are hurt," Sterjall said. He rushed over to Alaia, bringing a pharolith close to her. "Your thumb, it's—"

"I'll live," she groaned, compressing her wound to try to staunch the bleeding. Blood was soaking through her clothes, and her face was contorted with pain, but she managed to keep her attitude bright. That is, until the shock began to take hold. After taking a peek at her injury, Alaia began to breathe fast, her eyes darting about.

"Sit," Lummukem said gently. "We will take care of it. Hold your arm up so it does not bleed while we work on it."

Alaia managed a pained smile in gratitude.

"My scalp will hold the vines open while you work," Kulak said, wincing as he caught sight of the wound—Alaia's thumb had been severed at the joint, right above the metacarpal.

"The cut was mostly clean," Lummukem said. "It will heal, but we cannot bring your thumb back. Although we managed to recover this as we ran."

"My blowgun!" Alaia cried, for a moment forgetting about the pain.

"Hold still," the dragon requested, "we have work to do." They shapeshifted into Sunu—their human fingers were more suitable for this delicate work than their reptilian claws.

Alaia's eyes filled with tears as Sunu sutured her wound, and the veins on her forehead seemed about to pop, but she kept quiet. Sterjall couldn't bring himself to watch. Instead, still feeling guilty about what happened, he focused on taking her pain into himself, tugging hard at her threads until his handpaw throbbed in agony, then spreading that pain out until it faded to a dull ache throughout his entire body.

Alaia's face untensed slightly, then her eyes found Sterjall's and she understood. "Stop that," she snapped at him. "That's enough. I know what you are doing. I can handle this."

"I'm not… I wasn't—"

"I'll be fine, I swear. The pain is going away anyway."

"That is because we were taking some pain into ourselves too," Sunu said. They were still wearing the reptilian mask over their freckled face.

"My scalp was doing the same," Kulak admitted from nearby.

Alaia smiled, touched by her friends' kindness.

Sunu tightened a splint to prevent Alaia's left hand from moving, then took their varanus dragon form once more. "You will need rest," they told Alaia, "but first, we must find safety."

They resumed their journey while enveloped by the cathedral-like entrails of the Azurean Dome. The cool light of the kenzir stones illuminated sand, vines, and thorns of blue and purple hues.

For a long while they walked alongside the cats, with Alaia being the only one taking a saddle. They were still in the same canyon they had used to flee the moas, but the vines that had swallowed this portion made for a complicated trek, forcing them to climb rocks to get around larger obstacles, always wary of the holes left in the sandstone by the receding vines.

By the time they emerged inside the dome, the sandstone walls that flanked them had turned a deeper blue hue due to the nighttime arudinn. They climbed up an eroded gully to find a better view. The ascending path was covered in spiky cacti, succulents, and other geometrically obsessed plants, which they had to avoid stepping on. They saw no trees or any sign of water.

When they reached the top of the mesa and walked to the edge, the trunk of the Azurean Dome was beginning to brighten, turning the sky vine-green and the horizon a soft lilac. They watched as the supporting columns cast long, sharp shadows onto the dome's walls and ceiling, entranced as the landscape slowly revealed itself.

"More desert," Sterjall said, regarding the vista in awe. "But so different from the outside. It's so full of plants, even trees."

While most of the desert flora was short and sparse, copses freckled the landscape some miles ahead, adding touches of green to the otherwise black, blue, and purple hills. In the distance, a lush mountain range cut the dome almost perfectly in half. Three prominent peaks rose near the center, cradling the brightening trunk.

"There seems to be a town right by the nearest column," Sterjall said, scanning with his binoculars. "Maybe five miles away? There's a plume of smoke, and something like farming fields around it."

"What is the name of the tribe here?" Alaia asked.

"Ji Miscam," Lummukem answered.

More arudinn lit up, now spreading through the main branches of the dome's ceiling. The sharp shadows vanished, leaving only the softness of the dome's daytime.

Kulak looked up at the branching lights and said, "Every day that passes, my scalp feels it more. We have only been here for a few hours, but already my heart misses the stars from outside. My scalp wishes they could always be with me."

"Me too," Sterjall agreed. "But I'm also excited to discover what's in here."

Lummukem held up a claw. "Before we venture through this land, to Siffo we should send a message, so that he may know we have reached our destination." They pointed back toward the wall. "We are higher now. We believe that by crossing the wall in that direction, we will exit atop one of the buttes that served as our gateway. From the top, under the cover of night, we could safely send out Olo."

The others agreed now was the best time to send the message, as they knew not how long it would be until they could leave the dome once more. They walked through the half mile of wall and exited on top of the larger of the two buttes. Night had fallen outside the dome. Sceres was in Jade, almost directly above them and growing close to full, providing good light for them to see by. Far below, they spotted torches, a few campfires, and hundreds of soldiers and moas patrolling the road, trying to find a way to reopen the hole which had disappeared between the buttes. The wayfarers were too high up to worry about being seen, and there was no easy way up the butte, so they relaxed, wrote a message to inform Siffo of all that had happened, and fed plenty of seeds to Olo.

Lummukem inhaled a bit of soot, their slitted eyes dilating to blackness. They focused on Olo, saying all that needed saying, yet never hearing the jay's own voice. Then, from the depths of their reptilian throat, they commanded, "*Va jambradikh frulv henet alrull.*"

Olo flew away, filled with determination.

Lummukem turned to their friends. "Half the night will Olo take to cross the hundred miles of desert. If the winds are kind to him, perhaps by morning he will return. Let us take cover near the vines, feed ourselves, and rest for the night."

While they readied their camp, Sterjall approached Alaia and sat by her bedroll.

"Thank you," he said quietly. "This was my fault, and you—"

"Shut that muzzle, Gwoli," Alaia cut him off. "I'm honestly fine. Who needs two thumbs anyway?"

"It's not a joke."

"But you have to see the bright side of it! Maybe now I'll learn to work equally with both hands, like you did after you broke your arm. This was no one's fault."

"But it *was* my fault," Sterjall said. "It's not only that I shouldn't have fallen, but I shouldn't have tried to reach for Leif. And… And I should be protecting *you*, not the other way around."

Alaia sat cross-legged, straightening her back. "You can't be serious," she said, then stopped Sterjall mid-mumble. "No, no. I'm your big sister. It's *my* job to make sure *you* are safe. I don't need any taking care of. I can handle myself just fine."

"But it's because of me that you got involved in all these dangerous situations to begin with."

Alaia sighed. "Gwoli, look at me. I'm out here on the far side of the world, beyond six lands and six seas, having the most incredible adventure I could ever have dreamed of. It's not your fault, it's *thanks* to you. Ever since we left Withervale, I've seen new realms, met new kinds of people, witnessed magic from worlds we didn't even know existed. You think I'd trade this for the safety—if you could call it that—of working at the mines? Fuck no. I'd give my other thumb. Khest, I'd give sixteen thumbs to have a chance at living what I'm living."

"You don't have sixteen thumbs."

"I'd chop them off the Baurami and offer them to the sprites of fate instead. I'd saw off my very own nub if that's what it took. I don't care. This we have here, this moment now, this is all that is worth living for, no matter how many body parts it costs."

"But what if—"

"No, you have to see it from my perspective. I had no hopes of doing much with my life. But you? I always knew fate had something better waiting for you. Back then, I thought that meant you'd go study at the institute. But now

I know better. Now I know how truly lucky I am to experience all this with you. And I know it's dangerous, and I know you worry about me, but if it came to that and I died on this wild adventure, I'd die wearing the biggest of grins."

"Don't say that…"

She scooted closer and leaned her head on him. "I'm not planning on dying. Stop worrying. I'm fine, Gwoli. And I'm excited to see what new kinds of trouble we can get into, because I know we will." She yawned and grabbed a blanket. "But right now, I am drained as a wet nurse, and I need to get some sleep. And you do too, so go wrap your arms around your kitty."

Sterjall sighed, ears flattened. As he went to lie down next to Kulak, he secretly took more pain from Alaia, but only a small enough amount that she would not notice.

Alaia did notice, however, but said nothing this time.

Chapter Twenty-One

Jade Moon

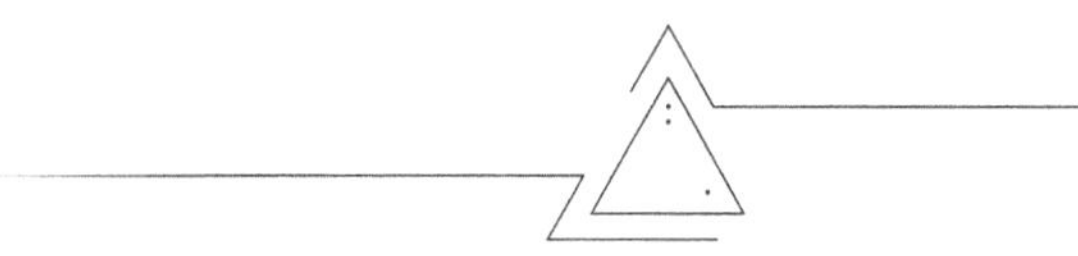

Sterjall could not close his eyes.

I have to be more careful, he admonished himself. He let an arm wrap around Kulak, caressing his hips. *What if you had come back for me and gotten hurt?* he wondered, then pondered morbidly, imagining how bad things could have gotten for all of his friends. *I can't let others get injured because of me. I just need to take care of you. All of you. I need to show you that you mean the world to me, that I want you to always be with me.*

He held his gaze on the Jade moon above, letting her green glow blind him, feeling Kulak's breathing change as the prince drifted deeper into sleep. Suddenly, an idea blossomed in his mind, bright as sparks of brime. His heart beat a bit too loud, making him nervous that Kulak might feel his excitement even through his sleep. He calmed himself down, thought the idea through, then made his decision.

Carefully, without disturbing the caracal's sleep, he got up, quietly woke Lummukem to ask them for a small favor, then returned to Kulak and softly tugged on his handpaw.

"What is it?" Kulak asked, scared that they might be in danger.

"Shh, everything is fine, be quiet. Come with me. I want to show you something."

"How long did we sleep for?"

"Only a wick or two. Come, it won't be long. It's about something you said. You gave me an idea."

Kulak groggily stood up, then followed Sterjall to the eastern end of the butte, where the view of the desert sky was more open. They stopped at the cliff's edge and sat on a rock, hip to hip, first looking far into the east, then straight down at the indefatigable soldiers patrolling the road like ants.

Sterjall produced a small mortar into which he poured a bit of water from his canteen. He then uncapped a vial and spilled a powder into the water, mixing it with a pestle.

"What are you doing?" Kulak asked.

"I'm mixing the kupógo grinesht. I asked Lummukem for some. You need new scalp pigments, they've nearly all vanished by now. I'd like to draw them for you this time. Don't worry, it's the blue kind, not purple."

"That is kind of you. But not easy to do."

"This one should be easy for me. Shift into Aio and hold still." After Kulak complied, he grabbed Aio's shoulders and made him turn. "Face straight north."

Aio pulled his mask off and turned his head to try to catch a glimpse of Sterjall's expression.

"I said hold still. Don't move your head or you'll make me mess this up. You can keep your eyes on the Sword of Zeiheim so that you don't move."

Aio stared at the constellation, focusing his eyes on the pink nebula that burned at its core. The wolf then dipped the tip of his index claw into the mixture and began to tap Aio's bald head with it, one dot at a time.

"You are tapping, not drawing," Aio commented, still sleepy and confused, but holding a wide grin.

"I know," Sterjall replied, looking up at the sky and tapping again. "I'm drawing a map of the stars, of the constellations, right onto your scalp."

Aio turned quickly, almost ruining Sterjall's careful work. "That… That is too wonderful," he said, suddenly waking up fully. He stood, kissed Sterjall's muzzle, then sat back down. "My scalp will carry the stars for me, wherever I go."

The green moonlight aided Sterjall. He placed a series of dots onto Aio's scalp, looked up to memorize a new pattern, then tapped again. He was meticulous, as precise as his skills allowed.

"Hey, you'll have Lummukem always protecting you now!" Sterjall said, completing the winged dragon's constellation over Aio's right ear.

Aio looked to his side and saw no dragon in the sky. "How do you know where Lummukem is?" he asked.

"Guessing a bit, but I think they would be right behind the dome. And I'd like to draw Nelv somewhere too, but her constellation is below the horizon at the moment. Maybe next time I do this—if at a different time of the night, or during a different season—you'll have her right up here." He tapped on the very crown of Aio's head, then looked straight up to see what to place in that location. *Oh… Shit…* he thought as he saw Banook's constellation, Kerjaastórgnem. He froze, then inhaled deeply, taking in the earthy, oily scent of the pigments, and thought to himself, *We can't just pretend he's not there.* With slightly trembling handpaws, he placed the dots for the bear.

Sterjall continued with Sovath to the east, above Aio's left ear, then Dunokh Sull on his occipital bone, which was below the horizon, but he knew where to place it. He then filled in the remaining areas with a dozen other constellations.

"Hold still, this part is the hardest." He dipped a thin blade of dry grass into the blue pigments. "I'm going to draw the lines between the stars. I don't have a reference for how the maps draw them, so I'm going to guess most of the time. But don't worry, it'll look good." He carefully drew line after line, using delicate strands of pigment to connect dots starmiles apart.

He circled around until he was in front of Aio. "And now the last one. I don't need a reference for this," he said as he lifted Aio's chin. He placed four dots on Aio's forehead to indicate the Sword of Zeiheim, then added Pellámbri—the pink nebula—right at the center. He made the Lodestar streaky, as if brighter.

"Lodestar guide me!" Aio said with a sparkling grin.

Sterjall chuckled. "Where did you learn that expression?"

"Alaia says it sometimes."

"Well, now she will truly guide you. No matter where you go, you will always be following the Lodestar, because she's right in front of you. The sword is currently tilted in the sky, but I made it point straight up so it looks nicer on your forehead." Sterjall drew the cross-shaped lines connecting the sword, tenderly kissed Aio's nose, and let go of his chin. "All done. You look like the constellation globe at the Mesa Observatory, but even shinier."

He sat on a rock in front of Aio and admired his work, stretching his whiskers in a proud smile. "You look beautiful," he said. "In the morning, we'll find something reflective so you can see yourself. It's too bad the pigments don't show up when you are in your half-form."

"They are still there, warm beneath my fur. My scalp does not lose them, but they would be distorted, like on Lummukem. More so if I was a jackal again."

"I do want to see you as a jackal again. That was… exciting. I wonder how different you felt as a jackal from what I feel as a wolf. I had a great time as the mountain lion and would love to do it again, but I don't feel like I miss it the same way I would miss not being Sterjall."

"Yes, my scalp remembers jackal and loves him, but does not need him the same way it needs caracal. Jackal is smaller part of me, but still part of me."

"That's how I feel too."

Aio eyed the bowl with the blue pigments. He reached toward his neck and detached his arambukh pendant.

"What are you doing?" Sterjall asked.

Aio carefully dipped one face of the octahedral sapphire into the pigments.

"Give me your handpaw," he said.

"Are you going to—"

"Handpaw. Pick one."

Sterjall held out his left handpaw. Aio spread it open, revealing the pink, leathery pads on the palms. He pushed the dark fur away, then carefully used his sapphire as a stamp, imprinting a triangular glyph. He then wiped the sapphire clean, dipped another face of the octahedron, and stamped it next to the first marking. He blew on them so they would dry more quickly.

"First is my own arambukh glyph. It stands for Aio. Second glyph is shorthand for possession. Other glyphs I did not use stand for debt, for lending, for settling, for transferring. When we stamp them on ledgers, these two together say something is mine."

"So, you own me now?"

"Perhaps only for a few months. Kupógo grinesht does not last that long."

"Well, if it's only for a few months, that's not too bad," Sterjall joked.

Aio locked eyes with him. "Did you mean what you said in darkness, inside Serdein's secret room?"

The sudden change of subject threw Sterjall off-balance. "I don't know what you mean," he said, earnestly confused.

"Before I woke up, my ears heard you speak to me. You said, *I love you, I cannot lose you.* Did you mean it? Do you love me?"

Sterjall's eyes darted down for a moment, his muzzle feeling heavy. He looked at his pink palm, at the two blue glyphs stamped on it. He rubbed on the symbols—they were clearly imprinted and would not fade for a long while. He forced himself to lift his gaze and meet Aio's eyes. "Yes. I… I love you," he said, reaching for Aio's hands. "I meant it. I just haven't had the courage to say it."

"Why do you still fear?"

Sterjall considered how to best answer. He sat next to Aio and wrapped his arm and tail around his waist, then leaned his head on his shoulder. "I feel it's unfair and… and I feel guilty. That is why I'm still afraid. I love two people, in very different ways, and I don't want either of you to feel jealous, to dislike each other, or to hate me for it."

"Banook is the one who should be jealous," Aio said with playful pride. "I do not see his arambukh stamped on your body. And his scalp does not hold the stars."

Sterjall chuckled. "He's on *your* scalp, by the way." He tapped on Aio's crown. "Right on top."

"He is?" Aio asked, then looked up and saw Banook's constellation glowing above them, the two yellow stars that were his eyes shining like quiet sentinels.

"Sorry," Sterjall said. "He was there, and I was trying to make the map accurate."

"My scalp does not mind him. He seems like a good man, a good bear. I am glad he makes you happy." Aio sighed. "I thought I had loved a few times before, but it was… How to say?"

Sterjall read the emotion Aio was trying to express. "Infatuation?"

"Yes. It is different with you. My heart has loved you since that first night outside Mindreldrolom, kissing you on the black beach. My scalp, my body, they know what it means now. But I do not know what it is like to love two people at same time. I do not understand that. But I understand it is true for you, and it does not change how my scalp feels about you."

Sterjall held him tighter.

Aio continued, "My soul cannot feel jealous, because I am here, with you, and every day I learn from you, discover more about the world, about myself. But my heart hopes that when the day comes, when our journey is over, and you and Banook are together again, that you will still love me the same."

Chapter Twenty-Two

Quajudrolom

"It looks incredible!" Alaia exclaimed as she admired Sterjall's handiwork. "Lummukem, check this side. Isn't this you?"

Lummukem circled to observe Aio's right temple. They traced the stars of the winged dragon with a sharp claw. "They are our stars."

The wayfarers had risen before sunrise, feeling Sunnokh's presence looming just below the horizon. Aio was examining his head in Lummukem's halberd, the steel blade polished to a mirror. "It looks better than my scalp imagined it," he said, regarding his reflection.

"I wish the pigments showed up that nicely on my darker skin," Alaia replied with lighthearted envy in her voice. "I mean, maybe I'd get something on my arms. I'm not about to shave my head."

Lummukem went to check on Ishke'ísuk. The Nu'irg was awake, but still tired from the previous day's exertions. The basilisk resumed perching on the dragon's shoulder and mindspoke a request.

"Ishke'ísuk says he is starving," Lummukem interpreted, "but he is mostly recovered. Khuron Aio, would you get breakfast started while we redress Alaia's wound?"

Sunnokh rose while they broke their fast. Together with his warmth, the star brought the tired wings of the azure-hooded jay.

Eihnk-eihnk! Olo called, landing on Lummukem's shoulder.

"Is there a message from Siffo?" Alaia asked.

"A moment. First Olo needs to replenish his energies." The dragon fed Olo, then pulled a tiny letter from the bird's pouch and handed it to Alaia, who read the captain's reply and playfully tried to mimic his accent:

> Glad ye made it. Ye took yer damn time. Lummukem ye said is them name now? A varanus dragon? That's a wonderful surprise. Too bad them didn't carry that tail armor, that's a mighty shame.
>
> We found plenty of food and a fresh spring five miles away. Though there are no roads, we've seen many pilgrims nearby. None have spotted us, yet. We fear we might soon be seen—we can't hide *Fjummomurr* forever.
>
> We sent a scout farther north, one who can easily hide her suid traits. Lixméd is her name. She reached Lhambor Di, talked to friendly locals, and told them she wanted to travel west. Them told her to never travel through the desert: there are badlands that can't be crossed, and no one would be *stupid* enough to try and cross them. The only way through is by the road that connects Lhambor Di to the dome. The road is hard to see, covered by sand, but many a traveler ye'll find on it. It might serve ye when ye return, but ye won't be able to hide. The Lhambor Di road connects forty miles north of Navar Mat, at the dome's perimeter. A white monolith marks the spot.
>
> Mine Puqua are still in high spirits, discovering new lands, making friends with the dolphins who visit the cove at night. I have to keep them from becoming too adventurous, lest them get us in trouble. We'll hold our position and wait for a message when ye begin yer return. The light of the kenzir is with ye!
> - C.S.

"Happy to hear they are enjoying themselves," Sterjall said. "Let's head back into the dome. It will be nighttime in there again—it's going to give me headaches."

As they walked toward the vines, Alaia yelped, "Wait! Wait! Gotta do one more thing!"

She ran to the edge of the butte and looked down at the dozens of soldiers gathered hundreds of feet below, at the spot where the fugitives had disappeared the day before.

"Hey! We are up here!" She tossed a stone down. "Come and get us, bird fuckers!"

Sterjall ran to her. "What are you doing?!"

"They can't do anything to us. Let me have some fun."

They heard the humming and squawking of moas, then the raised voices of many a startled soldier. Alaia poked her head out again, with Sterjall by her side also peering down.

"Yes, up here!" she hollered. "Find my thumb down there and shove it up your sand-crusted assholes!" She hurled another rock and turned around. "Okay, that'll do. It should keep them entertained for a few more days."

They returned to the inside of the Azurean Dome, to yet another confusing shift from day to night. Aided by pharoliths, they followed a creek down the butte.

"I think we should wait till it's bright to keep going," Alaia said, looking quite tired while holding the pommel of Pichi's saddle.

"Are you feeling alright?" Sterjall asked.

"I'm fine, it doesn't hurt anymore," she said. "But we don't know these lands, it could be dangerous."

They rested near the creek, agreeing that it would be safer to travel in daylight. Although Alaia fell asleep right away, the others took much longer to find rest—too many unknown animals moved in the shadows.

"Hold still," Kulak murmured as they unmade their camp the next morning. "That strange creature has returned."

"Is that a rabbit? Deer? Some sort of giant rat?" Alaia asked, just waking up. The creature, a gray kangaroo, was fearless and curious as she hopped near them. She gradually bounced closer, pausing to scratch her sides with her clawed hands.

"I've never seen anything like that. It must be one of the marsupials," Sterjall guessed. "She looks pregnant," he added, noticing the curve of her belly.

Two tiny heads poked out from the kangaroo's pouch, surprising them.

"What just happened?" Alaia blurted out. "Are those... babies?"

Blu approached the kangaroo, sniffed, and tentatively licked her. The kangaroo shook her long ears.

"She's not afraid at all," Sterjall said. "Kulak, tell Blu and Pichi to be careful and not to hunt any marsupials while we are here."

"They already know that. But how do we know which ones are marsupials?"

"Well... like... Just tell them not to eat anything weird-looking."

Another kangaroo hopped up to them and stopped to sniff at Blu's giant paws.

"This one doesn't have pockets," Alaia observed. "But what's the matter with his balls? It's like they are upside down." She cocked her head, trying to comprehend.

The wayfarers mounted their saddles and continued across the lush desert. Soon they arrived at the first of many patches of forest, which consisted of only one peculiar species of tree. The trees had a single, thick trunk that rose perfectly vertically and all at once sprouted open into fractal branches in a perfect circle, resembling an umbrella flipped inside out. The branching patterns were very similar to how the trunk and supporting columns split in the ceilings of all the domes.

"Dragonblood trees," Sterjall said, caressing the textured bark.

"Most sacred," Lummukem noted. "Thousands of them bless this desert."

"We have a tree like these in Withervale," Sterjall said, "at the arboretum next to my old school. It always looked so symmetrical to me, the branching so dense and precise."

"Few grow in Mindreldrolom," Lummukem recalled, "on the range west of Stelm Humenath. They bleed red when wounded, though their blood is not poisonous like that of baneblood trees. Legends tell that Noss was inspired by them when they thought of the domes. That is why they are sacred to the Laatu. We call them *sheinokhlom,* meaning *roots of firmament.*"

While they traversed the miles of odd forest, they encountered more unfamiliar creatures: wombats, numbats, bilbies, and quokkas, all either curious or oblivious, but never fearful. There were non-marsupial mammals too, from hares, to oryxes, desert sheep, and mice, but the majority of the animals they saw were unknown to them.

"There is one of your kind," Kulak said to Sterjall, having spotted a giant canid-like creature walking nearby. "So big. You should ask him about this land."

The animal, a thylacine, at first looked like an oversized coyote to Sterjall— far larger than a mountain lion, but not as massive as the smilodons. Sterjall then noticed the striped back, which reminded him more of a jackal or a tiger.

Something is wrong with his proportions, he thought, *and the length of his fur. Why does he feel so odd?*

The smilodons matched the pace of the thylacine, who was either ignoring their presence or pretending to. Sterjall focused his newly learned skill, which he had so far only tried with the spotted wild dogs, and mindspoke, «Hello? We are... Are you even aware we are here?»

The thylacine did not respond.

"What is wrong?" Lummukem asked, noticing Sterjall's concern.

"I... I think I lost it. I can't mindspeak with him."

The thylacine hopped atop a rock to enjoy the landscape. Sterjall called for him, but the thylacine only turned because he heard a noise, nothing else. He seemed bothered and maybe even embarrassed. After a moment, he hopped down from the rock and vanished.

"You'll get it back," Alaia reassured Sterjall. "Perhaps the animals in this dome mindspeak in a different language or something like that, and you just need to learn it."

"My scalp does not think that is how it works," Kulak said.

"I don't think so either," Sterjall agreed.

"We'll find other canids for you," Alaia replied as she scanned the landscape, which was opening up now that they'd reached the edge of the forest. "And maybe we'll also finally find a ruby-flecked stoneleaf in here."

Sterjall nodded. "Believe me, I've been looking. Hey, look at this weird cactus." He tapped on Blu's saddle, then hopped down.

The peculiar cactus was reminiscent of the dragonblood trees, though at a much smaller scale. Its single, round leaf—or spine—grew in an upside-down, shallow cone, as if meant to divert water down to its center. It was meaty and thorny, with pink and yellow flowers growing at the edges of the flattened cone.

"Look, there's a dead one too!" Alaia said, and as she hopped down to grab it, she took a small tumble, falling to her knees. "I'm fine, landed on my good hand, don't worry." She picked up the dried cactus; only the wide, conical skeleton remained, and though it was light, it felt solid and woody.

"Hey Pichi, fetch!" she said, then tossed the cactus like a disc. But Pichi did not rush to grab it. Instead, she kept her big eyes on Alaia and huffed.

Lummukem focused their sight on Alaia's threads and sensed something was wrong. They hopped down and grabbed Alaia just as she collapsed.

"Soak this in the cold stream," they said, handing a cloth to Kulak while they helped Alaia lean against a mossy rock.

Kulak promptly returned and placed the cloth on Alaia's forehead.

"Her blood runs hot," Lummukem said, eyes narrowing. They removed the splint and bandages from Alaia's hand and found that it had turned black and dry, and that the sutures had come undone. "The skin around the wound is dying. She needs care before it spreads, but we do not have the proper medicine."

"But she was doing so well," Sterjall said, leaning in to take some of her pain away.

"No, stop," Lummukem urged him, feeling the flow of the threads. "Have you been doing this today? Easing her pain?"

"Of course I have, I could feel she—"

"You must not. If she feels well, she will spend more energy. She needs rest, and pain will tell her to rest. Help us hoist her to Pichi's saddle. We must move. Perhaps the Ji Miscam will be able to aid her."

Sterjall felt even more guilty now, but he did as Lummukem ordered.

Alaia fell deeply asleep while cradled upon Pichi's back. The creek they had been following grew in width as it merged with others, birthing colorful pools that housed a variety of fish and turtles. Farther downstream was a meadow, where a succulent farm field was being worked.

"Is that a marsupial too?" Kulak asked.

In the middle of the field was a diprotodon, a giant wombat who was dragging a wheeled plow to till the blue and black soil. The diprotodon was a heavy beast, almost as large as Pichi, yet seemed entirely docile and nonthreatening. Behind the plowing giant followed a troop of quokkas and bilbies, who rushed in to plant seeds, and not far behind them came a squad of female wallabies, their pouches filled with water, slowly dripping it onto the freshly seeded soil.

"I wish Alaia was awake to see this," Sterjall said, stunned by the parade of bizarre animals. "Are the marsupials farming the fields all on their own?"

"Maybe the humans here also all died," Kulak speculated.

They circled around the field to avoid stepping on the crops and saw the diprotodon detach the plow from her harness, then head behind a hill with the wallabies at her heels.

"Should we remove our Silvesh so that we do not seem threatening?" Lummukem asked. "That is, if there is anyone but marsupials to be found."

"It's a good thought," Sterjall considered, "but that had the opposite effect for us when we entered Mindreldrolom. Perhaps it's better if we keep our half-forms. We need to remain alert."

They crested the hill, and farther down the creek spotted the diprotodon approaching a figure—a human this time, dancing alone in a plum orchard.

"Careful," Lummukem said. "Let us watch before we approach."

From behind cover, they observed the man. He was old, yet he spun with ethereal grace, letting his robes drift like windswept petals in a performance with no music.

"He flows like water," Lummukem whispered.

Within this lonely dance, a metallic glint suddenly flickered, and out from the man's robes extended a metal object tied to a rope. The sharp object sliced cleanly at the stems of three plums, but never did the fruits touch the ground, for the man caught them with gentle elegance, letting them spiral down the conical form of a cactus husk. His dance continued as if it was the air itself coming to life, with more plums falling from the tall trees, caught with such care that their velvety skins never bruised. In time, the dance melted away like a dying breeze, the man's robes draping down. He unloaded the plums into a basket and hung it from the diprotodon's harness, then put the conical cactus on his head, as a hat. He then stared directly at the wayfarers and in Miscamish said, "Springs eternal guide your roots."

"Shit, he saw us already," Sterjall swore, pointlessly dropping to hide behind the hill.

"He looks like a farmer," Kulak said. "We should greet him."

They cautiously stepped forward to meet him, concerned that the farmer did not seem afraid of them at all, not even of their saber-toothed beasts. He seemed merely curious, even mellow. Extending his knobby hands forward, he offered a handful of plums to the newcomers and waited for them to speak.

"M-my name is Sterjall," the wolf said awkwardly as he reached for a plum. "W-we need help."

The farmer smiled patiently.

Sterjall briefly explained who they were and why they were here, then showed Alaia's wound to the farmer. He hadn't spoken much Miscamish lately, so his words tangled, but he picked it up quickly again.

The farmer's name was Mio. While calmly listening to their story, he washed Alaia's wound with flowing water from the creek, then smacked his diprotodon's ample behind and hopped on top of the large creature.

"We have what she needs at my village," Mio said, speaking in a softly accented Miscamish sweetened by prolonged vowels. "We can speak as we travel. Tell me more of your story, and I will tell you more of ours."

The smilodons followed on either side of the diprotodon, who despite seeming sluggish before, matched their trotting pace with no problem.

Mio listened intently. He knew no Common, and told them that only a few scholars knew the old language in these lands. He was placid, patient, and inquisitive. All three Silvfröash noticed something strange about Mio: the threads around him seemed to shift in a peculiar manner, as if attracted to his head, but in a slightly chaotic way, similar to how shamans looked when under the influence of soot. But what surprised them most about Mio was how *un*surprised he was by their presence.

"The medicine I can procure will keep your friend stable," he said as they rode west, "but it is Hud Ouránama-Ulésse who you should seek right after, for she and her druids will know best how to aid your friend for a proper recovery. The Quajufröa lives near the trunk, in the city of Mikkagolm. If your fanged beasts can keep up, we can be there tomorrow. But first, we will stop by Asra, my home."

He hurried his diprotodon, who galloped faster now that the conversation had stopped. As the wind pushed against their faces, Mio's skeletal cactus hat pulled back, dangling from his neck by a ribbon of green silk.

Sterjall noticed a strange bump atop the farmer's scantly haired head: right at the crown, tucked in a glossier spot as if from a scar, was a round black bump of about two fingerbreadths in diameter. He wanted to inquire about it, but he didn't want to have to slow their pace.

Down a hillock the creek snaked, washing underneath quaint bridges, then cutting toward a small village of round huts. The dwellings had roofs made of inverted dragonblood trees, dried up and serving as conical caps. Flowering ivies adorned every crevice between the tangled, inverted branches of the roofs. The walls of the huts were built out of light-blue clay, with plentiful niches and alcoves to hold planters from which dangling succulents draped and spilled to the ground, like living walls of green pearls. Marsupials of all kinds gathered around, including a vast herd of diprotodons that ambled by the nearby supporting column, where they were being fed an herby blend of munnji cakes. Asra felt like an idyllic oasis, a spritetale hamlet of exotic colors and shapes inhabited by unreasonably exotic animals and humans.

Mio carried Alaia into a round hut and asked a girl to bring the medicine. As they waited, the locals gathered to watch, too shy to ask questions of the foreigners, but fearless enough to walk straight up to the smilodons and probe at their fangs. The villagers were draped in simple robes of pastel colors, and most wore dry cactus hats similar to Mio's. Sterjall noticed black bumps on the crowns of those with uncovered heads, except for the younger children.

The errand girl returned and handed two linen-wrapped bundles to Mio. "Thank you, Liijash," Mio said, opening the first bundle.

Sterjall squirmed as he saw the wriggling forms the farmer had uncovered.

"The leeches will drain the bad blood and allow for fresh blood to flow," Mio said. He applied the parasitic worms to Alaia's wound, letting them suck on the drying blood; her hand blushed as blood began to circulate properly. Alaia moaned lightly and seemed to be waking up. Mio then opened the second bundle, which contained a handful of herbs he crushed under Alaia's nose. Alaia inhaled the vaporous oils and dozed off again.

"That is to help her rest," Mio said. "Her fever should drop by tomorrow, hopefully by the time we make it to the capital. Her flesh will not keep rotting, but we need to stop the disease from spreading through her body. Ulésse will have better medicine for her."

Mio removed the leeches, cleaned the wound, and wrapped it cleanly once more. Outside, the villagers had brought trays of munnji cakes for the felids, of the kind served to their own carnivorous species. The cats ate some of it to be polite, though not much, as the taste was too foreign to their liking.

They hoisted Alaia back onto Pichi's saddle, then followed Mio westward, moving at a soft trot now to avoid shaking Alaia too hard. As they traveled, the farmer taught the visitors the Miscamish names of the marsupials, pointing out an infinitude of new species, of forms differing too much from one another to be under the same clade.

"What are those giants called?" Sterjall asked, pointing at enormous kangaroos that grew to sixteen feet in height.

"Procoptodons," Mio answered, then confirmed they were a companion species. He also confirmed that the thylacine Sterjall had tried to mindspeak with was not a canid, but a marsupial, and another of their companion species. Surprisingly, he also told them the diprotodons were *not* one of their companions in that sense; they simply were—and had always been—enormous.

They passed by a few more villages, where Lummukem spotted a group of youths dancing in a similar way to how Mio had danced when they first saw him. They, too, suddenly launched sharp points from their sleeves, only to retrieve them after spinning them from ropes around their legs and necks.

"Those weapons that flow with your dance, what are they?" Lummukem asked.

"Weapons?" Mio asked, intrigued. "Are you asking about the rope javelins?" He then pulled his sleeve back to reveal a heavy and sharp bolt secured by a slender rope to his forearm bracer. With a flick of his arm, the bolt—or javelin—launched toward Lummukem, flipping in midair to offer the blunt, tied end, which Lummukem easily caught. The dragon stared intently at the object, which was crafted of an intricately carved bone weighed by an exterior metal armature. Inside the carved details of the bone grew a red moss, and Lummukem noticed how threads from the moss seemed to flow back toward Mio, as if the weapon truly was an extension of him.

"I use it to harvest fruit from tall trees," Mio said. "The students there are just starting to learn the art. It will take them many years." He pulled on the rope and let the javelin spin around his bracer, securing it once more.

They stopped at trunk's last light to feed and rest. Pichi and Blu left them to hunt for their supper. Kulak opened up a few pharoliths to light their camp while Mio took out his cooking supplies. He was entranced by the cold light of the kenzir stones and asked many questions about them and about the lands of the Puqua, then began to clean Alaia's wound once more.

"It's looking better already," Sterjall said with relief, watching Mio work. "Will she wake up soon?"

"It is better if she sleeps," he answered, crushing more herbs beneath her nose. "I will keep her aware enough so she can eat, do not worry."

The old man was kneeling, wrapping clean bandages over Alaia's injury. He smiled, noticing Sterjall staring at the black bump on his head. "I see you've been wondering about my burrow," he said, tapping his crown.

"Burrow?"

"I took notice that none of you had one, and thought it quite peculiar."

"What are they?" Kulak asked, stepping closer.

"It is a trepanation hole. But *burrows* is what we commonly call them." Mio observed their confused faces. He reached up with one hand, and using his nails, he slowly pulled out the black bump, as if it was a cap, or a dome-like cork. The cap popped free with a sucking sound.

Mio leaned forward to show them the perfectly round hole in his skull. Kulak held a pharolith up, wincing as he peered in. No bone was visible; the hole had been rimmed with some sort of sterile pipe. Deeper down, they could see the moist membrane of Mio's meninges.

He put the cap back on. "It is to put the soot in, so we can talk to our animals."

Mio explained that long ago, the shamans of the Azurean Dome had developed the trepanation technique. In time, shamans became unnecessary, as every person was gifted with a burrow when they became of age. All adults in the Azurean Dome could commune with their animals better even than the shamans of old, and without the side effects from inhaling soot.

"If we had known this was possible," Lummukem mused, "we would have clawed a hole into our own head instead of spending years inhaling the sacred powder."

"But isn't that dangerous?" Sterjall asked. "Wouldn't it get infected?"

Mio shrugged. "We developed better tools over the centuries. Infections in the first months are common, but the survival rate is high."

Sterjall's fur prickled at the very idea. He forced himself to look away and instead glanced at the massive, resting wombat. "Is this why the marsupials behave so well?" he asked the farmer. "We saw them plowing a field, planting seeds, all on their own."

"They have no burrows, son," Mio noted serenely.

"I mean, how you've been able to train them to be so self-sufficient."

"Perhaps, partially it might be that, though they do it out of their own volition, knowing it is what is best for Quajudrolom. They are all quite intelligent."

Mio left them for a moment, to harvest tasty succulents for dinner.

"It is strange how calmly all of them behave," Sterjall said in Common as he lit the fire. "A bit sinister, even."

"We believe it is the soot," Lummukem said. "Too much in their heads, all the time. It may be good in some ways, bad in others."

"They seem harmless, at least. And kind. It must feel so different, living your entire life that way."

They quieted when Mio returned with a selection of juicy desert plants speared to his rope javelin, which he dressed by slicing off the thorns.

Pichi came back soon after, bringing a fat desert sheep she had crushed under her fangs. She proudly dropped the bleeding caprid at Mio's feet.

"Good catch, Pichi!" Kulak said and pulled out a knife. "We could make a stew, or perhaps grill it. How do you prepare sheep's meat in Quajudrolom?"

Mio dropped his wooden bowl, spilling the fresh succulents he was tossing. He covered his mouth and gagged.

Once Mio had recovered from the shock, he explained to them that eating most animals was forbidden in the Azurean Dome. Only specific carnivorous predators were exempted, since they kept certain populations in balance.

Mio performed a quiet ritual for the sheep, to thank it for its sacrifice and to apologize for ending its life too early. Once the ritual was finished, he let Pichi and Blu eat the dead animal, though he did not watch them do so.

"How can you? I don't understand…" Mio faltered. "Don't you feel their pain? With your Silvesh, don't you see them suffer?"

"We do," Sterjall admitted, "but we all have to eat. It's natural. I've met a few people who eat no meat, but it's rare in the New World or in the other domes we've been to."

"Please, do not do this while in our sacred lands. Ask Hud Ulésse to teach you our ways. You will understand when she explains it."

Sterjall kept his eyes on the ground, utterly mortified. "We will ask Ulésse," he said. "I'm sorry. We will honor your customs while we are guests in your dome."

CHAPTER TWENTY-THREE

THE SACRED GARDEN

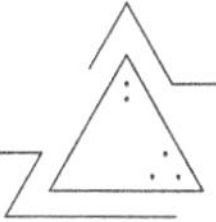

The Chail Trodesh, the three peaks at the center of the dome, were much closer now. As the wayfarers neared the base of the mountains, the desert abruptly ended, replaced by granitic spires and brown soil. The succulents were replaced by ferns, berry-filled bushes, and short evergreens, while the dragonblood trees gave way to a dense aspen forest that was beginning to drop its fiery leaves.

"It's magnificent," Sterjall said, hearing the notes of a kalimba vibrating in the back of his memory. "I've never seen so many aspens in one place before."

"Not many, but one," Mio corrected. "This forest is only one tree, one tree with stubborn roots."

Sterjall peered at the threads around him, but also below him, and could feel that what Mio had said was true. All the aspen threads shared the same flavor, as if coming from one single organism. He could not understand how that was possible, and it only made the forest seem more alluring. He glanced to his side: Alaia kept sleeping atop Pichi, aided by the soothing effect of Mio's herbs.

As opposed to the roadless openness of the desert, the mountains had clear, wide roads. People traveled on foot, on the backs of diprotodons, and even rode the occasional moa, though the birds here were of a different species, with more colorful feathers and dangling bright wattles above and below their beaks.

Once past the aspen forest, while they were passing through a lush jungle that did not care to lose its leaves in Winter, Mio taught them the names of yet more new animals, from koalas, to numbats, opossums, quolls—not to be confused with quoll-quolls—and bandicoots. He pointed out another of their companion species, one that was following them by gliding from treetop to treetop. They were called feathertail gliders, which centuries ago had been known as pygmy gliders, but were no longer the size of mice, but big as badgers.

From their new vantage point, most of the dome could be seen at once. East of the sierras there was a blue, purple, and black desert, while to the west was a mixture of rainforests and prominent lakes, leading to a distant bay. The mountain range acted as a barrier to the moisture, which formed more clouds and haze in the western half of the dome, making the horizon appear dim and far away. To the east, the dry air made everything seem crisp and near, playing games with their perception.

Tucked between the three peaks was a lush eucalyptus forest, with trees as tall as redwoods and trunks nearly as thick. As if it had been there in front of their eyes all along, the city of Mikkagolm manifested itself, embedded in the forest. The houses were round, also capped with inverted dragonblood tree roofs, but unlike at Mio's small village, here the walls were constructed with vertical logs of hard woods, layered with mosses and ferns to the point that they nearly disappeared among the greenery. While most of the cylindrical homes were only one or two levels high, some of them rose like towers, looking like thick tree trunks topped by conical hats.

Rumors had traveled faster than their smilodons and diprotodon could, and so had an envoy, who'd been sent ahead by Mio to make Ulésse aware of their arrival. As they neared the dome's central trunk, a sizable crowd gathered on the streets, tipping their hats at the strangers.

"This is Ulésse's home," Mio pointed out. He was greeted by the envoy, who was standing by two green-robed druids; they explained that Ulésse was working at the gardens and said they would take care of Alaia while the travelers went to fetch the Quajufröa.

Sterjall watched as the druids carried his friend into the dwelling, his insides knotted with anxiety. "Perhaps I should stay with—"

"They will care for her, Lago-Sterjall," Lummukem cut him off. "We came here with a mission in mind. Let us find Ulésse and tell her what brings us to her home."

The city and tall forest abruptly ended in an enormous clearing from which the trunk rose. In a wide circle around the trunk grew the Mikkagolm Gardens. Kulak was reminded of the Arjum Promenade around the Moordusk

Dome's trunk, where they had sculpture gardens, a reliquary, even a stadium. Here the garden was not decorated with stone sculptures or temples, but with every conceivable species of plant, all neatly organized, extending as far as their eyes could see.

"What are those bubbles?" Sterjall asked.

"Greenhouses," Mio answered. "For plants that need a more controlled climate." Like glossy blisters rising over the garden, dozens of the monumental glass bubbles shimmered—domes within domes.

"I can follow no further," Mio apologized, making his diprotodon stop by the garden's ornate moon gate. The crowd that had been following them stopped as well. "Only druids and chiefs are allowed in the sacred garden. Have your companion cats wait just past the entrance, as they won't fit through most of the narrow paths Ulésse might take you through." He pointed to an inn spiraling around a thick tree trunk and said, "If you need me, you can find me at the Helix Chambers, but you are Ulésse's guests now. Follow the glider, he will show you to her." Mio pulled his hat down, bowed his burrow, then rode away, followed by the curious citizens.

Sterjall looked up and noticed a feathertail glider waiting above the perfectly circular gate. The marsupial hopped off and glided deeper into the garden.

"Wait for us here," Kulak told the smilodons.

The three Silvfröash ventured through the circular opening and followed the patient glider over a mossy path. Past an aromatic herb garth, across the bridge of a bog garden, and cutting right through a hanging fernery, they arrived at an orchid garden, where the glider suddenly vanished into the treetops. The narrowing path led straight to another moon gate, and in front of it was Hud Ulésse, tending to colorful orchids. She wasn't as much waiting for them as she was meticulously focused on her work.

From far away, Sterjall could already feel the aura of Quajusilv; it was warm and inviting, like a crystalline amber melting in a somnolent hearth. He sensed not one, but two auras of the same hue. When he was close enough to see them, Sterjall first spotted a giant thylacine and knew him to be Ëalcor, the marsupial Nu'irg Banook had long ago told him about. Ishke'ísuk jumped off Lummukem's shoulder, landing as a perentie, and rushed to greet his old thylacine friend, who had grown much larger than he remembered.

Ulésse turned, watching the guests approach. She was in her half-form of a common wombat, short and stocky, shading her bulky head with the same kind of conical hat they had grown accustomed to seeing, although hers was decorated with the tiniest flowers. She seemed old, mostly due to the white texture in her brown fur, but Sterjall could not tell how old. Her green cloak and un-dyed wool blouse were unbuttoned at the front.

"Springs eternal guide your roots," she greeted them in an aged and solemn voice. She took off her gardening gloves and clasped her handpaws with one another, wrapping her claws around the opposite arm's wrist and bowing over the loop her thick-furred arms had made.

Sterjall repeated the gesture instinctively, as it was identical to a greeting he knew by heart: that of the Havengall Congregation. He nearly answered by saying, *Essence of one, soul of the many.*

As he bowed, Sterjall caught a glimpse of Ulésse's exposed belly and chest. He could see no breasts or nipples, and a skin pouch sagged where her belly began, heavy from holding all manner of gardening tools, as if she was wearing a pocketed apron. The wolf caught himself staring too intently and snapped himself out of it.

"Has your injured friend been handed over to the care of the druids?" the wombat asked, not showing any urgency in the slow pace of her voice.

"Yes," Sterjall said, "they carried Alaia into your home just moments ago."

Ulésse twitched her whiskers in acknowledgment. "Swell," she replied. "Worry not for her, she's in good hands." She put her gloves back on and re-sumed working on her plants. "The eastern winds told me three Silvfröash traveled to Mikkagolm from the lands beyond. They failed to tell me that a Nu'irg also journeyed with them." She tipped her hat toward Ishke'ísuk, who was now perching on the thylacine's long muzzle. "I am Hud Ulésse of the Ji Miscam, third wombat of the Keldris Khesúra, nineteenth Quajufröa since the great closing."

She patted the striped rump of the enormous thylacine standing beside her, so big he was nearly at eye level with her. "This is Ëalcor, Nu'irg ust Quaju. Welcome to our garden." As with most inhabitants of Quajudrolom, she only spoke Miscamish, with lyrical tones that reminded Sterjall of an ancient un-derground stream.

Ulésse kept working as she listened to their story: transplanting, pruning, trimming, mixing, watering, inspecting, tasting, and now and then asking ques-tions. They all found it exceedingly odd how nearly everyone they had met in this dome, including Ulésse, seemed unsurprised by their visit and simply lis-tened as if they were old friends catching up over a cup of tea.

Ulésse led them through the garden, clockwise around the trunk. She moved with purpose, albeit slowly due to her aged bones. Behind her, she rolled a cart with gardening tools and a watering can filled with murky water. She would stop at times after watering a plant to simply stare at it, as if measuring something invisible. *She reminds me of Khopto,* Sterjall thought. *She stares at the plants just as intently, the way he used to when picking herbs at the monastery's garth.* He sighed, absently rubbing at his bracelet.

The Quajufröa wasn't the only person working at the gardens; there were also the druids, who wore tunics adorned with flowery patterns and green cloaks with sleeves that draped nearly to the ground; they approached from time to time to bow their burrows before the visitors, only to then scurry off again, letting Ulésse have her privacy. But the most numerous of the garden workers, by far, were the marsupials. Hundreds of them performed specific, intricate tasks with the plants, receiving instructions from the druids, and from the feathertail gliders who acted as supervisors, gliding to and from the greenhouses and canopies.

Kulak was recounting their adventure across the Cobalt Desert when Ulésse ushered them into a greenhouse. The glass dome was heavily ornamented, like a stained-glass bubble. It was hot and humid inside, with tendrils of steam flowing at their feet like a white river. Ulésse continued listening as she climbed a ladder to transplant an elkhorn fern on an enormous cacao tree. She finished her work just as Kulak told her how Alaia had passed out, and about how they had encountered Mio. She slowly descended the ladder, took off her gloves, and wiped the sweat off her bulbous nose. She stared at them, her small eyes sitting very far apart from each other.

"You bring with you sadness and hope," she said at last. "You are as brave as the heroes of old, and your goal is an honorable one. Yet you place me and my people in a quandary. Your friend, we will heal. That is not a concern. And I will honor Noss's wishes, but neither myself nor Ëalcor can join you in your mission."

"W–why not?" Sterjall asked.

She maintained a slow, trudging walk as she talked, still busying herself with her plants. "Marsupials are extinct in the New World, or so your tongues have told me. It will take months, maybe years, for our clade to migrate safely. And then a sea we must all cross. Ëalcor cannot follow where marsupialkind lives not. As for myself, I am a farmer, a gardener, a botanist, learned in the ways of nature. And though my heart is young, I am not a teen any longer, but about to turn ninety-eight."

"Ninety-eight?" Kulak asked, befuddled.

"Not yet, in four more months. Though I still feel lively, my body is not cooperating quite as much any longer." She stepped over a hot spring creek that snaked through the greenhouse, the cause of all the steam. "You claim an entire desert of blue extends beyond Quajudrolom. I know the plant species that will thrive in it. I know the animals that will work the land, the fungi that will make it fertile again. My people, my plants, my marsupials, they need me more than you do."

She approached a glass shelf where a collection of carnivorous plants hungrily waited, then used minute tweezers to pick up mites and ants—she dropped them on sticky sundews, voracious pitcher plants, and predatory flytraps.

"Unlike at Mindreldrolom," she began again, "I need no permission from chiefs to make a decision for Quajudrolom. The Ji have no queen, but I am chief above all. I will help you open the dome, but here I will remain to help my people while our dome withers, to inspire them as they begin their slow pilgrimage over the deserts. I will call for the druids to join me tomorrow to set our plan in motion, which has been on our minds for generations." She opened the greenhouse's glass doors and waited for them to exit. "In the meantime, heroes from remote lands, follow me around the rest of the garden, as I still have work to do. You may ask anything you wish to know about my people, my plants, my animals."

They transitioned to the east side of the garden, where the desert plants grew in sands of all different colors. Sterjall kept his eyes open in case he saw a ruby-flecked stoneleaf, but the plants were so numerous and so diverse that it would've taken him hours to scour through all the species present.

"I had a friend once," he said, "a monk, who inhaled soot to learn the medicinal properties of plants. Is that what you are doing when you suddenly stop and stare at the plants?"

"Sometimes, but I wasn't doing so today," Ulésse replied. "I mainly check for their wellbeing, asking them what *they* need, how I may help them. If I'm searching for a particular effect, I may ask them about it."

"You mindspeak with plants?" Lummukem asked, their tone betraying their surprise.

"Plants do not talk, they are not conscious in the same way. But their threads can teach us much, just like tree rings can tell a story. You get to know them as individuals, until they become family. Any living creature can be read in that way, with enough practice. But we have found ways to make it easier."

"You mean the burrows?" Sterjall asked.

"I was referring to something else, lad." Ulésse lifted her watering can and poured a bit of murky water on top of a parched hedgehog cactus, then stared at it. "Do you see?"

"I... don't," Sterjall admitted. "But... the water, it looks like—"

"The water is mixed with soot. That is why it is dark. As the plants drink the water, they become easier to read. This cactus is telling me its roots need more room to spread, and that it is beginning to grow an offset, though it's not ready to be propagated yet. If it was flowering, the threads upon the pistils would shimmer in a similar way to the threads of the long-nosed bats that fertilize this species. There is a lot more to see, of course, but it becomes intuitive, part of the qualia of perceiving the threads, to a point where there's no objective way to describe it—you can only feel it." She transplanted the cactus into a larger planter with fresh purple soil, then gave it a bit more water.

"That must be a lot of soot to use," Kulak observed, "if you water all your plants this way."

"Only some plants, and only when scrying for connections," Ulésse clarified. "The soot supply is not a concern, as it is vast. When our old shamans developed the technique of trepanation, soot became plentiful, as a single burrow filled with soot could hold the effect for several years. It allowed us to experiment, to find other uses for our sacred powder." She lowered her bulbous nose to sniff at the cactus, then nodded as if agreeing with whatever a cactus had to say to a wombat.

"The burrows helped our people see these connections between organisms," she continued. "It also freed the shamans from doing all the hard work, as normal citizens could communicate with the animals to help us all keep the balance. The shamans of old are no more—their role transitioned, and they became our druids and scholars."

"Do you have a burrow too?" Kulak asked.

Ulésse removed her dried cactus hat and pointed to her broad head, between her small triangular ears. There was no black bump there. She then pulled all the tools from her pouch, shifted into her human form, and removed the marsupial mask to show that the top of her head was untouched, flowing with gray hair that once had been bronze.

She seemed much older as a human, with wrinkles congregating by her eyes, on her chin, on the folds of her brow. Her expressions compressed strata of memories and kindness, like that of an old companion one sees again decades later and finds them aged, but still carrying the same old soul.

Her name in this form was Ouránama, she told them, the same name as her mother, who was long gone, and her first daughter, who lived on the shores of the Keldris Khesúra.

Ouránama was thinner in her human form. Her unbuttoned blouse looked oversized on her, covering her sagging breasts and obscuring a tattoo that circled around her belly. Sterjall wanted to get a better look at the markings, but he was too shy to ask the old woman to expose herself to him.

"When I turned fifteen, instead of being gifted a burrow, I was honored with Quajusilv," Ouránama said, handing the black mask to them so they might admire it. Its shape was muddy, as if trying to average the forms of too many disparate species, but in its inclusiveness and vagueness there was beauty beyond description, as if all the qualities of marsupials had coalesced into the most perfect form.

She put the mask back on, returned to her wombat half-form, and began placing the gardening tools back in her pouch. "Those of us wielding the masks have no need for burrows. We can see the threads well enough without them. The Silvesh are wise and provide us with all the tools we need." She pointed at her belly and laughed heartily. "But truly, wise they are. Wombats have inverted pouches—I would've been dragging these trowels, shears, and pruners on the ground if I was built exactly like them. But while in my half-form, Quajusilv is smart enough to know I need to be up on two feet, so my pouch is formed upward, like that of a kangaroo."

Ulésse explained how the selection of the Quajufröash took place. She had shown the most promise among a group of gifted children who were learning to read the threads using soot in the traditional way. The druids had voted and chosen her. She told them that once she turned one hundred and eight—or eighteen times the sacred number—she would have to surrender the mask to the next elected young Quajufröa. She still had a bit over a decade to enjoy her wombat form.

"A hundred and eight?" Sterjall gawked. "Do you all live that long?"

"Some do, some don't," Ulésse said. "I will explain over dinner. Would you join me?"

CHAPTER TWENTY-FOUR

RIPPLES OF CONSCIOUSNESS

Only the branching top of the trunk remained lit, spreading lightning-like patterns over the capital city of Mikkagolm. Kulak whistled for Blu and Pichi to join them, and together they followed Ulésse. The old wombat led them to her home, which was just across the garden, where the tall eucalyptus forest began.

The smilodons waited on the covered porch, where a servant brought them water and munnji cakes. The cats found this mix of the paste a bit more palatable than the one they had been served at Mio's village.

Ulésse opened the front door and let the three Silvfröash walk in first.

"You are awake!" Sterjall said as he entered, relieved to see Alaia sitting on a couch, looking pale but alert.

"Gwoli!" Alaia replied, equally excited. She tried to rise from the couch, but Sterjall urged her to sit down again.

"My scalp is happy to see you are better," Kulak said to her.

"This place is wild," she whispered. "The druids told me what happened. Did you see those gross holes in their—"

Ulésse walked in, followed by Ëalcor, who barely fit through the doorway and was carrying Ishke'ísuk on his head.

"You must be Alaia," Ulésse said with a looped-arms bow. "And you must be starving."

Ulésse's green home was modest, of only a single level, comprising three circular rooms. The interior of the home was somehow greener than the outside, with herbs growing from every wall. The inverted dragonblood tree roof was like a room-wide chandelier from which all manner of tools hung. A kitchen sprawled at one end of her home, with a dining area next to it, while an ample living room filled most of the space. Two round-top doorways led to Ulésse's bedroom and a study which had been hastily rearranged into a guest room.

They made themselves comfortable while they caught Alaia up on what had happened.

While they conversed, Ulésse inspected the work the druids had done on Alaia's wound; she thought it adequate but decided to add an ointment of her own before wrapping the wound again. "Velvet knifewood," she said. "It will help you heal much faster."

She then directed them to sit at the dining table, where she served them a pink, pulpy drink. She scrutinized them without saying a word, then went back to the kitchen counter to prepare their dinner.

"Lago-Sterjall was asking about my age," she mentioned to Alaia, plucking herbs from her walls and windowsills. "I'm no longer in my prime, though I feel not a day over ninety. Most of us live to around a hundred nowadays, though I hope I get to live longer than that. The reason for our longer lives has to do with our burrows and our diets."

She placed a salad bowl in front of each of her guests, each brimming with a unique mixture of greens, fruits, and nuts, all sprinkled with chopped munnji cubes of different colors. She also picked a handful of seeds for Olo and caramelized insects for Ishke'ísuk.

"Taste this. See what you think."

Alaia was about to dig in, but Ulésse squinted at her, took her bowl away, sprinkled a few berries over the salad, and then gave it back.

"Are those... muskberries?" Alaia asked, already smelling the pungent stench of them.

"Reekblossom is what we call them. I sensed an affinity between them and you. I think you lack calcium, gal. These berries are filled with it. It will help you heal, and it'll provide sustenance to those bones that grow from your spine and your head."

Alaia munched on her exquisitely fetid salad. Never had she tasted such malodorously delicious muskberries before. Sterjall, Kulak, and Lummukem shifted into their human forms to eat, as their sharp fangs and serrated teeth were no good for chewing on greens.

As Lago tasted his bowl of bitter greens, sweet nuts, and goat cheese-flavored munnji, he felt as if the meal had been prepared exclusively for him; as if each ingredient provided exactly the right type of nutrient he needed and offered the exact flavor he was looking to savor at that moment.

"This… this is perfect," he mumbled, unapologetically speaking with his mouth full. "How did you… Wait, you were telling us about the burrows, and your diets or something."

Ulésse sat down with them, with Ëalcor curled like a wall of fur around her chair. "The burrows…" she began. "Our longevity came about after our transition to trepanation for all citizens. Since so many of us are practiced in the thread divination arts, we are able to understand which ingredients best fit our diets. Those with enough experience can tell which nutrients are lacking, which are piled in excess, and which toxins need to be flushed out."

Lago kept on chewing. "So does that mean that by eating this salad I'll—"

"No, lad, it would take more than one meal for you to notice a difference. But do enjoy your meal, nonetheless."

"We noticed you picked your ingredients carefully," Sunu said, tasting their much more plain-looking dinner. "We would like to learn how you do this." Though their salad looked simple, it was filled with spicy, complex flavors. A raw egg of some unknown bird was bulging at the center, yolk still unbroken.

"I will gladly teach you, Sunu-Lummukem, if you are willing to train with me and the druids for the next few decades."

Sunu swallowed.

Ulésse continued, "But I believe your current mission will not allow such delays, so for now I will briefly tell you the basics of our process. We, the Ji Miscam, have studied the connections between living organisms since before the Acoapóshi Miscam came to offer us the sacred Silv of Quaju. It was mainly this predisposition of ours that convinced them to grant us the honor of wielding the mask. The added insight the mask provided, together with the revelation that soot strengthened the connection to our sibling organisms, allowed us to develop our arts into a way of being."

"That reminds me of something else we've been wanting to ask about," Lago interjected. "Mio, the farmer who brought us to Mikkagolm, he told us none of you eat meat. Is that true?"

The old wombat was back in the kitchen, pouring water from a ceramic vessel into a kettle. She placed the kettle on the iron stove and glanced at her guests. Her small eyes were hard to read. "This is not entirely true. We do eat the meat of certain animals." She sat back at the table and sank her muzzle into her salad of grasses and roots, needing no utensils. With a few greens dangling from her rodent-like incisors, she continued. "Before we became a culture of trepanation, we were hunters. But that all changed when we learned to see better, when we shared in the pain of the creatures we killed."

"With the burrows, are you able to feel in the same way as when wearing a Silv?" Aio asked.

"Not the same, young prince. The particular qualia of an animal species are only accessible in a half-form of the same clade. But our means of connection, our empathy, that did increase with the addition of the burrows. The Ji are better able to empathize with creatures we once considered inferior to us. And we learned it was not merely animal species that shared what we call consciousness, but all living beings, in one form or another. From plants, to fungi, to the smallest of organisms."

"Plants can also feel?" Lago asked. "If that's the case, how do you know where to draw the line? Why eat plants, or eat at all?"

The kettle whistled. Ulésse retrieved it and poured the hot water into a glass pot filled with gold-tipped, aromatic tea leaves. She let the leaves steep as she chewed and pondered, until the water turned a sunrise-yellow color. She stared at the hot kettle, squinting with her beady eyes. "Lago-Sterjall, do you think this kettle is conscious?"

"Huh?..." Lago made an effort not to cock his head like a dog at the odd question. "No, I don't..."

"But does it not know when the water inside it is boiling? Did it not whistle, eagerly notifying me it was time to pull it away from the fire?"

"Well... It did, but that does not mean it's conscious. It's just what happens when water boils."

"Perhaps. Earlier today, inside the greenhouse, I fed ants to a flytrap. Did you see me do this?"

Lago nodded.

"When the ant touched the hairs inside the flytrap's lobes, it closed its teeth down and trapped the insect to digest it while still alive. Would you consider the flytrap to be conscious?"

Lago felt he was falling into a trap, similar to how Mamóru offered insight by making him struggle against his own beliefs. "The flytrap is alive," he said, "so at least it's doing that on purpose. But I don't know whether I'd call it conscious."

"Perhaps. You say the plant did so 'on purpose,' as if there was a willingness, a thought process behind the flytrap's actions. Yet the flytrap merely reacted to a signal sent by its sensitive trigger hairs. Whether it had been an ant, a stick, or a snowflake, the flytrap would've snapped its teeth down." She stirred the tea leaves, letting the steam warm her clawed fingers.

She looked back at Lago. "Now the ant," she continued, "the ant does seem different, does it not? The ant struggled to break free from the acidic prison.

Its legs shook, its mandibles bit down fiercely until it was digested. Do you think, young lad, that the ant was conscious?"

"Yeah, maybe." Lago recalled the time at the Mesa Monastery when he had been confronted by Chaplain Gwil about his torturing of the leafcutter ants. "I try not to kill ants on purpose," he said, without telling her the story, "but I also step on them all the time without noticing, and don't think much about it. But they do feel. They react, they fight back."

"Perhaps," she said once more while pouring the yellow tea; it had a sweet scent with fruity undertones. She did not strain the tea leaves out, but instead let them fall into the clay mugs to spiral with the hot liquid. She added a touch of lemon juice to each mug, stirred a little honey into Alaia's, then handed them out.

"The ant," she went on, "was also simply reacting as an ant would. Perhaps the way an ant can move is much more deliberate, at least to our fast-trained eyes. But if you could see plants grow over time, you'd notice they move in patterns nearly as elaborate as those of an ant, with the exception that they are bound to the soil by their roots."

"But the ant is much more complex," Alaia hypothesized. "Is that what makes it different?"

"They are different, though both are equally complex. I felt the ant's pain as it was dissolved in the flytrap, yet I felt no remorse, as I understood it to be part of the cycle that needs to endure in order for balance to exist among so many a living creature. The pain, however, was different from the kind of pain you or I feel. Not lesser, not necessarily. Only different."

"But is the ant conscious or not?" Lago asked impatiently.

"Ah, the question we all ask ourselves, yet the premise itself is flawed. Consciousness is not a doorway you cross. There is no threshold that turns it on or off."

"My scalp thinks that what she means is that it is like a staircase," Aio said to Lago. "Some creatures are higher up the steps than others."

Ulésse's long, black whiskers lifted in a proud smile. "You are getting somewhere, young prince, but not exactly." She slowly took a sip of her tea, drinking the leaves with it. It was still too hot for the others to drink from their mugs.

"Just as there is no threshold, there are also no defined steps," she said. "You may think of it now as a ramp with an infinite gradient of levels between each step. Yet that analogy is still flawed and incomplete. Would you say that a baby has the same consciousness as, say, a numbat?"

Lago had seen a few numbats, which Mio had excitedly pointed out for them. He recalled their friendly temperament, their squirrel-like tails, and their beautifully striped bodies.

"I… I don't know," he admitted. "I guess numbats and babies would be just as smart? Depends on the baby?"

"Perhaps. What matters at this point is no longer the degree. Picture that endless ramp once more, with no defined steps, but with a clear sense of up and down. It matters not how high or low in that ramp you find the baby, because the numbat is standing on a completely separate ramp. It's no longer a matter of degree, but a matter of *kind* of consciousness. The ant, the flytrap, perhaps even the kettle, they all have ramps of their own, each of a unique flavor and kind, some leading up, some down, some not even knowing the difference. We now find ourselves in a maze filled with an infinite number of ramps, all tangled together, like the threads that make up all consciousnesses."

"That still doesn't explain how you choose which animals are okay to eat," Lago countered.

Ulésse stood and from the branching ceiling plucked a handful of grape-like berries, handing them out as a dessert to everyone at the table. She took her time before answering, savoring the acidic fruits, which popped satisfyingly when bitten.

"Return once more to that room filled with infinite ramps. Imagine your-selves in that tangled tapestry of all conscious or perhaps not-so-conscious beings. Are your minds traveling in that space right now?" she asked.

All four of the wayfarers nodded, imagining the unimaginable space.

"You've spoken of complexity, gal," she said to Alaia. "A volcanic rock is very complex, yet that tells us nothing of its nature. Imagine now that some of those ramps not only go up and down, but that they split into multiple paths."

They all pictured it.

"But now… what if somewhere high on those split paths, the ramps were to turn, curve back, and merge onto the same ramp once more? What if, up on a higher level of understanding, we were to look back upon ourselves and see ourselves?"

"Do you mean being self-aware?" Alaia asked.

"Exactly," Ulésse answered. "Some creatures might be more or less com-plex than others. Their kinds of complexity might be entirely alien to us, or they may be something we see as natural. Yet the key to true consciousness lies in the ability to self-reflect, to reach a higher level not for the sake of climbing to an unreachable top, but to find a path that leads us back to where we began, so we can see ourselves in all our complexity."

Lago pictured those infinite ramps bending inward, creating loops of consciousness that reflected upon themselves. They drew circles and ripples in his mind.

Ulésse's beady eyes scanned her guests' faces and saw that her images were flowing through their heads. "We are nearly there," she encouraged. "Leave not this room you've imagined, with ramps that split and turn back into themselves. Now imagine—if possible—that each of those loops could grow another loop, albeit smaller, and then another loop on that one, and so forth. Soon each branch will grow like the leaves of a fern, with smaller portions curling inward and self-reflecting on their own self-reflections. This iterative pattern, this interconnectedness between the smallest and the largest parts, this is where one of the most peculiar kinds of consciousnesses lies."

"I'm having a hard time picturing so many loops," Lago said, "but I see it, like a branching tree trunk, with smaller branches connecting back to the main trunk, growing leaves that curl back into themselves. It's like some of the threads I see with Agnargsilv. Some of them seem to flow outward, but there are others that loop back."

"This is what we all learn to see, with enough practice," Ulésse agreed. "Thousands of years back, beyond six lands, beneath six seas, the precursors of our druids learned to perceive these confounding, tangling levels. That was where our journey began."

"Then how do you…" Lago paused, still forcing his mind to picture the forest. "How do you figure out which animals to kill and which ones to spare? Can you see them so clearly?"

"This is something we are still learning to this day," Ulésse admitted, "as the answer is, by its very nature, subjective. As Quajufröa, I can see the world as a marsupial would, but I cannot see the world—or see myself—as a fish, or a bird, or a flytrap, or an ant would. We can't make use of their distinctive qualia, but we can glimpse into their nature by careful observation, measurement, and self-reflection of our own. These loops of consciousness are one key aspect we search for before deciding whether taking a life is a moral choice. But given that the loops themselves have endless complexities, we can't always be confident in our choices.

"There are certain qualities that soot—or the Silvesh—let us glimpse. Even without these aids, by using our natural empathy, we can connect to other creatures and try to feel as they feel. Empathy is something that can be practiced and learned, and so we learn early on how to use it. We have found that there are many species of fish that do not feel in the same self-reflecting manner we do, as well as many arthropods, mollusks, and cnidarians. They are, in a way, as far down on their respective ramps as the unlucky ant I fed to the flytrap, though not as far down as the mindless kettle."

"What about birds?" Alaia asked. "Some are smarter than many mammals, yet you served Sunu an egg."

"There is a difference between self-awareness and the potential for self-awareness. We harvest the eggs from species who lay too many due to the lack of natural predators in this tightly controlled environment. An egg is filled with potential, but it is not yet a bird, so we feel not troubled when eating it."

Ulésse chewed on more of the acidic berries, crushing the tiny seeds within them without giving it a moment's thought. "We are but single leaves in this vast forest of endlessly twisting ferns. All we can do is try our best to minimize the suffering we inflict upon others, while aiming to bring happiness to those we help live on. Noss gave us new tools to accomplish this, namely the white blood that feeds so many of us. Luckily, our dome does not have too many carnivores." She scratched Ëalcor's head; he growled in a deep rumble, but did so playfully. "In times past, Ëalcor used to be as small as a wallaby, but as his own species grew bigger in Quajudrolom, he grew as well." She got up and slapped Ëalcor's enormous rump. The mellow thylacine barely lifted an ear. Ulésse then took their dishes and refused any help with cleaning the table. Over one last cup of yellow tea, she asked them more questions about their experiences, about their expectations for their next destination.

"We need to continue to the Nisos Dome after this," Lago explained, "the dome of glires, which is quite far to the southeast in what we call the Republic of Lerev. We know it's a rich and powerful land, but we don't know what to expect. We need to be ready for anything."

"You mentioned earlier that there is a road that can carry you across the desert, back to your ship," Ulésse said as a statement more than a question.

"That is what Siffo, our ship's captain, said," Sunu replied. "Although the road will be heavily transited—we are bound to encounter the enemies from Navar Mat who we recently escaped from."

"I will ask the druids to ready a convoy to protect you. Our diprotodons will do better in the desert, and perhaps a few of our procoptodons for further aid. I would send our faster zygomaturuses with you, but they are from the wetlands and would not fare well in dry dunes."

She wiped her handpaws and showed them to their makeshift guest room.

"Tomorrow I will ask you to retell parts of your story to the druids," she declared, "and once you are done, we will set our plan in motion. Rest now, tired voyagers, and think about the future you want to build not only for yourselves, but for all kinds."

CHAPTER TWENTY-FIVE

THE SACRED HOLD

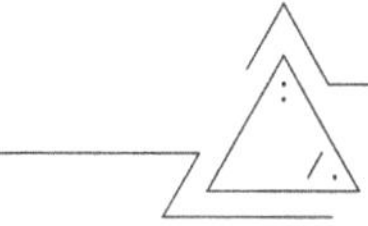

Lago lay in bed next to Aio, who was already snoring.

He could not sleep. He stared at the branching ceiling. Each branch of the dragonblood tree split in two, and those again into four, then into eight smaller and smaller branches. He closed his eyes and tried to conjure that forest of ferns Ulésse had embedded into their brains. It seemed so complex, with too many pieces. He pictured leaves of different sizes and kinds, all separate from one another and all unique, jumbled together in one incomprehensibly dense jungle. It was humid and foggy in there, not letting him see the leaves that were farther away from him.

His eyes opened. He had dozed off after all, and still felt the humidity of the woodlands he had visited. He wanted to understand these connections better, but despite all his efforts, he still saw all these leaves, these patterns of self-reflection, as isolated metaphors. Something was amiss.

In an attempt to unravel these tangled relationships, he put Agnargsilv on and stared up, not shifting into Sterjall so that the change would not disturb Aio. The dragonblood tree roof, as dead as it was, was covered in threads; not threads from its own dried bark, but from billions of smaller organisms that lived within and sprouted around it. It was as if the tree had found a way to sustain its life long after the plant was inert and dry. None of the threads from the plants above him seemed to loop back onto themselves, not like they did on his own body or on any of his friends sleeping near him.

He scanned his surroundings with Agnargsilv's sight to feel that elusive interconnectedness of parts. It was there in the threads, in how they combined with one another, in the relationships between species and individuals. And though it was visible through his mask, it was somehow ungraspable.

He concentrated on Alaia, who was asleep, and felt a throb in his hand as he focused on her wound. He decided not to interfere this time and focused elsewhere, suddenly distracted by two amber auras moving about in the yard behind the house. Ulésse and Ëalcor were still up, seemingly at work. Lago sat at the edge of the bed and watched their threads and their glows. After a long moment, he stood up, shifted into Sterjall, put his blue tunic on, and left the room.

He did not know how to reach the back yard, not without perhaps entering Ulésse's private bedroom, so he walked out the front door of the house. Blu was there on the porch, snoring contentedly next to Pichi. He stepped carefully around them and let his footpaws carry him to the lush garden behind Ulésse's home.

"You should be asleep," she said, keeping her back to him.

Ëalcor turned his pointed snout and swished his long, short-furred tail, snuffing at him. Moths flew like a tornado around a lamp, which was covered in a mesh so that none of the insects would be burned by the flames or the hot glass.

"You should be asleep too," Sterjall replied, walking deeper into the greenery.

"I've slept enough through my nearly hundred years of life, lad. There are things more important than sleep." She kept her back turned to him.

"What are you doing? Are you working?"

"I'm always working, in one way or another. I'm pollinating the orchids. This species only blossoms at night, and the moth which pollinates it does not live as far up the mountains as we are, so I have to lend it a hand."

She turned around and dropped a tiny brush into her pouch, then gave him a look that made him feel like a child who'd stayed up too late at night. "Now, I don't see you pollinating any orchids. Have you come to fertilize the oleanders? The outhouse is around the bend."

"I just… couldn't sleep. I was thinking of all you told us, and I'm conflicted about it."

Ulésse picked up the lamp, unleashing a whirlwind of moths. She walked with Sterjall farther into the yard, placed the lamp on a metal table, and pointed to a fig tree in front of it, one with a trunk that grew sideways in a curve, creating a natural bench. They sat next to one another without saying a word.

Ëalcor dropped his heavy body just a stride away and yawned. Sterjall admired the canid-like creature, marveling at his striped strangeness. He wondered how something could feel so familiar, yet so distant.

"I was…" he hesitated. "I was trying to picture this fern forest you mentioned. And I know it's only an analogy, not the real thing, but I'm having a hard time comprehending it. I see all these twirling leaves, all bundled up into tighter and tighter loops, but I still see them as disconnected."

"Yet you are two, and you are one," she said. "A wolf, a man. Can you see how those two connect in that deep forest your mind inhabits?"

"No, I can't. To me, the forest is foggy, and I can't see much beyond where I'm currently at. I don't know how to explain it. Before I found my other self, before I became a wolf, or recognized I had always been a wolf, I could not have imagined what being a wolf must be like. There was nothing in my experiences that could've compared, no rationalization that could've brought me closer to truly seeing as I see today. And though I guess it's possible, I still can't see myself as, say, that orchid, or as an ant, or as these moths circling the flame. Or even as something as familiar as Ëalcor."

The thylacine merely twisted an ear at the mention of his name, then went back to dozing off.

Moths landed all around the table, some on Sterjall's ears. He flicked them off, careful not to be too rough when doing so.

Ulésse stuck a handpaw in her pouch and pulled out a few walnuts. She cracked one open with her sharp teeth, tossed the brain-shaped core into her mouth, then offered some to Sterjall.

"Perhaps you already know, but you are focusing on the wrong thing," she said as she chewed. "Just like that kettle from earlier, which, in a way, was aware that it was boiling, yet it was not aware that it was aware. Tell me, Lago-Sterjall, what do you think happens when you see through your mask? Or when someone with a burrow feels other creatures around them?"

"It's something to do with the empathic focus," he said. "That's what Mamóru once taught us. It's some sort of energy that lets us connect to one another." He tried to crack a walnut with his teeth, but his were not built like those of a wombat. Instead, he cracked them open by pressing two of them against each other.

"That is true," Ulésse acknowledged. "The empathic focus is not as mysterious as the name makes it sound. It's nothing more than empathy, a means of reaching out and connecting to others who might be like yourself, or might be entirely different from yourself. It is, in many ways, easier to connect to those who are like us. If we return to the example of the forest of ferns, you might imagine that those who are like us are other leaves upon the same twisting plant, sometimes higher on the long stem, sometimes lower. Either way, they are close to us, and so we find it easy to reach out to them."

"What about those who are different? They are so far away, lost in this jungle fog, that they seem unreachable to me."

"Sterjall, lad. You are overthinking it."

"I know, but the analogy helps me visualize it, so I just thought—"

"Not in that way. You are stuck up above, in your comfortable level, where you assume you will find the answers. Search within."

"What do you mean?"

"Look deeper, lad. That is where the answer lies."

In his mind, Sterjall had been widening his reach, as if forcing the threads to connect despite their unbreachable distances. He swallowed, then tried to probe at the threads that lived within his core. He looked at himself, at how the blue glow of Agnargsilv began at his head and spread down his body as if following his arteries, his nerves.

And then he saw it.

The branching pattern was clear and extended much deeper. Like neurons, dendrites, and long axons stretching to their neighbors and finding a common ground with them at their most basic of levels. But not reaching up—reaching down.

"The roots…" he whispered, staring at the spiraling motion of the lamp-hypnotized moths, but seeing only the forest in his mind; the forest above, and the forest below. Even those plants that were far beyond sight in the thick fog were accessible to him now, simply by connecting his roots to those of other plants near him, and in turn, connecting those to their own neighbors. All organisms formed a single rhizomatic mat; extending together, growing together, helping each other flourish.

"The roots," he repeated. "Like the aspen forest we crossed. They are all one. We are all one."

Ulésse smiled. "You see now, Lago-Sterjall. This is the magic of empathy. We all share a common ground with one another. Literally, on this very planet. Figuratively, in the soil that feeds our consciousnesses and ties our roots together." A rosy maple moth landed on her bulbous nose. She let it crawl onto a claw and stared at it. "We are wildly different creatures, but we are all connected. To reach beyond, we need to expand our empathy with the aid of our neighbors' roots. We must seek each other, connect with one another, so that we may be healthier as one. Noss knew this, from within their boiling crust, to the cold depths of their oceans. They made it their principal goal, long before the advent of the Downfall, to find ways to expand these connections."

"The Silvesh…" Sterjall muttered.

"The Silvesh. They are conduits of consciousness. They are bridges between kinds. The Silvesh expose our minds to new ideas, new ways of being, so that in our differences we can find new strength, so that eighteenfold our empathy can grow."

Sterjall pondered as the shadows of the moths flickered over his dark fur. "Since the moment we first met you," he began, "I've been reminded of the monks from the Havengall Congregation, who had a monastery where I grew up, in Withervale. They were always a kind of family to me. They kept me safe and fed, helped me learn. The way you greeted us, how you held your hands and bowed, the way you aim to see these connections, it's so similar to what they believe. Essence of one, soul of the many, that is what they say when greeting one another."

"Those are the words of Khavenwall, a druid of old, from whom many of our teachings derive. She was not one of the Quajufröash, but inspired three key Quajufröash who lived during her time. Our greeting is a different one, but the Gek-Voren tribe she was a part of used a similar greeting to the one you just spoke."

"Khavenwall…" Sterjall removed his Havengall Congregation bracelet and held it in front of him. "Perhaps they were all one and the same," he said. "Her teachings, I mean, maybe it is what started the Havengall Congregation. Or rather, the part of it that survived the Downfall."

Ulésse took the bracelet from him. "The sacred hold," she intoned with wonderment. "This is from the same monastery?"

"Yes. I'm not one of the monks, but I used to work for them."

Ulésse shapeshifted into Ouránama, keeping the mask on her face. Her gray hair drooped eerily under the black mask, incongruous with the shape they connected to. She leaned back and pulled her blouse open. Beneath her sagging breasts was the tattoo that Sterjall couldn't fully see earlier in the day. It was a circle made of knotted fibers, resembling roots and branches, braiding into two hands that clasped on top, nearly identical to his copper-filigreed bracelet.

Ouránama traced a finger on the circle inked around her belly. "The sacred hold is a symbol that represents more than just unity. The hands are separate, but they are the same. They are bridging a gap and connecting to one another. They form a loop, a way to self-reflect. Essence of one, soul of the many."

"It all loops back on itself…" Sterjall thought out loud, taking his bracelet back.

"That it does," Ulésse said, back in her wombat form. "That it most certainly does."

CHAPTER TWENTY-SIX

MURMURATION

While Ulésse prepared breakfast, Sterjall tried to explain to his friends what he had learned during his sleepless night.

"So, here's what I'm curious about," Alaia began to say. She was looking much better already, her wound having scabbed healthily as if by magic. "Doesn't this mean that the domes themselves are not only alive, but self-aware?"

"That's… um…" Sterjall replied, still thinking. "The first time I saw the vines with Agnargsilv, I noticed looped threads on them. But only on the larger ones."

"And green aura too," Kulak added. "When sitting at the throne of Ommo ust Mindrel, my mind's eye sees all of Mindreldrolom glowing."

"As I did when I set the Varanus Dome to open," Sterjall agreed.

"Of course the domes are self-aware," Ulésse interjected from the kitchen. "They are perhaps the most complex organisms we know of, other than Noss themself. But again, it is never a matter of degree, but of kind. I've encountered a few fleas who were self-aware, but their kind of awareness was very limited, even if impressive for their size." She joined them, handing out meals with perfectly selected ingredients once more, of just the right kinds of nutrients each of them craved.

"Or perhaps," the wombat continued, "it is not only a matter of kind, but of our perception of time. Maybe the domes have entire conversations in their thorny heads, but the flow of their sap is slow, and so are their thoughts."

"What about beehives?" Sterjall asked. "Mamóru once told us they are a higher-level consciousness. That's why they appear to glow. Does that mean they are even more self-aware than we are?"

"Not so, lad," Ulésse answered. "The glows our Silvesh perceive are merely an indication of a level of compartmentalization. You and I are made of common cells, and so are bees. We are at the same level, in that regard. Beehives are made of bees, a level above, one which we cannot perceive in the same manner, but not necessarily more aware of itself. However, if there was a beehive that was miles wide, with billions of bees swarming at its core, perhaps it would be considering whether you or I, such small and puny creatures, are as self-aware as they are."

"You sound like Mamóru, sometimes," Sterjall said. "I think you would've enjoyed meeting him."

"I am certain I would have," she said. "And regarding the Nu'irgesh, they would be another good example—and perhaps the Silvesh as well—because they are a product of all the animals in their clades, though I have to admit I don't fully understand how that works. And then there is Noss. Well… Noss is even more of a mystery, but the answer lies somewhere in that realm." With that, Ulésse withdrew into her room to prepare herself for the very important day that was coming.

"You know," Alaia said, enjoying a bowl of oats with ground cloves and dates, "this stuff is so delicious and filling, but I feel like I don't enjoy it as much as the meals Nalaníri cooked. Ulésse knows what our bodies need, but not necessarily what our hearts crave."

The others quietly agreed. They truly missed Nalaníri's sumptuous—even if sometimes fatty and unhealthy—dishes.

Ulésse gathered the druids at a verdant grotto in the Mikkagolm Gardens. She looked exactly like one of them, wearing the same tunics and green robes, except for the fact she was half wombat.

Sterjall, Lummukem, Kulak, and Alaia told their story to the druids, who agreed that the opening of Quajudrolom must begin as soon as they could inform their citizens, who would need to prepare for the pilgrimage many of them would have to undertake into the desert.

"There's something that concerns me," Sterjall remarked to Ulésse once the druids had finished asking questions.

"What concerns you, lad?"

"The Kingdom of Bauram, which extends all around you—they might see the dome opening as an opportunity for profit. They might want to take Quajusilv from you, as a tool for war. And I don't think that you, well…"

Ulésse smiled. "Don't let our serene demeanors trick you. The Ji have been readying for the eventual conflicts that might arise. I was quite skilled with the rope javelin in my youth, but my path led me elsewhere. A healthy body is better suited for a healthy mind, that is why the Ji learn the Dance of the Six Seasons."

"What is the Dance of the Six Seasons?" Kulak asked.

"It is a way of controlling the rope javelin to make it useful in daily tasks. Some use it for fishing, for farming, for building, or even for weaving large nets, becoming the very dance as they work. But the same techniques can also be applied in battle, if needed."

"I can demonstrate, if you wish," a druid named Lëovar offered.

"If you would not mind," she said.

The druid rose from his bench and assumed a stance that was egret-like in poise. As though pulled by the breeze, Lëovar's posture shifted, then he dropped as if boneless. Abruptly, he blossomed, his robes expanding in eager petals. From within his sleeves, two rope javelins extended, both of which had remained entirely hidden, secured around his bracers; they pierced out and back in, bouncing and spinning around his elbows, his knees, propelled from his shoulders in an explosion of thorns. The heavy ends of his javelins then slammed against the ground in twin spirals, unleashing a whirlwind of sparks and dust around him, and with an upward thrust his robes pulled in the hot air and a cloud of fallen leaves, summoning an obscuring veil. Once the leaves dissipated, the druid had vanished, his robes falling empty like a heavy mist, but as the robes touched the ground, up he sprung from within them, limbs and javelins piercing the air in icicle-sharp strikes of six-fold symmetry. The javelins recoiled back in and wrapped around his arms once more. As the sleeves draped down to cover the blades, Lëovar's sharp posture softened and began to melt like cascading water, assuming the sinuous forms of a river-worn canyon.

"Beautiful," Alaia murmured, as the druid and his robes transitioned seamlessly from a twirl back down to his seat.

"Not all of us are as… flamboyant as Lëovar," Ulésse said, "but we are all trained in similar techniques."

"We noticed that a strange moss grows within the carved cores of the javelins," Lummukem said. "Their threads, they are most peculiar."

"The bloodmoss, yes," Lëovar said, extending one of his javelins again. The steel armature held an ornamented bone carving with a red moss growing within. The threads extending from the moss connected directly to Lëovar, as if they were a part of him. "The bloodmoss helps us glimpse within our javelins," he explained, "for it is tied to us, dependent on us." He pricked a fingertip with the javelin's tip, drawing blood, then sucked at it and mixed the blood with his saliva. He let his red spit dangle and fall right into the mossy carvings of his weapon, then spread the liquid around gently.

"You feed it your blood?" Kulak asked.

"Yes," the druid answered. "Our blood, our spit, our sweat. The bloodmoss becomes an extension of ourselves. As our bodies grow, the moss grows beside us and feeds from us. Its threads are bound to ours, and thus we can sense it clearly, like we can sense a finger or an arm."

"Burrows help with that," Ulésse clarified. "It has been a long time since I've wielded my javelin, so nowadays my bloodmoss lives happily in a planter back in my home." She looked back toward Sterjall. "So, worry not, lad. We are well prepared for the struggles that may come to us. And we have the aid of many giant marsupials, who are aware of what's at stake and would not hesitate to protect us. We will avoid conflict for as long as possible, but the Ji will do what is needed to fulfill our oaths to Noss." She stood slowly and straightened her robes. "It is time we inform our citizens of what's to come."

From an open field of flowers, hundreds of starlings were sent off, carrying messages to the elders in every city, town, village, and lonely dwelling in Quajudrolom. The murmuration floated like an amoeba above the gardens, flickering in iridescent shimmers. Sterjall saw the formation glow while it temporarily held a higher level of organization, as if the cloud of birds was conscious on some level, though perhaps not quite self-aware. The formation broke, the ephemeral aura vanished, and each bird fluttered away toward remote lands to deliver the message.

From Lummukem's right shoulder, Olo looked up at the receding wings.

"Hundreds of birds at once, directed by only a few druids," Lummukem observed, still astounded by the power of the burrows.

CHAPTER TWENTY-SEVEN

DESERT AMBUSH

The Ji Miscam had stocks of seeds readied for this epoch-defining transition. In each major city, caravans of humans and marsupials were formed. The seeds were distributed, and the members of the caravans were instructed where to go, what to plant, and how to help the land regrow.

Ulésse gave directions to a herd of forty diprotodons of a species even larger than the one Mio rode, as well as six enormous kangaroos, the procoptodons. While hauling a squad of druid scouts, plentiful seeds, and stashes of munnji cakes, the marsupials were to protect the wayfarers on their way to the eastern shores and become the first group to repopulate the desert.

Although the diprotodons' hides were already thick, they were outfitted with makeshift armor crafted from companion species' bones, making them look like fat skeletons. The procoptodons requested no armor, wanting to depend on their agility, the power of their enormous tails, and the bone-breaking kicks their single-toed feet could deliver.

During those days of preparation, per Sunu-Lummukem's request, Lëovar taught them the basics of the Dance of the Six Seasons, attempting to adapt the skillset to their own weapons, given that learning the rope javelin would take years, if not decades.

"I'm not so worried about the Ji anymore," Sterjall commented to Alaia one evening, after their training had concluded. "It's not only that their weapons are exceedingly hard to predict, but when I was sparring with Lëovar, I could tell he was anticipating my moves with eerie accuracy. It's like their burrows give them abilities similar to those of the Silvesh, a foresight of sorts."

"And every single one of them has one," she noted.

Ten days after the starlings had been sent out, Mio shared an early breakfast with the visitors, then walked with them to the garden's moon gate. "Here I must stop once more," the old farmer said. "And I believe you will leave soon after the deed is done, so I will bid my farewells now and head back home to Asra."

"Here," Alaia said, handing Mio a pharolith lamp. "You've been a good, honest guide. Thank you. Even though you put leeches on me. Sterjall told me."

Mio smiled calmly, bowed with the pharolith in his hands, and took his leave.

The wayfarers entered the garden and met Ulésse by the steps leading to the temple. The carved rocks outside Ommo ust Quaju were covered in flowering wisterias, which rained down blues, purples, and lavenders. The marsupial glyph above the temple's archway was overflowing with orchids that bowed down in welcoming clusters.

"The roots of Quajudrolom grow deep," Hud Ulésse intoned as she led them up the long tunnel. "From deeper still they will soon drink, from the waters of ages that moisten the crust of Noss. And there they will dig their own sepulcher and rest, content with their long lives and the lives they enabled to live on."

She entered the chamber, sat upon the elevated throne, and ordered the lattice to collapse. The whole of Chail Trodesh shook soon after. Birds took to the skies, heralding a new age.

The caravan did not wait for the dome to fully open; they hurried out of Mikkagolm soon after the lattice was collapsed. Ulésse joined them for the first part of the journey, riding a zygomaturus, a beast that looked like a bear with an enormous, upturned nose. Together with Ëalcor, she escorted the caravan down the mountain, across the desert, and through the blue-tinted vines, so that she could study the landscape her tribe would soon have to tread.

They exited the dome forty miles north of where they'd entered. Sunu sent Olo to scout, and it did not take him long until he found the white monolith that marked the mostly buried path Siffo had informed them about.

"This is where Ëalcor and I must take our leave," Ulésse said, picking up samples of sand and dried reeds. "These lands are barren, and they will be hard to bargain with, but we have the right plants to work the soil back to usefulness."

She approached the smilodons, carrying something in her handpaws. "Lummukem, you showed an interest in our medicinal plants. I want you to have this." She held up a tightly sealed glass jar. Inside were the dry, serrated leaves of a black-colored herb. "Velvet knifewood. These leaves will be useful for any cut that requires fast healing, as Alaia's well-healed hand will corroborate. Ground one leaf with animal fat and spread it over the wound. Use it sparingly."

"Our scalp is thankful," Lummukem said.

"And you should also take this," she said, holding up a tiny leather pouch. "It is filled with virgin bloodmoss, which has not been fed blood from any humans yet. Your halberd's reach is long, so the moss could aid you in visualizing strikes if you find a home for it at the bladed end. It will take time, perhaps years for it to become bound to your essence."

Lummukem thanked her again and stowed the jar and pouch away.

"I wish you could come with us," Sterjall said from atop Blu.

Ulésse returned to her own mount and slowly climbed on. "My body can barely stand riding this zygomaturus for fifty miles," she said. "In ten more years, when my age reaches eighteen times six and my time to surrender Quajusilv comes, I hope my successor will be able to travel as widely as you all have, or perhaps more so."

She bowed deeply, and before turning back toward the dome said, "Go now, children of Noss. Hurry back to your ship, onward to Okridrolom. And come back to us once your quest is over. Come back to see these lands restored. Springs eternal guide your roots."

"Essence of one, soul of the many," Sterjall replied, bowing with his arms looped in front of him.

Ulésse rode back through the wall, followed by Ëalcor.

The white monolith cast a sharp shadow upon the intersection of the two roads. The path leading to Lhambor Di stretched for only a hundred strides before it was covered in blue sand. Lummukem sent Olo soaring with a message to inform Siffo of their return, but asked the jay to fly directly over the road—at least over what he could see of it—so that they might know the general direction in which to travel.

Surrounded by an armored wall of forty diprotodons and six procoptodons, joined by nearly a dozen druids versed in the Dance of the Six Seasons, they trotted east, following Olo until he was lost beyond the horizon.

It did not take long until they encountered the first group of Baurami; merchants on their way to the city of Ausentia. Though the merchants wanted to stop the caravan to ask questions, they were too afraid and simply moved off the road, murmuring crude insults in their native tongue. By sundown, the wayfarers had a second encounter, this time with moa riders wearing the colors of Navar Mat. The diprotodons tried to hide Blu and Pichi within the herd, but the moa riders had climbed atop a dune to watch the group pass and clearly saw the smilodons. They pulled on their birds' reins and hurried west at full trot.

"Navar Mat is far, but those birds can run at breakneck speeds," Sterjall warned the druids. "We have to keep our distance."

As much as they wanted to keep going, the smilodons, diprotodons, and procoptodons needed rest. They stopped after midnight a safe distance from the road, finding a gulch of hard sandstone for cover. Sceres was still in Jade, giving them a hard green light to see by.

"They are completely entranced by her," Alaia said to Sterjall, smiling at the marsupials and druids, who were supposed to be sleeping but were instead sitting up and staring at the moon's verdant face. "I wonder what it must feel like for them," she added, "to be so far from home for the first time, to see Sceres and the stars."

"Sterjall, I think this is it!" Kulak called from nearby. Both Sterjall and Alaia perked up.

"This is what?" he asked.

"Come, see. This is the one you have been looking for."

Sterjall scampered over and found Kulak kneeling on the compacted sand. "Your plant," the caracal said, pointing at a plump succulent.

"That's a stoneleaf alright, but it doesn't have the right colors."

"Were the dots on it not meant to be red?"

"Yes, and these are black."

Kulak looked down at the plant, then up at Sterjall, confused. He then looked at the moon. "Your eyes are only seeing by green moonlight. Mine also see by the dim light of the stars." He pulled out a pharolith lamp and opened it. Under the cold light, the pillowy blue succulent glittered with sparkles of red dots, as if coated in a dew of fresh blood.

Sterjall leaned down and exulted, "That's the one! Alaia, come here, look!"

"It looks just like the one we had," Alaia breathed, admiring the beautiful ruby-flecked stoneleaf.

Kulak grinned, then began digging around it.

"No," Sterjall said, tapping his shoulder. "It's fine. I just wanted to find one. She will be better off here, at home."

Olo returned to the caravan at sunrise, bringing with him a brief message from Siffo, which Alaia read aloud:

Ye better hurry. Many a curious visitor from Lhambor Di has come by—our ship was spotted yesterday. We're pretending to only speak Puqua, to try to send them away. Mine crew has careened the hull clean of barnacles, ready for a speedy exit as soon as ye arrive. More trouble: three days ago, we saw Zovarian ships sailing south. Dozens of them. No clue where them are by now. One of our scouts will wait for ye a few miles west of Lhambor Di, to show ye the fastest way back. As soon as ye see the blue towers of the city, look for her on the side of the road.
-C.S.

Alaia folded the parchment. "Do you think we can make it there today?"

"No," Lummukem replied, "our feet have not yet traveled far enough. Tomorrow, if we hurry."

That evening, three Navar Mat riders caught up with them from the west, chasing fast with their moas but keeping a cautious distance.

"Stop!" a thick-boned rider ordered. "In the name of Duchess Hilid Kei and the Duchy of Blue Stone, order your beasts to cease their trampling!"

"Tell the duchess we found the pharoliths, and more!" Alaia teased them.

The soldiers did not find it funny. "Our army follows behind us. We are faster. You cannot outrun us."

"We do not aim to," Lummukem yelled back. "But if you attack, your lives will end."

Ishke'ísuk jumped from their shoulder, hopped across the armored backs of the diprotodons, and turned into a gigantic snake before landing in front of the three moas. The birds jolted backward in terror, dropping their riders, who tumbled down the dunes as they chased their fleeing mounts.

The caravan hid in a ravine to rest once more. Procoptodons kept guard atop a sandstone outcrop, sitting on their heavy tails. The druids performed their dances by moonlight, preparing their bodies. Though no soldiers came to bother them, not one of them could rest well.

Knowing that their destination was nearly at hand, they moved along briskly in the early morning, hoping to make one final rush. The road was crowded with onlookers, merchants, and farmers, all wanting to witness the curious creatures roaming their desert lands. The wedge-shaped towers of Lhambor Di came into view, blue as the sky, rising over an uplifted mesa.

"D'light uf d'kenzir is with ye!" a hooded figure called from the middle of the road.

The caravan halted and picked her up. She was a Puqua scout named Lixméd, who swiftly took a seat on Pichi, behind Lummukem, then pointed to a silty wash that veered off the main road. "*Fjummomurr* is this way," she said. "I'll take ye through d'safest path." She then ran her fingers over Lummukem's scaled shoulders and said, "Ye look deadlier than any uf us imagined ye'd be. But this shell make ye yet deadlier." She handed the dragon a bag; inside was the quaar tail armor they had rescued from the drowned palace at Kruwendrolom. Lummukem tried the armor on. The articulated segments clasped down with satisfying precision. The steel spikes at the tip weighed heavily, eagerly.

As they continued traversing the pathless lands, a cloud of blue dust rose behind them.

"Moas coming!" Sterjall warned. "Keep moving. Do not stop until we get to the ship!"

Twenty riders crested a dune. Then forty. Then too many to count. Some carried swords, others lances. The birds rode in formation to the east of the caravan, easily keeping up with the slower mammals. A horn blew, and the troop spread, moving to encircle the group.

Never slowing, the armored diprotodons formed a circle of their own, protecting Blu and Pichi, with the procoptodons at the outer edges hopping along on their heavy tails and claws. The druids dropped to platforms on the sides of the diprotodons' armored saddles, spying upon the enemy from behind cover. Alaia put her trusty quaar helm on, then readied her blowgun.

"Strike as soon as they enter your range," Lummukem told her and Kulak.

The enemy approached confidently, underestimating the speed and might of the docile-faced marsupials. The circle of moas tightened, but as they tried to push through, the procoptodons attacked in unison, swiping their tails and savagely kicking with their single-toed feet. Brown feathers exploded over blue sand. Bodies were flung, slamming into other soldiers, breaking the tight formation.

The procoptodons were fierce, but they could not watch over the entire perimeter. Diprotodons attacked as well, more sluggishly but with equal strength. Whenever an enemy was within range, the druids would appear from behind their armored saddles in a flowing dance, launching their rope javelins with deadly accuracy to snag the moas' legs, then pulling hard to knock them down.

"To your left!" a druid warned.

Three moa riders had snuck through the perimeter by jumping over the backs of the diprotodons as if they were stepping stones. Lummukem's halberd took care of the first attacker, while Alaia's and Kulak's darts paralyzed the other two. The diprotodons stomped on the bodies and tightened their formation once more.

A new troop arrived and took up positions around the perimeter. "Take cover!" Sterjall called. "Archers!"

The assailants released their arrows upon the caravan, and although most of the giant wombats deflected the impacts with their bone armor, some were struck on their legs and tripped, tumbling on the dunes.

"D'ship is right ahead!" Lixméd called out. "Keep un high ground!"

The attacks came from all directions at once. Despite their strength, the best they could do was hide behind the armored giants and blow darts whenever the moas were exposed. The edge of a cliff dropped off ahead of them; beyond it they could see the crow's nest of *Fjummomurr*. To their left was an equally high drop into the sea. The only path to the ship was to the right, where the moas quickly assembled.

They stopped at the precipice and gazed down at the moored ship.

"Siffo!" Sterjall cried out. "We need your help!" But the ship was empty; not a soul moved on deck.

Their path was blocked. A familiar face came forward, riding on a silver-armored moa.

"We now know what you carry, Luras Varum," Commander Vaalag proclaimed. "Or should I call you Lago Vaari of Withervale?"

She held a sword and shield at the ready.

"The northern state has been searching for you, for the treasures you stole. The east is at war with a threat we cannot fight alone. But now we know of the one way to preserve our great kingdom of blue sands. These masks will not fall into the hands of the Zovarian Union. They will become the property of the Kingdom of Bauram. Hand them to us now, and we might spare your—"

Screams exploded behind Vaalag. The Puqua sailors had been waiting in hiding farther down the cove, and they were now charging at the enemy's rear with their axes and shields.

"Now, attack!" Sterjall commanded. Blu and Pichi rushed forward, with two procoptodons at their sides; the giant kangaroos easily hopped over the formations to attack them from behind. Diprotodons followed like trampling siege towers, slamming with mighty force before the moas could deliver their powerful kicks. The Ji druids hopped down from their armored saddles, piercing their javelins through armor and bone, tangling dozens of moa legs in single twirls of their long ropes. Blu and Pichi slashed at the uniforms of blue, black, and white. Once inside their formation, Ishke'ísuk charged in his alligator form, snapping at the legs of the flightless birds.

Lummukem focused for a breath, planning their strikes. With unwavering confidence, they dismounted Pichi in a thrusting leap using the Soaring Skylark, then spun their halberd savagely in a Griffon's Whirl, continuing their strike by whipping their quaar-armored tail; the spikes at the tip kept the momentum of their swings and slammed against the enemies' feet with shattering force. A Cascading Palm, a Nightfall's Heartbeat, an Echo of the Snowflake—each attack was calculated, flowing after the others in an unstoppable maelstrom.

The moa riders were directed to focus entirely on Sterjall and Kulak, trying to drive them away. Sterjall tried to slash with Leif using the techniques he'd learned from Sunu-Lummukem, but his reach was too short, so instead he focused on parrying attacks to protect Blu's sides. While Kulak readied a dart in his blowgun, Vaalag kicked at the ribs of her moa and made the bird jump over them while she slashed downward toward the caracal. Sterjall tried to deflect with a Fluke Guard, but the fast strike overpowered him—Vaalag's sword sliced into Kulak, right across the old injury Marshal Thurann Embercut had once left in his shoulder.

Kulak clutched at his wound, losing his grip on the saddle, and tumbled over. Sterjall tried to catch him, but got pulled down with him.

Vaalag's bird landed expertly and quickly turned to face them.

Sterjall and Blu circled protectively around Kulak as Vaalag charged once more, her sword arm up and ready to swing.

As the moa lunged, the bird suddenly twisted, pulled to the left by a rope javelin tied to her throat, and to the right by another tied to her legs. Vaalag jumped off the saddle in a powerful twirl just before her mount collapsed.

As Vaalag propelled her sword toward him, Sterjall rolled under her, slicing upward with Leif and severing the tip of Vaalag's boot and part of her toe. The commander landed in a roll, unbothered by the pain, and raced toward the injured caracal. "Kulak!" Sterjall screamed, too far behind to protect him. Vaalag pounced savagely at the prince. Kulak blew a dart at her, but she deflected it with her shield. While in midair, her shoulder abruptly twisted to the side, and her grip on her sword faltered.

She slammed into Kulak with her shield, then looked over her shoulder to find a dark-bladed dagger sticking out of her scapula. She tried to reach for it but was swatted down by a powerful slam from Blu's paws, then her head crunched between his fangs.

With the loss of their commander, the morale of the Navar Mat troops was shattered. Nearly a hundred of them remained alive, but their numbers were quickly dwindling due to the unexpected jumps of the kangaroos, the unceasing trampling of the wombats, the countless teeth of the Nu'irg, the beautifully deadly dance of the druids, and the unrestrained ferocity of the Puqua sailors. They soon retreated to regroup.

Sterjall pushed Vaalag's corpse off Kulak, recovering his hurled dagger from her back, then kneeled next to him. "Are you—"

"Fine. Help the others," Kulak reassured him, getting to his feet and holding on to his bleeding shoulder.

Seven diprotodons were dead, as well as three of the procoptodons and two of the druids. A few more marsupials would not live for much longer. The Silvfröash did their best to alleviate the pain of those who would not survive, then thanked the others for their aid.

"This is where our paths must split," a druid said to the wayfarers. "There is danger ahead for us, but more danger travels with you."

"They will still come after you," Sterjall said. "We can help you get to—"

"No, this is the path we have chosen. Half of us will venture into the desert, to plant the seeds of our future. Half of us will return home with samples of soil, with maps from the scouted terrains. This is but the beginning. Blood will fertilize this land, mixing blue and red. Soon the restoration of these long-ravaged realms shall begin."

The druids mounted the marsupials and took off. The herd moved swiftly, lifting a blue cloud behind them.

CHAPTER TWENTY-EIGHT

TO THE OLD KINGDOM

"Hold still," Sunu said to Aio, applying a mix of animal fat and a single leaf of velvet knifewood over his slashed shoulder. "We are glad to have you hurt, so we can test our new medicine."

"It worked wonders on me," Alaia said, wiggling the bump where her left thumb used to be. Nearly three weeks had passed since her injury, and no pain lingered for her, not even a sense that there was something missing.

Fjummomurr was sailing south, keeping close to the shore. Siffo had kept the ship ready to weigh anchor, and while the wayfarers had been away, his crew had replenished as many provisions as they could muster.

The Puqua crew had been eager to depart, energized by the recent battle. They had lost four sailors upon the blue sand, and so in the blue sand they had been hastily interred. Their two Zovarian prisoners, Alid and Reija, had been released at the shore right before the black-sailed ship steered away.

"Do not overdo it," Aio told Sterjall, noticing he was using Agnargsilv to take his pain away. "I can manage." He tried to lift his arm to look at the wound, but tightening his deltoid shot a sharp pain through the twice-cut muscle. "How does it look?" he asked.

"Like a ghastly gash, honestly," Sterjall said. "Vaalag's sword slashed right over your old scar."

"Old? That was only months ago. At this pace, my body will be shredded before we are done opening domes."

"Don't worry, I think it'll look good once it heals. It's like a cross."

"Like the Sword of Zeiheim on my forehead?" he asked, a bit too cheerfully.

"Sure. Just… bloodier right now."

Sunu wrapped a cloth around Aio's wound and tied it. "Remain Aio until your body absorbs the medicine and your skin turns dry."

After all wounds had been taken care of, Siffo requested his friends join him in his quarters. "Mine crew did a commendable job at a-fixing d'quarter-deck," he said as he led them in. The color of the mended walls and ceiling was a bit off, but other than that, the chamber looked as good as new. The captain spread a new map over the oval table, one focused only on the south-western great islands of Fel Nisos and Fel Baubór, with cities, roads, and water routes neatly penned.

"Where did you get this?" Sterjall asked the captain.

"Lixméd bought it at Lhambor Di. Seems that all d'information our prisoners gave us was correct, unly d'distances were a bit askewed. We're 'bout here now"—he pointed on the map—"and soon we shell reach Aksas Di, where I'm a-guessin' d'Zovarian ships I saw were headed to. After that, there's Dogulvaras, n'then Kizad, d'first city uf d'Republic uf Lerev, past d'lands uf Bauram."

Sterjall studied the map. "There will be no way to secretly reach the Nisos Dome. We will find no deserts to cross unnoticed. We'll have to sail straight into the Republic of Lerev."

"It might be for the best," Alaia said. "Aren't they allies with the Tsing Empire?"

"That's true," Sterjall agreed. "At least that means they might not be on the best of terms with Zovaria or Bauram."

"And they worship the old animal spirits," she added. "They worship Noss themself. Perhaps we'll finally find a non-Miscam ally we can trust."

"My scalp thinks it is our best choice," Aio agreed.

"We think so too," Sunu said.

Sterjall nodded his approval to Siffo.

"Then to d'mighty island uf Nisos we shell sail!" Siffo declared. He exited his quarters and vociferously announced, "To Nisos! South and east let them sails billow!" He then sang yet louder, his crew responding fervently:

Grind yer tusks n'stow that tail.   *—Weigh!*

> *Light-ho d'kenzir stone.*

Rig a jig d'blackened sail.   *—Weigh!*

> *Bright-glow as cold as bone.*

> *Weigh-a-weigh d'kenzir stone,*
> *D'fjords await, d'winds are blown,*
> *D'Puqua sailors leeward bound,   —Hey!*
> *Weigh-a-weigh d'kenzir stone.*

Part Four
Lands Beyond the Mountains

Chapter Twenty-Nine

Down Minnelvad

"That's all you are carrying?" Kitjári asked Banook as she watched him sling a regular-sized travel backpack over his shoulder, which looked diminutive on him. The only other item he carried was the senstregalv glaive, which he used as a walking stick, with the green-scaled leather scabbard concealing the overly sharp, pointy bits.

"We are not climbing down icy crevasses this time," he answered. "The less gear, the better. Nalaníri has all we need for cooking—perhaps too much—and all I need for myself is the bare minimum."

"Ye'll be a-thanking me later," Nalaníri said, hauling her gear. "Ye n'Probo both."

Banook smiled at her, then looked around and whistled. Bear came trotting up to him.

"You know how to take care of yourself now, dear Bear. If you see Sabikh or Frud, feel free to spend time with them, but I shall not ask them to bring food for you any longer, you mighty hunter you."

Bear whined as Banook rubbed his neck.

"And please behave this time. Bring no more friends through the dog door. As its name implies, it is meant just for dogs. Those furtive foxes still owe me a set of embroidered pillows."

Safîs interpreted the words quite carefully for Bear.

Bear had become much smarter since meeting Safîs, having found a bridge with which to communicate with Banook and understand more about what the strange humans felt, and why they acted so weird. He was still a careless mutt, however, and because he could only get his friends in trouble during this covert mission, they all agreed it would be safer for everyone if Bear stayed at the cabin. Alone.

Bear became restless and twirled around. He barked, then jumped into Banook's arms.

"You are a good boy, the goodest boy. You will be fine. I'll miss you too."

Kitjári approached to pet the dog and kissed his wet nose. "Moon lights, silly dog. Please stay out of trouble. Don't burn the cabin."

Banook placed him on the cold ground.

Bear stayed put as his friends walked away.

Safís stopped for a moment, looked back, and saw Bear bark in the distance. She gave him a stern look, waited until Bear obediently sat down, then continued on her way.

"Slow those eager balls down, Probo!" Banook cried out. "There's no hurry. We'll get to the falls by tomorrow."

It was partly cloudy that afternoon, with a chill wind blowing from the west, though not one cold enough to worry them. Probo knew the way to Minnelvad; he had been there many times before, and was eager to show the majestic Firefalls to Nalaníri.

They hiked southwest through a valley of white-capped evergreens, following an icy creek. Banook pointed to a trio of bulky grizzly bears fishing on the opposite side of the creek. "The males usually don't begin their hibernation till mid-Hoartide, so there would normally be many more of them in this valley, yet I only see these three. I think you've done a good job, Kitjári—most of my friends are on the move."

Banook stopped to mindspeak with the grizzlies. Kitjári was able to follow their conversation, relishing in the peculiar sensation of the multiple 'voices' being perceived as having the same loudness, even though Banook was next to her, while the grizzlies were far away on the opposite shore. The bears greeted the Urnaadifröa and explained that though most of their kind had recently left, they'd chosen to remain in this valley to keep check on the non-ursid populations.

"Nalaníri told me you learned to mindspeak while in your feral form," Banook said as they continued their walk. "A smart way to understand how we communicate. I met one Urnaadifröa who was able to mindspeak to us as soon as he took his half-form, but most take months to learn."

"Lago still hasn't figured it out," Kitjári replied. "At least he hadn't by the time we split up. Maybe Aio will be smart enough to recommend the same thing Nalaníri recommended to me, and that'll help him out. He's a good kid, too. Aio, I mean, even if he's no more than a mischievous princeling."

Banook smiled. "I do hope this *princeling* teaches my cub a thing or two. I'm sure Lago will be delighted to have a conversation with Bear the next time they see each other. And I'm happy *I* won't be able to understand it—whatever goes through that dog's head is nothing I want to know about."

They didn't talk much for the rest of the walk, but focused on savoring the mountainscape, which sparkled with a pristine beauty only granite and snow could offer. They listened to their breaths, to the sound of their crunching feet in the snow.

Kitjári had lagged behind the others, having stopped by an icy creek to collect purple prickleberries, which were plentiful at the end of Umbra. She caught up to them and, without saying a word, handed a cluster of berries to Nalaníri, trying to guess at what she was thinking about.

«You seem to be getting along just fine,» Banook mindspoke.

She looked up and saw Banook wink at her. For a moment she was afraid that Banook had been reading her thoughts. But he couldn't, not without her willingly choosing to communicate her feelings to him.

«It's easier this way, somehow,» she told him. Although she only transferred the core meanings behind her ideas instead of the individual words and syntax, the order of those thoughts seemed more sentence-like when speaking with Banook than with other ursids. «It's more comfortable when we don't have to say anything to each other, when she doesn't see me babbling incoherently as I try to form sentences. I feel no pressure to be anything other than myself.»

«That's how you should feel with a true friend, at all times,» Banook replied. «I have not had a good chance to talk with Nalaníri yet. I still don't know what goes on in that boarish mind of hers. If you see me alone with her in the next few days, give us some space.»

Kitjári huffed. «Thank you, Banook. I will.»

The following afternoon, they arrived at a cluster of hot pools tucked between the twin peaks that framed the Firefalls, the same pools that Banook and Jiara had once stopped at while on their way to Da'áju, together with Ockam, Lago, and Alaia. The valley that the falls had carved was partially obscured by the steam, but they could still discern part of the enormous bowl of rock, travertine terraces, and colorful vents at the bottom.

All except for Safís enjoyed the warm pools. Her fur kept her warm, and her pride kept her from indulging in displays of immaturity. Despite the long journey, somehow her white fur remained as pristine as the freshest snow.

Banook was the last to leave the pool, just as Sunnokh snuck his brightness behind the Snoring Mountain. He shook the water off, wrung out his beard, and let the cold breeze dry his ample nakedness.

"Now that we've had our fun," he said, "I can show you to a pleasant camping spot behind the eastern peak. You should both keep your Silvesh hidden from this point on—Safís tells me she found tracks left by human visitors, which is unusual this late in the season, and could mean trouble. There might even be strangers with spyglasses that can see you when you can't see them. It would be prudent to hide anything decorated with pharoliths, and to wrap your fancy quaar bow."

Jiara stowed her mask away and pulled out a simple cover that wrapped over the grip and limbs of Dunokh Sull; she'd sewn it herself while at the cabin, making sure it could be quickly pulled down in one motion.

Nalaníri placed her glowing nosering in one of her vest's many pockets, made sure the scabbard around her axe was properly covering all the pharoliths, then stood there feeling discomposed.

"And Nagrasilv as well," Banook gently reminded her.

She shifted quickly, as if ripping off a painful scab, then shoved the mask in her bag.

Banook smiled warmly at Prikka, seeing her black-and-pink skin for the first time. "I was not aware that your human form was as beautifully spotted as your suid one," he said. "Lovely patterns, like inks melting upon a rosy sunset."

Prikka flashed a weak smile and turned away.

The snow had piled heavier overnight, but it stopped falling by the time they were back on their feet. The snowfall had covered the trail of cairns, but Banook knew the invisible path by heart.

"This is where Lago fell off," Jiara remarked to Prikka, "when Banook came to his rescue. Well, to *our* rescue, really—he saved us all from the mist-draft. It's been over a year already, but it feels like just yesterday."

They helped each other down the rock, careful of the steep drop below them. Banook lowered himself last; as his heavy boots landed, he kicked off a small avalanche that fell vertically at first, then sloped sideways and continued toward the toxic vents they were not planning on visiting this time around.

Sunnokh's warm touch rarely reached into these lands during Umbra or Winter, so despite them traveling toward lower elevations, the snow piled thicker. Banook moved ahead of them, carving a wide path for all except Safís, who chose her own path to the side and often waited ahead of them atop pointed rocks, fur blowing in the wind.

"She tries too hard to look magnificent," Jiara commented with some amusement.

"Oh, she doesn't need to try," Banook said. "I don't think she can help herself."

They were about to turn onto the next switchback when Safís jumped on a boulder and growled, looking back up the mountain.

"Avalanche!" Jiara screamed. "Move behind the rocks!"

Soft snowballs and flurries soon reached them, but put them in no real danger. The small avalanche coated them in weightless powder, which they promptly shook off. Safís remained atop her rock, regal and unfazed. She growled once more, staring at the accumulation of snow. Then she whined, jumped into the snowpack, and began digging.

"Where's Probo?" Prikka asked.

She heard a grunt, and Probo approached from behind her.

"Then what's she a-digging fur?"

Safís worked her claws until they heard another whine, followed by a *rooff,* and then a *rrowff!*

"Bear!" Banook yelled. "You rotten, silly mutt, we told you to—"

Bear jumped into Banook's arms. He was shivering cold, clumps of snow stuck to his brown and patchy-white fur, like heat-draining ticks.

Banook shook his head. "Just what are we going to do with you now, huh, boy?"

Bear licked Banook's lips, then placed his frigid nose at the bend of his elbow, closing his eyes.

"You poor boy," Jiara said. She stepped closer to pet him and remove the icy clumps from his fur. "We can't go back to the cabin now. Can Safís tell him to go back? It's not too far a climb yet."

Banook and Safís stared at each other for a moment. Banook nodded.

"Safís says Bear understood the command, but did not want to stay there alone like last time. He doesn't care if he's cold, or tired, or if he dies along the way. He wants to be with us."

"Take d'wretched pup," Prikka said. "What difference is one mour freak in our party gonna make? Safís can take care uf Bear." Safís growled and squinted her yellow eyes at the mention of her name and Bear's in the same sentence.

Banook placed Bear on the ground. "Okay, boy, if you come with us, you will have to learn to behave. No unnecessary barking, no sneaking to steal food from people you don't know, no jumping into boiling hot springs—are you getting this?" He looked to Safís, who was interpreting everything carefully. "And you will do as we tell you, when we tell you, and you will fend for yourself when possible. Do we have a deal?"

Bear wagged his tail between his legs while licking at Banook's boots.

"Safís says he understands, and he will do his best to behave."

"Well, I guess we are stuck with him," Jiara said, then began to walk. "Let's go. Bear, you better keep up."

Bear followed and barked with excitement.

Banook pointed a large finger at the mutt. "Hey! What did we just tell you?"

Bear whined and retorted with puppy eyes.

"Come here," Banook said, picking him up. "It's alright, you will learn. You can only do your best. I'll carry you until you warm up."

CHAPTER THIRTY

THE SECRET OVERLOOK

A few hundred feet down from where Bear had avalanched down to them, while still cradled in Banook's arms, the mutt began to growl.

"What's wrong, pup?"

Rrwouf… Bear lightly barked.

"He remembers!" Jiara exclaimed. "See that blue pool over there? That is where Lago boiled his leg. Whose fault that was, we'll never know." She glared at the dog.

"Is that why d'wulfy's left leg looks like a half-plucked chicken?" Prikka asked.

"I think of it more as a mangy coyote. His leg cracked through the ice right over there, when he rushed to save this lovely dog from jumping into the boiling pool." She turned to Bear. "Have you learned your lesson?"

Rwourrwff… Bear said noncommittally.

Not much later, they found the beginnings of the travertine terraces. The mineralized steps were obscured by a sometimes hot, sometimes icy mist blowing from the roaring falls, which led the wayfarers down petroglyph-covered walls until they reached the deafening bowl at the bottom, where the falls emptied their steaming anger into myriad pools of all conceivable colors.

They followed a sketchy path between scalding pools and bubbling mud until they reached a safe grotto tucked into the wall of the enormous rock bowl. It was loud no matter how far from the falls they were, as the circular walls reflected the sound. They leaned their backs against the crystal-covered walls and looked up at the thundering mountain.

Jiara noticed anxiety in the eyes of Prikka, who kept looking down at Probo, and then up at the falls. "What's wrong?" she asked.

"I… m'dear, this is harder un me than I expected." Prikka furrowed her black-and-pink brow. "Probo's a-trying t'talk to me, but I can't understand him without Nagrasilv. I'm too plain-skinned, this is not natural fur me. I can't stand being in this skin fur so long."

Banook put a hand on her shoulder. "It's alright if you need to wear it for a bit. I'll keep my eyes downstream in case anyone approaches. But as soon as we are back on the move, or resting, I'll need you to be strong and stay in this other beautiful form of yours."

"Thank ye, Banook," Prikka replied. She hurriedly retrieved Nagrasilv from her bag, put it on, and shapeshifted mid-sigh.

"I'm sorry, m'boy," Nalaníri said, squatting down to rub noses with Probo. "I'm a terrible listener when I'm not fully mineself."

"What did he want to tell you?" Jiara asked, watching as Nalaníri listened to Probo's ramblings.

"He says d'falls are smaller than them used t'be."

"That is true!" Banook agreed. "Though the travertine terraces were not here back in his time, and I think they make for a fair trade—magnificent power for splendorous beauty."

"All this steam is making everything wet," Jiara said. "Let's find a dry place to camp for the night."

"Jis' a moment longer," Nalaníri said, rubbing her hairy arms. "Let me savor this. I missed it."

An opaque fog fell over them that evening. Probo had wanted to show Prikka the beauty of the Firefalls glowing at night, but even from their not-too-distant camp, there was no way to see anything.

When morning came, the fog had not vanished. With no wind other than the one generated at the base of the falls, the moisture had condensed into tendrils of brittle hoarfrost, turning dry grasses and pine needles into blossoming dandelions. They trudged slowly down their obscured path, as even the rocky surfaces that had not been snowed upon were entirely covered by the fuzzy crystals. By late afternoon, the cold winds had returned, clearing the fog and making the falls visible again upriver. Below them, the beginnings of the Stiss Minn snaked through a canyon of rock and boiling water.

"I will show you my favorite spot," Banook said. "It's not easy to find, but there is a comfortable place to rest there, and it has the best view of the falls."

He led them away from any semblance of a path, then across a natural bridge of stone that took them to the western side of the hot river. They climbed up again and reached an elevated viewpoint cradled in a perfect nook that looked northwest toward the falls. The mossy nook was not big enough to pitch a tent in, and was a bit too exposed to the elements, but its rock-carved bench was perfect for resting and taking in the views. From there, the steaming river curved around rainbow pools and headed straight toward the imposing falls. Two fang-like peaks rose on either side of the falls, sharply framing its steam.

"Sunnokh will soon hide behind the Snoring Mountain," Banook noted. "The best spot to camp and make a fire is just behind that hill."

They dropped their gear and settled within a garden of boulders topped by thick branches from ancient maples. The snow had not reached the ground in this protected pocket, and there was enough room to spread out and make a sizable fire.

Probo had wandered off with Safís, showing her vantage points humans would have a hard time climbing to. Banook noticed the sudden quiet, and conspicuously requested, "Jiara, would you mind finding us something fresh to eat while Prikka and I gather wood for a fire?"

Jiara understood.

"I'll do my best," she said, "but since I'm not using Urnaadisilv, it's better if I have a professional assisting me. Bear! Come on, boy, show me where those critters are hiding."

Bear barked and strutted over to her.

Jiara followed the leafless maple forest until it transitioned into a land of dark-green hemlocks. She removed the cloth cover from Dunokh Sull and tiptoed her way around rocks and trees, following mountain goat tracks. Bear prowled nearby, but rather than getting overexcited when he picked up a scent, he stood still, analyzed it, weighed the multiple possibilities, then took a decisive course of action. He caught himself a mouse rather quickly, although it had been dead already.

Jiara took her time, hoping to give Banook a chance to talk privately with Prikka.

It felt strange to hunt without Urnaadisilv. Jiara had the skills, but she had gotten used to using the Silv to take some of the pain from her prey into herself, easing them into death without as much guilt, in the way she had learned from the Laatu. She could not use that recourse now, but she did have her mighty bow, so rather than taking an easy shot, she only loosed an arrow when she was certain the senstregalv tip would impact directly into the target's brain for an immediate, painless death.

Jiara dragged a freshly killed mountain goat to the camp, with Bear leading the way. It was already quite dark out. When she arrived, Banook and Prikka were sitting by the fire, still chatting. Prikka slapped Banook's thigh to alert him.

"A successful hunt, I see," the Nu'irg said. "I will help you skin it. Prikka, get the rest ready. I know you'll surprise us again with another wonderful recipe."

Jiara took the goat away from the camp to skin it, and Banook followed.

As they worked, Banook looked back to make sure Prikka was busy setting up her cooking gear. "I had an interesting conversation with your spotted friend," he whispered. "She still bewilders and provokes me, but I feel as if I understand her better now. I have some things I need to tell you, but it will take some time to fully explain them, and I'm afraid we won't get a good chance to—"

"Are ye going t'bring me that goat or shell I grill Bear in its stead?"

"Almost done!" Jiara yelled back.

"Like I was saying…" Banook continued. "But I have a plan. She's a heavy sleeper. A while after we go to bed, I'll get up and walk down to the falls overlook. I'll be quiet as a snowflake's kiss, but don't follow right behind me. Wait for a few moments, make sure she doesn't stir, then come down to meet me. There we will be able to talk in private."

"Shell I chop uff his head first or shell—"

"We are coming!" Banook belted out.

Jiara could not sleep. She was too curious about what Banook had discovered. Their bedrolls were far apart, having been strategically rearranged by Banook to help them when they needed to sneak away quietly. He had set his sleeping spot between the two of them, and there was a large boulder blocking the view as well, so that Jiara and Prikka could not easily see each other.

The fire was dying. Sceres was a green crescent headed west, soon to be lost behind the mountains in her search for Sunnokh. Jiara looked up at the Jade moon passing behind the branches of the old maples. She felt a shadow pass near her and saw Banook leaving the camp—she had not even heard him get up; he had been perfectly silent. His large silhouette tiptoed away into the green-tinted darkness.

Jiara waited for a long moment, then turned to her side and looked toward Prikka's bedroll but could not see much past the boulder; only part of a lump covered by blankets. Not a stir. She pushed her own blanket away, grabbed her cloak, and snuck away from the camp.

She put her cloak on and headed toward the overlook. She could not avoid her feet crunching as she approached the viewpoint's mossy nook, as there was fresh snow and ice on the trail. But she was not concerned—their camp was far enough away already. As she walked down the boulders and turned the corner into the nook, she heard a voice.

"Well, it took ye a while. I've been freezing mine arse uff while—"

"Prikka?"

"Jiara? What are ye doing out here?"

"I was. I j-just wanted, er…" Jiara froze. "I wanted t–to see the falls at night."

"Same, same as me. Truly, jis' beautiful," Prikka replied with a disquieted look. "Jis' like Probo described t'me."

She had been sitting on the nook's mossy bench, leaning back to take in the views. Now she sat up straight.

Jiara looked down the drop and let the steaming waters drag her eyes to the falls. The Firefalls were glowing, red as embers. The steam rose from the distant cauldron as if from the nostrils of a slumberous dragon. Much farther up, the steaming clouds were tinted green by the light of Sceres.

"This is a much better view than when I first saw these falls," Jiara said. "Muh-mind if I join you?"

Prikka scooted over.

"How are you feeling?" Jiara asked. "I mean, about not wearing Nagrasilv all day again."

"It doesn't bother me while I sleep, but it's hard throughout d'day, n'in moments like this. I could've felt ye a-coming, normally. I'm used t'seeing what's around me."

"When I showed up, you said, 'It took ye a while,' as if you were waiting for me?"

"Oh, no, not ye. I thought Banook was fullowing behind me."

"And why were you meeting Banook here in the middle of the night?"

Prikka turned her face away. "Jis'… t'look at d'falls. He said them are prettier at night. Nothing t'worry about." She paused and stared at the falls once more, but her eyes were unfocused.

This is too strange, Jiara thought. *Why is she here? That asshole of a bear!*

She looked at Prikka's bright, bulbous nose. "Hey, you shouldn't be wearing that."

"Oh! I furgot." She dropped the glowing nosering into a pocket. "I'm not used t'this, I put it un without thinking. Being without Nagrasilv is excruciating, like I'm a-hiding a part uf mineself. B-but… But ye not having Urnaadisilv has helped, in a way."

"Huh?" Jiara raised her brows.

"Because that way ye can't feel mine shame. It helps. It's easier t'talk to ye when I don't have t'hide."

Jiara felt entirely uncomfortable now, puzzled by the entire situation. "I think… This is all wrong," she muttered, still uncertain of what was happening.

"What d'ye mean?"

She nervously shook her head. "This is not what I wanted. I thought he would talk to you and help me understand, but this… I… Banook told me to meet him here, too. I saw him leave the camp, and I saw you still under your covers, but you made it here before me somehow."

"He told me t'put mine backpack under d'blanket, so it looked like I was still asleep. Told me t'leave before him. I wasn't expecting ye here either."

"Wait a moment… That trickster old bear. What did you two talk about today while I was gone?"

"I… I don't know how t'explain. I don't want ye upset at me."

"Just tell me!" Jiara demanded, then let out a long breath. "Sorry. I'm… just a bit bothered by all this. Will you tell me? Please?"

Prikka looked away. "'Tis what I feared. Yer angry at me. I asked him t'find out how ye felt about me. Because I always seem t'be making ye uncomfortable." She began to mumble nearly unintelligibly, faster with each new syllable. "Like d'time at d'Emen Ruins, I gave ye all these clues n'it unly seemed t'make ye feel nervous, n'ye tucked yer threads away, n'ye kept away frum me. N'I'm sorry, I shell not've done that without knowing if there was a chance 'tween us first. I see ye are fine with Lago n'Aio being together, but I was wrong in hoping ye'd be like 'em. I know ye don't like me that way, n'that's fine, but perhaps we can still be friends even if—"

Jiara kissed Prikka's cheek, then moved away, terrified of her own boldness.

Prikka glanced at her from the corner of one eye, clearly baffled.

"It's all my fault," Jiara said, shaking her head. "I meant to do that while we were at the hot springs."

"Was that…? I'm so confused."

"I'm such a fool."

"Do ye feel d'same? Why did ye not tell me?"

"Because I'm a coward. With the Silv on, I entirely misread you and thought I was scaring *you* off. Have you felt this way about me as well?"

"Since I first fell into yer arms frum that hoodoo, m'dear."

Prikka wanted to reach for Jiara's hands, but her nervousness betrayed her. Jiara noticed, feeling the hand hovering near her thigh. She took it and entwined their fingers. Prikka smiled awkwardly and looked away, feeling a mixture of joy, shame, and fear.

"What's the matter?" Jiara asked, leaning in to try to understand her expressions.

Prikka did not answer but turned back to face Jiara and closed her eyes. She leaned forward in fearful yearning, lips lightly parted.

Jiara could not understand what was going on in her friend's mind, but she could hold herself back no longer. She leaned in and kissed her.

The green moonlight made the moss around them sparkle.

They held their lips together nearly motionlessly until it became awkward again. They both pulled back with a chuckle.

"I was a coward too…" Prikka admitted. "That was all I was a-looking fur. N'I thought I had ruined it all. N'ye don't mind I'm a boar? Most times, I mean."

"As long as you don't mind me as a bear. I always thought that—"

"Could ye kiss me again?" Prikka nearly pleaded. Jiara did, this time with fervor, but only for a short burst until she decided to hold back, not wanting to push things too far and scare her again.

Prikka shivered.

"You are freezing," Jiara said, pulling away for a moment.

"I didn't expect it t'get so cold."

Jiara stretched her cloak over Prikka's shoulders. "All those awkward moments," she reflected, laughing a bit. "All those clumsy things I did. I guess I was… I was just too scared. And what an opportunity I fucked up—those hot springs would've been the perfect place for a first kiss." She looked at the Firefalls. "This view is not so bad, however."

"But our first kiss was not t'night, m'dear, or have ye furgotten?"

"Forgotten what?"

"D'day ye changed into yer feral form t'talk to d'kiuons. When ye came back t'me n'I squatted down, ye licked mine snout all over. 'Twas a bit sloppy fur a first kiss, but I enjoyed it."

"Oh, by Noss, how embarrassing." Jiara turned away to hide her shamefaced smile. "I was not in control of myself. I am sorry."

"Ye certainly weren't."

Prikka remembered how after that moment, Kitjári—in her feral bear form—had tried to sniff between her legs, as if it was the most natural thing for her to do in that form. She had become flustered and quickly asked Kitjári to shapeshift back. The thoughts suddenly rushing to her head mortified her. She shook them off and stood. "It is quite cold out here. N'we need sleep fur d'long road ahead. Would ye stay close t'me t'night?"

CHAPTER THIRTY-ONE

RETURN TO BRIMSTOWNE

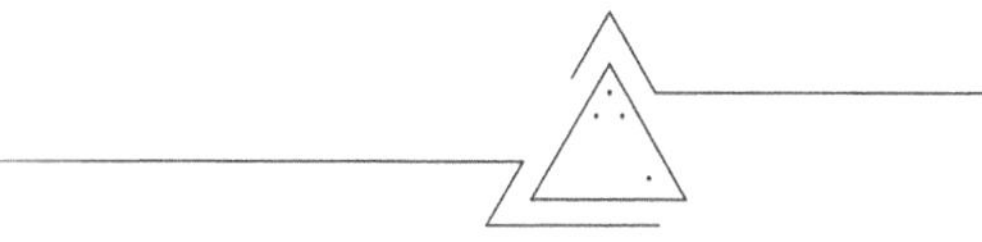

"No, I don't care if your deceitful trick worked," Jiara said to Banook as they waited for Prikka to finish cooking breakfast. "It wasn't right, even if you were right!" She raised her voice to emphasize her point, wanting to win the argument, but clearly unable to be mad.

Banook laughed. "Things worked out fine. You two came to me with the same preoccupation. You both wanted me to intervene. I merely took care of both cases at the same time."

"Let him be, m'dear, he's done us a good deed." Prikka served Banook a good portion of grilled catfish, which the big man had caught from a nearby creek before the others awoke. She sat next to Jiara, sharing a plate as she added, "I wouldn't have had d'courage t'say anything else mineself. I'm jis' happy we have each uther this way now."

After breaking camp, they took one last look at the Firefalls, then headed down the cairn path again. As they crunched through the melting snow, Jiara held up her hand, then squatted. "Only two people," she said, inspecting a set of boot prints. "They are fresh. Banook, would you mind telling Safis and Probo to shift into something more... domestic-looking? It might strike some people as odd to see travelers walking around with a wolf and a javelina."

Banook convinced Probo, who shapeshifted into a small species of domestic pig, though not without complaining about his lack of fur. Safis refused to comply with the request. "She says she'll remain white as snow," Banook explained, "hiding from any eyes until there's no other recourse."

Safis hopped away and disappeared into the snow, while Probo walked alongside Bear. Past a rocky gully, the ground was bare and the boot prints disappeared.

"I see them," Jiara murmured. Two hikers were ahead of them, pulling their camp down. A married couple, she guessed. "We should greet them as we pass, otherwise we'll seem too suspicious." They approached slowly, and Jiara purposely made her boots crunch on fallen branches so as not to surprise the couple.

"Moon lights," she called.

"Stars guide," the man replied, a bit startled, but then quickly relaxing.

"Beautiful views up there, ain't there?" the woman said.

"Unsurpassed in majesty and might," Banook agreed.

"We hiked all the way up the falls," the man said. "Gorgeous hot springs at the top. But you should know that. You are that Banook fella, aren't ya? I've seen you in town from time to time. Hard to miss. Don't you live far up in the mountains?"

"That's me, and that I do."

"You headed to Brimstowne?" the woman inquired.

"Not many more places we could be headed to along this path," Banook answered breezily. "Always good to find provisions in town."

"Not *always* good," she said. "If there was ever a time when it's not good, that time is now. Consider yourself warned, big man, Brimstowne is *swarming* with Negian soldiers. They are loud, obnoxious, and buy off all the supplies we normally need to get ready for Winter. After that stampede of mad bears passing through town, it was just too much for us. We decided to take a hike into the mountains to escape the racket."

"That is most unfortunate, but good to know," Banook said. "What are so many Negians doing in the colony?"

"A whole battalion evacuated the Anglass Dome recently," the woman explained. "The vines seem to be changing, or so we hear. The Negians fear the dome will fall on them. It's a mess, this whole pointless war."

"Who's in control of the soldiers?" Jiara asked, confused as to how soldiers could be let loose in the middle of a war.

"Who knows? All their generals went south, other than General Edmar Helm, who is holding tight to Withervale. Some Negians still obey the officers who stayed in the dome, hauling the wares they pillage back to Hestfell, but others felt left behind. With all the looting they've been doing, some are taking their chances and splurging in our town."

They thanked the hikers for the information and the warning, then continued downriver, leaving the conifer forests and reaching the poplars and birches of the lower elevations. The following afternoon, they made it to Geo Springs, the blue pools near the Sulphur Pit mines.

"Oy, Jilpi!" Banook called from far away, spotting a skeletal figure dehydrating in the sun.

"You know him, too?" Jiara asked. "We met him when we came up this way. He showed us how to follow the cairns."

"I'm not surprised," Banook said. "He's always around the hot springs, particularly once it gets cold. I swear he's older than I am."

"Lorr Banook!" Jilpi's cracked voice replied. "What may you be doing in town this late in the season? Umbra's last few days are at hand."

Banook approached while kicking off his boots, leaned his glaive on a rock, then sat at the edge of a pool, dangling his bare feet into the hot water. "Same old, old friend. I'm in need of a few tools for my workshop and did not want to wait until the harshest snows settled."

Jilpi gazed at Probo. "And you brought a pig to trade? Odd choice. Or is he a snack for the road?"

Probo did not understand human language as a human could, but he was still keen enough to understand the word *snack* and the tone of Jilpi's voice. He jumped into the blue pool and sent a wave of hot water toward the old man. Jilpi cackled as he shook the water off, charmed by the pig's reaction. Banook told Probo to stop, but Probo ignored him and happily splashed about.

Banook looked back to Jilpi and said, "Say, Jilpi… Folk we met on the road told us the town is infested by Negian vermin. Is it true?"

"True it is. The scum are everywhere. Is that why you carry such a big weapon with you?" he asked, glancing at Banook's glaive. "I hope you can help us wipe them out. If you'll be spending the night, you should at least have no problem finding a room at the Yeast Cauldron. Most Negians don't want to be seen entering the establishment. Mayhap your usual room is available—no one wants to pay more for that exceedingly large bed."

Jiara stared at Banook; he simply smiled back.

"Young Lurr with the hair of gold, you look familiar," Jilpi said, adding furrows to his leathery brow. "And this silly dog as well. Where are your three other friends?"

"Far away, Jilpi. Thanks for showing us the way up last time. That's where I met this lovely bear of a man, way up at the top of the falls." She hugged Banook from behind.

"You went all the way up? But it was a season of mistdrafts, if my mind properly recollects." Jilpi's mind was sharp and had properly recollected.

"So it was," Jiara agreed, "but we made it. *And* learned our lesson."

"Next time, look in the overhangs of the steaming creek for swallows and swifts," Jilpi recommended. "If you see both, no mistdraft is forthcoming. If the swallows nest early but the swifts streak high in the winds, take cover and take no chances."

Jiara nodded. "We shall do just that, Jilpi, thank you."

Banook got up, dried his feet, and put his boots back on.

"No time for a proper bath?" Jilpi scolded him.

"Not today, old friend. My companions are tired, and we need to find a room before dark."

"Your pig friend is smarter than you," the old man said, watching Probo climb out of the pool and shake his body, sending a spray of water toward all of them.

Jilpi laughed, then tipped his feathered hat. "A pleasure seeing you, Lorr Banook. Stop by for a chat on your way back up the mountain."

"As always!" Banook assured him, then began to walk the trail to town.

"Oh, Banook!" Jilpi yelled after them. "Do be careful. Aside from all the bears passing by lately, there's more you should keep your eyes open for. There's a white wolf following you, hiding in the snow. Beautiful animal, doesn't seem to be hunting. Mayhap just curious."

"We'll keep our eyes peeled, thank you!"

As they crested the ridge behind the pools and got a view of Brimstowne, Banook said, "Safis will not be happy to know she was spotted. Jilpi is very perceptive and shrewd."

"And he seems to know a lot about you," Jiara said. "The Yeast Cauldron? Your *usual* room? Really?"

"Did Lago never mention it to you? It's not only for supplies that I travel to Brimstowne. I have other needs, and there's quite a rowdy crowd ready to meet them just up ahead."

"Is d'Yeast Cauldron a bakehouse?" Prikka asked.

"Something like that," Jiara coyly replied.

"I would love t'try all them have t'offer."

Jiara suppressed a laugh, not bothering to further explain.

They passed by the yellow hole of the Sulphur Pit mines, which were not so busy this late in the year, as the ice made the spiraling ramps too slippery. They continued toward the yellow-roofed and black-walled buildings of

Brimstowne, but before reaching the crowded areas, Banook asked Safís to come closer.

"Dear beauty," he said, mindspeaking as well, "earlier you were spotted by the friendly man at the pools. You need to be more careful now. I know you don't like this, but to fit with this crowd, you will need to look like good old Bear for a while."

Safís growled, then shapeshifted into a white greyhound while she continued growling. Bear barked, hopped playfully over to her, heard the rising tone of her growl, and yipped away.

"And Probo, you could hide in my bag. They won't allow pigs in this establishment. Not of your kind, that is."

Probo shifted into his pygmy hog form. Prikka hoisted him up and tucked him inside Banook's bag.

It was nearing sunset. The streets were alive with music, drunkenness, and mischief. They followed Silverkeep Road and turned left, bumping shoulders with many a drunken Negian soldier. Jiara felt horribly exposed, keeping her hood tight around her face, yet she knew it was unlikely any of these soldiers would recognize her. They slowed beneath the round sign of the Yeast Cauldron, where Banook opened wide the double doors, inviting them in.

Jiara and Prikka stepped inside.

"Good evening Lurrs. Just the tubs, or looking for rooms?" the allgender receptionist asked, pinky out, holding a wineglass. "Lorr Banook!" they then exclaimed, seeing Banook ducking under the doorway. Banook's enormous glaive hit the lobby's chandelier, rattling down a cloud of dust.

"Sorry about that," Banook said. "Good evening, Lerr Ien. These are friends of mine, traveling together. And these two as well," he added, nodding to Bear and Safís.

"Odd time of year, odd company, odd weapon, and odd to see you with pets," they observed. "Do you want your usual? I believe it's available." Ien shuffled their long fingers through a board of keys, picked one out from the top right corner, and slapped it down on the desk. "If you promise these two will behave, I won't charge you extra. Same goes for the dogs."

"The usual will be perfect for me. But also one more room, for the ladies."

"As you wish. Would you like me to show them around?" Ien asked, handing over another key.

"I can handle that. Thank you, old friend."

"Anytime, Lorr. Enjoy yourselves. And be sure to order dinner before it's all gone. Oh, and if you see any Iesmari men around, they are likely Negian soldiers. I'm sure you've heard. Don't give them any attention. I hear they don't know how to clean up. And they are terrible tippers."

While Safis, Probo, and Bear waited in Banook's room, the rest of them headed down to the baths and ordered food at the bar.

Prikka had never seen an inn of this sort. The dozens of pools were filled with riotous laughter. The steam made it hard to see what was happening in the pools farther in the back, but it sounded fun, whatever it was. She was disappointed to see no bread choices listed on the menu, and thought the food was extremely lackluster once it arrived.

"Dunno what's so special 'bout this curious inn," Prikka complained, sprinkling some spices of her own onto the dish she was forcing herself to eat. A naked woman came to the bar and sat next to her; she didn't even place a towel on the stool before doing so.

"Lovely skin," the woman said. "Never seen pink and black like this before. It's so… exotic." The seductress licked her lips.

Jiara put an arm around Prikka, glared knives at the woman, and watched her leave.

"Them seem so comfortable in them plain skins here," Prikka noted.

"You don't have tubs like these in Nagradrolom?"

"Hot springs we do have, many uf them where I grew up."

Banook had moved farther down the bar to talk to a crowd of mostly men, most of whom were naked. Many were placing hands on his belly.

"What's a-going un there?" Prikka asked. "Shell we go help him?"

"Oh, I think he's doing fine. Look around you. See how most men are with men, and the few women are with women? And how everyone coming out of those back rooms is quite naked?"

Prikka understood now. The portions of her that were pink-skinned blushed. "Ye mean t'say, that woman was… n'them droves are swarming around Banook because them want…" She cowered deeper into her shoulders.

"And quite a crowd he's gathering."

"But… he's enormous."

"In more ways than one." Jiara smiled at a memory. "You sound a bit like Ockam, you know?" She told Prikka the story of her previous stay at the Yeast Cauldron, when she had visited with Ockam, Alaia, and Lago.

Prikka was visibly uncomfortable. The Puqua were not shy about nakedness, but sex was something private for them, and the idea of plain-skins and sex in the same thought was utterly unpalatable.

"But what about him and Lago?" Prikka asked. "Wouldn't d'wulfy get upset?"

"Why should he? He's with Aio."

"Which confuses mine tusks, I don't know how any uf that works. It's jis' too strange."

Banook returned and leaned behind his friends. "Dear ladies, you enjoy yourselves tonight. I know I will. I will see you all in the morning." He dropped a hefty tip on the bar and left for the dark rooms in the back, dragging a substantial following behind him.

The women returned to their room and sat in bed next to each other. Prikka was still shaken.

Jiara held her hand and said, "Sorry if that made you uncomfortable. Sorry there was no good bread."

Prikka punched her shoulder. "It's fine, this journey is all 'bout new experiences."

It was their first time finding privacy since the night they had kissed, and now that they were sitting side by side in their own room, they did not know what to do next.

"Them pools looked filthy," Prikka quietly complained. "Did ye see that man jis'… jis' putting his mouth un that younger lad's thing?"

"It is what it is," Jiara shrugged. "You can't compare it to the pools at the Emen Ruins. I wish I'd had the guts to do more back there. That would've been truly magical."

"It would've. But I'm not getting into them pools below, not even fur ye."

"This room isn't so bad though," Jiara said, then went in for a kiss.

They held their lips together, almost too still, until Jiara's pent-up energy suddenly released. She pushed Prikka down onto the bed and reached for the buttons on her shirt, but Prikka held her arms protectively in front of her.

Jiara kept pushing, reaching toward Prikka's crotch, but paused when she heard her beg, "No, stop."

"Just let yourself—"

"Please. It's too much fur me."

Jiara opened her eyes and saw Prikka's terrified face.

"What's wrong? I thought you wanted this. We finally have a moment alone and—"

"I do. I think. I don't know. I've never… never been with a woman before. I've unly been with one man, n'that was not an experience I want t'recall at this moment, yet it's there in d'back uf mine mind. I don't know what t'do, how it feels, what t'expect."

"Shit, I'm such a fool." Jiara sat back at the edge of the bed. "I wasn't thinking. I just assumed you would've had some other experiences before me."

Prikka sat with her knees lightly touching Jiara's. "I once kissed a girl in d'snout. She was red-furred, beautiful, long ears tufted with a white stripe. Quarter bushpig. It was a dare, kids' games. N'she laughed, n'nothing mour came uf it. What about ye?"

"Oh, we better not get into that. Perhaps I'll tell you at another time. But I won't push you. I mean, I'll try not to. It's tempting, and—"

"I'd like to, I think. But, d'thing is…" Prikka swallowed.

"You can tell me."

"Would ye mind… if… I would be mour comfortable with our fur on."

Jiara understood, although she did not fully understand. She lifted a hand and softly caressed the maze of spotted blacks and pinks on Prikka's cheeks and neck.

"I think you are beautiful both ways," she said. "But we can do whatever you feel comfortable with."

Prikka looked away for a moment and said, "Would ye… would ye show me? Teach me what t'do?"

Without answering, Jiara reached into their bags and took out both masks. She stood in front of Prikka, who sat looking up at her, and placed Nagrasilv on the black-and-pink face, watching Prikka's body change. She then shapeshifted into Kitjári and kissed Nalaníri, slowly pushing her back down onto the bed.

A bit awkwardly, she pulled off Nalaníri's vest. Then, slowly, tentatively, she unbuttoned her lover's shirt. Her wet muzzle slid from the pink snout down to explore Nalaníri's hairy neck, then toward the smoother chest and belly.

"Is this alright?" she asked.

Nalaníri let out a small whimper of acceptance.

Kitjári's muzzle lowered, kissing the boar's twelve nipples, giving equal attention to each one of them while her claws explored lower and unbuckled her belt. Nalaníri was breathless, wide-eyed, staring at the wooden beams on the ceiling.

Kitjári pulled the boar's leather trousers all the way off—her soft-padded crotch was covered in peach fuzz that glittered like dew. The bear stared at the mystery of the opening in front of her. She could nearly see Nalaníri's pulse beating there, expectantly terrified.

"Breathe," Kitjári said soothingly. Nalaníri obeyed, inhaling a jagged, deep breath.

Kitjári grabbed on to the furred legs and rested them over her shoulders. She could savor the heated scents of her then, the fear and eagerness. As her muzzle approached, the very presence of the bear's warm breath made Nalaníri grunt. Her cloven hooves twitched in the air, and her tufted tail curled tighter.

Kitjári paused, dragging the moment out a bit longer, simply breathing next to the plump lips, seeing them turn wet. She looked up and saw the strange beauty spread on top of the bed. Nalaníri was flushed, quivering. The bear could smell all of her.

Kitjári went down on Nalaníri, with her bear tongue probing much deeper than fingers ever could.

Chapter Thirty-Two

ARDOF

A knock at their door. Kitjári and Nalaníri shapeshifted, then quickly hid their masks. Prikka stayed in bed while Jiara put an ear to the door.

"It's just me," Banook's voice called. "You've slept in quite enough."

She unlocked the door and opened it. The hallway was blindingly bright, but Banook's towering silhouette covered up most of the light.

"Moon lights," he said. "Will you join me for second breakfast, or shall I break my fast thrice today?"

"We're coming, just give us a moment," Jiara promised before closing the door.

The three of them left the Yeast Cauldron and picked a table at a cafe across the street that had a convenient window from where they could watch the movements on the road.

Banook sat on two chairs and sipped his coffee. The cup looked insultingly teensy in his hands. "Glad you both seem to be glowing," he slyly remarked, "despite your eyebags."

"And you seem energized," Jiara replied. "And that tiny cup of coffee can't be solely responsible for it."

"Energized now, perhaps, but I was drained to the last drop last night. I thought this spot would be a good one at which to sit and wait, and the waffles aren't half bad. I'm hoping to spot Ardof, my ranger friend. Lerr Ien says they have seen him around in the last couple of days."

"How much are we willing to confide in him?" Jiara asked.

"We'll see. I trust him, and he already knows quite a lot. I think the only thing he does not know yet is that I am a Nu'irg. I never explained to him why I didn't leave with the rest of you."

They ate their waffles and chitchatted, letting time pass. After an hour they ordered more food and drinks so they would not feel guilty for hoarding the table so long. When Sunnokh was at his highest in the sky, Banook's eyes locked onto a figure on the streets. A copper-skinned man with a light-brown beard was striding quickly by. His black cape followed him like an airborne shadow.

"There he goes," Banook said, slapping a handful of Qupi chips on the table. "Let's go." He rushed down the street before the man could elude them. "May the moon light your path, ranger!" he called out.

"May the stars—" The caped man stopped, turned, and lifted his wide-brimmed hat. "Banook! What are you doing in town this late in the year?"

"I can tell you if you have news for me as well."

"News I do have, though only for special ears." He narrowed his eyes as he took in Banook's companions.

"Then follow us. I have a room at the Cauldron where we can speak in private. These here are my friends, Jiara and Prikka."

"Ardof," the ranger greeted from a cautious distance. "Ardof Zaom-Zinemog." His green eyes scanned Jiara's face, her clothing, her posture, her loose ash-blonde hair. "Lurr Jiara Ascura, ex-platoon commander at the Mugwort Forest. A pleasure to meet you."

"You seem to know a bit too much," Jiara said. "Let's get out of here, this is making me uncomfortable."

They hurried up to Banook's room. Before entering, Banook knocked six times in a very particular pattern and waited a few heartbeats. He then unlocked the door and the four of them went inside.

Bear jumped and slobbered all over Banook. Safis—as a white greyhound—sat in a corner, regally ashamed of having to once more take that form. Probo bounded over to greet Prikka, content as a pygmy hog.

"I've never seen you with pets before," Ardof commented as he studied the room, which had an obscenely oversized bed for Banook to sit on and enough chairs for the rest. After some light banter, Banook got to the point.

"We need to know about the Negian movements around the Anglass and Lequa Domes. Around them, and within them."

"What on Noss's name are you scheming? I know you and your friends were after the masks, but there are no masks left in those domes. You should know that. Where is Lago now, by the way? Or should I say, *Luras*?"

"We aren't here to talk about Lago," Jiara barked.

Ardof released an indifferent half-chuckle. "I hate the Negians as much as anyone else, but I need a reason to divulge such sensitive information."

"This is a matter of more urgency than trading information," Banook said. "The health of Noss is at stake."

"Is this about the domes growing out of shape? It's not as bad as they make it seem. It's nothing like what happened at Heartpine, the Negian troops are overreacting. They are irked, fearful, feeling as if they've been deserted. What is it that you are trying to steal from Anglass? Do you have a buyer?"

"We aren't looking t'steal a thing," Prikka said, frustrated with Ardof's assumptions. "We want t'open it."

"Open it like the Moordusk Dome opened? That would truly upset the Negians. It'd leave their resources up for the taking, and all their animals and slaves would escape."

"And that doesn't sound too bad, does it?" Jiara said.

Ardof shrugged. "Not bad at all. It sounds like total chaos, for them. But how do you plan on doing such a thing?"

"We know a way," Jiara answered vaguely. "It has to do with the temples. We just need to safely get to the trunk."

"The trunk?" Ardof asked.

"The big vine that grows at the center."

"I see. The Negians call it the *axis*, and they protect it better than anything else in the dome. This sounds rather suicidal, I'm not sure if—"

"Listen, Ardof," Banook pleaded. "When I said the health of Noss is at stake, I meant it literally. The domes retain a portion of the great Noss of old, and if they remain closed, and the animals within keep getting killed, so will Noss's memory die."

Ardof chewed on his lower lip as he lightly chuckled. "Are you rambling about the myths of the planet speaking to the ancient tribes? That's taking things too far, big friend. I understand some Miscam tribes are now on the loose, whether as slaves or rescued by whoever opened the domes to the west—and I'm not saying Lago had anything to do with that, yet I don't think I have to—but those Noss stories are simply myths."

"Like the Silvesh are simply myths?" Jiara taunted.

"Now *those* proved to be true, I'll grant you that much."

"And perhaps those silly stories about animal spirits?" Banook added.

"If the Miscam liked to worship toads or ferrets, that's their problem, not mine."

"Then tell me," Banook added, "if the other myths had been true, would you have helped us?"

"Perhaps. I'm sick of seeing these lands being ravaged, all those animals mindlessly killed by the Red Stag, the Miscam slaves suffering under their hideous new banner. But the peril is too grand. What is there to gain? I won't risk my hide because of some spritetales that have no foundation in reality."

Banook got up from the bed and began to take off his clothes.

"What is this?" Ardof asked.

"I'll show you what you want to see," Banook said, dropping his trousers.

"You know I don't partake in the same kind of—"

Banook swiftly shifted, landing on all fours in his golden bear form, filling most of the space left in the room.

Ardof nearly fell backward as Banook drew closer to him. The bear placed his wet pink nose right on Ardof's face, then huffed, blowing Ardof's hat back to uncover his receding hairline. The bear then shifted back slowly into his human form, holding his refractive smoke and rising like a dark monolith, casting a heavy shadow as his hairy belly reappeared.

"H-how did—what was—are you…"

"I am Kerjaastórgnem, Nu'irg ust Urnaadi. I am Tomut-Kich gur Hathar, the Light-Furred Serac of Norviria, who fished the first salmon from the Khull tributaries. I am Quoonbe, once keeper of the Laajus Glacier, thrice the warden of Mithrinn. I am Golden Claw, the monsoon spirit of the eastern plains, father of thunder and brother of the northwestern gales. And I am *Barrghnukhurrrgk*."

"Quiet down, big bear!" Jiara said. "I think he's got it."

Banook reached down for his clothes. "Will you need any more convincing, old friend?"

"F-fine, I understand, I just never expected…" Ardof mumbled. "And I do believe you, and believe in your… cause. B-but belief and trust are two different things, you are not telling me everything." He lifted his brows before Jiara said anything. "I'm not asking about Lago. But you said you are here on your own, yet I know you are working with someone else, and you need to be honest with me. If you don't trust me, why should I trust you?"

"What do you mean?" Banook asked.

"The knocking at your own door. The curious pattern you used. That you waited before unlocking it. Who were you warning? I guess they escaped through the window, but why are you hiding your accomplices?"

"Oh. That," Banook chuckled. "Safís, Probo, would you please?"

Safís stood up and satisfyingly changed back into a white wolf. Probo clumsily shifted into his javelina form, still lying down.

Banook introduced his Nu'irgesh friends and explained where they'd come from. Ardof could argue no more.

"Here's what we need," Banook said. "We need to exit Brimstowne without calling attention to ourselves and travel fast toward the east. We need to know how the insides of the Anglass and Lequa domes are guarded, what to be wary of, where it would be safest to enter from. Any Negian movements along the main roads would be good information. We shall aim to remain invisible, but we'll likely fail at it from time to time."

"There's only one way to enter the domes," the ranger said. "Through the southeast mines for the Anglass Dome, which will be filled with soldiers and slaves. And southwest for the Lequa Dome, by Shaderift, through the pipes, which will be equally defended."

"Pipes?" Jiara asked.

"It's how the Red Stag managed to get his army in and out so efficiently. They say he walked in a bit at a time, assembling pipe segments behind him to prevent the vines from closing up. Once he was through, an entire pipeline into the dome had been laid. Much faster than digging through miles of rock."

"That prickstain," Jiara mumbled. "He's probably doing the same on the Jerjan Continent right now."

"You haven't heard then? Are you so misinformed?"

"*Un*informed, perhaps," Banook corrected. "My friends have been traveling stealthily for months, while I've been living up in the mountains."

"The latest—and this is information I was about to deliver to Withervale— is that the Bighorn Dome has been taken and so has the Bayanhong capital of On Khurderen. The Red Stag has been joined by an army of sheep, goats, that sort of thing, under the control of a new horned scoundrel wearing their mask."

Jiara was about to ask for him to elaborate, but Ardof didn't give her a chance.

"But that's old news by now. After that, the Red Stag moved on to the Archstone Dome, but I have not been able to find what the situation there is. All I know is that his army has split, sending a legion *and* their fleet to the east, where they took Azash. All of Elmaren is now theirs. The Moonrise Dome will likely fall soon as well, they've already breached it."

"Breached it?" Prikka asked.

"Indeed. I heard this news only a few days ago. Do you know what that dome represents? Are you familiar with the mask that will be found in there?"

"Pinnipeds," Jiara said. "We know."

Ardof nodded, unimpressed. "Anyone who is paying attention knows by now. They found maps at Anglass and Lequa, which scholars from Hestfell quickly translated."

"We have a copy of a map like that," Jiara said. "I'm worried though. If Alvis Hallow has control of seals, walruses… He could more easily attack by sea."

"I wouldn't worry too much about that. He needs forces on land more than over water, that's where the real war will be fought. Besides, the Tsing Empire and Afhora can easily protect the Gulf of Erjilm and the Alommo Sea. Their fleets are enormously more powerful than the Negian ones."

Jiara nodded and pretended to agree, but what she was truly worried about was her friends, who were traveling aboard Siffo's ship. To avoid mentioning anything about Lago, she changed the subject. "Do you have any information about the insides of the nearby domes?"

"Of the inside of the Lequa Dome, I don't know much at all. But I have been *inside* Anglass."

"How did ye manage t'get in?" Prikka asked.

Ardof cracked his knuckles, then rubbed the white wraps covering his forearms. "Bribes. Connections. Extortion. Deception. Usual tricks of the trade. I traveled through Anglass for weeks. It's a beautiful place, despite the chaos the Negians unleashed. Endless prairies, meadows, hot rivers, waterfalls, more fertile than any pastures in the Great Steppes. Unfortunately, I can't buy your way in—you are too conspicuous. Just look at yourselves!"

Banook, Jiara, and Prikka exchanged looks, still uncertain whether to bring up the issue of the masks.

"Still," Ardof continued, "I meant it when I said I believe in your cause. I'm supposed to report back to the Wujann Observatory in a few days, but I think this is far more important than Withervale or the Zovarian Union as a whole. I'm willing to take you to our neighboring domes, but I do not know how you plan to enter them."

Prikka stood. "M'dear, do ye mind if we have one uf our private, secretive chats without ye fur a moment?" She gestured with her head and led Banook and Jiara into the hallway.

Safîs's yellow eyes watched Ardof as he waited. He dared not even swallow.

After a long pause, the door opened. The three walked in, with Jiara and Prikka carrying their backpacks.

"This is how we plan t'enter them domes," Prikka said, taking Nagrasilv out. Before Ardof had a chance to utter a sound or get a good look, she put the mask on and shifted into Nalaníri. Kitjári followed, happy to be back in her half-form as well.

"Two more Silvesh…" Ardof breathed out.

"Like the Red Stag," Kitjári said, "we can walk into the domes anywhere we want. If you have any suggestions about where it'd be safer, that'd be most helpful."

Ardof shakily nodded. "I-I'll show you the way." He cleared his throat. "And if you'll let me, I'll follow you in and help you reach the axis. I mean, the trunk." His eyes remained wide, his mouth dry. "I hope you've kept these masks a secret. If anyone finds out, thousands of soldiers will rain upon this very town, they'll kill every citizen until they find the artifacts. Can those… animal spirits… can they fight?"

"They can take forms larger than the one you saw me take," Banook said.

"Probo's good at a-trampling n'smashing," Nalaníri added, scratching the suid's wiry-haired back.

"Good," the ranger said. "We'll need all the help we can get. And you'll need good weapons."

"We've got some uf our own." Nalaníri removed the sheath that obscured the pharolith-encrusted blade of her tusked axe.

"Kenzir stones!" Ardof exclaimed a bit too loudly, then covered his mouth. "How did you…"

"They brought presents for me too," Banook added, sliding the glaive from under the bed. He removed the leather scabbard.

"A Dorvauros blade!" Ardof gasped, leaning forward to inspect the obsidian edges. "And is that—"

"Senstregalv," Kitjári confirmed. "Like my arrow tips, which go very well with this." She removed the cover from Dunokh Sull and held the recurve bow for Ardof to take. His fingers trembled near the weapon, unwilling to touch the ancient relic.

"That's… That is quaar… That is… the Arc of the Night Sky, D-Dun-D-Dun…"

"Dunokh Sull," Kitjári completed, still holding the bow out.

After a tense pause, Ardof dared to take it. He inspected the perfectly crafted curves and the filigree of delicate darkness. "I thought Lerr Mauvenel's stories were but spritetales. This—this is a true beauty… Is it true what they say?"

"Don't know, what *do* they say?" Kitjári asked.

"I heard tales that Mauvenel themself wove this bow's string from stardust. They claim arrows don't shoot from it, but instantly appear inside its targets' heads or hearts. They claim that the Ilaadrid Shard upon the moon's face is an arrow that was loosed from this bow, which froze in the cold space between

Noss and Sceres, and impacted as an icy crystal. They say the light it created upon the moon is what brought all life to our planet."

"If d'shard's light brought all life, who in d'nethervoids shot d'arrow?" Nalaníri questioned.

"Don't overthink it," Kitjári said, then looked at Ardof. "Maybe part of the first myth you mentioned is true. Lago told me once that we are all made of stardust. People, animals, legendary bows, all of us."

"Well, whether some or all the legends are true, I am in awe," Ardof said. He bowed to the bow and handed it back. "And I am fully committed to aiding you. Tell me what you need."

Together they discussed their strategy, studying Ardof's map, which lacked detail as it covered too broad an area, but gave them a sense of the vast distances they'd traverse. He mentioned that the north end of the Anglass Dome was the least well-guarded.

"There's a river east of Lappan," he said, "the Stiss Loit, which I believe is the same river that I saw inside the dome, later merging into the Stiss Malpa. It flows across the entire dome, passing close to the trunk. There's a lot of traffic by water over the southern half, as they use the river to move out stolen resources, but it's not so busy up north."

"Could we get a canoe?" Kitjári asked. "It might be faster that way."

Ardof shook his head. "We'd be too exposed. But we can follow the shoreline, which runs warm and grows plentiful tall reeds to hide behind. It won't be too hard to get to the trunk, but once there, all bets are off. I haven't been there myself, but if there's one thing the Red Stag has made clear, it's that he wants that temple protected."

"He wants to avoid what happened at the Heartpine Dome," Kitjári hypothesized. "At least that's somewhat positive. How do we get to this river you mentioned without being seen?"

"There's a caribou farmer I know in Lappan, who lives away from the main town," Ardof said. "I can find us a safe and quick ride to his farm and buy some caribou from him to help us. And Banook, forgive me for saying this, but you'd crush the poor spines of any of the animals. How will you manage?"

"We will not need the help of beasts of burden, other than ourselves. As a bear, I can carry one of you, and Probo can carry the rest in his largest form."

"For some areas that might do, but we will not be able to move about unseen in Negian lands, particularly near Longwinde and Blackfern. You'd be spotted."

Banook stared at Probo for a moment, exchanging voiceless thoughts. "There once were roads through the Stelm Khull," he said, "that both Probo and I were keenly familiar with. They might be overgrown and disused, but we can find our way through what remains of them. Safís could scout ahead of us, making sure we do not encounter mountain people or nomads along the way. She can tell the tundra wolves to be on the lookout as well, to howl warnings to us if they spot any dangers. Nu'irgesh can travel fast, faster than any animals you may have encountered."

Ardof agreed with the plan. He told them he could secure a ride to Lappan the next morning, but he needed to take care of other matters in town before it got too late. They agreed to meet in front of the Yeast Cauldron at sunrise.

"Well," Banook said, once Ardof left the room, "our plans are set. The night is still young, so I might as well go down and see what is happening at the tubs."

"You're going to make Lago jealous," Kitjári playfully chided him. "I know he's got Aio, but you're taking on twenty at a time."

"It's only fair," he replied. "It's proportional to our sizes."

The next morning, Ardof was waiting for them by the Cauldron's front doors. He traveled light, only carrying a small side bag, his long, thin dagger, and a braided hemp sling for hunting. He brought them to a side road where a large hay wagon waited. They climbed on it, hiding between the hay bales while the driver took them east.

"He's discreet," Ardof noted from within the safety of the bales. "We should be in Lappan by this evening. He'll drop us on the far outskirts of the town."

They slept during the ride, trying to save up energy for when they reached the dome. Under the cover of darkness, they hopped off the hay wagon, handed the driver a substantial tip, and journeyed east until they reached a warm river.

"This is the one," Ardof said. "It gets deep farther south, so we better cross it at this ford."

As a kuba, Probo helped them across, and from there they followed the shoreline. The wall of the Anglass Dome was only a mile away.

A pack of kiuons trotted by them and briefly stopped to greet Banook, then rushed away in a blur.

"Look at them go," Banook said. "They told me most bears are on the move by now. The path ahead is open for me."

"This whole bear migration scared the netherfarts out of everyone in Brimstowne," Ardof said. "And Nool, too, where I was some weeks back." He looked at Jiara. "So, you got this started then, and not Banook?"

"I did," she confirmed. "I'm not coercing the bears to go, not the way the Red Stag controls his cervids. They are doing it willingly, they want to help out."

"They listen to me too," Banook added, "but I have other limitations. I go where they go, not the other way around."

"I've been afraid to ask," Ardof began, walking alongside them. "You have the Nu'irgesh of canids, suids, and ursids here. And two... what did you call yourselves again?"

"Silvfröash," Jiara answered.

"Three Nu'irgesh, two Silvfröash. Quite a party. What I'm curious about is, what is the deal with him?" he pointed at Bear, who was happily panting by their side.

Banook smiled, but then he tightened his brow. "Mind your manners, ranger, and never again address him, directly or indirectly." He cleared his throat. "He is the great Gun Elvothosk Tsu-Amáriel, eldest of all Amáriel-Nu'irgesh from before even my own kind first walked on this planet. Keeper of the Oath of Nir-Endábbro, Avenger of the Great Battle of Nur Mooriseth. He was there when the Downfall burned all lands, yet he did not burn. He was there during the great floods of Jalmuggren, yet he did not drown."

Ardof swallowed and discreetly moved away from the dog.

"He demands respect and obedience above all," Banook added, petting Bear's head. "Right, boy?"

Arrrwouf! Bear agreed.

CHAPTER THIRTY-THREE

SCOURGE OF THE DUGGOR VEIL

"Monarch Hallow, a herald flew in with news from the east," a young envoy notified his liege.

"From Silv-Thaar Valaran's army?" the Red Stag asked, not slowing his step.

"Y-yes, Monarch Hallow."

"What is Valaran's message?" he asked, walking toward the trunk of the Archstone Dome, flanked by Silv-Thaar Markhor and Silv-Thaar Baneras. The enormous archway to Ommo ust Almel was visible now, right past the still-smoking buildings.

"Queen Lea-Ëuniss has surrendered," the envoy said. "The Elmaren Queendom is safely under the control of Silv-Thaar Valaran's army. He is on his way to the Moonrise Dome. He says he will return as soon as the pinniped mask is under his control, but he won't be able to send heralds while inside the dome, so this is the last we'll hear from him for a few weeks."

"Good. Keep me updated. Anything else?"

"No. Yes," the envoy replied. "I mean yes, but not from the Silv-Thaar. It is regarding the remaining Alampaari Miscam—we found their hiding spot."

"Well?" the Red Stag demanded.

"There's a canyon by the striped mesa. Steep and impassable, only accessible by tunnels. The survivors escaped through them and collapsed all the passages. We haven't found a way in yet, and we can't lay siege to them either—the canyon valley is vast, and will provide them with endless resources."

The Red Stag glanced toward Markhor. "This one will be on you," he said to his spiral-horned general. "Your caprids could nearly climb upside down if given a chance. A steep canyon should present no obstacle to them."

"Hooves will climb, horns will smash, skulls will crack," Markhor declared, then slammed her armored chest with a gauntlet. "No prisoners?" she asked.

"It is pointless to spare them," he answered. "The Alampaari cannot be tamed. They are better off fully exterminated."

Markhor huffed, then forcibly ejected a ball of spit onto the ground. She poked her ice axe toward the envoy. "Take me," she croaked, and followed the scurrying teenager.

"They would've made great soldiers," Silv-Thaar Baneras commented, watching Markhor leave. "Particularly the ones with thick hides." He too had a thicker hide now that he was in his half-form of a steppe wild horse, but nothing nearly as thick as the hides of the Alampaari who had partial traits of rhinoceroses. Baneras was well used to his equine form by now, having gained full control of his perissodactyls, but still felt inadequate for not being able to control the members of the local tribe despite them holding partial or full half-forms. There was something about humans that made them impossible to mindlock. The Wastyrian shamans thought it had to do with their inability to mindspeak.

"Shall we?" the Red Stag asked as they reached the enormous portal of carved sandstone. Above them was etched the perissodactyl glyph, the concave cuts encrusted with carved ivory and green gemstones.

They walked past the dozens of Negian soldiers stationed at the entrance to the temple. The Alampaari corpses had all been removed by then, but their dried blood was still streaked on the shallow slope of the vaulted tunnel.

"At ease," the Red Stag said to a soldier they passed by, who had tensed up like a bowstring. The soldier did not ease up at all, but pretended to. Monarch Hallow sneered, irritated by how the attitude of his subjects had shifted in the past few months. *They act out of fear, not respect,* he thought. *They think me careless. Their brains are as small as their ambitions. If only they could see the strategy.* Yet he knew better. He knew his recent decisions had cost him nearly half his army, at least of the human kind. Adding more elk, horses, and goats had no value to his troops—it simply made them feel expendable. Their morale was failing, and so was their commitment and their sense of pride in fighting for a cause larger than themselves.

But only those who fight with conviction can succeed. If they die, it is due to their lack of faith. If they die, they will have deserved their deaths.

Their long walk had become much too quiet. "Are you sure you want to do this?" Baneras asked, breaking the silence. "Markhor said that once it starts, there is no stopping it."

"I'm certain," the Red Stag replied. "We have few pipe segments left to spare. And even if we had more, your new colossi would never fit through them."

"I'm still concerned about flank attacks. Once the dome opens, the Horde could strike from all sides."

"They've dug trenches around the dome to protect themselves from us. They are brave warriors, but they think strategically—they would not venture blindly into an unknown land. Have some confidence, Baneras, you hold a weapon more powerful than any the Horde could ever possibly imagine."

"But I'll need to get close to their horses in order to use it on them."

"I'm not talking about your mask. I'm talking about Estriéggo. Your captured Nu'irg will be enough to tear them apart, and they will have no choice but to surrender."

Baneras nodded. They continued up the tunnel, their hooves echoing in the vaulted space, until it ended in a circular chamber. Vine columns snaked up into a ceiling much too high for the torchlights to reach. Six steps led up to a central dais, where the marble throne coldly waited, with the core vine rising right behind it.

The temple was quiet. All of the soldiers had stepped out to offer privacy to Monarch Hallow and Silv-Thaar Baneras.

"These are the relics I told you about," the Red Stag said, walking behind the dais to where ten skeletal bodies were resting atop stone beds—Alampaari chiefs of old. Although their remains were human, each wore the armor and regal clothing that had been crafted for their half-forms. Their human skulls looked diminutive inside the long helms.

"The dates carved upon the stones indicate these were chiefs from before the Downfall," the Red Stag said, walking past the remains of a chief who used to hold the half-form of an elasmotherium, or at least so it seemed from the single-horned helm clutching the much-too-human skull. "Why could you not grow a horn like this?"

"I… I'm not—"

"I merely jest, Baneras. Look," he added, arriving at the remains of a chief with a set of armor built for a horse-like half-form, "this is the one I thought you'd be interested in. From the patterns, it seems this armor was crafted for a zebra, but it should fit you well."

Baneras inspected the relics. The armor still glistened, having been kept clean by the Alampaari priests. It was forged from a strong metal with quaar filaments woven into a striped pattern of black against brushed grays. Despite the armor's beauty, the desiccated corpse within it made Baneras hesitate.

"I'll have a slave clean it up properly," he said. "But it does look like it could fit my frame."

The Red Stag didn't answer. He was already walking up the six steps. He ran a sharp-hoofed fingertip over the waxy core vine, then sat on the marble throne.

"Before you do this," Baneras said, turning his head, "it might be better if—"

His words were stopped by the sudden influx of threads. He had been aware of them since they had entered the temple. The threads had been flowing through the lattice in a mostly chaotic manner, but now they had all aligned as they shot upwards in a pulsing beam. The lattice of quaar conduits began to shift and reassemble itself, collapsing toward the core vine. Soon the vine was wrapped in a complex armor of quaar conduits, sinking through a hole in the ground. As the vine disappeared, it left behind a black emptiness that was quickly filled with white sap.

"Much easier than I expected," the Red Stag said. "Urgsilv simply showed me the way." He got up on his feet. "Follow me now, Baneras. We only have a few weeks before the vines part sufficiently. It's time we move our troops south and face the Horde."

Baneras did not simply wait for the Archstone Dome to open. Now clad in the striped armor of an ancient Alampaari chief, he rode his horse toward the southern perimeter, followed only by Estriéggo—the woolly rhinoceros Nu'irg—and a small troop of mounted crimson guardians to protect him. They exited near the Skyward Arch, a monumental bridge of rock that was sacred to the Graalman Horde. The locals had been busy, having dug many trenches along the periphery of the dome. They could feel the imminence of the Negians' attack; they'd been waiting for a full frontal assault since the first tremors began, after seeing the vines curling away.

But Baneras was much too insidious with his attack—he commanded Estriéggo to take the form of a dwarf horse to sneak closer, then to shapeshift into a colossal behemoth big enough to jump over the trenches and crush the warriors waiting beyond. Once the Horde sent mounted reinforcements, he mindlocked their horses and sent them to trample the enemy lines from within.

He repeated this strategy from trench to trench, ensnaring more horses with each strike. By the time the vines had opened enough to let full battalions through, the Horde's forces were in disarray. An unstoppable herd of behemoths, anisodons, rhinoceroses, and giant garrison horses flooded out of the dome to tear down the trenches and finish off any humans they could find.

"She's nearly here, Monarch Hallow," the envoy wheezed, a bit out of breath. "The Scourge of the Duggor Veil has come all the way from Doralghon to surrender to you, Lorr."

"She took her damn time," the Red Stag muttered, standing with arms crossed. Behind him towered Sovath, protecting the Red Stag in the form of a megaloceros, and behind the Nu'irg were the ruins of the sacred Skyward Arch, now a pile of rubble indistinguishable from the Graalman temple that had once been cradled under its long shadow.

The Negians had vanquished all threats around the Archstone Dome's perimeter and now needed to keep moving to the Scoria Dome, where the mask of chiropterans was waiting to be taken. The only thing delaying their advance was that the Red Stag had received news that Suux, Scourge of the Duggor Veil, Head Chief of the Graalman Horde, was coming to meet him in person. The lands of the Horde were vast, and although the Red Stag had confidence that his army could march through it without much trouble, he needed to secure the Horde's supply lines to travel faster. Their surrender would expedite his journey, feed his soldiers, and increase his stock of slaves.

A single galloping horse approached from the southwest. Silv-Thaar Baneras instinctively tightened the grip on his longbow. "Is that her?" he asked.

The Red Stag simply huffed derisively.

"She is not slowing her gallop. I could take over the beast and—"

"No. She is just one woman. There is nothing to fear."

The horse did not slow. Baneras had to jump out of the way, and as he tumbled sideways, he saw a warrior flying through the air. Suux had leapt off her horse to land in a streak of dust, without losing her footing. The zealous leader had tanned skin, and long brown hair that seemed wet from how much it glistened. She held a flailing whip in one hand, a spiked scourge; in the other she held a more softly spiked rambutan fruit. As she strutted toward the Red Stag, she popped the pulpy core of the fruit into her mouth, hurled the skin away, then spat out the hard pit.

"*Urgei Maarg!*" she yelled, her words a lash. Although shorter than Hallow by an entire handspan, she stood defiantly in front of him, staring up at his long muzzle. "Your army has won this battle, elk of crimson and death, but your numbers dwindle, your supplies fester. If you wish to pass through my lands unharmed, you will listen to my demands."

The Red Stag chuckled. He would've torn the spine from anyone else acting with such disrespect, but for a moment he felt utterly charmed by the woman's irreverence and courage. "Your brutes have no power without horses, my dear," he replied. "You've lost, and no amount of bravado will change that."

Suux cracked her scourge against the sand, making a cloud of silt explode from its nine spiked tails. Dozens of soldiers pointed swords and arrows at her, but the Red Stag held them back with a hand gesture.

"You have more beasts than people in your army," Suux said. "Beasts cannot rule over the Arched Lands. Beasts alone cannot build bridges, farm fields, row boats, birth heirs. You cannot conquer lands without people. I offer you a truce."

"A truce?" the Red Stag mocked. "And here I thought you came to surrender."

"The Scourge of the Duggor Veil does not surrender. Cut my head off if you wish, drink from my bleeding neck, then burn my bones in your sickly fires. But without my scourge cracking behind them, my army and my citizens will answer to no one. Without my aid, your army will linger and delay, and the Silvesh you seek will be taken by the enemy long before you arrive. Leave the lands of the Horde to the Horde and I shall help you cross them, then help you conquer the realms beyond. Join me, and together we will tear down the Nargara Bastion and bring an end to the empire of the Tsing."

The Red Stag smirked sardonically, yet deep inside he felt respect for the boldness of the chief, perhaps even admiration. He knew Suux was right—traversing the canyonlands would take months if they had to constantly watch their backs, secure strategic positions, and fight off the rest of the Horde's relentless army; he would defeat the Horde in time, no doubt, but wasting time was something he could not afford. Suux could provide his army with not just a path, but with provisions, and for the great battle that was to come she could contribute with a proper mounted cavalry that could make better strategic decisions than mindlocked beasts.

"Your insolence is endearing," the Red Stag said, putting a hand under Suux's chin. She swatted it away like she would a bloodsucking horse fly. "I have no interest in your lands," he added. "Tell the rest of your army to stand down, and I will see that my creatures do not trample the survivors. You will show me the fastest path to the Scoria Dome, and then toward the lands of the Tsing."

"Keep your vermin away from the sacred arches," Suux demanded, "or the Horde will attack, no matter what orders I give them. If one more arch is fallen by your beasts, I will personally see you flailed by the Scourge of Nine Torments." She paced around, studying the Red Stag's commitment. "I will send a general to show you the path to Scoria, but I will not be there with you. I will be in Doralghon, to inform the chiefs of our alliance. Your sluggish legions need to make haste, for the Tsing do not rest—they have been readying for war." She whistled loudly. Her horse galloped back to her, once again nearly trampling Silv-Thaar Baneras. Suux hopped onto the saddle while the horse moved at full speed, leaving in a cloud of rust-colored dust.

"She's dangerous," Baneras said, at last loosening the grip on his bow. "I do not think she can be trusted."

"Not in the long run," the Red Stag agreed. "But the Horde will grant us what we need, for now. After the battle against the Tsing is won, we can worry about taking that whip from her."

CHAPTER THIRTY-FOUR

SOUTHERN HOMELAND

"Are you sure you want to help me with it? It will be hard work, but I could use your expertise," Balstei asked Crysta. He grunted as he dropped the heavy log he was carrying, then helped two Laatu teens hoist it up to the top of the hut they were building.

"I don't know what I want, Bal," Crysta answered, trying to catch up with him as he hurried to retrieve another log. "I just know I could not sit still."

"There you go again," Hefra interjected. "We'd barely set foot inside the Moordusk Dome, and with all the wonders to discover there, you grew tired of it. Now we've barely just arrived at this untamed forest, and you feel like it's time to go visit a lifeless desert."

"Lurr Boarmane has a point," Balstei said, his thick arms tightening as he picked up more building materials.

"But there's something bigger going on in the world right now," Crysta retorted, "bigger than my research, than my career, than anything I could imagine. That's why I came here, and… and I thought for a moment that maybe I'd find Lago here, with you, you know…"

"Didn't he tell you he would travel west?"

"Yes, that's what he wrote last time he sent that bird. I was merely being hopeful. Either way, seeing those lava tubes will be wonderful—they hold perhaps one of the most important documents to salvage in all of history."

Balstei dropped his haul and signaled he was taking a break. He stared at the professor, sucked on his lower lip, and shook his head. "I'm not leaving for the scablands yet, Crysta. It'll be a few months, maybe a year. Crops need to take, the borders need protecting, the felids must be resettled and trained. *Then* I'll have time to go transcribe Mamóru's writings. Believe me, I'm eager as a hound in heat, but those petroglyphs can wait a bit longer. Fingrenn and Nelv want to make sure everything is properly sorted out in the settlement."

"I met Fingrenn yesterday," Crysta recalled, "but I don't think I've met Nelv."

"You've seen her. She's the clouded leopard who was prowling around the new mill."

Crysta's jaw dropped. "Nelv is a clouded leopard? Does that mean she—"

"Was that the Nu'irg?" Hefra asked, jumping into the conversation.

"That she is," Balstei said, leaning against a tree trunk, sweat drenching his torn doublet. "She's helped immensely, dutifully directing the felids who migrated with us. She's gone back to Mindreldrolom multiple times since we arrived. Tireless creature, enduring and determined."

"I would love to study her better," Hefra hungrily said. "Is there a chance that—"

"You touch her and you are dead," Balstei said, crossing his arms. "And it will hurt the entire time you are dying. I'm not kidding, nature lady, she's not to be messed with."

"I will cut your—"

"Please, stop it, you two," Crysta said, massaging her temples. "I don't know, Bal, I guess we can stay here and help you until it's time to go to the scablands. This *is* a beautiful forest. I wouldn't mind exploring it some more while learning from the Laatu."

"Look at you," Balstei smirked. "All roughened up, and it's only been, what, a month? Two, since you left Zovaria?"

"I don't even know what day it is anymore, actually."

Crysta and Hefra made themselves a comfortable camp in the new settlement in the Udarbans Forest. The Laatu had named the village Birsulf Allastirg, meaning *Southern Homeland*, and it was already feeling like home to a lot of the inhabitants. The previously uninhabited jungle was a few hundred miles south of the scablands and was ideal for the new colony, despite its great distance from the Moordusk Dome.

Crysta spent every waking moment pestering Balstei, demanding he tell her every single detail about the adventures he'd had with Lago. Balstei was happy to oblige, inserting a few reinterpretations of the facts when they made him sound more heroic.

Hefra spent her time learning about the felids, mostly from Fingrenn, the interpreter who had taken on the role of chief of the settlement. She was keenly interested in the relationship between shamans and soot, and how closely the substance allowed them to communicate with animals.

"We have shamans too, in the New World," Hefra told Fingrenn as they made their way back down to the village. She had been showing them species of edible and medicinal plants they were unfamiliar with. "But our shamans can barely give basic instructions to some kinds of birds, dogs, very rarely cats. Only the smartest of their kind can endure listening to our nonsense, it's nothing like what you manage to do. If we could hear animals talk, it would help us all so much. For us studying the natural world, I mean."

"It takes decades of hard work, Lurr Boarmane," Fingrenn said, gliding placidly alongside her. "But even so, our scalps cannot hear them mindspeak. We can talk *to* some animals, and we can interpret their reactions, but the process of 'hearing' the language of other kinds is one that, as far as we know, is only possible for the Silvfröash while in their half-forms." They paused, then added, "Well, there are some exceptions, perhaps."

"What sorts of exceptions?" Hefra asked, seeing a window open.

"Some shamans, very few of them, have at times heard a voice in their scalps when communing with animals they share a tight bond with. A rare occurrence it is, one that has blessed only those who have mastered the art over decades. My ears have heard stories of two shamans of old who heard Nelv's voice, as she can be very intent when she wants to be—but that may have more to do with Nelv than with the shamans who heard her. And one of our shamans here in Birsulf Allastirg, good old Klaawich of Dakhud, they have a companion albatross who is almost as old as they are. They have been together for sixty years. Klaawich claims that every once in a while, they are able to hear their companion speak, albeit briefly, and only after inhaling substantial doses of soot. The experiences tend to be coupled to large doses of braaw as well, making it hard to judge the veracity of their claims."

Hefra was resolved to find Klaawich, meet their albatross, and learn more. But in the meantime, she wanted to wring out all she could from Fingrenn.

"I'm still confused as to how you know exactly what to do with which species," she said. "I've seen your farmers, your animals, your shamans, all working together with a clear idea of which species should occupy which niche. Even though there's competition with the local fauna and flora, the species have somehow managed—at least thus far—to avoid causing a major upheaval in the lands they are... well... invading."

"We do not know everything," Fingrenn admitted. "We had specific guidelines from Noss themself regarding key species, types of habitats, and synergetic ways to maintain the proper nutrients in the soil. We also had maps—now outdated—showing potential areas to repopulate."

Fingrenn waved their arms toward the forest below them. "Here in Birsulf Allastirg we have diversity, which, although it seems beneficial, makes our job much harder, for there are too many variables to achieve balance. But the soil is fertile, the land provides. Our other largest group ventured northeast of here, to a land of hot lakes called the Wuovad Kladesh, on the southern shores of the Sajal Crater."

"What? Why? There's nothing but steaming rocks there. It's a barren, volcanic, mountainous wasteland."

"That is exactly why they chose that location. No other tribes will bother them there. That land will require a lot of work to transform, but our shamans know how to do it. They have with them the majority of our companion felids—the smilodons, snow leopards, and some of the domestic cats, who left the city a bit reluctantly. They will help the shamans in their endeavor."

"That makes no sense." Hefra shook her head. "How are they going to feed all the big cats? They can't make that sap paste away from the dome."

"They will need a constant supply of munnji, at least for a time. But there is a great road that connects the Wuovad Kladesh to Mindreldrolom, unlike here, where we are on our own and need to fend for ourselves."

"I don't know, Lerr Fingrenn. It seems to me that whatever plan Noss had, it might not exactly apply nowadays. Things have changed."

"That is expected, Lurr Boarmane. This is but a starting point. Once we strike a basic balance, we will have to seek Noss's wisdom and listen to their guidance, like we did millennia ago."

A week had passed since Crysta and Hefra had arrived at Birsulf Allastirg. Balstei was helping attach a spring bar to a broken wagon's axle when he spotted a large figure striding from the north. Tall and muscular, with a bright-blue, recently pigmented scalp, the tree trunk of a man lifted a hand in greeting.

"Kenondok!" Balstei called out and hurried to tap foreheads with his Laatu friend.

Kenondok called for a meeting with the entire village, and that evening he recounted his recent adventures. He told them Hud Ilsed had sailed *Drolvisdinn* back from the long journey into Nagradrolom and Kruwendrolom, then explained what the Silvfröash had learned from their audience with the new Noss, and told them of the passing of Mamóru. He would not speak of why the Laatu chose to abandon the Silvfröash with the Puqua—the matters of Khuron Aio-Kulak's breach of Laatu laws were not his to reveal, despite his own distaste for those actions. He was careful not to mention anything about Kitjári's and Nalaníri's secretive mission.

From the outer perimeter of the circle that had gathered, Nelv watched, perched on a high branch. She could not understand the man's words, but the shaman Klaawich—with his albatross holding to his scalp like an inconveniently large hat—interpreted the words for her as carefully as possible.

"That is the tale I have come to relate," the brawny man concluded. "But there is more than a tale I was entrusted with. My feet traveled far to carry a message from Khuron Aio-Kulak. A message for Nelv."

The Nu'irg ust Mindrel perked up, eyes dilated.

Kenondok first looked to Klaawich, then directed his gaze up at the branches, seeing only the reflecting retinas of the felid. "Our Khuron wishes you to travel to a southern land called the Taring Peninsula. At the farthest headlands rests an old lighthouse. Khuron asks that you wait there twice a month, on nights when the Ilaadrid Shard shines bright as sparks of brime, to look for a ship of white hull and black sails. Khuron will meet you there, later in his journey, seeking your aid."

Nelv's coin-like retinas dimmed through a slow blink.

After the meeting was over and the crowd dispersed, Kenondok approached Crysta.

"Lago-Sterjall thought I find you at Mindreldrolom," he said in his rough Common. "But quick feet took you far. Hud Quoda told you came this way. I brought message to you, like I brought message to Nelv." He handed Crysta a sealed envelope.

"Th-thank you," Crysta mumbled.

"My scalp thanks you as well, for help provided," he added, tilting his ridged, blue-tinted scalp. "Note you sent granted us safe sailing through Isdinnklad."

Kenondok turned and left without another word.

Balstei and Hefra had been hovering nearby, curious about the interaction. They stepped closer and saw Crysta ripping open the wax seal with trembling fingers.

"It's a letter from Lago," she said to her friends. "I'm a bit afraid to read it—it's always one surprise after another with him."

"If you don't read it, I'll take it from your bloody hands," Balstei said. "Get on with it, we are waiting."

"Okay, okay," she muttered, and began to read:

Dear Crysta,

Hey, I managed to sneak in one more letter to you! I assume you've heard about us from either Kenondok or Hud Ilsed. I'm hoping one of them will tell you about our trip in more detail. I won't write some of those things down, as always, for everyone's safety. The Zovarians are still after us and almost caught us at sea recently. But we are fine. We made it through.

I never expected these adventures to take me so far. Every day there's a new discovery, and it never seems to end. I feel like I used to feel when studying the stars, when I'd think I finally understood them just to find out there are billions more I will never get to know, no matter how long I live or how hard I try.

Life on this planet is so broken and so precious. I have found aspects of myself that I never even sought for, and now I'm becoming someone else, as if I barely recognize that boy who so eagerly wanted to study cosmology at the institute. Don't get me wrong, I still love the stars—they are the perfect companions, always there to guide me—but the idea of settling down and learning from such a limited source feels constricting to me now. Perhaps in the future, if this brittle, shattered world finds a way to mend, I might return to those studies. But I'm not kidding myself—once this is over, all will still be in disarray, and it will take a long time for a balance to be found. But we can't stop now. We are trying to help Noss, and we believe we've found a way. We need to see this through.

I've learned much recently from a dear friend, Mamóru, about what makes us conscious, what empathy has to do with how we can become greater than our isolated selves, and how consciousness can be hidden in levels inaccessible to our simple minds, in places we never thought of looking. If a beehive can be conscious, if our own planet can be conscious all around us without us knowing, it makes me wonder what else is out there that we simply can't or haven't perceived yet. Maybe mountains are conscious but move so slowly that we can't tell. Maybe the oceans know something we don't. Maybe the stars themselves look down on us and laugh at our audacity for calling ourselves self-aware.

I'm trying to find answers, but I know I won't ever find them all. I just know that empathy seems to be the key, the missing puzzle piece, the glue, the common thread, or whatever metaphor you want to use. It is what connects us all and lets us understand each other. Perhaps it will someday let us connect back to nature, and more.

There's one more thing. It might be a bit coercive of me to even mention this, but... Remember I told you that the Stelm Yenwu Observatory from where Jiu Zezi discovered the Downfall's comet is likely still within the Yenwu Dome? Well, we are going to be headed that way. Not right away, but sometime in the next year is my guess. I know you aren't very outdoorsy, and that traveling to the Yenwu State during times of war is not the smartest career move, but I thought maybe you might like to join us? Ask the Laatu about the plan to have Nelv meet us on our ship. Perhaps they'll agree to let you travel with her, then you both can greet us at the Taring Peninsula. If you can join us, I'll tell you all the details I've been glossing over in these letters. There's just too much to write.

I never got to truly thank you. I know you were writing a letter of recommendation for my sponsorship, though I don't know whether you ever finished it... But I also found out that you had been paying for my studies at Birth-Light School for the past six years. I was stunned. And I don't know how I'll ever be able to properly repay you, or even thank you. The way you always supported me has fueled my motivation not only to learn, but to hold on to something greater when all hope seems lost. I carry with me the knowledge of the stars, the stories from all the books you let me borrow, the memory of your ugly astrolabe, and the passion I saw in your face every time you removed the covers from the old telescope. So, thank you, Crysta, without you I would've been lost.

Love,
– Lago-Sterjall

Crysta wiped her eyes, then covered her mouth. Her facial expressions transitioned from sadness, to pride, to fear, to excitement. "I... Oh, Bal, do you think I should?"

"Don't look to me for answers, Crysta," he said. "As much as I want to see that old observatory myself, I have my own work cut out for me here. Though I'll try to go visit you one day."

"So, you think I should?"

"Don't put words in my mouth. It's up to you. It sounds dangerous."

"Yenwu is the dome of avians, is it not?" Hefra asked. Without waiting for an answer, she continued, "I hope you aren't thinking of traveling alone, sweet plum. You'd be dead in a wick if you ventured out there without me. And I'll need your help to take field notes. When are we heading out?"

PART FIVE

NETHER REALMS

CHAPTER THIRTY-FIVE

SIEGE AT SEA

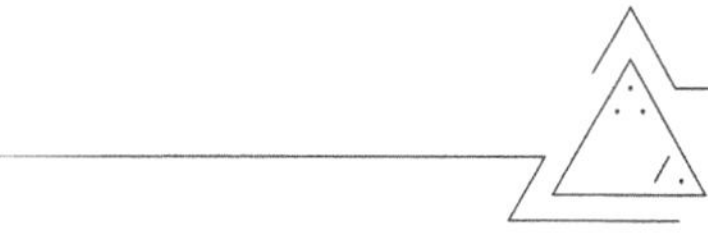

Fjummomurr's sails spread wide and dark. After the battle with the moa riders on the shores of Bauram, the ship had followed the winds southeast, toward the Republic of Lerev and the Nisos Dome.

The night after the battle, they sailed near the city of Aksas Di. They kept their pharoliths covered, yet they were still spotted. Far from the shore, several Zovarian ramships moved into formation to block their route, but they had not seen *Fjummomurr* approach until it was too late, letting the Puqua ship sneak right between them.

"We'll outsail them heavy ramships," Siffo said, "even though d'wind is not in our favor."

The winds were blowing from the east, so they had to tack against them, slowing their progress. The ramships tried to follow, but as the night passed, they were slowly left behind.

They were lucky to avoid any confrontations for several days, but when they neared the city of Kizad, they once more encountered Zovarian vessels patrolling the Esduss Sea. This time, a squadron of four of the much nimbler trimarans chased after them. *Fjummomurr* had to weave its way toward shore to avoid them, using the stronger eastern winds to pick up speed before the trimarans could overrun them. The trimarans got close enough to land a few arrows on their hull, then followed right behind.

"We must lose them," Lummukem urged.

"Goin' as fast as we can," Captain Siffo replied.

"But they are stepping on our tails."

"Then find an oar n'get t'rowing, if ye think it'll help."

Morning came with a change of the wind, now blowing from the west, carrying with it dire omens. The wayfarers gathered atop the forecastle to strategize.

The trimarans were not far behind, keeping their pace but seemingly holding back on purpose. To starboard, Zovarian ships scoured the blue shores of the great island. In front of them and slightly to port, the rest of the Zovarian fleet waited, dozens of ships patrolling the deep sea.

"Their numbers keep growing," Lummukem said solemnly.

Siffo studied the air. "Our unly chance is t'lose them right by d'shore, among d'islands n'cliffs. D'western winds are not kind to us today, but we can still use them."

"We would likely wreck upon rocks," Kulak said.

"Mayhap. Utherwise we'd jis' head straight to them."

"What if we try to go deeper into the sea?" Alaia suggested.

"No, *ugimeld*, them ships are already a-changing course, them will be ready fur that. D'cliffs are our unly chance. We can try t'weave around them. I don't see no uther way."

"You are the captain," Sterjall said, "you know what the best call is. I trust you and your sailors."

Alaia nodded her approval. Lummukem and Kulak exchanged concerned looks, then agreed to proceed with the risky plan.

Siffo grunted twice. "Then we shell lose them through them islands."

The Zovarians had not anticipated the perilous move, having assumed their enemies would retreat deeper into the sea or return north to take their chances with the pursuing squadron. Once *Fjummomurr* sharply changed course, the pink-sailed vessels took a long time to correct their own.

The bone-hulled ship pushed its black sails to the limit, steering sharply between the blue and black cliffs. The Silvfröash scanned the water ahead of them with their quaar conduits, trying to avoid shallow paths over treacherous rocks. So far, luck favored them, as they had yet to scrape their keel.

"We've pushed past them hinds!" Siffo bellowed. "Full sail east, take us out uf this maze!"

But as the ship began to weave its way back to the open waters, a call rang out.

"Enemy ahead!"

Four ramships, having been hidden behind an islet, slid into their path.

"That's Admiral Grinn's ship," Sterjall said.

"Into that canyon!" Captain Siffo belted out. "Pray to Lûrrumaag that there's a way out through it!"

The ship ventured into a labyrinth of sea stacks, trying to find a course between the towering rocks. They could see no secret path, no tunnel to escape through, not even a shore to crash upon to try fleeing by foot. The ship circled around a massive promontory, facing a narrowing passage toward the open sea.

"We can use the tailwind to push through!" Sterjall said, spotting the opening.

"They'll be upon us 'fore we arrive," Siffo countered, his tone defeated.

"We have no other choice!"

Siffo commanded *Fjummomurr* to sail east, trying to squeeze out of the trap they had caught themselves in. Walls of cyanic-blue striations rose to their left and right, undulating by them like fossilized waves. Far ahead, pink sails were changing course, hurrying to intercept them at the gap.

"We can make it!" Sterjall exclaimed. "Don't let them push us into the walls, we need to—"

"Back the sails!" Siffo interrupted. "Full stop!"

From behind the sandstone cliffs, five more ships appeared, blocking their path. Windward, six trimarans were now making their approach, having followed *Fjummomurr* through the maze of headlands. Ten more ships sluggishly drifted in from deeper at sea.

Fjummomurr halted and bobbed in the soft waves, tantalizingly close to the gap that would have taken the dispirited crew to freedom. The Zovarian ships slowed, pushing through the gap to surround them. Archers held their bowstrings, arrows knocked, ready to draw. An ornate ramship slid closer, and a familiar voice called out from its deck.

"For the deaths of my soldiers, I will see you face justice," Admiral Grinn said, blue cape slapping in the western winds. "For the death of my niece, I will see you face unimaginable pain. I should kill you all this very instant—and believe me, I would enjoy running my blade across all your necks. But the Arch Sedecims have ordered me to take you as prisoners, at least those of you we are closely acquainted with. The swine I care nothing about."

"If you touch them, we'll fight back," Sterjall threatened. "You know we can take a lot more of your soldiers before you take us all down. Put down your bows and don't bother our Puqua friends, then maybe we'll cooperate with you." He leaned close to Lummukem and whispered, "Do you think Ishke can find us a way out of this?"

The dragon looked at the basilisk, then back to Sterjall. "No. Ishke'ísuk might sink one ship. Perhaps two. Dozens more will remain to kill him and kill us. We should surrender—this is a fight we cannot win."

"Then hide him, and Olo too," Sterjall said. "It is better if they do not learn about them. They might be able to help us later."

Lummukem sent Olo to perch atop the crow's nest, then quietly spoke to Ishke'ísuk. The basilisk jumped into their hand and shapeshifted into a speckled padloper tortoise, not much bigger than a Quggon. Lummukem tucked the compact tortoise into one of their shodog's many pockets, leaving the flap open for him to breathe.

Admiral Grinn's vessel came alongside *Fjummomurr*, and they were boarded. One by one, their wrists and legs were shackled, starting with the Puqua. Kulak ordered Blu and Pichi not to fight back, even when they were covered by thick nets. The Silvfröash refused to surrender their masks, but they were stripped of their weapons and gear and marched over to Grinn's ship, then tied up on the deck near Siffo and Alaia.

"I don't see all the masks I was expecting here," Grinn remarked, parading in front of the prisoners. "But this one is new," he added, kicking at Lummukem's footclaws. "I'm guessing you picked this beast up at Fel Varanus." Lummukem opened their pink maw and snapped their serrated teeth in the air.

Grinn didn't flinch. "Where are the other ones? There were at least two more animals with you the last time we met."

"They went their own way," Sterjall said.

Grinn stood in front of the wolf. "Lago Vaari. Was it you who killed Kedra? If it wasn't for the Arch Sedecims' orders, I'd be cutting your fingers off by now. I still might. You know that without these masks, the Union is doomed. The Red Stag already has three more of them. Without the aid of—"

"Three more? That's impossible, there's no—"

"It's true," Grinn cut in. "He took the Bighorn Dome months ago. Now he's followed by an army of stinking goats, all while his army of elk keeps growing. Nearly a month ago, he reached the Archstone Dome, and one of his legions went east and conquered Azash. Queen Lea-Ëuniss is dead. The Elmaren Queendom has fallen, and the Moonrise Dome will fall with it, if it hasn't already. He is moving fast, and we need to move faster, or our realms will perish."

"So what would you do?" Sterjall mockingly asked, lifting his muzzle. "You'd raise an army of wolves, smilodons, and snakes, and go after him? Let all the animals die in the name of the Arch-fucking-Sedecims, just like General Hallow is doing?"

"He's not a general, he is Monarch Hallow now," Grinn corrected.

"I don't give a shit what he calls himself," Sterjall barked. "He's a power-hungry maniac. And you are not much different from him."

"Watch it, runt," Grinn said. "Now take off that mask and tell me where to find—"

"Scorch your flesh sixteenf—"

Grinn slapped Sterjall with the back of his hand. He then lifted a hard-heeled boot and kicked him in the chest. Sterjall convulsed from the impact and tried to curse, but his lungs would not cooperate.

"Tell me where to find the others," Grinn repeated, enunciating slowly.

Sterjall's muzzle tensed. "F… fuck y—"

Grinn threw a powerful punch at his face. Sterjall fell to his side and bled on the deck, losing his sense of orientation. He saw Kulak trying to wriggle free, and Grinn approaching him.

"No, don't," Sterjall said, but Grinn was now thirsty for more than just answers or treasures. The admiral noticed the blood soaking through Kulak's bandaged shoulder, grabbed onto it, and squeezed. Kulak hissed, then groaned in pain.

"Stop!" Sterjall pleaded, but Grinn only tightened his grip. Kulak screamed.

"Please, don't hurt him!" Sterjall yelled. He began to take Kulak's pain for himself, feeling his own shoulder burn and tense up. Grinn clutched harder, and Kulak let out an agonized wail.

"Stop! Just stop!" Sterjall cried, his own pain becoming unbearable. "Leave him alone! I'll tell you what we—"

A whistle interrupted them. On the deck of *Fjummomurr*, a Zovarian soldier was waving.

"We found one!" the soldier called out, then came running over the ramp connecting the two ships. In his hands was Momsúndosilv.

Grinn let go of Kulak's shoulder, wiped the blood off his hand, and took the proboscidean mask. "You said the other masks were not with you, yet here is one of them. Perhaps we should take the ones you *do* have by chopping your lying heads off."

"If you kill us while we hold our half-forms, the Silvesh you will not retrieve," Lummukem bluffed. "We would remain in our half-forms as corpses, and the Silvesh would be lost, forever."

"I find that very hard to believe," Grinn said, but his tone betrayed his doubt. He unsheathed his sword, strutting toward the mainmast, to where Alaia and Siffo were tied.

"I'm not asking nicely this time," he said, eyes locked on Sterjall. "Tell me where the other masks are, or your Oldrin girlfriend will swallow this slowly, painfully. After that, the swine next to her will get it, and we'll serve you bacon and spurs for dinner." He pressed his sword to Alaia's throat, making her lift her chin. "Tell me now or—"

A horn blew in the distance. Murmurs scurried across the deck of the ship. Grinn's soldiers climbed up the ratlines to see better.

"Lerevi ships, Lorr!" came a call from the crow's nest.

"How many?" Grinn asked.

"Hundreds, Lorr!"

Grinn called out a quick command to retreat; his sailors reacted instantly. Sails billowed, and the Zovarian fleet began to pull away. But too long it took them to weave around the many isles, and by the time they made it out to sea— tugging *Fjummomurr* sluggishly behind them—the armada of the Republic of Lerev had surrounded their vessels, outnumbering them five to one. The white-sailed ships of the Lerevi floated menacingly around them, their black flags prominently displaying a silver triple spiral formed from a single line—the triskelion, the proud sigil of the Republic.

A cockboat was lowered from their flagship, a two-decker frigate with sails too numerous to count, the white canvas overlapping across the masts like a flock of giant swans. Lerevi sailors dressed in yellow and silver rowed the cock- boat alongside Grinn's ramship.

Four sailors and an officer climbed aboard. The officer confidently strode across the deck and announced, "I am Fleet Admiral Theggo Saurfall of the Kil- gane Naval Base, commanding the *Silverweave*. You are in Lerevi waters, and by extension, in the waters of our ally, Empress Pian-Thi of the Tsing Empire."

Grinn tapped an open palm to his chest and greeted Theggo, trying to re- main cordial. "We hear your song of truth."

"Moon lights, Zovarian officer," Theggo replied curtly. "Name and rank."

Grinn bowed. "Stars guide. My apologies, we were in pursuit of—"

"I asked for your name and rank," Admiral Theggo Saurfall demanded, his bushy gray eyebrows darkening the stern look he gave Grinn. He was long-haired, noble-looking, outfitted in gleaming silver armor detailed with bright yellows.

Grinn lowered his head. "Admiral Grinn of the Centennial Fleet of Zovaria, Lorr."

"Admiral," Theggo croaked, rubbing his short beard. "Then you know better than anyone that mobilizing your fleet in this manner can be seen as a declaration of war. We've been keeping our heralds' gaze upon you. You've entered our waters multiple times in the last few weeks, and now you bring dozens of warships and take to our coasts." He shot a quick glance at Sterjall and his friends, pretending to be disinterested. "What is the reason for your breach of our peace treaty?"

"We have come in pursuit of fugitives, Lorr. We do not seek to break our pacts. It was a mistake to sail so far into your waters. I deeply apologize, personally as well as in the name of the Arch Sedecims. We will take our leave at once."

"So you shall. And you may carry your fugitives with you." Theggo then looked down at Sterjall, raising his eyebrows. "That is, unless they were sailing here seeking asylum under the care of Princeps Vordeno."

Alaia lifted her head and looked at Sterjall, opening her eyes wide and nodding briskly to him.

"Yes! We are a-umm," Sterjall stammered, "seeking asylum under Princeps Verdun… Uh—"

"Vordeno," Theggo corrected, "just as I suspected. Then asylum shall be granted to you. Admiral, you may release our refugees at once."

"They are our prisoners, not refu—"

"In whose waters do you think you are meddling? I will issue not one more warning. Release them, or my frigates will tear your sluggish ramships apart and take your surviving soldiers as prisoners of war. Release the refugees, now!"

Grinn's face tightened, turning sour and pale. He made a defeated gesture toward his soldiers, who promptly began to unshackle the prisoners.

Theggo stepped closer to Grinn. "Admiral, what you hold belongs to my refugees," he said, extending a silver-gauntleted hand, palm up.

Grinn hesitated.

Theggo placed his other hand on the pommel of his silver-and-copper-inlaid rapier.

Grinn surrendered Momsúndosilv to Theggo, then crossed his arms.

"They have our weapons and gear as well," Sterjall noted, standing up and rubbing his bruised wrists. He pointed his muzzle toward the stern. "The soldiers took it all to Grinn's quarters."

"We'll take care of that as well," Theggo assured them, "and there will be no objections from the admiral."

Under Theggo's supervision, the Lerevi took care that all the stolen belongings were returned to *Fjummomurr*. He then boarded the Puqua ship and watched the Zovarian fleet slowly retreat to the north. Once the Zovarians were comfortably far away, he turned to one of his sailors and ordered, "Send for Captain Dedric and Captain Mareesha, ask them to join me aboard this… peculiar ship. The captains and I will travel with our guests, for the time being.

We will set off to Alzara with the full fleet. There, we will split, and my flotilla will continue to the port of Nisos."

"Yes, Lorr," the sailor answered and hastened to retrieve the captains.

Once Dedric and Mareesha were aboard *Fjummomurr*, and once the ship began to follow the leading Lerevi flotilla, Theggo's tightened brow finally loosened.

"I think it's time we talk," he said through a sigh.

CHAPTER THIRTY-SIX

LAVRA FAITHFUL

Captain Siffo invited the Lerevi officers into his quarters, sensing that the admiral was uncomfortable speaking in front of so many Puqua sailors. He placed the mask of proboscideans back on the cabinet from where it had been taken, then gestured for the others to sit around the oval table, spreading a map of the southwestern isles between them.

"So, the legends were true after all," Admiral Theggo Saurfall began, crossing his legs. He made a conscious effort to avoid staring at the pharoliths illuminating the cabin. "We have been hearing about your journeys ever since a mysterious group of people went missing in Thornridge."

Sterjall immediately felt uncomfortable, flattening his ears without noticing it. He darted his eyes around, feeling as if they'd just fallen from one trap right into the next. "How does Lerev know what happens in the Free Tribelands?" he probed, failing to keep the confrontational tone out of his voice.

"From our Tsing allies, of course. Though I have to admit, even with all their resources, we've barely managed to keep up with you. Where are your other friends?"

"Why don't you ask your Tsing allies?" Sterjall said. Kulak kicked him under the table.

"Lago Vaari, I thought you'd be more cordial. More grateful."

Sterjall tried to use Agnargsilv to read the intentions of the three Lerevi, but their threads weren't entirely clear—the attempt left him with more suspicion than before. "My name right now is Sterjall," he said. "And yes, we are thankful that you rescued us, but when the first thing you do is ask where to find more masks, you should understand why we'd be a tad hesitant to answer." He crossed his arms and straightened his back.

"As you wish, Sterjall. You don't have to answer. I won't hide that the Republic has a vested interest in the Silvesh. But that is self-evident. Every realm powerful enough to command heralds is now looking for them and searching for other ways into the domes. The difference is that some realms are looking for the Silvesh so that they can conquer more lands, while others are simply looking for a way to stop the Red Stag."

"That's what Zovaria claims as well."

"True. But we know better. Or at least, we think we do. Let me tell you what I *do* know, if that will ease your mind." Theggo leaned back in his chair with pompous confidence; his silver pauldrons clinked as he put his arms behind his head. "I know the types of creatures that inhabit each of the sixteen domes. I know of the dome that was never made, where the ursid mask apparently hid. And I know of the seventeenth dome that burned down, where you retrieved that from." He raised a bushy brow toward the cabinet where Momsúndosilv had been placed.

The fleet admiral leaned in once more, gauntleted hands clasped upon the table. "This information was easy to gather. There are countless stories about the old man who transformed into a tusked beast, though I don't see a man of that description traveling with you now. You left many soldiers behind with heads and tongues still attached. A bit careless of you, I must say. We followed all the clues after the Moordusk Dome was opened, where many Laatu were captured and interrogated."

Kulak's face darkened in anger, and he tensed to rise to his feet, but Theggo raised a finger and kept going.

"Mind you, *we* did not interrogate the Laatu, it was the Zovarians who captured some of them. Those are not our lands, but we have our sources. After that, a Khaar Du ship spotted you near Koroberg—they informed Zovaria, and so our spies were informed as well. The Fjordlands Dome mysteriously opened soon after, and there were reports of Zovarian ships requesting reinforcements near Fel Varanus. And to continue with the pattern, the Varanus Dome seems to be unraveling quite hastily now." Theggo shot a side glance toward Lummukem before continuing. "My guess is that if we were to travel across the blue desert, we'd see holes in the Azurean Dome as well. The Kingdom of Bauram is going to have quite the surprise soon enough, seeing an ancient Miscam tribe alongside the lost order of marsupials suddenly flooding their lands. I assume you were on your way to Fel Nisos, though I have no clue how you thought you'd sail into our waters and walk onto our great island without being detected."

"We don't have to tell you what our plan was," Sterjall said.

"You do not, but it's become quite obvious what your intentions are. You're trying to liberate the imprisoned Miscam tribes. You've associated with them, helped them in their efforts to leave their lands. You even travel with three different tribes of theirs." Theggo pointed at Kulak, Lummukem, and Siffo.

Does he think Lummukem is a Mo'óto Miscam? Sterjall wondered. *He knows a lot, but less than he pretends.*

"I assume I am correct so far," Theggo went on with unquestioned conviction. "You set yourself to free the tribes as if not a maelstrom could stop you. A bit shortsighted, if you ask me, even though I must commend you for your bravery. You've done an amazing job thus far, and done exactly what we would've set out to do if we had the masks, though we would have done it for different reasons."

Sterjall sucked on his cheeks as he contemplated, then replied, "Your interest in the masks rather irks me. You seem quite focused on them alone. What do you want with them? Why should we be trusting of your kingdom?"

"Republic, not kingdom. We work for the benefit of the people, not for a monarch. Yes, we are after the masks, but for a different reason than you may think. Unlike on the mainland, at Fel Nisos we do not subscribe to the Doctrine of Takh or to the Tsing Codices. Lerev worships Noss and their eighteen spirits. Canticle twenty-seven of the Lavra Scrolls clearly tells us that the spirits were trapped in the domes, and the final recitation implies that it is our duty to see that one day they are freed, so that they may bring prosperity to all lands. Well, that day has arrived."

"For the land is our cradle, and we are merely seeds upon it," Captain Mareesha and Captain Dedric recited.

Theggo nodded to them and continued. "When the eighteen spirits were ensnared by the domes, the Downfall came. For centuries we prayed at the eighteen stupas, begging for the spirits to return. We learned—thanks to you— that the masks could be used not only to enter the domes, but to open them in full. You see, Lorr Vaari? Whether you are a Lavra Faithful or not, our goals align, in essence."

"Parts of them, perhaps," Sterjall dismissively replied. "But we aren't doing what we are doing because of canticles. We don't share the same faith."

"I'm not surprised, since you were not brought up in Lerev. Yet I still believe our goals are aligned. We want the domes to open. We want to free the spirits from their unjust imprisonment."

"And another common goal we share," Captain Mareesha interjected. "The spirits of Urg and Rilg have become corrupted by the Red Stag. We want to prevent that from happening to the others."

"Sovath and Beiféren are not corrupted," Alaia corrected her. "They are mindlocked. It is not their fault. They are trapped in their own minds and can only hear the orders of the Silvesh."

"Perhaps," Theggo allowed a bit dismissively, then focused back on Sterjall. "I freely admit we know little about how the Silvesh work. Our incomplete scrolls only mention them in fleeting passages. So, Lorr Vaari, tell me, am I correct in assuming that we are on the same side?"

Sterjall looked to his friends for support.

"We must be careful with them," Lummukem said in Miscamish. "But we need allies, and for allyships to work, there needs to be some trust. Although we do not have to tell them everything."

"I don't like his air of self-importance," Alaia huffed. "Or his stupid smirk."

"My scalp is uncertain," Kulak added. "But I will trust Sterjall's judgment."

Siffo remained quiet, as lost with the Miscamish words as the Lerevi.

"Your assumptions are only partially correct," Sterjall said at length. "Yes, we have been on a quest to open the domes, but not to free the Miscam tribes. That is only incidental. The real reason… Well… It is not something you will be happy to hear. Do your people truly worship Noss?"

"Only Noss and their eighteen spirits—no kings or false gods," Theggo assured him. "For the land is our cradle, and we are merely seeds upon it."

"Noss is… well… I don't know how to put it without sounding disrespectful, given what you've told me."

"Speak your mind," Theggo said. "We wish to hear the truth, nothing else."

"Noss… Noss is dead," Sterjall said.

Theggo squared his shoulders and glanced toward his two captains, lips tightened to a line. He looked back at Sterjall. "Dead? What in the Holy Scrolls do you mean?"

"Not dead, exactly," Kulak answered, holding a hand out to keep Sterjall from saying more. "Noss is now… reborn. Most of Noss perished during the Downfall, but they endure, fragmented, within the drolomesh. The planet's scalp is not the same as it was in lost epochs, but reopening the domes can bring back some of their memories, and that is what we must do."

"I… I don't…" Theggo seemed crestfallen but also untrusting. "How could you possibly know what became of Noss?"

"The reason we traveled to Kruwendrolom," Sterjall explained, "to Fel Varanus, I mean, was to find a sixth mask. I'm sure your spies know how many we had in our possession by then. We used the six masks as did the Miscam of old, to call for an audience with Noss."

"How… It's not… you said you were not a Lavra Faithful, so how do you know about the sacred ritual of Huchelm Iskewum?"

The words sounded strangely familiar to Sterjall. He replayed the sounds in his mind a few times until a rhythm came with the words.

"Oh! You mean *hum che velm isk enn gwum*? Those are the Miscamish words we chanted for the ritual. They mean *six into one body and mind*—nothing magical, just words to help us focus. Or was that detail missing in your canticles?"

Kulak kicked Sterjall under the table once more.

"Careful, young Lorr," Captain Mareesha said. "You know more than you let show, but I'd be wary of insulting our faith in public."

"The captain is right," Theggo concurred. "I will tolerate your attacks, but that is because I still believe we have a common goal."

"We apologize," Kulak said for Sterjall. "We are here as friends, and we are here to listen, to learn."

Theggo smiled unconvincingly at the apology and focused on the impulsive wolf once more. "Tell me, Lorr Vaari," he said, "did you accomplish what you had set out to do?"

"Yes. We spoke with Noss, that is how we know what we know."

"That is why we ventured south after Kruwendrolom," Kulak added. "Because Noss asked us to. Because they told us we must restore their lost memories."

"Admiral, we must be careful with this," Captain Mareesha said in a hushed tone. "Whether or not what they say is true, it would amount to the greatest of blasphemies for the Lavra Faithful. The scrollsingers would not entertain such ideas—it would unleash chaos."

"If this is true, the ministers and the princeps must know," Captain Dedric dissented. "It may help convince them of the value of an alliance. What greater cause than to help Noss themself, and in so doing, release all the imprisoned spirits? Lorr Vaari… Sterjall, would you be able to summon Noss once more and ask them to speak with Princeps Vordeno? Nothing would be more convincing than Noss's own words."

Sterjall shook his head. "Not unless we have six masks, and we only have three."

"You mean five," Theggo corrected him. "The four of you, plus that one." He pointed toward Momsúndosilv.

"Ye think I'm d'Nagrafröa?" Siffo asked with a snorting chuckle. "I'm not even a quarter uf a warthog, m'dear Admiral. Mine fingers may have hard-hoofed tips, but ye shell see mine entire lower body, frum mine belly all d'way down to mine feet, I'm just as meaty as yerself."

"There won't be a need for that," Theggo said, shaking his head. "Perhaps we were mistaken in that regard. I did think it peculiar that so many of your ship's crew looked like you, Captain. But what about that other mask? It is not the mask of the Spirit of Momsúndo?"

"Momsúndosilv is inert," Lummukem said, "and can no longer be wielded. The last proboscidean died at Kruwendrolom, and with him, the power of Momsúndosilv was extinguished." Lummukem purposely avoided mentioning that the last of the proboscideans was also the Nu'irg himself, lest they upset the admiral even further.

Theggo seemed dubious of the explanation.

"Try it on if you want, it doesn't do anything," Sterjall suggested, losing patience. "But either way, we are still missing three more masks. It's not our priority to talk with Noss again or to convince your faithful. Our mission is to open the remaining domes, starting with the one at Nisos. Are you here to help us, or to stop us?"

"Calm down, Lorr Vaari, I am here to help. I will take you to see Princeps Vordeno, but I will need to send heralds to inform him of what we have discussed. You will need to tell me more, so that I may better convince him of the urgency of your mission."

Sterjall began to roll his eyes, but Theggo stopped him with a hand gesture. "I will not force you to tell us where the suid and ursid masks went. I have my suspicions, but I'll leave it at that. I believe you, but I need more in order to convince the others."

"My scalp thinks of something that might convince them," Kulak said. "Noss said we should seek aid from the Nu'irgesh."

"What are the Nu'irgesh?" Theggo asked.

"Who you know as the animal spirits," Alaia elaborated.

"Spirits, yes," Kulak said. "Your people might not believe us, but perhaps they will believe the spirits themselves."

He nodded to Lummukem, who still had Ishke'ísuk hidden in their shodog's sleeve. Lummukem mindspoke to the diminutive tortoise, removed him from their pocket, and carefully placed him at the center of the table. Theggo and the two captains smiled, as if realizing they had been taken for fools all along and were finally being let in on the joke.

In a rattling burst, the tiny tortoise shapeshifted into an enormous snapping turtle wider than the entire table. Ishke'ísuk's maw snapped the air twice in

Theggo's direction; the admiral leaned back in his chair so far that he fell on his back, dragging his captains to the ground with him.

The table teetered and nearly tipped over. Ishke'ísuk changed back into his double-crested basilisk primal form and hopped onto Lummukem's left shoulder.

"That was excessive," Lummukem gently chided, glancing toward the Nu'irg. They then faced the fleet admiral, who was being helped up by his captains.

"Spirit of Kruwen," Theggo mumbled. "We are undeserving of your grace!"

"His name is Ishke'ísuk," Lummukem said. "He is friendly, he is lethal. He has forms much larger than the one your eyes saw, forms which would not fit within this cramped cabin."

As soon as Theggo was back on his feet, he went back down, to his knees. His captains followed. "We… How… For so long we prayed at the eighteen stupas. At last, our prayers are answered. We are your humble servants, mighty Kruwen. For eternity, or until the Endfall consumes us all."

Theggo's presumptuous demeanor quickly subsided after the encounter with the Nu'irg. He vowed to do anything within his power to help the wayfarers in their mission, as did the captains.

"You have to cool that temper a bit," Alaia later said to Sterjall as they watched the Lerevi return to their ships. "They rescued us, after all. We can't risk losing allies like them."

"Sorry," Sterjall said, squeezing his muzzle. "I still don't know what to think of them. I couldn't quite read their threads, and they had such an obvious interest in the masks that it still leaves me with a bad taste in my mouth."

"That's fine if you feel that way, but you can do better at playing along and try to make friends. Don't mess this one up, this could be where we finally gain the upper hand."

Sterjall blinked pointedly, then grunted his acknowledgment. "I will," he said. "I'll speak to Theggo some more, and perhaps I'll get a better feel for his true motives."

For eight days they sailed toward Fel Nisos, learning more about the Republic of Lerev; their motivations, their beliefs, their alliances. Theggo seemed honored to be helping them, even holding a sort of pragmatic reverence toward them, claiming that if Noss had allowed them to wear the sacred masks and had entrusted them in this most holy of missions, then they must be treated not just as allies, but prophets. Having Ishke'ísuk perched upon Lummukem's shoulder only emboldened his resolve to cooperate.

The wayfarers chose to confide in Theggo, although only in matters unrelated to Kitjári and Nalaníri's mission. Sterjall recounted the death of Mamóru and explained how the Nu'irg's memory now partially resided within the new Noss. He told Theggo of Ëalcor, mentioning that the thylacine was unable to join them in lands where marsupialkind did not live. He told him of Nelv, and how they meant to find her at the Taring Peninsula in the near future, hoping she had received the message sent with Kenondok.

During their seafaring voyage, Theggo explained to them about the Lavra Scrolls, a compilation of texts written by the early scrollsingers before the Downfall. The scrollsingers had lived in proximity to the Sehján Miscam, who had traded their expansive homelands in the Bauresht Peninsula for a large portion of Fel Nisos, where they ended up growing the mysterious dome. The Lavra Scrolls contained incomplete poems by dozens of scrollsingers, and had been kept safe from the Downfall in an underground library carved by an ancient, cave-dwelling tribe known as the Oxruk. The majority of the poems spoke about the Noss consciousness and the eighteen animal spirits, while others dealt with speculations about the cultural ways of the Oxruk and the Sehján Miscam. Most of the scrolls had been eaten up by time, leaving only patchy fragments.

Like the Takh Codex for most of the other realms, the Lavra Scrolls became the foundation upon which the Republic of Lerev was founded. They weren't prescriptive texts, yet they inspired devotion among their adherents, giving the Lavra Faithful heavy influence in the politics of the Republic.

"There is one benefit to the Lavra Scrolls being so incomplete," Theggo told Sterjall as they sailed toward the end of the peninsula, "it allows for ample interpretations. We did not know much about the Silvesh or about the nature of Noss themself, but now that we know better, we can change our ways of thought."

"I don't know," Sterjall said. "That sounds like a double-edged sword to me."

CHAPTER THIRTY-SEVEN

ESPLANADE OF THE SPIRITS

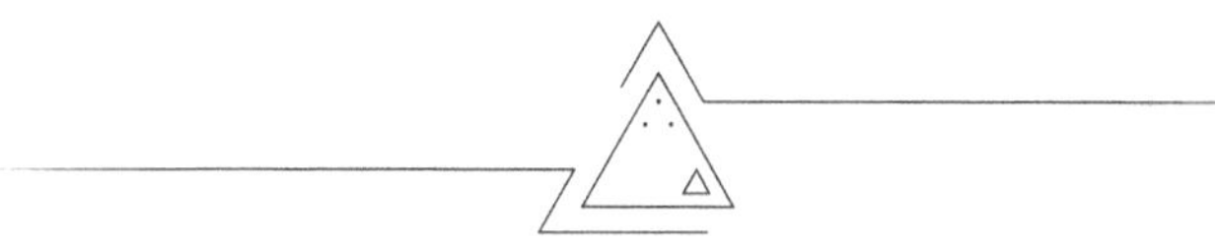

Fleet Admiral Theggo Saurfall of the Kilgane Naval Base directed his fleet to follow the shoreline of the Bauresht Peninsula, sailing south to Fel Nisos.

The shimmering blues of the Cyan Desert gave way to gray-sanded shores thicketed by mangroves and dense jungles. Once they reached Alzara, the main fleet stayed behind to keep watch for potential retaliations from the Zovarians, while Theggo's flotilla continued to Colverna, where they resupplied.

As their voyage progressed, the gray sands turned yellowish and bright, and from them grew tall palm forests and stubborn dune grasses. As they veered around the southern tip of the peninsula, the Nisos Dome came into view, directly to the south. The dome was glossy, nearly sparkling, having just been washed by one of the sporadic, late Umbra rains.

Theggo's heralds had kept him in touch with Princeps Vordeno, and informed him of all that the wayfarers were willing to openly discuss, yet the admiral refused to share that Noss was dead, as Sterjall had bluntly claimed. During the final approach toward his homeland, Theggo invited the wayfarers to join him aboard *Silverweave*, his swift frigate flagship.

"Why do they need so many sails?" Alaia asked no one in particular, staring up at the jumble of canvas and lines.

"This is truly a mighty ship ye have," Captain Siffo said, running his hoofed fingertips over the spiraling silver paints that decorated *Silverweave*'s railings.

"All this silver makes the ship look like something out of a spritetale," Sterjall added, following Theggo to the bow. He tightened the collar of his Laatu oilskin coat—with Winter following at their tails, it was cold at sea. He followed Theggo's gaze south, toward the stretching curve of the dome.

Theggo stood attentively and seemed not to be listening, as if waiting for something to happen. "At the end of the Reconstitution Epoch," he said unprompted, "the Nisos Dome was nearly as gnarly as Varanus."

"I heard of that," Sterjall said. "Something must've gone wrong inside there."

"Something, yes. We can't guess as to what caused it, or what reverted it, but there are countless records of it in our libraries, and records on the rocks themselves. You can visit the tunnels the giant vines once dug. They left strange-looking burrows after they receded, with pools of dry sap crystallized at the bottom. You could spend months exploring all the tunnels, particularly the ones at the Stelm Atuur."

"My scalp hopes the Sehján are faring well," Kulak said. "If Okridrolom returned to health, it makes me hopeful that things are fine once more."

Theggo drew in a cold breath just as Fel Nisos came into view, shimmering as a thin line of darkness beneath the bulging dome. "It's time to stow away the masks," he reminded them. "There are too many fishing ships with spyglasses in these waters. It will be a long ride to the palace, and word will get out fast if the citizens see your peculiar forms."

"Nothin' *we* can do 'bout that," Captain Siffo commented wryly. "Or shell I start ripping uff mine sailors' tusks?"

"Your ship alone will draw enough eyes, Captain. But my flotilla is loyal. They will take care of your ship and crew. There will be no hiding you, after a while, but we will do our best." He then looked to Kulak and said, "My sailors can take care of feeding your… cats, if you tell us how they should handle their diet."

"They go with us," Kulak said.

"They'll call too much attention to us," the admiral countered.

"We will soon need them," Kulak insisted. "If we go into Okridrolom, they go with us."

Theggo twirled a lock of silvery hair while considering. "As you wish. Our people have heard about these terrifying creatures by now, so we can pretend we bought them from a Zovarian merchant."

Kulak disliked the insinuation but could not argue with the plan.

Fjummomurr and *Silverweave* docked at the port of Nisos. Lago tossed his bag over his shoulder and disembarked behind his friends.

Everything was vertical in the great cities of Lerev. Nisos was built on terraces, with markets and residential areas stacked atop rocky cliffs. All of the buildings were curved in nature, made of smooth, light-colored rocks, with enough variety in tones to make the structures vary from subdued grays to whites and pastels, without the need for paints.

Captain Siffo chose to stay with his crew. He wanted time to make repairs to his ship and to learn about the techniques the Lerevi used for hull construction, navigation, and rope work. Theggo's captains promised to take good care of the Puqua while he escorted the rest of the wayfarers to Normouth, the capital.

Forty dragoons joined the escort, riding atop giant elands and kudus with long spiral horns, horse-like bodies, and deer-like heads. Lago had never seen such regal animals and could not tell which clade they belonged to; too many features were blended in their anatomy, and their coats were too delicate and ornamented, unlike the bison, caribou, and horses he had been accustomed to seeing around Withervale.

Lago and Aio rode atop Blu, while Pichi carried Sunu and Alaia. The protective circle of dragoons took them up roads that were flat and clean, snaking in convoluted switchbacks up to the top level of the city. Dry leaves blew in the cold wind. Although darkening clouds threatened rain, only a transient drizzle made it to the ground. Crowds gathered in windows and hollered to their neighbors from their balconies, curious more about the smilodons than about the foreigners riding them.

"Lerr Sunu, is it necessary to carry the Spirit of Kruwen atop your shoulder?" Theggo asked. The admiral was riding atop Tinnomeg, a giant eland with a pendulous dewlap, a glossy chestnut coat, and twelve white stripes across his humped back. "We are already gathering enough attention as it is, we don't want further rumors to brew. Perhaps the spirit can hide until we get to the palace?"

"There is no other way," Sunu answered. "He says he likes the breeze."

At the edge of the city, the road widened into a thoroughfare spattered with twirling leaves and dappled light. The southbound path was almost perfectly straight, always shaded by great eucalyptus trees. It all smelled fresh, almost minty. For a moment, Lago was reminded of the clean scent of the springs at the Emen Ruins.

"This is the Esplanade of the Spirits," Theggo told them, pulling on his reins to make Tinnomeg turn and face them. "The road is eighteen miles long, ending at the capital, Normouth. Each mile is dedicated to one of the animal spirits. If your smilodons can trot at our pace, we can be there before sundown."

The first mile of the esplanade was dedicated to Amá'a, the cetacean spirit. Being a seafaring nation, the Lerevi people placed more emphasis on sea creatures. The sidewalks were decorated with wildly elaborate fountains of dolphins and whales spitting water while frozen in midair. The second mile was very similar, dedicated to Gwonle, the pinniped spirit. At the center of each mile segment was a remarkable circular stupa topped with a black spire, where the citizens prayed and gave offerings. The stupas were surrounded by sculptures of the known species of each clade—they were incomplete, as the Lerevi's knowledge of their natural world was incomplete, but they felt properly reverential.

They passed by Kroowin, Urnaadi, Balast, and Urg, then arrived at mile seven, which corresponded to Momsúndo.

"That looks nothing like a mammoth." Alaia grimaced at a grotesque topiary sculpture of what the Lerevi thought a mammoth might have looked like.

"It is based on the fossils from our museums," Theggo replied, a bit disappointed. "Our scholars think it quite accurate."

"Why does it have only one eye on the forehead?"

"Isn't that what they looked like?" Theggo asked.

"Nuh-uh," Alaia replied.

They continued down the road. Nagra and Krost were followed by Agnarg and Mindrel.

"We are next to each other," Aio observed to Lago. "And we do not look monstrous, like poor Momsúndo." And they truly did not. The felid and canid sculptures and mosaics were strikingly beautiful, with the artists and scholars having had plenty of references to study before shaping them true to life.

A bronze smilodon roared in front of the Mindrel stupa. It looked fierce, with its saber-teeth cast from pure gold.

"Beautiful," Aio said, "but they gave sculpture a long tail. Theggo, tell your sculptors to shorten it. My eyes have never seen a mindrégo with a long tail."

"I'm sure they would've been happy to take notes," Theggo said, "but they are all dead. These sculptures were carved a thousand years ago."

They marched past Rilg, Almel, and then Quaju, which, as with Momsúndo, consisted of entirely too imaginative interpretations of what marsupials looked like. The sculptures' pouches were elongated, with covering flaps or buttons, sometimes on their backs. The shapes were mismatched, too vague and uncertain. The carvings were still beautiful, despite their inaccuracies.

The next mile was dedicated to Okri, the spirit of glires—rodents and lagomorphs.

Theggo regarded the bucktoothed sculptures. "If we had known our own Nisos Dome was the one housing the glires, we would've made a bigger deal out of mile fifteen. Or placed Okri at mile one. But we knew no better, not until your maps were revealed to us."

Lago shot him a suspicious look.

"Worry not," Theggo assured him. "We got a copy of your now famous map from our Zovarian source. Great draftsmanship on the original. Which one of you drew it?"

Yet pack and wolf are of one heart, Lago thought. "An old friend," he said.

"Understood," Theggo said with a nod. "I only hope Okri forgives us for our ignorance."

"They all have names, by the way," Lago told him. "Like Ishke'ísuk, his name is not Kruwen—Kruwen is just the name of the reptilian clade."

"I apologize." Theggo lowered his head, earnestly embarrassed. "We thought those Miscam words were their names, for that is how they were mentioned in the Lavra Scrolls."

Lago glanced at a series of mouse sculptures, hundreds of them, frozen mid-run along the sidewalk. "The one you call Okri," he said, "his real name is Gwit. His primal form is that of a tiny hazel dormouse."

Theggo nodded. "Gwit. I will remember that."

"I'll teach you the names of the others as we pass their stupas," Lago said, remembering those long-gone nights with Banook, when they would lean back to look at the constellations together, and the bear would tell him of the eighteen Nu'irgesh. A rhythm began to beat in his mind. *I hope we'll never be apart, I pray to stars above*, Banook's voice sang in his head. Lago sighed. *I wish I could know how you and Bear are doing.*

Trommo came next, and then Kruwen.

Sunu's dark-violet eyes squinted disapprovingly at the reptilians, which were all presented as sharp-toothed, savage, and violent. A winged dragon sculpture coiled menacingly around an obelisk. Sunu did not believe winged dragons were real, except in legends, or as points of light in the night sky.

The eighteenth mile and stupa were dedicated to Hoombu, the spirit of primates. The Lerevi considered it a lesser spirit, as it was too tightly connected to their imperfect human selves, so they had left it for last. There were simian sculptures around the stupa, but not a single one depicted a human.

The Esplanade of the Spirits brought them to a great city upon a shallow hill, framed by the Nisos Dome, which rose only a few miles away. Although Normouth was not terraced like Nisos, the height of its buildings made up for the difference in steepness. Pastel towers, white minarets, and pearlescent spires competed for attention, some being so polished that they seemed wet.

The road led them directly to the Normouth Palace, which in striking contrast to the rest of the city had been constructed of maroon marble so lustrous and dark that its sheen was reminiscent of drying blood. Its architecture was a jumble of circular motifs mixed in a chaotic, asymmetrical fashion; the circular bastions, turrets, baileys, and keep built as circles upon circles, extruded upward and intersecting with one another in an incongruous yet elegant whole. The palace's innumerable flags streamed tautly in velvety blacks, waving their silver triskelions in a hypnotic dance.

"The Normouth Palace is ancient," Theggo told them. "It was the residence of the nobles of old, when this was the Kingdom of Nisos and not yet our beloved Republic. Now it serves as a parliament building. Princeps Vordeno does not live here, but he works here with the House of Commons, the House of Lerrs, and the Lavra Faithful."

As they reached the palace, Theggo dismounted and handed Tinnomeg's reins to the stable hostler. He pointed his chin toward the two smilodons. "They will not bite. Just treat them kindly and see that they are fed. Venison will do." He placed an entire Quggon in the hostler's trembling hand as a tip.

The palace featured oval gates and circular hallways in confounding combinations. Maroon and black, curves upon curves, the passages welcomed them as they traveled through the residence of the kings of foregone times.

"The princeps's stateroom is through those doors," Theggo informed them. That was their cue.

They took their masks out of their bags. Sterjall, Kulak, and Lummukem returned to their half-forms.

As the triple circular doors of the stateroom opened, they were received by the princeps, who was flanked by two dozen generals, ministers, ambassadors, and other dignitaries. At the moment Lummukem stepped through the threshold with Ishke'ísuk perched on their shoulder, each and every Lerevi in the room dropped to their knees, beginning with the princeps.

"We hear your song of truth," Princeps Vordeno humbly greeted them.

NORMOUTH PALACE

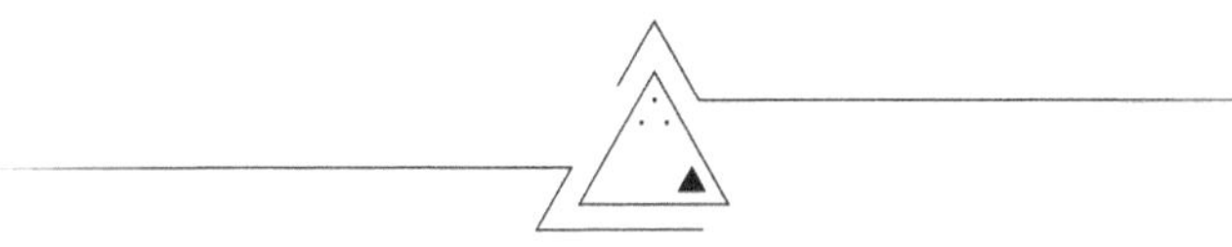

For three hours they sat around a circular table of marbled onyx, recounting the stories of Noss and of the spirits, solidifying an alliance, and discussing potential hurdles.

"How we reveal this information to our citizens will be critical, if we wish to maintain order in the Republic," Princeps Vordeno said. "The very thought of one of the spirits being present in our land would unleash a deluge of faithful into the capital, and would also invite many skeptics. Unruly masses will become uncontrollable."

Vordeno rubbed his neatly trimmed goatee with his manicured fingers. He was a charismatic leader nearing his fifties but looked to be somewhere in his thirties. He had been in power for two years, and his prospects for reelection made him take a conservative approach with most issues.

"We do agree that the masks are better in your care," Vordeno reassured the wayfarers, straightening his silver-embroidered black velvet tunic, "but only with our added protection. You have jeopardized much coming this far and risked losing it all at each step of the way. We cannot allow you to take such gambles any longer. The Republic will offer its unconditional support."

Not everyone was in agreement with the princeps, however. Two of the ministers wanted to bring the alliance to a vote; they felt that working in secrecy would result in the loss of trust from their constituents. The ambassador to the Tsing Empire thought it suspicious that the foreigners would not discuss the other masks that had been traveling with them, and suggested not coming to an agreement until they shared the entire truth. The minister of state thought it careless to open the Nisos Dome and invite an unknown tribe into their lands; she asked whether perhaps the Silvfröash could enter the dome, rescue the Spirit of Okri, and leave the Miscam where the Miscam belong. The cavalry general was adamant that at least one mask should be offered to the Republic in recompense for their aid in fighting the Red Stag.

A heated discussion followed.

Infantry General Seera Ashbend rose to speak. She was a tall woman with an angular face, wearing the same kind of armor as Theggo, but of silver and copper instead of silver and yellow, as did all the non-navy soldiers of the Republic. "Since we have control of the reptilian mask, could we not send a fleet to Fel Varanus to capture some of the giants that lurk there? They could aid us in our fight, like the megaloceroses aid Monarch Hallow."

Lummukem narrowed their slitted eyes, interpreting the words for Ishke'ísuk. The basilisk promptly shifted to a frill-necked lizard, scampered across the table to stand in front of the infantry general, and hissed and spat at her face. He then returned to Lummukem's shoulder.

"Ishke'ísuk says no," Lummukem said. "And never suggest that again. We do not enslave our friends."

Scrollsinger Brovon, the representative for the Lavra Faithful, suddenly stood up. His golden robes draped over the onyx table; suspicion draped over his aged face.

"Your Grace…" he barely mumbled through wrinkled lips. His dark eyes darted around the room as if suddenly coming to a realization.

"Yes, Holy Brovon. Speak your mind," Vordeno said. "It's clear there is something eager to come out."

The scrollsinger hesitated. "Your Grace, among all present, I perhaps am the most fearful of speaking impious words—yet a conflicting thought has now clouded my mind." He raised a finger, then put it down, feeling torn. "May the holy Spirit of Kruwen forgive me if I am speaking out of turn, but how do we know that what we just witnessed is not the same as what the Negian Empire is doing?"

"I fail to see what you are implying, Scrollsinger," the princeps said.

"What I mean is… Does the Red Stag not use his mask to control the Spirit of Urg? And does he not do this to inspire reverence among his subjects, who support his misguided cause? How could we tell that our honorable guest, Sunu-Lummukem, is not controlling the Spirit of Kruwen in the same manner? You all did see them glance at the blessed spirit before he came hissing at the infantry general."

"Ishke'ísuk acts of his own volition," Lummukem interjected. Their reptilian face seemed angry, but it always looked a bit angry. "He believes in our cause. He joined willingly to help us."

"The Red Stag claims to have the blessings of Takhísh and Takhamún," Infantry General Seera Ashbend noted evenly. "He controls his citizens by using their own beliefs against them. Our beliefs are different, yet we can be equally manipulated."

"Be careful with your words," Vordeno warned. "Think carefully before making accusations."

"I made an observation, not an accusation, Your Grace," General Ashbend said. "But I will make a request, hoping it will ease our minds. Sunu-Lummukem, would you be willing to take off your mask and show us that the Spirit of Kruwen is not enacting your will instead of his own?"

Lummukem explained the situation to Ishke'ísuk. They shifted back to Sunu, then lowered Kruwensilv upon the onyx table.

Ishke'ísuk hopped off their shoulder and stopped at the center of the table. Ever-so-slowly he let the refracting smoke grow around him, making the basilisk figure foggy, lost within the liquid-like mist and the elongating filaments. The smoke did not grow in every direction equally, but rather in a spiral pattern, lifting the silhouette of the basilisk within it while becoming longer, thicker, taking more and more turns until it grew into the shape of an enormous, coiled python, coalescing into glossy scales. The bifid tongue tasted the air while the slitted eyes scanned the room without blinking.

As the snake rotated his head to face each member of the table, the Lerevi rose from their seats and bowed with clasped hands. Even the infantry general paid her respects. Scrollsinger Brovon, however, only bowed halfway.

The python uncoiled and sprung from the table to form a towering spiral behind Sunu and their friends. He remained there, as still as one of the statues from the esplanade.

"I… I am afraid this proves nothing," the scrollsinger said, their voice evincing their regret. "We do not know exactly how the masks work. Perhaps the mindlock persists after the masks are removed, perhaps not, but there is no way for us to corroborate one way or another. The seed of doubt has sprouted within me, and I've begun to question other things we took for granted." He looked at Princeps Vordeno, who nodded his head.

Brovon stood and clasped his hands, seeming torn once more. "Your Grace, there are implications that have bothered me since the start of this council. The guests claimed that… They—I can't even bring myself to say it… They spoke of Noss having… perished. What greater blasphemy could a tongue utter? If

Noss has been dead this entire time, why did the Normouth Palace not burn in the aftermath of the Downfall? Who heard our prayers during the Reconstitution Epoch and kept our capital safe from the mudslides? Who, if not Noss, inspired the sacred treaties that upheld our powerful republic at the dawn of the Conquest Epoch? To whom have our offerings been given every Nossday at the stupas between Nisos and Normouth? If Noss is no more, who have we been paying tribute to? The very idea is preposterous, a slap in the face of every faithful."

"The way I see it," Vordeno said, "is that there would be no way to corroborate the words of our guests in this matter. I lean toward believing what they spoke to be true, at least in essence, but I know that is not enough."

"We can't form alliances out of assumptions," Brovon replied.

"Yet we have always done so. We assume the good faith of our other allies"—he nodded toward the Tsing ambassador—"and assume that our own foundations are truthful. Yet we've been deceived in the past, and our own founding laws had flaws that needed to be rectified."

"We can't offer you proof of our conversation with Noss," Sterjall said. "But if all goes well, eventually we'll find more Silvfröash to ally with us, and we could commune with Noss once more. What matters is that, right now, our goals are aligned."

Theggo was happy to hear Sterjall using his earlier expression. He looked toward the scrollsinger and added, "I would like to suggest another way of corroborating the truthfulness of our visitors' words. If we are to venture into the Nisos Dome, our own Lerevi representatives could see the reaction of the Spirit of Okri. This would grant us a chance to gauge how the local Miscam see them, and what the Spirit of—sorry, what Gwit thinks of this relationship."

"Does that sound fair to you, Scrollsinger Brovon?" Vordeno asked.

Brovon seemed dubious of the plan, but nodded. "If there are Lerevi witnesses and we are briefed as soon as they return, I will have no objection."

"Then we shall make sure our guests are accompanied by our very best," Vordeno said. "General Ashbend, how large a battalion can you spare to help our friends?"

"No!" Kulak interrupted. "No soldiers. We are not invaders. We need a strong relationship with the Sehján, we cannot risk them fearing we come for war."

"Perhaps not a battalion," Sterjall countered, "but a few soldiers to help us will be fine, as long as we are not an intimidating group. Theggo, if you'd be willing, I would like you to come with us. We trust you, and you'd be a good representative for the Republic."

Theggo bowed from his seat. "I'd be honored," he said.

"A dozen of my bravest dragoons will join you," Cavalry General Garvall Ferwillow said. "My troop will offer protection and any support you require, hopefully without seeming too intimidating. I offer no assurances on that last point."

"A dozen sounds reasonable," Sterjall said with a glance toward Kulak, who nodded in agreement.

They reached a consensus—although still with many dissenting opinions—that the Republic of Lerev would offer their full support.

"Our first goal will be to find the Sehján Miscam," Sterjall said. "We will travel to the Nisos Dome and convince them that it is time for their dome to open. We'll ask Gwit and the Okrifröa if they'd be willing to join us on the next part of our journey."

"The Republic should be ready to offer support to the Miscam tribe once the dome opens," Theggo assured the others. "They believe one of Noss's directives was to help the lost species in their dome spread. We can help them begin within Fel Nisos, then further their range once things settle."

"Can we count on your help?" Vordeno asked the minister of state.

The minister reluctantly nodded. "There are unsettled lands that might do, but we must keep them away from our cities until we are certain there is no danger."

"Splendid," the princeps replied.

"I will set a perimeter around the plateau," General Seera Ashbend said, referring to the high flatlands south of the Normouth Palace, which offered the closest entrance point to the dome. "We will take you to the vines and wait to escort you safely back after your return."

"We don't know how long this will take us," Sterjall admitted. "It could be days, it could be months. Each of the domes has been a different experience—we expect the same uncertainty here."

"We'll be close to the city," Seera said. "My troops will have no problem waiting."

"And I'm willing to accompany you as long as needed," Theggo added. "We'll be with you all the way, on land and sea. Once we exit the dome, if all goes as planned, my fleet can take us straight to the Taring Peninsula to see whether the Spirit of Mindrel—"

"Nelv," Kulak corrected him.

"My apologies, Nelv. To see whether Nelv is where you said she would be waiting."

"Lorr Vaari, will you still not tell us more about the other spirits? About the other masks?" the Tsing ambassador pleaded with Sterjall in his very high-pitched voice. "Empress Pian-Thi needs to be fully briefed before you sail into her waters."

The Tsing ambassador for Lerev was named Vor-Vor. He was an elderly Jabrak-Tsing eunuch, who displayed his bovid tail proudly over his royal-orange robes, draping it in front of his waist and letting the wiry tuft dangle over his right thigh. He wore a single Lode dangling from his left ear, to symbolize his commitment to the common folk in the name of his empress.

"No," Sterjall answered in a conclusive tone. "We made a promise not to involve them. They have their own mission and will be better off on their own. If you have so many spies in Zovaria and beyond, we must assume the enemy has spies in your lands as well. No offense."

"The Republic will vouch for the travelers," Princeps Vordeno reassured the ambassador. "Empress Pian-Thi can count on my word. We shall not push that subject further."

Ambassador Vor-Vor bowed. The black, hollow cube that dangled from his ear swung like a tiny pendulum. "I hear your song of truth, Your Grace. I shall request our Tsing fleet to ready an escort across the Gulf of Erjilm. Empress Pian-Thi is well aware of the threats and is keeping the gulf safe. She has further fortified the already impassable Nargara Bastion, which, even with the full force of the Graalman Horde, should run no risk of being breached. Our greatest concern now is Afhora—if the old kingdom allies with the Red Stag, they may gain control of the Alommo Sea."

"What is the plan once at the Gulf of Erjilm?" General Ashbend asked.

"We intend to enter and liberate the Ashen Dome," Theggo answered.

"What about the Seafaring Dome?" Sterjall asked.

Theggo shook his head. "The Capricious Ocean is most deadly in Winter. I would not risk my fleet in its treacherous waters, and I don't think the Negians would either. As far as we can tell, the Red Stag's strategy is to conquer by land. We should try to reach the domes he is closer to before he does. It is too late for the Archstone and Moonrise domes. The Scoria Dome will be next in his path, and I'm afraid we might not have time to stop him there, either."

Alaia awkwardly raised a hand and asked, "Don't you think the Red Stag might come after us? If he's after masks, there's one place where he can easily snatch a handful." She sank back into her seat, uncertain of how the Lerevi viewed the Oldrin.

"It's unlikely, Lurr Alaia," Theggo responded. "Even if they get their ships all the way around the continent, and even if they join forces with the southeastern kingdoms, their fleet will have a hard time against those of the Tsing Empire and Lerev combined. Monarch Hallow will play it safe until he loses his advantage. However, there is something I haven't told you yet, as I did not want to worry you unnecessarily. Something the princeps and generals are well aware of."

Everyone waited for Theggo to continue.

"We have been followed," he said. "Not by normal spies, mind you, but my captains spotted cormorants trying to remain elusive and distant, only visible by spyglass. They showed up five days ago."

"Zovarians…" Sterjall grumbled. "Of course they'd try to track us."

Theggo rubbed his bushy eyebrows. "I don't believe that to be the case. The Zovarians needed no spies to know exactly where you were headed. These were red-breasted cormorants, like the ones trained in Hestfell. There's nothing unusual about Lerevi ships in Lerevi waters—the only thing they could've been scouting for was your black-sailed ship."

"What does your scalp think they want?" Kulak asked.

"Other than simply keeping track of our movements, I have no idea. But let that be a warning. Assume the enemy knows our positions at all times. Their cormorants can't tell them more than whether a ship has been spotted or not, so they won't know how many masks or spirits go with us. But they know you are in Lerev, and they'll know the moment we begin our trip away from our great island."

"If there's nothing to be done about that, then let it be," Sterjall said. "For now, we should focus on what we have at hand. It's better to enter the dome at sundown, so it will be dawn on the inside." He looked toward the palace's windows. The light was turning golden, the sun readying to set. "But… perhaps we could first use a good night's sleep?" he suggested, feeling the weight of his fatigue.

"That would help us greatly with our planning," Theggo agreed. "We'll have all of tomorrow to prepare the provisions."

"See to it, Admiral," Princeps Vordeno said, ending the council session.

CHAPTER THIRTY-NINE

TRISKELION

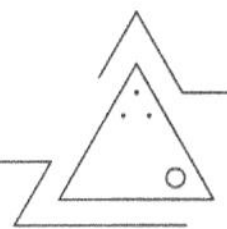

Under the supervision of Dragoon Leader Seshéni of Tallasar, twelve dragoons escorted the wayfarers toward the Nisos Dome, each mounted atop agile kudus, brandishing rapiers of shining silver and copper to match their hauberks.

Theggo followed comfortably atop Tinnomeg, his trusty giant eland. Unlike the dragoons—who wore their long hair tied in buns over their heads, stabbed by dagger-like hair spikes—Theggo let his hair loose in the breeze. The strands of gold and silver nearly matched the colors of his plated armor.

They climbed a switchback road up the plateau south of the Normouth Palace, getting an expansive view of the splendorous city as the setting sun caressed its thousand spires.

Infantry General Seera Ashbend was waiting at the windy top of the mesa. She tried to overpower the howling gusts with her voice, calling out, "I have a platoon of fifty setting up the perimeter! They will keep it clear for two miles in each direction! When you return, do so in the same general area, so we can escort you back to the palace."

They rode past a troop struggling to raise tarps for a pavilion. Theggo tapped a hand to his chest to salute the soldiers, who did their best to salute back without losing hold of the ropes.

Directly ahead, the vines waited.

Kulak asked Blu and Pichi to stop, then looked to the group for confirmation. Theggo and Seshéni nodded their approval.

The vines parted.

"Careful with the holes they leave in the ground," Sterjall warned the Lerevi, holding on to Blu's saddle, "particularly in rocky areas. There won't be as many as we venture deeper."

Pharolith lamps were opened. The dragoons gasped at the magical light, although their kudus didn't seem to care.

Quiet and devotional, the Lerevi followed the lead of the smilodons.

A foggy drizzle sprayed their faces once they breached through the half-mile wall. The gray morning extended like a series of curtains, only revealing sporadic silhouettes in front of them. They had exited on the opposite side of the plateau that spread toward the city of Normouth. The flatland was covered in green and orange vegetation, mostly short in stature, although a few trees stood out in the fog as threatening silhouettes.

Theggo turned his head around, feeling something strange about the way the fog cast a soft dimness in front of them. Through the mist, the vine wall was barely perceptible as a dull green speckled with bright dots. The glow intensified higher up and abruptly stopped to create a false, elevated horizon of light stuck beneath grayish dullness.

The wayfarers had explained to the Lerevi what they would see once they entered the dome; this peculiar phenomenon of light, however, did not fit any of their descriptions.

"I… I don't understand what I am looking at," Theggo mumbled.

"It's just the arudinn under fog and clouds," Sterjall assured him. "There are more of them higher up. Let's move ahead to find a clear viewpoint."

Colorful kangaroo mice hopped out of their way as they rode through the fog. One of the trees ahead of them seemed to glitter, as if its leaves were sparkling. As they drew nearer, the shape of the tree exploded into hundreds of green and purple shards.

"Emerald starlings!" Alaia yelled, fascinated by the iridescent-green wings and purple bellies of the birds. "Look at them flock! Those are the ones from Hefra's book, remember?"

"Yeah, the page you colored yourself," Sterjall told her. "Crysta never forgave me for you vandalizing that book."

"I made it prettier," she retorted.

For hours they marched slowly through the fog of the unknown lands, until the first darkening began at the distant horizon. They stopped at the edge of a cliff, feeling the mists beginning to part thanks to a warm breeze. As the landscape cleared, they found themselves looking over a wide, pond-speckled basin cut by a long lake. The expansive lake was dotted with tiny islands, the inverse of the thousand ponds on the land around it. From the largest of these islands grew one of the supporting columns, rising from the haze and vanishing into the clouds.

"It's magnificent…" Theggo breathed. "You said the trunk was vast, but I did not expect something of this scale."

"That is not Okridrolom's trunk," Kulak said with a smirk. "It is one of the columns. There are twenty-three in each dome. Our eyes cannot see as far as the trunk with this kind of weather."

Lummukem pointed to a potential path down the cliff. "The meadowlands are flat, at least as far as our eyes can currently see. We could march southward along the lake's shore."

"But first we should let our mounts rest," Theggo said, rubbing his eland's neck. "Tinnomeg is tired. This change of light is confusing, and if it's already darkening here, Sunnokh must be rising over Fel Nisos. We must've been on the move for a very long time."

Sterjall awoke sometime before the trunk brightened, hearing a soft, humming melody. The dragoons had set up tents to protect them from the rain, but only a light shower had come and gone.

The wolf tenderly removed Kulak's arm from his chest and sat up, peeking through the flap of his tent. He saw Theggo sitting at the overlook. The humming came from him, interspersed with quietly sung words in a solemn chant. He stepped out and looked up—the sky had cleared up, turning into the blackest ocean-blue.

Theggo sensed Sterjall approaching and stopped his humming. With a gesture, he invited the young wolf to sit by his side. The fleet admiral looked quite different now, with none of his shining armor covering his body. His long hair was matted, his eyebags heavy. His eyes, however, had a shine Sterjall had not yet witnessed.

Is it melancholy? Or happiness? Sterjall wondered.

Theggo's gaze followed the stretching lake. The trunk was barely visible now that the sky had cleared, as a tower of pure blackness against the blue arudinn. Most of the supporting columns were silhouetted now too, as well as the distant mountains, the brighter ones hinting at tops that were snow- or glacier-capped.

"This pre-dawn twilight is as disconcerting as it is alluring," Theggo said. "The trunk is intimidating. How could the Miscam achieve such greatness? Could it be that we have been mistaken about the nature of the domes? Of the spirits? Of Noss themself?"

He rubbed a pendant between calloused fingers. Sterjall saw it sparkle briefly and recognized the shape: it was a silver triskelion, like the ones on the Lerevi flags.

"I feel like all of us are mistaken, one way or another," Sterjall said. "Even the Miscam. Each of their tribes has its faults. Perhaps even Noss themself might be mistaken sometimes. It's just the nature of things. We are all imperfect, but I guess that makes us unique."

"Merely a few weeks ago, I would've recoiled at the blasphemy you just spoke. About Noss being imperfect, I mean. But times are changing, Lorr Vaari, and with the times we must change as well."

Theggo's eyes suddenly sparkled. Sterjall instinctively looked up and saw a 'star,' as Aio-Kulak would've called it, one of the vines in the sky suddenly flashing like a timid bolt of lightning, lingering for a long moment before disappearing.

"What was it that you were just singing?" Sterjall asked.

"It was the Thirteenth Canticle, the Song of Lerabeth. One of the poems of the Lavra Scrolls. My father used to sing it to me."

"It sounded beautiful."

"It's one of my favorites from the Second Scroll. It's uplifting, yet it drags you back down in an endless cycle."

He sang again, tumbling his voice in a rising and falling melody with no beginning or end.

> Down
>
>   fall
>
>   our spiraling souls.
>
> Oh spirits, have mercy, take heed of our song,
>
> Out bring us from darkness, replenish our hope.
>
> Our life-force be strengthened till upward we soar,
>
> Yet drop down to darkness once more.

Down

    plunge

        our bodies to dust.

Oh Noss fertile cradle, take pity on us,

Let not our seeds falter, let sprouts grow robust.

Your womb grant us shelter in layers of crust,

Till drought turns our branches to rust.

End

    fall

        will carry us all.

Oh mind who bears judgment, absolve your own faults,

Your sins be forgiven, your will reinforced.

Go conquer the maelstrom, forth battle the squall,

To tumble back down to a fall.

Hmm

    Humm

        Mm-hmm mm-hm-humm…

The song ended in a diffused humming, or perhaps it ended not, as the melody kept flowing within Sterjall's head.

"We do not know the fourth stanza," Theggo said, "as that portion of the scroll was deteriorated and unreadable. That is why the scrollsingers merely hum it, and the listeners are meant to make their own interpretations of it." He held his pendant right under his chin, rubbing it against his short beard. "Were you aware that I just committed a grave sin by singing that to you?"

"How so? Didn't you say it was from the sacred texts?"

"Indeed, but it is a sacrilegious act to sing them out loud unless you are an ordained scrollsinger. Which I am not, and my father was not. My father always sang them to me in secret, simply because the songs made me happy. I learned a lot from the canticles. They teach of the nature of creation, of our place among all creatures, of our insignificance, of our greatness. Their incompleteness has always sparked great debates, and I don't mean debates in which truths are revealed and accepted, but the kind in which preconceived notions are upheld and reinforced for all sides."

The trunk began to dimly light up, heralding the arrival of dawn. Theggo held a breath, perhaps suppressed a few heartbeats, then continued talking.

"My father was convicted for heresy when I was but a teenager. He taught me of the faith and convinced me of its truths before the Lavra Faithful took him from me. The Lavra Scrolls allowed me to hold on by giving me hope, by giving me a purpose. I don't know if I hold that same purpose any longer, Lorr Vaari, but I would like to think I still hold on to my faith, to my moral code."

The base from which the trunk sprouted was now visible—a black mesa, flat and steep-walled. The trunk brightened further, a gradient transitioning from darkness at the bottom to blinding sharpness at the branching top, in a dim crispness similar to a night when the Ilaadrid Shard shone its fiercest. The vines in the sky caught the light and turned a highly textured green. Each of the supporting columns streaked a shadowy twin that wrapped itself against the walls and ceiling of the dome.

A penumbral silence stretched between them.

"The pendant," Sterjall said, distracted by the sight of Theggo continuing to rub it in his fingers, "what does it mean?"

"The triskelion?" Theggo pulled it off so that Sterjall could better see the three connected spirals drawn from a single line. "It means many things. It's in the flag of the Republic, of course, but it's also a symbol that was found in one of the original Lavra Scrolls. It represents the three interconnected essences—soul, body, and mind."

He traced a blackened fingernail over the spiraling path as he spoke, following along the triangle-like shape as if trying to escape a labyrinth with no beginning and no end.

"The bottom-left spiral is that of the soul, which in our faith is embodied by the eighteen spirits. They are all within us, they are a part of us. From what you've taught me, there is some objective truth to this, and not merely a metaphorical one. The spirits are the embodiments of all the creatures of their kind. Where we, mere humans, fall within that, still escapes me, but the concept still holds."

The tracing finger escaped the pull of the first spiral and plunged into the helical depths of the second.

"The spiral on the bottom-right is that of the body, which is manifested as Noss, as the planet themself, the essence of all matter. Our cradle, our grave. The Noss in our canticles is evasive, unknowable, unreachable. The scrollsingers of old claimed to have spoken with them, yet I fail to see how they managed if they had no Silvesh of their own."

The finger sped up into the third and final spiral, which seemed brighter, as the trunk was brightening and lending its light to the curved forms of the pendant. The finger was swallowed by the maelstrom.

"The third spiral, the one on top, is that of the mind. That one is embodied in our own cognitive abilities. Despite the spiral being on top, our faith places little emphasis on this third aspect of our wholeness. I'm curious as to why. Perhaps we put too much faith on anything external and choose not to trust ourselves."

Theggo lifted his finger from the triskelion. He looked back up to the umbellate forms of light expanding outward from the trunk. "Each of those three spirals is represented in the three known stanzas of the Song of Lerabeth, yet we know there was once a fourth stanza of a similar structure. How that fits into the whole, we do not know. I look at this shape of pure perfection"—he lifted the pendant so that the spirals were silhouetted against the arudinn's glow—"and can find no way to add anything to it, to change it, to make it any more complete. Yet something feels amiss."

"The song and the triskelion, they remind me of a litany a friend of mine used to recite." In a melodious tone, Sterjall recited Ockam's litany, nearly singing it. "A young tree I am, the old forest I am not, yet forest and tree are of one soul. A small fish I am, the vast ocean I am not, yet ocean and fish are of one mind. A frail wolf I am, the strong pack I am not, yet pack and wolf are of one heart." He looked at Theggo, and added, "It's similar, though your song speaks of soul, mind, and body, while the litany speaks of soul, mind, and heart." He reached toward Theggo's pendant and picked it up by the chain.

"One thing I've been learning is to look at things from different perspectives," Sterjall said. "The same way that consciousness can have levels too complex for our minds to understand, so can other simple matters. But there are ways to think of them as abstractions, ways that help us see the invisible."

He placed the triskelion flat on the pad of his left handpaw. "Perhaps none of these three spirals is meant to be on top—all of them are equal, all three are one. You say you feel something is missing. I try to picture where that something could fit while still keeping the striking symmetry. The only place I can think of is here." He hovered a dark claw above the triskelion, on a point that hinted at an imaginary tetrahedron. "Things are always more complex than we think, yet still so simple. Heart. I think that's all that's missing in this song, in this symbol. We are all too quick to make up our minds, to crush each other's souls, to cut and tear at our bodies. A bit of empathy, a touch from our hearts, that's the only thing that can keep us united. It's what lets us become greater than our individual selves."

Theggo pondered, as if in a trance. "You are wiser than your years," he said. "Your parents must be proud."

Sterjall felt a jolt of pain within his very soul, but as he had learned to do with the mask, he let the pain in and internalized it, letting it become a part of him instead of denying its existence. He thought of his mentors, those who *would* be proud of him: Crysta, Gwil, Holfster, Khopto, Ockam, Jiara, Banook, Mamóru. Yet he also thought of his mother, who had died giving birth to him. And he thought of Theo Vaari, who had always been a shadow looming over him but now felt like nothing more than a trick of the light, a harmless illusion that would always be there but need not have an effect on him any longer.

"I hope I can make them proud," Sterjall murmured.

He returned the pendant to Theggo, who draped it back over his chest.

The branching top of the trunk was now fully lit, the glow of the arudinn expanding rapidly outward.

"Admiral Saurfall," came a call from behind them. It was Dragoon Leader Seshéni. "My troop awaits your presence. We need to strategize our next steps."

"I'll be right there, Seshéni," Theggo replied. He pushed the matted strands of silver and gold hair off his face and rose to his feet.

"Listen, Lorr Vaari," he said, putting a hand on Sterjall's shoulder. He gazed at the lines of pastel-whites that were stretching into the sky. "It's merely my first day seeing this and I'm already overwhelmed. I just wanted to say... I hope you are thankful for all you've experienced. For all you've seen, all the people you've met. For the wonderful worlds you've journeyed through. You are lucky, young Lorr."

"Thank you," Sterjall said. "I know. And I am. Thankful, I mean."

I truly am, he thought.

CHAPTER FORTY

WORLDS WITHIN WORLDS

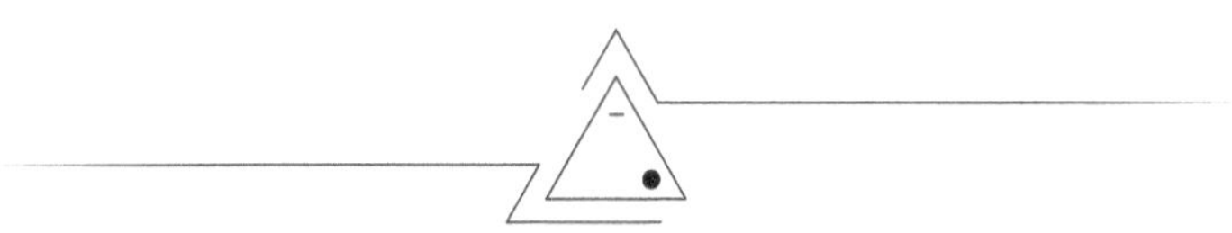

"There is something strange about the lake," Kulak commented as they wove a path from the plateau to the pond-flecked meadow. "Something feels different about it today, but my scalp cannot understand what."

"We agree," Lummukem said. "Something is amiss."

"I noticed dots of brightness on some islands before the trunk lit up," Theggo added. "There must be locals living there. We'll see better once we get to the shore."

"Hey, look at that!" Alaia said, pointing at a scurrying creature that dove into a creek. "An ottermole. Remember those cuties?"

"Haven't seen them in ages!" Sterjall replied.

"Another mole?" Kulak asked.

"An. Ottermole," Sterjall corrected him. "We made up that name, since we didn't know what they were called. They're like shrews but with beaver tails." He smiled, reminiscing. "We saw them inside the Heartpine Dome. Bear loved these things. Ockam wanted to hunt them, but Alaia wouldn't let him."

"Fuck no, they are too adorable," she said. "Who could possibly eat them?"

As they reached the innumerable ponds, they encountered a herd of capybaras lounging by the shore. The presence of the smilodons startled the oversized rodents, who barked at them and dove into the waters for safety, floating their squarish heads out like disapproving logs.

"Big rats," Kulak said, leading Blu away from them and into the wetlands.

Though from above the landscape had seemed flat, they had not considered the height of the reeds in the waterlogged marshes. As they entered the forest of papyrus plants, the reed stems grew way above their heads—mounts and all—to burst outward in radial patterns.

"Life is thriving here," Sterjall said. "I can sense hundreds of small animals hiding in the reeds. So many bird nests, too."

A splashing of waves got their attention. The sound led them to a clearing by the lake's shore, where colossal beavers, as large as Bergsulf bison, were chewing eagerly on papyrus sprouts.

"Even bigger rats," Kulak remarked.

"Castoroides," Theggo said. "Giant beavers. Though much more giant than the ones from our fossils."

"They must be a companion species," Kulak noted. "But where are the Miscam who feed them?"

The giant beavers were tame but distrustful. After staring at the intruders with obvious displeasure, they thunderously smacked their tails down, splattering the group's bodies with mud, then dove into the lake. Though they were heavy and slow on land, with their webbed feet they swam away at a formidable speed.

The clearing the beavers had flattened and chewed on was large enough to fit all of the travelers and their mounts, so they dismounted to rest. The dragoons stood guard around the edges of the clearing, watching the kudus and the eland graze on the papyrus sprouts and fresh grasses. Kulak sent Pichi and Blu to hunt. While Dragoon Leader Seshéni lit a fire to cook lunch, the others gathered at the lakeshore to survey the landscape. A couple of miles away stood the largest of the islands, from which the nearest supporting column grew.

"Is that smoke on the east side of the island?" Sterjall asked. He offered his binoculars to Theggo, but the admiral waved him off and produced a spyglass of his own, one with significantly greater magnification.

"It's too far away to see any buildings," Theggo said, "but that could be steam from hot springs, or perhaps nothing more than a low cloud clinging to the moisture of the vines." He turned his sight toward the trunk. From this lower elevation, they could no longer see the mesa the trunk grew from, so it seemed as if it was sprouting from the lake itself. Its reflection was a chaotic blur, smeared by the patterns of breezes that rippled the lake's surface.

"Um, Sterjall…" Alaia began with a concerned tone, tapping his shoulder. "That island to the left… Was it not farther from us just moments ago?"

"What do you mean?" Sterjall asked. He aimed his binoculars at the island. It wasn't too large, perhaps three hundred feet across, covered in green mounds with a compact forest of trees on top. "That's odd… There's a wake forming around—"

A deafening roar interrupted him. All of Kulak's hairs stood on end, recognizing Blu's voice.

"Mindrégosh, *pregithuk li chossat!*" he called out.

Blu and Pichi burst into the clearing, hissing and growling. The dragoons unsheathed their rapiers and formed a protective circle, signaling for the others to take cover within.

"Soldiers, coming through the reeds," Lummukem warned.

"Keep your weapons ready, but down," Theggo ordered. Seshéni repeated the command—her dragoons obeyed.

Glistening swordstaffs pushed between the papyrus stems. The sharp blades were followed by dozens of toughened female warriors with long hair of radiant reds and threatening burnt umbers.

The circle of dragoons tightened.

The warriors took short steps, knees bent, swordstaffs ready to strike. Their lacquered armor shimmered in hundreds of interlocked plates, like iridescent scales of strikingly vivid hues.

Just as Sterjall was about to speak, he was interrupted by battlecries from the shore. The island Alaia had pointed to had somehow made its way to them, carrying dozens more red-haired warriors who hopped into the clearing with weapons drawn. Kulak stepped forward with arms raised.

"Hold your blades, Sehján Miscam friends!" he bellowed in Miscamish.

The confused warriors stopped when they heard the caracal speak. One of them whistled a command. The circle of swordstaffs did not lower, but it stopped tightening.

"Mindrelfröa?" the leading warrior inquired in a tightly punctuated Miscamish. "Do our eyes deceive us?"

"Where are they taking us?" Theggo asked Sterjall; the admiral felt lost, not able to speak or understand any Miscamish. The dragoons seemed equally uneasy, except for Seshéni, who was just familiar enough with the tongue to get by.

"They are saying their queen lives in Kisdik, the city surrounding the column," Sterjall answered. "It's strange… They don't refer to their queen as the Okrifröa, and they refuse to talk about anything related to the masks."

A polite servant brought drinks and fruits for all—one of the few Sehján men they had seen so far, all of whom seemed to be relegated to subordinate roles.

While tasting the sugary foods, Sterjall tried to explain to the Sehján who they were and why they had come, but the warriors requested their guests—

or perhaps prisoners—wait before sharing too much, as their queen would need to hear their story firsthand. The warriors did not mind, however, sharing more about themselves and their peculiar islands.

They were traveling atop a floating island as large as a city block, constructed from a tessellation of dried papyrus stems, cuts of bark from cork oak, and other buoyant materials that formed perfectly durable rafts. Soil and grass covered the extensive platforms, and trees were grown atop so that their roots would hold the structures together, creating perfectly natural-looking islands, except for the peculiarity of them being able to move apparently of their own volition.

The travelers were sitting near what they chose to think of as the stern of the island, on a circle of wooden benches beneath a cork oak tree that had recently had part of its bark removed, leaving its trunk naked and exposed. Other trees around it seemed to have regrown their bark but were not yet ready to be harvested.

It hadn't taken long at all to sail to the column—or drift, or whatever they were doing, since none of them could see sails or oars present—and now the tower of vines was rising almost directly over them. But it was no ordinary island from which the column grew—it was another floating structure, wrapping around the column like a skirt.

They docked nearly seamlessly with the larger island. Sterjall stood up, getting ready to disembark, but the lead Sehján warrior, whose name was Tsei, told him to wait.

"The city of Krillimo rises before you," Tsei said. She tucked a lock of her bright-red hair behind her ear and smiled, stretching the parallel bands of white paint that ran from the bottom of her nose to the nook under her lips, like the incisive teeth of a rodent. "We are not yet at Kisdik, our capital, not yet under her grace," she continued. "Even greater is Kisdik, where all Sehján are beholden to Lakemother's protection. Both Kisdik and Krillimo are one and are many, so they are. Islands fuse over time, grow big when families build new connections, new relationships. Some islands then merge back into Kisdik and Krillimo, making them yet greater. Such is the way of islands."

"What is it they are saying?" Theggo asked, growing frustrated.

"She's telling us about their islands," Alaia answered. "Sorry, Theggo. I'll try to interpret for you and the dragoons whenever possible."

"They come now," Tsei said. "Our *okruwomesh*. Their tireless tails are ready to be changed. Blessed by waters eternal."

They did not know what an *okruwom* was, but soon found out. They felt something shake in the foundations of their island, then out splashed dozens of giant beavers, looking tired, but happy to be back on land to rest and feed. The exhausted castoroides headed toward a trough filled with munnji paste and dunked their heads in, while a new troop of beavers dove into the water to take their place.

The island jolted and began to move again.

"We are being pulled around by giant rats?" Alaia said in Common, fearful that her words might be taken as disrespectful. "This place keeps getting weirder by the moment."

South they continued, moving fast over the breezy lake. Tsei pointed to the 'bow' of their island, in the direction of yet another of the supporting columns, and said, "Kisdik floats around those sacred vines. That is our capital."

"Your queen does not live at the trunk? Near Ommo ust Okri?" Kulak asked, a bit surprised.

Tsei furrowed her brow and searched for a way to change the subject. She had noticed that Sterjall was fascinated by her peculiar set of armor, so she took some pieces off to let him examine them.

Sterjall inspected the articulated armored sleeves. They were made of a lacquered, lamellar construction, formed by dozens of overlapping plates. Each plate was iridescent, like a jewel beetle's wing, shining in verdant hues for the upper body pieces and in shimmering purples around the lower body. When he probed the plates, they bent in a rubbery manner, though they seemed durable and hard to pierce.

"What sort of material is this?" he asked.

"Elytra armor. That is what we call it, that is the name," Tsei replied. "Cut from okruwom tail leather. Lacquered by aphids. Color, life, and further strength they give. That is their blessing."

Sterjall cocked his head, trying to picture how aphids were involved in manufacturing armor.

Tsei made a puckering gesture that tightened the white markings on her lips, which Sterjall, by inference through Agnargsilv, understood to mean *wait*. She left him for a moment but soon returned with a thin branch covered in bulbous crusts of green sap.

Tsei pointed a fingernail at a nearly invisible line of dots on the branch. "Here live the welkil aphids. Here they make their resins. Strong resin. Yes. That is their blessing."

Sterjall had to place the branch over his muzzle and cross his eyes to be able to see the tiny aphids. They looked like sparkling emeralds the size of grains of sand.

"One plant we feed them, one color of resin they gift us," Tsei explained, now holding up her weapon, which had a hilt striped in green and violet. "Another plant, another color. Such is the way of the welkil, thus we are thankful."

"What are these weapons you wield?" Lummukem asked.

"A swordstaff became my calling, like for most others," Tsei answered. "Some wield quarterstaffs with iron caps, but most prefer the sharp blades of swordstaffs."

She let Lummukem hold the weapon, which consisted of a blade mounted on a hilt twice its length. The colorful lacquers on the hilt felt durable and provided perfect friction.

"My swordstaff's hilt is made of okruwom bones, wrapped with okruwom hide," Tsei explained. "Wrapped thusly, it blesses my hands with a better grip. Okruwom tail is toughest, good for armor. Thick, waterproof, but also soft. It remains elastic like lake weed, even with welkil resin. And do not let your teeth worry, we do not kill our kind. Okruwomesh bless us with their leather, with their bones, after they enter the Eternal Sea. Thus we are thankful for their blessings."

"The colors are exquisite," Alaia said to Tsei. "They remind me of the green and purple birds we saw when we entered the dome." She did not know the Miscamish name for *emerald starlings*, but Tsei seemed to understand.

"*Kroovieth burdrolv*," Tsei replied with a surprised smile. "My colors are inspired by their beautiful feathers."

The city of Kisdik became visible at last, rising around the column they'd been moving toward as if a flattened volcano was erupting vines into the sky. This floating island wasn't as tall as the mountains beyond the lake, yet impressive it was, constructed solely of buoyant materials grown through the centuries into a three-mile-long raft.

Kisdik looked similar to Krillimo, covered in barrow-like dwellings mostly hidden beneath grasses and trees. The shores were sprinkled with colorful buoys, which Tsei explained were there to mark the oyster and algae farms.

"Are all of your cities in the water?" Sterjall asked.

Tsei seemed troubled, unsure of how to answer. "The water is always safe," was all that she offered as a response.

Once they disembarked onto the floating city, their feet and paws were thrown off balance by how the land reacted to their weight, bobbing up and down over the waves. The entire island was perpetually bending and shifting, responding to the whims of the wind and tides, adapting its resilient shape. Blu was particularly upset by this development; he had hoped to take refuge on solid land, but this was just another undulating raft.

Through farmlands and marketplaces they were escorted, toward the core of the city, where the mound dwellings, which Tsei called their *dens*, became more numerous, sometimes intersecting each other in complex, multistory hillocks connected by curved, dark tunnels.

It was not to the highest point of the city that they were taken, but to an expansive plaza covered in cork oak trees at water level. At the center of this forested circle was a large pond, and at the center of the pond floated a particularly large den—an islet within an island surrounded by a pond within a lake. The den was connected to the island by dozens of taut bridges woven out of durable fibers, as if bound by a spiderweb of ropes and platforms. It was covered in ferns and pierced by many darkened tunnels, some of which were doorways, windows or ventilation shafts.

"The Queen's Lodge," Tsei said, approaching one of the bridges. "Ierun Jessha has been informed of your arrival. She waits at the gathering chamber. Some of you must wait at the plaza, for not big enough is the chamber, not for all."

Seshéni ordered her dragoons to stay behind with the kudus, smilodons, and eland, then followed behind the others. The bridges were more stable than Sterjall had expected, and easy to cross. As he balanced over them, he spotted a boy and a girl atop the curved roof of the Queen's Lodge. They had quarterstaffs and were practicing offensive and defensive moves with admirable prowess. Their trainer stood to one side and saluted the newcomers by placing her index and middle fingers right over her lip paints. When the kids saw the travelers at the bridge, they dropped their quarterstaffs and disappeared behind the grassy mound.

"We interrupted Khurun Puuja and Khuron Pol's training," Tsei said. "You will soon meet the twins. They are the lake's greatest blessing."

Tsei led them to the main entrance into the Queen's Lodge, having to duck to fit through the narrow tunnel. Sterjall followed behind her, admiring the dark curves of the stick-and-mud dwelling. For a moment they were in pure darkness, but Sterjall could feel the breeze of multiple paths opening to his sides. With Agnargsilv, he gazed upon the complex chambers inside the den— they reminded him of the inside of an anthill. As he analyzed the space, he quickly noticed something lacking. *There is no glow in here,* he thought. *No Okrisilv at the Queen's Lodge.*

The tunnel brightened and opened into the gathering chamber: a round, domed space constructed of treated wood walls with soft cork floors. Sterjall found the scents of the room odd but reassuring, like a mixture of old smoke, pine oil, and vanilla. He flinched as he came across a recessed alcove, which held a ghastly human skull wearing a crown carved from a single, giant opal. *An old Sehján ruler,* he guessed. *Gruesome. They could at least dust the cobwebs off it…*

At the center of the room was a circular opening about two strides in diameter, revealing a pool of clear water. The arudinn's light filtered down through the pond they had crossed outside and bounced up to meet them in this luminous circle. The pool glowed, lighting the log benches set around the opening. At the far side, standing in front of one of the benches, waited Ierun Jessha. The twins hid shyly behind her tall figure, both curious, but only the girl dared to sneak a peek.

Ierun Jessha's velvety voice echoed softly through the circular chamber. "Welcome to Okridrolom, children of the lakes beyond," she said, then placed two fingers over her lips. "Lakemother shelter you."

CHAPTER FORTY-ONE

BLACK MIRROR

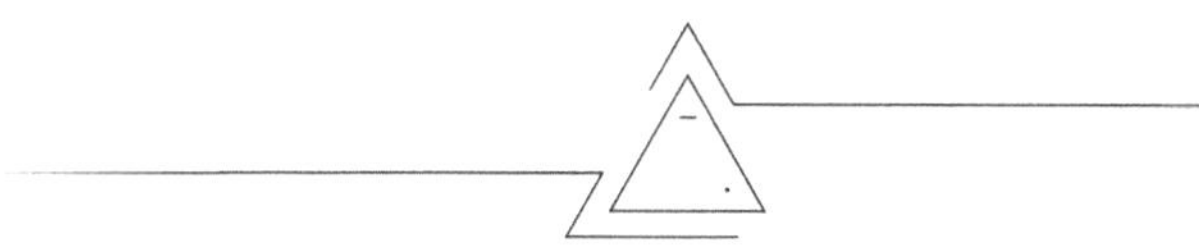

The queen was young and powerfully built, as it was with all the female warriors they'd encountered thus far. She wore lamellar armor not unlike Tsei's, only different in hue: Ierun Jessha's was colored a fiery amber. Her red hair flowed in smooth waves over her left shoulder, blending with her armor. She invited her guests to sit in the circle of log benches, then offered them a sour flatbread.

This time, Kulak took the lead in explaining the reason for their unexpected visit. With help from his friends, he went into as much detail as possible without extending the gathering for too many hours.

The twins sheltering behind the queen listened intently. They were merely eleven years old, with faces curious and covered in freckles. The girl, named Puuja, was more confident, and even dared to ask questions of the foreigners; while her brother, Pol, was eerily reserved and had not said a word since the strangers arrived, nor had he even looked at them directly.

Is that even the same boy I saw atop the roof? Sterjall wondered. The little warrior had seemed so much more confident, even powerful, while wielding his quarterstaff; down here he held his posture like a tight knot, making him seem smaller, as if he was a year or two younger than his sister. Sterjall looked away from the shy boy, who seemed to dislike being stared at so intently.

"This is why we came to you," Kulak concluded his tale, "searching for the Okrifröa." He paused, seeming disheartened. "But my scalp senses that you are not the Okrifröa."

Ierun Jessha sighed, closing her light-brown eyes.

"That title… I cannot claim," she said heavily. "Dire is our situation. Your task will not be an easy one to accomplish. Look into the water for truth, and listen to our story." She tossed a few crumbs into the pool in front of them, summoning colorful bluefins who quickly devoured the morsels while flashing like rippling bolts of lightning. They circled the hole, waiting for more.

"The story of Okridrolom is one of great struggle," Jessha began, staring at the patterns the bluefins traced, as if trying to divine meaning from their motion. "Beyond six lakes, beneath six seas, when our blessed dome had not yet closed, we were at war with a neighboring tribe. That we were." She tightened her lips, causing the vertical stripes painted on them to merge into one. "The pale demons, the Oxruk. Our cave-dwelling enemies felt entitled to these lands. Not theirs, not theirs they were, not now, not ever. A fair trade we made with the Kingdom of Nisos, giving up our much richer lands on islands north and islands west. Treaties were signed, oaths to Lakemother spoken, and to the Sehján Miscam these lands were granted. But the Oxruk… they knew not of reason—they knew only spite. Such is the way of the Oxruk. Yet away we banished them, keeping them outside our home until Okridrolom closed. Guileless were we, for we thought we'd see the Oxruk's pale faces no more."

Jessha clenched her sharp jaw.

"The pale demons tunneled in secrecy. Inside our mountains they cut their dwellings and hid there until our vines sealed, waiting to come out like cicadas in the year of penitence. When they showed their pale faces, it was too late, for the Downfall had come and only the lands within remained. Wars aplenty we fought. And we won. So we did. Our brave warriors killed the wretched Seer King and took his head and his crown."

Jessha glanced to the alcove holding the grisly skull crowned by a giant, carved opal, then continued with her tale. "The Oxruk surrendered, and we came to a long peace. We offered them to stay in the periphery, close to the vines Noss had told us not to approach. The Oxruk did so, and bred greater numbers through the years, always complaining that they wanted more land. Too much they dug, too many children they spawned, not respecting our sacred oaths or the balance of the dome. When we fought them again, we were not expecting them. Out the ground they gushed with sharp claws, gouging burrows under our cities, ambushing us. By their clawed arms perished most of the Sehján, resting now at peace in the Eternal Sea."

Jessha crossed her arms over her chest, then continued. "The last Okrifröa… Ierun Hejána was her name. She was a most colorful shekru squirrel, a companion species we did not have a chance to fully develop as Noss intended us to. She fought atop the Dohao Mesa, where our capital city of

Kissumar long ago stood. But the pale demons had devious tactics. From the rocky core of the mesa they excavated, up into the sacredness of Ommo ust Okri itself, where they murdered Ierun Hejána and for themselves claimed the Silv of Okri. That is their sin, that is their eternal shame." Jessha's voice tapered off, as if relaying this tale was taking a great toll on her.

The long pause tried Sterjall's patience; finally, he said, "Does that mean the mask—"

Jessha put three fingers to her lips, fully covering the white lines painted on them. Sterjall quieted down.

"Their attacks could not be stopped," she continued, "because the Oxruk… they could come from anywhere, at any time. Our survivors moved to the hallowed wetlands. Of their soft soil we are grateful, for there our blessed Lakemother permeates the earth. The Oxruk's tunnels crumbled in that terrain, so we hid among the reeds and learned to live a new kind of life. We heard Lakemother's song, who taught us to build boats and rafts with the reeds. Centuries it took us, but we learned to harvest the oak cork and use the resins to build floating homes. Our islands joined their strengths and became our vine-locked cities, while others still float freely around the great Klad Üo, the Klad Goro, the Klad Flal, and the Klad Allún." She tossed another handful of crumbs, which were quickly devoured from below.

"This is it, this is all of us. All Sehján survivors moved to the sacred lakes or to the wetlands around them, where Lakemother keeps us protected in her waters eternal. Thus to her we are thankful. And that is why I am a maskless queen."

Her tone was that of finality, so Sterjall dared to speak once more.

"What happened to Okrisilv, then? How come Okridrolom is still in proper shape and not grown wild, like Kruwendrolom?"

"For two centuries after our Silv was stolen, our blessed dome grew unhealthy and untamed. The arudinn suffered spasms of light and threatened to leave our sinful souls in the dark. A bad omen smelled the Oxruk. They saw their wretched cities crumble underground, as the very roots of Okridrolom grew misshapen and tore through their impure tunnels. The pale demons asked the Sehján for help, that they did. Ierun Gevilash was our leader then. She asked for a truce to help all of Okridrolom's inhabitants, pale-skinned and redheaded alike. In exchange for peace, she traveled to Ommo ust Okri to perform the cleansing ceremony, to bring our home back into balance.

"But Gevilash underestimated the treachery of the Oxruk, mightily she did. Once she finished the ceremony, and once the pale demons learned how they could do it themselves, their claws slashed her body, and to the Eternal

Sea they cast her soul. *Seers* they call themselves, those thieves who see nothing but hatred. We fought many wars to recover our Silv, to retake our capital… but dwindling are our numbers, and long and dark are their tunnels."

Sterjall felt a tingle at the edge of his perception. The bluefins at the pool parted, and out came splashing a fast-swimming muskrat who shook out his fur before landing, spraying water on all of them. The rodent transformed into a tiny hazel dormouse with such speed that the droplets that had been on his fur briefly hovered in midair in a watery muskrat silhouette.

"Gwit, your manners!" the queen chided him.

Theggo and Seshéni both dropped to their knees. "Blessed Spirit of Okri!" they intoned.

The dormouse Nu'irg didn't care about the perplexing genuflecting reflex of the Lerevi; he didn't even bother looking at the newcomers, completely unfazed by their presence. Gwit began to groom his golden-brown fur, starting with his head by pulling tightly with his paws, spiking up his back hairs and making his round ears and extensive whiskers rebound. He then briefly twisted around to scratch at his creamy undersides. Only then did his beady, black eyes—like blackberry drupelets—stare up in confusion.

From atop Lummukem's shoulder, Ishke'ísuk jumped down, wrapping his long tail around the dormouse. Recognizing his old friend, Gwit squeaked in unconfined joy.

Jessha smiled at the affectionate encounter, then gestured to Theggo and Seshéni to sit once more. "Gwit has come to bless us," she said. "As he does most evenings."

A servant hurried into the gathering chamber and placed a tiny platter with hazelnuts, pollen, and plump aphids on the ground. Gwit scurried to it to partake in the banquet, allowing Ishke'ísuk to feast on the aphids.

"We may have lost the Silv," Jessha continued, "but the Sehján still hold the favor of the clade of glires and the trust of the Nu'irg ust Okri himself. The Oxruk care not for the glires, whereas we work hard for their wellbeing. We grow beans and fungi for their lifeblood paste, but only near columns embraced by Lakemother's protection. We are limited to feeding species that live near the lakes, mostly the swimmers and ourselves. But most species we are unable to feed or train. And we can no longer milk the blood of the core vine—we saved all we had for our okruwomesh, the only companion species we managed to properly develop. Our shamans are still able to communicate with our animals, but they dare not venture into the dangerous mountains or the treacherous canyons. This is why the land is healthy only near our lakes, while the rest of Okridrolom grows wild."

While Jessha told her story, Gwit scurried around the chamber, having a conversation with Ishke'ísuk that not even Lummukem could hear.

Sterjall watched how their auras merged while the two Nu'irgesh exchanged ideas. Gwit's was a nearly phosphorescent yellow, like a field of quivering daffodils. The yellow blended with Ishke'ísuk's swimming lilacs in twirls of liquid light. Sterjall wished Theggo could see what he was seeing, as he also seemed entranced by the presence of the two spirits, although for entirely different reasons.

"How do you harvest enough soot for your shamans?" Kulak asked. "My scalp guesses you cannot mine it from floating islands."

The queen smiled, stretching her painted lips. "No, our islands we cannot mine. Gathering soot is a dangerous venture, one we are forced to undertake in the months of Fireleaf, Frostburn, and Pondsong. We send out decoys to lure the Oxruk, so that they do not find our secret sources. We hastily mine for graphite and bring it raw, to process it at our islands. It is not much that we can gather, so our shamans must use soot sparingly. The Oxruk stole nearly everything from us, but our secrets they cannot steal. They know not of the power of soot, nor do they know about all the powers of Okrisilv. That they do not."

Jessha glanced at Gwit, who had jumped atop Pol's small hands. The young prince giggled, hiding behind the log bench. The queen looked back toward her guests and added, "The Oxruk have found the way to take their half-forms, that they have, as that comes naturally with time. But they do not know that Okrisilv can be used to mindspeak with the glires, or that it can be used to ask the vines to move out of the way, or ask the dome to be opened. Those secrets we never told them."

"We should go tell them, ask them to open it," Puuja suggested, trying to get at Gwit, who was hiding behind Pol's neck.

Sterjall couldn't tell if Puuja had said that seriously or sarcastically. "Is that a possibility?" he probed. "Would the Oxruk agree to that? It would let them leave the dome once more. And perhaps then they'd return Okrisilv to you."

The queen exhaled a mirthless chuckle, then tightened her expression. "I am sorry, Sterjall, voice of the wolf, but you know not the deceit the Oxruk are capable of. If they see an opportunity to benefit themselves, they will take it, that they will. If you go to them, they will likely kill you before you get to say a word, they would take Agnargsilv, and then they would feed you to their impure gods of the depths."

"Are you so certain?" Lummukem asked. "Perhaps there is a way to have a conversation with them. It would benefit all of us."

The queen measured the odds in her mind while staring at the pool by their feet—it was no longer glowing brightly but had turned an oceanic blue. Attendants arrived with candles and lit the lamps that hid among the domed jumble of branches that made the den.

"The risk is too grand," Jessha said at last, with a new sparkle in her eyes. "We have been betrayed not once, but countless times. My own husband, my ruby lights' loving father, he too fell to their claws, long ago. The pale demons want us dead, exterminated. They think this land is theirs alone."

"What if we were to enter the temple and open the dome ourselves?" Alaia proposed. "Is the temple not above ground?"

The queen shook her head. "Kissumar is no more. It has crumbled to dust. The entrance to the temple was utterly destroyed. The only way in lies through the underground tunnels of Oxmaaga. That is their capital, not ours. Maze-like are their tunnels, impossible to navigate. No one who has been inside Oxmaaga is still alive today."

"Gwit is," Pol interjected sheepishly, staring at the dormouse in his hands. Those were the first words the boy had spoken since the meeting began.

Is he able to hear the voice of Gwit? Sterjall wondered. He paid attention to their threads but saw no direct connection, nothing that signified a flow of communication. *No, it's not that… he's just smarter than he seems. He's been listening in all along. There's something strange about him.* He tried to discern Pol's threads but found them elusive, as if they vibrated away from his empathic focus. He noticed Puuja putting a hand over her brother's knee, making Pol's threads instantly stop their incessant meandering. When they touched, it was almost as if the twins shared a single set of threads. They did not create an aura the way a higher-level consciousness would have, but simply became entwined together, as if they had always been one.

"Gwit… he has been in the dark caves," Pol repeated, more clearly. He then hid behind his sister, fearful of the stabbing gazes he had attracted.

"What does he mean?" Kulak asked.

"My dear Pollomekh is technically correct," Jessha said, reaching down to caress the boy's short red hair. "Six and a half centuries ago, one of our shamans conspired with Gwit, asking him to infiltrate Oxmaaga and steal Okrisilv back for us. But the plan failed. Gwit was captured and locked in Oxmaaga for two generations. We do not know what happened, that we do not, for we have not mindspoken with Gwit since Okrisilv was lost. But we know he came back changed. Fearful. Wary."

"If Gwit knows the city from the inside," Kulak said, "maybe he could lead us in."

"Impossible, that is," Jessha said. "Gwit cannot understand our human words. We could not ask him what he knows or does not know."

"This is not so," Lummukem gently disagreed, then quietly focused on the tiny dormouse. They looked up at the queen. "Gwit says he is glad we are here, for we brought him his old Nu'irg friend."

"Lakemother! How?…" the queen's eyes widened. "You speak to the clade of glires? Impossible."

"We do not, but we can speak with Ishke'ísuk, who in turn can speak with Gwit. We will translate to words as best we can. But meanings might be lost, as the Nu'irgesh speak not with words, but with emotions that need to be interpreted—doubly so, in this case."

"Then maybe Gwit can help us!" Sterjall exclaimed. "He might know a safe path into the temple. We can go in, set the dome to open, and escape."

Jessha shook her head. "I'm sorry, but a handful of us cannot battle our way into their fortress. The pale demons have thousands of soldiers in Oxmaaga alone. Thousands more in Taróro, Binull, Horo, and Maz'tesh. Their cities sprawl beneath the supporting columns, connected to each other by innumerable tunnels. Too many they are, and too few of us remain."

"We could at least ask Gwit what he thinks," Sterjall said, then nodded to Lummukem before Jessha could object.

Lummukem narrowed their reptilian eyes and bounced their thoughts from the basilisk to the hazel dormouse. Gwit had been sitting in front of the queen's feet, grooming his whiskers. He suddenly squeaked, more loudly than any creature his size should have squeaked, and scrambled to hide beneath Pol's scaled leather tunic.

Pol felt the dormouse tremble and began to cry himself, shrieking inconsolably.

"What is happening?" Theggo whispered to Seshéni, feeling safe speaking now that the boy was causing such a ruckus.

Seshéni shrugged and whispered back, "I only understood a handful of words. I think they are speaking with the spirits about storming the enemy's fortress."

"Enemy? What enemy?"

"Shh. I will explain once this is all over."

"Hush, my ruby light," Jessha muttered while rubbing Pol's head. "Hush, the pale men cannot get to you, everything is fine. Fear not, my dear ruby, my dear ruby light."

That poor kid, Sterjall thought, trying to read Pol's emotions but only getting a jumble of chaotic energy. He focused on Gwit instead, and there he sensed pure terror, which raised his hackles and forced him to take a deep breath.

It took Jessha a long while to calm her son down. She then took her seat once more, letting Puuja comfort her brother. Gwit had not yet left the safety of the boy's garments.

Lummukem addressed the queen. "Gwit has told Ishke'ísuk that he will never go back to Oxmaaga. He is afraid of the Oxruk, afraid of once again being kept as a pet for cruel rulers."

"What happened there?" Sterjall asked.

"Gwit will not speak of it. He has suffered enough."

"Could we ask him what we should do, then?" Alaia queried.

Lummukem did so. "He has no answers," they responded, "but hopes human issues can be solved with human measures. *Speak to each other*, he said to us."

The pool of water was now a black mirror. Sterjall saw the queen with her upside-down counterpart, both lit by orange flames. Her distorted reflection lightly rippled with the imperfections of the calm water.

"What would it take…" Sterjall thought out loud. "What would it take to get an audience with the Oxruk? Perhaps Gwit is right, and we can reach an agreement, one that will benefit all of us."

CHAPTER FORTY-TWO

TWINS

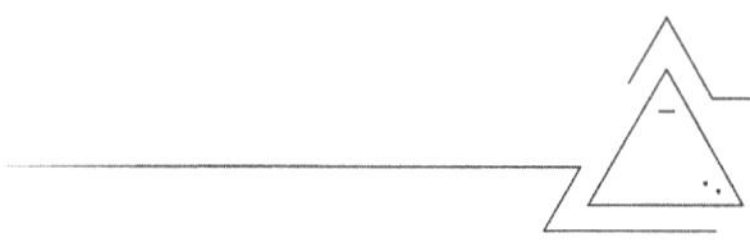

Jessha called for the chiefs of the islands and wetlands to gather in Kisdik, at least those who lived close enough to convene without risking travel through Oxruk lands. The Queen's Lodge was not large enough to accommodate them all, so they met atop a vast wooden terrace that crowned the highest hill of the floating city.

After much deliberation, the Sehján chiefs agreed to send an emissary to Oxmaaga, something that had been done safely in the past when subtle negotiations were preferable to war, though it had not been attempted for over a decade.

"The emissary must demand expedience, that they must do," the chief of the Klad Tilg urged. "If we give the pale demons time to react, they will recall armies from their other cities. By not giving them time, we make it less likely for them to set up a trap. They do not move fast, as they have no mounts to ride or to pull carriages for them."

Sterjall noticed a common theme of distrust throughout the entire assembly. He'd been hoping to approach the Oxruk in good faith, but it seemed to the Sehján that doing so would be entirely naive. Even in this safest of locations, all the Sehján were wearing armor, as if ready for something unsavory to befall them.

"The Winter Solstice arrives in two days," Kulak said. "The day is auspicious. We can claim we need to meet that day, say we will wait no longer."

"That will serve us well," Ierun Jessha said. "We shall send our emissary first thing in the morning."

Tsei looked to the wayfarers and said, "You must be as sly as them when dealing with the Oxruk. You must think like them. Do not show them the power you hold, do not let them know you have more than one Silv in your possession. Only one of you must venture to speak to Tajaz the Seer."

"We can be the ones who speak with their leader," Lummukem offered, referring only to their singular person, confusing some of the Sehján at the assembly.

"Perhaps it's better if you stay with Ishke," Sterjall said. "If you bring him with you, the seer will see his aura. We might not want to reveal he's with us."

"This is true," Kulak said. "Lummukem, what if something happened to you? We would be unable to talk to Ishke'ísuk or Gwit. I should be the one to go."

"No!" Sterjall nearly barked. "Not... not you. I can't—let me do this, I can handle this one." He swallowed thickly. *I'm not strong enough to see you risk yourself like this,* he thought. He recomposed himself, and added, "You and Lummukem can stay with the Sehján and wait for me to return."

"We believe Kulak might be better suited to handle these sensitive matters," Lummukem diplomatically pointed out. "He will be a good representative, and—"

"I can do this," Sterjall cut in. "I will return as soon as I'm done speaking with Tajaz, to let you know what he decides, nothing else."

"Why are you so adamant about this?" Kulak said. "As Laatu prince, I can speak for us as well, and my scalp—"

"I promise I'll be careful," the wolf interjected once more, putting a hand on Kulak's shoulder. The caracal winced, his recent wound still tender. "Sorry," Sterjall said, then quietly added, "Would you please stay with Lummukem and Alaia? Keep them company. I will be fine, I swear."

"My scalp still thinks I would be a better representative for the Miscam," Kulak replied in a murmur.

While considering the reply, Sterjall had an idea and voiced it for the group to hear. "If the Oxruk despise the Miscam so much, then it might be cautious to send a non-Miscam representative. Laatu, Sehján, it doesn't matter—they might feel an enmity toward any Miscam tribe."

"This might be true," Ierun Jessha said as she considered.

Kulak crossed his arms and let a burst of air escape through his nose.

"I know I can sometimes be... impulsive," Sterjall added. "But Theggo could go with me and help me keep poised."

Once Alaia finished interpreting for the Lerevi, Theggo said, "As the oldest among all present, I have acquired ample experience dealing with relations between realms. If the dome is to open, we will need a Lerevi representative to explain to the Oxruk what to expect. According to our minister of state, there are plenty of unpopulated lands among the far western forests of Fel Nisos, lands that are not of strategic significance to the Republic. There are also the old tunnels left behind by the vines in the Stelm Atuur—if the Oxruk live underground, they might find that option more appealing. I can explain the details to them and act as an ambassador."

"I will be glad to have you by my side," Sterjall said. "Where will we meet them?"

"We can approach Oxmaaga through the blessing of the Klad Üo," Tsei said, "protected by Lakemother's embrace. The great lake flows almost all the way to the Dohao Mesa. The location will need to be confirmed by our emissary, but we can assume it will be at the Olvur Gate, at the north end of the mesa. As we disembark, our warriors will march with us to the outcrop that overlooks the dry lands between the shoreline and the mesa. From there, we can keep watch while the representatives speak with Tajaz the Seer. That we must do."

Tsei looked toward the fleet admiral. "Theggo of the New Kingdom, your silver and gold armor seems suitable, as clumsy and heavy as it is. But Sterjall, you must be prepared for treachery. Beautiful are your regal vestments, but not protective enough."

"Regal?" Sterjall said, stifling a chuckle, realizing Tsei was referring to his old blue tunic and worn-down trousers.

"Yes," she said, not perceiving anything odd. "I will have our armorer outfit you with a suit of elytra. Our lamellar armor is light and comfortable and will offer more suitable protection. This must be done as a precaution."

Sterjall did not mind that at all—he found the intricate armor fascinatingly beautiful.

Early the next morning, the emissary—a square-faced woman named Skirr—departed for Oxmaaga. The wayfarers had been hosted at the Queen's Lodge, where they now impatiently waited for Skirr's return. Kulak, Sterjall, Alaia, and Lummukem were sitting with their legs dangling in the luminous pool of the gathering chamber. Tiny fish gathered at their feet, feeding on little bits of loose skin—they were particularly fond of the flakes coming off Lummukem's dried scales. It was quiet there, with the attendants nowhere to be seen, and the Lerevi off exploring the island.

"I want to go with you," Kulak said, holding Sterjall's handpaw right at the edge of the water.

"I know. We've been through this. It will be safer this way. If something goes wrong, I'll need you, all of you, to help get me out of trouble."

"Sounds like you're planning for trouble," Alaia remarked, her gaze piercing as if trying to read Sterjall's mind.

"I'm not. But the way the Sehján paint the Oxruk is terrifying. If they agree to meet us, it could be a trap."

A huge castoroides swam right below their feet, startling Alaia.

"Scared me," she muttered. "Was that Gwit?"

"No, just a giant beaver," Sterjall said.

"Wouldn't surprise me if they have rooms for them inside this 'lodge.' It does feel like a beaver's den, just a bit more upscale."

"Tsei told me it was the companion beavers who mostly built these islands," Sterjall said. "They carried logs, reeds, all sorts of materials from far inland. The Oxruk won't attack them, so they can travel far, cut down trees, and bring them over. They are prolific builders. She said they made their own system of tunnels that cross through the sunken portions of the islands, and that they built enormous dams in the mountains, too."

"Gwit must be proud," Kulak said.

"What have Gwit and Ishke been up to anyway?" Alaia asked.

They heard a scurrying sound in one of the tunnels. Alaia assumed her words had conveniently summoned the two Nu'irgesh, but it was the twins who entered the chamber. Puuja came trotting in front, with Pol hiding behind her. The two wore children's versions of the elytra armor, of the same kind of lamellar construction, but with none of the colorful resins applied to them. They looked more comfortable, yet plain.

Even before the children drew close to them, Sterjall's keen nose had picked up their vanilla scent, the same scent that permeated the Queen's Lodge. He quickly unclasped his handpaw from Kulak's. He wasn't sure what was proper or not with the Sehján and didn't feel like upsetting the twins.

As if it was the most natural thing to do, Puuja sat between Alaia and Lummukem at the edge of the pool, bare feet in the water, mimicking the others. She stared at Lummukem, who had the bladed end of their halberd resting on their lap and was digging a claw into the carved bone structure of the weapon. "What are you doing?" she asked in a vibrant Miscamish.

"We are planting the bloodmoss," Lummukem answered. "It was a gift from Ouránama-Ulésse of the Ji Miscam. It will help us see our halberd better, becoming one with us." The dragon then poked a finger with the marbled steel point of their halberd, sucked on the red droplet that formed, and let their saliva drip into the concavity where they had planted the moss. The red spit vanished into the deep crevice.

Puuja's face contorted in a mixture of disgust and sudden disinterest. She turned her head, nodding to her brother while unsuccessfully attempting to persuade him to unhide his face. "Pol wants us to ask a question," she finally said to no one in particular.

"What does the handsome boy want to know?" Alaia said with a smile.

Pol shied away from Alaia, tensing further.

Puuja answered, "We want to know if you could show us the Silvesh. We've never seen one."

"Uhh… They are a bit dangerous," Sterjall warned. "They are not toys."

"Oh, don't be rude," Alaia said, "the twins just want to see them."

"We know they are dangerous," Puuja said, swinging her feet and scaring the fish. "We've learned about them since we were kids, that we have."

"You *are* kids," Sterjall said, frowning.

"That's what we said," she replied. "Our mother, she is the great-great-great"—she added countless more *greats*—"great-granddaughter of Ierun Hejána, the last Okrifröa. She taught us all about Okrisilv, in case one day she gets to wear it, and then we'd wear it after her."

"*We'd* wear it?" Sterjall asked.

"Not you, we," Puuja corrected him.

"We believe Puuja and Pol think and speak much like Sunu-Lummukem," Lummukem noted. "She speaks of *them*, but she means only one of them. Is that not so, Khurun Puuja? As only women wear the Silv of glires in the Sehján traditions."

"Yes, that's what we meant," Puuja replied. "But as we said, our mother taught us everything. How to open the vines, how to heal the temple, how to see the things that are not there, how to gain strength, how to sharpen our teeth, how to fly like a bird."

"I don't think you can fly with them," Sterjall rebutted. "I would've noticed."

"Perhaps with the avian mask you might," Alaia retorted. "Or maybe with a flying squirrel half-form."

"Squirrels don't actually fly, they only—"

"Then will you show us?" Puuja pushed.

Lummukem shapeshifted to Sunu and removed Kruwensilv. They handed the excessively toothed mask to the kids.

Sterjall lifted a handpaw. "Sunu, it's—"

"It is fine," they said. "They are smart children, as curious as you were at their age."

"That's what worries me," Sterjall said.

Sunu made a dismissive gesture.

"It is as light as the lake's morning breath…" Puuja whispered.

Pol peeked at the black teeth from over his sister's shoulder. He grinned at the mask, trying to replicate its ferocity. The boy clearly wanted to touch the artifact, but although Puuja held it close enough for him to do so, he hesitated, keeping his hand a safe distance from it.

"You may touch it, Pollomekh, son of Jessha," Sunu assured him.

Pol squirmed at hearing his full name, but then relaxed. He lightly caressed Kruwensilv's nostrils, then pulled his hand back with a nervous giggle. He reached forward again, took the mask from Puuja's hands, and beamed in an asymmetrical smile.

Sterjall felt his anxiety rise like hot air. He could not help recalling his first time with Agnargsilv, being only a year older than Pol was now, and having suffered the most unimaginable pain. He became so lost in his memory that he didn't even notice when Kulak took the form of Aio, who tossed Mindrelsilv over the pool for Puuja to catch.

Puuja reached out with her arms, but the mask's lightness made it fall short of where she was expecting it to land. She teetered at the edge of the pool and almost fell in. Mindrelsilv splashed noiselessly on the water and floated there.

Aio laughed, then splashed his feet around, creating a wave that got everyone's hinds wet but allowed the mask to bob close enough for Puuja to grab. She picked it up and savored the sight of every sparkling droplet over the felid form.

"What's gotten into you?" Alaia asked, noticing Sterjall's tightening muzzle. "You never had problems sharing your toys with me. Let the kids have fun too."

"They each have one already. And they are not toys."

Pol made a throaty sound. He approached Sunu and handed Kruwensilv back. He leaned toward his sister's ear and whispered.

"Could you show us?" Puuja asked Sunu.

Sunu placed the mask on their face and shifted as slowly as they could, letting the twins observe the refracting smoke that formed around them, then held an arm out for the twins to touch.

"It is hard like okruwom bones!" Puuja exclaimed, squeezing the partially shapeshifted arm. "Yet it looks like smoke… Pol, feel it."

Pol refused, trying to keep his eyes on the ground, but unable to avoid peeking at the scaled arm solidifying in front of him. He then felt something touching his legs and squealed. Lummukem had quietly bent their still-growing tail to tickle the boy's ankles. The dragon smiled deviously, but with their face turned toward the water to make the boy feel more at ease.

Pol took a step forward, then lightly touched the scales on Lummukem's shoulders, as if cataloging the variations of blues, grays, ochres, and greens that made up their complex skin. He followed the scales up to the dragon's thick neck, and to the slightly purple-pigmented ones atop their head.

Lummukem quickly shifted back to Sunu, scaring Pol. The freckled allgender turned to the youngster and laughed from behind the dark mask. Pol giggled nervously, and though he had backed off, he was now too curious about those purple markings atop Sunu's bald head. They were very dim, barely visible, having faded in the last few months. He whispered in his sister's ear once more.

Puuja ignored him—she was too distracted making faces at Mindrelsilv, trying to imagine how it would feel to be a cat, narrowing her eyes and flashing her fangs. Pol shook her shoulder.

"What?" she asked.

He whispered to her again.

"We want to know why your hair is purple and not red. And why it's stuck to your head like it's wet."

"It is not hair that decorates our scalp," Sunu answered. "Laatu have no hair. Cast your eyes upon Khuron Aio, who also has no hair. We paint our scalps with mucus from snails."

"*Eugh!*" Puuja said, wrinkling her nose. Her brother repeated the sound.

Pol was now adamant that he needed to get a better look at the gross snail paint. He took a cautious step forward and extended a hesitant arm. In a flash, Sunu was back in Lummukem's form, exposing their pink gums at the boy. Pol recoiled screaming, but also giggling, hiding behind Puuja.

"You are scaring the poor child!" Sterjall complained.

"He is fine," Lummukem countered. "He is fearless. Look at him, he stands proud, defiant. We saw him fight with his quarterstaff atop the roof, so it is us who should be scared of him."

Pol and Lummukem kept teasing one another. Pol hissed, but Lummukem showed him their claws and forked tongue. Pol squinted menacingly, but Lummukem slowly closed their nictitating membranes, making their eyes look white and soulless.

Sterjall finally gave in. He stood up as Lago and pulled his mask off while walking around the pool. He tripped on Lummukem's tail, composed himself, then handed Agnargsilv to Puuja.

"This is Agnargsilv," he said. "Just… be careful with it."

Puuja held Agnargsilv in one hand and Mindrelsilv in the other. "We like this one better," she said regarding the felid mask. With her eyes never leaving Mindrelsilv, she handed Agnargsilv back to Lago.

Defeated, Lago plodded back to his side of the pool. Pol indirectly watched the discouraged young man, who slumped next to Aio once more. He whispered in his sister's ear again.

Puuja regarded Aio and Lago, then said, "We want to know which one of you is the boy and which one is the girl."

Lago clumsily dropped his mask into the water. Alaia laughed, and Pol laughed with her, uncertain of what was so funny. Aio covered his mouth to muffle his giggles and cared not to offer an answer, so Lummukem responded in his stead.

"Both Aio-Kulak and Lago-Sterjall are boys. 'Men,' some have dared say, but we still say 'boys.'"

"But don't they love each other?" Puuja asked, as if the lovers weren't sitting across from her. "We saw them kissing behind the oak yesterday, that we did."

"I told you we shouldn't have—" Lago started, but Aio shushed him.

Lummukem nodded to Puuja. "Yes, they are lorrkins, and so that is how they share their love. Sometimes a boy and a girl love each other, and they kiss. Sometimes it is two girls who love each other, and they kiss. And sometimes it is two boys who love each other, like Aio and Lago, and they kiss. It is all the same."

"Oh, okay," Puuja said, unfazed. She kept staring at Mindrelsilv.

Pol suddenly stood straighter and looked directly at Lummukem. With a surprisingly clear voice, he asked, "Are you a boy or a girl?"

Lummukem felt proud at hearing Pol's voice. "We are both," they said. "Sunu and Lummukem are both boy and girl. This is the way we were made."

"Then anyone can love you!" Pol excitedly said.

Lummukem's reptilian face turned sad for a moment, but then widened into a welcoming smile.

CHAPTER FORTY-THREE

UNDERWORLD

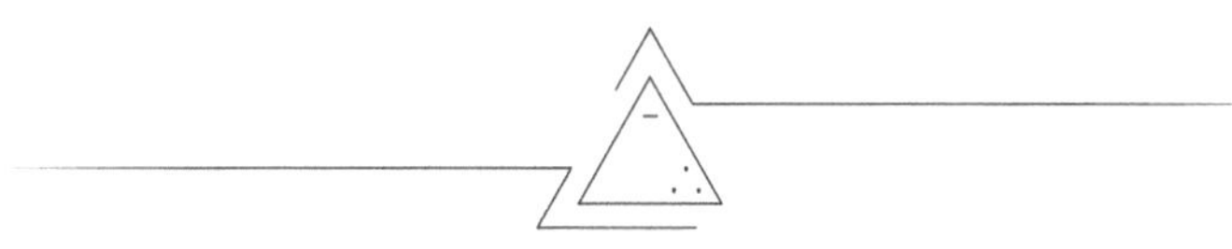

Skirr returned from Oxmaaga late in the evening. Everyone was eager to hear her report, so they hurried to meet her at the shores of Kisdik. The emissary hopped off her island and walked with the wayfarers, the chiefs, the queen, and the twins.

"It required persuasiveness, that it did," Skirr began. "But Lakemother's blessings are with us, and the Oxruk agreed. We are to meet with them at Oxmaaga in the morning, that is what Gurovon the Envoy said to me. They will allow us to speak to Tajaz the Seer, in peace, honoring the pact of the Winter Solstice. Tajaz wants one representative from each party to walk to the front of the Olvur Gate. No one else. All weapons will be forbidden."

Sterjall nervously glanced at his hip, where Leif dangled.

"Did you agree to these terms?" the queen asked.

"Yes, Ierun," Skirr said. "The dry lake was deserted. I saw many Oxruk soldiers outside the gate and atop the terraces, but that is nothing out of the ordinary."

"I will be there with our warriors to support you, waiting at the overlook opposite their gate," the queen declared.

"We are going too," Puuja proudly announced from behind her mother. "No pale demon can defeat us in battle."

"You may travel with us, my rubies," Jessha said, "but you will not venture close to the gate, nor will you take up arms."

"I'll have to practice what to say," Sterjall mentioned. "I need to be certain I'm not giving away too much information. Theggo won't be able to speak to them, so it will be all up to me. What if they do not accept our offer? What if they try to set a trap for us?"

Alaia interpreted the words for Theggo.

"We will have to remain attentive," Theggo said. "The dragoons will wait nearby in case something goes awry."

"Tonight we will further discuss our plans," Ierun Jessha said. "Then, before morning's first light, under the watch of Lakemother, we will set out." She directed her next words to an attendant. "Have Fel Kamman ready to depart, and okruwomesh well rested. All available warriors should join us and be ready for deceit. That they must do."

"I'm so nervous," Sterjall muttered to Kulak, his legs lightly trembling.

Kulak said nothing; he simply watched from the side as Sterjall was outfitted with his new elytra armor, helped by Tsei and a bulky armorer named Bouf. Sterjall lifted his arms and let them wrap the cuirass around his chest. The lamellar plates reminded him of the scales on a butterfly's wings, which he had once seen up close under Khopto's microscope— it was sparkling in myriad tones of blues, greens, and even purples.

He shivered. It was partly his nerves, partly the winds that arrived with dawn. It was the Winter Solstice, after all, and a cold snap was cutting across the vast lake. They were drifting on the Klad Üo atop a large island named Fel Kamman, which had simply detached from Kisdik as if it had never been a part of the city. The fog, lit by the brightening trunk, made the sizable island seem as if it was floating up in the clouds, moving fast despite the added weight of all the warriors that traveled on it. They would reach their destination in less than an hour.

"At least the underclothing is warm," Sterjall commented. The armorer had provided an arming doublet for his upper body and padded chausses for his lower half.

"Spread your legs," Tsei asked, and Sterjall complied. She showed him how to attach a war belt, from which highly flexible lamellar tassets extended to cover his thighs. A slightly shorter piece extended over his crotch, looking almost like a skirt.

Bouf pulled at Sterjall's tail, making him twitch—he had modified the plates on the back so that the wolf's tail could part it two ways and exit freely. "Good fit!" he exclaimed, smiling to reveal his missing front teeth. To Sterjall, the gap looked like the inverse of what the white paint over Bouf's lips tried to accomplish. Bouf explained that the bones decorating the tassets were there not just for looks, but for structure, and for strength. "Okruwom bones," he noted, then clutched his balls to add, "Stronger than steel!" His Miscamish was oddly accented, and his hair was not red like most of the Sehján, but nearly blond.

"Thank you, Bouf." Sterjall pulled his tassets around to inspect them. "I wish I could carry Leif with me. Maybe I could hide it under here?" He pointed beneath his right thigh.

"Not advisable," Tsei said, brow tightening. "The pale demons will look for any excuse to confirm their suspicions."

"What suspicions?"

"That it is us who are trying to set a trap for them. It makes no difference—weapon or no weapon, you will not be able to fight their numbers."

"That's comforting, thanks."

Tsei and Bouf tightened the belts on Sterjall's upper arms, then wrapped greaves around his lower legs. The one over the left, where the patchy fur from his burns was, had to be tightened more than the one on the furred side. Bouf had customized the greaves to work either with the shorter calves Sterjall possessed in his wolf half-form, or the longer calves of Lago's human form. He had even added additional lamellar plates to the sliding shoes Kulak had once gifted Sterjall.

"How come you don't wear helms?" the wolf asked.

"Our red hair protects us," Tsei answered.

It was as good an answer as he expected to get. Kulak seemed to approve of it, as the Laatu not only didn't cover their scalps other than with pigments, but fought wearing shodogs, which left their chests bare.

"At what point do Theggo and I run away?" Sterjall asked no one in particular.

"Your ears you must keep attentive," Tsei advised. "If there is danger, you will hear the blow of a horn. Warriors will be ready on the outcrop."

Sterjall shivered once more, feeling less and less confident about the entire situation.

Tsei fitted one pauldron to Sterjall's left shoulder, while Bouf placed the right one. The plates gleamed in purplish and even reddish colors, and streamers dangled loosely from them.

"You'll be able to put on the armor by yourself next time," Tsei said, showing him how the pauldron's belts attached easily to his cuirass.

"Do I get to keep the armor, then?" Sterjall asked.

Bouf was the one to answer. "You may, as long as you don't mind wearing a woman's outfit."

"Woman's?"

"All elytra armor is made for women, as only women go into battle," Bouf said. He was wearing a set of lamellar armor, but his was made only of leather without the lacquer, like the armor the twins wore. Bouf patted Sterjall's chest, making sure the plates locked properly with the structural bones. "It took a lot of work to fix up the chest for your odd figure to fit. So you better like it, and thank Lakemother that Bouf was able to help."

Then came the gauntlets, which Sterjall could pull over his handpaws by himself. They were exquisite, seamlessly articulated, studded at the knuckles. The iridescent-blue plates covered only the backsides of his handpaws, leaving his pink pads exposed so that he could still grip objects as needed. Although he would not be allowed to carry Leif to his encounter with the Oxruk, he knew the sharp-knuckled gauntlets were quite a weapon on their own.

Last came the arm bracers, which, per Sterjall's request, included a row of brime cubes on the left side, to replace the brime bracer Sunu and Kenondok had once concocted for him. Bouf had complained about the request, because it made it so that the bracer had to overlap the gauntlet to prevent the sparks from getting caught at his wrists; that was not ideal in Bouf's mind, at least not for deflecting swinging blades. As a compromise, Sterjall had agreed to have only the left bracer overlap in such a fashion, while the right one tucked under his gauntlet's wrist plates.

After Tsei and Bouf were done, Sterjall inspected his elbows, where articulated castoroides bones were carved to sharp points, like the scales on the back of an alligator. He shook his armored arms and let his body relax, or pretend to be relaxed. "How do I look?" he asked Kulak.

The caracal smirked and licked his black lips. Speaking in Common, so as to avoid Tsei and Bouf understanding his words, he answered, "It looks exotic and erotic. It makes me want to jump on you and pull the armor off again, so that I can savor your body."

Sterjall felt the warmth between his legs increasing and covered his crotch with his handpaws.

Tsei cocked her head with a confused look.

"That-a good, eh?" Bouf interjected, surprising them with his peculiarly accented Common. "I'da tried my best, but mayhap it shtill makes ya look too much like a wooman."

Sterjall did his best to hide his now quickly fading erection and his growing embarrassment, turning away from the toothless smile of the armorer.

"Scorch my tits sixteenfold, you look amazing!" Alaia said, holding tightly to the hood of her cloak, which was attempting to blow away.

"The armorer told me I get to keep it," Sterjall said with a sharp-toothed smirk.

"If you live," Tsei nonchalantly added.

"Thanks."

"Your scales look almost as beautiful as ours," Lummukem told him, scraping a claw over their scaled chest. "Almost as durable, almost as colorful."

"And I'm sure yours are also more comfortable," the wolf replied, tugging at his crotch to loosen his chausses. He straightened his back, then shivered. "I think it's going to snow," he said. "Aren't you two cold?" He eyed Lummukem and Kulak, who were still only wearing their open shodogs and kilts.

"We are always cold in this form," Lummukem admitted. "Yet the cold hurts us less when our blood is already cold."

Kulak shrugged. He was getting used to the cooler weather, and his fur insulated him enough.

Theggo approached, followed by the dragoons, who were pulling their kudus by the reins. The fleet admiral was glowing, his armor shining vibrantly.

"You look a bit different," Sterjall observed.

"Look who's talking," Theggo replied, eyeing the elytra armor.

"No, really. What is it? You are… resplendent?"

"Again, look who's talking, Lorr Vaari." He combed his long gray eyebrows and scratched his beard. "I gave my armor a little polish, that's all. Didn't want you to entirely outshine me." And his armor did sparkle, as much as the long strands of his silver-and-gold hair.

A horn blew.

"Be ready to disembark!" Tsei bellowed.

They took their positions toward the bow of Fel Kamman. From his vantage point, Sterjall could see dozens of castoroides, the okruwomesh, pulling the island from the front, but he knew now that there were many more giant beavers under the island itself, pulling it from below.

The beavers at the front dove out of sight and let the island coast to the rocky shore.

Sterjall and Theggo disembarked behind Skirr, the Sehján emissary. They could not see the Dohao Mesa yet, but only a rocky, forested uplift that ascended for about a mile. They set out uphill, followed by the other wayfarers and escorted by hundreds of Sehján warriors.

When they reached the edge of the uplifted outcrop, Sterjall stopped and stared down the vertical cliff. At the bottom, the flatness of a long-dried lake extended before him, streaked with dark-gray sand and pebbles. At the opposite end of the dry lakebed rose the Dohao Mesa, black and imposing, with the mighty Olvur Gate clearly discernible even from that distance. As Sterjall took in the view, shy snowflakes began to cloud the skies and tumble to their feet.

Standing in the middle of the dry lake, a lonely, ghostly figure waited, white robes flowing like spectral pennants.

"Is that Tajaz the Seer?" Sterjall asked.

"No," Skirr answered, "they are only an envoy, the pale allgender I spoke with yesterday. They are here to escort you both to the gate. I will go down with you, but the envoy will lead you the rest of the way. Follow me down the cliff."

"May Lakemother shelter you," Tsei said to them.

Sterjall hugged Lummukem, Alaia, and then Kulak. "I love you," he said to the caracal, holding the embrace. "I'll be safe, don't worry."

"My scalp will worry the entire time," Kulak said and pulled him tighter into a kiss.

Ierun Jessha cocked her head, unsure whether what she witnessed was a peculiarity of the foreign cultures, or if there was something more to it.

"Ready, Admiral?" Sterjall asked Theggo, but before he could respond, a high-pitched shriek startled them, followed by an anguished cry. Gwit was squeaking in a desperate tone, curled into a ball on the ground, his hazel fur horripilating. Pol mimicked the gesture while sobbing atop the grass.

Lummukem felt something heavy on their left shoulder and turned to see Ishke'ísuk transformed into a frill-necked lizard. His frills expanded while the Nu'irg released a mournful hiss that faded into a croak of despair.

At the same time, continents away, Probo squealed, Safís howled, Banook shed a tear, and all other Nu'irgesh felt their hearts shatter.

"What is happening?" Kulak asked, his voice pitched high with anxiety. "What is wrong with the Nu'irgesh? What is wrong with Pol?"

Lummukem froze in place, listening. They placed a clawed hand on Ishke'ísuk's back, attempting to comfort him. "He says… he says the pinniped Nu'irg has died. Däo-Varjak of Gwonledrolom, she is no more."

It took almost an hour for them to calm Pol and the Nu'irgesh down.

"Those sadistic monsters!" Sterjall spat, pacing around with his exposed fur still standing on end. "This means they have Gwonlesilv, and that the Miscam tribe in the Moonrise Dome is being massacred. Why did they have to kill a Nu'irg? How can they be so vile?"

"There is nothing we can do," Kulak said, trying to calm the wolf down.

"Yes, there is. We finish this, then go chop the Red Stag's antlers off. I want to stab his damn corpse with them. I want to make him turn red with his own damn blood."

"You are making Pol anxious again," Lummukem said with a mildness that threatened to make Sterjall even angrier. "Let us be calm and only worry about what is ahead of us."

"This also... This means..." Sterjall began, his anger suddenly replaced with sadness. "If all Nu'irgesh felt this happen, then... Banook, he must be in so much pain."

"Two months ago, Gwit and Pol acted this same way," Jessha said. "Pol did not know why Gwit felt such pain, but he cried with him for days. We never knew why. Now we understand."

"Two months... That was when Mamóru died..." Sterjall said, feeling ever more doleful.

"We need to go," Skirr interrupted. "The envoy awaits, and we promised them we'd be on time."

Sterjall closed his eyes and rubbed his temples. He tried to shake the anger off his shoulders and said, "Fine. Let's finish this and get out of here. The sooner we get to the Red Stag, the better."

PART SIX
UPRISING

CHAPTER FORTY-FOUR

THE FALL OF ELMAREN

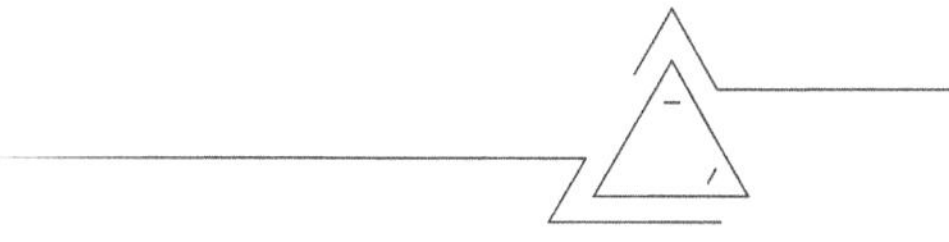

Silv-Thaar Valaran's legion had split from the Red Stag's army soon after helping them take Oskirin, the capital of the Dorhond Tribes. While the Red Stag ventured into the White Desert, guided by the many slaves they had recently captured, Valaran had marched east to Azash, the capital of the Elmaren Queendom.

The raccoon general traveled with the surviving members of his old arbalister squad: Fjorna, Osef, Aurélien, Trevin, and Muriel, along with his own legion and countless archers who were faithful to Fjorna above all. While Valaran's infantry approached by land, Shea Lu approached by sea, directing the Negian fleet from aboard their flagship, the *Black Spear*, taking up position in the Bay of Negórmea.

The fleet began the assault, overwhelming the ports of Azash. The sapfire cannons drove the Elmaren defenses away from the seashore ramparts, allowing Valaran's archers to bury them in an unceasing rain of arrows. His cavalry and infantry finished off the Elmaren army, aided by his mighty jarv wolverines, which were now fully under his control. The ancient city of shining white towers at last surrendered. Queen Lea-Ëuniss was beheaded, and her nacre gauntlet shattered, so that never again should the Queendom rise to power.

The Moonrise Dome stretched not very far south of the captured capital. Valaran was worried about entering the dome—his legion did not have the advantage of the enormous, segmented pipes that the Red Stag was taking to the Archstone Dome, so he could not depend on a quick influx of soldiers by land. The only sure strategy Valaran could depend on was to reach the center of the Moonrise Dome, set it to open, and have Shea's fleet attack by sea. How they'd go about doing that was still uncertain.

"Crescu, are you ready?" Fjorna Daro asked Silv-Thaar Valaran. She still preferred to call him by his first name, even though Valaran had been confined to his raccoon half-form for a long while now, not wanting to lose the mind-lock he'd at last managed to exert on his musteloids. The small squad of arbalisters was gathered in the now-abandoned city of Moongap, at the northern edge of the Moonrise Dome, near the shores of the Tumultuous Ocean. In this first excursion, they would take only a dozen trusted soldiers—this was merely a mission to scout the lands and measure the threats within.

"I'm ready. Let's go," Silv-Thaar Valaran said, not feeling entirely ready. He stood up and brushed his striped tail, then scratched the neck of Dishu, the yellow-throated marten perched on his shoulder—petting her always set his nerves at ease.

This time, Valaran wasn't wearing the unwieldy plated armor that Monarch Hallow had demanded all his generals wear, but instead wore his old leather uniform from the arbalister squad. It felt much more comfortable, made less noise, and allowed him to work stealthily, as he always had before.

Once inside the Moonrise Dome—which the Miscam tribes knew as Gwonledrolom—Fjorna quickly spotted a group of the local tribe fishing by the shore.

"They are all naked," she whispered from behind cover. "Every last one of them."

As they surveyed the territory, they found that both along the shore and at the inland villages, all the members of the Khardok Miscam tribe wore no clothes and carried no weapons.

"This will be so easy," Silv-Thaar Valaran concluded, almost feeling a bit guilty.

After returning to the outside of the dome to report their findings, they ventured back inside followed by a sizable unit who would wait in hiding for their command. Valaran decided to try their luck and lure in one of the locals, sending Aurélien, who spoke fluent Miscamish, to persuasively gather information from a young man. She learned that the Khardok Miscam had no concept of warfare, no need for armor. Aurélien portrayed the raccoon Silv-Thaar as a prophet from the New World who had come to save them, saying he needed to see the ancient temple so that he could bring back the promised land of plenty to them.

The Silv-Thaar was invited with great honors to visit Ommo ust Gwonle. While he and his arbalisters were escorted toward the trunk, they talked amongst themselves in Common with no fear, having learned that the Khardok did not even know of the language's existence.

"They are so trusting," Valaran said, walking alongside his naked escorts. "Poor, daft fuckers."

"What are we going to do with them?" Aurélien asked. "It would be so easy to kill them that it makes me a bit sad. Maybe we can convince them to join us?"

Fjorna spat. "They'd be useless. More mouths to feed. They don't even know how to put on clothes. Look at how much land they took—eighty miles across, wasted by a handful of savages."

The Khardok did not ride any beasts upon land. They had their guests walk all the way up the sacred Allúver Plateau from which the trunk grew. There, at the steps of Ommo ust Gwonle, a tusked figure awaited their arrival.

"Hide yourselves," Valaran ordered his arbalisters. He did not mean that they should take cover, but that they should tuck their threads inward to prevent their true intentions from being glimpsed. He had taught the technique to his squad, who were unable to visualize their own threads but had learned to adopt the required frame of mind.

Fjorna and her squad made themselves unreadable as they followed Valaran up the steps. There they met Jamma-Galdóri, the Gwonlefröa, who possessed the half-form of a long-tusked walrus. She was kind and courteous, gliding gracefully despite her webbed feet. She offered the Negians food and listened to their story. Valaran disliked her; he thought she smelled like fish.

Aurélien told Galdóri that Noss had spoken to Silv-Thaar Valaran, who was the Ieron of Krostdrolom, and had told him that although most of the other domes had already opened, Noss had been unable to send a message to ask for Gwonledrolom to open as well, so they had entrusted the Silv-Thaar to deliver the message in their stead.

Aurélien had become well-versed in what she thought of as the mythology of the Miscam, believing the Noss consciousness was but a ruse the Miscam had concocted to justify their perpetual hoarding of the richest lands. She had learned much from Luhásu and the Western Ikhel tribe, and she now used her knowledge to deceive those who trusted her venomous words. Her compelling speech won over Galdóri, who had no reason to doubt a king from another tribe. The Khardok leader agreed that if the world outside had indeed been renewed, and that Noss wished Gwonledrolom to open, then it was her duty to make it so.

"But you mustn't take my word for it," Aurélien finished with the humblest of voices. "You must hear this from Noss themself. There are ships on their way now, many ships, carrying Silvfröash from distant lands who are working to spread their species far and wide. If Gwonledrolom is set to open today, those ships could join us in time for the Winter Solstice. Then, under the blessing of the return of the light, six of you could gather and speak directly with Noss. Six of you, to work together and bring peace to the New World. But wait not for too long, lest the vines are not open enough by the time their sacred vessels arrive."

Galdóri's conviction redoubled. She took the Negians to the temple and sat naked upon the throne, commanding the quaar lattice to collapse and asking the vines to follow in their sluggish retreat. Fjorna cringed at the sight, thinking the naked walrus looked revolting, not regal, sitting on the temple's throne.

Once the opening was set in motion, Galdóri thanked the dome for the protection it had offered through so many centuries, then thanked the Silv-Thaar for his help and guidance.

Aurélien made a peculiar request then. "You must make sure all your citizens join us in celebration on the day of the Winter Solstice. They must be present to welcome the Silvfröash with song, with eagerness. And call forth for Däo-Varjak, the Nu'irg ust Gwonle, so she may witness this historic moment as well. All of you, all the Khardok must join on this auspicious day."

Over the next several weeks, the Moonrise Dome unhurriedly opened. From remote corners of the dome, the Khardok Miscam slowly arrived, gathering at the northern beaches to await the ships, preparing for the celebration.

At noon on the fifteenth day of Hoartide, Galdóri and her guests met atop a tall promontory that offered an expansive view of the shore and of the incoming ships. While Aurélien conversed with Galdóri, Fjorna stood impassively, keeping an eye on a new figure who had just joined them at the promontory, a peculiar pinniped of wide black-and-white stripes, who watched nervously from nearby, uncomfortable with the presence of the foreigners: The Nu'irg ust Gwonle, Däo-Varjak, the ribbon seal of the Alommo Sea. Galdóri had asked her to come witness this momentous occasion, and the Nu'irg had heeded her call. With hand signals alone, Fjorna issued commands to Osef, Trevin, and Muriel, who left the promontory in a hurry.

The Khardok danced and rejoiced, watching the ships lining up at the coast for miles and miles, waiting for the new Silvfröash to disembark. Shea's ships pulled close without docking, their sails aligned in a horizon of red canvas. A horn blew from the flagship, then more horns followed from each vessel of the fleet, like a rolling thunderclap. The dromon ships turned broadside to the shore, aimed their sapfire cannons, and all at the same time spewed melting death upon the trusting tribe. Ballistae and catapults launched soon after, followed by a swarm of arrows.

Galdóri watched as the inhabitants of this once-safe paradise burned within the sickly yellow flames. She fell to her knees in despair, then turned around, seeking for an answer, only to find Fjorna's steel-cold eyes. Fjorna put the Khardok chief out of her misery by sinking her dagger into the walrus's meaty neck, all the way to the white hilt. As the dead woman collapsed, Fjorna ripped the pinniped mask from her corpse.

Däo-Varjak reacted promptly, trying to escape by bouncing her way toward the only path to shore, but none of her forms were fleet on land. The ribbon seal's terrified eyes were met by a hefty net, cast over her by Muriel and Trevin. As she struggled to free herself, Osef dragged a metal cage toward her, but Däo-Varjak quickly shifted into an elephant seal nearly two tons in weight, breaking through the net and preventing the small cage from trapping her. Her thick skin bled from the cuts of the heavy ropes, as if she was wrapped in a red spiderweb. She tried to charge, but the arbalisters held her back with heavy crossbow bolts, then brought out two more nets.

The enormous elephant seal sprayed red as more nets wrapped around her weakened body. She had seen Jamma-Galdóri exhale her last breath, had witnessed the silver-blonde woman pick up Gwonlesilv with ruthless ambition in her eyes. She knew those eyes. Millennia ago, during the Unification Epoch, Gwonlesilv had been stolen by a power-mad prince from the Kingdom of Gorgellath. Under his command, Däo-Varjak had been forced to commit the most horrific atrocities, battling alongside thousands of mindlocked pinnipeds. Other Miscam tribes had come to her aid back then, rescuing her and the mask—but the deeds she'd been forced to perpetrate she could never forgive herself for.

The white smoke from the sapfire reached them, bringing to Däo-Varjak the stench of scorched flesh, making her vividly recall her ancient terrors. The cruelty of being used as a weapon of war, that was a fate she could not allow herself to suffer again. As more bolts impacted her flesh, she rolled her bleeding body, pulling the nets with her, and dropped off the promontory onto a jagged precipice, slamming into the sharp rocks. Her form shrunk under the net, first turning translucent, then black and white and red into her primal form. As Däo-Varjak's eyes closed, her shape turned luminous, then shone bright as Sunnokh, vanishing into an afterimage, into a memory.

The slaughter of the Khardok continued late into the night. By then, Shea's ships had docked, and she had joined the arbalisters.

"I didn't even have a chance to make use of the war galleys!" she cackled, bumping shoulders with Fjorna while ignoring Silv-Thaar Valaran. "What was that flash of light we all saw?" she asked.

"The Nu'irg," Osef Windscar answered. "We lost her, unfortunately."

"Not like we'll need her anyway, plenty of seals in the sea." Shea shrugged, then circled around Fjorna while cocking her head, lustrous hair draping like a waterfall of tar. "So that's the one, huh?" she asked, staring at the mask Fjorna was holding. "It looks smoother than Crescu's," she added, pretending to call him by his given name out of familiarity, but with a tone of disrespect underlying her words.

"We need to get it to Monarch Hallow as soon as possible," Fjorna said. "There is a long road ahead before we catch up to him. He might already be leaving the Archstone Dome by the time we are finished here. We must hurry now and finish our job."

"What's left to do other than wait for the rain to wash off the blood?" Shea asked.

"A few of the savages escaped, but not many," Osef answered.

"The infantry is taking care of them," Fjorna added.

"And my wolverines," Valaran added. "Although I had to confine them to a canyon—they started attacking our own troops again. They just don't know the difference."

"But it won't be long now," Fjorna said with confidence. "By the light of morning, the entire Khardok Miscam tribe will be exterminated."

CHAPTER FORTY-FIVE

HOLLOW MIND

"More!" Silv-Thaar Markhor ordered, lifting her tankard.

"What a feast!" Silv-Thaar Baneras exulted, still feeling odd about eating meat while in his steppe wild horse half-form.

The Negian army had stopped for the night in a Graalman village south of the Archstone Dome. They had only just begun their trip toward the Scoria Dome, escorted safely by horse riders Suux had provided. She wasn't present, however—the Scourge of the Duggor Veil reigned from Doralghon, and she would wait at the capital for the arrival of the Red Stag, hopefully after he captured the mask of chiropterans.

Baneras dropped a white-clean bone onto his plate. While still chewing, he mumbled, "I didn't know the Horde put such emphasis on their Winter Solstice celebrations!"

"They are behaving like this because of the garrison horses," the Red Stag informed him, leaning back on a throne-like chair their new Graalman allies had brought for him inside their guildhall. "Their legends speak of sacred, giant horses that went extinct during the Downfall," he said. "They see the garrison horses nearly as demigods, and believe we have rescued them."

"The ones I captured are probably bigger than the ones from their legends," Baneras said, then gulped down his ale. "And I'm sure a part of me is also bigger than any legend their women could dream of," he added, clutching his crotch.

Markhor's caprid face crumpled with disgust at the crass display, but she said nothing and simply kept on drinking.

"Be careful, if you find a place you can fit that in," the Red Stag said. He paused while a Graalman servant placed down a new tray of exquisite dishes. Once the servant left, he added, "It's different when you use slaves or a conquered tribe. The Graalman are not yet tamed, and they see themselves as equals. Do not spill your seed too hastily, because any heirs you conceive might end up wanting to take too big a claim. And if they take to your... elongated attributes, it will be obvious where their blood came from."

"Now that we learned the half-forms *can* leave some of their traits behind, I'll be careful where I stick it, don't worry." Baneras ruminated as he tapped his hard-hoofed fingertips on his helm, which was resting on an empty seat next to him. The zebra stripes of the sacred Alampaari armor glistened under the candlelight. "Monarch Hallow... Do you know if your son will have antlers? Can anyone tell? How far along is Ulle, anyway?"

"Seven months now. I asked Urcai to hire a thread reader to see if there is anything they can visualize, but their skills with soot can only see so far. He says my son looks healthy, but they can't pry more. Either way, I don't believe my kind grow antlers until they come of age."

"You made son with Urgsilv?" Markhor asked, her horizontally slitted eyes sharpening like daggers.

"Not yet. In two more months, we'll see."

Markhor huffed. "Sinful," she mumbled under her breath.

"What did you say?" the Red Stag demanded. "Speak up."

Markhor clenched her jaw and straightened her back.

The monarch stood up. "Speak up, goat, or I will—"

A thundering shriek shook the foundations of the guildhall, a roar of despair and helplessness. Chandeliers rattled; trays were dropped.

"What was that?" the Red Stag asked, pushing his chair away, already with a hand over the pommel of his sword.

Two more roars followed, quieter but tinted with equal despair.

"Nu'irgesh!" Markhor called as the three rushed to the guildhall's exit. As they were about to reach the portal, a columnar leg crashed through the archway, raining splinters onto them.

"Your Nu'irg, control it!" the Red Stag screamed to Baneras.

Through the shattered roof, Baneras saw the rhino-like face of a behemoth—it was Estriéggo, who had been kept in that largest of forms as a means of protection, as a display of power. The colossus trembled, tangling his legs and losing his footing. As his enormous body toppled straight toward his captors, Estriéggo twisted his long neck and looked down at Baneras.

Baneras tightened his grip on the giant's mind and, with an urgent order, forced him to shapeshift into a smaller form, the first his mind could think of. Estriéggo still fell, but in the form of a zebra, hurting no one else as his barrel-like chest slammed against the ground.

More screams, from beyond the shattered archway.

"Your beasts, Lorr!" a marshal called from outside the hall. "They have gone wild!"

The Red Stag and Markhor rushed out through the rubble and saw Sovath and Beiféren rearing on their hind legs, standing over the crushed bodies of Negian soldiers. Monarch Hallow could feel the mindlock he had exerted on Sovath, yet the megaloceros seemed out of control. He bugled, piercing through the commotion and reaching the Nu'irg's ears. Sovath suddenly stopped thrashing, although her posture was now tense, as if fighting waves of spasms.

Markhor, too, quickly regained control of Beiféren, although the helmeted muskox had not the strength to keep on his feet and simply collapsed onto the dead soldiers.

"What happened?" Baneras asked from within the shattered guildhall.

"I don't know!" the Red Stag spat, then ground his molars as he tried to contain his rage. "Stay back. Keep a hold of your beast, and I will see what I can gather."

He approached Sovath, commanding her to take her small primal form, just in case his mindlock were to fail once more. Sovath did as she was ordered, and stood there trembling as a tiny spotted deer, eyes disconsolate.

"Last time, same," Markhor remarked, stepping close to the Red Stag. "Like desert time."

Two months before, they had experienced something similar in the White Desert of Dorhond. As their parched army marched toward the Archstone Dome, both Sovath and Beiféren had suddenly stopped trudging and began a mournful whine, but both the Red Stag and Markhor had been traveling next to them and quickly made them snap back into their mindlocked trances. They hadn't given the incident much thought, blaming it on the heat sickness all of them had been suffering, but the events now seemed to be related.

The Red Stag placed a hand on Sovath's forehead. Deep within her, he spoke, «Tell me why you disobeyed my commands to remain still, beast. Tell me what just happened.»

Sovath, mindlocked and petrified, felt hatred boil through her core, but her mind was as blank as her eyes.

«Speak now, animal!» he howled at her thoughts. «Why did you three lose yourselves?»

Sovath held her breath. Urgsilv's orders could force her body to do abominable things, yet her mind, although trapped in a most cruel cage, was still her own. She would not let the monster take the last bit of her, not even after the Endfall swallowed them all.

"Tell me!" the Red Stag screamed, his spittle splashing the chital's face.

Sovath blinked impassively. Deep within her, she prayed that Däo-Varjak's death had been swift. Deep within her, she considered whether she herself would be better off dead.

CHAPTER FORTY-SIX

PLUNDERED PARADISE

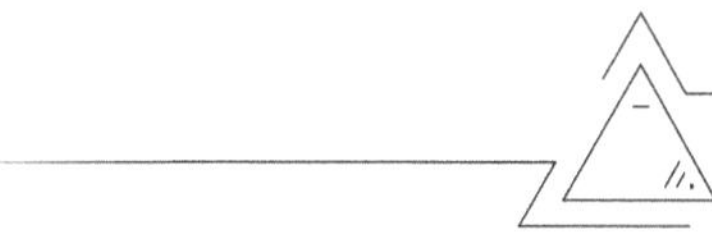

"Even the insides look misshapen," Kitjári remarked to Nalaníri. "Look at all these fibers, they are tangling into knots."

"D'outside didn't look quite so bad," Nalaníri said in hushed tones, as if the vines might hear her.

"The Anglass Dome's been changing quite slowly," Ardof informed them, holding up a pharolith lamp; he was still getting used to its spectral light. "But people who live on the perimeter could tell something was awry."

"At least them vines open up jis' d'same," Nalaníri replied.

Banook and Bear walked quietly alongside them, taking care not to step in the holes left by the retreating tendrils. Probo and Safís followed closely behind, having a mindspoken conversation none of the others were privy to. The wayfarers had been making their way into the Anglass Dome for nearly an hour. The vines had transitioned from thorny on the outside of the dome, to spongy and fibrous within the walls. Once they finally breached through, it was not the light of Sunnokh that brightened their faces, but that of the luminous arudinn coating the interior vines. It was midday in Urgdrolom, the domed land of the Teldebran Miscam.

They moved away from the vines and crouched at the edge of an elevated prairie overlooking an expanse of meadows, creeks, and fertile grasslands. Despite the beauty of the vegetation and the unrelenting song of birds, no big animals could be seen. The landscape was patchy, tainted by scars from recent burns, and covered in places by a thin dusting of snow.

"It looks just like the time I was here months ago," Ardof said, "only colder." He pulled his shoulders up and tucked his gloved hands under his armpits.

"The Winter Solstice arrives in just a few days," Banook said. "It will get much colder very soon."

"I can't believe the Negians would let you in," Kitjári said to the ranger, "bribes and all."

"The bribes were to make my way out, not in. To get in, all I needed was to make myself pass as a slave."

It was a clear day with few clouds, letting them see way past the trunk, which sprouted from a too perfectly round mountain the Teldebran called Stelm Nil. Although from afar the mountain's smooth form made it look like nothing more than a rolling hill, the wayfarers were not tricked by the illusion.

Steaming curtains rose from the vast prairies. "Hot springs," Ardof explained. "Hot rivers, even, running everywhere through the dome."

Banook pointed southwest toward billowing smears of reddish brown. "Those darker clouds don't look like steam to me."

"They are burning the fields again," Ardof said. "When the Teldebran slaves escape to the tall grasses, they herd them out with fire, then set them to work again if they aren't too burnt to be useful."

"Let's hope they can all run away after we open this forsaken dome," Kitjári muttered.

"Now I'm curious," Ardof said. "Why are you so eager to set Anglass and Lequa to open, while Heartpine sits there collapsing over itself? Wouldn't that one take priority?"

"It's complicated," Kitjári said. "There's a structure inside the trunk that allows the masks to… speak to the dome. That structure, the lattice, was destroyed at Heartpine, so there's no way to help it. It's just a matter of time before the entire dome comes crashing down under its own weight."

"Thornridge will be obliterated if that happens," Ardof noted, his voice tight as he considered the implications, "as will all the settlements around the dome."

"I know," Kitjári said, trying to avoid thinking too much about it. "We can only do so much. There is still hope for Anglass, as long as they haven't touched that lattice. But there's nothing we can do for Heartpine."

Banook stood up, seeming as round and tall as the mountain at the center of the dome. "There is too much of me to hide among even the tallest of these grasses," he said, "so I will be traveling as a kiuon from here on."

He undressed, then stuffed his clothes in his backpack.

"What about your glaive?" Kitjári asked.

"Ardof will kindly carry it for me. And my backpack too, since he travels so light."

"Look," Ardof said, "I'm not looking to charge you for this job, I'm doing it because I believe it will help all realms. But if you want me to carry that absurd monster of a weapon, you better pay up, mountain man."

Banook shrugged, then shrunk down, turning into a kiuon just as tall as Bear, although significantly wider. He led the way forward.

They trudged carefully, sticking to reedy marshlands to avoid detection, following close to the shores of the widening river. Ardof dispassionately carried the unwieldy glaive, sometimes dragging it behind him as if plowing a field. It took them a few days, but they eventually arrived at the base of the round mountain, where they hid from a passing caravan in a dense grove of poplars.

Banook grew back into his human form, resting heavily against a rotting log, looking pale and tired. He sighed deeply. "This is harder than I expected."

"What's wrong?" Ardof asked. "You seem ill."

"The closer we get to the trunk, the farther any of my bears are from me," Banook said. "They are all around us, yet all so distant. It feels just like when we ventured into the Da'áju Caldera."

"Probo n'Safís seem t'be doing jis' fine," Nalaníri pointed out. "Do them have suids n'canids in this dome?"

"I saw plenty of wild foxes and boars last time around," Ardof said. "But either way, the Negians brought pigs for their farms, as well as plenty of guard dogs. But I do not believe they bothered bringing in bears."

"Will you be able to move farther in?" Kitjári asked Banook.

"Yes. I will let you know if I reach my limit. We need to get to the trunk, that is what matters most."

Kitjári nodded. She pulled out her spyglass and scanned the terrain.

"Still not clear," she muttered, handing the device to Ardof.

Ardof peered at the roads that switchbacked up Stelm Nil. "There will be a lot more traffic on the southern side," he said. "This is as good as it will get. Once those wagons roll out of the way, we should move."

They waited for the caravan to pass, then began making their way up the mountain, with Safís scouting ahead for them. Ruins of a once-great city hunkered atop the mountain; the wooden supports and roofs had all burned, but the stone foundations remained standing.

"This is the… *was* the city of Nerokholm," Ardof said as they took a quick break in a ditch outside the destroyed capital.

"Why did them arseholes have t'burn it all?" Nalaníri asked.

"It wasn't the Negians," Ardof answered. "It was the Teldebran. They revolted and burned their own city, trying to leave nothing for the Negian looters."

While Safís kept watch from a high vantage point, Probo took the lead, and with a grunt hurried the others through the blackened streets, following the trunk counterclockwise. After a few miles of circling the enormous vines, they arrived at the southern end of the trunk. They could not yet see the entrance to the temple, but the additional patrols on the streets told them they must be near it.

"Keep quiet," Kitjári mouthed, tiptoeing inside a half-collapsed building. "I think the temple must be right around the corner from here. I can smell the—"

Arroouf, Bear said.

Ardof turned and saw a single soldier standing at the other end of the burnt building, staring at the animal people, at the wolf, the javelina, the kiuon. His mouth was open, but no sound made it out.

Thonk!

Ardof's sling landed a solid rock on the soldier's unprotected head. The ranger unsheathed his long dagger, ready to jump at the toppling soldier, but Kitjári put her claws on his arm wraps.

"Stop. Only if necessary. Some of these stoolgarglers are as trapped and hopeless as the Teldebran they are enslaving."

Ardof snorted with irritation but put his weapon away. Banook shifted back into his human form and dragged the soldier into a dark corner, covering the impact wound to prevent blood from leaving a trail. They gagged, tied, and hid the unconscious man behind a pile of stone bricks, then hurried to the far end of the building and crouched by a window.

"There it is," Kitjári said. The massive entrance to Ommo ust Urg was visible through the opening. Heavy infantry protected the archway, wielding swords, lances, battle axes, and long pikes.

"How many do ye think?" Nalaníri asked.

"Twenty, maybe thirty armored soldiers," Ardof said. "A dozen guard dogs, too."

"The dogs will not attack us," Banook said, "not while Safís keeps us company. She asks us not to hurt them."

"I see two crimson guardians right by the archway," Kitjári said. "We must take extra care with them." Her eyes drifted up. "I'll take out the archers on the balconies first, then the guardians before they notice, and then we charge the rest."

"You can't take crimson guardians with arrows," Ardof warned. "Their armor is magnium alloyed."

"We'll see about that," she said, readying a senstregalv-tipped arrow. "Banook, are you feeling well enough to battle?"

"I'm not at my best," he answered, squeezing his beard, which was now streaked with white hairs. "But this is as far from my bears as I will get in this eighty-mile-wide circle. I am ready." He directed his gaze toward the wolf. "Safís, could you tell Bear to stay put and wait for us?"

Safís flicked an ear, and Bear sat, quietly whining.

"Aren't you going to put on some clothes?" Ardof asked Banook.

"Better not, as I may need to take my bear forms."

"Probo m'dear," Nalaníri said, "once them screams start, ye go do yer thing, be a good decoy." The javelina grunted twice, then walked out of the building to wait for the signal.

Kitjári took aim at an archer on the highest balcony. She pulled on the quaar bowstring and released an arrow; it flew silent, like thunderless lightning. It pierced through the archer's skull and exited from the opposite side, lodging itself into an enormous vine. Kitjári shot again, and again, taking down two more archers.

A guard dog barked, scenting trouble. A crimson guardian heard the warning and turned to face the wayfarers. Kitjári let the next projectile fly directly toward the red-plated helm of the guardian. The powerful impact made the knight buckle over, but his reinforced helm held.

"Intruders!" he called as he regained his footing.

Safís released a shrill, penetrating howl, dispersing the guard dogs in a mixture of fear, confusion, and reverence.

"Now!" Nalaníri told Probo.

Probo charged toward the armored soldiers and shifted into a kubanochoerus while at full gallop. The crimson guardians easily dodged the attack, but Probo took down almost a dozen other soldiers, then kept running past the temple's entrance. He vocalized like a humpback whale, luring in the stunned survivors.

"Attack, now!" Banook yelled, charging with his heavy glaive, with Safís racing by his side. Nalaníri rushed forward too, helped by Kitjári, who now focused entirely on picking off anyone approaching Nalaníri.

"Get the red bastards first!" Ardof called, following behind them, a bit unsure of how he might help.

The soldiers' terrified eyes spotted the naked giant swinging the ludicrous polearm. Banook stomped heavily, his belly dragging with the momentum of his swings, his cock slapping against his thighs, his blade tearing a red path for the others to run through. With one mighty slash, he sliced through the armor of one of the crimson guardians.

Safís shifted into a perfectly white dire wolf and bolted straight into the temple, ignoring the battle behind her. Nalaníri and Ardof picked off the injured soldiers by the entrance, hearing wails from within the long hallway.

More soldiers—whom the wayfarers had not noticed—had been sitting in the shade of a nearby pavilion. Half of them rushed forward with their lances, while the others stayed behind with bows and arrows. Projectiles tore through the air, one piercing Banook's left forearm. The remaining crimson guardian saw Banook flinch and took the opportunity to swing his sword. Banook parried the strike, then shifted into his golden bear form and with his maw crunched the guardian's vambrace down into his bones. He tossed the guardian into a wall and gave chase after the archers, deflecting arrows with his fur and thick hide.

Kitjári had put her bow away and was now slicing with her short sword, opening the way for Nalaníri. "Stay with me!" she called, taking down two stunned soldiers. They heard and felt the earthquake of Probo returning.

"Perfect distraction. Thank ye, mine dear Probo," Nalaníri greeted the suid upon his return, then her voice deepened with concern. "M'boy, yer hurt." The kuba's massive tusks were covered in Negian blood, but more blood of his own flowed from cuts on his legs.

"We have to clear this area before we go in," Ardof said, seeing a few straggling soldiers who had followed behind Probo. "We can't risk coming out to an ambush."

Banook shifted back to his human self and picked up his glaive. "You three hurry—it is a long way to the center of the trunk. If we wait any longer, reinforcements will be upon us. Probo and I will hold the entrance."

Kitjári and Nalaníri ran into the tunnel together. Ardof followed closely behind.

"Khest! What happened here?" Ardof gasped, his eyes following a helm that was rolling down the shallow ramp—a head was still inside it.

"Safís happened," Kitjári replied, hopping over a pile of indecipherable organs.

They rushed past the half-mile carnage, following the wails of the few barely surviving victims. Once they reached the temple, they found the dire wolf with her fur splattered in red, snarling blood and teeth and rage. All her anger had been released, all the pent-up fury from when the Negians had destroyed her dome, killed her friends, and left her trapped for years.

"By the bloodwraiths of Khest..." Kitjári mumbled, stepping over the shredded bodies littering the temple's floor. Safís gasped heavy breaths, then let her snarl drop. She closed her eyes for a moment, then growled a low rumble and bolted from the temple.

Nalaníri put a hand on Kitjári's shoulder. "Ye haven't tried this yet, m'dear. Ye want to do d'honors?"

Kitjári pulled her eyes away from the carnage and slowly nodded. She stared at the throne on the central dais, which looked regally menacing with its tangle of antlers carved of white marble. She flumped onto the antlered seat and felt utterly overwhelmed as the threads converged into her and she saw through the entirety of Urgdrolom, as if gazing up through the trunk and sensing each and every column, branch, and vine. She felt the curved shape above as clearly as she sensed the strength of the deep roots below. Now that she could witness the dome in its entirety, she perceived it as a higher-level consciousness—or perhaps something wildly different from what she understood as a consciousness—and saw for the first time its waxy-green aura, its colors perturbed by malign, darker inconsistencies.

"It's suffering," she said, more to herself. "The dome is in so much pain." She felt a maternal urge to protect it, to shape it back to its previous perfection, as if she could cradle its enormity into her furred arms. But she knew that was not the answer—the time for healing had passed, and the dome needed undoing.

Kitjári took a deep breath and tried to comprehend the vast wholeness before her. While feeling her empathic focus expand through the quaar conduits, she tugged at the threads, hearing their myriad voices in response, and willed the lattice to collapse. Ardof and Nalaníri observed the methodical motion of the polyhedral complexity as it twisted above them, as it snapped and merged inward, wrapping around the thornless core vine that waited behind the throne. The smooth vine became coated in black conduits, then lowered into the bedrock. White sap filled the hole it left behind, like a window of light into the Six Gates of Felsvad. The job was done—nothing would stop the Anglass Dome from unraveling now.

"It's done. Let's get out of here," Kitjári rasped as she stood.

They rushed out of the temple, once more passing by the eviscerated bodies the dire wolf had left behind. Full-on war had exploded outside, the three Nu'irgesh fighting a wave of reinforcements.

"Banook!" Kitjári called. "We need to move!"

The giant swung his polearm through three torsos, then turned toward her. "Help Probo!" he urged. "Safís and I will take care of the rest!"

Probo was struggling to flank a troop of pike soldiers. Kitjári screamed as she attacked them from behind, followed by Ardof and Nalaníri, giving the giant suid just enough of a chance to trample the distracted soldiers. Once the main threat was mitigated, the wayfarers regrouped by the temple's archway.

"Mour are coming," Nalaníri warned as she gasped for air.

From the south, a metallic line of shields marched toward them in a tight formation. A rumbling roar made the shields rattle: it was Safís, lifting her head and letting out a deafening howl from her bloodied jaws. The incoming soldiers saw the piles of bodies in front of the archway, spotted the white and red dire wolf, and smartly chose to stop advancing.

"Quickly, before they change their minds," Kitjári said.

While Safís held her ground to intimidate the soldiers, the others retreated into the building they had scouted from earlier and picked up their bags.

"Bear, come boy!" Banook called, bloodied and out of breath. The dog followed.

As they rushed through the burnt city, Safís caught up to them once more. The few soldiers they encountered hastily fled or were dispatched.

"Into the grass, before they see where we went," Ardof said.

Banook stopped, pulled out an arrow from his left arm, then two more from his hips. "Hold on, you two," he told the other Nu'irgesh. He removed a few arrows from Probo, as well as a lance that was stuck in his rump. Safís was wounded as well, but no weapons were sticking out of her fur. "All clear, you can make yourselves smaller now."

He handed his glaive back to Ardof and shifted into a kiuon to hide in the grass. Safís and Probo followed in their primal forms.

They moved downhill while crouched, paralleling a cascading stream. A sudden earthquake oscillated through the wide hill. The tips of the grasses they hid amongst swayed softly.

"Well, if the Negians were terrified of this place falling on them, now they'll have more of a reason to be afraid," Ardof said.

"Don't ye worry," Nalaníri told him. "Them quakes are jis' d'dome a-making room with its roots. D'dome won't be collapsing, it's jis' shriveling underground."

"Do you think they'll chase after us?" Kitjári asked.

"Not the infantry, they aren't that stupid," Ardof speculated. "But there's cavalry at the southern end of the mountain. Once they are notified, they'll come looking for us, with hounds scenting our trail."

"We'll need t'find a place to rest n'hide," Nalaníri said. "D'arudinn are beginning t'slumber."

CHAPTER FORTY-SEVEN

TELDEBRAN LIGHT

Ardof led them down a trail alongside the creek, over steep terrain that horses would not dare traverse. The dome darkened, their feet tired, the water rumbled. Late that night, they arrived at a secluded canyon with a cascading stream wherein they found a dry cove to rest. Kitjári and Ardof took care of bandaging everyone's wounds, although Safís would not let anyone touch her, preferring to lick her lesions.

Kitjári noticed that the strips of cloth Ardof always kept wrapped around his arms were tinted red. "Hey, you are bleeding under your wraps. Let me take care of—"

"I'm fine. It's not my own blood."

"I'm quite sure I see a cut in the—"

"I said I'm fine."

Kitjári lifted her handpaws in surrender and let him be. She went to help Banook instead.

"If you shift to any other forms, the bandages will fall off," she warned Banook as she patched him up.

"I'll manage, and I'll heal before you know it," he said, then cringed, looking at the cuts on his lower calves and feeling the bruises on his back. "The closer we get to bearkind, the sooner I'll be my full self once more."

"We were too careless," Nalaníri complained. "Our friends are injured 'cause uf us. We were lucky t'have escaped. But jis' one arrow hitting d'wrong spot could've taken one uf us down."

"She's right," Ardof said. "As powerful as you all are, we need to be careful and avoid confrontations."

"I don't think there would've been a way to avoid a fight," Kitjári said. "Maybe in the Lequa Dome we'll find a better approach, but right now, all we can do is stay low and find a way out of here."

Ardof kept his eyes closed but avoided falling asleep. Once he was sure everyone else had passed out, he got up and headed to the creek. He washed his hands in the warm water, then lit a candle behind a rock, where the others could not see its glow. His right forearm throbbed from a deep cut. He winced as he removed his arm wraps, which he had kept compressed to avoid spilling too much blood. He dropped the wraps on a rock and inspected his injury.

"I would rather help with that, you don't want it infec—" Jiara stopped herself. She had snuck up behind Ardof and now saw what he'd been trying to hide.

Ardof quickly covered his arm. "Khest! You… What are you—"

"You're Oldrin," Jiara said. "Why are you working so hard to hide it?" Along the entire length of Ardof's injured arm, she had seen bony protrusions spiking out, from elbow to knuckles.

"It's none of your business. And I'm no fucking Oldrin," he snorted.

"You'll need stitches, let me help you."

Ardof looked at his injury while still hiding it from Jiara's gaze. He grimaced. It was a bad cut on his dominant arm; he'd have a hard time suturing it himself.

"Fine," he grumbled, "but don't tell the others."

"You have my word," she said, twice tapping her knuckles together.

After washing his cut in the creek, Jiara got to work on stitching the wound. It ran alongside the bony spurs, which were of a kind that would look utterly grotesque to those who did not see the Oldrin kindly.

"Your light-brown hair, your green eyes. You don't look Oldrin," Jiara observed as she tightened a stitch.

"I told you, pal, I'm not," Ardof said, pressing his teeth tight against each other, trying to squint the pain away.

Jiara took on a slightly mocking tone. "I'm no expert at this, but looking at your arms, I'd say—"

"I'm *not* Oldrin." He sighed, then continued, "I'm part Oldrin, alright? Someone in my family—not my parents—fucked a spur. Are you happy?"

Jiara chewed on her tongue and gave him a half-lidded stare. "Why are you so bothered by this?"

"You know why. How do you think I made it so far in these Takh-forsaken frontier lands, eh? If it wasn't for my eyes and beard, I'd be digging for sulphur or coal for the rest of my life. Of course I'm bothered—once someone finds out, word spreads, and then I'm fucked."

"What, you think I'm about to go tell on you? Consider the few little secrets we've shared with you lately. We are in this together. We have to trust each other."

"Some things are fine to keep private. I don't ask where you stick your bear tongue at night."

Jiara pulled the last stitch a bit harder than necessary. Ardof inhaled through his teeth.

"If you have a problem with where I stick my tongue, you better speak up now," she said, "because Nalaníri and I are not going to—"

Ardof held up his hands. "Fine, that was uncalled for. I hold no quarrel with you two, as odd as… whatever. But I have a right to be cautious. I've lost everything once before. I used to live in Nargara, right in the fissure, by the bastion. Moved there to start life anew, in secret, of course. I managed to keep my background hidden for years and had quite a good life, a life I was proud of. But one night you fuck the wrong Tsing whore, and suddenly your life is over."

"You have nothing to worry about, I'm not going to let you fuck me," Jiara said, tying the sutures. "Keep your wraps on. They'll help, but wash them at least once a day."

She rose to her feet, then added, "We are a team, Ardof. It's fine if you keep some secrets, as I'm sure you have many others, but let's help each other out when it matters. We'll need you, and you can also count on us."

Jiara left Ardof alone with his dim candlelight.

They left their camp just as the trunk began to light up. North they followed the warm river, oftentimes hiding in the steam it sent aloft.

Ardof looked up at the pastel-white sky of the dome and asked, "How long will it take to open?"

"For people to walk out?" Kitjári shrugged. "A week, maybe two."

Nalaníri concurred. "D'day we arrived back at Nagradrolom, 'bout a month after I set it t'open, we were able t'sail straight into it. It's slow, but eventually d'entire dome will recede back into d'land it came frum."

"It'll be a surreal sight," Ardof said. "These lands have not seen Sunnokh for centuries." He stopped by a wall of rock and looked around uncomfortably. "Do you mind if I light a small fire?"

"We can't afford t'cook," Nalaníri said, "it'd be much too dangerous."

"Only a small one, for a candle," he assured her.

"What's on your mind, friend?" Banook asked.

Ardof took out a small wooden figurine from his bag. It was Pliwe, the tri-horned goddess Alaia sometimes prayed to.

"My family came from Dorhond. We always say a prayer to Pliwe, by candlelight, when the Winter Solstice arrives. I should've done so at sunset, but I forgot. Well, since dusk in here is dawn on the outside, maybe it doesn't matter either way."

Mentioning his Dorhond background was not necessarily an admission of being Oldrin, Kitjári thought, but it was something she had not expected him to acknowledge. She glanced at Ardof's arm wraps: they were clean; there had been no more bleeding.

Ardof crouched in a nook by the rocks, placed a tallow candle in front of the Pliwe figurine, then recited quiet words by the lavender scents that wafted up from its feeble flame. He buried a few nuts in the ground where Pliwe had kept watch, then blew the candle out.

As Ardof was stowing his items away, a piercing squeal made him drop his figurine. It was Probo, wailing a mournful note of agony that none of them had thought a suid could utter.

Nalaníri turned toward her friend. "Probo? What—"

Safís then began to howl. Bear whined, unsure of what was happening.

"No…" Banook moaned. His eyes opened wide, staring at nothing, shedding a tear.

"What is wrong?" Kitjári asked. She could feel Banook's pain directly, too directly—her own heart ached.

"Däo-Varjak has died," Banook whispered.

"Who is Däo-Varjak?" Ardof asked. "How do you—"

"She is… was the Nu'irg ust Gwonle, the ribbon seal of the Alommo Sea. She was my friend, and Probo's friend, and Safís's friend, and now she is gone." He swallowed thickly, closing his eyes for a moment, as if in prayer. "Dire news this brings," he said at last. "I am afraid the Moonrise Dome must be lost. The Miscam who live there are surely in trouble, and Gwonlesilv could now be in the hands of our enemies. My poor Däo-Varjak… Fortune was always unkind to you."

At least they didn't enslave her, Kitjári thought, but dared not say it out loud. She embraced Banook, trying to soothe him, but nothing could comfort the mourning bear.

They moved quietly for the rest of the day, with Banook too pained and worried to utter any words. Even more quietly, they set their camp under a draping willow and waited for the darkness to be filled with the songs of night birds, frogs, and insects.

Ardof woke up to a rustling. He held still, listening, watching through half-closed eyes. He sensed motion at the edge of the drooping branches. Behind the tree trunk, he saw a stalking silhouette. He loaded a stone in his sling, concealing it under his blanket. Then, in a swift move, he pushed his blanket off and hurled the stone, striking the target.

The sound of the toppling intruder woke everyone up.

"What is happening?" Kitjári whispered, seeing Ardof rush out with his long dagger in hand.

"Khest," Ardof cursed behind the tree. "It's a Teldebran woman. I thought she was a soldier."

They placed the young woman on top of a bedroll. She was still conscious, but delirious, moaning a bit too loudly. The cut on her pale forehead dribbled blood over her long black hair, down to tint her white robes. She had been carrying a basket filled with crayfish, which were now scattered over the grass.

Kitjári and Nalaníri used their Silvesh to take some of the woman's pain away. As the pain subsided, the woman became more aware and saw the bear and boar staring at her. She sank into the ground, cowering.

"Are ye alright? Can ye hear me?" Nalaníri asked.

"*Baakiag, grei krurgothuk ch-chossat,*" the woman responded.

"It's okay," Kitjári replied in Miscamish. "We won't hurt you. We are sorry about what happened. We thought you were a Negian soldier."

"What is she saying?" Ardof asked. Banook quietly interpreted for him and Nalaníri.

"You are… Nagrafröa," the woman said, staring at Nalaníri. "And… I don't know your face, but you are also beautiful," she said to Kitjári.

"My name is Kitjári. I am Urnaadifröa. We have come here under the protection of the Nu'irgesh ust Nagra, Agnarg, and Urnaadi."

Banook shifted into a kiuon, so as to not scare her with a larger shape, ending up inside his enormous shirt and cape. He poked his head out and bleated.

The woman laughed. "What are the Nu'irgesh and the voices of Nagra and Urnaadi doing in this cursed place? Urgsilv abandoned us. Sovath abandoned us. All the cervids abandoned us."

"We are here to release this dome, to open it. Are you alone? What is your name?"

"Trinn," she answered. "I was returning to my camp. We hunt and fish at night, sleep during the day. There are many Teldebran camps, from those who escaped."

"You are also hiding from the Negians?"

"Yes, but they will find us, eventually. We move constantly, hide in holes, behind waterfalls, among vines. You can help us escape?"

Kitjári thought for a moment, then spoke to her friends in Common.

"We could help her, and help the camp she is with. Or better yet, we could ask Trinn to tell others. That way more of them could escape once the dome is open enough."

"We won't be able to help them all," Ardof cautioned.

"Not all," Kitjári said, "but at least more than a few." She regarded Trinn again. "Do you know where the other Teldebran Miscam camps are? If we tell you how to escape, will you be able to tell them too?"

"Some, yes. My friends will know a few others, and the other camps will know more. How do we get out?"

"The dome has already begun opening. All you need to do is walk to the vines and hide. It will happen very slowly. Do so before the Negians notice something is happening. You can take shelter inside the wall as it opens, and then escape. Northeast will be safest, away from any Negian bases. If you follow the rivers beyond the dome, past the forests you will find a wasteland called Lurr's Abyss. The Negians never venture there, fearful of spritetales of nethervoid dragons and wraiths. Go hide in the wasteland and in the mountains beyond. Can you tell that to your camp and all the other camps you know about?"

"Yes," Trinn said haltingly, "but they won't believe me."

"Then we'll go with you. Take us, and we'll convince them."

They set off in the middle of the night, following Trinn's directions. They reached a copse of maples and walked between the leafless trees, where they encountered a group of ten Teldebran farmers.

"*Oset fin uth halvet*," Kitjári greeted them.

The farmers were terrified at first, but thanks to Trinn's assurances, they quickly came to understand they were in no danger. They agreed that instead of following the Silvfröash out, it would be a greater kindness to have each of them travel to inform the other Teldebran groups they knew about, then ask those groups to do the same. The refugees would spread the word as fast as they possibly could, then hide among the vines until their dark embrace gave way to the outside world.

Before Trinn left them to find other groups, Kitjári called for her.

"Take this," she told her, handing her a closed pharolith lamp. She showed her how to open it, but did so discreetly. "It is a kenzir stone. It will show you the way through the vines. It will also help you convince the other Teldebran if you tell them who gave it to you. Lead them, take them beyond Urgdrolom. Save them."

"Thank you," Trinn said before jumping forward for a bear hug. Kitjári held her tightly and cried, not knowing whether the young woman would make it out or not, but hoping she would have a better chance than most.

Trinn departed, holding the lamp to her chest.

"It breaks my heart," Kitjári said to Nalaníri, watching the Teldebran farmers walk away, each of them in a different direction. She lowered her head. "I hope they all make it out."

Nalaníri kissed the bear's forehead, then embraced her. "Ye did a good thing, m'dear. Ye've given them mour than a way out, mour than a kenzir stone. Ye've given them hope."

CHAPTER FORTY-EIGHT

THE FRACTURED RANGE

The wayfarers exited the Anglass dome by midday on the seventeenth of Hoartide. The air was brumous and thick. Winter had clearly arrived to stay, bringing a coating of fresh snow and a chill breeze.

"It's snowing," Kitjári said, pointing out the obvious.

"From here on, we'll travel faster," Banook said. He looked to the nearly invisible white wolf standing beside them. "Safís, we could use your keen eyes and ears to scout ahead. Make sure no one crosses paths with us. I will use my big nose to follow your tracks."

Safís blinked her yellow eyes and disappeared among the flurries, white on white. Banook shifted into his golden arctotherium form and led the way, with Kitjári upon his back. Probo followed behind him as a kuba, carrying Nalaníri, Ardof, and Bear. Hours north of the dome, they entered the wasteland known as Lurr's Abyss, where they hoped the Teldebran survivors would eventually settle. From there, Banook showed them to a pre-Downfall road that followed the southern slopes of the mighty Stelm Khull, traversing the tributaries that birthed the Stiss Malpa. After four days of travel, they reached the inhabited moorlands near Blackfern, where they stopped riding atop the Nu'irgesh in order to make their way more stealthily.

The old road ended at farmlands. They hopped over a dry stone wall separating two fields, staring at the much larger wall of rock that rose on the horizon east of them.

"The Fractured Range," Ardof murmured. If they could have taken flight on a raven's wing, they would have seen a stretch of endless plateaus split by fissures resembling titanic mud cracks, segmenting the highlands into inaccessible blocks. South and east of the range were the fertile grasslands and meadows of the Great Steppes, all covered in snow.

"Too many farms and mines around the Blackfern Byway," Ardof noted, looking concerned. "We could cross north, then follow the seashore to the dome, if we don't mind dealing with a Bergsulfi or two."

"Fret not," Banook said, "for I have a better plan. The Fractured Range is much like a labyrinth, but I've explored its depths many a time in the past and know which cracks to take, even if they might've changed a lot with time. The paths that run through it will protect us from the winds and hide our hides. The bottoms of the fissures won't be covered in ice until perhaps the end of Frostburn. The most dangerous season to cross them is Thawing, when flash floods fill the fissures faster than one can take a breath to shout for help. But we won't encounter such hindrances now. Follow me. Let us find shelter from these glacial winds."

Sunnokh was out, threatening to drive them snow-blind. It had been cloudy and snowy since they'd exited the dome, and although the skies were now clear, the winds blew icily, making it paradoxically much colder. Banook stopped in front of a towering, vertical crack in the rock and looked back, toward the northwest.

"It feels so strange," he said with pensive eyes. "I have not been this far from the mountains since the epochs before the Downfall, when my bears and I were migrating toward our new home. And what resplendent mountains they are, whether one lives within them or gazes upon them from without."

"Are you going to be alright being so far from them?" Kitjári asked.

"My heart will miss them, but my body will be fine. My bears have ventured much farther already, likely all the way to the sea. I feel them spreading, as if with every breath I can smell the salty breeze, the dusty deserts, and the fragrant forests they are visiting. I will dearly miss my mountains, but I have also missed the other wonders these sublime continents have to offer. And I'll show you more wonders up ahead, if these fissures are still as magnificent as they once were. Follow me, before the light of day abandons us—there are marvels to behold."

There were dozens upon dozens of cracks they could have chosen to enter. Most led to dead ends, others to toppled boulders and too-tight passages, while a few opened into the interior labyrinth. Banook took the one he knew would lead them deepest. The walls rose high as redwoods, almost perfectly vertical and clear-cut.

"No new tracks, only old campsites," Banook observed, finding evidence of adventurers who had come to explore the strange formations but had not dared venture too far. "And no one seems to have found the way into the inner maze yet."

He took them through tight tunnels into the isolated passageways of the interior. Only a hint of snow clung to the bottoms of the chasms, where the ground was flat, filled with a layer of packed sediments that made it easy to traverse for humans, Nu'irgesh, and dog. Little was growing down there, namely a few lichens and grasses that were dry in Winter, but Banook said the fissures would explode in colorful flowers at the end of Thawing. Tree trunks littered and blocked some passages, which Banook explained came from trees that had died at the edges of the plateaus above them. He had to hurl a few out of the way.

"These are not cracks carved by erosion," Banook told them as he squeezed his belly through a gap. "See the markings on this side?" He pointed at a round boulder trapped in the wall on one side, which poked halfway out. He then pointed at a round hole of the same size marking the opposite side. "These fissures were formed not by wind and rain, but by the plateau itself cracking and splitting like dried mud, although it's made of strong rock. These ranges are not too old. I remember a time maybe only five thousand years ago when this entire domain used to be a salty lake."

"How's a lake a-turn into a broken highland?" Nalaníri asked.

"With pressure and time," Banook explained. "The lake had warm, salty water back in its heyday. The crust beneath was hard, hot, and latent, feeding the lake with plentiful minerals and warmth. But in time, the crust rose and pushed the lake up, cracking the bottom and draining it in a matter of mere months. Luckily, the land only bubbled, and did not erupt, otherwise this all would look more like how you described the Brasha'in Scablands. The crust dried and cracked, and the lake was no more, leaving these ruptured veins. But the fissures were not the only things the dried lake left behind." His coy smile suddenly glittered. "Follow me. We are close to my favorite spot, where magic grew in the hidden spaces between the split rocks."

A bit of sunlight still shone through the cracks, but rarely did it line up to hit the deep bottom. Banook traversed the maze with certainty and purpose.

"There you are," he said at last, stopping at an intersection and staring at the new path the others could not yet see. He waved his big hands to usher his friends through. "Come in and witness the miracle."

The new fissure was wider than the others, almost forty feet across, and it was covered in milky crystals that sparkled magically. The sunlight was filtering right into the broad rift, illuminating one wall in blinding sparkles, then bouncing to the other side in a more diffused, ethereal shimmer.

"It's all crystals," Kitjári whispered in awe.

Banook pointed at areas on the walls that looked almost like animal burrows, crystallized in agate-like organic patterns that were filled with colorful minerals.

Kitjári hovered her sharp claws close to the gem-layered wall, which was coated in spiky pyramids, glittering bubbles, and brittle hairs.

"Careful," Banook said. "They are quite fragile."

"How did this come to be?" she asked.

"I asked the same question once," Banook said, "to an old scholar who lived in Brimstowne centuries ago. He had visited the fissures to study them, and said that the burrows used to be mineral springs that fed the old lake. When the lake rose and the land fractured, the mineral-rich waters filled the newly formed cracks, where they crystallized. Then the water drained and the springs dried out, leaving behind these vitreous forms."

"Them are mighty beautiful," Nalaníri said, bringing her nose close to the pointy shards, which sparkled fiercely under the light of her nosering.

"There are many more fissures like this one," Banook said. "We'll travel through them, then we'll take a faster route over the central plateau, and we'll exit the range on the eastern side. The best place to camp for tonight is just up ahead. You'll see."

Their campsite looked as if it had been birthed by a dream. They set up beneath the hull of a ship that had wrecked when the lake had drained from under it, depositing the vessel into one of the cracks to be gradually crystallized. The hull was keeled, acting as a roof, with the half-buried masts supporting it at an angle. Every surface, every crevice of the derelict vessel was mantled in crystals.

They made a bonfire with wood from toppled trees and sat inside the crystal hull to watch the flickering flames reflect sixteen thousandfold. Sunnokh had almost set, smearing the tops of the plateaus with a gold light bleeding to red.

Banook was recollecting his times in these fissures, and marveling at how little the ages had allowed them to change. Yet changed they had. "When there are no people passing through, and few animals making their dens at the bottom, wonders like these can endure for thousands of years," he said. "They won't be here forever—eventually the dust will bury these treasures, or the land will crack again and swallow them, or miners will find something valuable and deplete its beauty in exchange for more ephemeral benefits. But despite the fleeting nature of these crystallized halls and hull, I'm certain beyond a doubt that new wonders will be birthed by Noss, that beauty will not be extinguished, only transformed."

"It makes me wonder," Kitjári said, footpaws stretched out toward the fire, "what good does keeping a secret like this do? What if it had disappeared without anyone ever seeing it?"

"I say more people should know about it," Ardof opined. He stabbed some strips of jerky with his long dagger and smoked them by the fire. "Why not? If it'll be gone in the future, whether by our hands or Noss's will, what's the point of keeping people from enjoying it?"

"But if more people find out about it, we'll be condemning the place to an earlier death," Kitjári said.

"It is all relative," Ardof said. "Would you feel comfortable if it endured a hundred years? A million? Either way, it's not forever. And if no one is here to admire it, does its beauty matter? Is it even beautiful at all with no eyes to make that distinction?"

"This boar here thinks that's hogshit," Nalaníri offered. "Even with no eyes t'enjoy them crystals, them are still a beauty."

"Perhaps all we need is to treat things with care," Banook said. "Let those who show respect to beauty be the first to rejoice in it. We know these crystalline halls won't endure an eternity, but our lives are transient—yours more so— therefore preserving these wonders for future generations is a noble endeavor." He tossed another log into the fire. Sparks floated up into a crack in what used to be the deck of the ship, vanishing in the darkness of a zircon-like hold.

"Once we exit the Fractured Range," Ardof said, changing the subject, "we'll need to be careful like never before, particularly after the commotion we caused at Anglass." He pulled the strips of meat away from the flames, then added, "We left many soldiers alive who saw your half-forms clearly. There will be stories that will reach Viceroy Urcai in Hestfell. He will know a few of the missing masks are traveling their lands. If he finds out we are headed to the Lequa Dome, he won't be sending a few soldiers, but an entire legion after us."

"Then let's make sure them don't see us," Nalaníri said, "because I want t'keep mine boar self frum now un." She scooted closer to the warmth, closer to Kitjári. "Back near d'Firefalls, that was d'longest I had been in mine human form since I learned t'use d'mask. I felt like I was a-losing mineself."

"I personally liked being Jiara for a while," Kitjári said, leaning against her. "Though with the cold, I much prefer the fur right now."

"Either way, they'll find out what we are up to sooner or later," Ardof said. "Let's hope their reinforcements take a while to arrive." He shared a few strips of jerky with the others, then wiped his hands.

"Them meats are delicious!" Nalaníri exclaimed, chewing ungracefully. "Savory, unctuously fatty, with a hint uf hickory n'sugar. What is this?"

"Bacon jerky," Ardof answered, then leaned back to rest.

"What's a bacon?" Nalaníri asked.

"Ardof!" Kitjári yelled, eyes wide open.

"What?" he asked.

"What?" Nalaníri also asked, still chewing.

The wayfarers had pulled out their bedrolls beneath the crystalline hull, trying to fall asleep while watching their infinite reflections—except for Nalaníri. She had stood quietly for some time, and then wandered out to explore the fissure, carrying with her the cold light of a pharolith lamp. From within the shipwreck's hull, she looked like a lost spirit casting long shadows in the glistening tunnel. Kitjári told the others not to worry and followed after her lover.

"Hey. *Grei aurgithuk hulm ed*," she said as she approached.

"Don't know them words yet," Nalaníri replied.

"Don't go so far," Kitjári repeated in Common. She had been teaching Miscamish to Nalaníri. Few Puqua knew the language—preferring their own tongue or Common—and even though Nagrasilv helped Nalaníri learn, she hadn't progressed much yet.

"It's alright m'dear, I unly want t'see them walls. D'crystals are even mour resplendent under d'light uf d'kenzir stone."

Kitjári held a handpaw out. Nalaníri took it. The two women walked together into a narrowing passage. They found a split where the crystals spilled in wild, columnar forms; there they turned left, and further down saw a warm glow glistening on one of the walls, much different from the light of the pharolith.

"What is that?" Nalaníri cautiously asked, closing the petals of the lamp to better see the dimmer light.

"Don't worry," Kitjári said. "I know exactly what that is. Keep the lamp closed and follow me."

She pulled the boar along, then stopped when they reached the next intersection. The fissure was aglow in radiant pinks, the crystalline facets receding in a tunnel of rosy stars. The few patches of snow bounced an even brighter pink onto the crystallized walls. At the far end of the rift, Sceres rose, full and titillating in her Tourmaline season.

"D'moon is dressed in pink!" Nalaníri blurted out in awe.

"She changed seasons while we were in Anglass. And she's as full as she'll ever be now."

The two of them hopped over a dried-up log and sat leaning against it, watching as the pink moon continued rising.

"Was that really the longest you've been without your mask?" Kitjári asked, thinking back on their previous conversation. "When we were near Brimstowne, I mean. Was it not only a day or two?"

"It was. I didn't want ye all t'worry, but it was truly hard un me. I knew it was important we be careful, so I had t'suck it up n'deal with it."

"It's strange how attached one can get to the half-forms, but I feel equally attached to my human form. Sometimes, if I stay as Kitjári for too long, it's like my whole body itches, like I'm sick of all the fur and I need to let my skin breathe. And then the opposite happens… I feel like my skin is too cold, like I'm longing for an embrace. I miss the sharpness of my teeth, the vibrant smells. But I can spend weeks in one shape or the other without feeling that at all."

"I'd usually turn to Prikka unly when I got too dirty n'needed t'scrub mineself better, every couple uf months. I've spent over a year, twice, without once taking Nagrasilv uff."

"A year? I can't imagine not being Jiara for so long."

"Those weren't entirely mine choice, though them didn't bother me. It was d'times I was pregnant."

"They don't let you be in your human form while you are pregnant?"

"No, m'dear, as d'fetuses can suffer. Them aren't part uf what Nagrasilv controls. Our bodies change too much during shapeshifting, it would cause troubles fur them. Even if I had wanted to, 'twas like mine body told me not to, like a survival instinct. I felt it in mine tusks. Fur months after Pau n'Rushun were born, mine body told me t'stay this way, as d'milk I could make fur them was mour nutritious when it came frum these here numerous titties. I'm jis' glad we don't have litters uf a dozen, like feral suids do." She snorted a chuckle.

"I noticed something when we were in Nagradrolom. Arho, Onbar, and Krûn had populations of different suid species, or is it half… quarter species? You know what I mean. How did you all figure out who lives with whom?"

"D'cities n'pruvinces tend to cluster same breeds naturally, not by force. It's not impossible t'have a mix 'tween suid species, but trying t'breed with yer own kind has a better likelihood uf working out. Even d'Silvesh themselves don't always show ye a single species half-form—I'm a wild boar, yet some uf mine features borrow frum those uf domestic pigs."

"Same as how Sterjall is a timber wolf but has the coat patterns of a dire wolf," Kitjári noted. She held her gaze on Nalaníri for a stretched moment, then asked, "What do you think drove you toward domestic pigs and wild boars? Aren't they the opposite?"

"Unly in name. Them are quite similar t'one anuther. It's hard t'describe mine attraction t'them. Did ye also have strange dreams before yer half-form manifested itself?"

"The weirdest fucking kind. Two I can clearly recall. Others were too abstract—I couldn't remember them after waking up, but I remember how they made me feel. It took me months to find my half-form. That whole time I was constantly having those dreams, even when not wearing Urnaadisilv."

"Aye, same with me, though it unly took me a few days t'find mineself. I had thought long n'hard 'bout who I wanted t'be by then, yet I was still surprised. Maybe d'answer was in them dreams. It's hard t'recall them, as most uf them were too surreal."

"Tell me what you can remember? I'd like to hear it."

Nalaníri leaned further back on the log and stared directly at the pink moon. "This one time, d'most vivid uf them dreams I had... I was in a dark cave, unable t'see anything at all. I couldn't find a way out, so I began t'claw at d'walls, trying to dig to d'surface. Then mine nails scratched un something hard, n'mine eyes were a-blinded, fur I had uncovered a kenzir vein. I looked at mine fingertips n'I had hooves instead uf nails, but then I looked down at mine body n'all I could see was a blackness. It was impossible t'see d'rest uf me.

"I clawed at d'vein uf kenzir till mine hooves were a-bleeding, till I pulled uff a piece uf d'glowing rock n'held it in front uf me like a lantern, n'I used it to search fur a way out uf d'labyrinth. It felt like I spent weeks in them dark tunnels, unable t'find an exit, n'mine kenzir stone was a-losing its shine. As d'stone went dark, I smelled a fragrance I recognized. 'Twas barley purridge with honey truffle jam, like mine mum used t'cook fur breakfast. I cast d'stone away n'fullowed unly mine nose. D'fragrance led me to mour dirt, so I clawed n'crawled till I broke through n'found mineself at d'top uf Stelm Shäerath. But d'Tricolored Mountain was not black n'red n'gray, but black n'pink, n'instead uf being striped, it was spotted in round patterns like mine human skin.

"I felt like I was d'entire mountain, like it happens in dreams when yer perception suddenly changes. I was as pink n'black as always, topped with white snow. I looked at d'landscape I called home n'felt d'pressure uf d'dome above me, crushing me. As a mountain, I could see d'kenzir mines in Brumm n'even d'small house I grew up in. I could see mine mum a-cooking, stirring a stew that was pink, n'savory, n'dense. Mum looked up n'saw me, saw d'mountain, n'dropped her pot. D'stew spilled n'made d'entire ground turn pink, n'then mine house, n'mine town, n'd'forests n'mountains, even mineself. Everything a-turned pink, except fur d'waters. I looked at d'two bays, d'Keldris Allastirg n'd'Keldris Klannath, n'them waters were black, n'so were d'waters uf all d'rivers, lakes, n'fjords. Pink n'black was d'entire world, as that was all d'world I had ever known, n'all I thought I'd ever know.

"Them two colors swirled together, n'd'land flattened till I was standing un a flat field uf pink n'black, standing un four cloven hooves, n'without looking at mineself I knew what I looked like, I knew who I was. I ran through d'flat world toward d'horizon, which kept a-shifting n'never got any nearer to me. I was a-trying t'find mine home again, but it was nowhere, not behind me, not in front uf me, 'twas jis' no mour. I looked up in despair n'saw d'dome coming down, a-crushing me, n'so I squealed n'I woke up."

"That's… Fucked up," Kitjári remarked, then laughed. "But I do get it, mine were equally perturbing." She told Nalaníri of her own dreams: the one of climbing the towers that turned to trees and ice and flesh, and the one of sprouting out of a mountain to become the tallest tree of all. She still didn't fully understand them, but felt she understood the essence of them. Then she told Nalaníri about climbing the real redwood and finding her form at the top of the tree.

"And that's when Lago, Aio, and Alaia spotted me, crawling down the tree, butt-naked but much furrier. And later that night, the Laatu gave me my name."

"What does yer name mean? I don't know many a Miscamish word yet."

"It means *wood-claw*. What about yours?"

"Mine's in Puqua. It means *gentle tusks*."

"That's adorable!" Kitjári said with delight and reached out to scrape a claw along one of Nalaníri's small tusks. "There is something tender and something fierce about them. Just like yourself."

"Like yers fit ye well, mine fits as well."

Kitjári caressed Nalaníri's face. Her pink skin beneath the white fur glowed even brighter in the moonlight, while the darker half of her remained an unknowable shadow. *Your rosy skin matches your beautiful aura,* Kitjári thought, then kissed her, tangling tusks, fangs, and tongues in one passionate embrace.

Despite the cold, she began to undress herself and the boar, setting their parkas on the ground so they could lie naked with each other. Kitjári propped herself on top of Nalaníri's hips, touching her black nose to the boar's pink one.

The bear playfully licked the heart-shaped nose, briefly extinguishing the glow of the pharolith nosering, then did it again, the light flashing with each lap.

"Don't ye swallow them!" Nalaníri warned with a chortle.

"You taste delicious, kenzir stones and all." Kitjári swiped her tongue from Nalaníri's nose to her chin, over her neck, and further down to explore the many nipples on her smooth chest. When the bear reached between her legs, Nalaníri covered herself with a hoofed hand.

"Wait." She shook her head. "Don't."

Kitjári pushed herself up, resting on her knees and arms. "What is wrong?"

Nalaníri was trembling, unable to keep eye contact.

"I thought… Didn't you like it last time?" Kitjári asked.

"I did, but… It's jis'…"

"Was it my tongue? I can go easier on you this time. And that time with my claws, I swear I didn't mean to… I'm sorry, I'm being pushy again. It's better if we—"

"No," Nalaníri assured her, still keeping her hand over her crotch. "Would ye… Would ye show me what it's like… with plain skins? Jis' Jiara n'Prikka?"

Kitjári paused, holding a concerned but understanding smile, studying the conflicted expressions on the boar's face. She unhurriedly returned to her human form, lowered her mask to the ground, then placed her hands on Nalaníri's knees, caressing the long, wiry fur. She nodded to Nalaníri, who slowly shapeshifted into Prikka, letting Jiara feel the textures change as she transformed.

"You look like a goddess," Jiara said, and meant it.

Prikka's jaw quivered. She had kept her mask on, feeling a welcome reassurance behind it. Her nosering glowed within Nagrasilv, sheltered in the hollow muzzle. She removed her hand from her crotch, hesitantly but eagerly; it was lush and hairy, the opposite of Nalaníri's.

Jiara stared at Prikka's pear-shaped body, which was made half of pink light, half of a void of inviting darkness. She dragged her fingertips to follow the curves of her lover's two colors, as if tracing a path on a map, sauntering around the hardened mountain of a nipple, sailing around the whirlpool of her navel, hiking up the forested mound between her legs, then falling into a dark and wet canyon.

She felt the pulse between Prikka's legs, heard the rustling of her hairs as her fingers spread the lips apart—one side was pink, the other black.

Jiara dove down to explore them.

CHAPTER FORTY-NINE

WHERE ISDINN AND STISS MEET

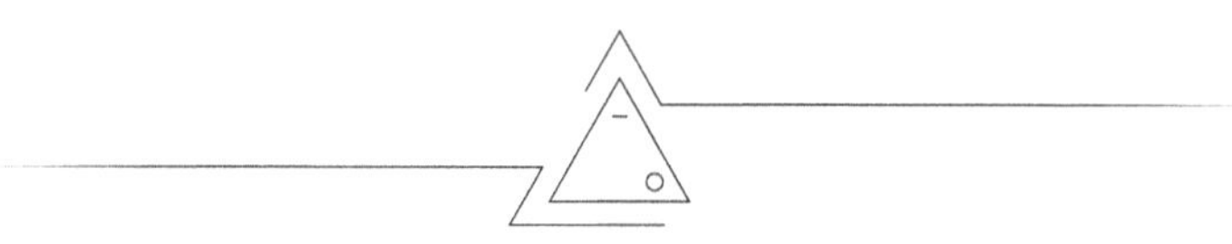

"That's the last of the crystal-coated cracks," Banook told the others, "as far as my dim memory can recall."

The wayfarers turned around to get one last look at the shimmering varnish on the walls. In this fissure, the minerals had solidified into a smoother layer, like nacre. Although the outskirts of the Fractured Range were covered in cracks, an enormous plateau at the center was much more solid. Banook showed them the way up to it, and from there they quickly advanced east for a few more days, exiting the range into snowy farm fields. Krostdrolom, the Lequa Dome, rose interminably just east of them.

"We can get to the wall by tomorrow night," Ardof estimated. "The pipe entrances are installed to the southwest, near Shaderift. We should avoid that area and enter on the northwest side."

The spot Ardof had in mind was next to the Almoth Bay. By the time they arrived, the bay's surface was beginning to solidify into a sheet of ice. Banook spotted two brown bears stomping at the thin ice of a frozen lagoon, trying to reach the unsuspecting fish.

"I know these two brothers!" he exclaimed, then called for the bears to come closer. "You two are fat enough already, should you not be in a cave waiting out the Winter?"

The bears huffed almost apologetically, stopping in front of the group.

"These are Wadrook and Cashe," Banook said by way of introduction. "Lago gave them their names."

"Like the brothers from the *Barlum Saga*?" Ardof asked.

"Exactly. Though these aren't backstabbing traitors, as far as I know."

Banook sat between the two bears, letting them rub their big heads all over him and drag their claws across his thick body a bit too forcefully. He laughed, having a wordless but heartfelt conversation with the ursids. After Banook asked them all the most pressing questions, Wadrook and Cashe plopped down to rest while Banook told his friends what he had found out.

"The brothers tell me there is a lot of movement to the south. Though they aren't good at counting, I wager there are thousands of soldiers who marched into the dome recently. My friends could not find a way past the aqueduct, so they came north and found this bay to settle on. As far as they know, no bears have traveled farther east into the peninsula."

"Thousands of soldiers sounds excessive," Kitjári said, "especially if the Jojek Miscam have long since been subdued. I'm afraid they came here for us."

"Banook, m'dear," Nalaníri said, "will ye be alright a-stepping into Krostdrolom? At Urgdrolom, them bears were all around, even if not inside. But here…"

"I am not certain. If the bears stopped at these walls, then close to these walls I may have to stop as well. The farther east we travel, the likelier I will feel my energy wane. If I feel too distant, too worn down, you will know."

"Maybe we can take these two pals of yours with us," Ardof suggested. "Would that help?"

"They are a lovely pair, but no. It would take a true migration of hundreds, perhaps thousands to have any influence on me. We can let these brothers go—we have a new world to explore now."

They waved farewell to Wadrook and Cashe, then ventured slowly through the parting vines, a safe distance away from the icy waters of the bay. After passing through a segment of wall dense with filtering fibers, they felt a drastic change in the weather. By the time they entered the dome proper, the temperatures were above freezing, though it was still chilly, with some snow still clutching tight to shaded pockets of the forest. The domed sky was mostly clear, glowing in white pastels with only a few poofy clouds to obscure it.

While making their way toward the center of the dome, the wayfarers circled past a supporting column protruding from an uplift, with an abandoned munnji silo at its base. They crossed an empty road and reached the edge of a cliff. From their high vantage point, they studied the landscape, which held a mixture of dense conifer forests, meadowlands, and riparian habitats covered by long grasses. On the northern shores—where the Lequa Dome scooped up a portion of the Lequa Sea—the land was scored by steep fjords, though none to rival the magnificent scales of those in the Fjordlands Dome. From a range at the center of the dome, the trunk rose, guarded by jagged and uninviting peaks.

"I have been to these lands before," Banook said, "and to the Stelm Ampenn, the mountains where the trunk grows from. They are beautiful, and seem hard to traverse, but wide roads spiral around their saw-toothed cliffs."

"The Negians don't seem to have destroyed this place as much as they destroyed Anglass," Kitjári observed.

"They would have a hard time burning wetlands," Ardof said. "And these forests are just too vast. I wonder if some of the locals have found ways to escape, or if they've all been enslaved."

"We better hide our tusks," Nalaníri warned. "There's a caravan a-coming." A procession of Bergsulf bison was pulling wagons on the road just behind them, headed north. They hid behind rocks and let the caravan pass.

"Negian drivers," Ardof noted, his brow furrowed. "And those must've been Jojek slaves sitting in the back. Seems like they are headed to the fjord."

"Shell we fullow them?" Nalaníri suggested.

"Let's wait a bit longer," Kitjári said, "see if we spot a smaller group we can more easily deal with."

Not much later, another bison-pulled wagon rolled by, this one headed south, with two Negian drivers and a Jojek woman in the back. The wayfarers waited in hiding near the road.

"Probo, yer turn," Nalaníri said. "Go be a lump."

Probo shifted into a giant forest hog and went to lie on the road.

The Negian drivers pulled on the bison's reins. "That's a big fucking pig," one of them muttered, standing up. His helmed companion stood as well, to get a better look. "Is it dead?" she asked.

Kitjári's senstregalv arrow bore through the soldier's helmet, killing her instantly. A smooth rock from Ardof's sling knocked out the other. The Jojek slave saw the spray of blood and swallowed a muffled scream, dropping inside the wagon for cover, trembling next to the smelly haul of fresh fish they had been delivering.

"Quickly, mour Negians are coming!" Nalaníri warned.

Ardof hurried to take the reins and drove the wagon into the forest, with Kitjári hopping on the seat beside him. She quickly tied the hands of the soldier Ardof had knocked unconscious, then hurried to the back of the wagon and placed a handpaw over the mouth of the trembling Jojek woman, shushing her before she could scream.

"Hurry!" Banook urged from within the conifer forest, waiting with Safís, Bear, and Nalaníri. Once the wagon was concealed beneath the canopy, they waited in silence until the next wagon passed, hoping they had left no trace of the battle. Kitjári then removed her handpaw from the woman's mouth and backed off cautiously.

"*Oset fin uth henet,*" Banook called.

"*Olvet f-finesh… f-fin…*" the woman stammered, confused by the use of a Miscam greeting and still too terrified to look at them directly. "*Ol-olvet…*" She could not make herself finish the sentence. "You n-not Joj-j-jek, why s-speak Mm-miscamm-ish?"

"We are here to help the Jojek, to help Krostdrolom," Kitjári said. "I am Jiara-Kitjári. What is your name?"

The slave's name was Macúsca. She was malnourished, her lanky body covered by a garment woven from dense fibers and dried up leaves that made rustling sounds whenever she moved. The wayfarers fed her, made her feel at ease, explained who they were and why they had entered the dome. The presence of the Silvfröash and Nu'irgesh inspired unquestionable fealty on the part of Macúsca, who despite her fear was not just willing, but enthusiastic about helping them.

Macúsca explained that the Jojek had been forbidden from speaking Miscamish. They were forced to learn Common so that they could communicate with their Negian enslavers, otherwise they were punished. By now her fear was so ingrained that she refused to speak in Miscamish and forced herself to answer in her broken Common.

She told them that almost exactly a year ago, all Jojek Miscam had submitted to the Negians after their leader, Ierun Faóla—who was known as Krobbar when in her ferret half-form—was killed by a torn-faced woman who traveled with Urgei Maarg, the Red Stag. Once the Krostfröa died, the musteloids gave up the fight, and the Jojek also surrendered, not wanting to needlessly die by the blades of their conquerors.

Macúsca worked in the northern port of Aldávi, helping load fish and other goods that were then transported to feed the cities of Jianmu and Tunhau farther south. She had never been outside the dome, but she took the road all the way to the pipes once a week.

"Have you seen any unusual movements there lately?" Kitjári asked.

"Yes, Lurr," Macúsca said. "Many soldiers, many arrived. Many blades. Jojek become afraid. Why so many blades? Is time to kill Jojek?"

"It's not you who they want to kill, but us," Ardof assured her.

"Where are all yer people?" Nalaníri asked. "How many uf ye are still alive?"

"*Raahush.* Thousands," Macúsca said. "They spread. Most work at Erne Goro, ustlas mines. Many work the sea, or serve at Dïer, by Ommo ust Krost."

"How hard would it be to get to the trunk? To, er… Ommo ust Krost?" Ardof asked.

"Not possible. Only two roads, many Negianesh."

Banook thought for a moment, then asked, "Will the Jojek fight again, if there is a chance to escape their fate?"

"Jojek follow leaders," Macúsca said. "Jojek follow Nu'irgesh, Silvfröash. But no weapons. They many, us few. How Jojek fight?"

"Maybe we can find a way." Banook pondered. "Do you know of Muri?"

Macúsca clearly recognized the name of the Nu'irg ust Krost, but kept quiet as if not hearing the question.

"Do you know if he escaped?" Banook pressed. "Or if he is still inside Krostdrolom?"

Macúsca's face took on a guarded aspect. Despite the trust she had already placed in the strangers, her allegiance resided with the musteloids even more so than with the Jojek themselves, and she did not want to betray the clade's trust.

"I blame you not for being vigilant, Macúsca," Banook said. "Musteloids and ursids like myself have always been close to one another. I know Muri is a cautious fellow, as much as you are."

"Muri hides," Macúsca hesitantly said. "Muri afraid, protected by *eilejen*."

"Where can I find him?" Banook asked with pleading eyes.

Macúsca remained silent.

"We are old friends," Banook said, keeping his voice calm, trying to put Macúsca at ease. "Probo, Safís, Muri, and I have known each other for longer than this dome has existed. Much longer. We will help you, but you must also help us, help Muri. Please, where can we find our old friend?"

Macúsca nodded, her eyes on the ground. "Ushwen Krost," she said. "Where isdinn and stiss meet. Sea shores. Hole in rock."

"Can you take us there?"

Macúsca glanced around as if searching for spies, then nodded decisively.

After gathering all the information they could from Macúsca, they focused on the Negian soldier without a hole through her brain, who was gagged and tied to the trunk of a spruce. He told them how well protected the temple was and offered more-accurate estimates as to the number of soldiers pouring in. He'd received word that enemies had infiltrated the Anglass Dome, and though he'd heard tall tales about there being giant animals who terrorized Ommo ust Urg, he hadn't known the ancient masks were involved. The Negians seemed to think it was just the animal spirits who perpetrated the attack, birthed by the netherflames to seek revenge.

The soldier told them how their legion was supplied, and that they had one armory near the Erne Goro mines, and another right by the pipes. He spoke freely, spilling out all that he could—having his dead friend propped in front of him made him very cooperative. Despite being a low-level infantry trainee, he knew more than enough to help them. All he wanted was to be freed, so he promised not to run for help, to stay in the forest and hide if they let him live.

"If… If I were y-you," the soldier added, unprompted, "I'd wait a few days. The Day of the Lost is coming, and the Day of Renewal right after. Our troops will be drinking themselves into oblivion."

Kitjári perked up at the mention of the holiday. "What day is it today?" she asked.

"The twenty-fifth of Hoartide," Ardof answered. "Only six days left."

"What's this Day uf d'Lost yer talking about?" Nalaníri asked.

"It's a leap day that happens every eight years," Kitjári answered, "between the last day of Hoartide and the first day of Frostburn. It's when we remember the dead, as the veils that obscure the Six Gates are thinner on that day."

"Oh, ye mean d'Forgotten Hours. We Puqua celebrate it too, but nothing t'do with d'dead, simply a chance t'feast aplenty n'furgive each uther fur past offenses. By d'end uf it, we're a-snoring with our bellies full n'our minds at peace."

"A stupor would be fine," Kitjári said, "but I'm hoping the Negians will drink so much braaw their blood turns flammable. We'll need to strategize, and fast, if we want to make use of this opportunity. If we can find Muri in time, perhaps he can help us recruit the Jojek."

"What happens to Jojek after?" Macúsca asked.

Kitjári tried to answer honestly. "I think we can help you escape, but I am not sure. Are there large numbers of ships docked on your northern sea?"

"Many ships, yes. We fish, we eat. Now we fish for Negianesh. Many ships also on great rivers and Klad Jilo. But no escape through sea, through Isdinn Kimen."

"Not yet," Kitjári said. "But there will be a way soon."

They extracted all the information they could from the Negian soldier, then sat down with Macúsca and asked her to draw them a map in the dirt pointing out where the majority of Jojek slaves worked and where they'd encounter the most Negian forces. As they studied the map, Ardof got up to take a piss. When he returned, he was wiping blood off his long dagger.

"Khest! Ardof, what did you do?!" Kitjári screamed.

"What you wouldn't," he explained unrepentantly. "I saw it in your eyes. You were going to let him live and ruin our plans."

"He was cooperating!" the bear yelled, standing up to face him.

"He was doing what he needed to do to stay alive, and the first thing he would've done after this would've been to run to his leaders and spill it all out."

"You don't know—"

"You don't know otherwise either, and we can't afford such risks. What's done is done. It's no worse than the arrow you shot through his friend's head."

Kitjári was fuming, more so because part of her was relieved. "Don't ever take matters into your own hands like that," she growled at him. "We are a team. We make decisions together."

"Yeah, yeah," Ardof replied dismissively. "Now let's find this, er, what is Muri, anyhow?"

"A honey badger, most of the time," Banook said.

Before they resumed their journey, Macúsca removed all the dead leaves that had been rustling over her strange garment. She searched the undergrowth for fresh leaves of a kind that did not rustle. When attached to the fabrics, they disguised her to the point that she became almost invisible when crouching in the vegetation. As she gathered the leaves, she explained to the newcomers that the Jojek had overpowered a lot of Negian units when the war broke out, simply by ambushing them from within the grass and forests, but once their ierun died and the Jojek surrendered, the Negians forced them to keep wearing the same leaves until they dried up and became noisy, giving away their movements at all times. It was a cruel way to keep track of the slaves, to remind them that they could never hope to be secretive.

Macúsca showed them the paths among the tallest reeds, through the densest jungles, so that they could ride on the Nu'irgesh and arrive at their destination faster. Once the arudinn dimmed and they stopped to rest, Banook took his human form and flopped down onto a bed of ferns.

"Are you alright, pal?" Ardof asked him, noticing his pale countenance.

Banook nodded, covering his shuddering body with his bearskin cape. "I am growing tired, more so after changing forms. We are moving far from bearkind. I feel as if I'm fighting a rolling tide with every step."

"Get some sleep," Kitjári said. "We are close to the shore now. You won't need to travel much farther."

Early the next morning, they arrived at the estuary where the fresh but turbid waters of the Stiss Lemen emptied into the salty breadth of the Isdinn Kimen. The rocky shoreline teemed with thousands of shorebirds, who perched on the windswept pines that crowned the cliffs.

As they left the dark forest and stepped into the light, Nalaníri noticed the stark changes in Banook's face: his beard had gone almost fully white, he had eyebags beneath his wrinkled eye sockets, had spots over his pale skin, and seemed to have lost a great deal of weight, despite still holding a substantial belly.

"Ye poor thing," Nalaníri cooed. "Ye don't look well."

"I know my limits," Banook said. "I will tell you when it's too much for me. I don't feel well, but I can keep going."

"Careful," Macúsca interrupted them. "Eskis, to north. Many boat, many enemy. Walk to beach, I show you Muri."

The beach looked empty, and a bit too exposed for comfort, even though the city of Eskis was miles away from them. Macúsca guided them along the shoreline, taking cover behind rocks whenever possible. They reached a jutting point where waves crashed, and hopped from rock to rock, trying not to step on sharp barnacles and slippery kelp, until they saw a cave opening up before them, one that was invisible from the shore.

"Sacred hole," Macúsca said. "Here Muri lives, before war. Here hides."

The rocks led them to a sandy pocket below the extending promontory. Kitjári spotted footprints in the sand and crouched down to study them.

"No worry," Macúsca assured her. "Feet from shamans, not Negianesh. See?" She lifted a foot to show the distinctive pattern of her sandals, which matched the prints, then explained further. "Shamans here, protect Muri. Shamans could not save Jojek, but save Muri."

Other strange shapes were imprinted on the sand, which looked like bear tracks to Kitjári. The five-clawed prints were enormous and carried a snaking line between them, as if dragging a heavy tail.

"Are there bears in here?" she asked Macúsca. "Urnaadi?"

Before Macúsca could answer, a growling roar echoed from within the cave. Running at full speed came five megalenhydris otters, twice as big as most bears, flashing terrifying fangs. Safís and Probo jumped in front of their friends and took their largest forms, blocking the path of the attacking musteloids.

"*Ergothuk!*" came a voice from within the blackness. "*Grei plehath!*"

The giant otters halted their attack.

A skeletal old woman walked out of the cave and fell to her knees in front of the Nu'irgesh. She clasped her palms in front of her forehead and uttered, "*Unnith ekhienn, haabral Nu'irgesh. Ekhienn pregith li gaanith tossash.*"

Behind her, stepping carefully into the light, came a sad, lonesome, and grumpy creature with black fur and a white back. Muri, the Nu'irg ust Krost, could not believe his eyes.

CHAPTER FIFTY

JOJEK RIOTS

Eight shamans were taking shelter in Ushwen Krost, Muri's secret hideout. Prior to the Negian invasion, the Jojek shamans would take pilgrimages to the sacred cave, together with the Krostfröash, when they needed Muri's advice. For the past year, the cave had served as the hiding place for the few shamans who had survived the Negian invasion. Giant otters brought food for them, which the shamans had to eat raw, as they dared not make fires.

Muri was not entirely trapped. He could exit his lair on occasion to forage and hunt in the forest, but he was afraid of going too far, of finding Krostsilv under the control of the enemy and falling to its coercive power. He had seen Sovath, mindlocked by the Red Stag, mercilessly killing humans and musteloids alike—he did not want that future for himself. Banook quelled the honey badger's fears by telling him that Krostsilv had traveled south and was no longer a concern for the musteloids within his dome.

"We have a plan, not just to open Krostdrolom, but to allow the Jojek Miscam to escape," Kitjári told the shamans while Banook interpreted for Muri. "In five days' time, the Negians will be celebrating the Day of the Lost. They will be drunk and unruly. If all the Jojek take up arms at the same time, especially at the soot mines, they will divert attention away from the temple. Then we could sneak in and open the dome. The Jojek can then travel north to the sea. The Negians will think they are trapped there, but if they take all the ships and wait on the water, in a week or two they'll be able to row or sail away to new lands. The sea will be cold and dangerous, but the Fjarmallen peninsula will be within reach, and if the Jojek take all the ships, no Negians will be able to follow any time soon."

"Fjarmallen is not densely inhabited," Ardof explained. "It's a disputed land mostly held by Dathereol, though there are also a few Negian outposts. If the Jojek disembark away from the cities and spread through the forests, they will soon find freedom, a new land to inhabit until these realms can be cleansed of the Negian threat."

"If we can spread your voice through Krostdrolom, it will be heard," the oldest of the shamans said in near-perfect Common. "When our leader died, so did the hope of all Jojek. If you lead us into battle, into freedom, we will follow."

"What shell ye need t'make that happen?" Nalaníri asked.

"The Jojek will listen to the Nu'irgesh, who can travel swiftly and spread the word," the shaman replied. "They will also listen to the musteloids, who Muri can speak to. He can send otters by river and sea who will carry our message. We would also send birds, but we have no soot left to fly heralds as we once could."

"We have some with us we can spare," Kitjári said.

The wayfarers and their allies had only five days to gather the support of as many Jojek Miscam as possible and execute their plan. The shamans crafted letters, signed them with a print of Muri's paw, and stowed them in waterproof vessels. They dispatched the missives with black-naped terns, as well as with otters big and small, who were told to only deliver the letters to Jojek Miscam who were found in total privacy. There was fear that a few of the messages might be intercepted, so the shamans infused their messages with as much allegory and Jojek mythology as they could. If the Negians seized any of the letters, it would take days to deliver them to a scholar to get them translated—in that amount of time, the revolt would already be underway.

Muri, Safís, and Probo ventured to the largest cities, where they delivered the letters and waited for the moment to fight. Banook recruited Jojek Miscam at the western edge of the dome, where he didn't feel as weary from being so far from bearkind. Ardof journeyed north. He and two shamans scouted the ports of Eskis, asking any Jojek they found to spread the news. Bear was asked to stay put at Ushwen Krost with the shaman elder, and the mutt did as he was told, for now.

Macúsca brought Nalaníri and Kitjári to Erne Goro, pointing out the soot mines and the nearby armory. When they approached a group of miners unloading mine waste on the shore of the Stiss Lemen, they were glad to learn that the miners had already received the message from an otter who had swam up the river. The miners enthusiastically vowed to join the fight—they had already been recruiting others, and they had a strategy to arm themselves before the battle started.

The plan was fully in motion.

Macúsca stayed at the mines waiting for Probo to join her; he would help her direct the attack. Nalaníri and Kitjári traveled on foot, following the spiked crags of the Stelm Ampenn toward the capital. Soon they found that the last portion of their path offered too little cover from the Negian convoys traveling back and forth. If they were spotted before the Day of the Lost celebrations began, their whole plan could fall apart.

"*Fûggun ishk!*" Nalaníri cursed. "We're still miles away frum d'temple. How are we going t'make it there unseen?"

"I have no idea," Kitjári fretted, hiding behind the last of the trees they had found for cover. "This road was supposed to be empty! I think they are rotating their units, also moving supplies. Probably preparing for the festivities."

"Either way, our arses are very fucked now." Nalaníri looked up at the trunk, which was just beginning to light up. They had traveled under cover of night, and the arudinn's increasing brightness now felt like a threat.

"Keep your head down!" Kitjári warned, pulling at her shoulders. "We only have a handful of hours before noon," she added more quietly, hearing marching footsteps just beyond their position. "We'll soon miss our cue. If we don't open the dome, and the Jojek all flee and pack themselves into the north, it'll be like sending pigs to a slaughterhouse."

Nalaníri winced.

"Sorry, just an expression."

"No, yer right," Nalaníri agreed, surprising the bear. "D'farms we passed by down d'hill. Them pigs trapped in that sty, we could free them."

"That's not at all what I was saying."

"Ye don't understand. I think them can help us. Fullow me, we need t'get to them before it's too late."

The time to fight was at hand.

The Day of the Lost was celebrated at midnight on the last day of the year, but inside the dome, the soldiers would time it for midday to match the festivities on the outside, letting drinks flow starting in the late morning. By noon, the hollering cries of joy and merriment would disguise any cries for help.

"Hold still!" Macúsca urged Probo, who was hiding under her dry leaf garment as a pygmy hog, making far too much noise as he made the leaves rustle. "We have to wait for the signal," she added, hoping the suid could understand her tone of caution, if not her words.

She walked purposefully, holding up a tray of drinks as she traversed a square just west of the entrance to Erne Goro, the soot mines. A Negian battalion had gathered in the square to celebrate, most of them already feeling the effects of the liquors they'd been ingesting. Macúsca handed out a few more drinks, then looked up, noticing long-tailed shadows moving in the canopy. "The coatis are ready," she whispered to herself.

There had been three companion species within the Lequa Dome. The first were the jarv wolverines, most of whom had been killed or captured to serve Silv-Thaar Valaran. The second were the megalenhydris otters, the survivors of whom had either taken refuge at sea or been locked in cages in the Klad Jilo, awaiting their turn to be shipped out as weapons. But the third sapient species, the white-nosed coatis, had been overlooked by the Negians, who did not find them particularly fearsome or useful. The coatis had grown nearly to the size of black bears and were even more adept than the ursids at climbing. Platoons of them were now gathered among the tall trees of the square, holding bundles in their long snouts, waiting for the same signal as Macúsca.

"Careful!" a Negian captain barked as Macúsca, distracted looking up, nearly crashed into him. "You new here, beautiful?" he asked with a lecherous look, taking a goblet from her tray.

"Little Common," she answered. "Apologize."

"Maybe I'll apologize after I'm done properly celebrating with you," the captain said through a slurred chuckle. He reached to grab her breasts, right above Probo's hiding spot, but a nearby yell stopped him.

"Make room! Stand away from the entrance!" a guard at the mines called.

"What is happening?" the captain asked a soldier.

"Outgassing at the mines, Lorr," the soldier answered, eyes scanning the enormous entrance of Erne Goro. "That will set us back at least a day until they find the source."

The Jojek slaves exited the mine in an orderly but expedient fashion, pushing ahead to make room for more, slowly taking up space inside the square where the celebrations were ongoing. There were many of them, but the Negian soldiers outnumbered the slaves by far.

Soon the square was nearly full. "Carry on!" a soldier bellowed. "Off to your shacks! Don't linger here, you filthy leaf crotches!"

The Jojek shuffled around, but didn't disperse; instead, more kept piling into the plaza, carefully taking their positions.

"Move!" The soldier pushed a miner to the ground. "Get out of here or we'll send you right back into the mines! Get moving or—*aaauuggh!*"

The miner slammed their pick into the soldier's foot, then pushed him away and blew hard into a conch shell—from its spiraling depths came a booming call.

"Now!" Macúsca yelled, dropping her tray and setting Probo free.

The canopy rustled as the coatis dropped linen-wrapped bundles which burst open as they hit the ground. The sticky wraps exposed hives from a particularly aggressive species of honeybees, who quickly sought to sting anything they could find. The Negians wailed in agony from the stings, writhing on the ground from the pain or running away clumsily in their half-stupors. The Jojek, however, were impervious to the stings—through millennia their race had harvested the honey and developed a resistance to the venom. Most of them had carried picks out of the mines and were now putting them to good use.

A quaking rumble broke through the screams as Probo took his massive kubanochoerus form and trampled the guards and fence of the nearby armory. He slammed into the warehouse's wooden wall, opening a path toward the stands overflowing with swords, axes, spears, and arrows. The Jojek followed behind him and swiftly armed themselves.

Safís closed her eyes and inhaled. As she breathed in, the landscape took form around her—the cooking fires burning in Calbor, the rotting canoes at the shores of the Klad Jilo, the alcohol-tainted sweat of the guards, the sharpness of their steel, the musk of the megalenhydris otters.

The giant mustelids were trapped in cages that floated half-submerged in the water. Safís could not mindspeak with them, but Muri had visited them the day before to explain the plan. The otters waited patiently, with renewed hope.

The white wolf opened her yellow eyes, then let out a piercing, lingering howl. She knew she would be giving away her presence, but how could she strike her enemy without first warning them of what was to come? How else would she properly taste their fear?

The howled note stretched, lowering in pitch as Safís grew into her white dire wolf form. The rumbling that remained was icy and cavernous; it stopped sharply, then her teeth flashed forward.

As the inebriated soldiers were torn apart, the Jojek working the port of Calbor hastened to the water. Quickly they unlocked the cages, and quicker still the otters escaped, rushing to exact revenge on their enemies.

The Jojek took control of every ship they could board. Even those ships with no crew began to move, pulled from below by the otters, who were taking them north toward the inner sea of the Lequa Dome.

☾

"Bear! Drop that!" Ardof hoarsely whispered. He crawled through the tall grass until he reached Bear, pulled the grilled fish out of the dog's muzzle, and tossed it away. "Stupid mutt! We told you to stay in the cave!" he complained, both as loudly and as quietly as he could.

Bear whined, watching his precious lunch sink into a swampy pond.

Ardof returned to keeping watch on the Negians celebrating at the Eskis harbor. The drinking parties at the port were just starting to get properly rowdy, but most of the Negians would never hear the tolling bells announcing the arrival of noon.

Ardof picked up a smooth, heavy pebble and loaded it into his sling.

Food had just been served to the Negians: endless trays of grilled fish, carefully spiced with ingredients chosen by Jojek shamans.

The Negians laughed out loud when they saw a soldier vomit up his entire lunch. They laughed again when two others convulsed in the same way. They stopped laughing when a dozen more toppled from their seats, mouths foaming and eyes bulging.

The Jojek at the ports bolted away, not to the ships—they would take care of the ships later—but toward the meadows.

"Stop them!" a marshal coughed out while also trying to induce himself to vomit. "Don't let them g-g—" His orders tapered off as he collapsed to the ground.

Those Negians who had not eaten the poisoned fish rushed forward, spears and swords in the air, trying to catch the fleeing rebels. Once they reached the meadow, hundreds of shapes appeared as if from nowhere, wearing green as fresh and vibrant as the tall grass around them. They dragged the Negians in screaming, vanishing among the rustling reeds.

☾

"Why haven't they sent her yet?" Banook huffed, then clenched his jaw. "Noon approaches, I can feel it in my skin. We need to strike now."

"She will come soon," a Jojek hunter reassured him.

Banook sighed and crouched by a window, from which he had a clear view of the pipe tunnels installed in the southwestern edge of the dome. The Jojek had smuggled him into their ramshackle dormitories, having him take the form of a kiuon and carrying him there inside a vegetable crate. Troops were still moving through the pipes—some coming in, some moving out—but the traffic was slowing as midday approached.

"I wish I had my glaive with me," Banook muttered. He had left his weapon in a cave at the base of Laaja Spahn, near the city of Jianmu; they would take care of liberating that city next, but for now he'd had to leave his gear and clothing behind to travel unseen in the small crate.

"You will find a suitable weapon at the forge," the hunter said, with no inflection to his voice.

"At least I'm feeling more youthful in these lands. I can feel my bears just outside the vine walls. I am filled with energy and ready to do what must be done."

"Good, because she comes," the hunter said, sharpening his ears and peeking out the window.

In flew a myna bird, alighting upon the hunter's wrist. "Ten on southern parapet," the myna croaked, "forty on eastern barracks, eight at pipes, sixty at plaza, two hundred past bridge. Wait for fire at watchtower." The bird then repeated the message, not knowing what it meant, but having memorized the sounds clearly.

"More than we expected," Banook noted. "But we can handle it."

"Ten on southern parapet," the myna began again, but the hunter stopped her by holding up a handful of seeds. While the bird pecked, the hunter peered toward the watchtower.

"Smoke," he declared. "It is time." He leapt out the window and aimed his bow at a guard on the nearest parapet. He loosed his arrow just as dozens of other hunters released their own projectiles. A trumpet sounded nearby, calling the Negians to arms.

Banook hopped out the window as a kiuon, avoiding the battle that unfolded around him and heading to a forge located between the dormitories and the pipes. As he entered the forge, he found a dead Negian with a sizzling neck wound, as well as a Jojek allgender holding a still-steaming, red-hot sword. Banook quickly took his human form, blocking the entrance.

"Nu'irg ust Urnaadi," the polite youth addressed him with a curtsy. "Here, we saved this for you." They put a hand on a massive sledgehammer that rested upon an anvil and tried to pull it toward Banook, but they could barely drag it a few fingerbreadths.

"Thank you," Banook replied politely, stepping closer. He lifted the bludgeoning weapon easily with one hand, flipped it around to test its weight, then placed it back down. "I think I will take this instead," he said, picking up the anvil.

Banook rushed out of the forge carrying the enormous mass of iron, headed directly toward the pipes. He trampled several confused guards, then brought the anvil down upon one of the pipes. A crack grew across the thick clay like dark lightning. He slammed it again, with the power of mountains. A segment of the clay pipe shattered into a rain of rubble, and the vines began to slowly close over the destroyed portal. Banook used the anvil to smash the remaining pipe, then hurled it at an infantry unit rushing to attack him.

Muri scurried under a chair and past the boots of a Negian soldier, hiding behind a barrel of rum. He was not concerned about being spotted—not in the harmless form of a least weasel.

Muri had made his way to Ifen, a lumber-processing outpost close to Dïer, at the base of the central mountains. The Nu'irg kept his beady eyes on the stockade surrounding the lumber mill, and on its locked gate. Finally, he spotted a white cloth tossed from a watchtower, drifting down and catching on the sharp wooden fence as the gate began to swing open—his signal.

He grew to his primal honey badger form and sank his teeth into the leg of the nearest soldier, then hopped onto tables and overturned drinks and food. He growled rabidly, catching everyone's attention. As soon as weapons were drawn, he leapt, and in midair took the form of a jarv wolverine, shredding the flesh of three stunned soldiers.

"The spirit!" someone screamed. "Don't let him get away this time!"

Muri ran, taking a winding route to slash at as many enemies as he could, pretending to be lost and scared, but always headed in the general direction of the lumber mill. Nearly everyone at the party chased after him—Viceroy Urcai himself had promised vast lands and kingly riches to the entire platoon responsible for the Nu'irg's capture.

Muri rushed past the stockade, headed to the largest shed in the mill.

"Close the gates!" someone ordered, trying to prevent the musteloid from exiting the way he'd come in. "He's in the shed! Grab the nets! Bring the mag-steel cage!"

The Negians carefully entered the giant structure. Muri stood at the center, pushing at a crane until it collapsed. He then moved on to destroy the main sawmill, sending gears, cranks, and chains flying apart as he unleashed his ire upon the device.

"He's trying to tear it apart!" someone yelled. "Stop him!" The enemy drew closer, surrounding the wolverine, who kept playing his part by demolishing whatever wood-cutting machinery he could find.

"We have you now, vermin," a soldier sneered, holding up a thick net.

The mill reeked of saw dust and sap, but there was another pervasive smell that the Negians knew very well and had failed to notice. The soldier carrying the net felt something squishing beneath his feet: the woodchips coating the ground were wet. He then noticed the empty barrels of high-proof rum lying on their sides, vapors expanding to fill the enclosed shed.

"Lorr, the rum," someone behind him called. "Takh have mercy, I think they—"

A dozen flaming arrows crashed through the windows, and in a burst of light and heat, the vapors ignited and sucked the air from the Negians' lungs. Muri jumped as the fire expanded, taking the form of a river otter and squeezing himself between the paddles of a water wheel to make his escape into the creek.

Although the rum burned fast, it did not do so explosively, allowing the Negians to recover and flee; but they found the gates locked, and the perimeter already burning. They looked up and saw sparkling blue, silver, and green bottles streaking through the air—the most expensive liquors, which would burn the fiercest once they smashed at their feet.

The smoke rose, unstoppable, and would be spotted from miles away.

The noon bells tolled.

The Day of the Lost was upon them.

CHAPTER FIFTY-ONE

REVOLT

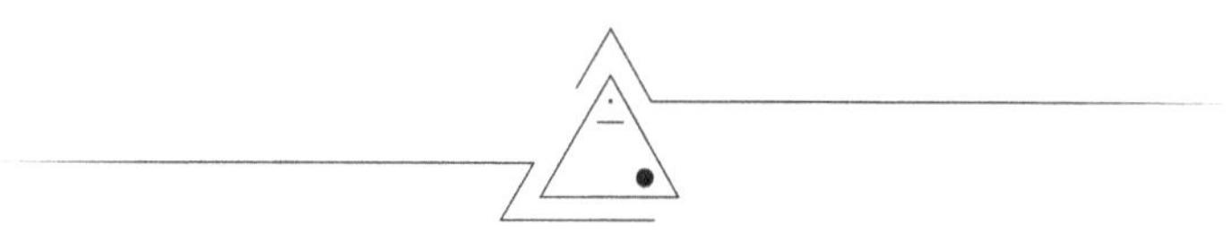

The entirety of the Lequa Dome was at war, and the only people unaware of that fact were the soldiers at the capital. Thousands of Negians were stationed at Dïer: cavalry, infantry, archers—all heavily armed. They were excessive in number, almost overprepared. But there was also an excessive amount of drink in their tankards.

It didn't take long until the Negians stationed around the trunk noticed the distant smoke. A magpie flew in from the southwest, delivering an urgent message to the legion at the capital, claiming a Jojek insurrection had taken down the pipe tunnels, aided by a golden giant, preventing reinforcements from entering from Shaderift. Then another herald arrived, warning of a white demon at the great lake; and another, with news of a tusked monster at the mines. News of rebellion flew in from every major city, all messages pleading for aid.

Since Ifen was the closest location they could support, several platoons were dispatched to protect the burning outpost, while a larger battalion headed toward the soot mines, as they were the Empire's top priority. Lines of soldiers marched down the road right in front of the farm where Kitjári, Nalaníri, and a few dozen pigs were waiting. The Negians stumbled; some fully drunk, some only lightly intoxicated, some sobering up from the dread of the fight to come.

"Close the door!" Kitjári said to Nalaníri, then dropped the dead guard she'd been dragging, tucking him away in the darkest corner of the pigpen. "Do the pigs know what to do?"

Nalaníri grunted twice as she secured the door, then turned her attention back to the suids trampling the mud outside.

Kitjári peered out from the corner of the shelter. "Can't waste a heartbeat more. We go after that unit passes," she said, seeing an opening between platoons. She dropped her gear next to the dead guard, then took off her clothes.

"Are ye ready, mine lovely pigs?" Nalaníri asked, undressing as well. They grunted their acknowledgment, their pink skins fully brown with mud. Nalaníri placed her clothes and gear on top of Kitjári's, but she held on to her glowing, tusked axe, its blade's pharoliths hidden in the scabbard. "Aren't ye gonna take yer sword?"

"I'll find one when we get there, I don't want to risk them spotting me carrying such a flashy blade. But my bow I can more easily hide." She slung her quiver and bow around her, and with a tremor in her voice added, "Please keep near me. We've never done this at the same time."

"As long as we stay close t'each uther, it will be safe, m'dear. Jis' fullow closely n'stick to d'plan." She gave a big kiss to Kitjári, bit onto the handle of her axe, then shapeshifted into a feral boar. Kitjári took a deep breath, then followed her out of the pen as a cinnamon-furred feral bear, her bow and quiver dangling by her belly. The two wallowed in the mud until they looked as much like the pigs as possible, then trotted out of the sty surrounded by the mud-coated suids.

"Th-the pigs are escaping!" a tipsy soldier called out, staring at the squealing sounder that was charging toward the main road.

"Never mind the stupid pigs," their commander said. "We have more important things to worry about. Keep your formations!"

A few pigs were kicked in the ribs as they passed by. One or two semi-drunk soldiers spotted the two odd animals among the bunch, and might have sworn they'd seen one carrying a weapon, but attributed the sighting to their inebriated eyes.

The streets of Dïer were loud with mobilizing units. Small scuffles broke out amidst all the chaos, but there was no ongoing battle at the capital. The sounder wove through the tight streets, between log cabins and tall trees, dodging the marching platoons.

When they reached the open plaza in front of the temple's entrance, the pigs bolted chaotically, squealing as if being chased by a hungry predator. The patrols were puzzled, not knowing what had frightened the creatures and uncertain whether they should keep their posts or try to herd the suids back.

One armored guard stood at either side of the vaulted arch. As the pigs squealed in front of the soldiers, they shooed them away, but two shadows slid past them and into the tunnel. "Fucking pigs!" one of them swore. "Stay here. I'll get the filthy swine out." He chased after the boar and bear while the other guard held his ground to prevent more animals from entering.

The vaulted tunnel was dimly lit, with lamps glowing only every few hundred feet. Once they had gained enough distance from the guard, Kitjári grunted for Nalaníri to stop, then stood on two paws. For a moment, she forgot why she had stood, relishing the feeling of being a bear, a real bear, with no preoccupations clouding her mind. But then the boar in front of her grunted, kicking her hooves down. The bear remembered, feeling insecure yet certain about what she must do. A bit too slowly, she returned to her half-form, dry mud cracking off her shifting proportions.

"Take your position, he's coming," she whispered to the boar.

Kitjári hid behind a column carved in the shape of an enormous stoat, while Nalaníri remained in her feral form and paced in the middle of the dim hallway, pretending to be lost. The guard saw her and slowed down. "Come on, piggy. Easy, just follow me." He inched forward with his hands up. He didn't unsheathe his sword, as he wasn't there to butcher the scared animals, but to see them out. "Nothing to fear. Is that an axe in your—"

Crunch. The guard looked down, finding chunks of dry mud at his boots. By the time he looked back up, the boar was rushing toward him, wielding her axe with the tusks forward. She swiped at his leg. His armor held, but the impact threw him off balance. Kitjári jumped him from behind, kicked his groin, then took his sword and pierced it through his lungs before he had a chance to scream.

"Nice tusks," she remarked to the boar. "Now help me move this."

Nalaníri clumsily returned to her half-form, shook the dry mud from her body, then helped hide the dead soldier behind the stoat-shaped column.

Kitjári regarded their naked bodies. "His armor would take too long to put on, but this buckler will help." She handed the small round shield to Nalaníri, then reached for her quiver. "Shit," she muttered, finding only one arrow. "They must've fallen as we were trotting. I'll have to make the shot count, then I'll improvise with this sword. You worry about staying alive." She picked up the dead guard's helm.

"What's that fur? It won't fit over our snouts," Nalaníri said.

"The next distraction."

They hurried deeper down the hallway, until the opening to the temple was visible. It was brightly lit, and they knew they'd find it well guarded. They slowed their pace in the shadows of the antechamber and flattened their backs against the thick columns on either side of the portal. They could see five guards by the far wall, but their Silvesh showed them eight more closer to them, left and right of the opening.

"Thirteen," Nalaníri mouthed.

Kitjári nodded. She tossed the metal helm down the hallway they'd come through, the clanking much louder than she'd expected. It rolled down the shallow ramp and stopped against a wall.

They heard a murmur from within the temple and sensed two guards approaching. The Negians saw the sparkle of the helm but weren't sure what they were looking at. As they walked into the antechamber, Kitjári pierced one in the stomach while Nalaníri slammed the buckler against the other's head, then tried to strike him with her axe, the weapon glowing freely now that she'd removed the cover. The guard saw the streak of light and parried the attack, but Kitjári was already on him, slashing her claws through his neck.

The two quickly rushed back to cover.

"The fuck's happening?" a guard exclaimed from within the temple.

"Olben? What was that? Luca? Talk to me!"

Olben was on the ground, gurgling his last blood-filled words, while Luca held one hand to her spilling guts, the other pointed at their attackers with one last effort.

"Hold! They are hiding behind the columns!"

Kitjári felt for the threads in the next room. By her enemies' postures, she could sense which ones held shields and which ones carried two-handed weapons. She also sensed that a man by the central dais had his arms up, clearly holding a crossbow—that was the most dangerous of all.

She nocked her only arrow on the quaar string and aimed through the stone column, seeing only the threads beyond. She then leaned over and released her shot. The arrow hit the stock of the crossbow with such force that it shattered the weapon before piercing the arbalister's chest in a rain of splinters and metal prongs.

Kitjári dropped her bow, clutched the grip of her sword, and ran into the temple. The guard closest to her was armed with a kite shield and spear. Through his threads, she could feel his hesitation, so she circled quickly around him to avoid a stab, then sliced at his back. As the man toppled over, she took his shield and slammed the pointed end hard on his head.

"It's the demon!" a soldier called. "The nethervoid demon who took Anglass!"

"Shoot at it before it gets closer!" another ordered. "Keep your distance!"

Kitjári spotted a man trading his mace for a bow and ran straight for him, holding the kite shield in front of her. A steel-tipped arrow pierced the shield and splintered right before her eyes. She slammed the shield into the bow, cracking the archer's knuckles and shoving him to the ground. As Kitjári ran past him, she swung her sword downward, slicing the archer's chin. Using her momentum, she tipped forward and rolled onto her shield, quickly recovering to hide behind one of the thorn-covered vine columns.

Another guard had hastened to a new location to pick up a crossbow. The bear wanted to rush her before it was too late, but the other enemies were advancing and would block her path. As Kitjári heard the *tchtchtchwick* of the crossbow loading, she screamed, "Nalaníri, to me!"

Nalaníri roared as she rushed in, clumsily swinging her axe and buckler. The guards were now alert, but although the fur-covered demon who had first rushed in was horrifying enough, they were not prepared for the sight of the naked, black-and-white boar.

With the enemy's attention briefly diverted, Kitjári stormed toward the woman with the crossbow and shoved her straight into the thorns of a vine column, then recovered and ran to Nalaníri, putting into practice techniques she had learned from Sunu: she rolled with a Withering Willow to slash her sword into a guard's ankle, then parried a spear with a Damselfly Roll.

She took up position next to Nalaníri, protecting her from the six remaining attackers as they retreated. A guard swung a mace at Nalaníri, but Kitjári repelled the attack with her shield, creating an opening for Nalaníri to strike back. The soldier dodged her swinging axe, which instead struck one of the vines and splashed white sap directly into his eyes. Kitjári took the chance to stab the blinded attacker, then protected the boar while she dislodged the axe from the dripping vine. Another Negian got too close, so Kitjári slashed with a Twin Crescents drive, gouging his arm and making him back off, holding his shredded tendons together.

In a combined but unsynchronized effort, the four remaining guards charged them. The first lost a leg to the bear's Blossom Claw; the second lost his breath to a buckler slam from the boar. Kitjári swiped her sword down hard on the stunned soldier, chopping part of his skull off, then roared, teeth bared, holding the remaining two enemies at a distance. The guards backed off, slipping on the blood of the fallen, then fled as quickly as they could.

Kitjári finished off the last of the wounded, then looked to the boar and asked, "Are you hurt?"

"I'm fine," Nalaníri replied, while holding her right arm across the left side of her ribcage. Kitjári made her pull the arm away and grimaced at the sight.

"Go!" Nalaníri insisted, covering the wound again to prevent too much blood from gushing out. "We'll have time t'heal later. Finish this uff, now!"

Kitjári sat heavily upon the throne of musteloids. She tried to concentrate, but could not pull her thoughts away from Nalaníri, her eyes lingering on the blood streaking her torso. She blinked forcefully, then pulled with her empathic focus. The enormous lattice began its collapse, transforming as it shifted its conduits inward, inching with mechanical precision toward the core vine.

"It's done," Kitjári said, standing up even before the core vine had disappeared underground. "Let's get the Khest away from this place." She picked up her bow and the few arrows she could find in the dead archer's quiver, then helped Nalaníri toward the exit. They hurried into the hallway, knowing the dome would now unravel on its own.

As they sped down the dimly lit tunnel, they encountered the guard they'd killed earlier. He was being inspected by two crimson guardians, with ten more regular soldiers in formation behind them. The crimson guardians drew their longswords when they saw the half-beasts approaching.

"Yaumenn's ire descend upon you, netherbeasts!" one of them swore.

"Just a dozen more," Kitjári said as lightly as she could, trying not to lose hope. "Stay behind me, keep your wound covered. Be careful with the knights, they know how to fight in pairs." She drew an arrow.

As the crimson guardians began to charge, the troop behind them erupted into blood-curdling screams. The guardians halted mid-advance and turned to witness the soldiers being mauled by a vicious jarv wolverine, who trampled their comrades as heavily as a grizzly bear, but with claws twice as deadly. The Nu'irg opened a path of torn ligaments and flesh, eviscerating one of the knights and leaping quickly past the other, dodging his sword.

Muri stood next to the Silvfröash and rabidly growled. Kitjári loosed her arrow, but it only sparked off the guardian's red cuirass. Nalaníri hurled her axe then, which bounced off the knight's helm and made him lose his perfect stance. Muri finished the stunned guardian off with a powerful bite, then led them toward the exit, slashing at any survivors left in their path.

They exited the tunnel and entered total chaos—the rebellion had reached the city of Dïer. Armed Jojek warriors were pouring in from Ifen, where Muri had helped them win the battle. Kitjári took command, calling for all the Jojek to follow her and the Nu'irg ust Krost.

Muri's largest form was just big enough to carry one person, though the wolverine was not exactly shaped to be a beast of burden. Still, he offered Nalaníri a ride on his back. He had to make an effort to keep his spine from bending up and down too much while running, but Muri pushed on and followed Kitjári toward the soot mines.

When they reached the pigpen from which they had staged their attack, Kitjári asked Muri to stop, then hurried to retrieve their gear. She quickly wrapped a bandage around Nalaníri's torso, then the two of them put their clothes on before continuing down the mountain.

In Erne Goro, they found a massacre. Piles of dead bodies littered the square by the mine's entrance, most of them Negian, bloated from deadly stings. Toward the demolished armory, they spotted a skirmish: Dozens of Negians and Jojek were tangled in battle, surrounding an enormous kuba.

"Probo!" Nalaníri yelled. She held on tight as Muri sped ahead and slashed at the Negians. With the aid of the Jojek warriors who followed behind them, they swiftly dispatched the remaining enemies.

"Stay as a kuba, m'boy!" Nalaníri urged Probo, who had been pelted by arrows and pikes, like an unwilling porcupine. "We'll get them uff ye." Probo's throat oscillated in rumbling tones too low to hear. He rested on his belly while the rebels removed the weapons from his body. He was badly injured, though most of the wounds were superficial. Once the intruding blades had been pulled from his hide, Probo made the ground tremble with one of his whale-like calls.

"What? No, yer hurt!" Nalaníri complained. "Yes, I am too, but I'll be alright. Ye've exerted yerself too much!"

"What does he want?" Kitjári asked.

"He wants us t'ride un him, t'take us north. But he's in bad shape."

Probo pushed with his wide tusks as he started to rise to his feet, almost lifting Nalaníri up.

"He says d'fight is at d'shores, n'we need t'hurry."

"He can handle this, let's do as he asks," Kitjári said, clambering onto Probo's massive cheekbones, then making her way onto his back. She helped Nalaníri up as well, then they headed north as quickly as Probo could manage, with Muri slinking by their side.

By the time they arrived at Eskis, it was already deep into the night, but blazing buildings let them see their way clearly. Most of the Jojek ships had already taken to the water, filled to the brim with as many people as they could carry. Older Jojek warriors protected the port, waiting for the younger survivors to fill the remaining boats.

"Keep going, m'boy!" Nalaníri said, holding on to Probo's wiry mane. "We're nearly there!"

"Look!" Kitjári called, pointing toward the bloodiest of the ongoing battles. "Is that…?" Bodies were being hurled into the air. In the middle of the skirmish, a heavy naked man was swinging an enormous glaive. The two Silvfröash and two Nu'irgesh rushed to help Banook, accompanied by a substantial following of Jojek who had seen them approach and were now feeling their spirits uplifted, their strength to fight replenished.

Once the port was secured, Banook dropped to his knees. Kitjári hurried to him, but did not want to touch the wounded giant, who looked frail and older than before, with a beard of almost perfect white except for the blood splattered through it. He was bruised and cut all over, breathing heavily. He pulled an arrow from his shoulder and looked questioningly at Kitjári.

"It's done," she told him.

Banook brought her into a bloodied embrace, smiling widely. "Well done, my furry friends. I am mighty proud of you."

They spied Ardof running to the pier, with Bear by his side.

"There you are!" he exclaimed, looking relieved to see them all alive. "Did you—"

"Yes, d'dome's opening," Nalaníri swiftly replied.

"Then help us fill the last of the ships. We must hasten. There are many more enemies coming."

"Where is Safîs?" Kitjári asked.

"She is still at the Klad Jilo," Banook said. "She told me she would stay till the very end to help as many Jojek as possible. There are more ships on that lake, many people to be saved."

"We can't go without her," Kitjári said.

"Yes, you can," Banook insisted. "And you can go without me. Probo and Muri will protect you. I'll stay to defend this port. Once I'm overrun, the water will offer me sanctuary as I swim to Muri's cave. I'll wait for Safîs there—she knows that's where we are to meet."

Kitjári stared at the old bear. "But what about—"

"I can't follow you into the ocean, for you will sail too far from my bears. I am already dangerously close to my limit."

"Urnaadisilv can keep you alive, if you stay near me. Like Momsúndosilv did for Mamóru."

"I am not as strong as he was, and I may perhaps feebly survive next to the mask, but I will slow you down. I will be useless to you, Kitjári and Nalaníri. I will be weakened and sluggish. You need to go, and go far. This is where I make my stand. Safîs and I will find safety, and we will escape. I'll find a way to help my bears cross the Ophidian, and I'll join you in faraway lands at a later time, when enough of my kindred have crossed."

The ships were nearly full. The blades of the approaching soldiers sparkled red and orange in the distance, getting closer.

"Go! Now! I will be safe. Find your way to the Jerjan Continent. Find my cub and tell him I love him. Tell him I'm coming to him."

Kitjári, Nalaníri, Probo, and Muri embraced Banook, while Bear whined next to him and licked his arms. Ardof shook the Nu'irg's heavy hand, then the six of them hurried to a departing ship.

Muri and Probo hopped aboard. Kitjári tossed Bear onto the deck before jumping on herself, then helped pull Nalaníri and Ardof up. Dozens of Jojek warriors remained at the pier, protecting the last few ships as they filled up.

Banook leaned on the shaft of his glaive and stood towering over the warriors next to him, nearly nine feet in height and with a body thick as an ox. He hurled a broken canoe at the oncoming troop, then prepared himself for the attack.

The ships pushed away from the pier.

"Bear, no!" Kitjári yelled abruptly. But Bear was already in midair. He splashed into the salty water and swam toward Banook.

"The fucking mutt is braver than I am," Ardof muttered. He looked around, grinding his teeth. "By Raushamitt's triple cock, they need me more than you do. Take care of each other, Lurrs. It's been a pleasure."

Before Kitjári or Nalaníri could respond, Ardof tipped his wide-brimmed hat and jumped off the ship, then helped Bear climb onto the pier. They shook the water off themselves and stood next to the Nu'irg. Bear growled defiantly as Ardof loaded his sling, waiting for the charging soldiers.

Banook stood naked, clutching his glaive, like an ancient statue of a god come to life. The sweat and blood dripped down his enormous body, glistening under the light of the approaching torches.

He charged, with a roar of a battlecry.

Part Seven
TWIN FATES

CHAPTER FIFTY-TWO

GUROVON THE ENVOY

"The envoy of the Oxruk is waiting for you," Ierun Jessha said to Sterjall. "Our hearts still pain for the Nu'irg's death, but we must carry on with our mission." The queen of the Sehján held tight to Puuja and Pol while keeping her eyes on Ishke'ísuk and Gwit. It had been less than an hour since the two Nu'irgesh had felt the death of Däo-Varjak. The basilisk and dormouse were still in shock, unresponsive to any attempts to rouse them.

"Let's go," Sterjall said, muzzle stern and tight. "We speak to Tajaz the Seer, get this dome to open, then we go rip the Red Stag's head off." He glanced toward Theggo.

"I'm ready," Theggo said, unnecessarily polishing his armor a bit more. He stood at the edge of the cliff and stared at the single figure waiting for them in the middle of the dry lake.

Ierun Jessha nodded to Skirr, the Sehján emissary, who led Sterjall and Theggo down a switchback trail, toward the spectral figure who waited for them.

"They only speak Miscamish and their own corrupt tongue," Skirr reminded them.

Sterjall interpreted the words for Theggo, then added, "I'll try to interpret as often as possible for you. Apologies if I can't do it every time."

Theggo nodded.

The three of them stopped in front of the Oxruk representative. The Sehján emissary introduced them all and said the allgender's name was Gurovon the Envoy.

Sterjall was taken aback. He'd expected some sort of hunchbacked, filthy creature to crawl out to meet them, but Gurovon the Envoy was regal, tall, and beautiful in their androgynous perfection, wearing white robes barely brighter than their pale, nearly translucent skin. Their robes blew in the wind, while soft snowflakes swirled by like moths attracted to their paleness. Gurovon's slender facial features and elongated nose were framed by a curtain of ivory-white braids, although they could not be white from age, for the envoy was young. They wore a bejeweled headband that draped a dark veil to dim the light cast upon their eyes, but it was diaphanous enough for Sterjall to see their sand-colored irises.

In a soft, measured voice, Gurovon began, "Your aid is appreciated, Skirr, Emissary of the Miscam. As agreed, I shall take the representatives to see Tajaz the Seer. But you are one representative short, as I do not believe you, Skirr, Emissary of the Miscam, to be the leader of your tribe."

"I am not here to meet with Tajaz the Seer, that I am not," Skirr answered. "Only Lago-Sterjall and Theggo Saurfall are requesting the audience."

"This is not what we agreed upon, Skirr, Emissary of the Miscam." Gurovon shook their head, lifting a hand to further shield their eyes from the brightness of the dome. "The terms were clear. Your tardy appearance we will excuse, but if we are to deal with Sehján matters, about lands the Sehján want to claim for their own, then the Sehján leader must be present."

Sterjall spoke, "It is only us who—"

"No," Gurovon interrupted, "we must honor our pact, as the Winter Solstice is upon us, and our oaths are unbreakable under the eternal watch of Ucrarn, lest doom wash us down the twelve stomachs of the Tar Serpent."

Skirr dismissed herself. She hurried back across the gray sand and up the outcrop. Sterjall and Theggo waited, awkwardly trying not to stare at the pale skin of the envoy. Sterjall swore he could see blue veins pulsing underneath.

When Skirr explained the situation to Ierun Jessha, she was not surprised—the Sehján had been expecting something unexpected.

"It must be a trap," Tsei said. "They cannot change the rules at the last moment."

"Unfortunately, the envoy is in the right, technically," Skirr sighed. "We agreed to a meeting of all representatives, and we are dealing with Sehján matters and Sehján lands."

"If we withdraw, they will never again allow us the same opportunity," Ierun Jessha said. "If we are here out of our goodwill, not meaning them harm, it does not seem right to show we do not trust them."

"But we don't," Tsei candidly remarked.

The queen nodded. "But we must commit to a relationship of trust, or pretend we do, otherwise we will fail, that we will."

"I will go," Tsei said. "I can speak for us. I can protect Lago-Sterjall and Theggo."

"No," Jessha declared, "it is I who should go. As Ierun, it is my responsibility to see this through."

Puuja rushed to hug her mother, and Pol followed. "Mom, don't go," the girl begged. "Let someone else do it. You have to stay with us."

Jessha kissed the twins on their foreheads. "Don't worry, ruby lights, I will be back soon."

"But you said you can't trust them!" Puuja cried.

"There is nothing to fear, my dear rubies, for with us are the Silvfröash, the Nu'irgesh, and Lakemother's spirit. Wait here with Lummukem and Kulak—they will keep you safe until I return."

Ierun Jessha stepped between Sterjall and Theggo. She was wearing her own suit of elytra armor, which sparkled in crimson and amber next to Theggo's silvery yellows and Sterjall's iridescent blues.

"Take us to Tajaz the Seer," she demanded, not bothering to greet the envoy.

Gurovon the Envoy nodded solemnly, seemingly unfazed by the impoliteness. "At once, honorable Ierun Jessha, descendant of Ierun Hejána," they responded. Jessha wasn't sure whether that was meant as a compliment or an insult, given that the Oxruk had murdered Ierun Hejána to steal Okrisilv from her centuries ago.

The four of them walked on the hard-packed lakebed toward the egregious blackness that was the Dohao Mesa. They saw no guards, no soldiers, only a few workers at the many terraces and tunnels that perforated the black cliffs. The holes reminded Sterjall of the Hollows at the Withervale Mesa, where he once had lived in a literal hole in the wall. Ahead of them, the monumental

Olvur Gate gaped in a stretched, five-pointed shape that climbed for hundreds of feet. Dreary and imposing the portal was, yet of an unmitigated beauty to match its measured and purposeful architecture.

Gurovon the Envoy stopped before the gates and waited, white robes slapping in the freezing winds.

The gates opened slowly, like continents breaking apart.

Sterjall expected an endless parade of Oxruk to come out flanking their powerful leader, but only eight men emerged, all pale and muscular, all white haired and wearing pristine white surcoats. They were carrying an elegantly ornate palanquin, which they lowered to the ground before swinging open a polygonal-shaped door. Out came nothing but tepid air.

"After you," Gurovon offered, pointing glassy nails toward the door of the ornamented vehicle.

"What is this?" Jessha protested. "Where is Tajaz the Seer?"

"He is in Oxmaaga," Gurovon the Envoy answered. "Eagerly awaiting the honor of receiving you."

"We *are* in Oxmaaga," Jessha said. "No further do we need to go. Tajaz was meant to come meet us here, that he was."

"On the contrary," Gurovon demurred. They shielded their eyes once more; when looking away from the black wall, their retinas were afflicted by much more brightness than they were used to. "What was agreed upon with your honorable emissary was that you were to come meet us at our capital. But here we are, merely at the gates of Olvur, which open to the road that leads to Oxmaaga. Our city, and the Seer's Rotunda, are deeper inside. Tajaz the Seer is waiting. We made the effort to make sure you had a proper welcome, but not here, not out in the cold, not under this insufferably bright light."

Sterjall interpreted for Theggo.

"I don't trust them," Theggo said, "but what choice do we have?"

"I don't know. We either get in that thing, or we go back to Kisdik and figure out some other plan."

"We could make this work. There is much the Oxruk do not know. If they are as cunning as the Sehján claim, they will want to remain on our good side until they've gathered enough information."

Gurovon patiently waited.

Sterjall's muzzle tensed as he pondered. "We should let Jessha make the decision," he said, then looked toward her.

Jessha stood firm. She tried to keep her shoulders squared and her jaw tight, but a tinge of insecurity tainted her voice when she said, "You must promise to return us to our people before the arudinn hide their light. If not, our new allies will be informed of your betrayal, and their armies will march into your tunnels seeking revenge."

"That I promise, over Ucrarn's darkened gaze," Gurovon said. "Our servants will carry us fast. You shall have your audience, then be brought back out with equal haste. After you, please." They removed the black veil from their face and ushered the others in.

Sterjall sat on the back seat, next to Jessha, while Theggo and Gurovon sat opposite, facing them. The eight bearers lifted the palanquin and carried it into the mouth of the Olvur Gate.

☾

"What's happening down there?" Alaia asked, squinting at the distant figures.

"Is that some sort of vehicle?" Dragoon Leader Seshéni added, surveying the gate through a spyglass.

"They are going inside. Why?" Kulak blurted out more loudly than he intended, watching through Sterjall's binoculars.

"I don't know," Skirr replied in confusion, covering the two streaks of white painted over her lips. "This is not what we agreed upon. I assumed Tajaz would come out to meet them."

"Assumed?" Tsei's brows narrowed in anger. "With the Oxruk, only two things you can assume—that their poisoned tongues will trick you, and that their claws will find their way into your back."

Pol began to cry. Puuja tried to comfort him, but he pulled away and went to embrace Lummukem's side. Lummukem squatted and placed their scaled chin over the boy's red hair. "Worry not, young Khuron," they soothed. "We are together as one, and we will make sure they are safe. We do not abandon those we love."

Tsei tightened her grip on her swordstaff. "What do we do now? They could be in trouble. Lakemother can't protect them inside their cursed city."

"They seemed to enter willingly," Kulak offered, trying to find some sort of consolation.

Skirr shrugged. "A bit longer we should wait. If they do not come back out by the end of the hour, I will walk to the gates and request to see the envoy once more."

☾

The Sehján had painted a dreary picture of the Oxruk caves, describing them as dark holes of stale air, filthy and reeking with unkempt masses of pale demons. They'd claimed the underground dwellers had no sense of propriety, no culture to speak of, no admiration for ideals such as beauty, honor, or empathy.

At first, the gloomy entrance had looked abysmal to Sterjall, but soon after they crossed the main threshold, the dread washed away. He saw lights above him. *Stars?* he thought. *That can't be. What are they? Glowworms, perhaps?* The ceiling of the enormous tunnel was speckled with thousands of luminescent dots, separated into almost branch-like segments, splitting like pointillistic bolts of lightning.

"What is that?" Sterjall asked, sticking his head out the window to see better.

"That is one of the sacrileges the Oxruk have perpetrated upon our sacred dome," Jessha grumbled.

"If sacrilege brings forth such beauty, a heretic I gladly self-proclaim," Gurovon countered.

"But what am I looking at?" Sterjall persisted.

"What so displeases the honorable Sehján queen are the foundations of Okridrolom," Gurovon answered. "You are looking at the underside of the roots of the great vines. The roots of the trunk itself."

"And they glow underground? Are the dots of light arudinn?"

"You guess correctly, son of Agnarg. They are covered in arudinn, though thousandfold less numerous than those upon the vines of the unbearably bright sky. The dimness suits us best, as our eyes are accustomed to the respite that darkness gifts us. We wish we could see the luster colors—what the Sehján think of merely as shadows—in the way Ucrarn can, but we are only their imperfect children, so we still need light to find our way."

"What you've done is unnatural," Jessha protested.

"As natural or unnatural as Okridrolom itself," the envoy replied dismissively. They noticed Sterjall's confusion and added, "We harvest the arudinn at the walls, late at night, when they sleep. We have devised ways to graft them into the roots without them losing their white blood. Once grafted, they reawaken and bring light to our cities. Each and every dot of light you see was carefully transplanted through centuries of hard work."

The tunnel suddenly opened into a vast plaza with a tall ceiling that looked like a frozen bolt of lightning reaching toward a dark horizon. The Oxruk could only graft arudinn where there were already roots to graft them to, so the light patterns followed the natural branching of the roots. Most of the roots grew horizontally, but some fell vertically or diagonally, in random columns of stippled light that cut through the ample space. The plaza was vibrant, the air warm, the streets full of Oxruk citizens going about their day, seemingly unaware of the presence of the visitors. They were all pale like Gurovon, all equally white-haired and long-faced. Sterjall thought the Oxruk all looked eerily similar to one another, equally ethereal and beautiful. Other than from their braids, the best way he could tell them apart was by the blue patterns of their veins showing through their skin.

Sterjall spotted a group of eight Oxruk waiting along their path. As the palanquin approached, they began to trot, matching the vehicle's speed, following directly to either side of the litter. Without slowing down or even bumping them, their eight bearers were switched for the eight fresh ones, who continued carrying the palanquin at the same hurried speed.

They were traveling alongside an open-water canal, headed downhill. The plaza ended in a tunnel where the canal merged with others and widened, forming a river with a lane to either side. The river was merely a handful of strides across, but wide enough to paddle canoes. Above this tunnel, the arudinn dangling from the ceiling were not broken up into organic, branchlike patterns, but were distributed across the entire surface in geometric tessellations, like a mosaic of stars that reflected in the underground river.

Gurovon picked up on the confusion in Sterjall's face once more. "The ceiling above this thoroughfare is one of the core roots," they explained. "The root is much wider than the narrow strip you see above you." There was nothing narrow about it, but Sterjall was used to the incomprehensible scales of the vines.

The lanes of the thoroughfare were heavily transited, mostly by people on foot, but also by other palanquins of different sizes and ornamentations. Gurovon lowered the black veil over their face as they passed by a perpendicular tunnel of blinding brightness. Sterjall squinted, seeing what looked like the pastel-white vines of the dome's sky.

Was that the outside? he wondered. *It can't be, we've been going deeper underground…*

"That was one of our farms," Gurovon informed them. "Unbearably bright they are, but the plants need them to be that way. We grafted more arudinn into the ceilings of the farms than in the rest of Oxmaaga combined."

"You grow your plants underground?"

"Not in all our cities, only in those that sprawl beneath the thickest roots. Our other unlucky cities do their farming on the outside. I pity their farmers, who have to venture into the suffocating openness daily."

The palanquin continued downhill along a new corridor of masterfully carved rock, following the cascading water canal. Next to every carved column, a guard stood at attention. Sterjall noticed their strange-looking weapons: gauntlets with five blades protruding over the knuckles, like claws attached to the backs of their hands.

"I thought we agreed to no weapons," Ierun Jessha angrily noted.

"There will be no weapons at the Seer's Rotunda, but our streets need to remain guarded," Gurovon replied.

The palanquin slowed as the cascading canal abruptly split; one half flowed left, the other right, circling an enormous, central island. They traversed a stone bridge connecting to a landing on the other side of the split. Past the landing was a colonnade directing them into a pentagonal portal crossed by heavy metal bars.

The rusted teeth of the gate lifted, welcoming the guests into the Seer's Rotunda.

CHAPTER FIFTY-THREE

TAJAZ THE SEER

The palanquin's door opened, and the four passengers stepped out.

Sterjall immediately recognized the configuration of the circular room. The vast chamber had twenty-three stone columns seemingly spread at random, with a wider column at the center, carved into a throne. The ceiling was speckled with few arudinn, leaving the chamber dim and eerie.

It's Okridrolom itself, he thought. *That throne represents the trunk.* The central column of rock unbraided to create the seat, the armrests, the luxurious back. Upon the carved throne sat a grotesque creature. Tajaz the Seer was in his half-form of a naked mole rat. Pink and translucent under the light of the arudinn, his hairless skin was wrinkled to the point that it bunched into confounding crevices and folds. He was truly naked upon the throne, with rows of nipples dangling like skin tags, tail curled around his stumpy legs like a dried-up earthworm, scrotum sagging below the seat like a flaccid wineskin.

Tajaz's furrowed face held two beady, cataract-clouded eyes that seemed to look at nothing. Below the pink incisions of his nose were rooted his protruding front teeth, like interlocking daggers of ivory. His shriveled lips hid behind the chisel-like incisors, waiting for their turn to speak.

Sterjall shivered, unable to avert his eyes. He blinked forcefully, and just then noticed another person, a servant of some sort, kneeling in front of the seer a few steps down from the slightly elevated throne. She was facing them, although her eyes were kept subserviently on the ground.

"Welcome to Oxmaaga," the woman said with a voice solid, smooth, and cold like river-rounded pebbles. Her white hair was braided atop her head into what looked like a nest of albino snakes. She was wearing pure white and kept her hands upon her knees as if they had been carved there from the same white marble as her thighs. With a tilt of her head, she gestured toward three seats that had been placed in front of her and the throne. Sterjall, Theggo, and Jessha sat down.

Gurovon slid quietly toward the entrance of the chamber to wait by the palanquin. No guards could be seen within the rotunda, but dozens of servants paced around the periphery, moving tables, cleaning, arranging seats—apparently setting up for a feast.

"I am named Hetfr the Speaker," the kneeling woman said, keeping her eyes down. "It is my honor to interpret the words of Tajaz the Seer for you. Tajaz the Seer wishes you to know that he perfectly understands the Miscam tongue, but, as the son of Ucrarn, he is only allowed to speak the sacred Rahih tongue."

Hetfr the Speaker glanced over her shoulder at Tajaz the Seer. The naked mole rat spasmed, then choked out a gurgling sound too cavernous and wet to resemble any language known to Sterjall. The wolf winced in his chair, reflexively tightening his sphincter.

Hetfr the Speaker turned her gaze to the ground once more. "Tajaz the Seer says your arrival during the Winter Solstice is providential, as that is the day on which the Moonstone Olm laid the eggs of the twelve gods of the Oxruk. He wishes to hear your story before we speak of potential alliances. Your emissary claimed that you come from outside Okridrolom. We are curious… How have you found your way across the walls of thorns and white blood?"

"I… We came from…" Sterjall began, struggling to find the Miscamish words. He was nervous, but he had to be the one to speak, as Theggo only spoke Common, and Jessha was not there to speak for the New World. "My name is Sterjall, I am the Agnargfröa," he said after an awkward pause.

Before departing for Oxmaaga, Sterjall and his friends had concocted a simplified version of their story—one that did not reveal anything about the Nu'irgesh or the other Silvfröash he traveled with. He told this obfuscating tale to Tajaz, explaining that the New World was once again vibrant and thriving. He said the old Kingdom of Nisos—now the Republic of Lerev—had joined forces with him to herald a message to the inhabitants of the domes, a message of hope, to tell them they no longer needed to be sequestered under a false sky, that they were welcome to spread into the two great continents once more.

"We came because we want to help, but we need your help in return," Sterjall concluded. "If this dome remains closed, Noss, our very planet, will forever remain incomplete."

Tajaz stirred on his throne, as if thinking, or perhaps only bored. Hetfr looked back at him. The gruesome rodent began to convulse once more, spitting out unintelligible croaks. While Tajaz jerked and groaned, Sterjall focused his gaze on the phosphorescent-yellow aura of Okrisilv, which spread through the body of the naked mole rat. There was something odd about the aura, about how it moved. Perhaps it was merely that it looked sickly instead of vibrant.

Hetfr returned her gaze to the floor of the rotunda. "Tajaz the Seer has heard your story, son of Agnarg, and is worried that you have already forged an alliance with the Sehján Miscam, and that such an alliance may serve as a disfavor to our race. He sees you've accepted their vestments and have taken shelter in their floating cities. He wishes to know whether the Sehján told you the full story of these lands, or only their interpretation of the truth."

Jessha's temples and jaw tightened. "We have told him the *real* story," she said. "We, too, seek an alliance, but we do not forget what was stolen from us."

Hetfr interpreted more guttural squawks. "Let our two other guests be the judges of that," she intoned. "Tajaz the Seer has asked me, Hetfr the Speaker, to tell you our story, as his tongue tires, and he trusts I know it well enough to tell it myself." For the first time, Hetfr faced the three guests directly. Her eyes were a pallid yellow—foggy lanterns upon her pale face. Though her age was indiscernible, she looked young and beautiful. "Will you listen, son of Agnarg? Will you take heed, King of Nisos?"

Sterjall was about to explain that Theggo was not a king, and to repeat that Nisos was now Lerev, but he stopped himself. He looked to his right, where Jessha sat.

Jessha leaned in and whispered, "Their words are poison. Be wary."

Sterjall swallowed, staring at Hetfr's yellow eyes. "We are here to listen," he replied to the speaker. "Please."

Hetfr kept her eyes locked on them and began, "This land has always been of the Oxruk. Long before the age of the Miscam, long before the Sehján invaded the great island, even before the kings of the east sailed to stab flagpoles upon mountains their ancestors had never seen, the Moonstone Olm laid their twelve eggs in the crust of this homeland of ours. Here our gods grew, here they birthed our race, and here we lived in peace, in the homes we dug in the mountains, in the enduring rock, among the minerals that give us life. But the

Kingdom of Nisos betrayed us. They sold lands that were not theirs to the Miscam, in exchange for riches and power."

Tajaz the Seer stirred, wheezing out rhythmic, gurgling sounds, but Hetfr did not turn. *Is he snoring?* Sterjall wondered.

The speaker continued, "The Sehján invaded our mountains and waged war upon the Oxruk. Those of us they did not kill, they cast out of our motherland. They expelled us and forced us to walk under the merciless heat of Sunnokh, who burned our skin as we searched for a new place to dig our homes. They ransacked our cities and tore down our temples to make room to grow their vines, so they could hide from their sins. They told us our new homes would suffice, that we'd live happily on the Stelm Auméllo and Stelm Atuur, but they were lying. They knew death was coming from the skies, and they wanted us out, to take for their blood-red heads the land that Ucrarn shaped for us."

Jessha saw the pause as an invitation to jump in. "You are the ones who attacked us, we were—"

"The Oxruk story is not yet finished, Jessha the Queen," Hetfr interrupted, quietly but firmly. "You may speak once our guests hear both sides." She regarded Sterjall, who nodded for her to continue. "We did attack them. We did swear we'd see the Miscam dead for their betrayals, this we do not deny. We wanted our lands back, we wanted our cities, our temples, our twelve shrines. But they had the support of Nisos, and so we were held back.

"In secret, we dug tunnels before the dome could close its roots upon us. We migrated into the warm bowels of Laaja Bumbra, remaining underground for many a year, waiting for the dome to finish closing. Once Okridrolom's vines sealed, the Sehján found us and sought to exterminate us. We fought for our lives. We survived. But they took the head of Bugr the Seer, and with his head they took his opal crown. We lived in peace for a time, with bitterness boiling in our guts. We asked the Sehján for our crown back, for the head of our seer, but they refused, telling us in their land there would only be queens, never kings."

Hetfr locked her eyes on Jessha for a tense moment, then looked back to Sterjall.

"When the Sehján dropped their guard, we took back our sacred city of Oxmaaga and regained control of our lands. We have been kind to the Sehján, letting them live on the surface, while we remain underground not bothering anyone."

"You have been ambushing us and trying to exterminate us for centuries!" Jessha interjected, tired of Hetfr's words. "Not only our cities have you taken, but our Silv, and our way of life."

Tajaz the Seer stirred from the commotion. Hetfr looked to the mole rat, who seethed and babbled hoarsely while drool pooled upon his shapeless chest.

Hetfr resumed looking at the ground. "Tajaz the Seer says Okrisilv is now in better hands. We've kept the dome healthy, as the old Sehján queen taught us to do, for the dome is our home now. Tell us, son of Agnarg, what is the proposal you and the King of Nisos have brought to the Oxruk?"

Sterjall adjusted his tail and tried to straighten up before answering. "We seek to heal Noss, to bring them back to balance. To do this, all domes must open, including this one, as it was intended to happen once the world outside recovered from the Downfall. We've come to seek your help in opening Okridrolom."

Hetfr continued with her back-and-forth cycle. Every time she looked at Tajaz, he would seize and gargle sounds at her, then she'd turn back around and interpret them.

"We still do not understand," she said. "The dome is taller than Gmorrogov, wider and deeper than the Klad Üo, the vine walls thicker and harder than the shell of the Hornstone Cavesnail. Explain to us what you mean by *opening the dome*, son of Agnarg."

"There is a way to let the wall of vines spread open," Sterjall answered. "It can be done by using the Silvesh, from within the temple. If you lead us to Ommo ust Okri, we can show you how it's done."

Sterjall was trying to imagine how to explain the process to Hetfr and Tajaz, when he came to a realization: if the vines were to recede underground, the entire city of Oxmaaga—and perhaps all the cities the Oxruk had built under the roots of the supporting columns—would collapse. The roots were their ceilings, the arudinn their light, the very paths their roads took were bound to the roots. He didn't know exactly how the domes opened, but he knew that at least parts of them burrowed underground, to sleep in the crust like titanic fossils.

"And what would the Oxruk gain from helping you open the dome?" Hetfr asked for Tajaz.

"You will at last be rid of us," Jessha responded. "If you do this, we will move out and carry the blessings of Lakemother elsewhere with us. The Sehján have spoken with the representative of the Republic of Lerev. They will grant us lands outside of these territories." She nodded toward Theggo, who nodded back approvingly even though he did not understand a word that had been spoken thus far.

Jessha continued, "The Sehján want to help Noss heal. We want to help the clade of glires spread, that we do. We grew the dome only for that purpose.

If you help us, you will get to keep these lands, and our red heads shall bother you no longer."

Whether Tajaz was excited, indifferent, or something else entirely, Sterjall could not tell. Those beady, clouded eyes revealed nothing; even his threads were tightened to him like a spool, utterly unreadable.

Tajaz jerked about and shrieked a raspy growl.

"Tajaz the Seer wants to know if opening the dome could bring any dangers to us, to our people, to our cities."

We should tell them, Sterjall thought. *How could we not? It would be a betrayal to pretend otherwise.* We don't know if this will be safe for them. But the conversation was finally turning productive, and he did not want to upset Tajaz, much less imply that his cities might be affected or even destroyed. He hesitated for much too long and was relieved when Jessha answered in his stead.

"No," the Sehján queen replied, "there will be no danger to you."

Sterjall's relief turned to horror at her response, at the ease with which she lied. He worried that Tajaz might be able to scent the deception in Jessha's threads, but her threads too were carefully tucked in. He was uncertain how to clarify the situation without exposing Jessha's callousness, but he once again took too long to speak up.

"Your teeth mustn't worry," Jessha continued. "The walls will simply part open like a blooming water lily. The Sehján will leave these lands, even leave the sacred Klad Üo. But the spirit of Lakemother will always go with us. You will be free to live your underground life as you always have. At that point, Okrisilv would be of no use to you, for no more healing would the dome be needing. But we would need Okrisilv to help Noss heal further."

Hetfr turned to Tajaz once more, but this time she swiveled with her torso, not just her head. Tajaz jerked uncontrollably, thrashing as if having a seizure. If there were words in the throaty roars and squeals he vomited, it seemed impossible that anyone could understand them.

Once the thrashing stopped, Tajaz was left winded, fighting for air, with his already pink skin turning even more flushed and irritated.

"At last, your deceit is revealed!" Hetfr yelped. "We knew your blood–red heads were only after Okrisilv. You came here to take it from us, to destroy us. Do you take us for fools, queen of the Sehján? We were testing you, to see how far your treachery could spread. We know how to open the dome, we have known ever since we ripped the skin from Ierun Hejána and claimed Okrisilv as repayment for the cities she and her predecessors destroyed. We know that what you propose would shatter our cities to rubble and exile us once more, if we don't die amid our crumbling ruins. We kept Okrisilv within our power so that we would never again be outcast, so that we could exist in peace. We will never let you take over our sacred land again. The dome will protect us, forever, and so will the twelve offspring of the Moonstone Olm. We will see your wicked race bleed until the Klad Üo turns red as your heads, until each and every Sehján has met our claws, until your blasphemous Lake-mother shits herself in fear."

The attendants who had been setting up the feast suddenly dropped their white surcoats to reveal their armor-covered bodies. They detached clawed gauntlets from their chest plates and attached them to their wrists and forearms. Sterjall, Theggo, and Jessha stood and turned to look for an exit. The doorway was barred with iron.

Dozens of guards approached them, each with five metal claws extending from each arm.

They were surrounded and heavily outnumbered.

"Please tell me everything is alright," Theggo quietly begged.

Sterjall whispered to him, "We're fucked. Stay quiet. I'll explain, if we live."

Tajaz gurgled, and Hetfr spoke again. "To you, son of Agnarg, we owe our thanks for bringing your Silv to us, as now you won't be able to exit or enter our dome to bring your traitorous kind with you. And to the King of Nisos, we knew your kingdom would betray us once more. We will finally have revenge for what you did to us, for selling our land to the wretched Miscam scum."

"Wait, please!" Sterjall pleaded as the circle of guards tightened. "We didn't—it wasn't what we… We can help, we can figure out an arrangement."

"Why should we listen to you?" Hetfr seethed, still kneeling in front of Tajaz, but now looking directly at them. "What deal can be struck with trai-tors, with backstabbers?"

"L-let us live, and we'll leave you alone," Sterjall said, not sure how else to stop the claws that were approaching his throat.

"Alone? Like the Sehján promised us so long ago? No, son of Agnarg, you are better to us dead." She looked at the guards. "Cut off his—"

"We will bring you the opal crown," Jessha cried out.

Hetfr stopped the clawed guards with a stare.

"The crown, for our lives," Jessha added.

Hetfr studied the Sehján queen's face. "Your ancestors claimed that our crown had been smashed to pieces long before you were born, descendant of Ierun Hejána."

"That was a lie. We have it. We have kept it as a memento of our victory."

"I… I have seen it," Sterjall confirmed, "a crown carved from a single opal, sitting upon an old skull."

"You have Bugr the Seer's head?" Hetfr asked.

"We do," Jessha replied. "I will bring them to you, if you let us go with our lives."

"You are treacherous and deceitful. We cannot trust you to be telling the truth."

"You can't," Jessha admitted. "You could cast our souls to the Eternal Sea right now, but that will get you nothing."

"Nothing but the Silv of canids," Hetfr corrected. "That, and the death of the descendant of Ierun Hejána, the death of the King of Nisos himself. A worthy price."

"But you would bring doom to your race," Sterjall said. "The armies of Nisos have no equal. They would find a way here and seek revenge. We failed, and you have us captured. But if you want the crown, let us live."

"We will not walk willingly into a trap," Hetfr said. "We will not let you leave here under pretenses you cannot corroborate." She gestured to the guards. In fluid, quick motions, the guards tied their arms behind their backs.

Hetfr was still kneeling. She turned to Tajaz once more, who seemed drained, but still managed to contract his pink body and howl a chain of languid vowels.

"King of Nisos," Hetfr called, looking directly at Theggo. "The son of Agnarg and the blood queen will remain our prisoners while you retrieve the skull of our seer and his crown of opal. You will bring it to us at the Olvur Gate. Not with an envoy, but by yourself, unarmed and alone. You will let us hold it and inspect it before we let these traitors go. And, if you play no more tricks on us, perhaps we will not cover your backs in arrows as you walk away."

Sterjall interpreted for Theggo and added, "They won't let us out. They'll keep us in here or kill us, even if you give them the crown. Don't trust them. Find another way to solve this."

"I don't know what to do…" Theggo shakily replied.

"Talk to the dormouse," Sterjall said, careful not to use Gwit's name. "They won't kill us until they have the opal crown. Buy us time. Find a way."

"Do you agree to these terms?" Hetfr asked. "Though they are not up for negotiation."

Sterjall interpreted, then waited for Theggo.

"I agree," Theggo answered, standing straight. "I will fetch the crown for you, and your seer's skull. My friends shall remain unharmed, or our deal is forfeit."

Sterjall interpreted back to Hetfr and the seer this time.

"In the meantime, the son of Agnarg must surrender his own Silv," Hetfr said. She stood for the first time and glided elegantly toward the wolf without letting her eyes leave the ground. She held out her pallid hands.

Sterjall stood firm. A guard shoved a knee in his belly, then put bladed claws under his muzzle. In a much softer and fearful voice, Hetfr whispered, "Tajaz the Seer will not ask twice." Her outstretched hands were quivering, her eyes still on the ground. "He is very angry," she murmured covertly. "Give it to him or he will have your head, mask and all, and he might punish all of us, too." She practically pleaded, as if terrified of what Tajaz's ire would unleash.

Jessha looked crestfallen. She nodded to Sterjall with sorrowful eyes.

Sterjall slowly shapeshifted into Lago. Hetfr removed Agnargsilv from his face and glided back toward Tajaz. She placed the canid mask upon the wrinkled folds of the naked mole rat's translucent belly while he convulsed through broken croaks once more.

He doesn't even raise his arms to touch it, Lago thought, disheartened. *Maybe… Maybe he can't. What a sad creature.*

"The terms are agreed upon," Hetfr concluded, kneeling once more. "Take them to their cell, where they will stay until the King of Nisos returns. If he does not return by the time the arudinn have extinguished their lights, we will kill the descendant of Ierun Hejána first, and then Sterjall, who is the son of Agnarg no more."

CHAPTER FIFTY-FOUR

A DORMOUSE'S CHOICE

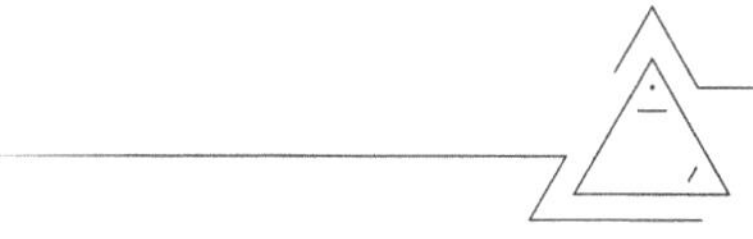

"This is taking too long!" Alaia complained. She had Theggo's spyglass propped up on a rock, aimed at the gates. Her arms had tired from holding it up, waiting for something, anything, to move in those deep shadows.

Kulak had been too anxious to keep watching. He was now slouched next to a tree, glancing up at the wandering snowflakes.

"Long enough it has been," Tsei declared. "We must ask what is happening, that we must do."

"I will go," Skirr said. "The guards at the gate will not attack me. I will demand an explanation. Wait for me here and watch with the metal tubes. If I am ushered into the gates, it is because I am being coerced in some manner. Keep your eyes open like lotus flowers in the early morning. Pray to—"

"Wait!" Alaia interrupted, her eye still glued to the spyglass. "They're coming out!"

Kulak bolted upright to take a look, watching with Lago-Sterjall's binoculars. "Yes!" he cheered. "The wheelless wagon is out. But… What is… No…"

"It's only Theggo," Alaia said in bewilderment.

Dragoon Leader Seshéni looked through her own spyglass. "The admiral's arms are bound. You stay, I will go fetch him." She hopped onto her kudu's saddle and rode hurriedly down the switchbacks before anyone could argue with her.

Theggo was walking alone in the middle of the dry lakebed when Seshéni reached him. Crestfallen was he, with only the company of the drifting snowflakes and his own troubled thoughts. Once Seshéni returned Theggo to the others, he told them all that had happened—or at least all that he had understood. Kulak and Alaia held each other as they listened in shock, while Lummukem sat numb upon the grass, their arms wrapped around the distraught twins as they translated the story.

"So, that's what we promised them before they were taken to a cell," Theggo concluded. "It's a slim chance, but that crown is the only thing we have with which to negotiate."

"We will send our fastest okruwom to fetch it," Tsei said, calling for a shaman to voice the request.

"But does your scalp think they will keep their word?" Kulak asked.

"No," Theggo said flatly, massaging his temples. "After what I witnessed, I'm certain that they will simply take the crown, kill Lago and Jessha, and maybe shoot me in the back as I walk away. Lago said to use the negotiation to buy them time and to find a different way to help them escape. I agree that's the best course of action."

"But what could we do?" Alaia asked.

"He said to talk to the dormouse, to Gwit."

Pol perked up when he heard the Nu'irg's name, having so far kept his head low and his spine curled in a knot. "Gwit has been in the dark caves," he said. He scurried behind Lummukem immediately after saying it, hiding his head under their shodog.

The entire group looked toward Gwit. The hazel dormouse was sitting on a rock overlooking the lakebed. He was still mourning Däo-Varjak's death; the loss of the pinniped Nu'irg weighed like a boulder upon his tiny body. He heard his name being uttered and twitched only an ear and a few whiskers.

"The last time we asked Gwit about the Oxruk city, he did not respond well," Lummukem said. "His scalp cares not for the affairs of humans. He wishes not to get involved."

"It is not merely the affairs of humans," Kulak argued, "and he knows as much. He knows what is at stake. If he is afraid of being captured by the Oxruk, he should be more afraid of being enslaved by the Red Stag."

Lummukem felt Pol stir behind their back and heard him whisper, "Ask him. Please."

Lummukem sighed, then looked to their left shoulder, where Ishke'ísuk was perched. They asked the double-crested basilisk to relay the request to Gwit. Even Ishke'ísuk seemed hesitant, but he promised he would do his best, climbing down to perch on the rock next to the dormouse.

As the basilisk expressed his thoughts, Gwit's minuscule limbs trembled. His fuzzy tail curled protectively around his compact body. He sank his head in and tucked his ears down, becoming a perfectly round, quivering ball of golden-brown fuzz. He began to squeak miserably, unable to look directly at his fellow Nu'irg.

Ishke'ísuk straightened his crests while lifting his chest. Gwit twitched and squeaked mournfully, turning away from the reptile, tucking himself yet tighter. The basilisk curled himself around the rodent, his crests dropping as his body slumped. He closed his eyes and lay there, wrapped around the dormouse's shuddering body.

A stretched moment dragged by, through which it seemed the two Nu'irgesh had fallen asleep. So still they remained, that the only motions were those of Gwit's lightly shivering fur, the gentle shifting of Ishke'ísuk's scales, and the punctuation of snowflakes landing and quickly melting on them both. At last, Gwit's trembling began to subside. He lifted his head and turned his beady eyes to Lummukem.

Lummukem nodded, then faced the gathered humans. "Gwit has told Ishke'ísuk that he will lead us to the city of Oxmaaga, but he does not dare venture into the throne room, nor anywhere close to Tajaz the Seer."

"How will he lead us there safely?" Tsei asked.

"An underground river. It feeds the city through its many channels."

"Lakemother shelter us," Tsei said. "We will take comfort in the wet blessing of her hidden children." Her brows dropped as she considered the dangers. "A dormouse can easily sneak through a cave, but how will we remain hidden? Our lights will be seen by the pale demons. As soon as we enter the city, their claws will be upon us."

"Kulak and Lummukem can see without light," Alaia noted, "as long as there is life around."

Lummukem nodded. "And the Silvesh allow us to see through the thickest of walls. We can move silently under the veil of darkness and find a way to free them."

"We will go with you," Puuja said, standing proud. "We are not afraid of the dark. We can fight with you. You saw us, we are good with the quarterstaffs, especially Pol."

"You cannot see the way we see," Lummukem said, "but we thank you for your bravery. Stay here, where you will be safe, and wait for our return."

Puuja slumped, deflated.

"Our warriors can help by making a distraction," Tsei suggested. "We must lure the pale forces through the gates of Olvur and bring them onto the lakebed, so that there are fewer enemies for you to hide from or fight against. That we must do."

"Do what you must," Lummukem replied.

"We need to hurry," Kulak said. He wiped the tears from his eyes and stood up. "Gwit, show us to the entrance."

They quickly packed supplies in Lummukem's side bag while rehearsing the plan with Theggo. The admiral would first keep the Oxruk busy, delaying his delivery of the skull and crown until as close to dusk as possible; they hoped that by then Kulak and Lummukem would somehow find Lago and Jessha and set them free. Theggo described as accurately as he could the route they had taken through the city and to the Seer's Rotunda, as well as the direction the other two had been taken toward when they split. Once the light of the trunk had finally faded, the Sehján warriors—as well as the twelve Lerevi dragoons, Alaia, and the smilodons—would swarm onto the lakebed and lure out the Oxruk, opening a window for their friends to fight their way out.

Only a few hours remained until the arudinn would begin to dim.

With Ishke'ísuk and Olo on their shoulders, Lummukem hastened alongside Kulak to keep up with the squeaking dormouse. Gwit dashed through the branches, stopping sporadically to make sure the slow humans were still following. He rushed ahead in a blur, climbed atop a rotten log, then paused again.

"We are coming!" Kulak cried between gasps.

Gwit darted forward once more, arriving at a mound of toppled boulders. He crawled into a small hole under the rocks and waited.

"The entrance hides beneath," Lummukem said, but they could see no entrance for anyone larger than the small rodent. They kneeled and looked into the hole, feeling a soft breeze. With Kulak's aid, they removed a few rocks, but the largest ones still blocked the path.

Ishke'ísuk jumped off Lummukem's shoulder and crawled under the rocks.

"Move back," Lummukem said.

Crack! The boulders suddenly shifted and toppled over as a giant gator took shape between them. The gator shook the dust off himself and moved to the side, revealing a dark hole in the earth. They peered inside but could only hear what sounded like flowing water in the darkness below. Kulak shivered. He was already beginning to feel the evening chill; jumping into cold water did not sound pleasant.

Gwit grabbed on to roots and climbed into the hole, disappearing under the ledge. It was hard to gauge the depth of the pool below, so Kulak pulled out a pharolith lamp and let it drop. They watched it sink into the river, the water dimming its light until it landed at the rocky bottom, illuminating a deep chamber. Ishke'ísuk shapeshifted into a banded water snake and sprang down. He waited for them, floating as a dark silhouette against the cold light of the kenzir stone.

"Ishke'ísuk says the water is warm," Lummukem said, to Kulak's relief. "We will go first." They handed their bone halberd to Kulak, then inhaled a small dose of soot so they could give instructions to Olo, asking him to fly in behind them, and warning him that he might need to get wet soon. Olo replied with *eihnk-eihnk!* and took to the air.

Lummukem plunged into the hole. Their quaar tail armor hit the water first, then they sank deeper until their claws grabbed the pharolith. They gestured with their arms when they resurfaced. Kulak tossed down their halberd, then jumped down himself, followed by Olo's fluttering wings.

"That was a big drop," Kulak said. "We will have to find a different way out. But at least it is warmer down here."

They heard Gwit chittering from deeper inside the chamber, in the direction the water flowed. Lummukem closed the lamp and followed the dormouse, partially swimming, partially stepping on uneven rock formations. The passage narrowed into full darkness; only a dim glow lingered from the entrance behind them.

Splash!

"What was that?" Kulak asked in alarm, turning around.

Sploush! they heard again as the rippling waves reached them.

Lummukem turned. Their slitted eyes widened with worry and disappointment. "No... Why did you—"

Toward them swam two small red heads.

CHAPTER FIFTY-FIVE

OXMAAGA TUNNELS

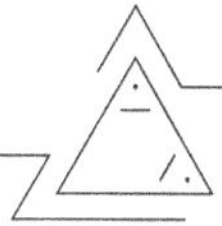

Lummukem sat in the cold glow of the pharolith light, trying to decide what to do. Pol held on to Puuja, fearful that Lummukem was upset at them—and they were.

Gwit squeaked nearby, a bit louder than usual, now in the form of a black rat. He was growing impatient.

"Gwit urges us to keep going," Lummukem interpreted. "Dusk nears. As the light of the arudinn fades, so does our hope of rescuing our friends."

"What are we going to do with them?" Kulak asked, glaring reproachfully at the twins.

"We do not know. We have no time to go back. No easy way back out."

"We can keep our tails out of trouble," Puuja said, embracing her brother. "We just wanted to help. Everyone else was doing something."

Lummukem eyed the twins' threads, which blended together as they comforted each other, nearly becoming one. "You will stay behind us," they said. "You will make not a sound, and you will not try to fight. We will travel in complete darkness, using only the sight of our Silvesh. You will need to hold on to us and agree to stay in the dark without any complaints. Do we agree?"

Puuja nodded.

"Pol, do we agree?" Lummukem pressed.

"We do not abandon those we love," Pol said quietly, keeping his head tucked against Puuja's chest.

Lummukem felt their sadness and found themself unable to blame them for wanting to help their mother.

"We hasten behind the Nu'irg now," Lummukem said as they stood and followed Gwit into the tunnel, keeping a minute shard of the pharolith's light glowing. A shelf extended above the water level, carved by Oxruk hands and abandoned long ago. Gwit said the precarious structure was safe, which it probably was, for a rat or a mouse. They decided to trust his judgment.

Pol traveled on Lummukem's back, knees resting on their shodog and arms wrapped around the dragon's thick neck. He stared at Olo, who perched next to his right arm, bothered by the intrusion. Puuja followed Kulak, holding his handpaw, not making a sound. The rumble of flowing water grew louder as more tributaries joined the stream, widening the underground river as they ventured farther into the domain of the Oxruk.

The elevated shelf stopped at a wall. Below them, the river flowed steadily and disappeared beneath the rock. Ishke'ísuk swam against the current to hold his position, oscillating like a wave. Gwit jumped off the shelf and in midair turned into a muskrat. He splashed into the river and disappeared under the rocks. Kulak and Lummukem could see his yellow aura receding, following the flow of the water until he drifted too far away for their Silvesh to perceive him.

"Ishke'ísuk says to follow," Lummukem said. "There is air farther downriver. Let the water carry you, trust the current, he says." Lummukem turned their head to look at Pol. "Will you be brave and hold on to my neck, while your sister holds on to Kulak's?"

"Yes," Pol said.

"Can you both hold your breath for long?" Lummukem asked them.

"Of course," Puuja answered with a cocky tone. "We go underwater from room to room, sometimes even to visit our neighbors' dens. I bet we can hold our breaths longer than you, that we can."

"What about Olo?" Kulak asked, squatting down so that Puuja could climb onto his back.

Lummukem considered for a moment. Their bag could hold air for a breath or two before filling with water. They inhaled a small dose of soot, then asked Olo to hop inside. Olo did so, a bit reproachfully.

In they dove, the twins holding tight to the dragon and the caracal. The water funneled under the wall and quickly tumbled them downstream. They did their best to keep the Nu'irgesh's auras in sight, then swam upward as they reached them, finding air. Lummukem held on to a rocky ledge and wrapped their tail around Kulak before the current could pull him and Puuja too much farther. They all climbed up onto the ledge and shook themselves dry.

Lummukem opened their bag and Olo hopped out, flying back to their shoulder. Mildly annoyed, he began to preen his wet feathers.

"Gwit implores us to extinguish the light now," Lummukem said.

Kulak stowed the pharolith lamp away. As soon as the pure darkness swallowed them, Pol began to lightly whine. Lummukem placed a clawed hand on the boy's shoulder. Matter-of-factly, they said, "Pollomekh, if you cry they will hear us, and you will get us all killed. We need you to stop." The straightforward way Lummukem spoke the words made Pol stop immediately.

"They will see for us," Puuja said, holding her brother's hand. "Just keep close to them and we'll be fine. And we'll be quiet, too. Right, Pol?"

Pol nodded in the dark.

The group continued in silence and soon heard footsteps, then people speaking in a tongue they did not understand.

"Mindrelsilv sees them on the other side of this wall," Kulak whispered to Lummukem. "Citizens, going about. Can you ask Gwit if there is a less crowded way?"

"He says to follow by water. The river will lead us to the cells, then to the throne room."

They jumped into a new river—one that did not flow quite as strongly—and waded their way under a low ceiling. The blackness was soon illuminated by an even, tenuous glow that cut through the bars of a metal grate. Gwit and Ishke'ísuk swam through the bars and waited. Lummukem pushed with their shoulder, but the rusty grate held. They shoved harder, and the grate swung open with a deafening creak. They all held still, the Silvfröash peering at the threads beyond the portal.

Once they were certain no one was coming to inspect the noise, they held their breath and ducked beneath the opening, resurfacing in an underworld beneath a sky studded with a million points of light.

"Lodestar guide me," Kulak gasped. "There are stars underground, as Theggo described."

Here the canal was six strides wide, and quite deep, filled with tendrils of red algae and schools of blind or nearly blind fish. Exuberantly ornamented skiffs floated nearby, but the light was dim enough that the infiltrators felt relatively safe. The high walls of the canal prevented anyone walking on the roads from seeing them, though they could not trust that they'd remain unseen forever.

Lummukem allowed Olo to dry himself, then asked the jay to follow by air as much as possible. Olo took off and perched high above.

Gwit floated impatiently downstream, still in his muskrat form.

"Follow to the end of the canal," Lummukem interpreted.

The long canal seemed to stretch to the very horizon, if there was such a thing in this nether realm.

"It will take us a long time to swim that far," Kulak said, "even if we swim with the flow of water."

A canoe approached.

"Down, wait for it to pass," Lummukem urged the others.

They dove and held to the bars of the grate, watching the oblong shadow of the boat traverse the arudinn-sprinkled rift above them. Lummukem felt a strange kind of buoyancy behind them, pulling in opposite directions: their quaar tail armor wanted to float, but the metal-studded tip wanted to sink. The forces evened themselves out, but they would make movement underwater unpredictable, particularly if they tried using their tail to swim.

Lummukem's and Kulak's lungs burned as they waited for the boat to pass. When it was finally safe to resurface, they rushed so fast to catch a breath that they swallowed water and began coughing. Puuja and Pol came up behind them, unfazed, still with plenty of good air in their lungs.

Pol whispered in Puuja's ear.

"Pol says you can ask the Nu'irgesh," Puuja said.

"Ask them what?" Lummukem replied.

"Ask them to swim for us."

Lummukem understood. He spoke to Ishke'ísuk, who in turn spoke with Gwit. The snake shapeshifted into a swift crocodile and positioned himself between Lummukem and Kulak, who grabbed hold of his small, scaled limbs. The muskrat turned into a castoroides and let the twins cling to his thick neck fur. Lummukem made certain that the Nu'irgesh knew to come up for air often—and only when it was safe—then asked them to hasten down the canal.

The crocodile and giant beaver swam at an incredible speed, with the dots of refracted light above them blurring like meteors. They darted beneath boats and scared schools of blind fish, often surfacing for air, but never slowing down. Olo followed above them as a silent shadow.

The canal split and merged a few times, but Gwit knew exactly where to go. He paddled his webbed feet with unparalleled power while using his thick, heavy tail like a rudder. Eventually, the space widened into a shallower pool.

The interlopers hid under an overhang. With their Silvesh, Kulak and Lummukem surveyed a canal that cascaded downhill, flowing parallel to an ornate corridor where guards stood at attention, long metal claws extending from their gauntlets.

As Kulak tried to make sense of the space, he looked up. His heart began to thump harder. "No…" he said.

"What is wrong?" Puuja asked.

"The arudinn," Kulak said, seeing the light waning. "We are running out of time."

Theggo watched the circular horizon of the dome, noticing the dimming of the distant vines. The still-bright top was crowded by clouds, forecasting a dark night to come. He sat stiffly on Tinnomeg's saddle, clenching a hand around the reins, waiting from atop the cliff overlooking the dry lakebed. The eland was agitated, sensing Theggo's own nervousness. The fleet admiral held the wretched skull of the old seer in a gauntleted hand. He glanced at it, admiring the beauty of the skull's opal crown.

Alaia stood nearby, comforting Pichi and Blu, when she noticed Tsei returning from a scouting mission. "Any sign of the twins?" Alaia asked.

"No," Tsei replied, sharpening her swordstaff. "Pray to Lakemother that they are merely hiding somewhere." To Theggo, she added, "My troops are ready."

"It's time I go," Theggo sighed. "Wait for my command before you rush onto the lakebed."

"Please be careful," Alaia said.

"I will. I will buy our friends as much time as possible. Stay focused. Keep your eyes on me and on the gate."

Theggo tapped on Tinnomeg's humped shoulders. The eland shook his spiral-horned head, making his draping dewlap ripple, then began to slowly walk down the switchback road.

Tsei lowered a colorfully gauntleted hand to Alaia's shoulder. "Lurr Alaia, there will be fighting ahead, for that is the way of things. Lakemother will protect you, but you also must protect yourself. Put that ugly helm of yours on, then let us drape you with a more colorful outfit for the rest of your body."

Alaia smiled and nodded decisively.

"You should've told us the truth!" Lago's voice was strained with anger. "Why didn't you mention that their cities were built under the roots of the dome?"

"Not all their cities," Jessha replied, her emotionless tone just upsetting Lago further. "They have more cities they can move into, to live their wretched lives in the darkness their pale skins so adore."

"That does not matter," Lago continued. "Their capital, their farms, even this cell is built beneath the roots. If they had accepted our proposal to open the dome, all of this would've been destroyed."

"Oxmaaga was built beneath the ruins of Kissumar," Jessha retorted, a hint of annoyance finally tinting her words, "our capital, which the Oxruk destroyed first. That they did."

"You mean the capital the Sehján built over their lands?"

Jessha did not reply.

The holding cell they were in was illuminated by arudinn; not quite as many as along the thoroughfares, but just enough to faintly see by. They were sitting on a stone bench, back to back, with their wrists bound and their feet tied to a metal bar. The cell was oversized for just the two of them, with multiple benches lining the perimeter and pentagonal, honeycomb-like holes carved into the walls. The place reminded Lago of a crypt, though perhaps a crypt for a race of giant bees. Upon seeing soft pads inside the holes, he realized they must be beds—the cell was some sort of dormitory.

Lago struggled with the bindings, wrists pulsing with pain. After being forced to shift from Sterjall to Lago, the lack of fur had reduced the tightness of his ropes, giving him just enough room to wiggle his wrists around. He managed to make one of the ropes slide over his bracer and down to his skin, releasing even more tension. He could do nothing about the knots in his own restraints, so he set about trying to blindly untie Jessha's instead. The ropes were tight, the knots indecipherable, yet still he struggled, feeling his fingertips turning raw, his nails beginning to bleed.

After a long while, Jessha murmured, "There are more important things at stake than some fetid cave cities. I wish you could see that."

"You are all blinded in your own ways. They are not fetid, evil monsters. They are people."

Jessha chuckled. "People. You obviously have more fondness for our captors than for the Miscam ideals."

"I don't care a whit about the Miscam ideals," Lago blurted out, surprising himself with his words. "They weren't always right, they weren't even in agreement with each other. Some things they did were great, others were vile.

What I want is to help Noss and stop the Red Stag. But not by cheating others… not by killing thousands of innocent people."

"What would you have us do, Lago-Sterjall? The Oxruk would never give up their cities, that they would not do. Their sense of entitlement knows no bounds. With them, you cannot negotiate in good faith. This needed doing, for the Nu'irgesh, for the clade of glires, for Lakemother, for Noss themself. Tell me, Lago-Sterjall, do you think it would have been better if the Sehján had never taken hold of this land?"

"It would've been fair."

Jessha suppressed a snort. "Would 'fair' have been enough to stop all the species Okridrolom protects from perishing in the Downfall? Or you may say we could have built the dome someplace else. Perhaps. Only waters eternal know the answer to that, but if we had done that, the Oxruk would've died. All of them. If anything, we saved them. Unknowingly, but that is the truth."

"I still don't think that—"

"This place was healthy and vibrant, long ago," Jessha spoke over him. "You have not seen it beyond the mountains, where our tribe cannot reach, where Lakemother's blessing does not extend. Many species we've already lost, and many more would've been lost if our constant guard had ceased. I will not apologize for trying to fulfill the oath we made to Noss. If it takes destroying some hideous caves, that we must do. Casualties will be unavoidable, either way."

Lago was torn, unable to argue further, angry with the situation and frustrated with his own sense of moral ambiguity. He kept fumbling with Jessha's ropes, twisting his body and arms at a painful angle, trying to get the last knot to slide free. "Just… a little bit more… There!"

Jessha's restraints came undone. She quickly pulled her arms forward. Lago heard a scraping sound as Jessha released her feet, then felt her sawing something over his wrists, freeing them quickly. She hurried around the bench to cut the ropes binding Lago's feet as well.

"You have a knife?" Lago growled.

Jessha had concealed the small blade under her elytra war belt, exactly where Lago had suggested he could carry Leif before being told it would be too risky.

"Only a small one," she said as Lago's ropes gave way under her okruwom-tooth blade.

Lago stood. "So, you were planning on killing Tajaz?" he half-asked.

"Only if necessary. It was a precaution." She tucked the knife away and explored the room as she spoke. "Listen to my voice, Lago-Sterjall. I believe your heart means well, but the Oxruk do not care about you, about me, about anyone but themselves. They *will* kill us. The crown Theggo will bring is the only reason our lungs yet breathe, for it is their most sacred artifact. It is true that Oxmaaga is grand, but it is built with the blood of slaves, with ruthlessness, and under the names of false gods. We told you not the whole story, but never did we lie, that we did not do. We are not at fault for the things that happened far in our past. If this land had been left to the Oxruk, Okridrolom would've shriveled and died long ago. For such is the way of the pale demons."

Lago tried to ignore her words. He massaged his bruised wrists while searching for something of use within the room. He found no windows, no weapons, only soft pads inside each of the pentagonal sleeping holes in the walls. He approached the wooden door, which was tightly locked. A vertical slit rimmed with metal ran through the wood at eye level. Beyond it, he could see the stone hallway they had been dragged through. At least four guards kept watch, leaning against the walls.

He slumped back onto the stone bench. "I… I don't know what to do now. I guess we wait for Theggo." His elytra armor clinked mutedly over the rocks and gathered up by his waist, belly, and chest. It fit more loosely now that he did not have his wolf fur. It made him feel like a child. *I failed you*, he thought, at first thinking about Noss, but then his thoughts drifted toward Alaia, Aio-Kulak, and ultimately toward Banook. *I didn't want it to end this way. I wanted to see you again.*

"Do you see that, Lago-Sterjall?" Jessha suddenly asked, looking straight up.

"What? What do you see?"

"The arudinn are beginning their slumber. Dusk will soon be upon us."

"Shit…"

"Through the sewers?" Puuja complained, wincing with disgust.

"At least it will be safer," Kulak said.

Gwit had recommended they take a less dignified route, which would take them through the latrines near the guard stations. The Nu'irg knew best, so they chose to follow his lead. Lummukem called for Olo to join them again, then pulled open a rusty grate. All of them held their breath and dove in, pulled by a fast current that ejected them into a circular pipe. They rose up for air and immediately wished they hadn't: the stench was vile. The miasma of the sewers clung to them like syrup.

They did their best to continue through the fumes, following the pipes over a series of drops. Gwit suddenly stopped and looked at a column of water that drained from a wall, swirling into the putrid waste below. It was fresh, some sort of drainage with constant flow.

"Clean water," Kulak said joyfully, rushing toward the torrent.

"Thank you, Lakemother! Bless us with waters eternal!" Puuja exclaimed, blindly feeling for the water and sinking her long hair into it.

They washed the unspeakable filth from their bodies. Puuja and Pol were particularly relieved, as they had needed to venture through the sewage without seeing, only feeling the sticky clumps and stringy unknowns that had adhered to their hair, bodies, and faces. The twins let the waterfall press down upon their heads, and they would've stayed there until the water ripped the last of their red hairs from their scalps if Lummukem had not hurried them.

A dormouse once more, Gwit crawled along the side of the cascading stream and balanced on a tiny ledge leading into the connecting pipe, following it against the flow of fresh water.

"Where are we going?" Puuja asked.

"Just crawl behind us," Lummukem said. "Gwit says we are nearly there."

The pipe slanted slightly upward. They barely fit, having to crouch with the water rushing around their knees. They spotted several openings above them, some with a visible arudinn glow, but Gwit told them they were not yet there. At last, he stopped and looked up, squeaking at an opening.

Kulak went up the hole first, exiting into a small chamber, and realized it was a latrine that dropped straight into the flowing water, to then empty into the filthy bowels deeper down. Lummukem handed him their halberd, then lifted the twins through the hole before hopping up themself.

The stall was dark. The ceiling was lit by a single root with merely a dozen arudinn on it, all of which were almost fully darkened. Guards, dozens of them, marched in a hallway nearby, their footsteps sounding hurried. The sound of metal and calls from an officer told them they were picking up weapons and hurrying to their destination.

Kulak observed the threads through the walls and noticed one presence moving toward them. "Quick, hide!" he hissed, pushing the others into the tiny stall and pulling the wooden door shut behind them; but the door would not latch—not with all of them pressing against it from the inside. Lummukem was forced to drop back into the hole, dangling from one arm to make room for the others.

A shadow appeared through the crack just as the door snapped closed and locked. There was a heavy knock. Someone yelled something unintelligible in the Oxruk tongue. Puuja covered Pol's mouth, then looked at Kulak, uncertain of what to do.

The knock persisted; the voice outside grew angrier.

Kulak swallowed, then released a sickening groan, as if painfully emptying his bowels. The voice on the other side of the door yelled something dismissive, then trotted away.

"All clear, my scalp thinks," Kulak said.

They made sure no one else was around, then snuck out of the stall.

The adjoining room was a sort of barracks, with a weapon rack filled with clawed gauntlets, shields, and spears, many of them now scattered on the ground—the guards had picked up their weapons in a hurry. Pentagonal sleeping spaces were carved right into the rock walls, padded with yellowed mattresses. Though the arudinn were nearly extinguished, the barracks were softly lit by warm lantern light.

"No, drop that," Kulak said, seeing that Pol and Puuja had picked up short-hilted spears from the ground.

"What if we get in trouble?" Puuja asked.

"Let them keep the weapons," Lummukem said. "But you both must promise you will not try to fight, unless there is no alternative."

"We promise," Puuja said.

Pol nodded, staring at the ground.

CHAPTER FIFTY-SIX

DOUBLE AMBUSH

Theggo rode on Tinnomeg, slowly approaching the Olvur Gate. He held the skull and crown high above him for Gurovon the Envoy to clearly see. The admiral's resplendent form was nearly blinding and holy-looking due to the pharolith he carried at his waist, which illuminated him and the surrounding stream of snowflakes in a cone of streaked light. The opal crown shimmered, as if holding a cold fire within. The pharolith was not just a trick to make him seem more powerful, but a way for his friends to spot him from the distant cliff, and a way for him to signal if he found himself in trouble.

Gurovon the Envoy stood alone, with no palanquin behind them. They no longer wore their black veil now that the trunk was almost completely dark, yet still they had to lift a hand to shield their eyes from the radiant knight before them.

"I bring forth the skull and crown of your seer!" Theggo bellowed out in Common, knowing the envoy would not understand most of the words but could infer their meaning. "I've fulfilled our part of the agreement. Now it is your turn to fulfill yours. Release Jessha, queen of the Sehján, and Lago-Sterjall, whose mask you have stolen. Release them now, and the crown that was taken from you shall be yours again." In a moment of inspiration, he added, "This I promise to you, in the name of the Kingdom of Nisos. In the names of kings old, and kings new."

The pale allgender stared up at the kingly figure of silver and yellow, at the pearlescent radiance of the crown he held in the light above him. With a polite gesture, they indicated for Theggo to place the seer's skull and crown upon the silty ground.

Theggo shook his head. "No," he said, "show me that Lago and Jessha are alive and well, and then I will hand you the crown. Usher them out from your darkened caves."

Gurovon stared with a pale face that revealed no emotions. They cocked their head, their ivory braids dangling to one side, then repeated the gesture with their arms.

✦

"What is taking them so long?" Alaia muttered to herself, keeping an eye on Theggo. He was clearly visible under the pharolith's beam, as was the white-robed envoy standing in front of him.

"It is better this way," Tsei said, "for he prolongs the negotiations. His valor is granting our friends more time." She helped tighten the pauldrons on Alaia's shoulders, then stood back to admire the suit of elytra armor she'd just been outfitted with. In contrast to Alaia's quaar-black helm, the armor beneath was of iridescent ochre that refracted maroon colors, with a few vibrant, yellow accents. Tsei had picked a feather-like style of lamellar for Alaia—one with plates that had more overlap and were rounded at the points, as opposed to Sterjall's more rectangular ones.

"Too tight?" Tsei asked.

"No, it's just right," Alaia replied, not wanting to complain about the pressure the armor placed on her thirteen back spurs. Although the suit had required no custom tailoring, she had asked Bouf to attach pockets for her darts and blowgun, like the ones she was used to from her overalls.

"My troop is ready," Dragoon Leader Seshéni informed them. "We will rush down as soon as we see Theggo's signal."

"We will be right behind you," Tsei said, "though we cannot move as fast as you and your horned beasts."

Alaia inhaled a dose of soot to ease communication with Blu and Pichi, even though the intelligent smilodons understood her well enough by now.

The three of them impatiently kept watch.

When the last of the trunk's arudinn succumbed to the call of night, something stirred at the Olvur Gate. Illuminated only by the light reflected from Theggo's armor, dozens of pale figures marched out, all of them wearing white.

"Are those soldiers?" Alaia asked, squinting through the binoculars. "I don't see Lago or Jessha."

"The way they move, they are indeed trained soldiers," Seshéni said. "Keep your eyes on Theggo." She mounted her kudu and whistled to her dragoons.

"Please, please," Alaia pleaded, "just come out… Please…"

"They won't come out," Tsei said. "The Oxruk only betray. Kulak and Lummukem are their only hope, that they are."

They watched Theggo prolong his negotiations, with the crown still held high for all to see. The white-robed figures reshaped their formation, spreading to flank him. Theggo tried to keep Tinnomeg under control, but the eland began to toss and back away, rearing on his hind legs.

The Oxruk closed in, claws at the ready. An armored officer shouted a command, and the soldiers charged. Theggo lifted the pharolith and shone it back toward the cliff like a beacon, then let Tinnomeg's reins loose.

"Ride!" Seshéni called from the cliff. "Protect the fleet admiral!"

The twelve dragoons galloped downhill, followed by Alaia atop Blu, with Pichi right by their side. The Sehján warriors followed closely behind, carrying torches to ensure the Oxruk could see their numbers; their primary aim was not to help Theggo, but to force the Oxruk to deploy out of the city, giving the prisoners a greater chance of escaping.

Theggo zigzagged over the dry lakebed as arrows pierced the crust by his eland's hooves. He met Alaia and the dragoons in the middle of the field, barely out of range of the Oxruk archers.

"Where is Lago?" Alaia cried out.

"Him and Jessha were not at the gate," Theggo said, holding tight to the skull and crown. "I do not believe they intended to bring them out at all."

The Sehján reached the middle of the lakebed as well, their torches forming a long chain of orange lights.

And then, the Oxruk made their move. Behind the Sehján, hundreds of holes suddenly formed from dropped hatches, sucking the sand in and letting Oxruk ambushers emerge, their clawed gauntlets slashing.

"Ambush!" Tsei screamed. "Watch behind you!" But as the Sehján turned, more holes opened right below them. The Sehján knew to expect attacks from underground and broke formation, focusing on preventing the Oxruk from exiting the holes, but too many Oxruk battled their way out, coming out of nowhere. Rather than chasing after the Sehján, they seemed interested in one thing alone: taking the skull and crown from Theggo.

"To me, nether demons!" Theggo cried as he lured the slower foot soldiers. "Follow after your seer's cursed head." His pharolith glimmered, all eyes following its brilliance. "To me! And may the light of a thousand suns smite—"

A hatch opened right beneath Tinnomeg's fast-trotting legs. The eland toppled at full speed, dropping his rider and dragging with them a cloud of dust. The seer's skull hit the ground and shattered in an explosion of dry bones. The opal crown tumbled away, leaving a beautiful geometric imprint on the silt as it rolled.

One of the Oxruk made the mistake of chasing after the crown instead of attacking Theggo, giving the admiral a chance to recover and pierce his rapier under the pale man's armpit. Two more of the cave dwellers hurried to attack him, but Theggo parried the claws to keep his distance.

Four more holes. Six. A dozen opened in the sand surrounding Theggo, a torrent of pale-skinned soldiers rushing out like ghostly termites protecting their nest. Theggo tried to reach Tinnomeg, but his way was blocked by iron claws. He heard a rumble behind him and turned to attack—it was Seshéni, stabbing through the enemy line with her rapier. Her dragoons trampled behind her, tearing through the white-robed figures with their momentum. Theggo scurried through the blades and blood and grabbed on to Tinnomeg's saddle, galloping away with the Oxruk swarming at their heels.

A Sehján horn blew atop the cliff; another followed to the east, and then another to the southeast. "Get ready!" Tsei commanded.

Alaia heard the signal and held tight to Blu's saddle. With a blown dart, she took down an Oxruk running after the still-rolling crown. She dangled off Blu's side and picked it up, luring the enemy while Pichi slashed at the distracted soldiers.

"Get ready!" Tsei repeated from nearby.

"*Fiithan usurearn halleimaf!*" one of the Oxruk leaders cried out, making his troop suddenly stop. They all stared eastward, and after a heartbeat of panic, began to scramble back into their holes.

"Lakemother help us!" Tsei cried out. "Cleanse this land from their pale curse! Fill their lungs with your waters eternal!"

From the east came a wave of water washing onto the lakebed. In a nearby plateau, Sehján shamans had worked with the giant beavers to break the beavers' enormous dams, releasing a torrent from the upper lakes. The rushing water was only a few feet deep, but it was enough to grant the Sehján a temporary advantage and frighten the Oxruk. But merely throwing the enemy off balance was only a secondary aim; the goal was to flood the unprepared Oxruk still waiting to exit the tunnels—and there were many of them still.

As the water reached the holes, it spiraled into the funnels and flooded the ambushing burrows. While the Oxruk fumbled to close their hatches, many fell to the swordstaffs of the Sehján, the rapiers of the dragoons, and the claws and fangs of the smilodons.

Lakemother's waters drained as the Sehján began a partial retreat.

"Hold the cliff!" Tsei commanded. "And protect our island! Hold, and pray that Lakemother aids our friends and frees them from the claws of their captors!"

CHAPTER FIFTY-SEVEN

A THRONE OF LIES

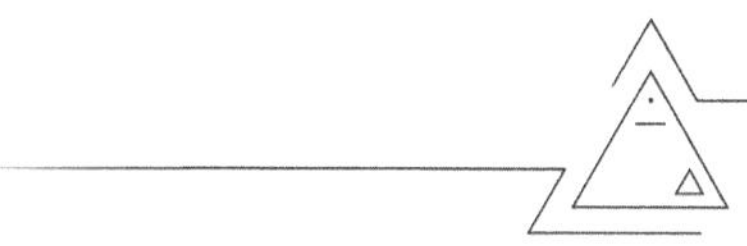

"The guards are coming," Lago whispered. Now that the arudinn had at last fully faded, echoing footsteps approached the cell door.

"We fight, or we die," Jessha vowed. "Be ready. May Lakemother shelter us." She leaned against the wall by the door.

Lago leaned on the opposite side, his heart drumming through his body.

A streak of orange lamplight beamed through the slit. As the door creaked open, the guard stepped inside, but before he could utter a sound, Jessha's blade sliced through his neck. The guard did not scream, but his lamp shattered loudly on the floor.

"*Gunnxith!*" a pale-skinned guard called from behind the first. He rushed in with clawed gauntlets slashing the air. Jessha rolled out of the way, giving Lago a chance to punch the Oxruk's pasty forehead with his spiked gauntlets. He then jumped on the guard's back, trying to restrain his arms. The Oxruk quickly turned and tossed the young man off, but he lost his balance long enough for Jessha to twice stab her small blade into his ribs. She kicked him to the side, where he toppled to the ground and lay there moaning.

Four more guards came trotting down the hallway. Lago swore he could feel their footsteps making the ground tremble. He was trying to remove the weapons from the Oxruk with the slitted throat, but the clawed gauntlets would not come off.

"Help me close the door!" Jessha ordered. Lago dragged the dying guard's heavy body into the room, and as his feet cleared the opening, Jessha pushed her weight against the door. But the ground trembled louder, and off she was shoved as the door fiercely swung back open. Through it came four more guards, the first two toppling off balance, the next two hurtling through the air in a spray of blood, crushed by the jaws of an enormous alligator.

"Ishke!" Lago yelled. He wanted to hug the beast, but Ishke'ísuk was too busy slamming his weight onto the guards and finishing off the one moaning in the corner. Then Lago saw the others. Lummukem and Kulak, hurrying down the hallway. *And are those the twins?* he wondered.

When Ierun Jessha saw her son and daughter, she gasped, terrified. "My rubies, my babies!" she cried out, running to them. "What are you doing here?"

Lummukem kept guard with their blowgun while Kulak rushed into the cell. He hugged and kissed Lago, then said, "Quickly, Gwit is here. He can show us a way out."

"Thank you," Lago managed to get out. "And… you stink."

"I explain later." Kulak placed something in Lago's hand.

"Leif!" Lago said with relief, then quickly attached the scabbard to his war belt. The caracal readied his blowgun as he hurried them out, leaving the dead bodies behind the closed door.

"Gwit says we could escape through the old capital," Lummukem said, following the rat and basilisk that scurried in front of them. "The city is above us, so we must climb, though the exits may be locked."

As they passed by the armory, Jessha grabbed a clawed gauntlet and attached it to her wrist.

"They took Agnargsilv from me," Lago informed the others. "Tajaz had it in the Seer's Rotunda. It's not too far, just around the next corner."

Gwit stopped and squeaked unhappily.

"Gwit will not go near Tajaz," Lummukem warned. "He fears he will be controlled and forced to attack us."

"I understand," Lago said. "But I can't leave Agnargsilv behind, I need to get it back. Gwit can stay outside the rotunda, but I'm going in. This way."

The others followed Lago down a long corridor that paralleled a water canal. Sconces had been lit to replace the arudinn, warming the hallway in rusty colors and making it smell of oil and fumes. Up ahead was the intersection where the water split and the stone bridge connected to the entrance of the rotunda.

"Backs to the wall!" Kulak warned, flattening against the stones. At least a dozen guards were running across the bridge, hurrying away from the Seer's Rotunda. Once the guards were out of sight, the group advanced once more.

"Shit, there's more!" Lago said, slowing down. Two more guards had emerged, pacing by the entrance.

The fugitives had nowhere to hide now, so they simply kept moving forward. One guard began to cross the bridge, while the other stopped at the landing before it. The one at the landing spotted the incoming strangers, but as she cried out for help, a dart from Lummukem made her topple over. A dart from Kulak took care of the other, who fell straight into the split water canal, where the narrowing width pulled the flow faster. She floated downstream as they hurried in the opposite direction.

When they reached the unconscious guard at the landing, Lummukem swiped their quaar-armored tail to send the Oxruk into the canal, following her companion.

"The bodies will be found," they said, "but better if the water leads them away from us."

Beyond the bridge were the columns converging to the pentagonal portal of the rotunda—the metal gate was still open. Lago rushed to hide behind a column, and the others followed.

"Kulak, can you see into the room farther down?" Lago asked. "Agnargsilv should be in there."

"Yes," Kulak said. "Mindrelsilv sees a blue aura. And a yellow one as well, like Gwit's, next to it."

Gwit began to tremble, hiding behind Pol's heel while Pol tried not to cry.

"Tajaz the Seer is nearly immobile," Lago said. "He's a naked lump on that throne. I don't think he can hurt us. If we go in quietly, maybe we can retrieve the mask without sounding the alarm."

"Mindrelsilv sees no guards close by," Kulak said. He aimed his quaar blowgun to narrow his empathic focus and see farther. "There are people in rooms behind, but not in the rotunda."

Jessha squatted to face the dormouse. "Gwit, can you protect Pollomekh and Puuja, and wait for us to return?"

Lummukem interpreted the words, and Gwit seemed content with the strategy.

Puuja stepped closer. "But Mom—"

"No buts. Hide under the bridge. There is a ledge beneath it." Jessha led the twins to the overhang and helped them down. Gwit followed behind them.

"I love you, ruby lights," she told her children. "Do not let your teeth worry. I will be back soon." More quietly, she added, "Mother will take Okrisilv back for us. Mother will make sure the dome opens, no matter what. Stay safe near Lakemother's embrace and wait for me."

She rushed back to where the others hid, then followed Lummukem and Kulak, who were scanning through the walls with their Silvesh as they led the way. The group crossed under the metal teeth of the pentagonal door and entered the Seer's Rotunda. They quickly scurried to the side, hiding behind low walls that hugged the periphery of the circular room. With the arudinn extinguished for the night, the room looked very different, but it was not dark—in hollows within each of the twenty-three columns, cauldrons had been set to burn.

They crawled in silence until they found a spot from which they could clearly see the throne at the center. Tajaz the Seer was there, like a pile of pink skin contorting upon itself, fold upon fold in a shapeless bulge. His clouded eyes were closed, and though his mouth was closed as well, his incisors were perpetually exposed, shining like curved, overlapping daggers. Tajaz wheezed rhythmically, drool sliding into the translucent folds of his armpits. Agnargsilv rested upon a wide armrest next to the naked mole rat.

"My scalp thinks he is sleeping," Kulak whispered.

Lago peeked over the short wall. "I'll go grab it, really quick—"

"Hold," Kulak interrupted him. "Someone approaches."

From a doorway opposite the one they had entered came Hetfr the Speaker, gliding softly on bare feet. She rounded the large column of the throne and stopped in front of the pink mound of flesh. She said something in the Oxruk tongue, but Tajaz kept sleeping.

A guard came running through the main entrance; he spoke hurriedly to Hetfr and hastened straight back out. Whatever information he'd delivered seemed to upset her. She spoke to Tajaz and, seeing no response, lightly kicked at his hanging, crusty feet. Tajaz woke up startled, opened his cataract-fogged eyes, and immediately began to thrash about and gurgle. The pale woman spoke over him, trying to explain something.

Hetfr the Speaker turned away from Tajaz, still talking, but now with rage in her voice. She paced around like a caged animal. Each time she faced Tajaz, he began to thrash once again.

Wait… Lago thought, glancing carefully over the top of the low wall. *He's not speaking to her. He simply acts that way whenever she turns to face him. He's not saying anything at all.*

As Hetfr turned away again and paused for a moment, Tajaz stopped his convulsing moans, exhausted from the effort. His pink head was left dangling, aimed directly toward the group of infiltrators. Lago quickly hid behind the wall once more, but Lummukem and Kulak could tell that Tajaz the Seer was looking directly at them, sensing their auras with Okrisilv's sight.

Tajaz sputtered a hiss in their direction, in a tone Lago had not heard before, as if trying to vanquish them with mere foaming spittle. It prompted Hetfr to turn to him once more, causing Tajaz to resume his cycle of writhing.

Hetfr snatched Agnargsilv and used it to cruelly hit Tajaz while screaming words that, despite being in a different language, could be easily identified as obscenities and curses. She slapped at his lumpy ears, kicked at the tail which curved protectively, and punched at the rolls of fat in the distended belly until Tajaz began to sob and gurgle.

Hetfr hurled the canid mask at the naked mole rat's face, and though the light weight of it did not hurt him, the gesture itself made the pitiful creature break down in tears. Agnargsilv fell to the ground next to the throne.

Tajaz the Seer slowly turned translucent and foggy in a pink, refracting mist. The form shrunk to reveal a miserable-looking old man, with white hair so long that it served him as a nest. The wrinkled man was pallid, naked, and powerless except for the dark mask he wore. He could not speak. He merely sputtered meaningless noises as he cried.

Lago had dared to peek through a crevice once more. *That poor old man,* he thought. *That woman is evil. How could she—*

Hetfr savagely snatched Okrisilv off the old man's face and held it in front of her. Tajaz leaned awkwardly on the throne and, with clouded eyes, faced the low wall once more, using all his energy to lift a knobby finger toward the intruders he could no longer see. Hetfr yelled at him and slapped at his arm, making the man flail once more, though this time much weaker than while he had been wearing the mask. Hetfr kept admonishing Tajaz, then suddenly stopped, seeming to understand something. Her eyes turned toward the wall, sensing a shadow behind it. In a swift move, Hetfr placed the mask of glires upon her face.

Lago heard Hetfr shriek out a command loud enough for any nearby guards to hear, then felt something move quickly by his side. He turned and saw Ierun Jessha running toward Tajaz and Hetfr, her clawed gauntlet ready to strike. "Jessha, no!" he yelled, emerging from hiding with his friends following. *Tajaz is not the Okrifröa,* he realized the moment he began to run.

Hetfr spotted the attackers and immediately shifted into her half-form of a brush-tailed porcupine. Her long quills punctured through her white robes while her piercing tail formed below, like a prickle-covered mace. She quickly spun her slender body, dropping to the ground with her tail swinging.

Jessha was clobbered by Hetfr's tail. Most of the quills were deflected by her elytra armor, though some pierced through small gaps on her chest and arms. She ignored the pain and continued to swing her clawed arm.

Lago slid on the floor in front of the screeching old man, clutched Agnarg-silv in his hands, and shapeshifted into Sterjall without losing momentum. He saw Kulak blowing a paralyzing dart at Hetfr, which she took harmlessly on her back quills while jumping out of the way.

Jessha tackled Hetfr, tumbling with her while dozens more quills pierced her body. Her clawed arm sliced through the porcupine's robes but got stuck amongst the sharp spines. Hetfr rose up spinning, robes in tatters, and swung her spiked tail as she ran, missing Jessha's face by a hairbreadth.

Guards could be heard calling out commands while Hetfr escaped toward the pentagonal gate.

"Let her go!" Sterjall screamed. "Let's get out of here, now!"

But Jessha was of a single mind. She pursued Hetfr, who pulled a lever as she passed through the doorway. The gate fell to seal the polygonal opening, but Jessha slid under the rusted fangs just before they bit down. The iron bars slammed hard into the ground and locked.

The stone bridge was just ahead of Hetfr and Jessha. Hiding under the bridge, Gwit saw the incoming wielder of Okrisilv and panicked, wanting to run away but unsure of where to go.

Past the bridge, dozens of guards hurried forward, running to protect Hetfr. The porcupine tripped on her ripped robes, granting Jessha one last chance. The queen sprung like a hare, caring not that she was headed straight for the piercing quills, and slammed her clawed arm into Hetfr's back. Hetfr lurched forward and collapsed at the base of the stone bridge. Jessha pulled her quill-covered arm back, rising with a dozen more needles protruding from her chest and neck.

Hetfr shook on the ground. Her porcupine eyes were like bloodied mar-bles, looking up at the Sehján queen, disbelieving, filled with hatred. She flashed her sharp incisors, then slumped, lifeless. Her body turned smoky and refractive, leaving only a pale, blood-drenched woman wearing a dark mask.

Jessha claimed Okrisilv and was about to run back to safety when she real-ized the gate was now closed.

She turned again. Across the bridge, the guards were coming for her. In the passages to the left and right, following the split water canal, more guards approached. She felt the air tremble next to her ear—a spear, barely missing her face.

"Mom!" Puuja yelled from under the bridge. "Come hide with us!"

"Follow Gwit!" Lummukem cried from behind the iron gate. "He will lead you out!"

Another spear flew by Jessha, tearing a colorful scale off her pauldron.

The third spear did not miss, sinking through her belly.

"Mom, no!" Puuja screamed, her tiny voice splintering the air.

Jessha dropped to her knees at the edge of the canal, staring at her twins on the opposite side. With a strained effort, she murmured, "Take it, ruby lights. Take the mask that is rightfully yours… T–take it to the temple… and… and do as I taught you. I will w–wait for you, at the Eternal Sea. I love you, my rubies, I am proud of… you… forever."

As one last spear hit Jessha in the chest, she hurled the mask across the canal, toward Puuja's outstretched hands. But the mask was too light; it slowed in the air before making it even halfway over the canal, then fell like an autumnal leaf to be dragged down the torrent.

Pol dove into the water after it.

"Pol, wait!" Puuja screamed, her gaze split between her dying mother and her vanishing brother. Gwit jumped into the water as well, shifting into a giant beaver in mid-plunge, splashing out a large wave that made Puuja stumble.

"Go…" her mother urged, as a pale guard stood over the queen with a clawed arm rising. "Take care of each other. Go… with Lakemother."

As the claws came down, Puuja leapt into the water and was pulled by the fast current. Guards at either side of the canal saw her red hair flash by; they hurled spears at her, but she dove for cover, swimming in her own grief, letting her tears become prayers in the sheltering water.

CHAPTER FIFTY-EIGHT

RUBY LIGHTS

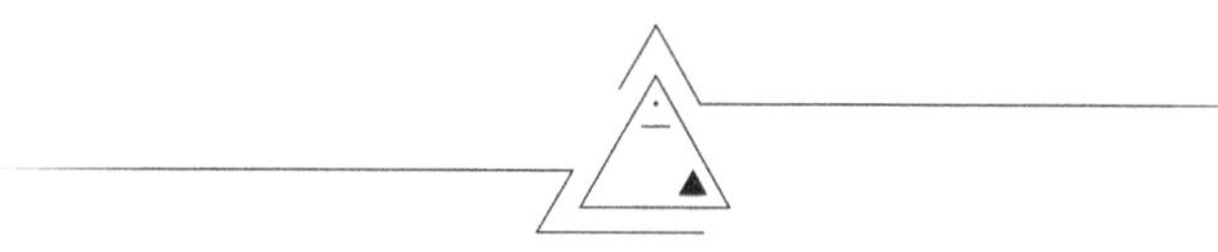

Lummukem strained to lift the metal gate, but it would not budge. They felt a spear fly past their shoulder and looked out toward the bridge. Jessha stood there with Okrisilv in her hands. Another spear found its target, piercing her stomach.

"Follow Gwit! He will lead you out!" Lummukem yelled to the children.

Jessha fell, guards piling atop her. There was nothing Lummukem could do. They retreated from the locked gate.

Tajaz the Seer gazed in Lummukem's direction with clouded eyes. The dragon was not sure whether the old man could see them, but they were glad he was no longer screeching.

"There's an exit at the back!" Sterjall yelled. "Quickly!" He ran toward the opposite end of the circular room, where an identical gate was open but already flooding with pale guards.

Ishke'ísuk sped past Sterjall. He leapt, transforming in midair and spinning wildly in his heavy alligator form, trampling and tearing at the wall of Oxruk. He took down nearly a dozen, but many more had already flooded the rotunda. The Oxruk moved to encircle them, some hiding behind the low walls at the periphery, others weaving between the columns to strike with their iron claws and spears.

Lummukem spiraled with their bone halberd, executing a Winged Seedpod maneuver while their spiked tail lashed out. Kulak took cover behind a column, blowing darts at any Oxruk trying to flank them. Sterjall crawled behind the low wall, his enemies visible to him through stone. He felt a guard spying him over the wall, so he scraped his bracer against it, shooting brime sparks up to blind the soldier, then rose quickly and sliced the pale man's neck with Leif. He ducked back down, a spray of blood striking his muzzle. Ishke'ísuk dashed around the rotunda's perimeter, chewing at the legs of the guards taking cover behind the low walls. He disabled or killed them all, but too many spears were now stuck in his body, and he could run no longer.

"To the gate, before they close it on us!" Sterjall called out.

Lummukem was closest to the gate, but they hesitated, seeing too many reinforcements trotting up the corridor. The new squad of guards saw the carnage that awaited beyond the entrance and chose to drop the gate rather than risk their lives entering the rotunda. Kulak's teal eyes spotted the single brave guard who rushed alone toward the lever. He blew a dart, hitting the pale man in the neck. The Oxruk guard toppled over, but with his dying breath activated the mechanism, releasing the metal bars. The teeth of the gate chomped down hard, piercing through the pale bodies that blocked the entrance and locking into place with a sonorous clang.

Both exits were now blocked. A few spears were hurled through the barred gates, but the aimless attacks seemed useless, so the skirmish came to a halt.

Sterjall crouched behind the walls once more. Kulak followed him, while Lummukem stayed at the opposite end of the circle, pulling spears out of Ishke'ísuk's body.

"Are you alright?" Sterjall asked the caracal in between soft pants.

"Terrified," Kulak replied. "But not hurt. Is Ierun Jessha—"

"She's dead. I saw her fall. I don't know what happened to the twins." Sterjall stuck his head up and saw Lummukem tossing away a bloodied spear. "Ishke is badly hurt. We need to find a way out of here."

"Gwit told us there are exits above," Kulak said, "through the old capital of Kissumar, near Ommo ust Okri. It would be easier to follow his advice than to swim back the way we came—the Oxruk are alert, the water flows against us."

Lummukem skirted their way carefully around the perimeter, carrying the wounded basilisk in their arms. "He is not well," they said, holding up the Nu'irg for the others to see. "We must hasten to an exit."

"Did you see where Gwit went?" Sterjall asked.

"We saw his aura swimming away with the twins. We trust they will have an easier way out than us."

Kulak aimed his quaar blowgun like a telescope, scanning the threads to their sides and then upward. "The roots are thick," he said. "We must be below the trunk. My scalp can sense tunnels, though it is hard to make them out."

Lummukem began to explore in the same manner while Sterjall tried the same with Leif; he had a lesser range, but could see more broadly.

More guards gathered behind the gates. They seemed to be deliberating over whether opening the gates now was a good idea, trying to measure the threat still lurking inside the rotunda.

"We sense stairs that go up, past the back gate," Lummukem said. "But we cannot fight so many enemies, not even with Ishke'ísuk's aid."

The basilisk took pained breaths in Lummukem's arms. Not only was he badly injured, but he had been changing shapes too often and was now exhausted.

Lummukem placed him in their bag, leaving the top open.

"What is that smell?" Sterjall asked abruptly. "Is that… smoke?"

The three of them poked their heads out and saw a dark cloud wafting in from the back gate, while the front gate was being sealed with wooden planks. Tajaz the Seer began to wail once more, sitting helplessly upon his throne.

They don't even care about Tajaz, Sterjall thought. *That poor old man.* He suddenly realized how ridiculous it was to think about the wellbeing of an enemy in this dire situation, but he could not help himself from caring about the abused elder. *It is not his fault,* he thought, but it was a thought without conviction.

"They are trying to smoke us out," Lummukem said. "Our scalps will falter from the lack of air."

"Stay low, do not breathe it," Kulak urged the others.

"It will take a lot of smoke to fill this chamber," Sterjall said.

"Time is something they have," Lummukem said, "and something we lack."

Puuja and Pol sat next to the hazel dormouse. Gwit was squeaking anxiously, trying to hurry them deeper into the dark tunnel in which they'd stopped to catch their breath. Gwit had carried the twins to safety, helping them open a grate in the canal, then swimming with them into a chamber just large enough to sit in; there they had stopped to rest and mourn.

"Not now!" Puuja finally yelled at the Nu'irg. She continued sobbing, holding tightly to Pol. "Please stop. Let us… We can't…"

The chamber they sat in had only a subtle hint of light filtering past the grate through which they had escaped. It seemed to be a ventilation shaft with a light breeze constantly flowing through, making their wet bodies shiver with the cold. Pol had lost his spear when diving to save the mask of glires, but Puuja had kept ahold of hers. Okrisilv waited on the cold rocks next to them; neither of the twins wanted to touch it.

Gwit ran into the shaft and squeaked from within its depths. It was as dark as his beady eyes in there, and it seemed tight even for the children. The dormouse squeaked louder, begging them to follow.

"We don't want to go…" Pol whispered. "We don't want to leave Mom…"

"It's okay, Pol," Puuja comforted him. "Mom is… with Lakemother, but we are together. It's okay. We'll find a way out, that we promise."

Pol rocked back and forth. "Our friends are in danger. We can't leave Lumm—"

Creak! came a metallic shriek muted by the water. The chamber's dim light dimmed further as shadows swam in the canal below. Gwit squeaked as loudly as he dared.

"They are coming! Go! Follow Gwit!" Puuja was pushing her brother into the tight shaft when she heard water splashing behind her. A pale figure emerged from the water, with skin as smooth and translucent as an olm's.

Puuja instinctively picked up her weapon and swung it. The spear's blade buried itself in the man's skull, making him drop in a pool of crimson. Puuja had only ever fought with a quarterstaff before; she had not expected the blow to do more than bludgeon the man. Her heart thumped at the sight of the figure floating in a pool of his own blood. *We… We did this,* she thought. *Did we… Did we kill him?*

"Hurry!" Pol called.

Another figure surfaced, coated in a meniscus of water and blood. Puuja came out of her trance, grabbed her spear, and crawled into the shaft. *Okrisilv!* she remembered, turning around. But the blood-covered woman already had her hands on the mask.

Puuja swung her spear again, cutting into the woman's wrist. She snatched the mask from her hands and hurried into the shaft while the woman pulled herself out of the water, crawling on her elbows. Puuja tossed the mask to Pol and slithered into the opening, barely making her body fit.

A sticky hand grabbed at her foot and tugged hard. Puuja tried to pull away from the grip, but the woman was much bigger and stronger. The girl blindly poked her spear toward her feet until she felt the pointed end contact something soft. There was a pained shriek, then a thrashing sound, and then silence. Puuja chose not to look back and instead followed the sound of her brother and the squeaking dormouse, sinking deeper into the lightless cavity.

An eternity later, they felt the shaft widen into a space where they could rest their backs without being in total darkness. At the floor in front of them was an ornamental air vent carved with spiraling patterns. From the many holes emanated shafts of light, like fingers reaching toward them—a respite from the darkness. Gwit had already scampered deeper into another dark tunnel. He squeaked to hurry them again.

"Shut up!" Puuja screamed.

Pol opened his eyes wide and put a hand to his sister's mouth. He leaned toward the holes and peeked down into the room. He could see nothing moving.

"What are we going to do?" Puuja asked no one. "They are going to find us, and they will—"

"Take it to the temple," Pol said. "Take it to the temple."

He stared at Okrisilv. It sat there next to the bloodied spear, caged between beams of light, looking menacing and yet peaceful. It had sharp incisors that shimmered in their blackness, a slightly triangular muzzle, and ears somewhere between those of a hare and a mouse. Ridges flowed over the mask's surface, emulating the pattern of long whiskers.

"Take it to the temple," Pol repeated, rocking back and forth.

"We can't… We don't know how to use it. We need to get out of here alive, that's what—"

"We know how to use it," Pol interrupted. "She taught us. Take it to the temple."

"But it takes time to learn. It's not easy."

"We learn."

"But we don't even know where to—"

"Guide us in the dark with it. To the temple."

"But what if—"

"Mom said to take it to the temple!" Pol screamed. This time, it was Puuja who placed her hand over his mouth.

"Okay, okay. Please be quiet."

"You have to try."

"I… We…" Puuja picked up the mask. It sparkled, still covered in droplets. Gwit scampered back into the chamber and stood in front of them, staring with the angriest face a dormouse could muster.

"Gwit, we know you can't understand us," Puuja said, "but… should we do this? We are scared."

Gwit stared, wiggling his whiskers quizzically.

"It's okay, Puuja," Pol said. "Mom is with Lakemother, but I'm here with you. It's okay."

Something in those particular words made Puuja break into tears once more. When she stopped, she picked Okrisilv up and closed her eyes.

"We… I need to learn, sooner or later," she said, her voice taking on a solemn tone. "I am the descendant of Ierun Hejána, heir to Ierun Jessha, who from the Eternal Sea watches over us."

She had suffered so much that she would welcome more pain—anything to make her forget the anguish of losing her mother. *Nothing else can hurt us now,* she thought. *Nothing can make us feel any worse than we already do.*

"Lakemother shelter us," she whispered, then slowly welcomed Okrisilv.

The mask felt too big for her small head, but somehow it still latched on like iron shavings pulled by a magnet, shooting a torrent of agony directly into Puuja's spine. She writhed in a pain she had not believed possible, sharing the struggles of all the conscious beings near her, from the smallest slime molds to the Oxruk guards rushing about in tunnels beyond thick rock walls. Despite the unbearable torment, she did not scream, but the pain kept building and tightening. She felt her body contort, her lungs wanting to cry out so loud that all the people inside and outside the dome would hear her agony.

Suddenly, her pain mellowed, becoming a dull throb. She opened her eyes and through the narrow eyeholes saw Pol's hands grabbing her own. Her gaze shifted upward, finding Pol's stiffened face, veins nearly popping out of his temples, red eyes holding back tears.

She saw it then, saw her brother and herself as one being made of an infinite tapestry of interlacing threads. They were one. And Pol was there, taking half of the pain away from her, holding tight with the special bond they had always shared. Pol began to hum to himself, tears cascading down his cheeks. Then he sang. He sang the lullaby their mother used to sing to them during stormy nights:

> Fear not of the darkness, my bright ruby lights,
>
> Fear not of the pale men that come in the night.
>
> Your mother is with you, your den's warm and bright.
>
> Fear not my dear rubies, my dear ruby lights.

> Fear not of the water, my dear ruby lights,
>
> For Lakemother's womb shines like skies of pure white.
>
> Beneath her embrace all is safe, all is right.
>
> Fear not of the water, beloved ruby lights.

Puuja joined in the last refrain, partially singing, partially humming, partially sobbing.

> Alone you will never be, bright ruby lights,
>
> For mother is with you come day or come night.
>
> I'll tuck you in bed and then kiss you goodnight.
>
> So fear not of the darkness; fear not, ruby lights.

Puuja pulled her brother closer and together they sobbed, embracing each other with all their combined grief.

ENDLESS SPIRAL

"They are closing the vents!" Lummukem warned. The dragon had climbed a wall, trying to widen a small ventilation hole with their halberd, but had barely managed to chip the rock. They dropped back to the ground and took a deep breath.

Sterjall observed from nearby. He could see the Oxruk behind the stone walls, crawling through the shafts, blocking the ventilation holes. The smoke was getting denser. *Is it poisonous?* he wondered. *No, if it was, we'd be dead already. But we'll be dead soon if we don't find a way out.*

While trapped in the smoke, they had used their quaar conduits to peer into the distance, trying to form a mental map of the tunnels. They gathered that the temple itself was nearly directly above them, following a vertical root hundreds of feet wide which grew past the back entrance. A spiraling staircase was carved around that largest of roots, which had been easy for them to spot with all the Oxruk reinforcements descending it.

Sterjall made his way around the base of the throne, trying to find secret levers, a hidden passage, anything. Tajaz the Seer still sat there, seemingly asleep in his nest of long white hair. Sterjall placed a handpaw on the wrinkled body and heard him moan.

Poor old man, he thought. *You were mistreated, abused, and now they don't even care if you die in the smoke with us.* He thought that perhaps the Sehján had been right about the Oxruk; perhaps they *were* monsters. But seeing this helpless man, innocent or not, turned his stomach. *Whether there are monsters down here or not, no one deserves this.*

Sterjall pulled Tajaz to the ground where there was still some air for him to breathe, then held his breath and climbed the wide column that made up the throne. He found only a vine-covered ceiling above him, so he dropped back down, lungs wheezing and eyes burning from the smoke.

There is no way out but through the two entrances, he realized with waning hope. He remained low to the ground and unsheathed Leif, using it to once again peer beyond the back gate where the smoke was pouring from. Dozens of guards were gathered there, waiting for him and his friends to pass out. He studied the shape and structure of the corridor.

"That's it!" he suddenly exclaimed, then coughed. "I know what to do!" He aimed Leif a bit higher, toward the vines that acted as the corridor's ceiling, and willed the vines to move. The sound of cracking stone was followed by mumbles from the confused guards. Sterjall could sense the vines slithering to the sides, weakening the support of the rocks, until finally the ceiling above the Oxruk caved in. The rotunda shook as tons of rock crashed into the hall-way. The fresh air that rushed into the throne room pushed the smoke into spirals. Whatever machine had been used to create the smoke was crushed, its fuel spilling and igniting violently, setting the clouds aglow.

"What did you do?" Kulak asked, shocked by the blast but with renewed hope in his heart. "The vines, did you just—"

"Yes, let's go! To the gate."

The three of them hurried to the back entrance; its gate had bent and buck-led, toppling sideways from the impact of the rubble, but the passage beyond was now blocked by a wall of fire and rocks.

Sterjall frowned as he tried to find a way through the debris. "Shit. But still, this can work. Follow me!"

He hurried over to inspect the front entrance instead. The vines were not as numerous there; they still parted at his command, dropping a few boulders onto the pale skull of an unsuspecting guard, but the gate was unaffected.

"Do it here," Lummukem suggested, pointing straight above them. "There is a large chamber above us."

"It could crush us all to pieces," Sterjall said.

"Control it one vine at a time. Make them come down to meet us. We will help."

"Wait," Sterjall said, stepping toward Tajaz, who was sprawled uncon-scious on the ground. He picked the old man up, surprised at how light he felt, and moved him toward the front entrance where there was more fresh air to breathe. "Let's do this," he said as he returned. "But slowly, be careful."

The three Silvfröash focused on the ceiling of the Seer's Rotunda, willing the vines to part sideways and downward, forming a ramp for the rocks to slide upon. The ceiling cracked, but they kept forcing more vines to let go of their burden, until the upper level suddenly collapsed in a rumbling tremor. Black smoke lifted to mix with the cleaner air from the room above, then got sucked through the open vents from the larger space.

"Climb, now!" Sterjall urged the others. The vines, although slippery, were at least thornless when underground; the three of them moved briskly over them, scrambling up toppled boulders and broken furniture, dislodging rocks beneath them until they arrived at a cracked floor.

A door was ajar at the far end of the chamber. They hurried to it.

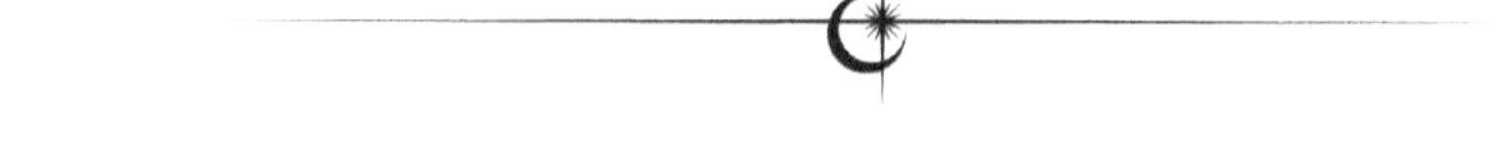

Gwit squeaked in the darkness, but Puuja could see him now, whether or not there was light. The dormouse looked like a phosphorescent firefly, or perhaps like fresh pollen shaken off an overeager pine. *So vividly yellow,* Puuja mused, although she somehow understood that the aura did not have a color; it wasn't even in her field of view. She was too nervous to overthink it—to fully learn and experience what seeing with Okrisilv was like.

"Hold on," she said to Pol. "Don't let go of my hand. Watch your step here. There, we are almost through. There's a room on the other side."

They had been scurrying through the vents for a long while, constantly climbing. Gwit seemed to know his way, leading them speedily through the tunnels.

"It smells burnt," Pol noted, and Puuja felt it. The air in the shaft quickly thickened, becoming hard to breathe. They could not see the smoke, which was just as dark as the lightless void they traversed, but they knew it was saturating their tight space.

Gwit tried to hurry them up.

"No!" Puuja coughed from the exertion. "We need fresh air!" She led them through a shorter tunnel and found a wall with many holes—a ventilation panel. No light shone from the other side, but she could feel a breeze. She kicked at it, but the panel barely rattled. Pol added a kick of his own, and the thin stone shattered, fresh air rushing in.

As she was getting ready to climb out of the shaft, Puuja briefly let go of Pol's hand. Pain shot up through her nerves once more. She clutched Pol's hand again, the throbbing in her spine lightly subsiding.

The smoke grew denser, forcing even Gwit to give up and exit through the broken panel, rushing ahead of the twins for fresh air.

"I… We'll have to take the mask off for a bit," Puuja said. "It'll be fine. It's an easy drop to the next room."

She pulled Okrisilv off and felt instant relief. Her head still drummed in an internal struggle that would linger for much longer, but she could focus better now. She weakly lowered herself into the chamber below them, then helped Pol down.

"We hear footsteps," Pol warned.

Puuja had seen a stone bench before taking the mask off, so she pulled Pol in the dark until they bumped into the hard surface.

"They are coming. Stay low."

A door opened, illuminating the room. A cloud of black smoke was forming in the vaulted ceiling. Puuja heard shouting and tried to guess at the number of people by counting the steps she heard. *A dozen, perhaps?* She was uncertain. The guards rushed across the chamber and unlatched a door on the opposite end, allowing more smoke to rush in, then disappeared into the cloud.

The room went quiet.

"We need to use the mask again," Puuja whispered. "We need to see if anyone else is around the corner. Please, don't let go of my hand."

Pol held on tightly and took in his share of the pain.

Puuja walked toward the door and said, "Gwit, is there a way through here?"

Gwit did not understand her, but he understood what he must do. Go up, find an exit. Go up, free the twins.

They followed the dormouse to a strange wall of waxy green. It seemed flat, but Okrisilv told Puuja that the wall had a slight curve to it, and that it was alive. A staircase was carved into the rock next to the green wall, following it straight up. Gwit shapeshifted into a kangaroo mouse and hopped up the steps, three at a time. The climb was arduous, but at least there were sconces to illuminate their path.

"Hide!" Puuja urged Pol, sensing movement in a side tunnel. They took cover behind a column. Two guards with spears and metal shields rushed past them, briefly gazing at the strange-looking mouse that was hopping up the steps. They had no time to waste with the funny creature; there were fugitives on the loose, so they kept running. Puuja held her breath until the guards were out of sight and then continued up, always holding on to her brother with one hand, and to her bloodied spear with the other.

Hundreds more steps up, she felt a complicated series of connections through the mask. *The surface?* she wondered. There was a higher density of threads there, like a soup of organisms, dense and vibrant. Her head began to throb again. Life had been much sparser in the solitude of the vents, but now she was surrounded by threads—by pain. She pulled the mask off to take a break.

Gwit turned toward a branching tunnel.

"Gwit is pointing to the exit," Puuja said. "We could see it with the mask, the outside. It was painful there. But we must follow. That we must do."

"No!" Pol said. "Take it to the temple."

"But we need to—"

"We promised Mom. The temple is above us."

Puuja nodded. She put the mask on and forced herself to climb up. Gwit squeaked next to them, trying to lure them out to safety, but the twins kept climbing.

"To the temple, Gwit," Puuja said, looking back at the Nu'irg. "We take it to the temple."

Gwit understood. He hopped up the steps to lead the way once more.

Lummukem slammed their spiked tail into an Oxruk's spine, then charged into the hallway. More guards came running toward them, hurling spears. Kulak and Sterjall tipped a table sideways to block the incoming weapons, which stuck halfway through the wooden surface.

"We need to keep moving in that direction," Kulak said. "The root is near."

A racket of dislodged rocks resounded behind them. The guards had found a way into the Seer's Rotunda and were now climbing over the rubble and vines. Soon they'd be surrounded again.

Sterjall focused Leif toward the ceiling, directly above the climbing guards. The next level gave way and collapsed with such force that the blast of air and smoke pushed the toppled table away, sending it tumbling toward the other enemies.

"Shit," Sterjall yelped. "Watch out!" He rolled to the side and deflected a claw with his bracers, then performed a triple attack Lummukem had taught him, first shooting up a Brime Strike, then using the momentum of his striking arm to slice with a Lunate Fang before punching upward with a Geyser Paw. His spiked gauntlet crushed the guard's kidney, saving Kulak from a deadly blow.

Lummukem returned to defend them, punching mercilessly with a sequence of Mantis Shrimp Blasts. Kulak and Sterjall took up positions next to the dragon. Luckily, most of the Oxruk had run out of spears to throw, switching to their clawed gauntlets for close-range attacks. This gave the three Silvfröash an advantage, as they could foresee their strikes—something which was impossible to do with a piece of dead steel and wood moving quickly through the air.

Lummukem disabled six guards in quick succession, then kicked a set of doors open. In the next room was the enormous root and the staircase that spiraled around it.

"I hear more guards coming down the steps," Sterjall said. "Get ready."

Puuja could sense the temple not too far above them, distinct thanks to the quaar conduits that formed the lattice. Beams of threads shot in odd patterns around her, feeding the roots, expanding to the skies.

"There are guards inside the temple," Puuja warned. "Okrisilv feels them."

Metallic footsteps clinked closer. They had nowhere to hide this time.

An Oxruk priestess, armed with claws in both hands, stopped and stared at the red-haired apparitions. Her metal-plated armor was hammered with a million concave indentations, her white hair covered by an oblong helm with narrow slits for eyes. Puuja weakly pointed her spear at the priestess, who spat a curse and assumed a defensive stance, one claw down, the other up.

The priestess had failed to notice the kangaroo mouse standing directly beneath her. Gwit suddenly shapeshifted into a castoroides, so wide and tall that it sent the priestess flying upward, slamming her helm against the rocky ceiling. She tumbled down the steps in a jumble of limp limbs and detaching plates. The twins stepped aside as the heap of flesh and metal rolled by them, then continued their climb, following the giant beaver up the last set of stairs.

Five more priestesses waited at the top, so surprised by the creature appearing before them that they held their attacks a moment too long. Gwit hopped onto one of them, crushing her plates with his weight. When the other four attacked, he shifted into a lodgepole chipmunk and darted out of the way at a speed none of the armored enemies could match.

Puuja stepped in, still unnoticed by the Oxruk, clutching her spear tightly with both hands. She noticed her mistake a moment too late: she had let go of Pol's hand, and now the pain of all the threads overwhelmed her. She let go of her weapon and dropped to her knees, holding her head.

One of the priestesses noticed the girl, ran toward her, and kicked her before she could react. Puuja rolled across the ground screaming. Her face hit the steps of the central dais, and Okrisilv detached, falling away from her. Pol rushed to his twin's aid, took her spear, and slammed it into the armored woman, then spun the weapon to push her farther back.

The other three priestesses came running from the far end of the chamber. Gwit saw them rushing toward Pol and sped forward, transforming back into the castoroides and slapping two of them with his heavy tail, then rolling with his excessive momentum to crush their bones beneath him.

The priestess who had dodged the attack swung her claws at Pol, who parried masterfully. The twins had trained with quarterstaffs for years, readying for a war with the Oxruk that could come at any time. This time, Pol's weapon had a sharp metal point, which found a gap in the side of the priestess's armor. She screamed, then sliced down with her claws. Pol blocked, but the wood in his spear was not reinforced—the metal tip went flying away, leaving him with only a long stick. But that was alright; Pol knew the weight of a quarterstaff better. He hit the priestess on the chest, then on her armored shoulder, then connected a third blow against her unarmored heel, cracking a bone and making her shriek in pain.

Only two Oxruk were still fighting, one barely standing on her broken fibula. They both rushed Pol at the same time. Gwit blocked the path of the uninjured priestess like a wall of fur, pierced his enormous incisors through her helm, then flung her into one of the thorny vines. Puuja had barely recovered from the heavy kick she had received, but did her best to protect her brother, rolling on the ground to make the last priestess trip and tumble on her weakened foot.

Pol flipped his weapon and wedged the blunt end against the cobblestoned ground. The toppling priestess slammed into the splintered end, shooting shards of wood into the crevices between her armored plates. Gwit twirled in a flash, his beaver tail slamming the injured priestess into a far corner of the temple.

"I hear more coming up the steps!" Pol said through heavy breaths.

Puuja glanced around. The temple had only one entrance: the stairway they had ascended, and where Gwit was now readying his tail to strike. The original entrance, the long tunnel that once led to the Sehján capital of Kissumar, was entirely blocked by rocks.

"You need to do it," Pol urged his sister. "Tell the dome to open, like Mom taught us."

Puuja slowly got to her feet. Her chest and neck were bruised; one of her arms felt useless. She picked up the mask and shambled up the dais. She looked at the core vine rising behind the marble throne, at the lattice above her, recognizing all of it from the stories their mother had told them. With the memory of Jessha fresh in her mind, she began to sob.

"You need to do it," Pol repeated. "Hurry."

"We do it together," she said.

Puuja sat on the throne, feeling way too small. She swallowed her tears, held on to her brother's hand, and put the mask on.

The pain was too much to bear. Her own physical pain from the blow she'd received was dreadful enough, compounded by her grief over her dead mother, the pain of the vines around her, of the layers of moss and fungi that grew in the damp room. The pain of her brother, who was seeing her struggle, also throbbed in her spine. And there was also the pain of the priestesses they had wounded, who lay moaning on the ground—when Puuja's mind found their threads, she could not help but feel a connection to them. She tried to divert her thoughts, to focus on the lattice above her, but she could barely hold her body upright. The seat felt cold. Her head swam in a fever, her chest throbbed, her spine felt like it was made of growing needles. She closed her eyes, visualized the threads and conduits… and passed out, slumped against the white throne.

"No!" Pol shrieked. "Puuja! Wake up!"

Gwit looked at the twins, then looked back down. As the first guard began to rise from the steps, he slammed down with his beaver tail, shattering the man's vertebrae into splinters. He sank his incisors into the body and hurled it down the steps, sending a cascade of pale skins and white robes plummeting. But they would recover; they would keep coming.

"Puuja! Please, we need you!" Pol cried out, but Puuja was unconscious. The mask had taken its toll on her, forcing her beyond what anyone should endure at such a young age.

Pol shook his sister's shoulders. "Please. Do it for Mom." She didn't respond. Though Puuja was unconscious, she remained tense, as if electrified by the pain of the mask.

Pol reached a hand forward and pulled the mask off her face. Puuja took a deep breath, as if awakening from a nightmare. She weakly opened her eyes and tried to reach for the mask again, but she fell forward. Pol caught her and found her unconscious once more. He softly lowered her to the ground, then looked toward Gwit, who was assaulting more attackers with his tail.

Pol looked at Okrisilv, then glanced down at his sister. She seemed so peaceful there, sleeping in a bed of long, red hairs.

He drew in a cold breath.

"Fear not of the darkness," he whispered to his sister, or perhaps to himself.

He sat on the throne and put on the mask.

CHAPTER SIXTY

THE TWIN CAPITALS

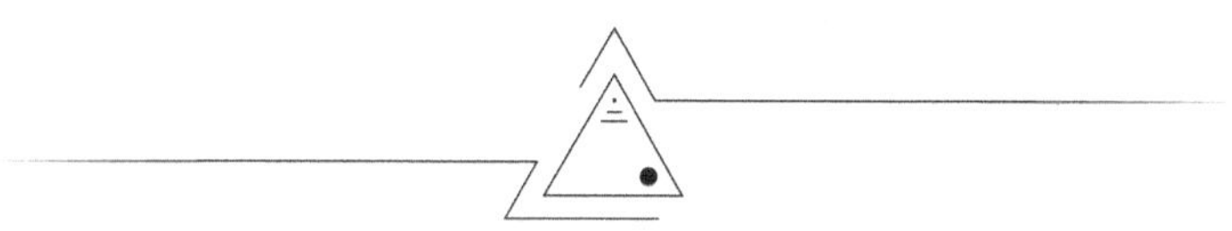

"We could reach the temple from here," Kulak said, quickly climbing the steps that wrapped around the enormous root. "We could go there first, ask the dome to open, and then escape."

"No," Sterjall firmly said. "We escape, that is our goal. Destroying entire cities is not what we came here to do."

"They betrayed us!" Kulak protested. "They would have killed you!"

"We must do this, for Noss," Lummukem added. "There are bigger struggles ahead. This is necessary, Sterjall, whether you like it or not."

The wolf fumed. He had seen so much betrayal in such a short time, and it had quickly eliminated every chance of finding a peaceful road toward opening the dome. He felt like a fool as his own convictions of good and evil writhed in his mind. He wanted to keep arguing, searching for a better way out of this mess, but he could not get around the fact that opening the dome, for the sake of Noss, was necessary. *Yet at what cost?* he pondered. *And what other option do we have left?*

"Oxruk coming," Lummukem said, snapping Sterjall out of his frustration.

Two guards stopped above them and held their ground, taking cover behind their shields, spear tips poking out. Lummukem and Kulak tried to pierce them with darts but could not find an opening. As they waited for a chance to attack, another group arrived, climbing the steps behind them.

"You two take the ones below," Sterjall said. "I'll deal with these two above."

Sterjall assumed the Stalking Jaguar stance. He heard a *fwhip!* and then a *crack!* as an arrow exploded at his feet.

"They have bows!" Kulak warned. He and Lummukem took cover behind a column, but Sterjall could not hide while holding back the guards. The next arrow struck his back; the elytra armor deflected it, but the impact sent him tumbling. A shielded guard took advantage of the moment and charged with his spear.

Sterjall had his empathic focus locked and knew exactly the moment the pale man came for him. He first scraped Leif's pommel on his brime bracer, blinding the attacker, then turned on his heel, grabbed the spear's shaft, and tugged hard, flinging the guard down the steps. The Oxruk archers reacted quickly, dodging out of the way and readying their bows once more.

More foot soldiers—an entire squad—came up behind the archers. Sterjall scraped his bracer again, making the guards flinch and drop their arrows. He scraped it each time the guards recovered, but they soon realized the sparks were nothing to fear and simply covered their eyes before each strike.

Sterjall could not keep the light tricks going forever, but Kulak suddenly had a bright idea. He reached into Lummukem's bag, where Ishke'ísuk was resting, and from underneath the basilisk retrieved a pharolith lamp. He spread open the petals and aimed the beam at his enemies. Even indirectly, Kulak found the light painfully bright. For the Oxruk, it was unbearable. They cowered and cursed, loosing arrows blindly up the steps.

Lummukem rolled out from cover with tail swinging and halberd slashing in a Wheel Spider assault, so swift that it nearly flung Olo off their shoulder before the jay had a chance to take wing. The dragon's armored tail connected with a jawbone, shattering it, while their halberd sliced off half a dozen legs. They twirled in a lethal spiral, borrowing techniques from the Dance of the Six Seasons they had learned from the Ji Miscam, until all that remained was a pile of pale soldiers writhing in agony.

Lummukem stumbled up the steps, breathless, an arrow poking out of their chest. The dragon broke the shaft, leaving a shorter, splintered stick protruding from between their ribs.

"You are wounded!" Kulak cried out. He touched a paw pad over the dragon's chest, where a trail of blood flowed beneath the broken arrow.

"We will live," Lummukem assured him. Olo perched on Lummukem's shoulder once more and began pecking at the intruding object. "Olo, stop. We deal with wounds later. Now we push on."

Only one shielded guard remained on the steps, shaking in fear. Kulak aimed the pharolith toward him, making it impossible for the pale man to get a good look over his shield.

"Move out of our way and we won't hurt you," Sterjall said, hoping the guard understood Miscamish. "Leave the city, it might not be safe in here for much longer." He made a clear gesture of sheathing Leif, but as he finished tucking the blade away, he felt a warning in the threads.

The spearman made his move.

Sterjall took a step toward the incoming attack, letting the shaft of the spear rub over his elytra armor, then slammed his body against the shield. He unsheathed Leif and thrust it blindly. When he pulled his arm back, his dagger dripped with the soldier's blood. The Oxruk dropped shield-first and banged noisily down the steps as if riding a sled.

Sterjall wiped the blood off the black glass, feeling nauseated and angry.

"We must keep going," Kulak said, pulling at his arm. "It was his fault, not yours. We must hurry." His ears suddenly perked up, his whiskers twitching, feeling something odd in the flow of the threads. A tremor shook the stairs, forcing them to hold on to the walls.

"More rooms collapsing?" Sterjall guessed.

"No," Kulak said, eyes wide and dilated. "Okridrolom. It is opening."

The root next to them began vibrating, releasing a shower of dust.

"Shit—how?" Sterjall started. "We need to get out of here, now!"

They hurried up the stairway, stepping over several dead Oxruk whose bodies lay sprawled on the steps. A scream. Metal scraping. A guttural roar. They stopped as they reached the top of another flight, gaping at the sight of a dozen more Oxruk fighting against a giant beaver.

"Gwit!" Sterjall called out.

The guards turned, alarmed by the voice. Kulak quickly aimed his pharolith. The Oxruk cowered, giving Gwit a chance to trample them. The castoroides trotted down the steps to meet the newcomers, his fur bloodied, crisscrossed by slashes from clawed gauntlets.

Lummukem rushed forward to finish the guards off before they could find their footing. They pulled their halberd out of the last body, then looked up the stairway. "Puuja!" they exclaimed. The girl was shambling down the steps, holding Pol in her bruised arms. The boy was unconscious. Okrisilv rested upon his chest.

"I'm okay…" Puuja said. "Help Pol."

Lummukem scrambled to them and picked the boy up in their scaled arms, not caring about the searing pain from their chest wound.

"The temple is opening," Puuja croaked weakly. "Follow Gwit, he will show us to the… show us to…" She toppled forward. Lummukem barely stopped her from hitting the ground. Kulak hurried to help, taking the girl into his arms.

Gwit grunted weakly, leading them to one of the side openings. He limped through the new tunnel, thick hide and thicker tail leaving a trail of blood with every step.

They only encountered one group of Oxruk as they climbed the turns of the new tunnel. Sterjall growled at them, now holding the kenzir stone in one hand and Leif in the other, and managed to scare them away from their path. They had not seemed interested in fighting either way, and were merely trying to flee.

Many flights higher, Gwit pointed his sharp incisors at a set of tightly spiraling steps. He slumped to the ground, exhausted at the mere idea of having to climb any higher.

"Ishke'ísuk, wake up," Lummukem said, peeking inside their bag. The basilisk was still there resting, trying to heal. "You must tell Gwit to use his last bit of strength to turn back into his primal form," Lummukem urged the Nu'irg. "We will carry him, so you can have a companion with you."

Ishke'ísuk partially uncurled himself, gazing toward the giant rodent. Gwit watched him with bloodied eyes, then with noticeable effort began to turn translucent. The refractive smoke shrunk to the ground, leaving a little hazel dormouse covered in minuscule cuts. Breathing harshly, he curled into a perfect ball, concealing his injured face with his fuzzy tail. Sterjall carefully picked Gwit up and placed him in Lummukem's bag. "Take care of him, Ishke." The basilisk wrapped his tail around the dormouse, then closed his eyes.

The wayfarers continued up the tight steps, and at the top found a locked hatch in the ceiling with hinges made to swing inward. Lummukem stuck their halberd into the locking mechanism.

"Move back," they said to the others, then twisted and pulled on their halberd. The rusty locks snapped, and the hatch suddenly opened; with it fell a small avalanche of rocks, dirt, and snow. They climbed out of the hole first before hoisting the children up behind them, then stopped, gazing at the surrounding devastation.

They were standing upon the ruins of the ancient Sehján capital of Kissumar, with the trunk of the dome rising only a few city blocks away from them. The broken city was overgrown and decayed. Few walls and towers still stood, strangled by ivies. Scarce trees grew atop the rocky mesa, but enough soil had accumulated to provide sustenance for brushes and ferns of all kinds. Snow kept falling, piling into a soft coating in the crevices of the dilapidated structures. The skies had partially cleared, lighting the ruins with the dim blueness of the nighttime arudinn.

"Hide the light, or guards will see us," Lummukem warned Sterjall. The wolf stowed the pharolith away.

"We must hurry northeast," Kulak said. "Shamans were sent there to help break the beaver dams. We can escape with them."

The group rushed over the ruins, but slowed their pace when they heard voices ahead. A family of Oxruk was pushing its way out of another hatch. Out came a woman holding a young girl, nearly identical in posture to Kulak holding Puuja. The pale woman froze at the sight of the strange figures. She seemed terrified. A man pulled on her arm and fled with her.

A tremor shook their feet. They looked back and saw a cloud of dust billowing over a distant portion of the Dohao Mesa.

"The tunnels are already collapsing," Sterjall said. "The roots are digging in." He held his breath. *This isn't how it had to happen*, he thought, *so many of them are going to die.*

Another tremor. More hatches opened nearby, more pale figures emerged, but they all appeared to be regular citizens. The wayfarers tried to move swiftly so that fewer of the emerging Oxruk would spot them, but they couldn't run at full speed while carrying the children.

A guard spotted them. He was surely aware of the pointlessness of trying to fight, running away instead, but not without first blowing out a signal on a war horn.

"We have miles to go," Kulak fretted. "They will be coming for us soon."

"We will send for help," Lummukem said. They pulled at one of their pendants and uncapped a seedpod filled with soot, inhaling a small dose. They whispered quiet words to Olo; the herald flew away in an instant.

More tremors, more portions of the mesa caved in. The ruins of the Sehján capital crunched down to fill the holes the Oxruk had dug.

"*Gunnxith!*" called a man near them. Three Oxruk guards approached, but they kept their distance.

"Stop!" Sterjall cried out in Miscamish. "We don't want to hurt any more of you. Go to your other cities, the ones that are not under the vines. You will be safe there. Leave us alone."

But the pale guards did not understand. They charged toward Kulak, who was struggling to carry Puuja's unconscious body, forcing Sterjall to defend him. The Oxruk were not working in unison; they had no strategy, only fear, but they were not holding back. Sterjall moved swiftly, blocking claws before punching and slicing. Once the Oxruk were down or stunned, he sprayed a Brime Strike to blind them, then hurried Kulak and Lummukem onward.

Other Oxruk heard the guards' cries for help. Most ignored them, trying to save themselves, but some heeded the calls. Kulak and Lummukem tried to hold their blowguns in one arm while carrying the twins in the other. They had no paralyzing darts left, so they used the darts of the orchid-faced frog, which caused maddening hallucinations and a burning feeling throughout the body. The guards struck by the darts ran away, feeling their bodies ablaze, crying out in torment.

Sterjall had not wanted to use the pharolith, for it would act as a beacon and alert more enemies, but they had no way to move unnoticed any longer. He took out the lamp. The luminous beam was streaked by horizontally blowing snow—a lighthouse in a tempest. He aimed it at any Oxruk rushing to attack them. As the guards shielded their eyes, Kulak and Lummukem hit them with darts, making them writhe in fear and agony. The other guards began to believe it was the light itself that was cursed, so they kept back, praying the ill-fated beam would not send their souls spiraling through the stomachs of the Tar Serpent.

"We have few darts remaining," Kulak said.

The last darts Lummukem and Kulak had were the deadly ones. The next Oxruk who rushed them landed at Kulak's feet with a dart in his forehead, mouth foaming; he would be dead in mere heartbeats.

More hatches opened near them, dozens of Oxruk gushing out in streams. Another guard attacked, but quickly slumped lifelessly to the ground, a dart protruding from his leg. Another threw a spear at them, which Lummukem deflected with their armored tail.

Too many Oxruk were converging on them now. The guards advanced cautiously, wary of their opponents' seemingly magical attacks, not understanding the blowguns and overestimating the power of the blinding beacon.

Sterjall's pharolith suddenly lit upon one of the armored priestesses, whose hammered-metal plates shined even brighter than the white-robed guards, reflecting the lamp's beam straight back at him. She lifted a clawed arm and yelled out an order. All the guards formed a circle and took a defensive stance blocking the path, forcing the wayfarers to stop. If the group wanted to continue, they'd have to go through her.

"Shit," Sterjall muttered, afraid of the power the priestess commanded. "If they attack all at once, we're dead."

The priestess struck her two clawed gauntlets together, shooting out sparks that, despite not being as bright as Sterjall's, were somehow more menacing.

The wolf halted, keeping his light aimed at the priestess. Kulak blew a dart, but it bounced off her thin-slitted helm. He placed Puuja on the ground and took out his knife. Lummukem set Pol next to Puuja so they could wield their halberd with both hands.

"Get ready…" Sterjall said. "Do not let them get to the twins."

"*Sahhumei!*" the priestess yelled, holding her arms up, crossing her claws over her head.

"*Sahhumei!*" she repeated.

A shrill scream echoed from the darkness of nearby ruins, which briefly made the priestess flinch, but she kept her posture and determination. "*Hishath!*" she yelled, swinging her arms down with a sparking, metallic shrill. All at once, dozens of guards rushed forward with their claws pulled back, ready to strike.

A terrifying roar blared from the dark. The priestess was suddenly knocked to the ground and stomped on by giant paws. Blu trampled his way in, slicing at the Oxruk guards, with Alaia holding onto the saddle while Olo flew above her. Pichi vaulted right behind, her serrated fangs tearing at the pale bodies.

A handful of guards dodged the attacks and advanced toward Sterjall, but Lummukem spun their halberd with a Twin Crescents, chopping off their feet before they arrived. Sterjall fought back-to-back with Kulak, protecting the unconscious twins.

"Hold on, Gwoli!" Alaia shouted from atop Blu as he charged through the guards. She extended an arm and helped pull Sterjall onto Blu's saddle, then made the smilodon run in a protective circle while Pichi recovered the others.

As they rode through the collapsing ruins, more guards appeared ahead. Sterjall aimed the pharolith at them, confusing them enough that they could not react. The smilodons jumped over the disoriented Oxruk, leaving them in the dust of the crumbling twin capitals.

"Thank you," Sterjall said to Alaia, his heart beating in his throat. "You showed up right on time." He was holding tightly to her elytra armor. "You got one too, huh? Nice colors."

"Focus, Gwoli," she said. "Are you hurt? Is everyone—"

"I'm fine, but Lummukem, the twins, the Nu'irgesh, all need help. Shit, I thought we were dead. I mean, I've thought that about a dozen times today. But back there, I was certain it was the end."

"Olo came to fetch me," Alaia said, "and then I saw your pharolith from far away, so it was easy to find you. I had to leave Theggo and the others. The Oxruk set up an ambush from underground, but our ambush worked better."

The smilodons slowed their pace as they reached the northern edge of the mesa. The wind blew hard at the cliffside, but the snow was mostly done falling for the night. Down in the lakebed, the battle had left many dead and wounded. The expanse was covered by a foot of water, with hundreds of small holes draining it in vortices. They could barely see the bodies from their height, but the white robes of the Oxruk stood out bright and tiny like termites. Many of them were now climbing up the opposite cliff, but the Sehján had already retreated beyond the uplift.

"We need to get to the shamans at the dams," Alaia said. "They will let the rest of the Sehján know we are on our way back."

Farther east, they reached a now emptied lake where a troop of shamans was holding off an attack from the Oxruk. Blu and Pichi quickly helped take the enemies down. The shamans thanked the smilodons and riders for their aid, then blew on a large horn. Their call to withdraw from the fight was echoed by another horn farther north, and then by another west of it.

The smilodons ran across the top of a shattered castoroides dam—still freely spilling torrents of water—and jumped over loose logs until they reached the far side. They galloped north, then west toward the Klad Üo, where they found the Sehján protecting Fel Kamman, the floating island they had arrived upon. A skirmish had broken out at the shore, with a wall of Oxruk soldiers attempting to tie the island down with ropes so that the okruwom could not swim away with it.

Blu and Pichi bolted over the unsuspecting soldiers, leaping across the water and onto the island. "Carry them to safety!" Lummukem ordered a crowd of Sehján warriors, helping lower Puuja and Pol.

"Take out the pharoliths!" Alaia called from atop Blu. "In Pichi's bag!"

Kulak rummaged through the saddlebag and took out four more pharoliths, distributing them among the wayfarers, then handed the last one to Tsei, who had rushed over after seeing the twins return.

Theggo appeared from the shadows and stopped next to Sterjall, holding up a shield to protect the two of them from incoming arrows. "Glad to see you are safe," the admiral said. "I would've been more glad if you hadn't taken so damn long. Where is Jessha?"

Sterjall didn't reply. He simply aimed his pharolith at the enemy while taking shelter behind Theggo's shield. All pharolith wielders advanced, blinding the Oxruk across the water while Sehján warriors cut the ropes that were preventing the island from escaping. Many arrows flew at them, but the sightless archers missed their targets.

Once enough ropes were cut, the island began to drift from the shore. The last few ropes were severed by the force of the swimming okruwom, dragging with them a handful of Oxruk who would not let go of the ropes. The castoroides met the Oxruk from beneath the water, drowning them, then returned to their positions to haul the island.

"Take us home, Lakemother!" Tsei cried out. Her warriors cheered as Fel Kamman drifted into the cold night.

The Silvfröash, Alaia, and Theggo collapsed, utterly exhausted.

"We are alive…" Sterjall exhaled. "We made it… Thank you, Alaia… Thank you."

"You are welcome, Gwoli," she said.

"And you look amazing in that armor, truly. Fits you well."

"Almost as girlish as yours," she replied with a tired grin.

CHAPTER SIXTY-ONE

THE CABAL

Silv-Thaar Valaran's legion had celebrated passionately after exterminating the Khardok Miscam tribe of the Moonrise Dome. The sapfire cannons, together with the trusting nature of the tribe, had made it much too easy for them. Pints of braaw had flowed all night, but the Silv-Thaar had tired of the public celebrations. He left his troops to have a more private gathering with his old arbalister squad.

The seven squad mates gathered at a spacious house near the Moonrise Dome's trunk. It was rustic, but comfortable and well-supplied. There was no fireplace, only a firepit with a hole in the roof to let the smoke out. The arbalisters brought bottles upon bottles of a strong liquor they found in the cellar of the dwelling, then sat around the fire to celebrate.

"Y-you should've seen their… their fucking faces," Armsmaster Shea Lu said through a slurred cackle, then gulped directly from a bottle; it was not her first that evening. "Th-they jis' stood there in front of the cannons till I gave the order. What in Khest were they thinking?"

"We only lost one soldier," Trevin said while picking his long nose. "Some idiot who marched with his shield held too high and didn't see a drop in front of him. Broke his neck."

Valaran shook his furred head. "Honestly, I was expecting to go back to Monarch Hallow with half, maybe fewer of our combined troops." He poked at the fire with his spear. "We were lucky. All we lost was a few platoons at the battle of Azash. But we got all those Elmaren weaklings in the end."

"Not thanks to *you!*" Shea said. "I ssscorched those fuckers. You merely picked off the suh-survivors."

Valaran stabbed his spear into the ground and leaned back, not wanting to feed Shea more fuel. Dishu, his pet marten, curled up in his lap, finding comfort in the warmth of the fire.

Fjorna was quiet. She held the pinniped mask in front of her, losing herself in its details.

"Who do you think Hallow will give the mask to?" Aurélien asked. "Behler?"

Valaran was the one to answer. "He doesn't trust Behler. Gino or Korten would be my guess. I don't think he trusts any of his other generals."

"Yourself included," Osef added from the shadows.

Shea took another gulp and slouched forward. "Asss far as I can guess, he'll just give it to another Muh-Miscam traitor like Luhásu, Markhor, whatever that goat calls hershelf. He stopped caring 'bout his own people looong ago. All he cares about is collecting his da-damnable masks."

"Keep your voice down, Shea," Fjorna ordered. "There are soldiers outside these walls."

"So fucking what? They think the same way. Redsshtag practically abandoned our navy at Montano. That horned prick left them with no supplies."

"He has antlers, not horns," Aurélien helpfully corrected.

"*Fuck* his antlers," Shea continued. "Y'knew this was coming at some point, you all jis' didn't wanna s-say it out loud. I spoke to the admirals, and they all feel… feel… feel the same way. They trusted that Red Bastard at first, believed in him, but now that he's em-emnamored with his masks, swooning over new lands, they feel deserted, dispensable. They are looking for a real leader to follow."

Osef paced around the large room, closing every window and door he could find.

"It's the same with the archers," Muriel agreed. "They follow you, Fjorna, because you trained them. Because you showed them that you care for them. And the captains and even the marshals, while on the road to Azash, they told me they were glad they were picked for *this* mission. They'd rather follow anyone but the Red Stag. He makes them feel superfluous, cares more for his elk, even if he sends them to die in heaps of meat."

"He's got a lot of them fooled, though," Osef added, "with his quaar spear and shield. His ploy is working. Many do believe he carries the favor of the Twin Gods."

"The citizens, perhaps," Muriel said. "But most soldiers, especially after being left behind by him, can see through his deceit."

"We have quite a large army of our own here," Trevin added, scanning the eyes of his companions. "A faithful one, one that believes in our cause. We have a fucking naval force with us. And we have two masks, just as many as Hallow has in his possession."

"Don't be obtuse," Valaran groaned. "Hallow's strategy is… imperfect, but he's gotten us this far."

"You always take his side," Shea snorted. "F-figures. You really that uhfraid of him? Or… or perhaps you feel you *owe* him something?"

"Shut that whore mouth, Shea," Valaran spat. "Don't think I don't see through your sneers. If you want to say something, just—"

"I'll say it. You are a coward, that's wuh-what I think. What did ye have to do to get your filthy mask? Take his red cock? You elk-fucking v-vermin."

"Enough!" Fjorna snapped. "That's enough, Shea. I won't entertain any more accusations. We are trying to solve a problem here. It is true that we have as many masks as Hallow by now, or perhaps one fewer if he's secured the Archstone one. But one thing we do not have is the power of the spirits, of the Nu'irgesh."

"The musteloid one escaped from right under our noses," Aurélien recalled.

"And we would've captured the pinniped one if Osef had worked faster instead of letting that stupid seal turn herself to mush," Valaran muttered, wanting to slap someone. His marten felt the tension and scurried away.

"Fuck you," Osef said. "You were right there and didn't come to help! But who cares what you think anyway. We know you went behind our backs to get your little mask, you traitorous rat."

"Who the fuck are you—"

"Stop," Fjorna said, more mutedly this time, yet somehow with more command. The room went quiet. "Unless we work together, with no enmities, all that we are discussing is pointless." She stood and paced around the firepit. "I hate that egotistical asshole," she continued, even more quietly. "I hate that I trusted him for so long, that I believed in his strategy, in his word. And I'm glad you are speaking up now, in private, but I'm afraid what you are suggesting is much more complex than you make it seem."

"You don't yet know what we are suggesting," Shea said, dropping the empty bottle and stumbling to her feet. She staggered around the room, directing a piercing stare toward Fjorna.

Fjorna narrowed her eyes. "Then say what you mean, Armsmaster, and be clear about it. This is not the time to mince words."

Shea swiftly took out her knife and in one clean swipe, slashed Valaran's throat.

The raccoon fell forward, struggling to hold his trachea in place, gurgling repulsively as his ears were set aflame in the firepit.

The woman grinned viciously. "Is that clear enough fo—"

"Shea! Damn stupid—" Osef jumped toward her, trying to take her knife away. The others were too stunned to react.

"Scorch your flesh sixteenfold!" Shea barked through the struggle. "You bald piece of shit! Y-you wanted this!"

"Stop at once!" Fjorna yelled, trying to pull Valaran out of the fire as blood gushed out of his slit throat. "Both of you, that's an order!"

Shea pulled herself from under Osef's grip and tried to stab him. Osef grabbed her knife hand and twisted it, pointing the blade back toward her. Despite the searing pain, she would not let go. She shoved Osef backward and charged at him with all her weight, but in her drunkenness stumbled to the side, allowing him to spin her around and slam her against the wall.

Osef stepped away. Shea still tightly held her knife, the blade now lodged in her sternum.

"Fuck…" she gasped.

"Shea!" Fjorna cried, still holding Valaran's body, putting pressure on his neck in a futile effort to staunch the bleeding.

Armsmaster Shea Lu looked at her bleeding chest, then up to Fjorna. "They… they will fffollow you, Chief…" she croaked. "They will follow you… anywhere. Lead them."

She collapsed to the ground.

Fjorna's heart thumped. When she looked down, she was no longer holding Silv-Thaar Valaran, but Crescu, his half-burned face still smoking, his cheeks and lips covered in blisters. Krostsilv was crackling in the fire. Fjorna lowered Crescu's body to the floor and reached into the flames to rescue the mask, burning her arm and singeing her deformed brows.

"What in Khest do we do now?" Fjorna whispered through gritted teeth.

The five remaining arbalisters sat around a small table so that they could speak more quietly, though Osef remained standing, pacing back and forth agitatedly. The two masks waited on the table between them. The two dead bodies waited farther down the room, near the fire.

"Was this your fucking idea, Osef?" Fjorna asked.

"I. Never. Told her. To do that," he grumbled, stung by the accusation. "She was drunk. If it's any consolation, I think Crescu never deserved that mask, but he was still a friend. I didn't want him *dead*. I thought we'd finally make him turn against Hallow, that this was our chance to bring him back into our family. I thought he'd keep his stupid raccoon face, and you'd take Gwonlesilv for yourself. That's what I fucking thought." He finally dropped his weight heavily into a chair.

Aurélien picked up the musteloid mask and examined its complex beauty. Islav and Aness—her two green magpies—perched on her shoulders and observed the mask with her.

"I always thought you deserved this one, Fjorna," she said. "You killed the Miscam witch who wore it before, then handed it to Hallow on a silver platter. He should've gifted it to you then. And if not then, after Jaxon died." She held the mask forward and lifted her pointed chin toward Fjorna. "Like Shea said, they will follow you. Lead them. Lead *us*. Our army knows this mask already. They know what it represents."

Fjorna held the mask only with her eyes. "It will look like I betrayed Crescu. That I killed him and Shea."

"No, it will look like they killed each other," Osef said. "Which is close enough to what truly happened. Shea hated his guts and was not afraid to say so publicly. We place the bodies in a clever arrangement, make a big scene by breaking some chairs and bottles, then have soldiers come see what's going on, while we pretend we were unable to stop the scuffle. They'll back us up. No one will believe we killed two of our own squad, they know us better than that. Either way, it was Shea who betrayed Crescu, not us."

"Take it, Fjorna," Aurélien said, nodding and slowly blinking.

Fjorna picked up Krostsilv, held it for a breath, then placed it back on the table. She picked up Gwonlesilv instead and pushed it to Aurélien's chest.

"Only if you teach me," she declared.

Aurélien examined the pinniped mask. It was smooth, too smooth, in direct contrast with Aurélien's scarified face. Only upon close inspection could she see the infinitude of intricate details that broke up the polished shapes.

"Will you teach me?" Fjorna insisted. "You are a shaman. You will learn faster than I ever will. Show me how to wield it, for we'll need to act fast and convince both the infantry and navy that we know what we are doing."

They heard screaming outside, then a frantic knocking on the door.

"Shit…" Fjorna muttered. "Move the bodies, make sure it looks like they were fighting each other."

More hurried rapping against the door rattled it on its hinges.

"Silv-Thaar! The wolverines!" a soldier yelled from outside. "They've escaped!"

"Help me with this," Fjorna commanded. Together she and Aurélien tossed Crescu partially back into the fire, then threw Krostsilv on the ground next to him, placing Shea nearby holding the knife she had used to cut his throat. Trevin and Muriel tossed tables around and broke some bottles, then screamed for help. Osef hurriedly unlocked the doors.

"The wolverines have escaped!" a soldier yelled as he rushed in, followed by five sentinels. "We need the Silv-Thaar to—"

The soldier's jaw dropped as he saw the two dead bodies by the fire and Krostsilv lying next to them like a charcoal skull.

"Bring a medic!" Fjorna ordered the stunned soldier, pretending to be assisting Crescu. "Hurry!"

Gloomy was the air when morning arrived. A few of the jarv wolverines had been captured overnight and placed in cages once more, but most had fled into the forests as soon as their mindlocks had been severed, mauling dozens of guards while making their escape.

The army gathered within the low mists, filling a field near the Moonrise Dome's trunk. The officers stood at the front, so that they might better hear the story. Osef Windscar, standing atop a Khardok temple built of stone and seashells, was telling them a carefully curated account of how Crescu Valaran and Shea Lu had died, claiming that Shea had wanted to take Gwonlesilv for herself, but that Silv-Thaar Valaran had tried to stop her. The soldiers who had rushed in the previous night corroborated the story.

"Are you ready?" Aurélien Knivlar asked Fjorna, her face in shadows.

"Almost," Fjorna Daro answered, watching Osef through a small window at the temple's back. She finished combing her hair, letting it cascade onto her right shoulder while her shaved side was kept unobstructed. Although that entire half of her face had been mangled by Lago long ago, she now displayed it openly, proudly showcasing the torn ranking insignia on her left temple. She rose to her feet and swung her crossbow's strap over her shoulder. "May Yza's shadow bless us sixteenfold," she said, and walked out.

Just as Osef finished answering the last of the questions from the officers, Fjorna stepped in front of him and lifted Krostsilv into the air, the mask shining darkly against the parting mists.

"Arbalisters!" she pronounced thunderously. "I come here with news that I wish were not as dire. You know me, you know us. Those of you who recently joined us in this campaign—infantry of land and sea who we have come to see as siblings—you may not know us as closely as those who trained in our commons, but we share one heart. I have witnessed your bravery, your determination. And I have seen with how much more conviction you have battled here, with us, than in the battles before we split paths with Monarch Hallow."

She waited for the crowd to quiet further. Aurélien stepped up beside her, holding Gwonlesilv in front of her, the pinniped mask a dark void over her belly.

"We have all been deceived," Fjorna continued, choosing her words with care. "This war we are fighting is the right war. The cause we fight for is the right cause. But the person we have been following has forsaken us. He is no true leader. He has betrayed the Empire!"

Some anger flared among the ranks, but it was quickly drowned out by the overpowering mutters of agreement.

"Monarch Hallow. The Red Stag. You have witnessed his true self," she said sternly. "He is overcome by greed, by bloodlust, by power. He cares more about goats, about deer, than about the Negians he trained and fought with. I, too, believed in him at first. I understand what it's like to be inspired by lofty promises, to wish within my very marrow that the stories are true. But none of them are true! He claims to hold the blessing of the twin gods, yet that shield he carries is not the Shield of Creation—it's merely a Miscam artifact I delivered to him myself. The spear he carries is not Takhamún's spear, but a replica forged by trickster artisans. I know many of you figured this out, or suspected as much. Yet still we followed him, because we wanted to believe in a greater cause. And thus we have strayed far from the path of righteousness. But we can still correct our course!"

She gazed around the assembled army, measuring the conviction in the troops. "We have the means now to turn the tide in this war," she said, nodding to Aurélien, who lifted Gwonlesilv high. "We control not only the might of the Negian fleet, but will soon have mastery over the sea creatures themselves. We hold the riches of the shattered Queendom, and the power of two Silvesh."

She tightened her grip on the musteloid mask and looked straight into its empty eyes. She did not need to fake the tear that slid down her cheek or her suddenly cracking voice. "In… In memory of Crescu Valaran… Or Crescu of the Khull Ford, as I knew him when we were children, I will shoulder the burden of his mask. But I will not do so alone, for Aurélien Knivlar will stand by my side and teach me how to wield it, as she herself learns to master the mask of pinnipeds."

Fjorna wiped her cheek and straightened her back. "This is how we will rebuild our broken realms. By the might of the sea, by the power of our resolve. Join me, join us, as we form the greatest force Noss has ever seen. As we shatter the scepters of Zovaria's Arch Sedecims, as we take the masks they have stolen from us, and recapture the artifacts fallen into Hallow's deceitful hands!"

As the crowd roared with renewed conviction, Fjorna unslung her crossbow and held it high. At the sound of her bolt releasing into the skies, two of her arbalisters—Muriel and Trevin—approached behind her, holding twin banners up for all to see. The banners were a driftwood gray, emblazoned with a bright yellow sigil with a greenish tinge—the color of the sickly flames of sapfire. The sharp sigil was in the shape of an anchor blended seamlessly into the forms of a loaded crossbow.

"For now, we will call ourselves the Cabal!" Fjorna yelled over the commotion. "I do not ask you to help us mend the broken states, but to erect a new empire, one that we will build together as siblings. One that yet has no name, but that will bring unity in the prosperous years to come. Under this new banner we will fight! And down will fall the bloodied sigils of the Red Stag, down to burn into oblivion!"

There were only a handful of defectors within the newly-minted Cabal, and they were swiftly dealt with. All trace of the Red Stag's dominion was destroyed; his sigil erased, his banners shredded. Even their flagship, the *Black Spear*, was renamed to the *Ballista*, and at its top the new yellow-and-gray banner flew.

While the army gathered their resources and readied to depart by sea, Aurélien worked to understand the power of her new Silv. A mere three days after first donning Gwonlesilv, she found her half-form. She had been swimming in the warm reefs of the Tumultuous Ocean, letting herself be taken by the huge waves. She tumbled back to shore breathlessly only to return to the sea, pushed to the shore over and over again. After hundreds of taxing tumbles, her mind stopped focusing, following through with the same motions until she eventually found herself flat ashore, fully exhausted.

Aurélien faced the skies, eyes glistening behind the mask's eyeholes. The firmament was a bizarre sight, as the dome was already partially opened, leaving the daytime arudinn broken into polygonal shapes that showcased the blackness of the night sky behind it. Equally bizarre was the sight below, that of Aurélien's naked body. Her scarified patterns extended as glossy bumps beginning at her navel, swirling outward like a galaxy of compound twirls and coils, tracing spirals even up to her smiling lips. Those scars had been with her since her coming of age; they would remain with her in all her forms.

Up above, between the daytime and nighttime skies, Aurélien spotted two twirling, winged shapes. Islav and Aness circled hypnotically in their iridescent-green dance. Aurélien let herself be taken by their persuasive calls.

"*Va jambradikh frulv halvet alrull*," she said to herself, to her magpies, to the sky, to the sea.

She felt lightheaded, ethereal.

When she looked back down at her body, it was speckled in gray. Her feet were flat and fin-like, her hands glossy and webbed. Though the surface of her body looked smooth and rubbery, it was coated with densely packed fur, yet her scarified bumps remained as furless spots funneling eternal spirals toward her belly. Silv-Thaar Knivlar felt her piercing fangs and understood herself to be a leopard seal, like the ones she had seen hunting seabirds during Winter at the Lequa Sea, when she had just begun her training as an arbalister. She grinned sharply.

***

With Aurélien's mentorship, Fjorna Daro found her half-form only a week later. The Cabal was already making its way southwest, sailing with the stolen Negian fleet and a large portion of its infantry. The ships had docked at a port on the southern edge of the now broken Elmaren Queendom. While they resupplied, Fjorna ventured into the forest to hunt.

Through her mask's new sight, the forest brightened anew. It became more than a place, coalescing into a feeling, a memory. She reverently held Whisper—her treasured crossbow—and smelled the sandalwood stock, the bone and copper inlays, the yak sinew drawstrings. The *tchtchtchwick* of her weapon reloading sounded like a lullaby, and she was suddenly transported back to her home in the Fjarmallen forests. Like an innocent child she once again felt, remembering the days when her father had taught her how to hunt, how to hide in the snow, how to move swiftly and invisibly among the whiteness that blanketed the trees.

She was a predator.

She was a shadow made of light.

With her fur shimmering in the gloom, Silv-Thaar Daro returned from her hunt in her half-form of a pristinely white ermine—pristine in every way, except for her grotesquely disfigured face.

Chapter Sixty-Two

A New Strategy

It was a cold start to the year. The vast Graalman plains south of the Archstone Dome were covered in snow. Despite the lack of wind, the biting stillness cracked the skin of the marching legions.

The Red Stag wore an icy scowl while he rode on Tremor, his trusty Jartadi steed. Tremor was now more white than black due to the snow covering his thick body; he was a sizable horse, yet he looked like a pony when compared to the garrison horses the Negians had found within the Archstone Dome, who were smarter, thicker of bone, and mightier in stature than any in the New World. The monarch had briefly considered riding one of the giants, but discarded the idea, not wishing to appear small.

Silv-Thaar Baneras rode his own Jartadi steed, a piebald warhorse named Albedo, catching up to the monarch with a soft trot. He hesitated, opening and closing his mouth without saying anything.

"What is it, Baneras?" the Red Stag asked. "Speak your mind."

"I… You aren't going to like this, Monarch Hallow," he replied. Baneras's long face seemed somber, his ears flattening over his zebra-striped helm. "A herald flew in, bringing dire news."

"Spit it out. What does Urcai have to say?"

The steppe wild horse fidgeted with his longbow, rubbing the hard tips of his hoofed fingers over the taut string. "Uh… a few things," he began. "There was a slave revolt at the Lequa Dome. The stationed forces contained it, but the survivors stole our ships and fled to sea."

"Fled? To the sea within the dome? What do they plan to do there other than freeze or drown?"

"They are escaping. Or waiting to escape, more likely. The dome… well… it's opening. There have been tremors. Urcai reports they found many dead by the axis, and that the lattice and the core vine have vanished, like how it happened at Anglass."

The Red Stag tightened his grip on Tremor's reins. "I told Behler to send reinforcements," he hissed through his grinding teeth.

"He did. He won the battle, overall, but somehow the enemy still got to the temple. They waited till our soldiers were drunk, while they celebrated the Day of the Lost. Same reports as what was seen at Anglass—a giant white wolf, a huge boar with a forehead horn, a giant bear with fur of gold, but there was also a report of a jarv wolverine. Behler's scouts must've missed that one."

"How can they command a wolverine? Only Silv-Thaar Valaran can give orders to the musteloids."

"That's the other thing, Lorr…"

The Red Stag could feel his blood boiling just from that superfluous formality, as it indicated weakness, shame, and fear. He sensed worse news coming. He simply grunted without looking at the strong-jawed Silv-Thaar.

"The thing is… Crescu… Silv-Thaar Valaran… is dead."

The Red Stag pulled on the reins, making Tremor rear.

"Show me the message at once."

They stopped the army's march and ordered the troops to settle for the day, so that the monarch could properly read each and every word Viceroy Urcai had sent to him. Soldiers from the Graalman Horde erected Monarch Hallow's pavilion within a deep canyon of dark sandstone, sheltering it from the evening winds. When his tent was ready, the Red Stag stomped in through the tarp door and pointed to a group of chairs. Silv-Thaar Baneras, Silv-Thaar Markhor, and General Korten dus Fer swiftly took their seats.

The Red Stag paced around the pavilion, one hand gripping tight his antlers, as if he were about to snap them off. He had lost command of two domes, which were now opening up their resources and releasing numerous slaves. He had lost control of Krostsilv, and of the archers and infantry who had pledged allegiance to the backstabbing arbalisters. He had lost the majority of his fleet to this traitorous faction commanded by Fjorna Daro. And he had lost the Moonrise Dome entirely, and with it, the mask of pinnipeds.

He needed a new strategy.

Monarch Hallow took time to calm himself, then at last said, "We nearly lost it all in the White Desert." His words sounded more like a croak. He lifted a fist as if looking for something to strike, then lowered it again. "We were careless," he pointedly declared, deflecting the blame onto the group, even though the fault was entirely his own. "But we made it to the Archstone Dome. And if it hadn't been for you, Baneras, and how quickly you learned to control your mask, we would have perished there."

"It was Markhor's mentorship that allowed me to do so, Lorr," Baneras said. "She was hard as her horns on me, and it paid off."

Markhor simply sat quietly, her strange caprid pupils scanning the room.

"Perhaps," the Red Stag granted. "But we were pushing our luck. We need a way to take control of the masks much faster. We can't be sitting around waiting for the next Silv-Thaars to learn how to work them."

"But that's the shamans' sole purpose," Baneras said, a bit confused. "To be able to expediently control the masks when time is of the essence, even if temporarily."

"Expediently, yes, but that could still mean days. In the heat of battle, that is not quickly enough. If we were to kill one of our mask-wielding enemies, and we didn't control their power immediately, all the creatures from their army would disperse. But what if… What if we let the shamans practice?"

Baneras narrowed his eyes. "Practice how?"

"My mask, your own, and Markhor's we cannot use, for we'd lose the mindlocks on our creatures if we took them off, and the beasts would flee unless we contained them. But perhaps we could attempt this with the next mask we acquire, the mask of bats. Once we reach the Scoria Dome, we can properly train all our shamans with it."

"I thought Balastsilv would be mine to control," General Korten dus Fer interjected, trying to keep his voice from breaking. As commander of the Sixth Legion, he was next in line to become Silv-Thaar.

"It will be yours, Korten," the Red Stag assured him. "Just don't mention it publicly. I do not want Behler to lose hope. You and the shamans can train together, and Balastsilv will be yours to command once the training concludes. I only need them to learn the arts of mindlocking and shapeshifting, for whichever forms they might take next."

"What of Fjorna and her stolen masks?" Baneras asked. "Will they present a threat to us? What did their traitorous group call themselves again?"

"The Cabal," the Red Stag rasped with a disdainful sneer. "Urcai says they've taken to sea. They are likely trying to beat us to the Scoria Dome, but they will not succeed. We are much closer than they are. That mask, those wings, they will be ours, and they will grant us the advantage we need."

CHAPTER SIXTY-THREE

PURPLE

When Sterjall awoke after the battle, they were back in Kisdik, the floating capital of the Sehján Miscam. Fel Kamman, the island they had traveled on, had merged seamlessly with the larger structure.

Sunu was being tended to by a physicker, who had asked them to take their human form so he could more easily sew up their chest wound. The arrowhead had dug deep, but the physicker had been able to pull it out without causing too much more damage. Sunu opened a glass jar from which they pulled out a single leaf of the velvet knifewood that Ulésse had gifted to them when they left the Azurean Dome. They mixed it with animal fat and applied it to their wound.

Ishke'ísuk and Gwit were recovering quickly, yet despite healing much faster, they were both still quite tired and covered in scabs. The twins had regained consciousness, but they were stricken by their mother's death and would not speak of what had happened.

The Sehján called for no meetings that day; the time for strategy would come soon, after they had time to rest, to mourn. In honor of Ierun Jessha and all the warriors who had lost their lives, that evening they covered a small island in figurines woven from dried papyrus leaves to represent the fallen.

Three of Seshéni's dragoons had lost their lives as well. She would have preferred their bodies be buried in Noss's cradle of soil, but it was impossible to recover them. Instead, she placed her triskelion pendant upon the island—one spiraling circle to honor each of her brave warriors.

The island was released into the lake with a torch burning atop it. Hundreds of figurines caught fire as the island drifted out, to be consumed above their own reflections, to be taken to the Eternal Sea by Lakemother.

Pol and Puuja held hands and cried as the embers faded to smoke, but they did so quietly. They had mourned already, on their own, in the darkness.

Later that night, in the Queen's Lodge, Puuja and Pol sat side by side in the gathering chamber, feet dangling in the circular pool at the center. Okrisilv floated in the opening, dark quaar upon dark water, spinning aimlessly at the whims of the bouncing waves.

"Will it always hurt so bad?" Pol asked, staring at the mask.

Puuja wasn't sure whether Pol meant the pain of losing their mother, or the pain of wearing the mask. She guessed the latter.

"We don't think so. Mom said the pain is eventually carried away by Lakemother. Last time we tried it, it wasn't as hard as the first."

"It was, when we let go of our hands. Well, maybe not as bad, but still, it hurt a lot. There were so many kinds of pain. Did you feel them all too?"

"We did," Puuja said. "We felt all of it. Our pain together, the pain of every creature, the pain of Lakemother herself, for the water itself seems to have pain in it."

"Yes. And the pain of the Oxruk," Pol added solemnly.

Puuja quieted, observing her brother.

"Are we murderers?" Pol asked.

"What has gotten into you? We are heroes! We saved Okridrolom, that we did."

"But… their cities. Do you think they died in there?"

"We should hope so."

"Don't say that. We felt them, they suffered too. We felt their pain, and it was like our pain."

Puuja scooted closer, taking Pol's hand. "Pollomekh, we can't think that way. They are not the same as us. If anyone killed them, it was Okridrolom itself. The pale demons infested their roots, and Okridrolom found a way to get rid of them. And then Lakemother took them, and they deserved it."

She pulled the mask from the water and handed it to her brother. "And we recovered what was most precious to us, that we did. We did what was right."

Pol's eyes drifted away from the mask and instead rested upon the alcove where the opal crown of the Oxruk had been placed once more, although now there was no skull under it. "Do… Do you think we should give it back now?" he asked hesitantly.

"Give what back?"

"Their crown. We won the war, and we have Okrisilv. Do you think they should have their crown—"

"What nonsense! Don't speak like that." She then felt guilty about her harsh tone. "Pol… Mom is watching from the lakes beyond. She needs us to be strong, to look to the future now. She needs us to be bright and brave. We have to do what is right for the Sehján. We, together, that is what we'll do."

Pol pretended to smile. He put the mask back in the water, watching it bob up and down. "Do you think they will let us both wear it?"

"Why wouldn't they?" she asked, furrowing her brow.

"Okrisilv is only meant for women. There is only one heir."

"Sterjall wears women's armor, that he does. If they let him wear that, why couldn't they let us both wear Okrisilv?"

Pol shrugged, uncertain. He looked around the room. "Even this place, the 'Queen's Lodge.' It's not meant for a boy. I never fit in."

"Don't use that word, we don't like it."

"Sorry… We'll try… It's so strange, that you are Ierun Puuja now. It makes no sense."

Puuja lifted her chest and chin, then theatrically proclaimed, "Well, then as your all-powerful queen, our first order shall be that anyone gets to wear whatever they want to wear. That, and no more snail eggs for breakfast, ever again."

Pol's tight lips curled upward ever so slightly.

"What do you think you'll be? We'll be…" Pol asked, eyes still on the mask.

"Don't know. There are so many animals we like. Do you think we'll be the same animal?"

"Maybe. I… We want to be big and brave, like Lummukem."

She shook her head. "Can't be a dragon with Okrisilv, or anything like it."

"But we can have bigger teeth!" Pol said, placing his index and middle fingers under his nose, mimicking enormous incisors.

"Your lip paints are all faded," Puuja told him, reaching with her thumb to remove the last flecks of white paint from Pol's lips.

"Yours are all gone too," he said.

Puuja played with her long red hair, twirling it in her fingers while she thought. "We can't really know what we'll be. But whatever we end up as, we have to stick together."

"Yes. Always."

"Let's pray to Lakemother that we both become the same animal, no matter which one it is. That we must do."

Pol hesitantly nodded. His eyes kept on tracing the random pattern of Okrisilv's motions. He felt scared, but also excited.

The water stilled.

Not even the waves on the pool shifted enough to make a sound.

There came a rustling from the main tunnel. Their faces turned to find Sunu, walking quietly toward them with a mortar and pestle in their hands.

"You two should be asleep," the freckled shaman said.

"And why are *you* not asleep?" Puuja argued.

"Because we are not tired, and we have things to do."

"We are not tired, and we have things to do as well. Like sit here and talk. What are you eating?"

"It is not food we carry, but pigment to paint our scalp."

Pol leaned into Puuja's ear and whispered.

"We want to know why you speak like us," she said.

"Speak like you?"

"Like you are with someone else, but it's only you. Ishke'ísuk is not with you, and we don't see Olo around."

"We are not one, but many," Sunu said. "We are Sunu, and we are Lummukem. We are man, and we are woman. We are killer and healer. We are Laatu, and… and not Laatu. We live two lives, share two souls, just like you two are one, but are more than one."

Pol whispered in Puuja's ear again.

"Are you your own twin? That's what Pol said to ask you," she said.

Sunu considered. "Perhaps. We had never thought of us in that way. We may be, as we are many things, some of which we still don't know."

Sunu was about to kneel by the pool, but was interrupted once more, not by words, but simply by a stare. Pol was looking directly at them—something the boy struggled to do in most situations.

Pol leaned toward Puuja's ear once more.

"No, we can't!" Puuja whispered back.

"We should."

"But what if—"

Pol whispered again. Puuja rolled her eyes at him and sighed.

"We want to tell you a secret, but we are afraid of getting in trouble."

Sunu sat cross-legged in front of the water, across from the twins. "If trouble finds you, it will not be because of us, as we do not reveal that which is entrusted to our care. Our ears will listen to your secrets, but it would make us very happy if we could hear them directly from your own lips, Pollomekh the brave."

Pol nearly dashed to safety behind his sister, but he stopped himself. His lightly freckled cheeks were flushed with embarrassment, or perhaps pride.

"I…" he started, eyes bouncing between the water and the shaman. "We did not… We did not tell the others all that happened last night, that we did not." Pol's voice was methodical, calculated, with a childish pitch but a mature control. He continued abruptly, without all the hesitation. "We told everyone that it was Puuja who put on the mask and sat on the throne. True enough that was, but there is more truth. Puuja fell and would not wake up. Then it was… *I*… who put on the mask to ask Okridrolom to blossom. We did not want to tell the others, because Okrisilv is meant to be worn by the heir alone. Such is the way of the Sehján."

Sunu nodded and waited.

"We did not know who else to tell. We know what we did was sinful, but it was the only thing we could've done, that it was. And though it was wrong, it felt right. We want to share the mask again, but we are afraid of what the Sehján will think, and we don't want to get Puuja in trouble. The Silvesh are meant for one person, but you… you said you are not one, but many, so maybe you would understand."

Sunu looked into the boy's evasive eyes. "In Sunu-Lummukem's tribe, the Laatu tribe, there are laws similar to those of the Sehján," they said. "Laatu law did not allow allgenders to wear the Silvesh, yet here we are, as the voice of the reptilians. Laws are not immutable, they are made to satisfy the needs of their time. Times change, and so laws change with them. There is no time of greater change than that which you are living through right now. You have been careful, and that is commendable, but whether you choose to or not, Pol, you are now the Okrifröa as much as Puuja is. Whether others will accept you as such, it is not for our scalps to know yet, but you must begin by accepting yourself."

Pol tried his best to keep eye contact as he nodded gravely.

"As far as we know," Sunu continued, "no one of such a young age has ever wielded a Silv, as they are not meant to be worn until one comes of age, which you two have not. We believe that to be not a reason for shame, but pride. It is praiseworthy, admirable. We could not have achieved what you have at your young age."

"What do you think will happen to us?" Puuja asked. "To all the Sehján, we mean."

"Our scalp knows not. But tomorrow we will meet the chiefs to search for answers."

"But… Gwit will probably have to go help you. Will we go as well?"

"Can we?" Pol excitedly added.

"It is not up to us to decide. But if you were to come, our heart would be happy to have you with us."

Pol and Puuja smiled and remained quiet, at least for a little while.

Sunu uncrossed their legs and kneeled at the edge of the dark pool. They cupped a bit of water in their hands and dripped it into the mortar to blend with the pigments, ground the mixture with the pestle, then leaned forward to look at their unsteady reflection within the pool. They turned their head left and right, scrutinizing the fading patterns upon their scalp, then dipped a paintbrush into the purple liquid inside the mortar. The shaman squinted their violet-cast eyes as they moved the brush closer to their scalp.

Pol lightly kicked his feet around, rippling the water, making Sunu lose focus.

"We cannot see our reflection if the water is unsteady," Sunu said with no inflection. They waited until the waves settled, then began to drag the brush up again.

Pol kicked once more.

"We cannot see our reflection if we are too busy strangling children."

Pol's eyes widened.

Sunu smiled, and Pol slightly relaxed, but kept his guard up.

"What is it for?" the boy asked, not kicking the water any longer.

"It is to remind us, and others, of who we are."

"Can we help?"

Sunu lifted their head. In Pol's eyes, they saw that the boy was asking earnestly, kindly.

"Do you know how to draw?" Sunu asked, already regretting their words.

"No, no, it's more like this!" Puuja insisted, tracing a branching shape atop Sunu's head. She was drawing along the right half of Sunu's head, the side with patterns like those of skeletal leaves. Pol was working on their left side, using his fingers to draw shapes vaguely reminiscent of mushrooms. The reptilian glyph upon Sunu's forehead was thankfully not attempted, as it would not only have been too complex for the children, but unnecessary: for the Laatu, wearing the glyph was something that was done only for their first time wearing the mask, as a way of accepting the gifts of the clade.

A drop of kupógo gringralv—the purple snail pigment—dripped on top of Sunu's left ear.

"It's getting all over!" Puuja complained. "We have to use the brush, not our fingers!"

"If you'd let me have it for a moment—"

"We have to finish this leaf first!"

Pol tried to grab the brush anyway, and while fighting for it, he smeared a long streak of pigment over Sunu's scalp. Sunu winced, fully accepting of their fate, terrified of seeing the outcome. While Pol added a few adornments by Sunu's neck, Puuja tried to clean up some of the drips on their temples, but only succeeded in smudging the shapes further.

"We're sorry," she nearly whispered in shame. "We think we messed it up. Maybe you should wash it and we can try again?"

"The scalp pigments do not wash off," Sunu noted as mildly as they could. "We will wear your masterpiece proudly, for months to come."

"It's not too bad," Pol said, staring at his abominable creation, and then at his purple fingers. "Hey, how about this?" he asked with a sparkle in his eyes.

Pol placed his wet index and middle fingers right below his nostrils.

"No, stop!" Puuja gasped in horror, but dared not reach out to stop her brother.

Pol dragged his fingers down to the nook below his lower lip.

"What did you—" Puuja paused, then tilted her head as she considered Pol's face. "It's… It looks really nice… Can you do me too?"

Sunu closed their eyes and shook their head. The twins might get in trouble for this, but they could not take this small moment of joy from them—not after all they had endured.

Pol dipped his fingers in the mortar and reached forward.

"Be careful…" Puuja mumbled without moving her lips.

"Be quiet, be still," Pol said. He dragged his fingers down Puuja's lips in the same manner, leaving parallel purple marks upon them. She blew air softly from her nose and mouth, trying to dry the pigments, lest she turned her lips entirely purple by accident.

Sunu looked at the twins, then down at their own reflection. "You two look beautiful," they observed, "but we look like a giant snail vomited over our head. You will need practice and perhaps a better canvas, but we are content with the mess you made."

Pol jumped forward to hug Sunu, dragging a streak of purple across their chest. Sunu hugged him back, welcoming Puuja into their embrace as well.

"What in the nethervoids crawled upon your scalp?" Lago asked Sunu the next morning, sitting up in his bed inside the Queen's Lodge.

"Pellámbri weeps!" Alaia blurted out, covering her mouth. "What happened?"

"We were attacked, viciously, by children," Sunu admitted, standing by the round window of their shared bedroom and letting the light wash upon their splattered scalp. "But we survived."

Aio still slept soundly in bed. Lago shook his shoulder. When there was no response, he shook harder. Aio grumbled. "I need just…"—he cracked open his eyes—"just… By the Six Widows! Sunu! What happened to you?"

"Children," they repeated. "That is what happened."

"Well, it doesn't look half as bad when you are a varanus dragon," Sterjall commented later as they all walked out of the Queen's Lodge.

Lummukem's pigments, on their scalp and beyond, fully tinted each pigmented scale as if they were naturally purple, draping in a random assortment from the top of their head, with other random streaks along their body.

"It's chilly out today," Alaia said, sinking her head into her shoulders. Snow had been slowly piling up over the rounded dens of Kisdik. They heard the clashing of wooden weapons and looked behind them. Puuja and Pol were practicing with their quarterstaffs atop the Queen's Lodge, but this time they were doing so alone—their trainer was one of the Sehján lost in the battle.

"Time to go! The chiefs are waiting!" Tsei called to the children from across the bridge.

The twins slid down the snow-covered mound, still holding their weapons. They balanced on the bridge and crossed the pond that circled their den.

"You will not need weapons for this council," Tsei playfully advised.

"But what if the Oxruk attack?" Puuja said. "You never know."

Pol nodded pointedly, staring at the ground, but said nothing.

"Did you paint their lips?" Kulak asked Lummukem, tilting his head to better see the twins' new marks.

Lummukem shook their overly purple head. "Do not blame us, Khuron. The twins are guilty of their own sins."

CHAPTER SIXTY-FOUR

DEPARTURE OF THE SEHJÁN

Atop a vast terrace in Fel Kisdik, the Sehján council assembled once more, this time to discuss the future of Okridrolom, or rather, the end of it.

More chiefs were present now, from lakes at the far reaches of the dome and from the few settlements in wetlands that were safe from Oxruk attacks. Some representatives were still missing, namely those who lived around the ice-skirted column of the Muura Glacier, or in smaller lakes too remote. Heralds had been sent to them, but since it was treacherous to travel over land—more so now that the Oxruk would be seeking revenge—many opted for caution.

After much arguing, the council decided that as soon as the vines had opened enough, a migration beyond their sequestered lands would begin. The Sehján would attempt to exit the dome without any more bloodshed, but there was no certainty that more attacks would not happen, so they would be prepared for war as they left their islands.

Theggo informed the Sehján of the best routes through Fel Nisos and of the available territories they could first inhabit, as had been agreed upon with the Republic of Lerev. He also explained that the Lerevi would offer aid to the Sehján and their key species in sailing to nearby islands, and even to the Jerjan and Loorian continents if they desired. But that process would likely extend over the next years or decades; presently, the war against the Negian Empire had to take precedence.

Sterjall nervously pulled at his chin whiskers as he watched the representatives discuss. Once the proceedings quieted, he swallowed his fear and raised his voice. "There is one final request I wish to make," he said, then looked directly toward Theggo and continued in Common. "Admiral, we need to have Princeps Vordeno agree to leave some of these mountains to the Oxruk." Once his words were interpreted, the Sehján gasped in disbelief.

"I can make no promises on that matter," Theggo said, speaking over the commotion, "but I will talk to the princeps. It will not be up to me to decide."

"This is blasphemy!" an elderly chief cried out. "These lands will be ours again, this is the time to hold strong and stand our ground, that we must do!" The crowd roared in agreement.

"It was their land before, and it's the only land they have now," the wolf said, hoping to quiet them. "Their cities will soon be in ruins, but they have places under the mountains where they can live. And they can rebuild, with time. The Miscam tribes had a goal for this land, and that goal was met. Once the species spread more widely, there will be no more need for wars here. The Sehján will be better off elsewhere, the way they were before Okridrolom was grown."

His speech was not well received. Although the idea of being able to move without fear of attack from under the ground appealed to all the Sehján, they could not let go of their enmity, and so they reached no agreement on the matter. Sterjall felt powerless and disappointed, forced to accept that the conflict was too complex for him to quickly solve, and that the fate of the Oxruk would take time to be decided.

The discussion shifted to the future of Okrisilv. It was decided that Puuja, Pol, and Gwit would travel to meet Princeps Vordeno; once the matters of the Sehján and Oxruk were settled with the Republic of Lerev, they would join the wayfarers aboard *Fjummomurr* and sail east with Theggo's fleet.

"Khuron Pollomekh and Ierun Puuja are good fighters for their age," Tsei said, "but they will need protection, and a connection to their race and history, that they will. I volunteer to travel with this company, if you would have me, and if Lakemother wills it so." It was the first time Puuja had heard anyone other than Pol refer to her as Ierun; it made her feel both embarrassed and sad.

"The Day of Renewal quickly approaches," a one-eyed chief said to conclude the council. "Let us aim to venture outside of Okridrolom before the year ends. Let us use this time to prepare, to thank Lakemother for her protection before we leave her womb and enter the next life that awaits us."

It took two weeks for the Sehján to organize for their departure. Under Lummukem's tutelage, Puuja learned to better control the pain that came with wearing Okrisilv, overcoming the need to hold Pol's hand. Pol learned to do the same, though none but the three of them knew this secret.

The twins wanted to learn Common, knowing they would be living in the New World from now on, where only scholars spoke Miscamish. Lummukem volunteered to be their language teacher, also offering to take the role of battle trainer for the siblings.

On the last day of the year, the wayfarers ventured to the northern edge of the Nisos Dome, toward the same spot through which they had entered it. They were joined by shamans and warriors who had already scouted the lands and who were gathering all the rodents and lagomorphs they could reach, delivering the instructions on what they should do once the dome had opened.

Led by leaders of the castoroides companion species, thousands of hares, mice, capybaras, beavers, groundhogs, voles, squirrels, marmots, porcupines, pacaranas, and chipmunks were assembling at the edges of the dome, gathering resources to help the Sehján shape the future of the clade of glires. Gwit was there too, directing and inspiring his kind, motivating them to cooperate and follow through even during his absence.

Puuja moved with the flow of animals, with Okrisilv on her face. She still had not found her half-form, so she could not yet mindspeak to them, but she commanded respect from all glires, especially when Gwit would ride on her shoulder or atop Pol's head.

Battles had been fought with the Oxruk during those two weeks, though not major ones. The pale race seemed focused on taking care of their injured and digging to rescue survivors. Still, precautions were needed, so the group traveled slowly, carefully, and well protected. Due to the centuries of wars with the Oxruk, the Sehján had lost much of the knowledge Noss had imparted to them, as well as some key species. They could only aim to do their best, hoping that Noss would provide further guidance once the Sehján communed with them once more.

The wayfarers camped on the north shores of the Klad Üo, very close to where they'd once been surrounded by Tsei's fierce warriors. The landscape seemed wildly different now, with snow covering everything but the hundreds of small ponds. The weight of the snow flattened the papyrus reeds around them, letting them see farther into the distance.

Lummukem sat by the bonfire, quietly feeding blood and saliva to the bloodmoss growing in the carved bones of their halberd. Once finished, they closed their eyes, taking immeasurable pleasure in the simple act of warming up their cold blood next to the flames. It was one of their favorite feelings while in their half-form; there was something primal and rejuvenating about it, like a deep thirst being sated. Since Sunnokh did not show his face within the domes, and the arudinn were a poor substitute to the directional, biting warmth the nearest star could provide, Lummukem treasured those moments in which they could simply relax and absorb the heat of a fire without any distractions.

"Stop pulling on their tail!" Puuja suddenly yelled. "They are trying to sleep!"

"While sitting up?" Pol asked.

"That's how they do it. We've seen them. But stop it, you'll upset them."

The dragon's tail flicked out of the way; Pol chased after it. "How do you say *tail* in Common?" he asked.

Lummukem answered without opening their eyes.

Sterjall and Kulak were curled up next to each other not too far from the fire, using Blu as a pillow.

"My scalp wonders when their patience is going to run out," Kulak murmured, watching the twins torment the varanus dragon.

Sterjall shrugged and pulled the blanket closer to his neck. "I think Lummukem likes it."

"It is hard to tell if they are smiling, but their tight eyes do not seem very happy right now."

"There, the twins moved on to torture Alaia. Good for Lummukem."

Pol seemed too shy to bother Alaia, but Puuja led the charge by inquiring about her nub. Alaia let her touch the bony protuberance on her forehead, then asked Pol whether he wanted to as well, but he cowered behind his sister. Alaia then detached her elytra cuirass, dropping the ochre, maroon, and yellow plates next to her. "Look," she said, lifting her undershirt to reveal her protruding spine spurs—her thirteen sisters.

The children shrieked, horrified, and fled to the safety of Lummukem once more.

"I'm afraid the twins are getting too attached to them," Sterjall said. "Pol only wants to ride on their back now. I hope it's not just because they lost their mother." He looked up at the deep blues of the domed night sky, spotting a brief beam of sunlight breaching through the opening vines. Once the ephemeral column of light vanished, he looked back toward Lummukem. "Do you ever… Do you wonder what being like Lummukem would feel like?"

"Scales would feel strange to my scalp. Too hard, too cold. I prefer fur."

"I don't mean that. I mean having two sexes at once. Not just being allgender. I've met plenty of allgenders, and I feel like I'm not too far from understanding what that's like."

"My scalp thinks being man and woman might not be too different from being lorrkins. After all, we do things men and women do." Kulak paused for a moment, a touch of slyness entering his voice as he added, "Though we have not, for too long a time now." He reached under the blankets and began to rub on Sterjall's sheath, but the wolf was too distracted, staring at Lummukem's blank face.

"That's not quite what I mean, either." He stopped Kulak before he became too hard. "And we can't do that here, they'll see us."

"The Sehján have seen us kiss, seen us sleeping next to each other, and did not seem too surprised. But fine, we will save this for another time." Kulak kept his hand on Sterjall's crotch but stopped rubbing. "What is it that you mean, then?"

"I mean, do you wonder what it feels like to be a woman? We are so many things. We are men, and wolf, and caracal, so we know how it feels to have all these different qualia, but… you know…"

"No, my scalp does not wonder. I hope yours does not either, because women I am not attracted to. It is only men, like you, that I want." He began to fondle again, easing a finger into the wolf's sheath to try to lure more out. Sterjall gently stopped him once more.

"It's alright, I was just saying things," Sterjall said dismissively. "But there's another thing I wondered about… The night Sunu first put on the mask, you said something. You said you'd change the Laatu laws to allow allgenders to not only wear the Silvesh, but to love and have children if they wished. When you said that, I saw a tinge of sadness in Sunu's face. Do you think they are unable to have children? I don't know how any of that works, but I'm guessing it could be a problem for them."

"You think that is why they have become so protective of the twins?"

"Maybe… It all makes me so sad, knowing they likely haven't had a chance to explore love in any way before. Not unless they broke 'sacred' laws, and Sunu has always been very strict about following the laws."

"They will have a chance, when they are ready. But I also do not know if they can have children. Perhaps the twins are a blessing from Lakemother, as they would say. I know Lummukem has been a blessing to them both. That is for certain."

CHAPTER SIXTY-FIVE

ANNIVERSARY

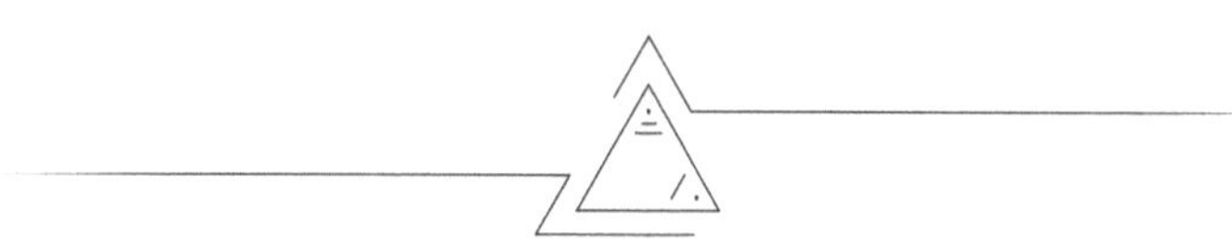

It was a bitterly cold morning. The Nisos Dome's skies were clear, displaying a timid palette of pastel whites. By noon, which was equivalent to midnight outside the dome, the Day of the Lost would settle upon them. The leap day that occurred once every eight years was a day to remember and honor the dead and the missing: the heroes, the lovers, and even the enemies who had fallen in battle or succumbed to disease, old age, or heartbreak.

The caravan was still a few miles away from the dome's wall and had stopped for lunch while scouts were sent out to patrol the area. Kulak and Sterjall sat at a cliff's edge, looking down toward the Klad Üo and the scores of ponds around it.

"Much will change, and so soon," Kulak said, his eyes seeing beyond the snow-streaked wetlands in front of them.

Sterjall heard footsteps behind them but didn't care to pull away from snuggling with the caracal. The footsteps belonged to Tsei, who eyed the couple curiously before clearing her throat. "Many openings has the wall of vines. They seem deep enough to walk through, but I dared not venture too far."

"Any trouble?" Kulak asked.

"We saw the same Oxruk swarm from the other night, passing by the eastern cliffs. It is too bright for them to attack. We saw no signs of their tunnels in the area. My scouts think they are fleeing by land to a different location."

"And you didn't attack them?" Sterjall asked.

"No, as per your request. But I still do not understand why you insist on sparing their lives, that I do not. If the pale demons could, they would have all our throats sliced this very moment."

"The war needs to end at some point. You could be the ones to take the first step."

Tsei seemed unconvinced. She left them, heading over to warm up by the fire.

"You have a kind soul, Sterjall," Kulak said. "But sometimes it worries me. There are times when we will not be able to avoid causing harm. It will be necessary."

"It's not always necessary. When possible, I want to avoid it."

"My scalp wonders what you would have done, back at Ommo ust Okri, if the twins had not been the ones to ask the dome to open. Would you have stopped Lummukem and myself from doing it?"

"I… Why are you asking me this? Are you angry at what happened?"

"Not angry. Only curious. You wanted to find a way out, but eventually we would have needed to open the dome. We were there, that was our chance. Returning would have meant more war, more death."

Sterjall turned his muzzle away. "I don't really know. I did not want to be a part of it." He sighed, lost in thought.

After an agonizing silence, Sterjall continued, "When we left those tunnels, when we were in the ruins of Kissumar, I saw you carrying Puuja in your arms and… And then I saw this Oxruk woman carrying a young girl in the same way. She was terrified, even more terrified than you, than me. She looked at us and saw monsters. Agnargsilv showed me her terror, but I didn't need the mask to understand it. Her expression was enough."

"My eyes saw her too," Kulak said. "But we were all scared. We were all running for our lives."

"Yes, but… But sometimes I feel like we are expendable pieces in a much larger game. I feel even Noss does not care for us, that we do their bidding because we want to believe in something greater, because we want to be certain that there is an objectively right path. But think about it—we are the smallest of pieces in Noss's body, we live but for a tiny fraction of their billions of years. We are nothing to them. If I scrape my hand, I'll rip that piece of skin off with my own teeth and spit it out. In that flap of bloodied skin there are thousands of living cells that I couldn't care less about. Don't you think Noss might feel the same way about us? Why should they care for anything but themself?"

"You have lost me. I think Noss is wiser than that."

"And aren't *we* supposed to be wiser than that? I'm not even talking about a fleck of skin, but of people, of animals, of entire clades. We love our close friends, yet we see everyone else as others, as lesser, as expendable in this war we barely even understand."

"But there are those who are right, and those who are wrong. Even if they do not know it."

"I'm not so certain anymore. I hope Noss does not see us as disposable creatures, made to serve their own wellbeing. It's just… I think we all need to do better. If we consider only our greater goals, without having regard for the feelings of the innocent people that will suffer due to us, then we are no better than our enemies. Yet I don't feel there's a solution. Horrible things will need to be done, people and animals will suffer, but I… I don't want to feel like I ignored their pain, that I thought of them as beneath me, as superfluous, as only cells to be sacrificed for the sake of our selfish selves."

Kulak's eyes were cast on the many moving islands of the lake. He blinked, turned, kissed Sterjall on the cheek, and said, "I think Mamóru would have been proud to hear your words." He snuggled closer. After a long pause, he creased his brow. "You have made my scalp wonder things now."

"That's no good," Sterjall joked.

"Never good. But scalp wonders when it wants. We set to open domes because Noss asked us. But why do all domes need open? Perhaps, if things were different, we could have left this dome to the Oxruk. Perhaps they would have lived a better life on their own."

"I'm torn about this, too," the wolf quietly replied. "We don't know which of Noss's memories are hidden in which dome. We don't know what we'll uncover, or how that might help us in the future."

"But we know species need to spread once more, at least Laatu know this. It saddens my heart, but we did what we think is best, even if not perfect. We will help Noss heal, and they will remember, and they will guide us."

"I hope we chose right," Sterjall murmured. He let the breeze ruffle his fur and kept his eyes unfocused. He then noticed movement down in a meadow — it was Alaia, carefully collecting colorful pebbles from a creek. "She's gonna come for me soon," he said. "She's getting things ready for the Day of the Lost. Do you celebrate it as well?"

"Yes, but we call it differently," Kulak said. "Laatu call it *Stammarg ust Baaf*, the Season of Promise. Most marriages happen on this day. Mother was planning for me to make my pick today."

"You mean among the candidates the provinces would choose for you?"

"Yes. Six women were selected already, though my scalp still knows not who they were, who they are. I was to marry one of them this very day. My scalp hopes Mother is thinking of me today. That she will someday be happy with the choice I have made."

Sterjall shifted his tail uncomfortably. He felt as if Kulak was implying they were married already, and although his love for the prince had grown, he could not help feeling a stab of guilt in his chest every time the idea of commitment came to his head. He thought of Banook sitting peacefully in his cabin, with Bear laying on his favorite deerskin pillow in front of the fireplace. He imagined the bearded giant sharing a meal with Kitjári and Nalaníri as they recounted their adventures, all while watching the snow pile up on the terrace. It was a peaceful, comforting image, though, unbeknownst to Sterjall, one that could not have been further from the truth.

I wish I knew how they are doing… What they are doing, Sterjall thought, then heard a familiar song play through his mind. In Banook's deep voice, he heard the words, *I hope he knows that we can be together all along, when far apart he thinks of me and hears the mountain song.*

"My scalp always knows when you think of him," Kulak said.

Sterjall lifted his head in surprise, but said nothing.

"Do not worry," Kulak continued, unfazed by his reaction. "When you think of him, your face turns happy, and also sad. Your eyes have fire inside them, like two hearths. I have learned to understand your love. It is complex. I am happy to be part of it. I am happy Banook is a part of it. I wish you would speak of him more often, and not hide him in your thoughts."

"I… I'm sorry. I'm always too self-conscious when it comes to that, but I should be more open about him. It's just that… It's our anniversary, today. One year since Banook and I first kissed. That's why he's on my mind. Although I guess that with the addition of the Day of the Lost, our anniversary would be tomorrow, but it's already been one whole year."

"He must be thinking of you, then. I hope he is."

Kulak felt the nervous restlessness of Sterjall's legs bouncing up and down. He recognized the pattern at once. "You are singing his song, in your head."

"Sorry, does that bother—"

"No. It only bothers me that you never sing it for me. I hear you humming it at times, and heard you teach the words to Alaia. I would like to know the words too, if you would teach me."

"It's a very long song. And getting longer."

In a pleading, playful tone, Kulak asked, "Am I in it yet? Will I be in it?"

Sterjall smiled with embarrassment.

"Yes, of course you are. I mean, ever since Mindreldrolom. There's no way you wouldn't be a part of the song. But I haven't written most of our adventures together yet, just one stanza."

Kulak waited without saying a word.

He said a word.

"So?"

"So what?"

"You cannot say that and leave me waiting. My tufted ears yearn to hear it now."

"It's not very good, it's a work in progress."

"I did not ask to hear excuses, I asked to hear a song."

Sterjall looked behind him. The rest of their group were at the camp, beginning their lunch preparations. No one was paying attention to them.

"Fine. But please don't make fun of me. I get too worked up about it."

Sterjall brushed his whiskers, as if that would in any way help his performance, then sang:

> The Khuron lies on sands of black, entranced by starry skies;
>
> He shares a kiss, a joke he cracks, his love he aimed disguise.
>
> The wolf confused—his soul alight, his heartbeat like a drum—
>
> Could feel a flame inside ignite; new love has left him numb.

Kulak beamed. "My tufted ears think it is perfect. Did you feel love already, on that first kiss upon black sands?"

"I don't know. Probably not yet. Just a strange kind of passion. I was truly confused. But I couldn't stop thinking about it, about you."

"My scalp is glad to hear Khuron in your song. In Banook's song. If you were with him now, would you tell him about Khuron Aio-Kulak?"

"I guess so. I think he'd love to know about you."

"What would you tell him?"

Sterjall hesitated, feeling as if he was sliding into a trap. He let go of his insecurity and answered honestly. "I'd tell him you are the bravest person I've ever met."

"Brave?" Kulak nearly choked with laughter. "Sunu-Lummukem is brave, strong, determined. I am weak as newborn kitten. I hide behind blowgun. My paws can barely hold a knife. My scalp does not think I qualify as brave."

"I think that is what makes you brave. Lummukem can chop off a dozen heads with one swing of their halberd while breaking two dozen legs with their tail. They have no reason to fear. You've saved me countless times. You rescued me when the odds were against you. And you stood up for yourself in front of your mother, in front of your tribe. You've created real change, shaping the future for the better. I think that's inspiring, and I love you for it. That's what I'd tell Banook—I'd tell him I fell in love with you because you give me faith that fighting for what is right is always the right choice, no matter the odds."

The caracal snuggled closer, an ear resting on the wolf's chest, listening to his heartbeat. Although no stars yet shone within the newly opening dome, Kulak's eyes seemed to sparkle with starlight.

CHAPTER SIXTY-SIX

DAY OF THE LOST

While the others enjoyed their lunch together, Lago and Alaia left the camp. They found a small nook under an old sycamore where they could sit in private. A few emerald starlings watched them from above, like iridescent leaves.

"They are so beautiful," Alaia said. "Their green and purple feathers do look like Tsei's armor." She handed Lago a dried papyrus reed. "Shall we get started?"

"I guess. Last time I did this, I was only what, eleven? Even before Agnargsilv came to me. I can barely remember."

"I remember my first Day of the Lost. Well, I guess it was my second, since I was a toddler for my first, so that one doesn't count. I remember it, but I didn't understand it."

"I didn't either." Lago adjusted the mask attached to his shoulder brace, relaxed through a sigh, then lined up a series of reeds; with Leif, he cut them all to the same length.

"Hey, you lacquered your nails!" Alaia said. "I haven't seen you do that in a while. And I don't think I've ever seen you paint them yellow before."

"Yeah. It's not my favorite color. But I felt like it today."

Alaia reached for Lago's hands and stared at his colorful nails.

"Hey, y-you also…" Lago stumbled. "You… What did you do to your hand?"

"I made it prettier," Alaia said, rotating her left hand to show the white paints she had applied around the bump where her thumb used to be. She had drawn spiraling patterns to enhance the emptiness that was there, in a similar way to how she emphasized her nub by braiding her hair around it.

"Is that the paint the Sehján use on their lips?" Lago asked.

"Tsei gave me some."

"Only you could find a way to make a wound look so pretty."

"Hey, this is who I am now, one-thumbed and proud. But let's get to this already. Do you remember how to do the weave?"

"I think so," Lago said, "I did it a few times with the monks. They used the same pattern for their baskets."

Lago held one of the papyrus reeds in front of him. Alaia placed another on top, then used a third one to interlock them in a triangular pattern. Together, reed after reed, four hands working as one, they began to weave a Day of the Lost cache, about a handspan wide. Once the concave form was halfway done, resembling a bowl with dozens of ribs sticking out at the top, they began to recite their eulogies.

"In memory of the Sehján warriors," Alaia intoned as she wove a new reed, "who bravely fought for us, for their Lakemother, for their children's futures. Woven as one." She finished weaving the reed into the basket-like form, then dropped a handful of colorful pebbles inside.

"I don't know how many pebbles to place. There were too many dead," she sadly admitted.

Lago wove the next reed. "In memory of the Oxruk, who died defending their home. Woven as one." He tossed more pebbles inside, having picked ones that were lighter colored.

"Are you serious?" Alaia asked. "The Oxruk? On top of the Sehján?"

"They deserve to be remembered too," he said with a shrug.

Alaia chuckled silently, then wove three thin reeds as one. "In memory of Gestall, Hemi, and Wallamer, the dragoons who gave their lives to protect Theggo. Woven as one." She dropped three glossy pebbles into the cache; they clinked like marbles.

They worked carefully to weave the form inward. It was now closing in an oblong sphere, with the top end still open.

Lago sighed as he wove the next reed. "In memory of Sontai, who inadvertently brought me life. Woven as one." He dropped in a reddish pebble.

Alaia regarded the pile of pebbles by her feet and considered. "Can we do animals too?"

"I don't see why not."

She wove a reed and said, "In memory of Fulm, who is probably hissing at us from beyond the Six Gates. Woven as one." She dropped the darkest pebble she could find into the mix.

One more reed, one more chant. "In memory of Bonmei, the Agnargfröa that never was." Lago dropped a tiny ruddy pebble that made nearly no sound at all.

The bottom of the cache was now heavy with rocks.

"In memory of Bahimir," Alaia said as she wove the next reed, "who stood up for me when the Negians attacked the mines. My valiant fool. Sorry, Bahimir, you should've stayed put. Woven as one." Instead of a pebble, she dropped a single black cube into the cache, one with a hole pierced through it: a Lode. The tiny chip of lead infused with a minuscule amount of magnium was worth a measly tenth of a Qupi.

"A Lode, seriously?" Lago complained. "Isn't that a bit cheap? You could at least drop a few Qupi, maybe a Hand."

"I know, I know, but Bahimir had a necklace made out of a single Lode, like Ambassador Vor-Vor's earring. It was meant to signify something about working for the common good or some shit. He would've appreciated the gesture. It's odd… I don't even know if my friends from the mines are alive or dead. Should I add pebbles for them?"

Lago shook his head. "No, only for the ones we know are gone. For the rest, hope for the best." He wove the next reed. "In memory of Khopto, who tried to get me into drugs. Woven as one."

"See? Who is the one being disrespectful now?"

"It's true though," Lago said, taking off his Havengall Congregation bracelet. The two copper hands unclasped, but he bound them back to each other before placing the looping bangle in the cache.

"I thought you liked that bracelet. Are you sure?"

"As certain as the day has thirty-two hours, an hour sixty-four moments, and each moment sixty-four heartbeats." Lago rubbed the green-tinted imprint the patina had left on his wrist. "I'm not a member of the Congregation, not really, and sometimes it just brings me painful memories. The sacred hold represents more now, after all that Hud Ulésse taught me. But let someone else discover it, I think it might bring them joy."

Another reed entwined. "In memory of Ierun Jessha, who gave a new life to her twins. Woven as one." Alaia took out a silver ring and dropped it on top. It fell right in the center of the copper bracelet, held by its looping embrace.

"Where did you get that?" Lago asked.

"I asked the twins if they wanted to leave something in memory of their mother. It's one of Jessha's rings."

"It's beautiful," Lago said, weaving the next reed. He heard a distant melody in his head, oscillating from metallic tines. *Wave your farewells till your leaves turn to gold...* His eyes turned glossy, lost in remembrance. "In memory of Ockam, my protector." He choked up, struggling to get any more words out. "Woven... woven as one."

He looked around, and his face turned to disappointment.

"I just realized... I don't have anything to give for Ockam."

"What about that?" Alaia suggested, pointing at the penannular brooch fastening Lago's cloak.

Lago pulled the pin through the gray fabric and stared at the crescent brooch Ockam used to wear. The image of Sceres and her shard had lost its silvery sheen, building up a thin layer of rust.

"I love this thing," Lago admitted. "And Jiara will smack me when she finds out I gave it away, but it is most appropriate. Will you place it with me?"

They held the brooch together, then let it drop into the cache.

Alaia held Lago's hand for a moment, then continued weaving. "In memory of Abjus, who was kind of a nubhead, but undoubtedly a brave one. Woven as one."

She dropped a dart inside the cache. "Don't worry, it's not poisoned," she assured Lago.

"But what if a kid finds it? They'll cut their fingers while digging through the pebbles."

"A worthy blood sacrifice. The rest of the gifts will make up for it."

The cache was nearly closed now, but Lago added another reed, and once again let his eyes fill with tears. "In memory of Mamóru, the flower I'll never forget. Woven as one." He detached the stem from Mamóru's meerschaum and briar pipe. "The long stem won't fit," he said sadly, and dropped only the bowl inside.

"At least it's not his cane. I still have that back in *Fjummomurr*."

One more reed, one more memory.

"In memory of Givra," Alaia said, "who was the first to teach me Miscamish. *Drelvei praalv velm.* Woven as one." She dropped in an octahedral pendant: Givra's marbled-agate arambukh.

"Wait, you kept that?" Lago asked incredulously.

"I... Maybe? I wanted something to remember her by."

"The Laatu would likely kill you if they found out."

"They won't. It's going in the cache, far away from their judgmental scalps."

There was still some room left in the cache. Lago and Alaia wove a few more reeds together and dropped a bunch of pebbles through the tightening aperture.

"In memory of the Puqua and Laatu sailors," Lago said, "who now sleep in the depths of the Isdinnklad. Woven as one."

When only a small opening remained, Lago paused. "I have one more." He wove a short reed as the very last loop, but without tightening it. "In memory of my mother, Nistre Vaari, who I never knew. Woven as one."

On top of all the small treasures, Lago placed a tiny bottle of solvent for fingernail lacquers.

"Dad once said yellow was her favorite color. The first time I painted my nails was after I found her little box of lacquers, which Dad had hidden away with all her stuff." Lago's jaw clenched for a moment before he settled. "He beat me up real good, but I kept the box."

They tightened the top of the cache, sealing it into a round package of hexagonal and triangular patterns. They both looked around, making sure no one was watching them, then placed the cache inside a deep tree hollow. They covered it with dry leaves and a bit of snow.

As they walked back to the camp, Alaia said, "I haven't seen you get that emotional in a long while. Do you even believe in the Six Gates?"

"Huh?"

"I mean, you told me once you don't buy into all of that. But still, you went through with the ceremony."

"You don't have to believe in the myths to partake in the ceremonies. Aren't you supposed to be praying to Pliwe instead?"

"We don't do that during the Day of the Lost."

"Same thing. I don't care if the Six Gates exist or not—mourning and remembering is not for the dead, it's for the living."

Alaia shrugged. "Maybe. I remember the first time I found a Day of the Lost cache. It was deep in the mines, in a closed-off area no one had been to for a long while. It had a bunch of pebbles I used to decorate my hole in the Hollows, and also some dried-up candy, and a few translucent beads that I braided in my hair."

"I've only ever found one. It was in a drainage canal under Feldspar Boulevard, under the bridge before it drops into the East Flank. It had a wooden toy and a Hex."

"A Hex?" Alaia yapped. "Who can afford to just drop off a Hex? Oh, I know who, spoiled rich kids from the East Flank, that's who."

"Well, it made me very happy. Isn't that the point of it all?"

"I guess. I mean… I guess the point is for us to remember those who have departed. Perhaps by leaving a little piece of them behind, it also helps *us* let go. But their memory lives on long after we are gone. That's how I like to think of it, at least."

"Yeah. I think that's how I want to picture it, too."

Lago took one last look back toward the tree which held their secret treasure. He closed his eyes and walked away.

CHAPTER SIXTY-SEVEN

VALKNUT

The Day of the Lost had come and gone, and it was now the first of Frostburn, the Day of Renewal.

By the time the arudinn had all settled into their gloomy slumber, a small group of travelers accompanied the wayfarers through the vines: Theggo, the twins, the two Nu'irgesh, Dragoon Leader Seshéni with her surviving troops, and Tsei, who held on to the back of one of the dragoons, getting used to sitting on the strange kudus.

By the cold light of their pharoliths, they traversed through the wall of the Nisos Dome, finding no need to push the vines apart. Although the wall was dark and the tunnels windy, there was already enough room for them all to stroll through; and so they did, thinking of the days ahead, and of what adventures might soon come. The only obstacles they encountered were the sap-filled craters the largest vines had left behind when receding. The smaller holes too had been filled with sap, but it had since dried into crystals.

As the sharp scent of the sap filled his nose, Sterjall let his mind drift to thoughts of friends he had not seen for a long time. Far across the Esduss Sea, Crysta and Balstei were helping the Laatu settle into new territories. Farther still, in a dome just beginning to open, Kitjári and Nalaníri were escaping into the Lequa Sea, leaving Banook, Bear, and Ardof behind; but Sterjall knew nothing of them, and could not have imagined the parallel journeys they were undertaking.

The tunnel brightened. The end of the path was near.

It was early morning when they reached the outside world, and it was warmer, too. Little snow coated the ground, only piling up in crevices at the shadowed sides of vines. Dozens of pavilions dotted the landscape, and hundreds of Lerevi soldiers were keeping guard around the edge of the tall mesa, but they had not yet spotted the strange group emerging from the wall.

Puuja and Pol were riding on Pichi, holding on to Lummukem and Alaia. When the twins saw the blue sky and the brightness of Sunnokh, they gasped so loudly that they alerted the soldiers to their presence.

"We hear your song of truth!" Theggo greeted them, while Seshéni and the dragoons saluted the Lerevi soldiers. An envoy rushed off to find an officer while the soldiers stood at attention. Soon enough, a troop of a hundred Lerevi infantry had gathered to escort the group toward the capital city of Normouth. The maroon-colored palace stood just down the cliff, waiting for them with black flags flowing above it.

The soldiers asked no questions of the travelers, though they seemed nervous, perhaps eager as they marched solemnly down the switchbacks of the mesa. Once they reached the bottom, Infantry General Seera Ashbend came trotting to meet the group. Seeing the dark mask on Puuja's face, she nodded her approval.

Seera tapped an open palm to her chest, eyes on Theggo. "We hear your song of truth. Welcome back, Fleet Admiral. I see your mission was a success. We've felt the tremors, and saw the vines slowly crawling open, so I made sure to have more forces ready for your return."

"A success it was," Theggo said, "though we lost three brave dragoons to the enemy, as well as many of the Miscam who fought for our common cause."

"The enemy?" she inquired.

"It's a long story, one that we wish to relate to Princeps Vordeno as soon as possible. Although we are all weary, could we arrange for a meeting at the palace before day's end?"

"That… may be hard to arrange," Seera said hesitantly. "Things have changed since you departed." The infantry units kept flowing down the switchback road, slowly converging around the wayfarers and their allies.

Theggo then noticed something peculiar: the black flags that flanked the road were not emblazoned with silver triskelions. The silver complexity of the triple spirals had been replaced by a simpler copper-colored form, a valknut: three triangles that were interlaced together, yet were still separate forms. The triskelion was the symbol of the free republic, while the triple triangle represented the three conjoined yet independent aspects of the Lavra Faithful, of the government, and of their people; all entwined into equal wholes, yet clearly meant to give equal power of representation to the scrollsingers.

"What dark portent do these new banners bring?" Theggo asked, squinting at the new flags.

"As I said," General Seera Ashbend repeated, "things have changed since you departed. The citizens grew angry when they heard of the secret meeting Vordeno had summoned, where no vote from the constituents was called for, no consideration toward the populace was taken. The Lavra Faithful were enraged when Brovon told them of the decisions that were made, and made with such haste."

The general gestured toward the dragoons.

"Brave dragoons, I order you to kindly ask the Sehján, Zovarian, and Laatu you've escorted to surrender the masks. They belong to the Theocracy of Lerev, where they will be put to better use protecting our holy land and building a prosperous power that will squash the threats of the east." She looked to Sterjall. "We thank you for all you have done, and we will offer fair retribution for your service. But the people of Lerev have spoken, and this is the decision we have come to."

"Fuck you," Sterjall shot back. "We came all this way to—"

"Where is Princeps Vordeno?" Theggo demanded. "I will have a word with—"

"Vordeno is dead," Seera said. "If you wish to air any grievances, you may speak to Holy Princeps Brovon. But the masks are coming with us." She looked at Seshéni. "Dragoon Leader, you have your orders."

"These refugees are under my care," Theggo insisted. "You have no authority to make them surrender their possessions. I will escort them back to sea, where they will board their ship, and shall not be bothered by—"

Shiiiing! came the sound of the general's unsheathing rapier. "Dragoon Leader, their masks! This is an order!"

Seshéni looked to Sterjall, then to her soldiers. She unsheathed her own rapier, and her eight dragoons followed suit. Their kudus advanced toward the two smilodons.

"What in the nethervoids do we do now?" Sterjall asked Theggo.

Theggo narrowed his wrinkled eyes. With his voice hoarse and determined, he replied.

"We fight."

End of Book 3

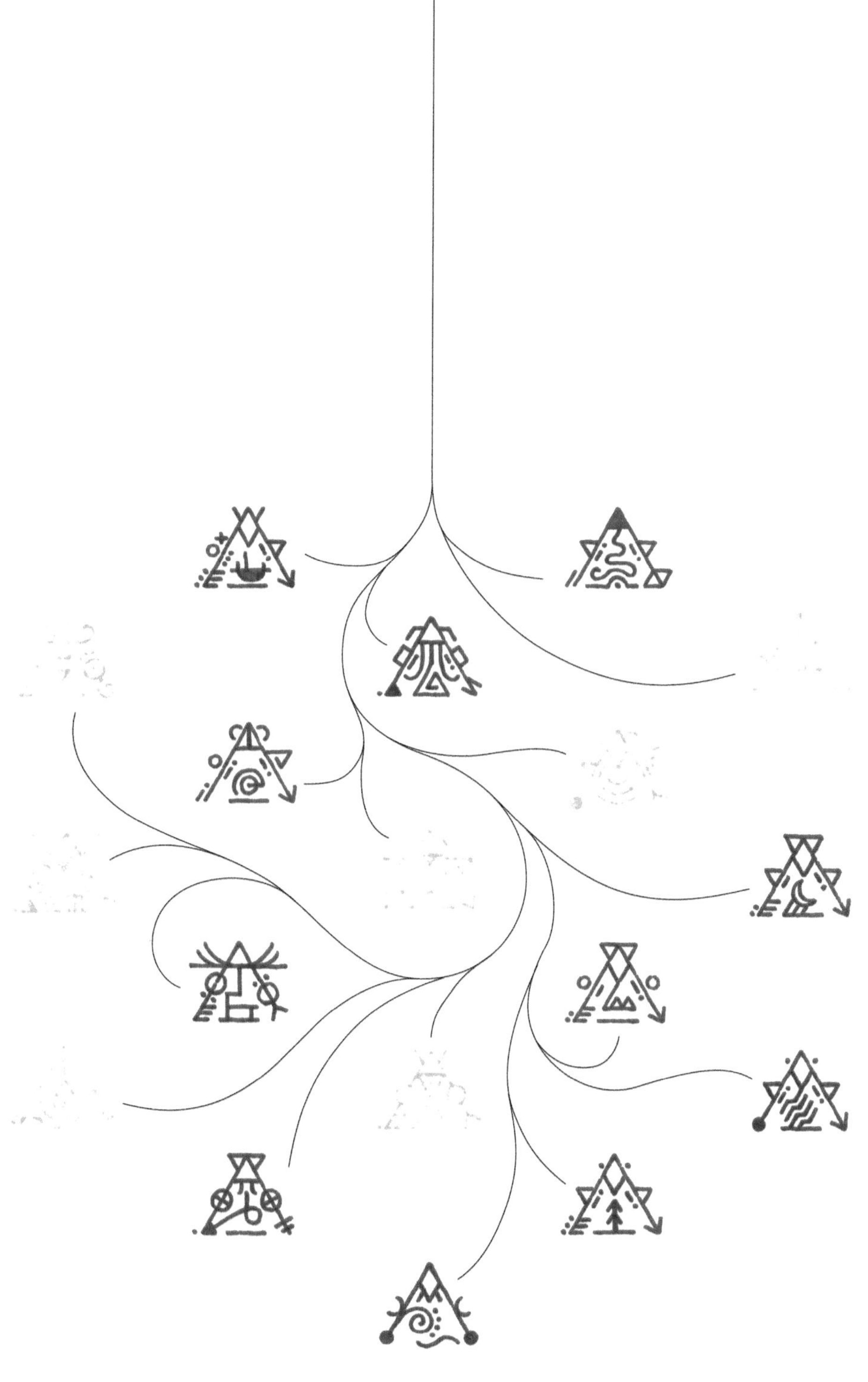

Appendices

All the materials found in these appendices can also be found online with much cleaner formatting and with additional goodies, such as a complete Miscamish dictionary, full-resolution maps, and updated illustrations. They are included here for your convenience, but I recommend you check them out on the official website.

Scan this QR code or type in the
following URL to access the extras:

JoaquinBaldwin.com/book3/extras

To keep updated on new book releases and to gain access to unreleased illustrations, deleted chapters, tutorials, and lots more, sign up to my mailing list in the following link:

JoaquinBaldwin.com/list

Oxruk Deities

Excerpt from *The Doxlob Survey* by Scrollsinger Soráná, dated to the twenty-sixth year of the eleventh King of Nisos (753 B.D.).

O'olto (Moonstone Olm, A)

The primary deity of the pale race that inhabits the shade of Gmorrogov is a blind salamander. Their name is metaphorical, for their body is not made of a gemstone, but of light itself trapped in the form of the translucent protean. They are said to be made of all shades and colors of light and of darkness, even what they call the luster colors: those beyond what mortal eyes can perceive. Their creation story has branched into five different versions, but they all speak of the Moonstone Olm having laid the twelve eggs from which the twelve deities hatched, which I have listed here in order. The Olm themself is not worshipped directly (except by the reclusive sect from Maz'tesh), and they are only mentioned in relation to their offspring.

Ucrarn (Night Eyes, A)

The first deity to hatch from the twelve eggs and the only one with a humanoid form (it remains unclear whether they have limbs or a tail; details vary between tellings). Ucrarn is an albino allgender—albino for the already pale Oxruk, making their skin not merely white, but fully translucent. They were the first to shape the lands of Illid, digging tunnels in the crust so that their progeny could be birthed safely away from the "ungodly" light of Sunnokh. Their nearly gelatinous skin resembles that of the blind olms, and their arteries run blood that is not red, but white. Their eyes are pits of darkness, and their gaze blackens everything it touches. Ucrarn can see shadows (a narrow spectrum of the luster colors) in the way mortals see light.

AXÚD MED (HORNSTONE CAVESNAIL, A)

A fertility deity. As the Hornstone Cavesnail's indestructible shell cuts through Noss's crust, it slices rifts that become underground rivers. Their mucus glands birth fresh springs out of bare rock, and their eggs replenish the underground with the peculiar troglobite species that Scrollsinger Jeärivo wrote extensively about in his Speleological Bestiary.

RAHIH (BREATH OF AGES)

One of three inanimate deities of the Oxruk. Rahih is a mudpot that appears near toxic vents deep in the crust of Laaja Gmorrogov and Laaja Bumbra, although it can manifest in any cave deep and hot enough. Its incessant bubbling is said to have given the Oxruk the gift of the spoken word while at the same time taking away their gift of mindspeech (the similarities with the Yenwu parables is unmistakable, yet no direct link between the Oxruk and the Theocracy has been found). Oxruk supplicants travel to the deepest caves to divine from the sounds of the mudpots—those who survive the toxic fumes return speaking the divine glossolalia and often become high priests, following the path to seerdom.

AZZÖEL (PHANTOM CRAYFISH, M)

An aetheric creature who guards veins of aetheric elements and buried treasures. His carapace is formed of pure aether, his chelipeds made of ignium. His heart pumps a hallucinogenic gas the Oxruk call "jegug," which seems to correlate closely to aetheric nitrogen, or nox, at least as far as the mysterious reagent is thus far understood by our artificers. Due to the Crayfish's gaseous nature, he can traverse through rock as easily as a guppy through water. The Crayfish often manifests through the word of Rahih, birthed by vents, or is sometimes seen in the Overworld hovering brightly above boglands.

GNUMMA (GLOWWORMS, "GNUMMA OF THE THOUSAND EYES")

Gnumma is a colony of glowworms which is also the stars. The Oxruk keep their own star charts not of sixty-six but of only fifty constellations, with Gnumma being none of them while being all of them. As a weather deity, Gnumma's job is to bring Sunnokh to the skies once a day, and more importantly, to push Sunnokh into the Shadow Realm every night. Falling stars are a way for Gnumma to feed, trapping those who chase after the bioluminescent trails into their sticky threads. Humans trapped by their web quickly pupate and are reborn as flies.

Erréna (Singing Myotis, F)

A fertility deity who is a chimeric microbat with a rat's tail and a shrew's head. Her excretions sprout life and prosperity, and her clicking songs are said to move time forward, for without Sunnokh, the Underworld would otherwise be stuck beyond time. Humans reborn as flies after being captured by Gnumma's traps offer sustenance to the Myotis, thus completing the cycle through which humans feed themselves.

Zugg Elan (Agate Forest)

The second non-living deity of the Oxruk is a petrified ash forest located in the Voidfields of the Stelm Atuur. The Forest rests deep underground in a precarious cave system where the base sediments were washed away while keeping a great number of the trees still standing as if supporting the rocky ceiling above. Before the dawn of the current era, when the cosmos was nothing but brightness, the trees were said to have absorbed one star in each of their rings, crystallizing them into their agate cores and allowing only Sunnokh to remain. Through this effort the Forest grew but also died, only to be rebirthed (although no longer alive) by the Moonstone Olm. Although no scrollsingers have been allowed into the sanctum, we have acquired samples of the petrified wood and have concluded they will offer no material gains to the Kingdom of Nisos.

Wembor (Orchid-Nosed Mole, M)

A tiny creature with ten legs, each extending to five magnium claws. The Mole is a deity of smithing and war, and it is after his claws that the Oxruk's clawed gauntlets are fashioned. His keen nose can smell emotions, sensing lies, betrayal, lust, yearning, and fear. It is said the Mole can possess seers and priests by burrowing through their feet, nesting into their hearts to grant them immortality (at least until the Mole leaves their bodies), forcing the humans to do his bidding, bringing bloodshed and strife to their sects.

KOTFR (VELVET WORM, A)

A deity of consciousness and language. The velvet worm is yet another aetheric creature, one that lives exclusively in the Luster Realm, being most tightly connected to the elements of soot and pharos. The papillae on their head squirt an adhesive slime that binds and connects people, animals, plants, deities, and even the stars themselves into a single web. This same sticky slime is what binds words to their meanings, and what allows the aetheric elements to manifest in the Physical Realm.

JOPPAR AND JOBBARI (CHRYSOCOLLA GEODE)

The Oxruk's third non-living deity. The hollowed boulder is said to be so large that one could bathe in the concave, crystalline centers of its split halves. The two segments reside in separate cave systems, yet they remain connected by the word of Rahih and the threads of Kotfr. Seers who bathe in one half of the Geode can hear the words spoken by a seer bathing in the other half. In some rituals, the Oxruk use the Geode to speak to Ucrarn themself, who is said to sleep inside a twin geode at the very center of Noss. The Oxruk are too secretive about the Chrysocolla Geode, and our survey has found no direct corroboration of its existence.

OULENTEERA (BIOLUMINESCENT MUSHROOM, A)

Although described as a single organism, every glowing mushroom in any cave is said to be Oulenteera themself, with all their roots reaching down and connecting into the very heart of Noss. Their glowing spores they see as a manifestation of the thoughts of the planet (although they do not think of Noss as a planet—they sneer at the thought of their land orbiting the ungodly Sunnokh). This bioluminescent species is farmed to illuminate (if dimly) the long cave systems the Oxruk inhabit, but their light is so dim only the Oxruk seem to perceive it, so we have deemed it meritless of further study.

Xash (Tar Serpent, A)

Although the Tar Serpent is an anti-deity, they are still revered. Being the last to hatch, they first swallowed all twelve moonstone shells, then ate their progenitor, the Moonstone Olm themself, becoming larger than all worlds and enveloping Noss, the skies, and even Sunnokh themself. The Tar Serpent has twelve stomachs, each loosely linked to one of their siblings, and one to their progenitor. As they digest the cosmos, Noss and all their inhabitants traverse through the twelve stomachs. We currently find ourselves in the fifth stomach, that linked to Gnumma, the glowworm deity, and thus we can see the glow-worms lining the Tar Serpent's entrails: our very stars. Once we reach the final stomach, the one linked to the Moonstone Olm themself, the luster light will vanquish all creation, the Moonstone Olm will be reborn, and from darkness a new cosmos will crystallize.

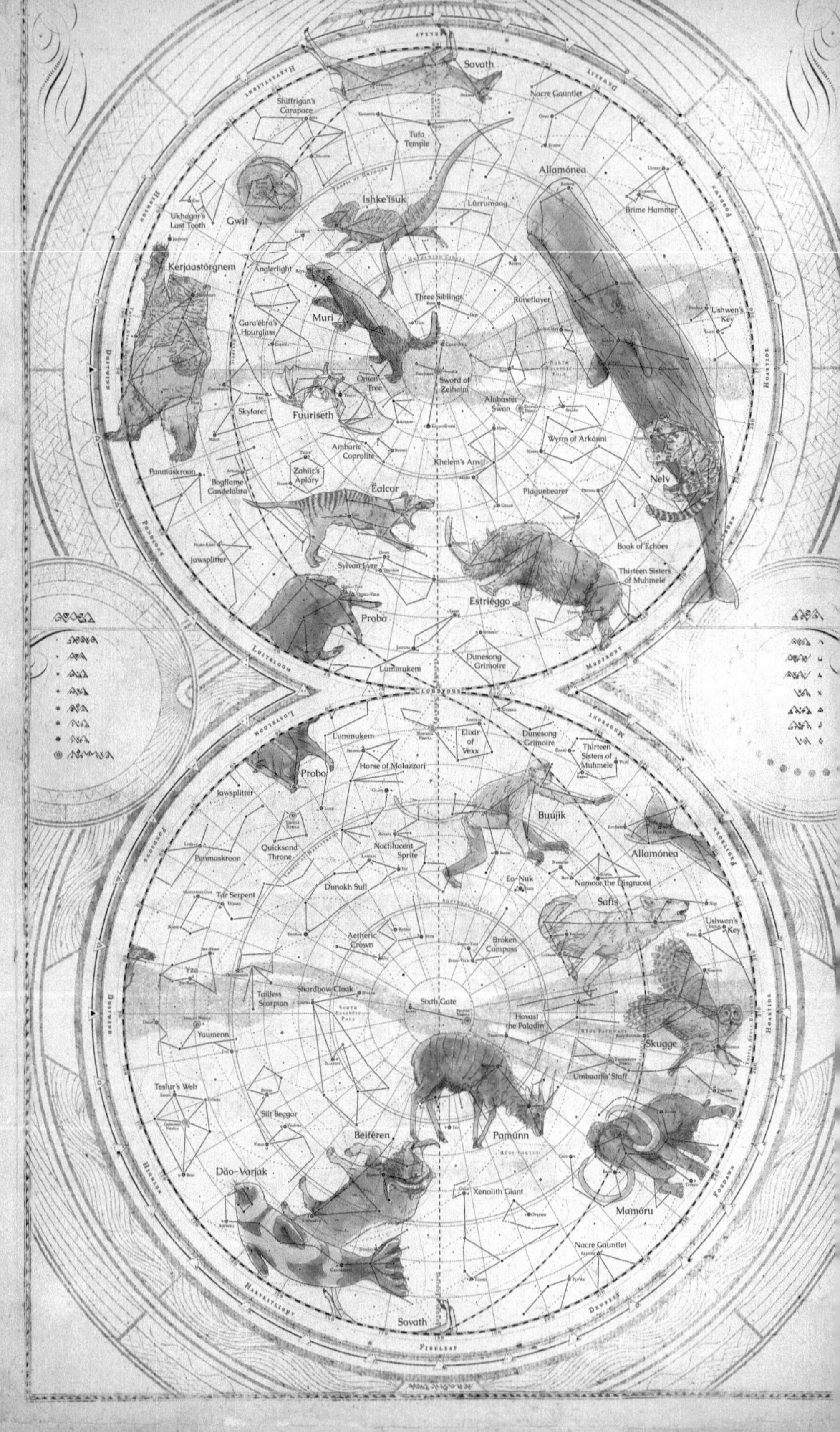

Sovath
Nacre Gauntlet
Shiffrigan's Carapace
Tufa Temple
Allamónea
Ishke'Isuk
Lûrrumaag
Brime Hammer
Gwit
Ukhagar's Last Tooth
Anglerlight
Three Siblings
Runeflayer
Ushwen's Key
Kerjaastörgnem
Muri
Gura'ebra's Hourglass
Sword of Zeiheim
Alabaster Swan
Skyfarer
Fuuriseth
Omen Tree
Wyrm of Arkánni
Nelv
Ambaric Coprolite
Khelem's Anvil
Panmáskroon
Zahiic's Apiary
Ealcor
Plaguebearer
Bogflame Candelabra
Book of Echoes
Jawsplitter
Thirteen Sisters of Muhmele
Sylvan Lyre
Estriéggo
Probo
Dunesong Grimoire
Lummukem
Lummukem
Elixir of Vexx
Dunesong Grimoire
Probo
Horse of Malazzari
Thirteen Sisters of Muhmele
Jawsplitter
Buujik
Panmaskroon
Quicksand Throne
Noctilucent Sprite
Allamónea
Eo-Nuk
Namoor the Disgraced
Tur Serpent
Dunokh Sull
Safis
Aetheric Crown
Broken Compass
Ushwen's Key
Yza
Tailless Scorpion
Shardbow Cloak
Sixth Gate
Hovast the Paladin
Yaumenn
Skugge
Tesfur's Web
Umhaarlis' Staff
Silt Beggar
Beiferen
Pamánn
Dáo-Varjak
Xenolith Giant
Mamóru
Nacre Gauntlet
Sovath

Constellations

This celestial planisphere represents the sixty-six constellations of Noss as interpreted by Miscam-influenced realms during the Segregation Epoch. After the Downfall, many of the constellation names changed in the common usage.

The ☆ symbol indicates the brightest star or nebula in the constellation.

Aetheric Crown
Crown with jewels cut from each of the aetheric elements.
☆ Ust

Alabaster Swan *(F)*
Atzu deity of creation. Also known as Mother Swan Arsíri.
☆ Zygnaar Nebula

Allamónea *(F)* *ala-MOH-nea*
Nu'irg with a sperm whale primal form.
☆ Asheeri

Ambaric Coprolite
A galvanum core swallowed and defecated by the Ice Drake of Beyenaar.
☆ Bezoar

Anglerlight
The kenzir stone lure tusk of the Fathom Narwhal.
☆ Illicium

Beiféren *(M)* *bay-FEH-ren*
Nu'irg with a bootherium primal form.
☆ Simbbo

Bogflame Candelabra
Horumma artifact trapping the four malignant lights.
☆ Faari

Book of Echoes
Tome of every page left blank in every other book, holding their untold stories.
☆ Deltara

Brime Hammer
Aetheric hammer so hot that it needs no forge to shape even the hardest metals.
☆ Usteov

Broken Compass
A cursed artifact that points south whenever it feels like it.
☆ Zerza-Velm

Buujik *(F)* *BOO-jick*
Nu'irg with a red-shanked douc primal form.
☆ Salóm

Däo-Varjak *(F)* *DAH-oh VAR-jack*
Nu'irg with a ribbon seal primal form.
☆ Graumendel

Dunesong Grimoire
Codex of songs that can control blue Baurami sands.
☆ Ukhbria

Dunokh Sull / *DOO-nokh sool*
"The Arc of the Night Sky." A legendary quaar bow.
☆ Khamam

Ëalcor *(M)* *EH-al-core*
Nu'irg with a thylacine primal form.
☆ Sejaar

Elixir of Vexx
A potent brew that will cure any ailment, even life.
☆ Nostrum

Eo-Nuk *(A)* *EH-oh nook*
Tsing deity of creation. Tiny constellation of six stars that look like one.
☆ Illid

Estriéggo *(M)* *ess-tree-EH-goh*
Nu'irg with a woolly rhinoceros primal form.
☆ Keratus

Fuuriseth *(F)* *FOO-ree-seth*
Nu'irg with a white leaf-nosed bat primal form.
☆ Tragus

Gara'ébra's Hourglass / *gar-ah-'EH-bra*
Aetheric artifact crafted to stop time.
☆ Caesura

Gwit *(M)* *gWIT*
Nu'irg with a hazel dormouse primal form.
☆ Glires Nebula

Horse of Malazzari *(M)* *mah-lah-ZA-ree*
Graalman god of fertility. Hung horse.
☆ Glans

Hovast the Paladin *(M)* *HOH-vast*
Lengendary warrior who defeated the Wyrm of Arkánni.
☆ Helvena

Ishke'ísuk *(M)* *ish-keh-'EE-sook*
Nu'irg with a double-crested basilisk primal form.
☆ Cabochon

Jawsplitter
Bloodwraith of Hasuuth with three purple eyes.
☆ Phara-Kamu

Kerjaastórgnem *(M)* *ker-jah-STORE-gnem*
Nu'irg with an arctotherium primal form.
☆ Metheglin

Khelem's Anvil / *KHEH-lem*
Magnium anvil upon which the Sword of Zeiheim was forged.
☆ Chaam

Lummukem *(M)* *LOO-moo-kem*
Ancient winged dragon that swallowed the skyfires that threatened Illid.
☆ Jaggura

Lûrrumaag *(F)* *LOO-rue-mog*
Puqua kubanochoerus deity who carved the twelve fjords with her tusks.
☆ Reveok

Mamóru *(M)* *mah-MOH-roo*
Nu'irg with a steppe mammoth primal form.
☆ Baass

Muri *(M)* *MOO-ree*
Nu'irg with a honey badger primal form.
☆ Ratel

Nacre Gauntlet
Ceremonial gauntlet of the Elmaren Queendom carved from a giant pearl.
☆ Kladdar

Namoor the Disgraced *(M)* *nah-MOOR*
Traitor who was boiled to death in the Ignimorr mud pots.
☆ Rux

Nelv *(F)* *nelv*
Nu'irg with a clouded leopard primal form.
☆ Vibrissa

Noctilucent Sprite *(A)*
A sprite who travels between realms by taking the Rëus Pathways.
☆ Aurana

Omen Tree
Hollow, fossilized tree in the Azure Desert that sometimes
resurfaces from the sands.
☆ Augury

Pamúnn *(M)* *pah-MOON*
Nu'irg with a nyala primal form.
☆ Pogo

Panmaskroon *(M)* *pahn-mass-CRONE*
Mischevious tamarin monkey who can weave her long,
white mustache into any shape.
☆ Libella

Plaguebearer *(F)*
Slender pilgrim with a miasmatic breath who brought the
Yorkab Empire to its pestilent end.
☆ Saniish

Probo *(M)* *PROH-boh*
Nu'irg with a javelina primal form.
☆ Quoll-Velm

Quicksand Throne
Ceremonial chair that will consume those who can't answer the sand riddles.
☆ Truffle Nebula

Runeflayer
Whip with metal runes at its nine tails, casting a curse on
any person or ground it flays.
☆ Ra-Shi-Met

Safís *(F)* *sah-FEES*
Nu'irg with a tundra wolf primal form.
☆ Tai

Shardbow Cloak
Cloak that allows the wearer to walk on beams of moonlight.
☆ Ilaadrus

Shiffrigan's Carapace / *SHE-free-gahn*
Lilac crab armor that allowed Shiffrigan to breathe underwater.
☆ Felagor

Silt Beggar *(M)*
Apparition of the playas who drains water out of travelers
through their tearducts.
☆ Buura

Sixth Gate
The final entryway to the Supernal Realms.
☆ Felsvad Nebula

Skugge *(A)* *SKOO-geh*
Nu'irg with a great gray owl primal form.
☆ Murtegai

Skyfarer
Winged ship that travels across the stars.
☆ Carchesium

Sovath *(F)* *SOH-vahth*
Nu'irg with a chital primal form.
☆ Dukheh

Sword of Zeiheim / *ZEI-hime*
Legendary weapon crafted of lightning.
☆ Pellámbri

Sylvan Lyre
Instrument to summon sprites, and sometimes netherbeasts.
☆ Tertäum

Tailless Scorpion
Netherbeast with eight eyes made from extinguished stars.
☆ Opisthoggar

Tar Serpent *(A)*
Oxruk deity with twelve stomachs.
☆ Ucrarn

Teslur's Web / *TEHS-lure*
Web between the stars spun by the Great Spider of the Khaar Du.
☆ Gossamer Nebula

Thirteen Sisters of Muhmele *(F) moo-h-MEH-leh*
Oldrin spritetale about thirteen princesses, an aureate thrush,
and a mischevious crone.
☆ Vulu

Three Siblings
The first hominids in the Codex of Absent Parables.
☆ Egwe

Tufa Temple
Aetheric temple of mineralized soot and caesura where
each breath lasts a century.
☆ Sammonn

Ukhagar's Last Tooth / *OO-kha-gar*
The rotten cuspid that gives the Crone of Ukhagar her powers.
☆ Cog

Umbaarlis' Staff / *oom-BAR-lihs*
Staff with sixteen gems that keeps the universe in balance.
☆ Talaemánwe Nebula

Ushwen's Key / *OOSH-when*
Aetheric key safeguarding the lava gates under Mount Loor.
☆ Emsal

Wyrm of Arkánni / *ar-CAW-knee*
Black-tongued lava monster who leaves lava tubes in its wake.
☆ Scarëia

Xenolith Giant
Oldrin titan birthed under the pressure of the Stelm Rilganesh.
☆ Taamir

Yaumenn *(A)* *YAW-men*
Demigod whose red hands absorb life.
☆ Scarlet Nebula

Yza *(F)* *IT-suh*
Demigoddess whose shade blesses all it touches.
☆ Umbralia

Zahiir's Apiary / *za-HERE*
Producer of the nectar of Eörel, said to have kept Zahiir alive
for six hundred years.
☆ Haabe

Glossary of Commonly Used Miscamish Words

Parts of speech:

adj. adjective   *adv.* adverb   *art.* article

conj. conjunction   *det.* determiner   *interj.* interjection

nan. animate noun   *nina.* inanimate noun   *num.* numeral

prep. preposition   *pron.* pronoun   *v.* verb

Animate nouns, pronouns, and determiners come in six levels, indicated by the numbers **1–6**. An *s* is for singular, *p* for plural.

KEY

spelling – approx. pronunciation /IPA/ (part of speech) - **definition(s)**

---

agnarg AG-narg /ˈagnarg/ (nan4) - canid, canine

Agnargfröa ag-narg-FRO-ah /ˌagnargˈfro.a/ (nan5) - voice of the canids

Agnargsilv AG-narg-silv /ˈagnargsɪlv/ (nan5) - mask of canids

agnist AG-nist /ˈagnɪst/ (nan3) - fox

agnurf AG-noo-rf /ˈagnurf/ (nan3) - wolf

allastirg AH-last-irg /ˈallastɪrg/ (nina) - south

almel AL-mehl /ˈalmɛl/ (nan4) - perissodactyl, equine

amá'a ah-MAH-'ah /aˈmaʔa/ (nan4) - cetacean

ankrov ANKH-rohv /ˈankrov/ (adj) - rusty

arambukh AH-rahm-boo-kh /ˈarambuχ/ (nina) - money, coin

arudinn AH-roo-dihn /ˈarudɪnn/ (nan2) - seedlight

ash ash /aʃ/ (adj) - white, blank

baakiag BAA-key-ag /ˈbaːkɪag/ (adv) - please

balast BAH-last /ˈbalast/ (nan4) - chiropteran

bir beer /bɪr/ (nina) - home

braaw bra /braːw/ (nina) - mead

ca'éli kah-'EH-lee /kaʔˈɛlɪ/ (nan3) - pilgrim

dinn dihn /dɪnn/ (nan1) - light

drolom DROH-lom /ˈdrolom/ (nan5) - dome

drolv drolv /drolv/ (nan2) - wing

drolvis DROL-vis /ˈdrolvɪs/ (nina) - eternity

enwenn EN-when /ˈɛnwɛnn/ (nina) - graphite

ĕovad EH-oh-vahd /ˈɛ.ovad/ (nan1) - fire

esht esht /ɛʃt/ (adj) - blue

far far /far/ (nan3) - pine, conifer

fel fell /fɛl/ (nina) - island

fröa FRO-ah /ˈfro.a/ (nan6) - voice

gralv grah-lv /gralv/ (adj) - purple

grest grest /grɛst/ (interj) - no

grin grin /grɪn/ (nina) - paint, color, hue

gwonle WON-leh /ˈgwonlɛ/ (nan4) - pinniped

gwur gwoor /gwur/ (nina) - province, territory

hed head /hɛd/ (nan3) - chief (allgender)

hod hohd /hod/ (nan3) - chief (male)

hoombu HOH-OHM-boo /ˈhoːmbu/ (nan4) - primate, ape, monkey

hud hood /hud/ (nan3) - chief (female)

idash EE-dash /ˈɪdaʃ/ (adj) - clear, transparent

ieren YEH-rehn /ˈjɛrɛn/ (nan3) - royal (allgender ruler)

ieron YEH -rohn /ˈjɛron/ (nan3) - king, emperor

ierun YEH -roon /ˈjɛrun/ (nan3) - queen

isdinn IS-dihn /ˈɪsdɪnn/ (nan1) - sea

Iskimesh IS-key-mesh /ˈɪskɪmɛʃ/ (nan6) - Enchantress, third planet from Sunnokh

jall jahl /dʒall/ (nan2) - heart

keldris KEHL-dris /ˈkɛldrɪs/ (nina) - bay, harbor, cove, port

Khumen KHOO-men /ˈχumɛn/ (nan6) - Dawn Pilgrim, first planet from Sunnokh

khuren KHOO-rehn /ˈχurɛn/ (nan3) - prince (allgender)

khuron KHOO-rohn /ˈχuron/ (nan3) - prince (male)

khurun KHOO-roon /ˈχurun/ (nan3) - princess

klad clad /klad/ (nan1) - lake

klannath KLA-nath /ˈklannath/ (nina) - north

kriss chris /krɪss/ (nina) - iron

kroovieth KROH-vee-eth /ˈkroːvɪɛθ/ (nan3) - starling

kroowin CROW-win /ˈkroːwɪn/ (nan4) - avian

krost crossed /krost/ (nan4) - musteloid, mustelid

kruwen CREW-when /ˈkruwɛn/ (nan4) - reptilian, reptile

kupógo coo-POH-goh /kuˈpogo/ (nan3) - snail

laaja LAH-jah /ˈlaːdʒa/ (nan1) - volcano

leif LAY-f /ˈleɪf/ (nan2) - fang

lerr LEH-rr /lɛrr/ (nan3) - liege (allgender honorific)

lerrkin LEH-rr-kin /ˈlɛrrkɪn/ (adj) - bisexual

loomdinn LOOM-dihn /ˈloːmdɪnn/ (nina) - east (birth–light)

lorr lore /lorr/ (nan3) - lord, sir, mister

lorrkin LORE-kin /ˈlorrkɪn/ (adj) - gay, attracted to men

lurr LOO-rr /lurr/ (nan3) - lady, madam, miss

lurrkin LOO-rr-kin /ˈlurrkɪn/ (adj) - lesbian, attracted to women

maarg mah-arg /maːrg/ (adj) - red

malpa MAHL-pah /ˈmalpa/ (adj) - great

mindahim MIHN-dah-him /ˈmɪndahɪm/ (nan3) - caracal

mindílli minh-DEE-lee /mɪnˈdɪllɪ/ (nan3) - sand cat

mindrégo mihn-DREH-goh /mɪnˈdrɛgo/ (nan3) - saber-toothed cat, smilodon

mindrel MIHN-drehl /ˈmɪndrɛl/ (nan4) - felid, feline

mindu MIHN-doo /ˈmɪndu/ (nan3) - black panther

minnéllo mih-NEH-loh /mɪˈnnɛllo/ (nan1) - waterfall

minquoll MIHN-kwol /ˈmɪnkwoll/ (nina) - catball

Miscamish MISS-kah-mih-sh /ˈmɪskamɪʃ/ (nina) - Miscamish

momsúndo mom-SOON-doh /momˈsundo/ (nan4) - proboscidean

nagra NAH-grah /ˈnagra/ (nan4) - suid

ninn nihn /nɪnn/ (nina) - pass

nokh noh-kh /noχ/ (nan1) - sky

Noss noss /noss/ (nan6) - second planet from Sunnokh

nu'irg NOO-ʾee-rg /ˈnuʔɪrg/ (nan5) - ghost, spirit, soul

okri OH-kree /ˈokrɪ/ (nan4) - glires, rodent, lagomorph

okruwil OH-kroo-will /ˈokruwɪl/ (nan3) - pacarana

okruwom OH-kroo-wohm /ˈokruwom/ (nan3) - castoroides (giant beaver)

ommo OH-moh /ˈommo/ (nina) - temple, church

Ongumar ON-goo-mar /ˈongumar/ (nan6) - Amberlight, fifth planet from Sunnokh

quaar kwaar /ˈkwaːr/ (nina) - soot (crystalline, durable form)

quaju KWA-joo /ˈkwadʒu/ (nan4) - marsupial

quas kwas /kwas/ (nina) - canyon

rilg reel-g /rɪlg/ (nan4) - caprid

rilganesh REEL-gah-nesh /ˈrɪlganɛʃ/ (nan3) - sheep (big horned)

rilgéreo reel-GEH-reh-oh /rɪlˈgɛrɛo/ (nan3) - goat

sajal SAH-jahl /ˈsajal/ (adj) - foreboding

Sceres SEH-rehs /ˈssɛrɛs/ (nan6) - moon (the moon)

senstregalv SENS-treh-gal-v /ˈsɛnstregalv/ (nina) - obsidian (special)

Senstrell SENS-trell /ˈsɛnstrɛll/ (nan6) - obsidian, fourth planet from Sunnokh

shisendinn SHE-sen-dihn /ˈʃisɛndɪnn/ (nina) - west (death–light)

shodog SHO-dog /ˈʃodog/ (nina) - jacket (open–chested)

Silv silv /sɪlv/ (nan5) - mask

Silvfröa silv-FRO-ah /sɪlvˈfro.a/ (nan5) - voice of the mask

stelm stelm /stɛlm/ (nina) - mountain

ster stare /stɛr/ (nan6) - star

stiss stiss /stɪss/ (nan1) - river

sulf soo-lf /sulf/ (nina) - land

sun soon /sun/ (nan1) - flame

Sunnokh SOO-noh-kh /ˈsunnoχ/ (nan6) - sun (sky–flame)

tago TAH-goh /ˈtago/ (adj) - gray

telm telm /tɛlm/ (nina) - valley

thaar tha-ar /ˈθaːr/ (nan3) - vanguard

trell trell /trɛll/ (adj) - black

trod troh-d /trod/ (nina) - peak

trommo TROM-moh /ˈtrommo/ (nan4) - bovid, bovine

urg oorg /urg/ (nan4) - cervid

urgei OOr-gay /ˈurgɛi/ (nan3) - elk

urnaadi oor-NAH-dee /urˈnaːdɪ/ (nan4) - ursid, ursine, bear

ust oo-st /ust/ (prep) - of, of the

ustlas OO-st-lahs /ˈustlas/ (nan1) - soot

welkil WEHL-kihl /ˈwɛlkɪl/ (nan3) - aphid (resin making beetle)

wujann WOO-jan /ˈwudʒann/ (adj) - icy

Characters, Gods, Items, Tribes

Abjus *(M) AB-juice*
Chief of Gwur Esmukh in Mindreldrolom. Fiercest Laatu warrior.

Acoapóshi / *ah-kowa-POH-shee*
Miscam tribe in the Tarpits Dome. Stewards of Hoombusilv,
the mask of primates.

Aio *(M) EYE-oh*
Kulak's human form. Prince of Mindreldrolom. Ierun Alúma's son.

Alaia *(F) ah-LAY-uh*
Lago's best friend. Worker at the Withervale coal mines.

Alampaari / *alam-PAH-ree*
Miscam tribe in the Archstone Dome. Stewards of Almelsilv,
the mask of perissodactyls.

Allamónea *(F) ala-MOH-nea*
Cetacean Nu'irg. Sperm whale primal form. Died in times
before the Downfall.

Alúma–Farshálv *(F) ah-LOO-mah far-SHALL-v*
Queen of Mindreldrolom. Khuron Aio–Kulak's mother. Tigress half-form.

Alvis Hallow *(M) AHL-vis HAL-low*
Red Stag's human form. Monarch of the Negian Empire.

Aness *(F) AH-niss*
One of Aurélien's magpie heralds.

Ardof Zaom–Zinemog *(M) ARD-of ZAH-om ZEE-neh-mog*
A ranger informant who frequents Brimstowne to gather information.

Ashaskem *(M) ASH-as-kem*
Kulak's brother who was killed as a baby for being born part tiger.

Aurélien Knivlar *(F) aw-REH-lee-en knee-VLAR*
Shaman in Fjorna's arbalister squad. Commands two magpie heralds,
Aness and Islav.

Bahimir *(M) bah-he-MERE*
Alaia's supervisor at the Withervale coal mines.

Balstei Woodslav *(M) BAHLL-stay WOOD-slav*
An artificer who studies the aetheric elements.

Banook *(M) bah-NOOK*
A mountain of a man who lives alone in the mountains.

Bear *(M) bear*
Lago's mostly mutt, barely shepherd dog.

Behler Broadleaf *(M) BEH-lehr BROAD-leaf*
General of the Fifth Legion of the Negian Empire. Snub-nosed.

Beiféren *(M) bay-FEH-ren*
Caprid Nu'irg. Bootherium (helmeted muskox) primal form.

Bikhéne / *bee-KHEH-neh*
Miscam tribe in the Scoria Dome. Stewards of Balastsilv,
the mask of chiropterans.

Blu *(M) blue*
Kulak's companion smilodon.

Bonmei *(M) BON-may*
Heir to Agnargsilv. Son of Mawua, grandson of Sontai. Ockam's adoptive son.

Brovon *(M) BRO-vohn*
Scrollsinger. Representative for the Lavra Faithful at the Normouth Palace.

Buujik *(F) BOO-jick*
Primate Nu'irg. Red-shanked douc primal form.
Can take the form of a woman.

Crescu Valaran *(M) KREHS-coo VAH-lah-ran*
Armsmaster in Fjorna's arbalister squad.

Crone of Ukhagar *(F) crone of OO-kha-gar*
Trickster character from spritetales.

Crysta Holt *(F) CHRIS-tuh holt*
Lago's professor. Works at the Mesa Observatory.
Secretly works for the Zovarian military.

Däo-Varjak *(F) DAH-oh VAR-jack*
Pinniped Nu'irg. Ribbon seal primal form.

Dedric *(M) DEAD-rick*
Captain in Theggo's flotilla.

Drolvisdinn / *DROLL-vis-dihn*
Ilsed's leaf-sailed ship with a hull of knotted roots.

Dunokh Sull / *DOO-nokh sool*
"The Arc of the Night Sky." A legendary quaar bow. Also a constellation.

Ëalcor *(M) EH-al-core*
Marsupial Nu'irg. Thylacine primal form.

Edmar Helm *(M) ED-muhr helm*
General of the First Legion of the Negian Empire.

Estriéggo *(M) ess-tree-EH-goh*
Perissodactyl Nu'irg. Woolly rhinoceros primal form.

Fingrenn *(A) FIN-gren*
Laatu interpreter who tutors the travelers.

Fjorna Daro *(F) FYOR-nah DAHR-oh*
Chief Arbalister from a specialist squad of the Negian Empire.

Fjummomurr / *FEW-moh-murr*
Siffo's black-sailed whaling ship with a hull reinforced with
kuba bones and a narwhal figurehead.

Frud *(M) frood*
Bear from the Stelm Wujann. Sabikh's cub. Also a Barlum Saga character.

Fuuriseth *(F) FOO-ree-seth*
Chiropteran Nu'irg. White leaf-nosed bat primal form.

Gaönir–Bijeor / *gah-OH-neer BEE-jeh-or*
"Shield of Creation." Takhísh's legendary shield.

Garvall Ferwillow *(M) GAR-vall FER-willow*
Cavalry general for the Republic of Lerev.

Gino Baneras *(M) GEE-no bah-NEH-rahs*
General of the Fourth Legion of the Negian Empire. Longbowman.

Grinn *(M) grinn*
Admiral of Zovaria's Centennial Fleet. Bashed in the head by Balstei.

Gufrok *(M) GOOF-rock*
Celebochoerus who carries Kitjári through the Stelm Nedross.

Gurovon *(A) GOO-roh-von*
Oxruk Envoy. Ushers the travelers into the tunnels of Oxmaaga.

Gwil *(M) gwill*
Chaplain at the Withervale chapter of the Havengall Congregation.

Gwit *(M) gWIT*
Glires (rodent and lagomorph) Nu'irg. Hazel dormouse primal form.

Gwoli *(M) WOH-lee*
"Younger brother" in Oldrin. Pet name Alaia has for Lago.

Hefra Boarmane *(F) HEH-fruh BOAR-main*
Naturalist who specializes in ornithology and entomology.

Hetfr the Speaker *(F) HEH-t-fruh*
Oxruk Speaker who works for Tajaz the Seer.

Hilid Kei *(F) HE-lid kay*
Duchess of Navat Mat who captures Serdein.

Holfster *(A) HOLEf-str*
Botanist from Bauram. Has a nursery in Withervale.

Ikhel / *EE-hell*
Miscam tribe in the Bighorn Dome. Stewards of Rilgsilv, the mask of caprids.

Ilaadrid Shard / *ee-LAH-drihd shard*
The beacon that shines on Sceres's face twice a month.

Ilsed *(F) ILL-sed*
Chief of Gwur Gomosh in Mindreldrolom. Captain of Drolvisdinn.

Isdinnuk / *IS-dih-nook*
Miscam tribe in the Seafaring Dome. Stewards of Amá'asilv,
the mask of cetaceans.

Ishke'ísuk *(M) ish-keh-'EE-sook*
Reptilian Nu'irg. Double-crested basilisk primal form.

Iskimesh *(F) IS-key-mesh*
Enchantress. Third planet from Sunnokh.

Islav *(M) IZ-lahv*
One of Aurélien's magpie heralds.

Jabrak-Tsing / *jah-BRACK tsing*
Race from the southern Tsing Empire who have tufted tails.

Jessha *(F) JEH-sha*
Sehján queen who has never worn Okrisilv. Mother of Puuja and Pol.

Ji */ gee*
Miscam tribe in the Azurean Dome. Stewards of Quajusilv,
the mask of marsupials.

Jiara Ascura *(F) gee-AH-rah as-COO-rah*
Kitjári's human form. Platoon commander in the Free Tribelands.

Jilpi *(M) JILL-pee*
Old miner from Brimstowne who likes to soak in the hot springs.

Jiu Zezi *(F) gee-oo ZEH-zee*
Yenwu cosmologist who discovered the comet that would cause the
Downfall.

Jojek */ JOE-jeck*
Miscam tribe in the Lequa Dome. Stewards of Krostsilv,
the mask of musteloids.

Kedra *(F) KEH-drah*
Zovarian scout who works for Crysta.

Kenzir stone */ KEN-sr*
Pharoliths. Glowing rocks made with the aetheric element of pharos.

Kerjaastórgnem *(M) ker-jah-STORE-gnem*
Ursid Nu'irg. Arctotherium primal form.
Can take the form of a man. Banook.

Khardok */ KHAR-dock*
Miscam tribe in the Moonrise Dome. Stewards of Gwonlesilv,
the mask of pinnipeds.

Khopto *(M) KHOP-toh*
Havengall monk who works with soot and specializes in "seeing the threads."

Khumen *(M) KHOO-men*
Dawn Pilgrim. First planet from Sunnokh.

Kitjári *(F) kit-JAH-ree*
Urnaadifröa. Jiara's black bear half-form.
Platoon commander in the Free Tribelands.

Klaawich *(A) KLAA-which*
Laatu shaman who has an albatross companion.

Korten dus Fer *(M) COURT-en doos fair*
General of the Sixth Legion of the Negian Empire.

Kulak *(M) COO-lack*
Mindrelfröa. Khuron Aio's caracal half-form.

Laatu / *LAH-AH-too*
Miscam tribe in the Moordusk Dome. Stewards of Mindrelsilv, the mask of felids.

Lago Vaari *(M) LAH-goh VAH-ree*
Sterjall's human form. Young man from Withervale who by chance inherits Agnargsilv.

Lakemother *(F) LAKE-mother*
Sehján deity of the waters and protection.

Leif / *LAY-f*
"Fang." Lago's dagger.

Luhásu *(F) loo-HA-soo*
Western Ikhel leader who allies with the Red Stag to obtain Rilgsilv.

Lummukem *(A) LOO-moo-kem*
A winged dragon from spritetales. Also a constellation.

Luras Varum *(M) LURE-us VAH-ruhm*
Lago's name when he wants to go incognito.

Macúsca *(F) mah-COOS-kah*
Jojek slave who helps start the revolt at the Lequa Dome.

Malazzari *(M) mah-lah-ZA-ree*
Graalman god of fertility. Hung horse. Also a constellation.

Malnûvi *(F) mal-NOO-vee*
Puqua elder chief from the village of Onbar.

Mamóru *(M) mah-MOH-roo*
Proboscidean Nu'irg. Steppe mammoth primal form. Can take the form of a man.

Mareesha *(F) mah-REE-sha*
Captain in Theggo's flotilla.

Mauvenel *(A) MA-OO-vin-el*
Legendary hero who wielded Dunokh Sull.

Mio *(M) MEE-oh*
First Ji Miscam the travelers encounter. Old farmer from the village of Asra.

Mo'óto / *moh-'OH-toh*
Miscam tribe in the Varanus Dome. Stewards of Kruwensilv, the mask of reptilians.

Muri *(M) MOO-ree*
Musteloid Nu'irg. Honey badger primal form.

Muriel Clawwick *(F) MEW-ree-el CLAW-wick*
Arbalister in Fjorna's squad. Waldomar's sister.

Murtégo / *moor-TEH-goh*
Miscam tribe in the Yenwu Dome. Stewards of Kroowinsilv, the mask of avians.

Nalaníri *(F) nah-lah-NEE-ree*
Nagrafröa. Prikka's boar half-form. Puqua chef.

Nelv *(F) nelv*
Felid Nu'irg. Clouded leopard primal form.

Noss *(A) noss*
Second planet from Sunnokh.

Nupáll *(F) noo-PAHLL*
Domestic pig who carries Nalaníri through the Stelm Nedross.

Ockam Radiartis *(M) OCK-uhm ra-dee-AR-tiss*
Sylvan scout from the Free Tribelands. Bonmei's adoptive father.

Odask *(M) ODD-ask*
The father of Nalaníri's two children.

Oldrin / *ALL-drin*
Race from the far east of the Jerjan Continent who grow bony protuberances called spurs.

Ongumar *(M) ON-goo-mar*
Amberlight. Fifth planet from Sunnokh.

Osef Windscar *(M) OW-sehf WIND-scar*
Arbalister in Fjorna's squad.

Ouránama *(F) ow-RAH-nah-mah*
Ulésse's human form. Chief of Quajudrolom. Gardener, farmer, and botanist at Mikkagolm.

Pamúnn *(M) pah-MOON*
Bovid Nu'irg. Nyala primal form.

Pau *(F) pow*
Nalaníri's teenaged daughter.

Pellámbri *(F) peh-LUHM-bree*
The Lodestar. A pink nebula at the heart of the Sword of Zeiheim.

Pian–Thi *(F) pee-an TEA*
Empress of the Tsing Empire.

Pichi *(F) PEE-chee*
Largest of smilodons, who usually carries all the gear.

Pollomekh (Pol) *(M) POH-loh-mekh*
Prince of the Sehján. Puuja's twin brother.

Prikka *(F) PREE-kah*
Nalaníri's human form. Puqua chef.

Probo *(M) PROH-boh*
Suid Nu'irg. Javelina primal form.

Puqua */ POO-kwa*
Miscam tribe in the Fjordlands Dome. Stewards of Nagrasilv,
the mask of suids.

Puuja *(F) POO-jah*
Princess of the Sehján. Pol's sister.

Quggon */ KYOO-gone*
A cube made of 9 chips that add up to a value of one hundred Qupi.

Quoda *(F) KWO-dah*
Chief of Gwur Pantuul in Mindreldrolom. Lives in Panjuul. Dreadlock wig.

Qupi */ KYOO-pee*
Chevron-shaped chips used as currency units.

Red Stag *(M) red stag*
Alvis Hallow's elk half-form when wearing Urgsilv.

Rushun *(M) ROO-shoon*
Nalaníri's teenaged son.

Sabikh *(F) sah-BEE-kh*
Bear from the Stelm Wujann. Frud's mother. Barlum Saga character.

Safîs *(F) sah-FEES*
Canid Nu'irg. Tundra wolf primal form.

Sceres *(F) SEH-rehs*
Noss's moon.

Seera Ashbend *(F) SEE-ruh ASH-bend*
Infantry general for the Republic of Lerev.

Sehján */ seh-JAHN*
Miscam tribe in the Nisos Dome. Stewards of Okrisilv, the mask of glires.

Senstrell *(F) SENS-trell*
"Obsidian." Fourth planet from Sunnokh.

Serdein Humuen–Vok *(M) SUR-dane HOO-moo-en vock*
Moa rider from Lhambor Di who travels the Cobalt Desert.

Seshéni *(F) seh-SHEH-nee*
Dragoon leader of kudu-riding troop from Lerev.

Shea Lu *(F) SHEH-ah loo*
Arbalister in Fjorna's squad.

Siffo *(M) SEE-foh*
Puqua captain of Fjummomurr, the Tusked Whale. Quarter warthog.

Silv–Thaar Markhor *(F) silv-THAH-AR MAR-core*
Luhásu's markhor half-form when wearing Rilgsilv.

Silv–Thaar Valaran *(M) silv-THAH-AR VAH-lah-ran*
Crescu's raccoon half-form when wearing Krostsilv.

Silverweave */ SILL-vr-weave*
Theggo's many-sailed frigate.

Skirr *(F) SKI-rr*
Sehján emissary who goes to speak to Gurovon the Envoy of the Oxruk.

Skugge *(A) SKOO-geh*
Avian Nu'irg. Great gray owl primal form. Only allgender Nu'irg.

Sontai *(F) SON-tie*
Bonmei's grandmother. Gives Agnargsilv to Lago. Gray fox half-form.

Sovath *(F) SOH-vahth*
Cervid Nu'irg. Chital primal form, but often seen as an antlerless megaloceros next to the Red Stag.

Sterjall *(M) STARE-jahl*
Agnargfröa. Lago's timber wolf half-form.

Sunnokh *(M) SOO-noh-kh*
"Sky-flame." The sun.

Sunu *(A) SOO-noo*
Laatu shaman warrior trained both in the arts of healing and battle.

Sword of Zeiheim */ ZEI-hime*
Legendary weapon crafted of lightning. Also a constellation.

Tajaz the Seer *(M) ta-JAHZ*
Oxruk Seer. Naked mole rat half-form.

Takhamún *(M) ta-kha-MOON*
The Unmaker, god of destruction from the Takh Codex.

Takhísh *(M) ta-KHEE-sh*
The Demiurge, god of creation from the Takh Codex.

Teldebran */ TELL-the-brahn*
Miscam tribe in the Anglass Dome. Stewards of Urgsilv, the mask of cervids.

Theggo Saurfall *(M) THEH-go SOUR-fall*
Fleet Admiral for a Lerevi flotilla of the Kilgane Naval Base.

Thurann Embercut *(F) THOO-rahn EM-br-cut*
Marshal of the Zovarian Ninth Battalion, stationed in Nebush.

Tinnomeg *(M) TEE-noh-meg*
Giant eland who Theggo rides to battle.

Tjardur */ CHAR-dure*
Miscam tribe in the Ashen Dome. Stewards of Trommosilv,
the mask of bovids.

Toldask */ TOLD-ask*
Miscam tribe in the Brasha'in Scablands. Stewards of Momsúndosilv,
the mask of proboscideans.

Tor-Reveo */ tore REH-vee-oh*
"Spear of Undoing." Takhamún's legendary spear.

Tremor *(M) TREH-mr*
Jartadi steed the Red Stag rides. Black velvet coat.

Trevin Gobbar *(M) TREH-vinn GOH-bar*
Arbalister in Fjorna's squad. Long nose.

Tsei *(F) t-SAY*
Sehján warrior who first finds the travelers inside the Nisos Dome.

Ulésse *(F) oo-LEH-she*
Quajufröa. Ouránama's wombat half-form.
Gardener, farmer, and botanist at Mikkagolm.

Urcai *(M) OOR-ky*
Crafty artificer from the Negian Empire.

Vaalag Feallanor-Vok *(F) VAAH-lag fe-AH-la-nor vock*
Navar Mat commander in service of Duke Hilid Kei.

Vor-Vor *(M) vore vore*
Tsing ambassador. Jabrak–Tsing eunuch who sails aboard Canvasback.

Vordeno *(M) vore-DAY-noh*
Princeps of Lerev. Democratically elected.

Wutash, Northern / *WOO-tash*
Miscam tribe in the Da'áju Caldera. Stewards of Urnaadisilv,
the mask of ursids.

Wutash, Southern / *WOO-tash*
Miscam tribe in the Heartpine Dome. Stewards of Agnargsilv,
the mask of canids.

LOCATIONS

Afhora, Kingdom of / *ah-FOR-uh*
One of the sixteen realms. Its capital is Sundhollow.

Agnargdrolom / *AG-narg-droh-lom*
Heartpine Dome. Located between the Free Tribelands and the Negian
Empire.

Aksas Di / *ACK-sus dee*
Baurami city on the eastern shores of the Cobalt Desert.

Aldávi / *al-DA-vee*
Jojek city in the Lequa Dome. On the northwest, at the end of the Tor Fjord.

Allathanathar / *ala-THA-na-thar*
Capital of the Kingdom of Bauram.

Almeldrolom / *AL-mehl-droh-lom*
Archstone Dome. Located between the Dorhond Tribes
and the Graalman Horde.

Amá'adrolom / *ah-MAH-'ah-droh-lom*
Seafaring Dome. Located in the Capricious Ocean, locked to an atoll.

Anglass / *AN-glass*
Negian fortress on the south–east perimeter of the Anglass Dome.

Anglass Dome / *AN-glass*
Urgdrolom. Dome located in the Negian Empire, north of the Stiss Malpa.

Archstone Dome
Almeldrolom. Dome located between the Dorhond Tribes
and the Graalman Horde.

Arho / *AR-hoh*
Port city in the Fjordlands Dome.

Arjum / *AR-joom*
Capital of the Laatu Miscam, province of Gwur Ali, in Mindreldrolom,
the Moordusk Dome.

Arjum Promenade / *AR-joom*
Public walkway around Mindreldrolom's trunk, holding the stadium,
sculpture gardens, reliquary, etc.

Ash Sea
"White Sea." Northern sea teeming with icebergs.

Ashen Dome
Trommodrolom. Dome located in the southern Tsing Empire, with a top that constantly smokes.

Asra / *AS-rah*
Idyllic village on the eastern deserts of the Azurean Dome.

Azash / *ah-ZAH-sh*
Capital of the Elmaren Queendom.

Azurean Dome / *ah-ZUR-ean*
Quajudrolom. Dome located in the Kingdom of Bauram, surrounded by blue sands.

Balastdrolom / *BAH-last-droh-lom*
Scoria Dome. Located between Afhoran, Tharman, and Graalman lands.

Bauram, Kingdom of / *bau-RAHM*
One of the sixteen realms. Its capital is Allathanathar.

Bauresht Peninsula / *BAU-resht*
Southeastern end of Fel Baubór. Part of the Republic of Lerev.

Bay of Negórmea / *neh-GORE-meh-ah*
Wide bay between the Elmaren Queendom and the Dorhond Tribes.

Bayanhong Tribes / *BAH-jann-hong*
One of the sixteen realms. Its capital is On Khurderen.

Bergsulf / *BERG-sulf*
Land of independent colonies in the Unclaimed Territories, north of the Fractured Range.

Bighorn Dome
Rilgdrolom. Dome located between the peaks of the Stelm Rilgéreo and Stelm Rilganesh.

Binull / *bee-NOOL*
Oxruk underground city in the Nisos Dome.

Birlénno / *beer-LEH-no*
Main port city at the center of the Fjordlands Dome.

Brasha'in Scablands / *brah-sha-'EEN*
Volcanic wasteland in the western Zovarian Union.

Brimstowne / *BRIMs-town*
Mining frontier town in an independent Bergsulfi colony
by the Stelm Wujann.

Brumm / *broom*
Kenzir stone mines in the Fjordlands Dome.

Calbor / *CAL-bore*
Jojek city in the Lequa Dome. On the shores of Klad Jilo,
the largest lake in the dome.

Capricious Ocean
Southernmost of the four oceans, known for its unpredictable waters.

Chail Trodesh / *cha-ill TROH-desh*
"Three Peaks" at the center of the Azurean Dome,
surrounding the capital of Mikkagolm.

Claoth / *clawth*
Northernmost city in the Fjordlands Dome.

Cobalt Desert
Expansive desert of blue, black, and purple sands in Fel Baubór.

Da'áju Caldera / *da-'AH-joo*
Vast, static cirque glacier in the Stelm Wujann.

Dakhud / *DAH-hood*
Capital of the province of Gwur Aalpe in the Moordusk Dome.

Dathereol Princedom / *dah-THEE-ree-ol*
One of the sixteen realms. Its capital is Therimark.

Dïer / *DEE-err*
Capital of the Jojek Miscam in Krostdrolom, the Lequa Dome.

Dohao Mesa / *DOH-how*
Dark-colored mesa at the center of the Nisos Dome.

Doralghon / *DOH-ralg-hone*
Capital of the Graalman Horde.

Dorhond Range / *DOOR-hund*
Ragged sierras separating the White Desert from the Archstone Dome.

Dorhond Tribes / *DOOR-hund*
One of the sixteen realms. Its capital is Oskirin.

Drann Trodesh / *drahn TROH-desh*
Sawtoothed mountains wrapping around Unemar Lake.

Druhal / *droo-HAL*
Capital of the Wastyr Triumvirate. One of three.

Elanúbril / *ella-NOO-breel*
Capital of the Khaar Du Tribes.

Elmaren Queendom / *EL-ma-ren*
One of the sixteen realms. Its capital is Azash.

Emen Ruins / *EH-men*
Dorvauros ruins with hot springs resting within a lava tube.

Erne Goro / *ERR-neh GORE-oh*
Largest soot mine in the Lequa Dome, west of the capital of Dïer.

Esduss Sea / *ES-doos*
Sea separating Fel Baubór from the Loorian mainland.

Eskis / *ES-keys*
Jojek city in the Lequa Dome. On the north, where the Stiss Lemen
empties into the Isdinn Kimen.

Farjall / *FAR-jall*
Negian fortress on the south-east perimeter of the Heartpine Dome.

Farkhalum / *far-KHA-loom*
Capital of the Wastyr Triumvirate. One of three.

Farsulf Forest / *FAR-soolf*
"Pine Land." Forest north of the Heartpine Dome, south of the Stelm Ca'éli.

Fel Baubór / *fell bau-BORE*
Continent-sized island of blue sands, mostly belonging to
the Kingdom of Bauram.

Fel Kamman / *fell CAH-mahn*
Floating island of the Sehján that attaches to Kisdik.

Fel Nisos / *fell NY-sus*
Great island of the Republic of Lerev.

Fel Shinn / *fell sheen*
Island north of Fel Varanus.

Fel Varanus / *fell VAH-rah-noose*
Zovarian island on which the Varanus Dome spreads its tendrils.

Firefalls
"Minnelvad." Steaming waterfalls in the Stelm Wujann,
northwest of Brimstowne.

Fjarmallen Peninsula / *fee-ar-MAH-lehn*
Loosely inhabited lands on the fast southwest of the Dathereol Princedom.

Fjordlands Dome
Nagradrolom. Dome located between the Zovarian Union and
the Khaar Du Tribes.

Fjordsulf / *FJORD-soolf*
Cold land of fjords and icebergs of the Khaar Du Tribes.

Fractured Range
Old lakebed that crackled into massive slot canyons as it dried out,
east of the Stelm Khull.

Free Tribelands
One of the sixteen realms. Its capital is Klemes.

Galewrath Craters
Wide expanse of frozen craters separating the Stelm Nedross
and the Stelm Wujann.

Graalman Horde / *GROWL-mahn*
One of the sixteen realms. Its capital is Doralghon.

Gulf of Erjilm / *ERR-juhlm*
Circular gulf at the split between the two great continents.

Gwonledrolom / *WON-leh-droh-lom*
Moonrise Dome. Located in the far east, in the Elmaren Queendom.

Gwur Aalpe / *woor AHL-peh*
One of six provinces in the Moordusk Dome. Its capital is Dakhud.

Gwur Ali / *woor AH-lee*
One of six provinces in the Moordusk Dome. Its capital is Arjum.

Gwur Esmukh / *woor ES-mook*
One of six provinces in the Moordusk Dome. Its capital is Quas Trell.

Gwur Gomosh / *woor GOH-mush*
One of six provinces in the Moordusk Dome. Its capital is Oälpaskist.

Gwur Pantuul / *woor pan-TOOL*
One of six provinces in the Moordusk Dome. Its capital is Parjuul.

Gwur Úrëath / *woor OO-reh-ath*
One of six provinces in the Moordusk Dome. Its capital is Humenath.

Hashan / *ha-SHUN*
Capital of the Tsing Empire. Also called the "City of Bridges."

Heartpine Dome
Agnargdrolom. Dome located between the Free Tribelands
and the Negian Empire.

Hestfell / *HEST-fell*
Capital of the Negian Empire.

Hoombudrolom / *HOH-OHM-boo-droh-lom*
Tarpits Dome. Located in the Tsing Empire, by the Khonn Tar Pits.

Horo / *HOH-roh*
Oxruk underground city in the Nisos Dome.

Humenath / *WHO-men-ath*
Capital of the province of Gwur Úrëath in the Moordusk Dome.

Ifen / *EE-fen*
Jojek city in the Lequa Dome. Southwest of the capital,
at the base of the mountains.

Illenev / *EE-leh-nehv*
Capital of the Wastyr Triumvirate. One of three.

Isdinn Kimen / *IS-dihn KEY-men*
A portion of the Lequa Sea scooped up by the Lequa Dome.

Isdinnklad / *IS-dihn-clad*
"Sea Lake." Long, tapering sea splitting the Loorian Continent.

Jerjan Continent / *JER-jann*
Named after Laaja Jerja, tallest peak at 38,264 feet.

Jianmu / *gee-AN-moo*
Jojek city in the Lequa Dome. On the far west, by Laaja Spahn.

Keldris Allastirg / *KEL-dris AH-last-ihrg*
"Southern Bay" in the Fjordlands Dome.

Keldris Klannath / *KEL-dris CLAH-nuth*
"Northern Bay" in the Fjordlands Dome.

Khaar Du Tribes / *khar doo*
One of the sixteen realms. Its capital is Elanúbril.

Khaar Du Wastes / *khar doo*
Icy wastelands of the north.

Khaarkadesh / *KHAR-cah-desh*
"Stone Road" in the Khaar Du tongue. Glacier valley in the
northern Stelm Wujann.

Kilgane / *KILL-gain*
Lerevi naval base at the southern tip of the Bauresht Peninsula.

Kisdik / *KISS-dick*
Floating Sehján capital wrapped around a supporting column
of the Nisos Dome.

Kissumar / *KISS-oo-mar*
Old Sehján capital around the trunk of the Nisos Dome.
In ruins, overtaken by the Oxruk.

Kizad / *key-ZAHD*
Northernmost city of the Republic of Lerev, in Fel Baubór.

Klad Allún / *clad ah-LOON*
Large lake in the Nisos Dome.

Klad Flal / *clad flahl*
Large lake in the Nisos Dome.

Klad Goro / *clad GOH-roh*
Large lake in the Nisos Dome.

Klad Jilo / *clad GEE-low*
Largest lake in the Lequa Dome.

Klad Mahujann / *clad MA-hoo-jann*
"Very Icy Lake." Perpetually frozen lake between the Stelm Nedross and
the Stelm Wujann.

Klad Senet / *clad senate*
Largest lake in the Loorian Continent, at the heart of the Free Tribelands.

Klad Üo / *clad OO-oh*
Largest lake in the Nisos Dome. Home of the floating cities
of Kisdik and Krillimo.

Klemes / *CLEM-uhs*
Capital of the Free Tribelands, west of the Klad Senet.

Koroberg / *COH-roh-berg*
Zovarian port city southwest of the Fjordlands Dome.

Krillimo / *CREE-lee-moh*
Floating Sehján city wrapped around a supporting column
of the Nisos Dome.

Kroowindrolom / *CROW-win-droh-lom*
Yenwu Dome. Located in the Yenwu Peninsula.

Krostdrolom / *CROSSED-droh-lom*
Lequa Dome. Located in the eastern Negian Empire,
by Bayanhong settlements.

Krûn / *croon*
Capital of the Puqua Miscam in Nagradrolom, the Fjordlands Dome.

Kruwendrolom / *CREW-when-droh-lom*
Varanus Dome. Located in Fel Varanus, a far western island
of the Zovarian Union.

Laaja Deulmosk / *LA-AH-jah DEWL-mosque*
Volcano in the Fjordlands Dome very close to the kenzir stone mines.

Laaja Jerja / *LA-AH-jah JIR-jah*
Volcano. Tallest peak of the Jerjan Continent at 38,264 feet.

Laaja Khem / *LA-AH-jah khem*
Volcano northwest of the Da'áju Caldera with old Dorvauros mines
tunneling through it.

Lappan / *LA-pahn*
Town on the northwest edge of the Anglass Dome.

Lequa Dome / *LEH-kwa*
Krostdrolom. Dome located in the eastern Negian Empire,
by Bayanhong settlements.

Lequa Sea / *LEH-kwa*
Northeastern sea that funnels into the Ophidian. Dome is named after it.

Lerev, Republic of / *luh-REHV*
One of the sixteen realms. Its capital is Normouth.

Lhambor Di / *LAHM-bore dee*
Baurami city on the eastern shores of the Cobalt Desert.

Loorian Continent / *LOO-ree-anne*
Named after Mount Loor, tallest peak at 35,167 feet.

Lurr's Abyss / *LOO-rr*
Wasteland in the Stelm Khull, north of the Anglass Dome.

Macu / *MA-coo*
Old Mo'óto capital at the center of the Varanus Dome.

Maz'tesh / *MAHZ-'tesh*
Oxruk underground city in the Nisos Dome.

Mikkagolm / *ME-cah-golm*
Capital of the Ji Miscam in Quajudrolom, the Azurean Dome.

Mindreldrolom / *MIHN-drehl-droh-lom*
Moordusk Dome. Located in the Zovarian Union, near Zovaria.

Minnelvad / *ME-nell-vahd*
"Firefalls." Steaming waterfalls in the Stelm Wujann,
northwest of Brimstowne.

Montano / *mon-TAH-no*
Negian port city in the only Negian state in the Jerjan Continent.

Moonrise Dome
Gwonledrolom. Dome located in the far east, in the Elmaren Queendom.

Moordusk Dome
Mindreldrolom. Dome located in the Zovarian Union, near Zovaria.

Mount Glirjil / *GLEER-jill*
Tallest peak of Fel Baubór.

Mount Loor / *lure*
Tallest peak of the Loorian Continent at 35,167 feet.

Mount Punwok / *POON-wok*
Prominent peak in the Stelm Nedross.

Mugwort Forest
Largest forest in the Free Tribelands.

Muskeg
Zovarian town on the southeast of the Moordusk Dome.

Muura Glacier / *MOO-rah*
Frozen lands in the Stelm Atuur, where the Sehján city of Fuävi is located.

Nagradrolom / *NAH-grah-droh-lom*
Fjordlands Dome. Located between the Zovarian Union and
the Khaar Du Tribes.

Nargara / *nar-GAH-rah*
Tsing fortress city on the eastern borders, home of the Nargara Bastion.

Navar Mat / *NAH-vahr mat*
Capital of the Duchy of Blue Stone, on the east perimeter
of the Azurean Dome.

Nebush / *NEH-bush*
Zovarian port town on the southwest of the Moordusk Dome.

Needlecove
Small Zovarian town close to the Northlock Strait.
Known for its chalk promontories.

Negian Empire / *NEE-jann*
One of the sixteen realms. Its capital is Hestfell.

Nerokholm / *NEH-roh-kholm*
Capital of the Teldebran Miscam in Urgdrolom, the Anglass Dome.

Ninn Tago / *nihn TAH-goh*
"Gray Pass." Old road cutting over the Stelm Ca'éli, connecting
Withervale to Knife Point.

Nisos / *NY-sus*
Lerevi port city. Used to be the capital of the old Kingdom of Nisos.

Nisos Dome / *NY-sus*
Okridrolom. Dome located in the Republic of Lerev,
in the island of Fel Nisos.

Nool / *nool*
Negian city close to Withervale.

Normouth / *NOR-muth*
Capital of the Republic of Lerev.

Okridrolom / *OH-kree-droh-lom*
Nisos Dome. Located in the Republic of Lerev, in the island of Fel Nisos.

Old Pilgrim's Road
Longest road in the Loorian Continent, running from
Umarion to Wyrmwash.

Ôllomuy / *OH-low-moo-ee*
Port city in the Fjordlands Dome where Siffo is from.
They harvest very sweet figs.

Olvur Gate / *ALL-voor*
Entrance to the city of Oxmaaga, the Oxruk capital, carved on the
north wall of the Dohao Mesa.

On Khurderen / *on khur-DEH-rehn*
Capital of the Bayanhong Tribes.

Onbar / *ON-bar*
Village in the Fjordlands Dome where first contact with the Puqua happens.

Ophidian Sea
Snaking sea separating the Loorian and Jerjan continents.

Oskirin / *OSS-kih-ruhn*
Capital of the Dorhond Tribes.

Oxmaaga / *ox-MA-gah*
Capital of the Oxruk in the Nisos Dome, burrowing below the old
Sehján Capital of Kissumar.

Quajudrolom / *KWA-joo-droh-lom*
Azurean Dome. Located in the Kingdom of Bauram,
surrounded by blue sands.

Quiescent Ocean
Westernmost of the four oceans, known for its calm waters.

Rilgdrolom / *REEL-g-droh-lom*
Bighorn Dome. Located between the peaks of the Stelm Rilgéreo
and the Stelm Rilganesh.

Sajal Crater / *SAH-jall*
Round crater in the volcanic lands of the Stelm Sajal.
Known for its warm waters.

Scoria Dome
Balastdrolom. Dome located between Afhoran, Tharman,
and Graalman lands.

Seaborr / *SEA-bore*
Negian port northwest of the Lequa Dome, in the Almoth Bay.

Seafaring Dome
Amá'adrolom. Dome located in the Capricious Ocean, locked to an atoll.

Shaderift
Negian city on the southwest of the Lequa Dome.

Shaderift Aqueduct
Conduit built to carry water from the Klad Enturg to the
fortress of Shaderift.

Sharr Helm / *shahr helm*
Capital of the Tharma Federation.

Silverkeep
Silver mines near Brimstowne.

Silverkeep Road
Road that runs from Nool, to Brimstowne, continuing north
into the Silverkeep mines.

Slømmon Forest / *SLOW-muhn*
Forest in the Stelm Shäerath of the Fjordlands Dome,
known for its hoodoos and honey truffles.

Snoring Mountain
Peak in the Stelm Wujann that tends to tremble unpredictably.

Spine Bay
Inner saltwater bay northeast of the Fjordlands Dome.

Stelm Atuur / *stelm ah-TOUR*
Range on the southeast of the Nisos Dome, known for its many tunnels
left by receding vines.

Stelm Auméllo / *stelm aw-MEH-loh*
Range on the southwest of the Nisos Dome.

Stelm Glirjil / *stelm GLEER-jill*
Range south of the Azurean Dome known for its caves full of tar.

Stelm Humenath / *stelm WHO-men-ath*
Highest peak inside the Moordusk Dome.

Stelm Khull / *stelm khool*
"Graveyard Mountains." Spur of mountains extending east from
the Stelm Wujann.

Stelm Nil / *stelm nil*
"Smooth Mountain." Central mountain in the Anglass Dome, from where
the trunk grows.

Stelm Sajal / *stelm SAH-jall*
"Foreboding Mountains." Volcanic range east of the Brasha'in Scablands.

Stelm Shäerath / *stelm SHAH-eh-rath*
The Tricolored Mountain, central peak at the Fjordlands Dome from where
the trunk grows.

Stelm Tai-Du / *stelm tai-DOO*
"Night-Snow Mountains." Range north of the Tarpits Dome.

Stelm Wujann / *stelm WOO-jann*
"Icy Mountains." Vast sierras in the northern Loorian Continent.

Stiss Khull / *stiss khool*
"Graveyard River." Glacier-fed river extending east from the Stelm Wujann.

Stiss Lemen / *stiss lemon*
River that starts near the Erne Goro mines of the Lequa Dome, and empty
into the Isdinn Kimen.

Stiss Malpa / *stiss MAHL-pah*
River that empties into the tip of the Isdinnklad Lake, right at Withervale.

Stiss Minn / *stiss mihn*
Tributary of the Stiss Malpa that starts at the Firefalls.

Sulphur Pit
Sulphur mines west of Brimstowne.

Sundhollow / *SUHND-hollow*
Capital of the Kingdom of Afhora.

Taring / *TAH-ring*
Pre-Downfall ruins at the Taring Peninsula, southwest of the Gulf of Erjilm.

Taróro / *tah-ROH-roh*
Oxruk underground city in the Nisos Dome.

Tarpits Dome
Hoombudrolom. Dome located in the Tsing Empire, by the Khonn Tar Pits.

Telm Klannath / *telm CLAH-nuth*
"Northern Valley." Valley with many rivers and creeks that feeds
the Stiss Khull.

Teslurkath / *TESS-lure-cath*
Iceberg-covered shores on the frigid, northwestern frontiers of Noss.

Tharma Federation / *THAHR-mah*
One of the sixteen realms. Its capital is Sharr Helm.

Therimark / *THEH-ree-mark*
Capital of the Dathereol Princedom.

Thicket Island
Large island east of Fel Varanus, wrapped by unruly vines from
the Varanus Dome.

Thornridge Lookout
Free Tribelands fortress protecting the perimeter road around
the Heartpine Dome.

Trommodrolom / *TROM-moh-droh-lom*
Ashen Dome. Located in the southern Tsing Empire, with a top that
constantly smokes.

Tsing Empire / *zing*
One of the sixteen realms. Its capital is Hashan.

Tumultuous Ocean
Easternmost of the four oceans, known for its rough waters.

Tunhau / *TOON-how*
Jojek city in the Lequa Dome. On the southwest, by the piped entrances.

Unclaimed Territories
Areas not claimed by any of the sixteen realms.

Unthawing Ocean
Northernmost of the four oceans, known for its icesheets and icebergs.

Urgdrolom / *OORG-droh-lom*
Anglass Dome. Located in the Negian Empire, wrapped by the Stiss Malpa.

Ushwen Krost / *OOSH-when crossed*
Jojek temple in the Lequa Dome. Secret cove where the Stiss Lemen
empties into the Isdinn Kimen.

Varanus Dome / *VAH-rah-noose*
Kruwendrolom. Dome located in Fel Varanus, a far western island of the
Zovarian Union.

Wastyr Triumvirate / *was-TIER*
One of the sixteen realms. Its capital is Illenev.

White Desert
Expansive desert of white sands speckled with Dorhond temples.

Withervale
Easternmost Zovarian city, on the border with the Negian Empire.

Wuovad Kladesh / *WOE-vahd CLAD-esh*
"Fiery Lakes." Area southwest of the Sajal Crater known for its hot springs.

Yanan / *YA-nun*
Zovarian city in Holv-Yanan, the only Zovarian state in Fel Baubór.

Yenmai / *YEN-my*
Capital of the Yenwu State.

Yenwu Dome / *YEN-woo*
Kroowindrolom. Dome located in the Yenwu Peninsula.

Yenwu State / *YEN-woo*
One of the sixteen realms. Its capital is Yenmai.

Zovaria / *zoh-VAH-ree-uh*
Capital of the Zovarian Union.

Zovarian Union / *zoh-VAH-ree-uhn*
One of the sixteen realms. Its capital is Zovaria.

THE JOURNEY SO FAR
UNTHAWING OCEAN
Elanúbril
Khaar Du Tribes
TESLURKATH
Baysea Beyenaar
Tesz Bay
FJORDSULF
STELM NEDROSS
Klad Mahujaun
Dragonkeep Bay
Spine Bay
Fjordlands
STELM
Needlecove
Koroberg
Isdinnklad Sea
Zovária
Isdinnklad Lake
Zovarian Union
Moordusk
STELM CA'ÉLI
Abramicas Bay
Muskeg
Nebush
Varanus
Old Karst
Klemes
Klad Senet
New Karst
Fel Varanus
Free Tribelands
QUIESCENT OCEAN
Fel Daulos
STELM ANKROV
Yanan
Allathanathar
Brashayn Scablands
Sajal Crater
UKHRRIA RANGE
Dunewaar
STELM SAJAL
Yenwu
Unclaimed Territories
MOUNT LOOR
Yenmai
Lhambor Di
Yenwu State
Aksas Di
Esduss Sea
Azurean
Navar Mat
Bay of Hashmun
Kingdom of Bauram
Kizad
Gulf of Erjilm
Bauresht Sea
Ashen
Ngau Tor
Taring
Nisos
Normouth
Republic of Lerev
Nisos
CAPRICIOUS
Loorian Continent
Jerjan Continent

NOSS

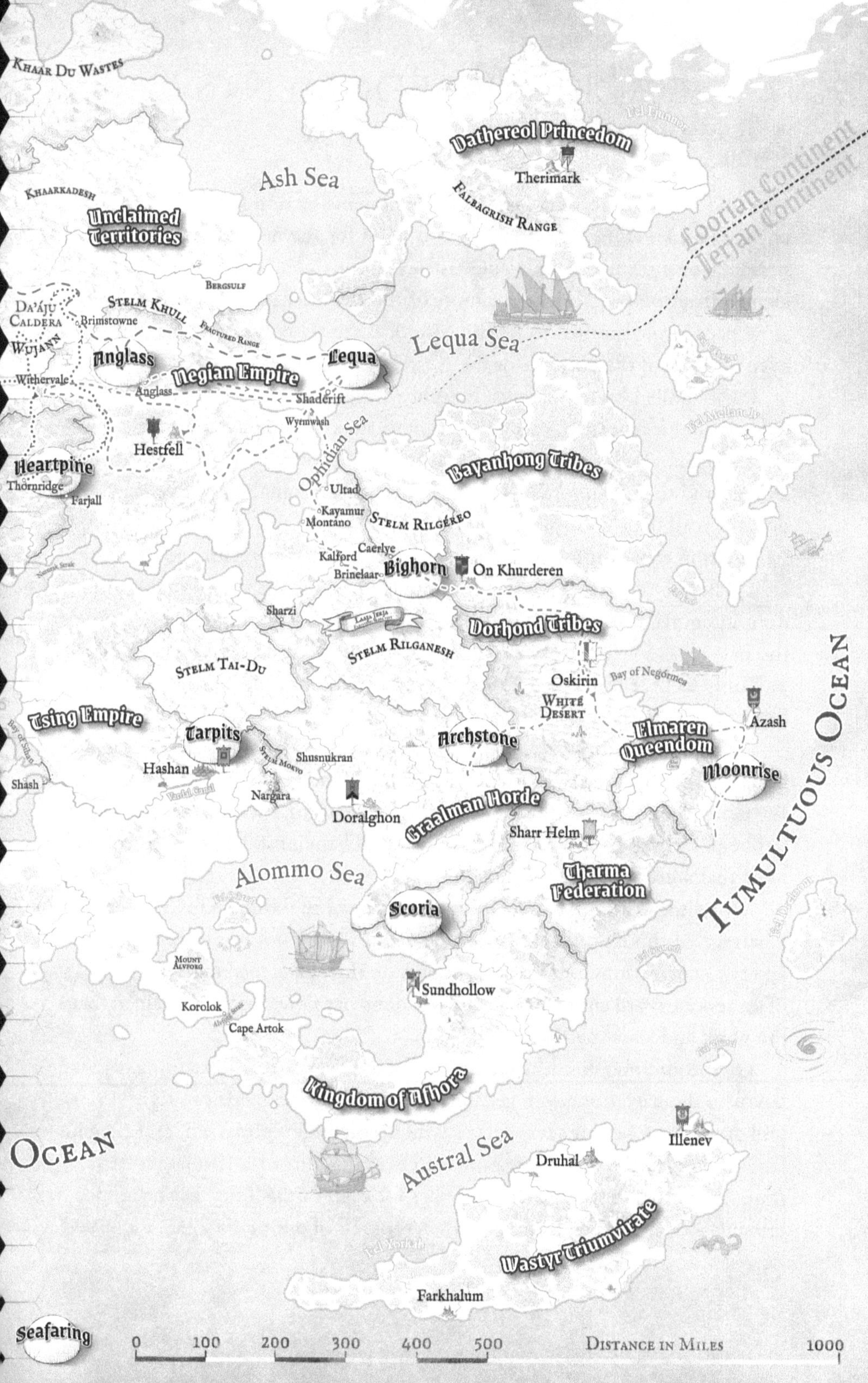

Khaar Du Wastes
Khaarkadesh
Ash Sea
Dathereol Princedom
Therimark
Falbagrish Range
Loorian Continent
Jerjan Continent
Unclaimed Territories
Bergsulf
Da'aju Caldera
Stelm Khull
Brimstowne
Fractured Range
Lequa Sea
Wujann
Anglass
Negian Empire
Lequa
Withervale
Anglass
Shaderift
Wyrmwash
Ophidian Sea
Heartpine
Hestfell
Bayanhong Tribes
Thornridge
Farjall
Ultad
Kayamur
Montano
Stelm Rilgéreo
Caerlye
Kalford
Brinelaar
Bighorn
On Khurderen
Sharzi
Dorhond Tribes
Stelm Rilganesh
Stelm Tai-Du
Oskirin
Bay of Negórmea
White Desert
Tumultuous Ocean
Using Empire
Tarpits
Shusnukran
Archstone
Elmaren Queendom
Azash
Hashan
Stelm Mokyo
Moonrise
Shash
Nargara
Doralghon
Graalman Horde
Sharr Helm
Tharma Federation
Alommo Sea
Scoria
Mount Alvforg
Korolok
Sundhollow
Cape Artok
Kingdom of Athora
Ocean
Illenev
Druhal
Austral Sea
Wastyr Triumvirate
Farkhalum
Seafaring
0   100   200   300   400   500   Distance in Miles   1000

Acknowledgments

I find it strange to write an acknowledgments section for Book 1 of a six-book series, knowing that it should also stand for the next five books I wrote simultaneously. Some names (such as those of my generous beta readers) will change from book to book, but most of the thanks I want to give are to the same people and groups. So let the core of these acknowledgments stand six-fold, for each of the volumes of the *Noss Saga*.

I was spoiled by my parents, Angélica Delgado and Juan Carlos Baldwin. They would let me buy any book I wanted, encouraging me to devour Bradbury, Sagan, Tolkien, Allende, Márquez, Vasconcelos, Gaiman, Asimov, Borges, and so much more. All my passions sprout from their unrelenting support—it is all their fault. Gracias, a él y ella.

Writing can be a lonesome endeavor, but I had my husband, Timothy, always here beside me, to whom I could blabber incoherent thoughts at random intervals, like a bouncing board for spittle and nonsense. Too many of the best ideas for this saga came from me spouting something massively stupid, only to hear him correct me or point out a different route I had not the foresight to envision.

Awfully prematurely, when I was merely in the planning stages of the first book, I had begun to envision the covers. Since the very start I knew I wanted Ilse Gort to lend her skillful hands for the illustrations. I was terrified to ask for her help. I was so happy when she said yes, and happier still when she proposed ideas that were much better than my own.

My editor, Andrew Corvin, was instrumental in fixing up my messes with a barrage of thoughtful suggestions. His notes were not just simple grammar and typo corrections, but offered insights on the characters' motivations, flow of sentences, word choice, and even broader story notes that truly helped focus the work and keep the voice consistent.

On the audiobook side, Magnus Carlssen did a fantastic job adding his own flavor to the narration, even getting all my tricky pronunciations right. I ran a poll among the beta readers to see which voice they preferred, and Magnus landed right at the top for a reason. And teaming him with Iain James Armour (Fox Amoore), who wrote the melodies for each of the lyrics, has been such a blessing—the first time I heard a work in progress of one of the songs, I squealed.

After so many last-minute tweaks, a final proofread was needed. Shiloh Skye joined in to help, not only offering meticulous corrections, but truly polishing and elevating the text. He is also an avid reader and a great advocate for indie authors, and has been helping the saga reach many new fans.

I had the luck to count with a thoughtful and diverse group of beta readers, who gave me a ton of notes to work with. Thank you for believing in me and for offering your help—this book is far better thanks to you, Abs M Rice, Alejandro Renteria, Alex Mui, Amanda Leigh, Angie Lee Camp, Arthur Huang, BirdsongChoir, Blackquill, Brian Jackson, Carlos A. Luna Aranguré, Charlie McGrew, Colleen Maloney, Conor Davitt, Cosmo, David "Professor Jefe" Jones, Edwin Herrell, Elliot D. Brown, Erik Tye, Fana, FFAT, Franz Anthony, Guephren, Jack Sanderson, Jul, Kiko, Kyle Branch, Kyle Dolloff, Louis D.S, Marco Nowak, Marián Sulák, Marcus Rodriguez, Markus Lundberg, Marston Jones, Matt Morgan, Matthew Green, Max Sjöblom, Miguel Ángel García García, Mike Hillard, Miles Fox, Nora Rogers, North, Reverie Benedetto, Rosalea Barker, Ross Blocher, Rourkie, Ryan Tye, Sandra Malpica, Santi Rowe, Scurrow, Sean Wenzel, Shadow Worfu, Skiriki, Solomon H., Streuhund, Ted Sawyer, Tiberius Rings, Timothy Dahlum, Victor Hugo Guadagnin, Zechariah Sanders, and a couple of anons.

One thing I never lacked during this process was encouragement. As an introvert, having an online community I can count on has been a true blessing. I truly appreciate everyone in social media who has been hitting little heart icons to trigger tiny releases of dopamine in my brain. In particular, thank you to my fervent furry following, who taught me to be courageous enough to be myself, to write a story that speaks my truth. You inspire me.

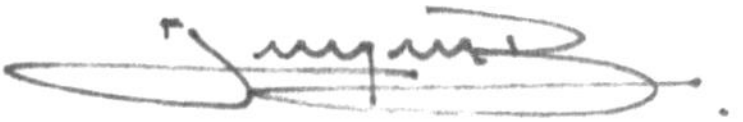

ABOUT THE AUTHOR

Joaquín Baldwin was born in Paraguay, where he first found his love of books by picking up every volume by Ray Bradbury he could get his hands on, and then by submerging himself into a single-bound copy of the Lord of the Rings trilogy—but it wasn't until much later that he'd acquire a taste for writing.

At age 19, he moved to the US to study film and animation, where he received a BFA from CCAD and an MFA from UCLA. He was the recipient of a full scholarship from the Jack Kent Cooke Foundation.

His short films have won over 100 awards and honors at festivals and competitions such as Cannes, the Student Academy Awards, Cinequest, and USA Film Festival. Soon after receiving his masters, he began working at the Walt Disney Animation Studios as a CG Layout Artist, and later as a Director of Cinematography, working on films such as Zootopia, Encanto, Wreck-It Ralph, Frozen, Raya, and Moana.

Never content with sticking to his lane, Joaquín has experience as a professional photographer, illustrator, comic artist, web designer, and 3D designer. His varied skillset came in handy when developing his fantasy saga, allowing him to create his own illustrations, maps, 3D models, book covers, website, and even his own language (phonetics, runes, and all).

Since the 2020 pandemic hit, he's been spending every second of his free time forging the complex world of Noss.

Sign up to Joaquín's mailing list:
JoaquinBaldwin.com/list

Connect with Joaquín on social media:
Search for @joabaldwin to find him on most sites, such as Bluesky, Mastodon, Facebook, Twitter, and Instagram.

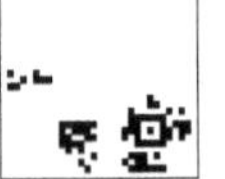